Susan Mallery is the #1 *New* ___ f
novels about the relationship ___ -
romance, friendship, family. Wi ___
keenly observes how people think and feel, in stories that take
readers on an emotional journey. Sometimes heartbreaking,
often funny and always uplifting, Susan's books have spent more
than 200 weeks on the *USA TODAY* bestseller list, thanks to her
ever-growing legions of fans.

Susan lives in Seattle with her husband, two ragdoll cats and a
tattletale toy poodle. Animals play a big role in her books, as
well, as she believes they're an integral component to a happy
life.

The Vineyard at Painted Moon

SUSAN MALLERY

MILLS & BOON

Mills & Boon
An imprint of HarperCollins*Publishers* Ltd
1 London Bridge Street
London SE1 9GF

www.harpercollins.co.uk

HarperCollins*Publishers*
1st Floor, Watermarque Building, Ringsend Road
Dublin 4, Ireland

This paperback edition 2021
1

First published in Great Britain by Mills & Boon,
an imprint of HarperCollins*Publishers* Ltd 2021

Copyright © 2021 Susan Mallery, Inc.

Susan Mallery asserts the moral right to be
identified as the author of this work.
A catalogue record for this book is
available from the British Library.

ISBN: 978-1-84845-817-8

MIX
Paper from
responsible sources
FSC
www.fsc.org
FSC® C007454

This book is produced from independently certified FSC™ paper
to ensure responsible forest management.

For more information visit: www.harpercollins.co.uk/green

Printed and bound in Great Britain by
CPI Group (UK) Ltd, Croydon, CR0 4YY

To Barbara—
this one is for you.

The Vineyard at Painted Moon

one

"Not that what you're wearing isn't great, but the party starts in an hour."

Mackenzie Dienes looked up from the grapevine she'd been studying, her mind still on the tight clusters of small, hard grapes that would, come late September, be ripe and sweet and ready for harvest. Between now and then, she would monitor their progress, willing them to greatness and protecting them from danger, be it mold, weather or hungry deer.

She blinked at the man standing in front of her, tall and familiar, with an easy smile and broad, capable shoulders.

"Party?" she asked, letting her thoughts of the vineyards go and remembering that, yes, indeed, it was the evening of the annual Solstice Party, hosted by the Barcellona family. As she was a Barcellona, by marriage if not by name, she would be expected to attend.

Wanted to attend, she reminded herself. It was always a good time, and Stephanie, her sister-in-law, worked hard to make it a perfect night.

"The party," she repeated, her voice slightly more panicked this time, then glanced down at herself. "Crap. What time is it?"

Rhys, her husband, shook his head. "You really don't listen when I talk, do you? We have an hour. You'll be fine."

She pulled off her gloves and shoved them into the left front pocket of her coveralls, then stepped behind Rhys and gave him a little push toward the flatbed truck he'd driven out to the west vineyards.

"You say that because all you have to do is shower and get dressed. I have to do the girl thing."

"Which takes you maybe ten minutes." He put his arm around her as they hurried toward the truck. "Happy with the grapes?"

"I think so," she said, glancing toward the healthy vines growing on either side of them. "We might have to do some thinning in a couple of weeks, but so far, so good."

As they slid onto the bench seat of the old truck, he glanced at her. She smiled, knowing there was a fifty-fifty chance he would call her out on her thinning statement. He was, after all, the vineyard manager. Technically all the decisions about the vineyard were made by him with her input, but not her instruction. As winemaker, she managed the grapes from the moment they were picked until the wine was bottled.

But at Bel Après, areas of responsibility often overlapped. Theirs was a large, boisterous family in which everyone had opinions. Not that Mackenzie listened to a lot of other ideas when it came to her wines, although as Rhys often pointed out, she was very free offering hers when it came to *his* work.

He drove along the dirt path that circled the vineyard, stopping by her truck. She slid into the cab, then followed him back to the family compound. The main road leading into Walla Walla was thick with tourists who wanted to enjoy the longest day of the year. She merged into the slow-moving traffic, doing her best to keep from glancing at the clock on the truck's dashboard as she inched along.

Vineyards stretched out on either side of the road, flat on the left and rising toward the hills on the right. Bright green leaves topped sturdy trunks that had been carefully trained to grow exactly as she wanted them to. The rows were long and neat, and the spaces between them were filled with native grasses that held in moisture and protected the roots from the heat.

Looking at her healthy crop kept her mind off the fact that she and Rhys were going to be desperately late.

Twenty minutes later, she followed him off the highway onto a less crowded secondary road—a back way home. Five minutes after that, they parked the trucks by the processing buildings behind the big tasting room. Rhys had already claimed one of the golf carts the family used to get around. She slid in next to him and they took off toward the center of the property.

Bel Après Winery and the surrounding land had been in the Barcellona family for nearly sixty years. Rhys and his siblings were third-generation. The original main house had been updated several times. When Rhys and Mackenzie had married, Barbara, Rhys's mother, had suggested they build themselves a house close to hers, rather than commute from town. Eager to stay in the good graces of her new mother-in-law, Mackenzie had agreed.

A large two-story home had been built. Barbara and Mackenzie had decorated every room, the act of choosing everything from light fixtures to doorknobs cementing their affection for each other.

A few years later, Stephanie, the second of Barbara's four children, had gotten a divorce and moved back home with her two kids, requiring another house to be constructed. When the youngest of the three girls had married, the last house had been added. Only Lori, the middle daughter, still lived in the original home.

All four houses faced a huge central courtyard. Mexican pavers were shaded by vine-covered pergolas. The extended family used the space for big dinners and as a kids' play area. If one of the women baked cookies, a cookie flag was hung out the front door, inviting anyone to stop by. At Christmas, a large tree was brought in from Wishing Tree, and for the annual Summer Solstice Party, dozens of long tables were brought in to seat the two hundred or so guests.

Rhys swung the golf cart behind the large main house, circling counterclockwise. Normally he would cut across the courtyard, but with all the party preparations, he had to go the long way. He pulled up at the rear entrance to their house and they dashed inside.

Mackenzie paused to unlace her boots and left them in the mudroom. Rhys did the same. They raced up the stairs together, separating at the landing to head to their individual en suite bedrooms.

Once in her bathroom, she started the shower. Thankfully, she'd already picked out the dress she would wear. She raced through a shower. After she dried off, she wrapped her hair in a towel and dug out the scented body lotion Rhys had given her a couple of years ago. Why anyone would want to smell like coconut and vanilla was beyond her, but he liked it.

She walked into the large closet and opened her underwear drawer. To the right were all the sensible bikini panties she usually wore—to the left were the fancier ones for special occasions. She chose a black pair and slipped them on, then went to the second drawer and looked for the matching push-up bra. When it and the pads were in place and doing the best they could with her modest curves, she pulled on a robe and returned to the bathroom.

After plugging in her hot rollers, it took her only a few minutes to apply eyeliner and mascara. She was flushed from the day working outside, so she didn't bother with any other makeup.

Her hair took a lot longer. First she had to dry the dark red shoulder-length waves, then she had to curl them. While the rollers were in place, she searched for a pair of black high-heel sandals that wouldn't leave her crippled by the end of the night.

Those found, she opened her small jewelry box and pulled out her wedding set, sliding both the engagement ring and the wedding band into place on her left hand. Diamond stud earrings followed. She'd barely stepped into her sleeveless black dress when Rhys walked into the closet, fully dressed in black slacks and a dark gray shirt.

She sighed when she saw him. "See. You have it so much easier than me."

"Yes, but in the end, you're more beautiful. That should be worth something."

"I'd rather have the extra time."

She turned, presenting him with her back. He pulled up the zipper, then bent to collect her shoes. They retreated to her bathroom and together began removing the curlers.

"We're late," Mackenzie said, catching sight of his watch. "Your mom is going to be all snippy."

"She'll be too busy welcoming her guests."

The last of the curlers was flung onto the counter. Mackenzie fluffed her hair, then pointed to the bedroom.

"Retreat," she said, reaching for the can of hair spray.

Rhys ducked to safety. She sprayed the curls into submission before running into the bedroom to escape the death cloud. Rhys was on the bench at the foot of the large bed. She sat next to him and quickly put on her shoes.

"Done," she said, pausing to reacquaint herself with the seldom-used skill of walking in heels.

She grabbed her husband's wrist. "Seven fifteen. Barbara's going to kill us."

"She's not. I'm her only son and you're just plain her favorite."

"We weren't ready exactly at seven. I can already hear the death-march music in my head. I want to be buried on Red Mountain."

Rhys chuckled as he led the way downstairs. "In the vineyard? I'm not sure your decaying body is going to be considered organic."

"Are you saying I'm toxic?" she asked with a laugh as they walked toward the front door.

"I'm saying you're wonderful and I'd like us to have a good night."

There was something in his tone, she thought, meeting his gaze. She'd known this man her entire adult life. They'd met over Christmas her freshman year of college. Her roommate, his sister Stephanie, had dragged Mackenzie home to meet the family. Grateful not to have to spend the holiday by herself, Mackenzie had gone willingly and had quickly found herself falling not only for her best friend's hunky older brother but for the entire Barcellona family and the vineyards they owned. Barbara had been like a surrogate mother, and the vineyards, well, they had been just as magical as Rhys's sexy kisses.

Now she studied her husband's expression, seeing the hint of sadness lurking behind his easy smile. She saw it because she hid the same emotion deep inside herself. The days of stealing away for sexy kisses were long gone. There were no lingering looks, no intimacy. They had a routine and a life, but she was less sure about them still having a marriage.

"I'd like that, too," she murmured, knowing he wasn't asking them not to fight. They never did. Harsh words required a level of involvement they simply didn't have anymore.

"Then let's make that happen," he said lightly, taking her hand in his and opening the front door.

The sounds of the party engulfed them, drawing them into the rapidly growing throng of guests. Mackenzie felt her mood lighten as she took in the twinkle lights wrapped around the pergola, the tables overflowing with food, the cases of Bel Après wine, stacked and ready to be opened. Servers circulated with trays of bruschetta. There was a pasta bar and a dessert station.

Music played through speakers hidden in foliage, and the delicious smell of garlic mingled with the sweet scent of summer flowers.

Mackenzie spotted Stephanie talking to one of the servers and gave Rhys's hand one last squeeze before separating from him and walking toward her sister-in-law.

"You outdid yourself," she said, hugging her friend.

"I'm pretty bitchin'," Stephanie said with a laugh, then waved her hand toward the twinkle lights. "Those will be a lot more effective when the sun goes down in two plus hours."

Because the longest day in their part of Washington State meant nearly sixteen hours of daylight.

"You exhausted?" Mackenzie asked, knowing Stephanie had spent the past three weeks making sure every detail of the party was perfect.

"It's been the usual challenge with a few extras thrown in," her sister-in-law said lightly. "I won't even hint at what they are, but brace yourself for a surprise or two."

Mackenzie immediately scanned the crowd. "Is Kyle here?"

Stephanie, a petite, curvy brunette with beautiful brown eyes and an easy smile, groaned. "What? No. Not that. I told you. I'm over him. Totally, completely, forever."

"But he's here."

"Yes. Mom invites him every year because he's Avery and Carson's father. The fact that he's my ex-husband doesn't seem to faze her. You know how she gets."

Mackenzie did. Once her mother-in-law made up her mind about something, she could not, would not be moved. There was no evolving of an opinion over time. Barbara was a human version of the immovable object.

"Kyle is her oldest granddaughter's father, and therefore a member of the family." Stephanie wrinkled her nose. "I deal with the awkwardness of it. On the bright side, she refers to him as 'the sperm donor,' which I like."

"If only he'd fought the prenup, Barbara would have turned on him like a snake." Mackenzie paused. "You're sure you don't want to start back up with him?"

"Yes. Totally. I'm done with that. He strung me along for years after the divorce. No more sex with the ex. It's been eighteen months since our last bump and grind, and I'm standing strong. I'm horny as hell, but standing strong." She glanced around at the guests. "Maybe I'll hook up with someone here."

"Have you ever hooked up with anyone?"

"No, but there's always a first time." Stephanie wrinkled her nose. "I just don't know how it works. Do we slip away to the barrel room and do it on a desk or something? I can't take him home—the kids are there. And a car is just so tacky."

"Because the barrel room isn't?" Mackenzie asked with a laugh.

"I don't know. It could be romantic."

"Or, at the very least, intoxicating."

Stephanie waved away that observation. "Fine. Not the barrel room, but then I'm still left with a lack of location, not to mention any prospects." She sighed as they walked toward one of the wine stations. "This is why hooking up has never worked for me. It's too complicated. They make it look easy in the movies and on TV, but it's not."

"I have zero experience. I'm sorry. I'll read up on it so I have better advice next time."

"Which is why I love you." Stephanie shook her head. "Obviously I should let the whole man-slash-sex thing go and focus on other aspects of my life."

They each asked for a glass of cabernet. While Stephanie simply sipped her wine, Mackenzie took a moment to study the color, before sniffing the aroma. She swirled the wine twice, then inhaled the scent again, liking the balance of fruit against the—

"For heaven's sake, just drink the wine, I beg you," Stephanie said with a laugh. "It's fine. It was fine when you watched the grapes being crushed, it was fine in the barrels, it was fine when it was bottled and it was fine when it won what I'm sure is a thousand awards. Okay? It's good wine. Relax and stop being a winemaker for one night."

"You're crabby." Mackenzie took a drink and smiled. "For the record, it's much better than fine."

"You would say that. It's your wine." Stephanie looked over Mackenzie's shoulder and smiled. "Here comes your handsome husband. I'm guessing he wants your first dance."

Mackenzie turned and watched as Rhys approached. He enjoyed the dancing at the Solstice Party and took all the female guests for a turn around the dance floor, but he always saved the first one for her.

"Shall we?" he asked, holding out his hand.

She passed her wineglass to Stephanie, then followed her husband to the small dance floor. No one else joined them, but she knew that would change as soon as they got things started.

"We need to check the Seven Hills drip system," she said as they moved in time with the music. "The forecast says we're going to get hotter and drier in the next few weeks, and I want to control the exact amount of moisture."

One of the advantages of "new world" vineyards was the ability to control quality by providing exactly the right amount of irrigation. Once the fruit was established, she could stress the vines, causing them to focus more intensely on the fruit.

"I know better than to point out we walked the vineyard last month," Rhys said lightly.

"That was a general check. Now I have a specific concern."

"As you wish." He spun them in a tight circle. "Maybe the rest of the work conversation could wait until tomorrow."

"What?" Why wouldn't they talk about— "Oh. The party. Sorry."

"Don't apologize. You're never truly off duty, but if we could put it on hold for the night, I would appreciate it."

Because he enjoyed events like these. He liked talking to his friends and meeting new people and generally being social. Rhys was much more extroverted than she was. If someone new joined the tight circle of vineyard owners in the area, he was the first one to go introduce himself.

She nodded her agreement and tried to think of something to talk about that wasn't vineyard or wine related.

"I hope Kyle leaves Stephanie alone," she said, thinking that was a more neutral topic. "She's trying hard to move on."

"She has to figure out what she wants. He's always going to ask—it's up to her to tell him no and mean it."

She knew he was right, but for some reason his blunt assessment irritated her.

"That's not very understanding," she said before she could stop herself. "Kyle's a big-time Seattle sportscaster with the ability to find a different woman every night. Stephanie's a small-town single mom working at the family business. Where, exactly, is she supposed to meet someone?"

Her husband stared at her. "What does her dating someone else have to do with whether or not she's still sleeping with Kyle?"

"There aren't any other options for her. She's lonely."

"She's going to stay lonely until she gets herself out there."

"What *there* are you talking about? The giant singles scene here in Walla Walla?"

They stopped dancing and stared at each other. Mackenzie realized this was the closest she and Rhys had come to having an actual argument in years. She had no idea why she had so much energy about the topic or what was causing her growing annoyance. But whatever it was, the Summer Solstice Party was not the place to give in to unexplained emotions.

"I'm sorry," she said quickly. "You're right, of course. Stephanie has to find a way to change her circumstances so Kyle is less of a temptation."

His tight expression softened with concern. "I want my sister to be happy."

"I know you do."

"I want *you* to be happy."

There was something in the way he said the words. As if he wasn't sure that was possible.

"I am," she said quietly, thinking she was almost telling the truth.

"I hope so."

She faked a smile and waved her hand toward the growing crowd of guests. "You have a lot of women to dance with tonight. You'd better get started."

He studied her for a second, as if assessing her mood. She kept the smile in place until he turned away. When he was gone, she looked longingly toward her house. Disappearing into the quiet tempted her but wasn't an option. Tonight was a command performance and there was no leaving early. But soon, she promised herself. In the quiet of her room, she wouldn't feel the low-grade unease that had haunted her for the past few months. Alone in the dark, she would be calm and happy and think only of good things, like the coming harvest and the wine she would make. Alone in the dark, she would be herself again.

two

Barbara Barcellona observed her guests as they laughed and talked. The Summer Solstice Party was a ten-year-old tradition, and one she enjoyed. She liked being the generous hostess and being able to show off her glorious estate and her attractive adult children. She liked how everyone dressed up for the evening and how the invitations were highly sought after, and how those who were not invited schemed to be included the next year. She liked the music and the food and even the twinkle lights her daughter Stephanie always insisted on, even though the sun was still visible at seven thirty in the evening.

The large crowd was a tribute to her, but more important, it was a tribute to Bel Après. People came to show their respect for the winery and all it represented, and that was what Barbara enjoyed most of all.

Forty-one years ago, when she'd married her late husband, Bel Après had been struggling to stay solvent. She hadn't known the first thing about wine or winemaking, but she'd learned as quickly as she could. She and James had grown the business together. Eventually she'd taken over as general manager. She'd been the one to find the winemakers who had created the wines that had slowly, oh so slowly, brought Bel Après back from the brink.

Her gaze moved across the crowd until she found her daughter-in-law. Barbara watched Mackenzie talking with some of the winery owners and she smiled as she saw how they all listened attentively. Mackenzie had been a find, she thought warmly. A shy but gifted young woman who had immediately understood Barbara's vision of what Bel Après could be. Even if Rhys hadn't married her, Barbara would have hired her. But he had and Mackenzie had joined the family.

Barbara's warm, happy feelings vanished as Catherine, her youngest, joined Mackenzie. That girl, Barbara thought grimly, taking in the flowing tie-dyed dress most likely created from a couple of pillowcases and a yak bladder. Catherine's mission in life was to not be ordinary and to annoy her mother as much as possible. Happily for her, the quest for the former naturally led to the latter.

She felt a hand on her waist, then a kiss on her bare neck. She turned and smiled at Giorgio, who pulled her close.

"You're looking fierce about something," he said, pressing his body to hers. "Tell me what troubles you, my love, and I will find a solution."

"How I wish that were true." She nodded toward Mackenzie and Catherine. "My daughter's a mess. Can you fix that? And while you're at it, can you make her stop being an artist and find an actual career?"

Giorgio, a tall man who, despite being sixty-five, was still vibrant and handsome, said, "She's lovely. She'll never have the beauty her mother possesses, but she is a sweet, caring young woman."

"You're too kind." She smiled at him. "I mean that. Stop being so nice. What is she wearing? At least her husband had the good sense to put on a decent shirt, and the kids look fine."

He took her in his arms and spun her in time with the music. "Let her be who she is, at least for tonight. Think only of me."

She laughed as she moved with him onto the dance floor. "That's very easy to do."

As they danced, Catherine once again came into view. Her daughter smiled at her and raised a glass of wine, as if in a toast. Something really had to be done about her, Barbara thought, although she had no idea what.

"May I cut in, or would that break the mood?"

Barbara smiled at Rhys, her only son. "You may."

Giorgio pretended distress. "Fine. A single dance, but then I must reclaim your mother."

"I'll bring her back to you unharmed," Rhys promised, guiding her through a series of quick steps. "Great party, Mom."

"It is. Stephanie did an excellent job, much to my surprise. The bruschetta bar is very popular. She was right about that." She looked at her son. "Have you seen what Catherine is wearing?"

"Mom, let it go."

"She looks terrible."

"Jaguar doesn't seem to think so."

Barbara followed his gaze and saw Catherine and her husband slow dancing, despite the fast pace of the music. Typical, she thought with a sigh. God forbid Catherine should dance to the same beat as everyone else.

As for Jaguar—actually his real name. Barbara had insisted on seeing his birth certificate before agreeing to the marriage— he wanted whatever Catherine did. The woman practically led him around by the nose.

"Stop," Rhys told her. "You're getting your 'my daughter is annoying me' look. Enjoy the party."

"I am. It is a lovely night. I'll even pretend I didn't notice that you and Mackenzie were late."

"By fifteen minutes, Mom. She was in the west vineyards communing with the grapes."

"Is she still happy with how things are progressing?"

Her son smiled. "You know she is. Otherwise, she would

have been in your office, telling you every little thing that was wrong."

Barbara knew that was true. Mackenzie always kept her informed. They were such a good team.

The song ended and Rhys led her back to Giorgio, who was chatting with several guests. As Barbara walked over to the bar to get a glass of wine, her youngest joined her.

"Barbara," Catherine said pleasantly. "Wonderful party."

Barbara did her best not to bristle. At the beginning of high school, Catherine had insisted on changing her name to Four, of all things. As in the fourth child. Barbara had refused to accommodate her, so Catherine had started calling her by her first name, to be annoying.

Barbara simply didn't understand where things had gone wrong. She'd been loving but fair, had limited TV and made all her children eat plenty of greens. Sometimes parenting was such a crapshoot.

She motioned to her daughter's dress. "One of your own creations?"

Catherine spun in a circle. "It is. Don't you love it?"

"With all my heart."

Catherine grinned. "Sarcasm? Really?"

"What did you want me to say?"

Catherine's good humor never faded. "What you said is perfect."

As her daughter drifted away, Barbara moved closer to Giorgio. He put his arm around her waist, the pressure against her back both comforting and familiar. She nodded as he talked, not really listening to the conversation. Whatever he was saying would be charming. He was like that—well-spoken, always dressed correctly for the occasion. He had an enviable way with people and a natural charm she'd never possessed. She supposed that was what she'd first noticed—how easy he made everything when he was around.

This night, she thought with contentment. It was exactly right. Her children and grandchildren were around her. Giorgio was here. The vines were healthy and strong and come September there would be another harvest.

She spotted Avery, her oldest grandchild, talking to her father, Stephanie's ex. Kyle was too smooth by far, Barbara reminded herself. Their marriage had been a disaster from the beginning, but Stephanie had been pregnant, so there had been no way to avoid the entanglement or the subsequent divorce.

At least Avery and Carson hadn't been scarred by the breakup. Barbara couldn't believe Avery was already sixteen. She was going to have to remind Stephanie to keep a close eye on her daughter when it came to boys and dating. If she didn't, there was going to be a second generation with an unplanned pregnancy, and no one wanted that.

She often told people that children and vineyards meant constant worry. Just when you were ready to relax, a new season started with new challenges.

Stephanie walked over to her. "Mom, it's about time for the toast, if you're ready."

"I am."

Barbara excused herself to follow her daughter toward the DJ and the small platform by the dance floor. She took the microphone the young man offered and stared out at the crowd. Stephanie called for quiet and it took only a few seconds for the party to go silent.

"Thank you so much for joining me and my family at our tenth annual Summer Solstice Party," Barbara said, pausing for applause, then holding up her glass of chardonnay.

"To my children—may the next year be one of happiness for each of you. To my grandchildren—know that you are loved by all of us." She turned and found her daughter-in-law, then smiled at her. "To my special daughter of the heart—the day you came into our lives was a magnificent blessing."

There was more applause.

Barbara looked at Giorgio and smiled. They'd discussed

whether or not she should mention him, and he'd asked her not to. After all, he was just the boyfriend and he'd said tonight was about family—yet another reason she loved him. The man understood her and wasn't that amazing.

She waved her glass toward the crowd. "To the rest of you, here's to a wonderful summer and a happy life."

"Happy life," they all echoed.

"How does it feel to be a magnificent blessing?" Four asked with a grin.

Mackenzie did her best not to groan. "It's better than last year when she said I was a miracle brought into the family to take Bel Après to greatness. Although technically I'm pretty sure she said I brought a magnificent blessing, not that I was one." She looked at her youngest sister-in-law. "Sorry about her enthusiasm."

"Don't be. We love you just as much. Or maybe more. Our love isn't conditional."

Four was right about that, Mackenzie thought. Barbara always claimed Mackenzie was her favorite, but that affection was very much tied to her work in the winery. If she hadn't been interested in Bel Après, Mackenzie wasn't completely sure Barbara would have allowed the wedding to take place.

"She is a challenge," she murmured.

"She is," Four agreed. "She's my mother and I love her, but there is something deeply wrong with her. I can't figure out if she was traumatized as a child or if she was just plain born mean."

The stark assessment surprised Mackenzie. "You think she's mean?"

Four's eyes brightened with amusement. "Do you think she's nice?"

"I wouldn't say nice. She can be…exacting. But she's always been good to me."

"She has, and you deserve her affection." Four hugged her. "You have an open and giving heart that warms us all. You are the fairy dust that allows us to fly." She waved her glass. "Oh, and you're magnificent."

"I agree."

The male voice came from behind her. Mackenzie turned to see Bruno Provencio walk up to join them. The man knew how to dress, she thought. Like Rhys, Bruno wore slacks and a long-sleeved shirt, but somehow the clothes were more elegant on him. Barbara said his clothes were all custom—a concept Mackenzie understood intellectually but made no sense to her on a day-to-day basis. Why take the time when you could buy stuff online and have it delivered with just a few clicks?

Something she would guess that Bruno had never done in his life, she thought, trying not to smile. Bruno came from money. He was good-looking, with dark hair and brown eyes, and carried himself with an air of confidence that added to the appeal.

One day she would be confident, too, she told herself. If not in this life, then maybe the next.

She groaned. "Don't say magnificent, please. Barbara was just being..."

"Her usual charming self," Bruno said, taking Mackenzie's free hand in his and leaning in to kiss her cheek. He did the same with Four.

"Successful party, as always," he said.

"It's all Stephanie," Mackenzie told him, setting her empty glass on the passing server's tray.

Bruno held out his hand to Mackenzie. "A dance?"

She smiled and nodded. She wasn't sure if she gave off a non-dancer vibe or if it was her position as Rhys's wife and Barbara's daughter-in-law, but almost none of the men at the party wanted to dance with her. But every year, Bruno asked and she happily agreed.

They moved toward the dance floor and joined the other couples there. Rhys was dancing and chatting with the owner of a local fashion boutique. Barbara and Giorgio were wrapped in each other's arms.

Bruno put his hand on her waist, keeping a respectable distance, and they began to move to the music.

"Perfect weather for the party," he said.

She glanced toward the setting sun. "It is. We were lucky it wasn't too hot." The high eighties were manageable, but a day in the nineties would have made for an uncomfortable event.

"We're seeing more of you than usual," she added. "Do you have new business in the area?"

Bruno was a wine distributor—at least that was how he described himself. She knew he also invested in a few wineries and had more money than God, and when he flew into town, he did so on a private jet. But aside from that, he was a mystery. A handsome mystery, but still, an unknown.

"I'm thinking of buying a winery," he admitted.

"You are? I knew you were an investor, but I didn't think you wanted more than that."

He gave her a half smile. "I like being in charge."

"Can you tell me which one?" she asked, then shook her head. "Never mind. I'm sure you can't. Still, I'll have to speculate."

"Text me your guesses. I'll tell you if you figure it out."

She laughed. "There are nearly five hundred wineries in a hundred-mile radius. You'd be forced to block me before I got even close to figuring it out."

"I promise not to block you."

"Buying a winery. That's exciting. All the possibilities."

"Interested in being my business partner?" His voice was teasing.

She laughed. "You flatter me, but Bel Après is my home. So you'll be living in Walla Walla permanently? What about your family? I know your parents are still alive and you have siblings."

"They are all perfectly content on the East Coast and I like life here. I get home to see them often enough."

Now it was her turn to tease. "So you don't want to be *too* close."

"Best if I'm not. My mother likes to set me up on blind dates. They never go well."

"So distance is your friend." Mackenzie looked around. "Speaking of dates, you didn't bring anyone tonight, did you?"

"No."

She met his gaze. "At the risk of sounding like your mother, you never bring a date. Why is that?"

"I'm not seeing anyone in particular."

"Why not? I would think finding women would be easy. You're a successful, good-looking guy. I would think women would be all over you."

"Are you flirting with me?"

She laughed. "I think we both know I'm not capable of flirting." A thought occurred to her. Maybe the problem wasn't women at all. "Unless you'd rather not date women and you're concerned we'd have an issue with that. We wouldn't."

She paused, not sure how to navigate the socially awkward conversation she'd inadvertently started.

His half smile blossomed. "I'm not gay. I do like women. I'm not seeing anyone seriously because I can't seem to find someone who interests me enough to make the effort."

"Have you been married?"

"Yes."

She stared expectantly. "And?"

"We got a divorce. It was a long time ago."

"I'm sorry."

He shrugged. "I was at the time. Not anymore." He looked into her eyes. "I can't have children. We found out when she couldn't get pregnant. She didn't want to deal with that and she left."

Mackenzie came to a stop. "How could she be so awful? There are other ways to have children."

"She wasn't interested in any of them."

"I'm sorry, Bruno. For prying and for reminding you of a difficult time in your life. I should stick to small talk."

He pulled her a little closer and spun her. "I don't mind that you know."

"Still. I'm sorry."

"We'll change the subject. How much does Barbara hate what Four is wearing?"

Mackenzie looked at her sister-in-law. Her flamboyant dress was all bright colors, with an uneven hem and a short sleeve on one arm and a long sleeve on the other.

"I haven't talked to her about it, but I'm sure it's not her favorite."

"Four enjoys tormenting her. If Barbara would stop engaging, Four would stop being so outrageous."

She turned back to Bruno. "That's insightful."

"I'm a good observer."

"What else have you figured out?"

He looked at her for several seconds. His gaze was so intense, she was sure he was going to say something that would shock her, or maybe just keep her up for three days. Instead he stepped back, squeezed her hand, then released her.

"I should let you get back to your party," he said. "Have a good night."

He walked away, leaving her alone in the crowd, uncertain about what had just happened and what it had all meant. If anything.

The party was getting louder as more wine was consumed. Delicious smells from the buffet made her stomach growl. She was just about to grab something to eat when she spotted Rhys talking with a pretty blonde whose name Mackenzie couldn't remember.

As she watched, the woman reached out and touched Rhys's forearm. The flirtatiousness was clear, and she waited to see how her husband would respond. He gave the woman a brief smile and took a half step back.

Mackenzie doubted his movements were the least bit planned—no doubt he'd reacted involuntarily. Rhys wasn't the type who cheated. He was a good man who took his responsibilities, whether to her, his family or the winery, seriously. She could depend on him. She trusted him.

But they hadn't shared a bedroom in nearly five years, and it had been at least that long since they'd made love. So if he wasn't sleeping with her, who was he sleeping with? And even as she asked the question, she wondered if she really, truly wanted to know the answer.

Stephanie Barcellona wanted to state—for the record—that ex-husbands were a very bad idea. Especially good-looking ones with easy smiles and knowing glances. She'd spent the past hour ducking and weaving to avoid Kyle, but no matter how she busied herself with the party, he kept circling closer.

If only her mother hadn't insisted he be invited. Perhaps more to the point, if only Stephanie had the backbone of a goldfish, she would walk up to him, look him in the eye and say that it was over. O. V. E. R. She was done being his booty call whenever he found himself in Walla Walla with a few hours to spare. They had been divorced over a decade. Nearly twice as long as they'd been married. They needed to be finished with each other for good. Having sex a couple of times a year didn't help either one of them. Though she was pretty sure it didn't faze him at all and only she was left feeling like an idiot.

It had been eighteen months since her last, um, encounter with Kyle. She'd gotten through last year's party and the holidays without giving in to his whispered "Hey, beautiful, let's go somewhere quiet." She told herself that if she could stay strong for the rest of the night, she would have broken free of him. She was determined, she had a plan. Unfortunately, she was also horny.

Betrayed by my hormones, she thought glumly as she circulated around the guests, making sure all was well. While she checked the flow of food and double-checked there was plenty of wine at the bar, her girl parts began to ache. Kyle always knew exactly how to make her come in, like, eighteen seconds. Humiliating but true.

She spotted him out of the corner of her eye, headed in her direction, and quickly walked the opposite way. If he got within touching distance, he would do that shoulder-to-wrist strokey thing with his fingers. The one that made her all shivery. Then he would lean in and tell her she had a great ass, because Kyle was just that much of a romantic. Then he would corner her so he could lightly brush against her nipples and she would be lost.

"Not happening," she breathed. "I can't do this anymore."

She continued the duck-and-weave dance, feeling like a character in a very badly written play, when she saw Giorgio nod at her. It was time.

All thoughts of Kyle fled as she checked her pocket for the small cloth bag tucked there, before walking directly to the DJ.

"Stephanie," Kyle said, his tone low and suggestive, as he closed in behind her.

She didn't bother looking at him as she said, "Not now."

When she reached the stage, she smiled at the DJ. "Ready."

He gradually lowered the volume of the music, then handed her the microphone. All the guests turned toward the small platform.

"If I can have your attention for just another moment," she said, looking at Giorgio, who appeared incredibly calm, despite the momentousness of the occasion. "A certain gentleman would like to have a word with his very special lady."

She passed both the microphone and small cloth bag to him, then stepped back into the crowd that had gathered.

Avery, her sixteen-year-old daughter, slid in beside her. "What's going on?"

"Watch. It's going to be epic."

Avery sighed. "Mom, I've talked to you about trying to use slang. It's not a good look."

"I just do it to annoy you."

They linked arms and leaned in to each other. Stephanie didn't care if the word was too young for her. It was perfect—because this was going to be 100 percent epic. She could feel it in her gut.

three

Barbara had no idea what was happening, and she didn't like that one bit. She looked between Stephanie and Giorgio, hoping they weren't going to do something ridiculous like sing a duet. Stephanie didn't have much of a voice.

Still, she trusted Giorgio. The man took care of her the way no one ever had, so she should just relax and pretend to enjoy whatever silly thing they had planned.

Giorgio smiled at her as he spoke into the microphone. "Hello, my love."

She smiled back without speaking. He knew she didn't like to be played for a fool and she trusted him. Whatever misgivings she had, she should ignore.

He glanced at the circle of people around them. "For those of you who don't know me very well, I met this wonderful woman two years ago, in Italy. We were tasting wine at a little place outside of Tuscany. The day was beautiful, but the woman next to me was even more appealing. I found myself unable to look away."

"You were very charming," she said, relaxing as he spoke.

"On the outside. On the inside, my heart was beating so quickly. At my age, that can be a dangerous thing."

Everyone laughed.

"I introduced myself and suggested we share a glass of wine." He smiled again. "She agreed and I was so happy, I could barely speak. You told me about Bel Après and your children and Mackenzie, and I could hear the love and pride in your voice. Within the hour, I was smitten."

Barbara felt herself getting lost in the memories of that first meeting. He'd surprised her by talking to her. She hadn't known what to think. Handsome men simply didn't ever talk to her—not the way he had. He'd been funny and kind and the afternoon had flown by.

"I was married before," he said. "My wife passed away five years ago, and it never occurred to me that I would find love again, but I have. A great, glorious love that has filled my heart."

She placed her hands on her chest and mouthed, "Me, too."

He handed Stephanie the microphone and took something out of a small bag, then stunned her by dropping to one knee.

"Barbara Barcellona, you are the love of my life. I love you and adore you. I want to make you happy, and spend the rest of my days with you. Will you marry me?"

She hadn't seen it coming, she thought, genuinely stunned by the proposal. She stared at Giorgio, trying to take it all in. The sound of the music retreated until she could hear only her own heartbeat.

Happiness swelled, becoming joy, and she knew that she would never again experience a moment so perfect.

"Yes," she said, fighting tears. "Oh, yes, Giorgio. I'll marry you." Around them, everyone began to cheer and applaud.

He stood and slid a large diamond solitaire onto her finger, then cupped her face and kissed her. The feel of his warm lips on hers was magical. She felt like a princess. She felt thirty years younger.

"I love you," he whispered into her ear.

"I love you, too."

Around them, the clapping continued. Her children gathered around, hugging her and Giorgio.

"Did you know?" she asked Rhys.

Rhys grinned. "He asked for my permission. It was very honorable of him and I'm happy for you both, Mom."

"I didn't know," Mackenzie said, kissing her cheek. "Barbara, congratulations. You're going to be a beautiful bride. I know Giorgio will make you so happy."

Four and Lori rushed in to hug her.

"No one told us," Four said with a laugh. "What a wonderful surprise."

"I'm happy for you," Lori added, sounding slightly less than thrilled.

Barbara supposed the living arrangements would be a problem. Lori had never moved out of the large family home at the center of the compound. It was one thing to have Giorgio staying there when he visited, but another to have him a permanent resident. A problem she would deal with tomorrow, she told herself, determined to enjoy every moment of the very perfect evening.

The music resumed and Giorgio drew her to the dance floor. She laughed when she heard the opening notes of "Lady in Red," then glanced down at her red cocktail dress.

"So that's why you asked me to wear this," she said, gazing up at him.

"It was all part of the plan."

She leaned her head against his shoulder. "I was surprised."

"I'm glad. Rhys knew, of course, and Stephanie."

"They kept the secret."

"Barbara?"

She looked at him.

"I don't want you to worry about anything," he said, his gaze filled with affection. "I'll be happy to sign a prenuptial agreement. I want no part of Bel Après."

"You will?"

She hadn't even thought of a prenup. She would have, probably before midnight, which would have kept her up the rest of the night. "Thank you for that. I'll sign whatever you want, as well."

Giorgio had plenty of money from the aerospace manufacturing firm he'd run in upstate New York.

"We're a very modern couple," he teased.

She raised herself on tiptoe and whispered in his ear, "Yes, and later, we're going to have lots of modern sex."

He chuckled. "How is it modern? I think of our lovemaking style as more traditional."

She grinned. "We keep the lights on."

"That we do."

They danced for another three songs before going to get something to drink. Several of the female guests stopped her to admire her ring. Barbara hadn't had much of a chance to study it herself. She would guess the diamond was at least three carats. A little large and flashy, but she was confident she could carry it off.

Stephanie met them by the bar.

"That was amazing," she said with a happy sigh. "I'm so thrilled for you both."

"You did a very nice job," Barbara told her, doing her best to keep the surprise out of her voice. "The moment was perfect."

Stephanie hugged her. "Next, the wedding. Let me know if you want my help planning that, Mom. It's one of my skill sets."

A wedding? Barbara hadn't thought that far ahead. Obviously she and Giorgio would have some kind of ceremony. At their age, it made sense to make it small—family and a few close friends.

She immediately recalled her first wedding. She and James had been young and there hadn't been any money to waste on something as frivolous as a wedding. They'd been married in a small church and the reception had been in the old farmhouse where they'd lived. It hadn't been the wedding of anyone's dreams.

She looked at the ring glinting on her left hand, then at the crowd enjoying themselves. She was the matriarch of Bel Après, and the owner of a successful business. Money was no object.

"Giorgio, what do you want for a wedding?"

He drew her hand to his mouth and kissed her knuckles. "I want whatever makes you happy, my love."

He was such a good man.

Barbara considered her options. Having the wedding at Bel Après made the most sense. There were spaces for large events. Even though the winery wasn't gauche enough to pimp itself out as a destination anything, they did host parties for major customers or special occasions. Still, a wedding required planning.

Barbara looked at her oldest daughter. Stephanie managed the retail store and tasting room. She could, in a pinch, manage the wine club, as well, and she planned whatever parties were held on the property, including a handful of weddings. While Stephanie didn't have anything that could be considered talent, she was organized, and honestly, how hard could it be to plan a wedding?

"All right," Barbara said. "Stephanie, you can plan my wedding. I want a real one," she added. "Traditional. Nothing ridiculously modern. I'll accept fun and elegant and a little over-the-top, but that's all."

Stephanie grinned. "We can make that happen. We can even talk about a lot over-the-top."

Barbara held in a sigh. "We'll talk about it later. Right now I want to dance with my fiancé."

She turned to Giorgio and held out her hand. He pulled her close, then led her to the dance floor. So much happiness, she thought, leaning against him. The night was perfect, and the rest of her life was going to be just as wonderful.

Two hours and what Stephanie would guess was half a bottle of wine later, she was still processing what had happened. She was happy—of course she was happy. Giorgio was a wonderful man who adored her mother. There was also the happy side effect of Barbara being just a little easier to deal with when he was around, and who didn't want that?

She'd known about the engagement. She'd been the keeper of the ring and the decider of the timing. She was excited to be helping her mom plan a wedding. It was all good. Great, even. But—and it was a big but—she couldn't quite seem to wrap her mind around what she was feeling.

It wasn't just happy, she thought. It was something else. Something that made her uncomfortable and sad and maybe a few other things she couldn't or didn't want to name.

She stood by the bar, working on yet another glass of wine, when the truth hit her, like a sucker punch to the gut. All her air rushed out as she blinked back unexpected tears.

She wanted a different life. Her kids were great and she loved her family, but she wanted more. She wanted a job she loved—she wanted to be excited about how she spent her day, instead of just going through the motions. She wanted to be proud of herself and strong and brave, and that meant she really had to get off her ass and do something. Wishing was a waste of time. She'd spent the past five years talking about leaving Bel Après and going to work somewhere else and she'd done nothing to make that happen.

"Hey, babe."

The low words were accompanied by a finger sliding from

her bare shoulder to her wrist. Stephanie turned and saw Kyle smiling at her.

"Stellar party, as per usual," he added with a wink.

"You're still here," she said, struggling to resurface from her confusing thoughts.

"Sure. I thought maybe we could spend a couple of hours together."

His tone was suggestive. As if to emphasize the point, he put his hand on the small of her back and then slid it down to cup her butt.

"No. Just no."

She spoke without thinking, taking a step away and staring at him, fighting the oddest sensation of having no idea who he was. Yes, they'd been married, but they'd divorced over a decade ago. What was she doing, having sex with him a couple of times a year, whenever it happened to fit into his schedule? She didn't want that, or him.

Why had she agreed to their sad arrangement? Ignoring the gross thought that she had no idea how many other women he slept with on a regular basis, didn't she deserve better? Didn't she deserve to be happy, with her own robust life? Instead she'd settled on ex-husband crumbs tossed her way. Kyle was a distraction, and one she'd allowed to go on for too long.

"You don't have to say it like that," he grumbled, sounding defensive. "Just tell me you're not interested."

"I'm not interested." Her voice was firm. "We talked about this before, Kyle. I said I was done and I meant it. Stop trying to get me into bed. I won't do that anymore. We're divorced. We should act like it."

With that, she walked away, looking for a safe group to join, then smiling when she spotted her kids talking to Lori.

"Having a good time?" she asked as she slipped between Avery and Carson.

"We are." Her daughter laughed. "Mom, I can't believe you

didn't even hint about the proposal. It was so romantic. Even if they are, you know, old."

"Ancient," Stephanie teased. She turned to Carson. "What did you think about what happened?"

Her fourteen-year-old surprised her by grinning. "It was cool, Mom. Romantic, like girls want. Plus, it takes some, ah, courage to ask that in front of everyone. What if she'd said no? He would have been humiliated for life."

"Love gives you courage," she told him.

Avery sighed. "Great. Now she's going to make you watch that old movie she loves so much. What's it called?"

"Say Anything," Stephanie and Lori said together.

Avery groaned. "That's the one."

"I am kind of feeling it's time," Stephanie admitted.

"Do it quick," her daughter said. "Before Carson goes off to baseball camp. I don't want to get stuck being the only one who has to see it."

"You loved it."

"You wish."

Carson yawned. "It's late, Mom. I'm going to bed." He hugged her.

Her baby was four inches taller than her already and he still had a lot of growing to do. Of course, she was short, but still.

Avery hugged her, as well. "See you in the morning, Mom."

"Night."

She watched as they made their way across the patio and went into their house, then she smiled at her sister. "Having a good time?"

"I was until the engagement." Lori's tone was sharp.

"I thought you liked Giorgio."

"I do, but now everything is going to change."

"I don't think he'll mind you living in the house, if that's what you're worried about. Besides, Mom would never make you move out."

Lori's expression tightened. "Oh, please. We both know she'd throw me out in a heartbeat if it served her purposes, or if Mackenzie asked her to." She exhaled sharply. "It's not that. Did you see how in love they are? I knew they were happy, but the look on her face when he proposed...I want that."

"To get married?" Stephanie tried to keep the surprise out of her voice.

"Of course. Everyone wants to belong. Some of us know when we should keep what we have rather than throw it away."

"Are you talking about my divorce?"

"You had something with Kyle. Maybe you should have stuck with what you had."

"A cheater who was never home?"

"It was a marriage."

"We were both miserable. Besides—" Stephanie pressed her lips together. She didn't need to defend her position to anyone. "It's better now," she said. "With us apart. But if you're interested in dating, I hope you meet someone."

"Nothing good ever happens to me."

With that, she turned and walked away. Stephanie watched her go, wondering how she and Lori and Four could be sisters when they were all so different. She supposed it was just one more thing that proved God had sense of humor.

She walked over to an empty chair and sat down. While the rest of the family were allowed to leave any time after ten, she was stuck for the duration. The party was her responsibility and she had to make sure everything was cleaned up and put away. She would be up until at least two in the morning.

On the bright side, she was apparently done with her ex. It had taken ten years and a cosmic slap in the face, but at least it had happened. First thing tomorrow, she would start looking for a job that excited her. She'd finally escaped from the trap of casual sex with her ex. Now it was time to escape from the family business and strike out on her own.

four

Mackenzie carefully studied the wine in the glass before taking another sip. This time she let the liquid sit on her tongue a bit longer before swirling it in her mouth and then spitting it into the coffee mug she'd brought with her.

Barrel tasting was essential so she could keep track of the progress of the wine, but getting drunk while doing so was a rookie mistake. She'd learned early that spitting came with the job. She picked up her clipboard and made a few notes. Later she would transfer the notes to a computer file. Old-school, for sure, but it was how she preferred to work.

This corner of the barrel room held her personal wines—blends she'd created because she'd had an idea and had wanted to see how it played out. The first three times that had happened, Barbara had flat-out refused and then had told Mackenzie to stop asking. Frustrated, Mackenzie had told Barbara that if the wines didn't do well, she would cover the losses with her salary. But if they sold the way Mackenzie expected, she would get a cut of the profits for as long as the wines were made.

Barbara had agreed, drawing up a contract they'd both signed. Two years later the first of the Highland wines had been released. Highland Thistle—named in tribute to Mackenzie's Scottish ancestry—had sold out in two weeks. She'd used a more French style of blending the cab and merlot grapes, giving Thistle a softer finish that was appealing to a younger crowd.

The following year Highland Heather, a nearly botanical chardonnay, had sold out before the release. Last year, Highland Myrtle, a Syrah, had done the same. At that point, Barbara had stopped telling Mackenzie no on pretty much anything wine related. Still, the three wines provided a steady flow of money every quarter. The proceeds were currently just sitting in an investment account, but someday she would do something with them.

She reviewed her notes, then tucked the clipboard under her arm and headed for the offices on the second floor.

Bel Après had grown significantly over the past sixteen years. They'd always had enough capacity to produce more wine, but previous winemakers had sold off hundreds of tons of grapes rather than risk creating a new wine that failed. When Mackenzie had come on board, she and Barbara had come up with a strategic plan using the best of what Bel Après produced.

As she took the stairs to the second floor, she glanced at the awards lining the wall. Bel Après had started winning awards with Mackenzie's very first vintage, and Barbara had been giddy with the success. She'd wanted to enter every competition, but Mackenzie had insisted they be more selective. Better to place in a few prestigious competitions and get noticed rather than win awards no one had heard of.

Bel Après had been written up in journals and magazines, driving sales. Every year they'd expanded production. Ten years ago, they'd tripled the size of the barrel room.

She reached the top of the stairs and paused to look at the pictures mounted there. They showed Bel Après as it had been a generation ago, when Barbara had been a young bride. From there, all the way down the long hallway, photographs marked the growth of the winery and the family.

She smiled at a photograph of Rhys with his three sisters. He looked to be about ten or eleven with the girls ranging from nine to maybe five. The girls were all smiling and mugging for the camera, but Rhys looked serious, as if he already knew how much responsibility he had waiting for him.

He'd grown into a good man, she thought. He worked hard, was a fair employer and came home every night. Rhys was her rock—his steadiness freed her to send all her energy into the wines.

Mackenzie's parents had died when she'd been young, and her grandfather had raised her. He'd been a winemaker up in the Spokane area of the state, and she'd grown up understanding what it was to wrestle magic from the soil.

He'd gotten sick when she was fifteen—a cancer that could be slowed but not cured. Sheer will had kept him alive until she'd graduated from high school. He'd died that summer. Mackenzie still remembered the first day she'd moved into the residence hall, meeting her new roommate. Stephanie had been friendly and upbeat and exactly what Mackenzie had needed.

That first Christmas, Stephanie had brought her home. Mackenzie had been overwhelmed by Bel Après, dazzled by Barbara and swept away by Rhys.

He'd been so steady, she thought, smiling at the memory. Kind and strong, but with a sly sense of humor that made her laugh. Her second night there he'd knocked on her door at two in the morning, telling her to get dressed. He'd taken her outside, where unexpected snow fell from the sky. There, in the cold, dusted by new snow, he'd kissed her. It had been a perfect moment. She might not have fallen in love with him then, but she'd certainly cracked open her heart to the possibility.

She was still smiling at the thought when she walked down

the hall, through the open door and into Barbara's large office. The corner space had huge windows that overlooked the property. The other two walls were covered with maps of the various vineyards owned by the family.

The Barcellona family was a dynasty. If Mackenzie and Rhys had had children, her blood would have blended with theirs, adding to the whole in some way. But they hadn't, so when she was gone, there would be no legacy. No piece of her to be found anywhere.

Except in the vineyards, she reminded herself. She had made her mark there. The wines of Bel Après owed what they were to her.

"Tell me good news," Barbara said, motioning to one of the chairs pulled up in front of her desk.

Mackenzie took a seat. "Rhys has been checking the Seven Hills drip system. The weather's getting hotter and I want to make sure there's enough water to protect the vines. I've spent yesterday and today barrel tasting. I'll get you my notes by tomorrow."

"We have that very expensive software system for your tablet," Barbara told her with a gentle laugh.

"Yes, and maybe one day I'll want to use it."

"You can be stubborn, Mackenzie Dienes."

"I get that from you."

The teasing between them was familiar—they both often mentioned sharing traits, despite the lack of blood relationship. Even looking at the two, a stranger would assume they were related.

Both were about five six, with dark red hair. They had strong, lean builds and wore an air of confidence. Mackenzie's eyes were green, while Barbara's were brown, but otherwise, they could easily pass for mother and daughter.

Stephanie, Lori and Four all took after their father in looks, as did Rhys. They had dark hair and brown eyes. Rhys was tall, but the sisters were on the shorter side, and curvy, with Lori the closest to plus-size.

Mackenzie flipped through her notes. "The '18 reserve cab is coming along nicely. It's already lush, with plenty of forward fruit. It's going to be dense, and it will cellar at least fifteen years. It's going to be big. We'll want to put some aside for competitions and at allocations for wine club. I'll want at least ten percent of the bottles for the library. This wine is going to score high and get snapped up quickly. We can sell the remainder in five years for at least double the original price."

Barbara leaned back in her oversize chair and smiled. "You said it was a great year."

"It *was*. We had perfect conditions and a harvest to match. I want to hold it an extra three months before we sell it."

"What? No! You can't. The reserve is already scheduled to be bottled and we've told our wine club members when to expect it. There are events that—" Barbara pressed her lips together. "Mackenzie, you're being overly cautious."

"Three more months. I promise, it will be worth the wait."

"It had better be," Barbara grumbled. "Do you know the costs of keeping that many barrels in storage?"

"As a matter of fact, I do." Down to the penny. She might not run the business side of the winery, but she knew all the numbers.

She heard familiar footsteps in the hallway and smiled. Seconds later, Rhys walked in. He crossed to her, bent down and kissed her lightly on the mouth, before greeting his mother.

As he took his seat next to Mackenzie, he said, "You were right about the Seven Hills irrigation. Several of the drip lines had been chewed through. How do you know when stuff like that happens?"

"I just get a feeling."

Bel Après had acreage all over southwestern Washington State and into Oregon, from Red Mountain to the Walla Walla Valley and south to Seven Hills. The different areas had distinct characteristics that influenced the grapes. Mackenzie liked working with the various topographical challenges each vineyard offered.

Everyone was hot for Red Mountain, and she thought the vineyards there were special, as well, but she could make her magic just about anywhere. She supposed her ability to go with the flow, so to speak, was because she didn't own any of it. She was married to Rhys, but as for her work at Bel Après, she was simply an employee. She got a paycheck twice a month, along with quarterly royalties from her Highland wines, but at the end of the day, she worked for Barbara.

Her house was part of the Barcellona family compound, her truck was winery property. She supposed if she were to suddenly pack up and leave, she could fit everything that was actually hers into a handful of moving boxes and be gone in a few hours.

An unexpectedly sad thought. Not that she was going anywhere. This was home. Rhys was her husband, Stephanie was her best friend and Barbara was pretty much the closest thing to a mother she'd ever had.

She was a Barcellona, she reminded herself. In spirit if not in name. She was a part of the fabric of the family. If sometimes she thought about how nice it would be to buy a few acres just to play with, well, that wasn't going to happen.

There were more footsteps on the stairs. Stephanie and Four joined them. Stephanie sat next to Mackenzie and immediately started talking.

"Carson leaves tomorrow. I don't think I can let him go."

Mackenzie grabbed her friend's hand and smiled. "You do this every summer. He's been going to baseball camp since he was eleven. Yes, you'll miss him, but it's for the greater good. Let him go. It's what he wants."

"You're being rational. I find that offensive."

Mackenzie laughed. "No, you don't."

Stephanie's mouth turned up at the corners. "Okay, I don't,

but why is this so hard? I thought it would get easier. But every summer it's just as painful to know he's leaving."

"You love him and you like having him around."

"I know. I suppose part of it is that he's gone the whole summer. When he gets back, we're two weeks from school starting. Why does camp have to be so long?"

Barbara turned toward them. "Dear God, Stephanie, let it go. We're all aware that you have trouble setting your children free. Catherine, say something about the cycle of life or the universe having angels to take care of teenage boys."

Four smiled. "You'll have more time with Avery. Maybe plan a girls' weekend in Portland or something."

Stephanie brightened. "You're right. That would be fun. Thank you."

"Order restored," Barbara said dryly. "Hallelujah."

She waved her hand as she spoke, her new engagement ring catching the light. Mackenzie leaned forward and touched her hand.

"I didn't get to see your ring up close, at the party. It's lovely."

Barbara splayed her fingers. "I'm still getting used to it, but yes, it is fabulous. Giorgio chose well."

"In his choice of bride as well as his choice of jewelry," Rhys said with a grin.

Stephanie glared at him. "Suck-up."

Barbara sighed. "Children, please."

"Have you decided on any wedding particulars?" Mackenzie asked.

"Something with the family over the holidays," Barbara told her. "I'm not sure. I was thinking small, but now I'm leaning toward ostentatious."

"You should," Mackenzie told her. "You're so very much in love. Everyone can see it."

Barbara's expression softened. "What a lovely thing to say. Thank you."

Lori walked in with five folders in her hand. Mackenzie didn't bother waiting for Barbara's pointed look. She rose and excused herself.

"I'll be home right after," Rhys said, taking the folder from his sister and opening it.

She nodded and waited to see if he would look up from the family's monthly financial report, but he didn't.

"Close the door behind you, Mackenzie," Barbara called.

She did as requested, then retraced her steps to the first floor. As she stepped outside, she calculated how many of those meetings had taken place since she and Rhys had gotten married.

And it was just family. Mackenzie had never attended a single meeting, nor had Jaguar, Four's husband. Nor Kyle, when he and Stephanie had been married.

She selected a golf cart and drove past the tasting room and onto the private road that led to the compound. Vineyards stretched out for as far as the eye could see. The sight of clusters of hard green fruit filled her with anticipation. In a few short months, the grapes would turn color and ripen, and then they would be harvested. An intoxicating scent would linger over the area, sweet with promise of what was to be.

As she approached the compound of four houses in a loose circle, she paused to collect the mail, then drove toward the house she shared with Rhys. In the distance, she saw Jaguar outside playing with his kids.

Overhead the sky was a perfect blue. The temperature had hit ninety, but it would cool off at night. She hit a button on her key chain, and a golf-cart-size garage door rose slowly, allowing her to zip inside.

The house was still and cool. After taking a glass from a cupboard, she filled it with water and ice, then opened the refrigerator to check what was for dinner.

A baking dish held chicken with sun-dried tomatoes and artichoke hearts. Next to that was a salad. On the counter she found a three-by-five card with heating instructions and a peach pie.

The four families shared the services of a professional chef. Chef Betsy came in five days a week. Dinners were left daily, along with the next day's lunch.

Mackenzie turned over the card and saw the next day she would be eating a shaved roast beef and arugula wrap with asiago cheese and a horseradish dressing for lunch. She put the card on the counter and took her water with her as she headed upstairs.

Like many of those who worked outside, she showered at the end of the day. As she tossed her clothes into the hamper and pinned up her hair to avoid the spray, she told herself she was really lucky. She had a pretty amazing life. A husband, a beautiful house, family and friends, a job she loved. Even someone else to do most of the cooking. She was truly blessed, in every way possible. As for those times when she found herself wondering if maybe there was something else out there—well, she should just suck it up and get over herself. Nothing could be better than what she had.

five

Stephanie opened the closet by the front door and pulled the rolled decorative flag out of the corner. As she opened the front door, she gave the pole a little shake to unfurl the flag, then stepped onto the porch and slid the pole into place. A light breeze caught the fabric, causing the print of the giant cookie to ripple slightly.

In addition to the six dozen cookies she'd baked for Carson to take with him, she'd made four dozen more for the family. A few years ago, Mackenzie had started the tradition of putting out a flag whenever she baked cookies. Avery and Carson had gone running to grab a few and bring them home. Now that Zeus, Galaxy and Eternity were big enough to roam the compound, they watched for the cookie flag, as well.

Stephanie went back inside and carried two disposable containers up to her son's room.

Carson's large suitcase was ready to go. His carry-on backpack stood open on the desk. Her son was stretched out on his bed, his gaze locked on his tablet.

"I made you cookies for the trip," she said. "And the first few days of camp."

"Thanks, Mom."

When he didn't raise his gaze, she sighed heavily. "Look at me, Carson."

He did as she requested. She waved the two containers. "These are your cookies. The ones in the red container are peanut butter. You're fourteen, Carson, so I'm trusting you to be responsible with them."

The corners of his lips trembled as if he were trying not to smile. "With cookies, Mom? I think I'm up to the challenge."

"Peanut butter cookies. Just the thought of you carrying them with you makes me break out in a sweat. Remember that some kids are allergic. It's a real thing. Do not go passing them around without talking to everyone first. Peanut butter cookies can trigger nut allergies."

His dark eyes crinkled as he grinned. "Didn't you put walnuts into the chocolate chip cookies?"

"What? Crap. What was I thinking?"

He dropped his tablet onto the bed, stood and wrapped his arms around her. "Mom, don't sweat it. No one I know is allergic to nuts."

"What about at camp? Forget it. You're not taking these with you. No kid is dying on my watch—not because I made cookies."

He took the containers from her hands and dropped them into his backpack. "We'll be fine. I'll make sure everyone I bunk with is okay with nuts. There's four of us in a suite, Mom. The cookies won't last the night."

She knew he could be trusted to be responsible. "Okay, just be careful. Maybe I'll text your counselor."

He winced. "Don't set me up to be that freaky little kid who can't be away from his mommy."

"That's so judgmental."

"You know I'm telling the truth." He zipped up his backpack, then slung it over his shoulder and grabbed his suitcase. "It'll be fine. Have a little faith."

"I should go with you to the airport," she said.

"Mom, stop. I'm driving to Seattle with Grandma and Giorgio. Dad's meeting me there and getting me to my gate. I'm fourteen years old. I'll be fine."

She wanted to protest that he was still her baby, only she knew he wouldn't appreciate that. So instead of telling him he had to stay little forever, she followed him downstairs and found Rhys sitting on a stool by the island. Four and her three kids were there, as well, all eating cookies. Because in this family everyone came by to say goodbye. Mackenzie had stopped by that morning, as had Jaguar, and Avery had seen her brother before she'd gone off to work.

"Excited?" Rhys asked his nephew.

Carson grinned. "Can't wait."

They hugged. Four was next, whispering something in his ear. Carson chuckled but didn't respond. He hugged and kissed his cousins before heading out front. Stephanie went with him.

Right on time her mom and Giorgio pulled in front of her house. Giorgio popped the trunk of the late-model Mercedes and helped Carson with his luggage. Stephanie hugged her youngest.

"Text me the second you get to California," she said. "From the airport and then again when you arrive at camp. If you don't text me, I'll call your counselor and pretend that I'm crying and then you *will* be the freaky little kid who can't be away from his mommy."

Carson sighed. "Mom, you don't have to do that. I'll text you, I swear."

"Threaten to fly down and stay with him," her mother offered from the passenger seat in the car. "Remember when I had to do that with you?"

Stephanie did her best not to shudder at the memory. She'd been a bit chatty in high school and was constantly in trouble for talking to her friends. When the usual punishments—detention and being grounded—hadn't worked, her mother had told her that whatever was happening at school must be so very interesting, what with Stephanie unable to stop talking about it. So Barbara would come with her to every class, unless she could learn to be quiet.

Stephanie hadn't spoken for nearly four days.

"Text me or I'll come stay with you," she told her son. "Look into my eyes and see how much I mean that."

"You're scary sometimes," he told her as he kissed her cheek. "Love you, Mom."

"Love you, too."

She waved at the car until it was out of sight, then walked back into the house to find only Four still in her kitchen.

"They took cookies and ran," Four said cheerfully, pointing at the empty plate. "Sorry if you didn't get any."

Stephanie pulled a second, overflowing plate from the cupboard and placed it between them. She poured them each a cup of coffee from the pot, added cream, then settled next to her sister and picked up a chocolate chip cookie.

"You don't have to stay with me," she said conversationally.

"I'm just here to make sure you're okay."

"I'm fine."

"You're actually not fine. You're sad and worried." Four sipped her coffee. "I don't know how you do it. I couldn't let any of my kids go away for the summer."

"Zeus is only eight. He's too young to go away overnight. But later, if he wants to, you'll let him."

Four shook her head. "Never."

Stephanie smiled. "You will because it will be the best thing for him and you're that kind of mom."

"Don't try to sweet-talk me with rational thought. It doesn't work on me."

"Yes, it does."

"You're very contrary today."

"No, just pensive. I know they're supposed to grow up and have their own lives, but sometimes it's hard. Still, as you've often reminded me, there is a season for everything." She paused, thinking about all that had happened in the past few days. "I'm ready for a new chapter in my life."

Four looked at her speculatively. "What does that mean?"

Even though she'd seen her mother drive away not five minutes before, Stephanie still looked over her shoulder to make sure they were alone.

"I need to get a new job."

Four nibbled her cookie without speaking.

"What?" Stephanie demanded. "You have to say something. You always have an opinion."

"You've made this announcement before," her sister said gently. "I'm not sure you want to leave."

Ugh—there was an assessment she didn't want to hear. "I can't stay. Mom treats me like I'm an idiot. She's always double-checking my work and dismissing any ideas I have about how to make things better. I'm thirty-eight years old. It's time for me to strike out on my own, don't you think?"

"If it's what you want."

Stephanie supposed her sister's inability to believe in her was her own fault. She was the one who had been whining about leaving Bel Après for the past five years and to date she'd done exactly nothing. Zip. Zero. Nada.

"I'm pathetic," she said, pulling her phone from her jeans front pocket. "Or I was, but not anymore."

She scrolled through her emails, stopping when she found the one she was looking for.

"Here." She held out her phone to Four.

Her sister read the note. "You have an interview next week."

"I know. Marington Cheese. It's a small company, but they're determined to grow, and I'd like to be a part of that."

Four glanced back at the email. "Really? Cheese?"

Stephanie tried not to wince. "They make it and sell it. They're artisans. I know it's not wine, but going into that business feels like cheating or something." She took back the phone. "I haven't told Mackenzie."

Four's eyebrows rose. "That's almost more surprising than the interview itself."

"Yes, well, I'll tell her after the fact." Her shoulders rounded as she hunched forward. "It's just she's so damned brilliant at what she does. I think about that and I feel like a failure."

"Everyone is gifted in their own way."

"I'm not. I'm ordinary. Worse, I've settled. She has her wine, you're an amazing artist. If I don't have a special talent, at least I can be brave and get off my butt and do something."

"Then, yay cheese."

Stephanie laughed. "Thanks. I'm doing a lot of research on the industry and coming up with a few marketing plans. It's time I actually used my degree, you know?"

"You'll be brilliant."

"I'd accept getting a decent job offer."

Four tucked her long hair behind her ears. "You should start dating."

"Absolutely not. The last thing I need is a man in my life. I'd be forced to compare that relationship to the one Mom has with Giorgio. I don't need another place to feel that I'm lacking."

"It was a beautiful proposal," Four said. "I wish it was going to work out for them."

Stephanie nearly slid off the stool. "What do you mean? Of course it's going to work out. Why wouldn't it? They're so in love."

"She won't let go. The more she should, the harder she clings to whatever ridiculous idea she has. Giorgio is all about letting go. He loves her, but I don't think he understands who she is. Not really."

"That's really deep."

"I'm feeling a connection to Mother Earth today. It's powerful."

Stephanie reached for her coffee. "Want to give me some lotto numbers? There's got to be a Powerball somewhere."

Four patted her arm. "A, it doesn't work like that and you know it, and B, you don't need the money. Let someone else win. You'll find your joy and happiness in less material ways."

"I think anyone could find joy in fifty million dollars."

She owned her house outright and she had some savings, but she needed to work to pay the bills. Fifty million dollars would—

She held up her hand. "I take it back. I'm going to work to find my place in the world, not wish for it to be given to me. Someone else needs to win that money."

"Personal growth. I'm so proud." Four rose and hugged her. "I'm going to go meditate. I want to take advantage of my connection to Mother Earth today."

"Love you," Stephanie called as Four crossed to the door. "Say hi to Mother Earth from me."

"You could tell her yourself."

"She only likes you."

Four was still laughing when she shut the door behind her.

As far as Barbara was concerned, the Four Seasons Hotel in downtown Seattle was just about perfect. She loved the location, the views, the understated luxury, the staff. She always stayed at the hotel when she came over for business or shopping, but these days the hotel seemed even more wonderful than usual. A fact that had nothing to do with the hotel itself and everything to do with the man who shared her room.

Giorgio, handsome in a hotel robe, pointed to the bottle of champagne resting in the ice bucket. "More, my love?"

She waved her half-empty glass. "In a minute. I'm still trying to catch my breath."

They'd checked in two days ago, after dropping Carson off at the airport. In that time, they'd been to museums, seen a show at the 5th Avenue Theatre and tried new restaurants. But their afternoon trip to Nordstrom had derailed when Giorgio had suggested they order in rather than shop.

After making love, they'd had champagne and small bites sent up to the room. Decadent, she thought with a smile. It was barely one in the afternoon and she'd already had champagne and a man in her bed. Let the millennials have their avocado toast—she would take sex with Giorgio instead, any day.

"What makes you so happy?" Giorgio asked.

She tucked her feet under her, adjusting her silk robe around her legs. "You."

"Good. That's what I want to do."

She studied the lines in his face. She could see the man he'd been when he was younger. He would have been difficult to resist, she thought. Not just because he was attractive, but also because he was strong and caring.

"Tell me about Beth Ann," she said, thinking about how lucky his late wife had been to have so many years with him.

"What do you want to know?"

"Did you have a big wedding?"

He smiled. "We each came from a large Italian family. Yes, it was a big wedding. Three hundred people. Grandparents, aunts, uncles, cousins, friends. The church was overflowing. Our mothers and aunts cooked for days."

"That sounds nice." She sipped her champagne. "James and I had a small wedding. I didn't have any family and we didn't have any money. Do you mind if we have a big wedding?"

His eyes crinkled as he smiled at her. "Your happiness is my happiness, my love. I will be there regardless. I've talked to my children and they are excited to fly in here."

"Thank you for asking them."

"Of course. You remember we'll be flying to New York in a few weeks for Rosemary's birthday."

"I do. I'm looking forward to it."

She'd met his children a few times on their quick visits back east. His two sons were running the family business and his daughter was a pediatrician. Unlike her, he got to be proud of *all* his offspring.

"I'm thinking late fall or maybe over the holidays," she said. "Everyone is too busy around harvest and I don't want to wait until the new year."

"I agree. The sooner I claim you as mine, the better."

She laughed. "I think you do plenty of claiming, Giorgio. Sometimes twice in a day."

He grinned at her. "You know what I mean. I want to spend time with you, Barbara. Just the two of us." He waved his hand toward the walls of the suite. "I appreciate that we get away for a few days, but that's not enough."

She held in a sigh. "You mean work."

"I mean the lack of work. You said you'd start cutting back."

She had said that, she reminded herself. She was supposed to be handing off her responsibilities so she and Giorgio could travel. But who exactly could she trust to run the company? Rhys was busy managing the vineyards, Stephanie had an average skill set, at best. Lori would jump at the opportunity but had the imagination of a flea, and Catherine wasn't worth discussing.

"I should talk to Rhys about hiring someone to take over his job," she said, thinking out loud. "Then he could step in for me."

"You haven't talked to him about that yet?" Giorgio sounded more hurt than angry.

"I've meant to."

He set down his champagne glass. "Barbara, do you want us to spend more time together?"

"Of course. We've talked about traveling together. I look forward to that."

He took her hand in his. "Then I'll make you a deal. You plan the wedding of your dreams and I'll do the same with the honeymoon."

All of which sounded perfectly fine, she thought warily, but wasn't the same thing at all.

"What did you have in mind?" she asked, trying not to sound cautious.

He slid closer. "I've been thinking about a cruise."

"I've never been on a cruise."

"You'll love it. I'll find a wonderful itinerary. I was thinking of Australia and the South Pacific. Maybe we can sail from Los Angeles."

He lowered his head and began to kiss along her neck.

"From Los Angeles," she said, trying to ignore the tingles and heat he evoked. "That's a long cruise."

"Two months."

"What?" she asked with a yelp. "You want us to be gone for two months?"

He straightened and smiled. "No, three months. After that we'll fly to Italy and rent a villa, then explore."

Three months! Was he insane?

"I can't be gone that long," she began. "Bel Après needs me."

He took her champagne glass from her and set it on the coffee table. "You have good people, my love. Give them room to succeed."

Which sounded like something Catherine would say, she thought, fighting a flash of annoyance.

"Three months is ridiculous," she told him.

He untied her robe. When he put his hands on her breasts, she was much less interested in the argument.

"We need to talk about this," she said, but without much conviction.

"We will," he promised as his mouth settled on hers.

She really should insist they talk now, she told herself, then decided it could wait. It seemed that lately sex was always the answer, and why would she want to change that?

six

According to Stephanie's research, the Marington family had been making cheese in eastern Washington for about a hundred years. The milk used to make the cheese came from local cows and nearly half of it was certified organic. They had a good reputation for quality and taste, and from what she could tell, they were looking to expand their brand beyond the local markets and specialty stores. The fourth-generation Maringtons, fraternal twins Jack and Jill—Stephanie had confirmed the unfortunate names—were using social media to make that happen, and they were looking for someone to help with that.

To that end Stephanie had spent the past week studying the company and researching the market. She had three solid campaign ideas and a lot of numbers on cheese consumption, market entry and partnerships. Her plan was to dazzle and get the job offer of her dreams. The fact that the thought of telling her mother she was leaving Bel Après made her slightly sick to her stomach was something she was going to have to ignore. She needed more than she had, and the only way to make that happen was to be proactive. She was hopeful and nervous, but mostly hopeful.

After parking in front of the low, one-story building, she gave herself a twenty-second pep talk, grabbed her handbag and briefcase, and walked inside.

There was no receptionist. Just an open space with a couple of chairs and a hallway leading to several offices. She couldn't see or hear anyone, which made her wonder if she'd gotten the date or time wrong. She called out, "Hello?"

"Hey, Stephanie?" A tall, slim man walked out of one of the offices. He smiled when he saw her. "Right on time. I'm Jack."

They shook hands.

Jack had blond hair and blue eyes. His features weren't unattractive, but there was something very bland about his appearance.

"Good to meet you," he said. "Come on back and let's talk."

She followed him into a cluttered office. Papers were stacked everywhere, including on the only visitor's chair. She waited while he cleared that, trying not to flinch as she inhaled the smell of what could only be called bad cheese.

"There you go." He took the seat on the other side of the desk, glanced at his computer screen, frowned, then turned his attention to her.

"You work at Bel Après," he said. "That's wine. I'm not much of a wine drinker myself, but I know enough to put together a pairing. We send out suggestions of what wines to drink with our cheeses. Our customers like that sort of thing." He stared at her intently, his pale blue eyes watering slightly. "Wine is easy, just so you know. Cheese is hard. I hope you understand that."

She had no idea what to say to that comment, so she settled on a faint smile and nod.

"We're looking to grow the company," he said. "Find different markets, have a bigger online presence. Our cousin Bing has been doing our website. He's a great kid. Computers are his thing, but he doesn't always take care of everything, you know."

"Kid?" Stephanie asked faintly. "As in, he's young?"

"Fourteen. He took over the website when he was eleven. He prefers robotics, but family is family, right?"

Stephanie was saved from having to respond to that by the sound of footsteps in the hall. Seconds later a woman walked into the office. A woman who looked exactly like Jack. Same features, same coloring, same size, same blue shirt and khaki pants. They were identical—except for the whole man-woman thing.

"I'm Jill," the woman said, moving papers off the credenza and sitting there. "You're here about the marketing job, aren't you?"

"Yes."

Jill looked at her brother, her expression peevish. "I've told you, I can handle it."

Jack shook his head. "We've been over this. We need someone with training."

"Oh, please. So she has a college degree. Big whoop. I can do the job in my sleep."

"And yet you don't."

"I'm going to tell Dad what you're up to."

Jack offered Stephanie a tight smile. "You've worked in a family company, so you understand the push-pull dynamics, I'm sure."

Jill turned to Stephanie. "Are you married?"

"I...what?"

"Married. A lot of women try to work here because they want to marry Jack. That's not going to happen. He's not going to be interested in you. He doesn't need you in his life. He has me."

Okay, so now the creep factor was a bigger deterrent than the cheese smell. Whatever hope she'd had crashed to the ground and crawled away. If the interview was going this badly, there was no chance the job was going to work out.

"Jill, come on. She's not here to marry me. She wants a job." He looked at Stephanie. "Why do you want to leave Bel Après?"

"I wanted to challenge myself with something new. Your

expansion plans are exciting, and I was thinking I could help with that."

At least she *had* been thinking that. Now she was much less sure.

Jill stood up. "You're not right for the job. I don't care what Jack says. You can't have it."

Jack glared at her. "This is my interview, not yours. You don't get to say."

"I get as much say as you get. We're equal partners. Besides, you know what Mom and Dad are going to think. They don't like outsiders. I don't know why you even brought her in for the job." Jill looked at Stephanie. "You're not going to get it."

"Okay, then." Stephanie rose and smiled at both of them. "Thank you so much for your time. Good luck with the expansion."

With that, she walked out the way she'd come. Once in her car, she breathed in non-cheese-smelling air and told herself at least there was a bright side. She'd wasted—she glanced at her watch—only eight minutes of her life, not counting the research she'd done and, hey, the drive over. But better to know now rather than quit and take the job only to discover she couldn't make it work.

Which all sounded great but didn't shake her sense of disappointment. She hadn't even had a practice interview. Walla Walla wasn't a big town, so there weren't a lot of marketing jobs available, especially with her excluding the wine industry. So she was back to where she'd started—working for her mother and wishing for something more.

Mackenzie poured single malt Scotch into two glasses and carried them into Rhys's study. He stood behind his desk, sorting through the mail. She'd already looked at it herself, and there was nothing to concern her. A utility bill that he would pay and some flyers for local real estate for sale. The Walla Walla area was growing and the housing market had heated up.

When she set the glass on his desk, he smiled at her. "Thanks."

They moved to the sofa and sat at opposite ends.

"The drip system is fixed," he told her. "You'll want to drive out in the next few days and look it all over."

She smiled. "Because I don't trust your work?"

"Because you like to be sure."

She did and she *would* check. Her need to oversee all aspects of the vineyards had nothing to do with his ability and everything to do with her slightly obsessive nature.

"I heard one of the big grocery store chains applied for a permit," he said. "They're building down by that new development."

"That will make the people who live there happy. I was just thinking how the area is growing."

"It is."

They looked at each other, then away. Silence descended, making her uncomfortable. She and Rhys had always ended their days together, talking about what was going on in the vineyard and in town. But lately, conversation seemed harder to come by and she wasn't sure why. They were married, they loved each other. Surely there was something to talk about that wasn't work.

"Your mom texted," she said to fill the empty space. "She and Giorgio are staying an extra day in Seattle."

"Good for them."

She nodded. "They seem really happy and in love."

"They do."

She glanced at her husband and was surprised to find him looking at her with unexpected intensity.

"What?" she asked.

"Nothing. Just thinking about my mom. Who would have guessed she would meet someone so many years after my dad died?"

"You're not upset, are you?"

"No. I'm glad she won't be alone. Giorgio takes good care of her. It's just…" He looked away and the silence returned.

She set down the glass and wondered when everything had changed for them. They had been happy once.

"Do you think we—"

"Are you ever—"

They both stopped talking.

"You first," Rhys said.

She drew in a breath, wanting to ask the question and yet terrified of his answer. "Was it ever like that with us? The way they are with each other?"

He didn't meet her gaze. "I don't know. Maybe."

There was no maybe, she thought. If it had been like that, wouldn't they both remember? Would it be helping them now? A past filled with that much love and passion would smooth over the rough spots.

"I know you're not happy," he said quietly.

"Neither are you."

There was a finality to those words, she thought sadly. Or maybe just hopelessness.

He glanced at her, then away. "I still love you, Mackenzie."

"I love you, too."

Which should have been enough, she thought, suddenly over-whelmed with a sense of sadness so profound, she had trouble breathing. But it wasn't enough, because the love they were talking about wasn't passionate or even romantic. Not anymore. They were friends, not lovers. Companions rather than a ro-mantic couple, and while marriages ebbed and flowed, theirs seemed to be draining away on a daily basis.

Rhys stood. She thought he was going to walk out of the room but instead he moved in front of her and pulled her to her feet. His arms came around her and he kissed her.

The action was so unexpected, she didn't know how to react.

The pressure of his mouth was insistent and she instinctively parted her lips.

He plunged his tongue into her mouth, stroking and seeking. At the same time, he moved his hands up and down her back before cupping her butt and pulling her against him. She was shocked to realize he had an erection.

She had no idea what to think or feel or how to act. Nothing he was doing was the least bit arousing but it was clear he wanted to have sex, and it had been literally years and they were married and saying no felt mean and punitive, somehow, even though that wouldn't have been how she meant it.

She ignored the awkwardness and the need to withdraw, instead putting her hands on his shoulders and kissing him back, leaning into him, rubbing her belly against his arousal, wishing she felt something. Anything. But she didn't. There was only a sense of duty and not wanting to hurt Rhys because, honest to God, the man hadn't done anything wrong.

He raised his head and stared at her. His eyes were dilated, his breathing heavy. She knew what he wanted. Nothing extraordinary—just sex with his wife. It had been so long since they'd been intimate. Guilt at that fact made her smile at him and hold out her hand. He took it and led her upstairs.

He led her into his bedroom. They went to opposite sides of the bed and quickly undressed. Mackenzie tried to remember the last time they'd done this. Had it been four years? Five? She wasn't sure which had come first—the separate bedrooms or the not having sex. Not that it much mattered.

They slid into bed. Rhys pulled her close and kissed her. As his tongue tangled with hers, he cupped her breast and began teasing her nipple. After a minute or so, she felt the first flicker of interest low in her belly. A whisper of desire and the thought that maybe this really was a good idea. She relaxed into the sensation, willing it to grow. Maybe sex would help them find their way back to each other.

"Are you ready?" he asked eagerly, shifting her onto her back and moving between her legs. Before she could answer, he was pushing inside.

She wasn't close to ready. The first two thrusts were painful, but then her body adjusted. She moved in time with his movements and tried to get into what he was doing, but there wasn't time. As he moved faster inside of her, obviously getting closer, she thought briefly about faking an orgasm, but before she could decide or get started on the process, he groaned and was still.

For nearly a minute, his rapid breathing was the only sound in the room.

He withdrew and looked at her. "You didn't come."

"It's okay."

"Let me get cleaned up and I can do something."

He moved to his side and took a box of tissues out of the drawer. He passed her a couple, then took a few for himself. After pulling on his underwear, he returned to the bed and faced her.

"Mackenzie, I want to make you come." He gave her a wry smile. "I was a little rushed before because it's been a long time."

He sounded so earnest. Because Rhys always took care of her. She thought about what it would take to get her over the edge and knew she didn't want to go there. What was the point? Whatever interest she'd had was gone, leaving only a sense of sadness and a ridiculous urge to cry.

"It *has* been a while, but I'm okay."

His smile faded. "You don't want me to?"

She shook her head.

He stared at her. Just when she was about to ask what he was thinking, she saw tears in *his* eyes.

"It's over, isn't it?" he asked quietly. "Our marriage. We're done."

It was as if he'd hit her in the stomach. She couldn't breathe and she fought the instinctive need to curl into a protective ball and cover her head. Her body went cold and she thought she might throw up. Even as she told herself to run, she knew she couldn't possibly stand without crumbling to the ground.

"I'm sorry," he said quickly. "God, I'm sorry. I thought that's what you were thinking. Mackenzie, I'm sorry. I take it back. I swear, I take it back."

He couldn't, she thought, stunned by what he'd said. There was no taking it back. Horror joined shock as the truth crashed into her. He'd breathed life into the very thing they'd both avoided for a long time and now it was alive and they had to deal with it. *She* had to deal with it. With what they no longer had and how the speaking, the acknowledging, would change everything.

She wanted to reach into the past and pull the words away, crumbling them in her hands so they no longer existed or had power over her, but it was too late.

When she was reasonably sure she wouldn't shatter, she sat up, careful to pull the sheet with her. The tightness in her chest eased enough for her to catch her breath, as she tried to make sense of what he'd said.

Rhys thought their marriage was over. He thought they were done. And if he thought that, then they were, because it took two people to be in a marriage. It took two people to—

"You're right," she whispered, staring at him. The shock faded enough for her to feel the sadness of the moment and maybe a little of the inevitability. It was done. They were done.

She sat with the truth, wondering how to get through this moment and the next and all the moments that would follow. Who was she if not married to Rhys? Being with him informed her life, the rhythm of her days. Without that, what did she have? He had been a part of her for her entire adult life. If that was gone, how would the hole he left ever fill in?

His tears returned. Without thinking, she reached for him. He did the same and they hung on to each other. She breathed in his familiar scent, felt the heat of his body and knew this was very likely the last time they would be naked together. Not in a sexual way, although that was true, too, but in a bared-to-the-soul kind of way. As soon as they let go, everything would change because there was no going back.

She didn't know how long they clung to each other or who leaned back first, but eventually they untangled and they were simply two people, staring at each other.

"I'm sorry," he repeated.

"Stop saying that. You don't have to be. You're right—it *is* over. I've known it somewhere inside, I just never articulated it, even to myself."

"I don't want to hurt you."

"You didn't."

"I did. I meant what I said before. I love you, Mackenzie."

She looked into his eyes. "But it's not enough anymore, is it? Our love is different. It's not what your mother has with Giorgio."

His mouth twisted. "You saw that, too?"

"How in love they are? Yes, and while I was happy for them, being around them made me feel sad."

He nodded. "The contrast. It made everything clear for me." He hesitated. "We don't have to do anything right away. We can take our time figuring it out. You know that a divorce won't change your position at Bel Après." He gave her a faint smile. "If my mother has to choose between the two of us, she's going to pick you. We both know that."

Divorce? Her position at Bel Après?

Reality gave her the second blow of the evening and she was no more prepared this time. If their marriage was over, of course they would be getting a divorce. That was what people did. And if she and Rhys weren't married, then she would have to move out and…and…

"Don't," he said quickly. "Nothing has to change."

"Everything has to change," she told him, feeling her chest tighten. "Everything."

He took her hand in his. "It doesn't. We don't have to decide anything tonight. Let's pretend we didn't talk about it."

"We can't." She looked at their hands, the familiar way they were clasped, then carefully pulled free. "You want a divorce."

He hesitated before nodding slowly.

She braced herself for the logical question. No, not the question. The answer.

"Is there someone else?"

Rhys drew back, his eyes wide. "Did I cheat? God, no. I wouldn't do that. I've never done that."

She believed him because of who he was. "But you wanted to."

"Haven't you?" He motioned to the space between them. "We haven't had sex in years. We're roommates, not a married couple. Yes, I've wanted to meet someone and fall in love. Hell, at this point, I would be happy just to have regular sex with pretty much anyone."

The words rained down like shards of glass, slicing her heart with wounds so deep, they would never heal.

"I'm sorry," she whispered. "I didn't know you were that unhappy."

"It's not your fault. We did this together. We're both to blame. Somehow everything we had got lost."

She nodded because her throat hurt too much for her to speak. Not just her throat—every part of her. She was shaking and sick and broken. Desperately broken.

"I can't talk about this anymore," she whispered. "I can't. Maybe tomorrow, if that's okay."

"Not tomorrow," he told her. "Take a few days, a few weeks. Like I said, nothing has to change, Mackenzie."

"You're wrong. Nothing can stay the same. We can't unsee this. What we've said... There's no going back. I just need some time to figure out what moving forward is going to look like."

He nodded. "What can I do to help?"

She shook her head and got out of bed. For the first time in sixteen years, she was uncomfortable being naked in front of him. She quickly pulled on her clothes, feeling the seeping dampness between her thighs—proof of the sex.

This had been their last time, she thought grimly, as she put on her bra. They would never do it again. Pain and regret clutched at her, making her wish she'd let him bring her to orgasm. Not because she wanted the release but because it would have been something good they would have shared. It would have connected them, at least for a moment.

Afterward he would have smiled at her the way he always did—that totally male "I'm the man" smile. A combination of pride and happiness that came with knowing he'd pleased his partner. She wanted to see that smile just once more and now she wouldn't.

After pulling on her shirt and fastening her jeans, she picked up her socks. "I'm going to go to my room."

"Don't you want dinner?"

"I'm not hungry." She held up a hand. "I'm all right. I just need some time alone."

"Okay. I'll be here if you need me."

They looked at each other. Tears filled Rhys's eyes again. Her own burned.

She wanted to throw herself at him, to have him hold her and tell her everything was going to be fine. Only she couldn't. Not anymore. And if he said the words, he would be lying. So instead, she hurried out into the hallway and made her way to her own bedroom. Once inside, she carefully closed the door behind her, then collapsed onto the floor and gave in to the pain. Cries turned to sobs, shaking her entire body as, deep in her chest, her shattered heart broke into a thousand pieces.

seven

Stephanie pulled the small glass jar of ginger-infused simple syrup from the refrigerator. She and Mackenzie went all out when it came to their monthly Girls' Nights. Drinks, snacks and plenty of honest talk. Tonight she would be confessing the interview debacle and letting her best friend's sympathy and caring help heal the lingering disappointment. Mackenzie would tell her she wasn't trapped and right now she needed to hear that.

"So you're going out but I can't?"

Stephanie looked up as her daughter walked into the kitchen. Avery had always been a pretty child, but in the past couple of years, she'd turned into a real beauty. She had dark hair and big brown eyes. Apparently the Barcellona chubby-female curse had skipped a generation because Avery was thinner than either of her aunts.

Not that she would say any of that. Avery had been nothing but annoying all week.

"You know the rules," she said instead. "No boy–girl parties unless I talk to the parents and confirm there will be supervision."

"That's not fair."

"It is to me."

Avery flipped her long hair over her shoulder and glared. "You're a terrible mother."

"You used to be a wonderful kid. I really miss your My Little Pony stage. You were so sweet and we had so much fun together." She smiled. "Disappointment is multigenerational. That should give you comfort."

"Not enough. I want to go to the party. Alexander said it's going to be the best party of the summer."

Alexander was Avery's current boyfriend. They'd lasted past two months, so it was serious. Something else Stephanie got to worry about.

"No party unless I talk to the parents. Give me their number or resign yourself to staying home." She picked up the small tote with the drink supplies. "I'll be back by eleven."

"Whatever."

Avery flounced out of the room. Stephanie sighed, knowing it wasn't the last time she would have to say no to a party. It was going to be a very long, difficult summer. She could only hope that her daughter would be distracted by her new job working on the retail side of the Bel Après gift shop.

She carried her small tote through the house and out the front door. From there it was only a few steps to Mackenzie's house, where they had their evenings. The kid-free zone made it easy, and while Rhys was usually home, he pretty much stayed in his office.

She let herself in the unlocked door and called, "It's me."

"In the kitchen."

Stephanie walked through the large two-story foyer and into the spacious kitchen. It was the mirror image of her own. Her house, Mackenzie's and Four's were variations of the same floor plan. Four's had an extra bedroom and a big workspace over the garage while Mackenzie and Rhys had fewer bedrooms but two offices.

Mackenzie stood at the refrigerator, pulling out a prepared cheese plate their chef had left for them. Betsy always put together delicious snacks for their evenings, including appetizers that could be heated in the oven and then served.

"Hi," Stephanie said, dropping her tote and holding out her arms. "I need a hug."

Mackenzie smiled, then obliged, holding her tight. "Bad day?"

"Just some snipping from Avery. She's such a teenager."

"She'll outgrow it."

"I hope so. We don't actually fight, but there's sure plenty of bickering." She stepped back. "You're lucky. Your grapes don't talk back."

"I know, but they can get mold, which is hard to deal with. Carson and Avery seem mold-free."

"I'll try to keep that in mind the next time she makes me want to scream."

Stephanie put the simple syrup on the island. Mackenzie already had out rum and ginger ale, along with glasses and plates.

"We have cheddar crab puffs in the oven," Mackenzie said. "They need another ten minutes."

"I'll mix the drinks while we wait."

She squeezed lime quarters into a martini shaker, then added mint and blueberries. After muddling the mixture, she added rum and some simple syrup. Mackenzie had already put ice into two glasses. Stephanie shook the martini shaker, then poured the strained mixture into the glasses and topped it with a bit of ginger ale.

"You want me to talk to her?" Mackenzie asked. "Four and I could take Avery to lunch and find out if there's anything specific bothering her or if this is just usual teenage stuff."

Stephanie handed her a glass. "I'd love that. Thank you. Right now I'm the last person she'll confide in. And while you're at it, try to find out if she and Alexander are having sex. She swears they're not, but would she really tell me?"

"I'll do my best," Mackenzie told her. "But I can't promise she'll say anything."

"I know, but I appreciate any help. You're so good with her."

Mackenzie was good with all the kids, Stephanie thought, still surprised she and Rhys had never decided to have any of their own. Early on in their relationship there had been talk, but nothing had ever happened. She wondered briefly if her friend ever regretted that, but she wasn't sure how to ask. Before she could figure out a way, the timer dinged.

"Crab puffs," Mackenzie said, grabbing a hot pad and opening the oven.

It took only a few minutes to carry their food to the family room. They settled in familiar seats on the large sectional sofa with their snacks on the glass table in front of them. Sunlight spilled in from the big floor-to-ceiling windows.

Stephanie raised her glass. "Happy Thursday. My life sucks."

Something flickered in Mackenzie's eyes. "That's not true. Your life is great."

"I wish. Ignoring the ongoing Avery issue, I had a job interview a couple of days ago."

"What? You didn't tell me. Where? What happened? Did you get the job? Are you leaving?"

Stephanie held up her hand. "Nothing happened. I don't have a job, I'm not leaving. In fact, I'm probably never leaving because I can't seem to motivate myself, and when I finally do try to do something else, it all goes to shit."

She paused and looked at her glass. "Wow, I have attitude and I haven't even tasted my drink. I apologize in advance if I get bitchy with the alcohol." She took a sip of the cocktail and sighed. "And I didn't tell you about the interview because I was embarrassed."

"Why would you say that?"

"It was with cheese."

Mackenzie smiled. "You had an interview with cheese?"

"No, with Marington Cheese. A brother and sister are running it, sort of. Jack and Jill. They're fraternal twins who look and dress alike and are way too codependent."

She told Mackenzie about the very brief interview. Mackenzie winced when she explained about the "You can't marry him because he has me" comment.

"That's scary. You wouldn't have been happy there."

"That's what I tell myself, but it's not like there are a lot of options in Walla Walla. Tri-Cities is bigger but that would mean an hour commute each way. Am I totally spoiled by saying I don't want to drive that far?"

"Yes, but it's understandable. Plus in winter, you'd be fighting the snow." Mackenzie put down her drink. "You know what I'm going to say, right?"

"Ack. Yes. Look at the wine industry."

"It's king. You could easily find a job if you were willing to work with what you know."

"It's not the knowledge thing, it's the Bel Après thing. I would feel like I was betraying my mother." She leaned back against the sofa and groaned. "I can't believe I just said that. Like she cares. I doubt she would even notice I was gone. I'm being stupid. Just say it. You think I'm an idiot."

She waited for a funny response, but Mackenzie only stared at her intently.

"What?" Stephanie asked. "What's wrong?"

"Nothing. I love you so much. I want you to know that. You're a wonderful friend and I'm grateful you're in my life. I don't want that to change."

"It's not going to. Me getting a job somewhere else, assuming I ever get off my ass and make that happen, won't change anything. I'll be right here." She studied her sister-in-law. "Are you okay? Did something happen?"

"I'm fine. It's just, you know, things change. Look at Avery. And you had an interview. That's huge. I'm so proud of you."

"Thanks. I just need to figure out what to do. It's weird, but I feel like Giorgio's proposal shifted my worldview or something. Does that make sense?"

Mackenzie stared at her drink. "I know exactly what you mean. There was something so powerful in that moment—it put all our lives in perspective."

"And not in a good way," Stephanie grumbled. "I have a meeting with my mother on Saturday. We're going to talk about her wedding. There are no words to describe my lack of joy at the thought of getting through the wedding planning with her. I have no idea why I said I would help."

"Because she's your mom and you love her."

"Maybe, but I don't like her very much."

Mackenzie grinned. "No one does, sweetie. Don't worry about it. You'll do great and the wedding will be beautiful."

"I should get you to plan it," Stephanie said. "She'd agree to everything and adore it because it came from you."

She expected Mackenzie to laugh, but instead her friend's humor faded and her face paled.

"What?" Stephanie asked, sitting up straight. "There's something."

"Sorry. My period. I'm cramping."

"You sure?"

Mackenzie looked at her. "I could show you proof but it would be gross."

"You're right. Okay, finish your drink and I'll make us a second round. We'll drink to the thrill of being women and try to figure out what God was thinking when he invented menstruation."

Barbara ran her hands across the front of the binder Stephanie had handed her. The picture of the happy bride and groom on a beach at sunset should have been far too obvious for her taste, but instead of being annoyed by the photograph, she found herself happy and excited.

"This notebook will help keep all the information about the wedding in one place," Stephanie told her. "I have the same thing on my tablet. Whenever we make a decision, we'll update both."

They were in Barbara's dining room. Stephanie had arrived with three overflowing tote bags filled with magazines, folders and what looked like several table linen samples. Barbara would never admit it out loud, but she was impressed. She knew her daughter had handled at least a dozen weddings at Bel Après over the past few years. She couldn't remember any disasters, and the Solstice Party had gone well. Maybe she should assume the best about Stephanie and relax about the wedding. If worse came to worst, she could step in to run things herself.

But for now, she would play at being the bride and enjoy being taken care of. She appreciated that Stephanie understood the importance of the meeting. Despite the fact that it was a Saturday morning, Stephanie had dressed in an office-appropriate floral-print dress. She had on makeup and her long hair was pulled back in a low ponytail.

She was the prettiest of her three girls, Barbara thought. Catherine could be a beauty, if she wasn't so damned odd all the time. Her taste was appalling. Half the time she wore overalls with some ripped-up T-shirt. As if she and her family couldn't afford normal clothing. And she didn't want to get herself started on how those children of Catherine's dressed. When she was younger, Galaxy had spent an entire summer wearing a ridiculous bumblebee costume and Catherine had let her.

As for Lori, well, she was an ongoing problem. She certainly dressed professionally enough at work, but she always looked so frumpy. Maybe it was because she was fat. That girl put on five or ten pounds a year. In another decade, she was going to be as big as a house. Barbara held in a sigh. Where had she gone wrong?

She shook off the question and focused on what Stephanie was saying.

"The flow of most weddings is fairly traditional," her daughter explained. "A ceremony, followed by a reception. The wedding can be family only, with a larger reception to follow, or you can invite everyone to both. The reception dinner can be a sit-down with servers or buffet-style. We can have a DJ or a live band. It's all available."

Barbara almost felt light-headed by the possibilities. "No buffet," she said firmly. "That I know for sure. Otherwise, I just don't know. What do you think?"

Stephanie dug in one of the totes and pulled out several very thick bridal magazines. "Start with these. Look at the dresses, of course, but read the articles. They'll talk about everything from the right kind of makeup to how to have a themed wedding."

Barbara glared at her. "Have you lost your mind? Why would I want to do that?"

Stephanie grinned. "You wouldn't. My point is it's been a long time since we had a wedding in this family. When Mackenzie and Rhys got married, they wanted something simple. Only friends and a few family members."

"I remember," Barbara said, remembering the small but elegant event. She and Mackenzie had planned it all together, from the menu to the music. Mackenzie had even recycled Barbara's old wedding dress into something more stylish. "It was beautiful."

"But small and low-key," Stephanie pointed out. "You're going to want to make more of a statement."

Her daughter's perception surprised her. "You're right—I am. Not gaudy, of course, but with maybe two or three hundred people." She drew her lips together. "Nothing rushed, like your wedding."

Stephanie startled her by glancing at her watch and chuckling. "Ten minutes, Mom. Impressive. I thought it would take you at least twenty to bring up the fact that Kyle and I got married because I was pregnant. It's nice that we can still surprise each other."

"Are you being smart with me?"

"Would I do that?" She was still smiling as she pushed the magazines across the table. "These will help you get into the wedding swing of things. Once we know when, where, and how many guests, we can start narrowing down options."

Barbara nodded. "I want the wedding and reception here," she said. "Of course if it's over the holidays, it has to be indoors and I'm not sure we have a big enough space for that. Yes, you're correct. Those are the three most important decisions."

She paused for a moment, then added, "Don't talk to your sisters about this. I don't want either of them influencing you. Lori has the taste of a kangaroo and we all know that anything Catherine suggests would drive me mad."

"Don't worry. You're the bride, so you decide."

Barbara eyed her. "Are you seeing anyone? If you're not, you might want to get on that. You'll want a date for the wedding."

Stephanie laughed. "So that's the reason I should start seeing someone?"

"It's as good a reason as any. Plus, it's nice to have a man in one's life. I'd forgotten." Giorgio made her feel so many wonderful things, and not just in bed. Although she wouldn't discuss any of that with her daughter. "Let me know if you get involved with someone and it seems serious. I'll have him investigated."

"I can't decide if you're kidding or not."

"I'm not kidding. Why would I kid? If you get involved with someone and there's a chance the relationship might go somewhere, we will need to know about his background. Who is he? Who are his parents and siblings? What about his past? Is he a criminal? Did he do drugs?"

"You're assuming I couldn't figure that out for myself. Why would I date a drug-dealing criminal?"

Barbara waved away the question. "This isn't about you, darling. It's about being safe. I had Giorgio investigated when I realized we were going to be seeing each other when we came back to the States. It's a sensible thing to do." She smiled. "Giorgio understands how things are. He's already offered to sign a prenup. I didn't have to ask."

"How romantic."

Barbara narrowed her gaze. "Despite what you think, it's very romantic. Giorgio loves me and wants to take care of me. Not just in bed, but in every way, including protecting the family and the winery. I would think you would appreciate that. The land and the children are what matter."

"In that order," Stephanie said dryly.

"Children leave. The land is forever. But speaking of children, is Avery still seeing that boy?"

"Alexander?"

"Is he the blond one? Is he the least bit intelligent? You've talked to her about birth control, haven't you? We don't need another unplanned pregnancy in the family."

"Wow, Mom. When do you slow down enough to catch your breath?"

Barbara heard the hint of annoyance in her daughter's tone.

"I know you don't appreciate me butting in," Barbara said sharply. "But I'm saying all this for your own good, and for Avery's. You've always been a decent mother. This isn't the time to relax and simply let things happen. You have to stay firm and guide her."

"Because that worked so well for us?"

Barbara stared at her daughter, not sure if the comment was meant sincerely. She looked at the wedding magazines and the linen samples and knew they still had the rest of the meeting to get through. Perhaps she should back off and make her case another time.

"You turned out very well," she said, trying to sound gracious. "I'm sure Avery will do the same."

"Interesting." Stephanie hesitated, as if not sure she was willing to pass on the fight. Then she nodded and pulled a large piece of paper out of her tote bag and unfolded it. After smoothing it on the table between them, she pointed to the floor plan of the tasting area, the retail space and all the private rooms.

"Having a wedding between harvest and late spring means it has to be indoors. We have the private event room, which is big enough for a reception of up to a hundred people." She pointed to the room on the drawing. Small circles represented tables.

"You said two to three hundred people, which makes more sense to me. This is the wedding of Barbara Barcellona—people will be fighting for an invitation."

Barbara hoped that was true.

Stephanie continued. "So I had a crazy idea. If we use the event room for the ceremony, we can easily fit in three hundred guests. Then we'd hold the reception in the tasting and retail space."

She put down another large sheet of paper, showing the floor plan of that area and where the tables would go.

"We can move out all the inventory and the shelves, and empty most of the wine. I think it will take three days to get everything ready and three more days to put it all back. Assuming the wedding is on Saturday and no one works on Sunday, we're talking about having the tasting room closed for just over a week." She smiled. "It's up to you, but knowing how much Bel Après means to you, I wanted to find a way to give you the wedding of your dreams right here."

Barbara touched her daughter's hand. "It's lovely. A wonderful idea. Yes, let's do that. Then I can have my holiday wedding."

Maybe the Saturday before Christmas, when the tasting room

was decorated to look like a winter wonderland. She and Giorgio could then have a beautiful tropical honeymoon for a couple of weeks. Three at the most.

She thought briefly of his claim to want to have her to himself for three entire months. How ridiculous. There was no way she could be gone that long—she had responsibilities and a life. But three weeks would be perfect. Maybe they could go to that place with the little huts on the water. She would like that.

"Great," Stephanie said. "I'll start working on specific dates and pulling together some ideas. You'll want to start thinking about your dress." She tapped the magazines. "You'll get a lot of ideas in these."

Barbara eyed the magazines and enjoyed her sense of anticipation. "I'll start looking at them tonight."

"I look forward to hearing what you ultimately decide." Stephanie scanned her tablet. "Do you want bridesmaids?"

Barbara tilted her head. "I never thought about that. I could have my four girls." Her mouth tightened. "But only if I get to pick what everyone wears."

Stephanie would look good in anything, she thought. As would Mackenzie. "Avery is old enough to be a bridesmaid, but Galaxy and Eternity are too young. No, just the adults in the ceremony. When does Avery start applying for college? Is it this fall?"

"She's only a junior. She applies next year."

"What is she thinking? I know WSU is the closest and most obvious, but it might be good for her to go out of state. Get some fresh ideas. UC Davis has an excellent wine program."

"She hasn't said she wants to go into the family business, Mom. Let her come to that on her own."

"Don't be ridiculous. It has to be Avery. Carson isn't going to have anything but baseball in his head. If not her, then who? Do you really expect me to turn Bel Après over to Catherine's wild children?"

"One of them might have the passion for it, Mom."

Passion my ass, Barbara thought grimly. The way those children were being educated, she wasn't sure any of them even knew how to read. There was no way they would be prepared to run Bel Après.

"Back to the wedding," Stephanie said, waving a picture of a large four-tiered cake. "There are so many options with cakes these days. Traditional, of course, but also cupcakes."

Barbara looked at her. "You can't distract me with cake. I'm not five."

"But I can try." She put down a picture of a wedding cake made up of cupcakes, which was much nicer than Barbara would have thought. "These could be super cute."

Barbara raised her eyebrows. "Does anything in my life inspire the phrase 'super cute'?"

"No, but it could become a thing."

Barbara surprised herself by laughing. "Fine. We can talk about cupcakes as much as you want, but I'll be ordering a traditional cake."

eight

Monday morning Stephanie walked through the retail area that shared space with the tasting room. It was early—barely after eight. The tasting room didn't open until ten and the staff didn't arrive until nine. For the next hour the lack of customers and employees meant she could work in peace and get a clear idea of what had sold over the weekend.

Summer was busy at the winery. Tourists flocked to the area, standing four and five deep at the tasting bar and snapping up the glasses, tea towels and other kitchen and barware they offered. Printed inventory sheets gave her an up-to-the-minute accounting of sales. The more expensive glassware moved briskly, as did the wine openers, foil cutters and stoppers. But the real winners in terms of volume were the tea towels.

They regularly stocked six different designs, with a rotating seasonal stock. All the towels had an excellent markup, so much so that even on sale they were profitable. Barbara hated the tea towels, but she couldn't argue with the money they brought in. Sometimes Stephanie chose an especially whimsical design—just to annoy her mother. More often than not, it sold better than any of the more traditional designs. This summer she'd gone with a floral and ladybug theme, and based on the numbers, they were kicking some serious retail butt.

The tasting room at Bel Après had been remodeled four years ago. They'd increased the square footage, doubled the length of the tasting bar and added more retail items. Stephanie had wanted to include a small café in the remodel. Nothing fancy— just delicious food that could be taken off the premises or enjoyed on a few tables she'd wanted to put outside, in the shade.

She'd put together a business plan, including costs and sales projections. She'd even come up with a sample menu that included picnic baskets filled with things like ham and figs, gourmet sandwiches, and grilled corn with flavored butters and salads.

A lot of the larger wineries in the area offered lunches to go and she knew they were successful. But Barbara had simply shaken her head and muttered something about Stephanie's delusions of grandeur before moving on to the next item on the agenda.

Stephanie supposed that was when she'd stopped trying to grow her end of the business. Her mother was in charge and all Barbara cared about was the wine. So Stephanie found pleasure in small things, like ladybug tea towels that her mother found annoying. Not her proudest moment, but sometimes it was all she had left. Occasionally she opened the idea files on her computer and researched things like how to expand into the Chinese market. She'd put together an entire package on enticing Chinese tourists to visit the area, with Bel Après as the highlight of the trip. She knew it was a waste of time—her mother would never consider it. But there were days when Stephanie wanted to do more than go through the motions.

Leaving was the obvious solution, she told herself. She thought about what Mackenzie had said—that in this part of the state wine was king. She did know the industry, but could she work for a competitor? That would be a fight to end all fights. She supposed the very sad but realistic bottom line was that she wasn't willing to take on her mother. Which left her completely trapped. And if that wasn't grim enough, she knew she had only herself to blame.

With that depressing thought on her mind, she retreated to the break room, where she'd made coffee when she'd first come in. She poured a cup and walked to the window that overlooked the shaded grassy area dotted with a handful of picnic tables the employees used on their breaks. She imagined the grass replaced with pavers, some kind of pergola providing additional coverings, an outdoor wine bar and nicer tables and chairs.

"Not this week," she murmured to herself. "Or ever."

"Stephanie?"

The sound of Mackenzie's voice broke through her self-pity party.

"In the break room. There's coffee."

Her sister-in-law walked in and tried to smile. Stephanie took one look at her and knew something was wrong. Mackenzie's normally bright eyes were red—as if she hadn't been sleeping or, worse, she'd been crying. Her skin was pale and there was a slump to her shoulders that wasn't anything Stephanie had seen before.

"What?" Stephanie demanded. "Something's happened. Tell me."

Instead of brushing off the concern, Mackenzie motioned to one of the tables. "We should sit down."

Stephanie's stomach dropped and her body went stiff. There *was* something and it was bad. She knew it. Her mind searched for possibilities. Mackenzie didn't have any family, so there wasn't an unexpected death. Was it medical? Had Mackenzie had a doctor's appointment with bad news? No, it was early on a Monday morning—she couldn't have gotten news today and if there'd been something last week, she would have mentioned it sooner. They'd seen each other like five times during the weekend.

When they were seated across from each other, Mackenzie cleared her throat. Tears filled her eyes before she blinked them away.

"You're scaring me," Stephanie said, reaching for her hand. "Just say it."

"It's not awful," Mackenzie said quickly. "I mean it is, but it's not lethal. No one knows and I don't want anyone to know. Not yet. I'm still processing."

Stephanie stared at her, waiting, her sense of dread growing.

"Rhys and I are getting a divorce."

The words took a second to sink in. Stephanie heard them but couldn't understand what they meant.

"You're not," she said. "You can't be. You're fine."

Mackenzie's mouth twisted. "I wish that were true. Things haven't been right between us for a while. We've drifted apart, and somewhere along the way, we lost our marriage."

"No." Stephanie pulled back her hand. "No, you didn't. You're fine. I've seen you together and it's like it always was. You were dancing at the party."

This wasn't happening. She didn't want it to be happening. "You can't get a divorce. That will change everything. We're sisters. You live here. You've always lived here. You can't change it."

Even as she spoke, she knew she was getting it all wrong. This wasn't about her—this was about Mackenzie—but no matter what she told herself, she couldn't get past how the news rocked her world.

"We're a family. We have traditions. We have Girls' Night and we work together. I see you all the time. What about family dinners and my kids? Are you just going to walk away from that?" Another thought occurred to her—one that was more shattering. "Are you leaving? Are you leaving Bel Après?"

"I don't know. I haven't thought that far ahead. This just came up a couple of days ago and I've been trying to deal with it. I wish you could understand that this is horrible for me. I'm devastated. Rhys and your family and Bel Après are all I know."

Stephanie stood. "Then make it stop. Get counseling. Fix it. Don't get a divorce. You'll change everything and it will be terrible. How could you do this to me?"

Mackenzie stared at her, wide-eyed. Anger replaced the sadness. "This isn't about you, Stephanie. I just told you my marriage is over and all you can talk about is how *you* feel? What about me? Rhys is the only man I've ever loved and we're splitting up. I might lose my home and my job, and you want to talk about Girls' Night?"

Mackenzie stood. "You're my best friend. How could you be so selfish? I thought I could count on you. I thought you cared about me. I've been wrong about everything."

The words were a slap. Shame overrode the shock, bringing Stephanie back to reality, but before she could say anything, Mackenzie was gone, leaving only the realization that nothing would ever be the same again.

Mackenzie couldn't decide if she felt more sick or more drained. She'd thought she was handling the situation well, dealing and trying to figure out the next step, but all that had gone to crap when she'd tried to talk to Stephanie. Her friend, her *best* friend, hadn't been there for her, leaving her feeling desperate, alone and afraid.

Despite the hot morning and sunny skies, she was cold. Every part of her still hurt and she couldn't quiet her swirling mind. Under other circumstances, she would have assumed she was coming down with something, but she knew her symptoms had nothing to do with a summer virus and everything to do with the painful realization that the solid ground she'd always counted on was about to become quicksand.

She fingered the lush green leaves of the grapevines. The canopy would soak up the sun and turn that light into nutrients to feed the clusters of grapes. It also protected them from the powerful rays. This she understood. This made sense to her. Everything else was a terrifying morass of confusion.

Her marriage was over. The bald truth had seeped inside of her the night she'd huddled on the floor in her bedroom, lost, sad and alone. There was no going back, no changing what had been said. Rhys had told her she could take her time but they both knew the outcome was inevitable. And if she wasn't married to Rhys, then who was she and where did she belong?

She walked toward her truck, trying to breathe deeply so maybe her chest would stop hurting, only to pause with her hand on the door.

Not her truck. The company truck she drove. She didn't own a truck or a car or a house or a stick of furniture. She supposed she owned her clothes and her jewelry, such as it was. A few knickknacks and some artwork she'd bought. She had her salary, her savings and the royalties from the wine deal she'd made with Barbara.

There was the postnuptial agreement, she reminded herself, signed three years after she'd married Rhys. She'd been heartbroken to learn that no matter how hard or long she worked or how successful she was, Barbara wasn't interested in giving her even the tiniest piece of Bel Après.

Barbara had claimed it was the terms of her late husband's will—that only blood relatives could be a part of Bel Après, but Mackenzie suspected much of what went on was Barbara's decision.

Rhys had found her crying and been desperate to chase the sadness from her eyes. He'd explained that a postnuptial agreement was like a prenup, but signed after the wedding. While he couldn't give her a vineyard, he offered her the value of half the house, along with a portion of his trust fund. Later they'd amended the postnup to exclude her wine royalties from any community property claim. The combined assets were worth a chunk of money, but she would give it all back to him if only things could stay as they had been.

But that wasn't an option. She might not know anything about getting a divorce or what it would mean or what happened next, but she was certain that her marriage was over. Nearly as unsettling was the fact that Rhys was further along in the process than she was. While she was barely able to breathe, he was ready to be done with them. With her.

She fought against the tears burning in her eyes. She'd spent too many days giving in to the pain and she was done with that. From now on, she was going to be strong—that was her promise to herself. She was going to make plans and get on with her life—even if she no longer knew what that meant. Even if she was alone, with no husband and no best friend. She could count only on herself from now on.

She drove back toward the compound, taking in the beauty of the landscape. Vineyards stretched out on either side of the road. The distant mountains were dark against the blue sky. There were things she could count on, she told herself. The changing seasons, for one. Harvest, the frenetic few weeks that followed. The anticipation of what the new vintage would bring and how she would craft it into a perfect wine.

She parked by the main building and started for the production building, remembering how different it was now from what it had been sixteen years ago, when she'd first started working here. Bel Après was bigger, more successful, and she'd been a part of that.

Barbara had hired her as an apprentice winemaker right out of college. She'd also been engaged to Rhys, so taking the job had been the obvious thing to do. Two years later, she'd been promoted to head winemaker.

Her whole life was here, she thought, pausing at the foot of the stairs leading up to the offices. She didn't know what life was like without Bel Après and the family. Probably more significant, she didn't know who *she* was without them.

She took the stairs two at a time. Rhys's office was at the end, across from hers. Because they worked together. In a normal day, she saw him dozens of times—from breakfast until they said good-night. They made decisions together, they discussed every aspect of the business. They were a team...or at least they had been.

She stepped into his office. He didn't see her at first—he was too intent on whatever he was studying on his computer. Everything about him was familiar. The shape of his nose, the strong line of his jaw. He was a handsome man who looked like what he was—a decent guy who took his responsibilities seriously.

She remembered when Stephanie had first invited her home for the holidays. They'd both been freshmen at Washington State University. She and Stephanie had been roommates and friends from the first day they'd met. Mackenzie hadn't been sure about the wisdom of thrusting herself on her friend's family, but the alternative had been staying on campus by herself—a grim prospect considering the university all but shut down for Christmas. But with no family of her own and no place to go, she'd been grateful to have an alternative.

They'd made the drive to Walla Walla, going slowly over the snowy, mountainous roads. When they'd arrived, everyone had rushed out to greet them. There had been too many faces and names, but everyone had made her feel welcome. Rhys, the only man in a household of women, had made her heart beat faster with his kind smile.

Over that first holiday, she'd gotten to know everyone. Barbara had shown her around the property, taking her through the processing areas and into the barrel room. Lori and Four had been like younger sisters—friendly and eager to hang out with their older sister and her friend, and Rhys had invited Mackenzie out to dinner in town where they'd talked and laughed for hours.

They'd made love on Christmas Eve, in front of the family's large tree. By the time she and Stephanie had headed back to college, she'd already been more than half in love with him.

Rhys looked up and smiled at her. "Hi."

"Hi, yourself."

She closed the door behind her so they could have privacy, then took a seat across from him.

"I was remembering that first Christmas," she told him.

"That was a good time."

"It was. I don't think I had much of a choice about falling in love with you and Bel Après. I was alone in the world and you offered me everything I'd ever wanted."

"Mackenzie," he began, then stopped.

"What?" she asked softly. "It can't be unsaid. More important, you're right. Our marriage is finished. It has been for a long time. I didn't want to admit it, but that doesn't change the truth."

He looked both pained and relieved. "What do you want to do?"

"I don't know. I'd like us to stay friends."

"We have to. You're my best friend and I don't want to lose that."

"Me, either. I just know nothing is going to be the same." She thought about her horrible conversation with Stephanie but knew talking about that would be a distraction from what mattered. "I'm still trying to figure it all out. I like my job here and—" She stared at Rhys. "Why did you get scrunchy face just now?"

"I don't ever get scrunchy face, as you call it."

"You were thinking something."

He looked at her, his expression intense. "Don't you think you deserve more than just a job? You're the most talented winemaker I've ever met. Shouldn't you have something of your own? Don't you want to stand on a hill and look all around you and say, 'This is mine'?"

While the words didn't hurt as much as his recent statement that their marriage was over, they were still dangerous to her well-being, poking at an open wound she didn't allow herself to acknowledge.

Rhys leaned toward her. "Whatever you decide, my mom will keep you on for as long as you want."

"I know. She won't care if we get a divorce." She paused. "I don't mean that in a bad way."

"I know what you meant. Is that what you want? A divorce?"

She wanted to say that she didn't—she'd liked being married to him. Only she wasn't sure they actually had a marriage, not anymore. Besides, she knew it was what he wanted. He was ready to move on to something beyond what they had.

"It's the next step," she said instead. "I'm just not sure of the logistics."

"You'll have money," he said eagerly. "Lots of it. I've been running the numbers, and based on the value of the house and the amount from my trust, you should have close to two million dollars. That's enough for you to do anything."

As he spoke, he pulled a folder from a locked drawer in his desk and opened it.

"It's all here," he told her. "And that amount doesn't take into consideration the money from the wine royalties and whatever part of your salary you've saved."

She told herself he was being kind, trying to reassure her, but she couldn't help thinking this was more proof he was ready to be done with her. As for the money, it wasn't anything she could wrap her mind around.

"You think I should leave," she said faintly. "You want me to go."

"I'm not pushing you out. It's just you're gifted. You should have something of your own. You don't want to work for my mom for the rest of your life. How would that even happen? You'd get a place somewhere else, drive to Bel Après, then drive home at the end of the day? That's not going to make you happy."

She knew he was trying to help, but his words only made her feel worse. The bleak picture of her life had her fighting tears.

Was that what was next? A sad little apartment and working for Barbara? Rhys got to keep their house and his family and everything else, while she lost everything?

Apparently her pain didn't show, because he kept on talking.

"There's no rush." He passed her the folder. "We'll move forward when you're ready and not before. Until then, we'll live together in the house." He smiled at her. "You can stay there forever, as far as I'm concerned. I like living with you."

Which sounded nice but wasn't true. He wanted her to leave. Maybe not today, but soon.

She had to clear her throat before she could speak. "I appreciate that, but I think there needs to be an end date." She forced a smile. "Eventually I would cramp your style. You don't want to have to explain why your ex-wife is in the living room when you bring home a date."

He chuckled. "That would be awkward, but I can always go to her place."

She tried to keep her expression from tightening. He spoke so easily, she thought, as if he'd already worked everything out. Which he had. What was it he'd said? He wanted to have sex with anyone who would have him? None of this should be a surprise.

"I need to think," she told him. "Just a few more days. If we could keep this quiet a little longer."

"As long as you'd like. Did you tell Stephanie?"

She tried not to think about their conversation. "Yes, and she was upset."

She was deliberately vague, not wanting to go into what had actually been said. She didn't think she could get through the telling without losing what little control she had. Better to let him think Stephanie had been sad but supportive.

She got up and waved the folder. "Thanks for this. I'll look it over."

"You'll want to run it past your lawyer."

She stared at him blankly. She didn't have a lawyer. Then she got it. He meant a divorce lawyer.

"Sure," she whispered. "I'll get right on that."

And she would. Just as soon as she found a way to collect the pieces of her shattered life and start breathing again.

nine

Stephanie alternated between self-pity and guilt for the better part of four days before realizing she had to talk to someone. She decided to confront the one person she could yell at in total safety.

She waited until she knew Mackenzie would be in an evening meeting with Barbara, then walked into her brother's house and called his name.

"In my office," he replied.

She made her way to the large bookshelf-lined room. He was sitting at his desk, laptop open. It was well after seven, but sunlight still spilled into the room, warming the hardwood floors.

"Hey, Steph, what's up?"

She stared at her older brother for a second, before putting her hands on her hips. "A divorce?" she asked, her voice a shriek. "You want a divorce? I know it has to be you. Mackenzie would never ask for one. Why are you doing this? We're a family and you're ripping us apart. Get some counseling and get over yourself."

She paused to draw breath, then realized she had nothing else to say, so she sank into the one of the chairs and braced herself for the pushback.

But instead of yelling, he only shook his head and said, "I'm sorry."

"That's it?"

"It's all I've got."

"Did you cheat? You can't keep your dick in your pants?" She fought against sudden tears. "Mackenzie's amazing and beautiful and smart and why don't you want to be married to her anymore?"

He stood and circled the desk. After pulling her to her feet, he held her close.

"I'm sorry," he repeated. "I didn't want to do this."

"Then don't."

"I have to."

He led her to the sofa and waited until she sat down.

"There's no one else," he told her. "I didn't cheat. What I did was let it go on too long. We're great as friends, but we're lousy in a marriage. We're roommates and we work together and nothing more. I can't live like that. I won't. I want more."

"So this is about you being selfish?"

"Dammit, Steph, I'm not the bad guy."

"Could have fooled me. What do you want that she's not giving you?"

"Love. Sex."

"Oh, please. Sex? Really? That's the reason? What, she won't put on a French maid costume for you? Grow up."

He sat on the sofa and faced her. After swearing softly, he said, "Mackenzie and I haven't had sex in five years. We sleep in separate rooms, in separate wings of the house. We only ever talk about business. Call me all the names you want, I don't care. I want more than that. I'm tired of being lonely and horny and trapped in a relationship that isn't working for either of us."

Stephanie felt all the mad whoosh out of her. She stared at

Rhys, unable to understand what he was saying. "You haven't had sex in five years?"

"Yeah. You know what really sucks? We did it last week. First time in forever, and that's when we knew it was over. Hell of a goodbye."

"But I thought you were happy. You were always together."

But not touching, she thought suddenly. They never touched. They didn't hold hands or hug. There was no secret communication or laughs or shared jokes. Not that she could remember. How could she not have seen that?

"I didn't know," she breathed. "She never said. You never hinted."

His mouth twisted. "A man doesn't like to admit he's not having sex with his wife. Besides, what was I going to say? We all like and respect Mackenzie. What happened is both our faults. It's over and you have to deal with that. It's not about you or the family, it's about us."

Even as she was unable to grasp it all, she knew he was telling the truth—about all of it. How could she not have seen through the facade? She and Mackenzie talked about everything—why had her friend kept this from her? Shame? Guilt?

"I'm sorry," she whispered. "About all of it." Oh, God, she'd been a horrible friend. She hadn't been supportive at all.

"I yelled at her," she admitted. "I said she was ruining my life."

"Not surprising."

"Hey, you're supposed to be sympathetic."

"You need to be there for her," he said. "I've got the whole family. I'm keeping my life, but not Mackenzie. She's not going to have anything. We're all she has, and she's about to lose that. You need to be her friend. You and Four. Lori's going to side with Mom, and depending on how this all plays out, you know how ugly things could get. If Mom turns on her, her life will be hell."

Stephanie nodded even as she began to cry. "Everything is

going to change. I hate that. But I don't want you to be unhappy and I feel awful about Mackenzie."

He slid close and wrapped his arm around her. "I know. Me, too."

"This sucks. And there's no good solution."

"Tell me about it."

Mackenzie sat on the ground, a small amount of dry soil clutched in her hand. About fourteen thousand years ago, the Missoula floods, caused by melting glaciers, deposited a smorgasbord of nutrients all across eastern Washington. To the east were the wheat fields, but here, by the Columbia River, were the vineyards.

In 1977 Gary Figgins established Leonetti Cellar as Walla Walla's first commercial winery. In 1981 *Wine & Spirits* magazine named the first Leonetti cabernet sauvignon—the 1978 vintage—as the best in the nation. By 2012, six wineries from the Walla Walla area were on the list of Top 100 Wineries of the World. Bel Après was one of them.

In the past, knowing the history had always helped, but not today, she thought, letting the soil slip through her fingers. Today she was sick and confused and lost, and no amount of history was going to make that right. Everything was moving faster and faster and she didn't know how to make it stop.

The worst was the fear, the uncertainty. She was getting a divorce, she no longer had a best friend, she might lose her job, she might quit her job. She wanted nothing more than to go home, but even that wasn't a sure thing. The house wasn't hers, it never had been. It was part of the Barcellona family trust and she wasn't a member.

She covered her face with her hands and braced for tears, but she was all cried out. There was nothing left inside but a sense of foreboding. She felt like a speck of dust being blown around by cosmic winds, and that thought terrified her.

She knew that the worry and stress weren't helping. She had

to figure out a way to get control. She had to decide on a first step, then the next one and the next one. She was thirty-eight years old, she was healthy and she was good at her job. That was a start. She needed to get off her ass and come up with a plan.

She'd spent the last two evenings reading articles online with subjects ranging from her rights in a divorce in Washington State, to how long it would take—a mere ninety days, assuming neither of them contested the settlement—to dealing with the emotional aftermath. She felt vaguely more knowledgeable but no more settled. Adding to her stress level was the question of her work. Did she stay? Did she leave? And if she left, where was she going to go and what was she going to do when she got there? Work for another winery? Buy a winery?

That last thought had been keeping her up nights. She'd tried to dismiss the possibility, but like the idea of the divorce itself, once thought, it couldn't be unthought.

Could she, would she, should she? Her own winery. There were so many things she wanted to do that Barbara had never agreed to. Styles she'd wanted to try, new trends in blending. At the same time, she'd wanted to play with going more old-school with some of the wines.

She rose to her knees and plucked a grape from the bunch closest to her. It was still hard and sour—more than two months from being ready. But the promise was there.

This she knew, she told herself. This was who she was and this was going to save her. She couldn't count on Rhys or Stephanie or anyone but herself. She wasn't a part of Bel Après—not really. So what did she want? What was her legacy? Was she willing to just work for someone for the rest of her life, or did she want more?

Rhys had told her the postnup would give her about two million dollars. That was enough to buy a small winery. Or be a down payment on a larger one. It was options and a safety net and very possibly the start of a dream. She could accept what was happening and do something positive or she could whine and complain and make herself sick with worry. The choice was hers.

"I don't want to live like this anymore," she whispered, coming to her feet. "I won't live like this. I want love and passion and something that matters to me."

She looked around. Vineyards stretched out to the horizon, the even rows a testament to the meticulous care they received. This was her passion, she thought. It always had been. This was who she was. She might lose everything else, but she wasn't going to lose that. She refused to.

Dropping the grape to the ground, she started back for the truck. Before sliding behind the wheel, she stopped to trace the Bel Après logo on the side. She was still dealing with a ton of crap, but right now the weight of it was just a little bit less than it had been.

When she reached the highway, she headed for Walla Walla. The sun was high in the sky and the afternoon was hot. A good day to grow grapes, she thought. She turned toward town, then made a quick right turn when she spotted a sign for a used car lot.

A first step, she told herself. That was all she had to accomplish today. One small step. Tomorrow, she would make another. That was the only way she was going to get through.

She climbed out of the truck and looked around. An old man walked over, smiling as he approached.

"Afternoon," he called. "You looking for a new ride?"

She sucked in a breath, then smiled back. "I am. Either an SUV or a pickup. I want low miles and four-wheel drive."

Two hours later she was the proud owner of a late-model Jeep. After parking her work truck in its place by the offices, she took a golf cart to her house only to realize she wasn't sure who could give her a ride back to the car lot to pick up her Jeep. She and Stephanie weren't exactly speaking and Rhys was working. She didn't have any friends outside of the Barcellona family— something she was going to have to deal with, just not now.

She considered her options for a second before crossing the

courtyard to Four's house. As she circled to the rear, she passed wind chimes and a miniature stone circle. The back steps were covered in hand-painted tiles. Mackenzie knocked once, then let herself inside.

"Four, it's me," she called.

"In the kitchen."

She walked through the mudroom and found her sister-in-law collecting flour and sugar. Several empty muffin pans stood on the counter, along with bowls overflowing with fresh blueberries.

Four smiled. "The first of the season. It will be a few more days until they're at peak ripeness, but these ones are good for baking. I'll bring by muffins later."

"Thank you." Mackenzie glanced around the kitchen. "I need a favor. Are you already into this, or can you take a break for about an hour?"

"I haven't started yet, so I'm available. What's up?"

Four wore a pretty summer dress. The pale flowy fabric was covered in rainbows and unicorns. She'd pulled her long hair back in a ponytail and had on dangling earrings shaped like green beans.

She was the youngest of the siblings, the most artistic and the one who made Barbara insane. Mackenzie had always liked her, and she admired Four's willingness to be exactly who she was, consequences be damned. While Stephanie was her best friend, Mackenzie and Four were also close. Mackenzie was godmother to her three children. She showed up for school plays and birthday parties. On the first day of school, she walked the kids to the bus stop.

What if all that was lost? What if she wasn't around for Galaxy to show her a new hair ribbon or to see Zeus's latest frog find? What if there were no more art projects or nights spent lying on a blanket to look at stars?

Four's breath caught, then she rushed forward and pulled Mackenzie into a bruising hug.

"Breathe," her sister-in-law told her. "Breathe deeply. Pull in the essence of the universe and exhale the broken pieces."

Mackenzie managed to laugh. "I appreciate the hug if not the advice. What are you talking about?"

"Whatever's bothering you. Tell me what happened."

"Rhys and I are getting a divorce."

She braced herself for judgment or anger or for Four to step away. Instead her friend just held on, offering comfort and warmth.

"I'm sorry," Four said at last.

"Me, too."

Four stepped back and sighed. "I'm not surprised, but I'm sorry."

"Why aren't you surprised?"

"Neither of you has been happy for a long time. There's no connection between you. You don't fight because that would require a level of passion you don't have anymore."

Mackenzie stared at her. "You didn't want to share any of these insights with me a year ago?"

"Would you have listened?"

"I don't know. Maybe."

Four smiled. "You make your choices in your own time. We all do." Her smile faded. "You're not just leaving him, though, are you? I'm going to miss you so much."

Mackenzie fought tears. "I don't want to leave, but I don't know if I have a choice."

"You don't. Bel Après isn't right for you. My mother has spent the last eighteen years using your talent while trying to control your spirit. That was never going to work. You deserve so much more." Four reached for her hands. "Know that whatever happens, I'm your sister and I love you. I'll always be there for you and I know you'll always be there for me and my family. I trust you completely."

The words were comforting and welcome. For these few minutes, Mackenzie felt nurtured and loved. If a part of her wished Stephanie had responded the same way, well, she was going to have to get over that.

"Thank you," Mackenzie said, drawing in a full breath for the first time in days.

"You're welcome. Now how can I help?"

Mackenzie laughed. "At the risk of sounding like one of your kids, I need a ride."

Stephanie wondered if she felt as bad as she looked. She hadn't showered in two days, she'd barely left her bedroom. Now as she sat in her kitchen, sipping coffee just after seven in the morning, she tried to tell herself she had to get over herself and do the right thing. Only she didn't seem to want to listen.

Her phone buzzed. She glanced down and saw a text from Carson.

Hey, Mom. Checking in. Things are great. I pitched a perfect 6 innings yesterday. Love you.

Despite everything, she managed a smile. At least she'd done one thing right. Carson was a good kid. Avery probably was, too, and she would notice just as soon as her daughter let go of some of the attitude, but as for the rest of it…she was a hideous human being.

She'd realized that at about two in the morning, had cried, stomped around her bedroom, then cried some more. But no amount of self-loathing was going to change what she'd done and now she was stuck having to fix it.

Only she was just weak enough to want to pass over that part—the apology—and go back to how things were with Mackenzie. Except she couldn't. There was a big, fat problem in the way, and that problem was her and what she'd said.

She forced herself to her feet and went upstairs. One shower and a change of clothes later, she was feeling half-human. She came out of her bedroom and saw Avery in the hall. Her daughter looked at her.

"Mom, what's wrong?"

"Nothing."

"You've been crying."

"I know, but it's not anything you did." She tried to temper the words with a smile. Avery didn't look convinced.

"Do you want me to do something?"

The unexpected offer gave her a brief respite from the voice in her head chanting endlessly that she was slime.

"Get better grades and tell me I'm your best friend?"

Avery grinned. "Anything else?"

"I'm okay. Just some stuff. I'll figure it out."

Avery surprised her by moving close and giving her a quick hug. "If you need me, I'll be around all day."

"That's sweet. Thank you."

Avery nodded and went downstairs. Stephanie pulled her phone out of her pocket and sent a quick text before she could talk herself out of it.

You home?

Yes.

I'll be right over.

She waited but there was no response to that. She would guess that Mackenzie wasn't sure what to say—especially after how Stephanie had gone off on her the last time they'd spoken.

"It's going to be different this time," she promised aloud before following her daughter to the first floor.

"I'm going to talk to Mackenzie," she called, heading for the front door. "Then I'll see you at work."

"Okay."

Once outside, Stephanie inhaled the already warm air. It was going to be a scorcher—temperatures well into the nineties. Mackenzie and her crew would be prowling the vineyards, looking for signs of stress. Some heat was good for the grapes, but too much, too early could be a problem.

She walked the short distance between the houses, trying to figure out what she was going to say about the divorce. Rhys's confession had completely changed her perspective and made her sad. Two people she loved most in the world had been in pain and she hadn't known.

She walked up the three stairs to the front door and let herself in.

"It's me," she called.

"In the kitchen."

She walked in that direction, stopping when she saw Mackenzie.

Her friend looked as bad as Stephanie felt. Pale and thin, with shadows under her eyes. They stared at each other, then Stephanie rushed toward her. Mackenzie did the same and they met in the doorway, arms wrapped hard around each other as they hung on tight.

"I'm sorry," Stephanie said, tears filling her eyes. "I'm sorry. I was terrible. I said awful things and I made you feel bad. I wasn't there when you needed me. I don't know how that happened. All I could think of was myself and how the divorce would affect me, which is wrong and makes me feel like a worm. I won't do it again. I swear. I love you so much. I want to be there for you. Please, please believe me."

Mackenzie continued to hold her. They clung to each other for a couple of minutes before stepping back and smiling. They were both wiping away tears.

"We're a mess," Mackenzie said. "We need tissues and coffee."

"Any liquor?"

"It's seven thirty in the morning."

"Not in Vienna."

Mackenzie laughed. "You are right about that. How about some toast, instead?"

"I'll eat toast."

They sat at the island, each on a corner, their knees bumping. Stephanie squeezed Mackenzie's hand.

"I really am sorry. I was so wrong. I reacted without thinking and I hurt you."

"It's okay."

"It's not. I'm going to do better."

"I appreciate the apology." She reached for a tissue and blew her nose. "It's been a hard few days."

"I'll bet. What's going on? Are you and Rhys talking about anything? Are you fighting?"

"No fighting. Some talking." She got up and poured them each coffee, then put bread into the toaster. "I'm trying to adjust to what's happening. I'm not surprised but it feels really fast, if that makes sense."

"It does." Stephanie hesitated. "Is the divorce a sure thing?"

Mackenzie nodded. "Rhys is more than ready and I'm getting there. I thought about asking him to go into counseling, but there isn't anything for us to save. Not really. We haven't been truly married in a long time."

Stephanie thought about her brother's confession that they no longer slept in the same room or had sex, then wasn't sure if she should mention that.

"So what are you going to do?" she asked instead.

"Get a divorce lawyer. Figure out my life." She faked a smile. "You know—the easy stuff."

"Are you going to keep working at Bel Après?"

Mackenzie hesitated and Stephanie felt her stomach knot.

"You're not."

"I don't know," Mackenzie told her. "I haven't decided. I'm pretty sure Barbara would keep me on, regardless of the divorce, but then what? That's what I've been thinking about. Do I get an apartment in town, or even a condo, and drive here every day to do the job I've been doing? Do I want to be an employee here for the rest of my life? Before I felt like I was part of the family, but without that, what do I have?"

A legitimate question, Stephanie thought, trying not to be bitter. The fact that she'd never bothered to get her own life in order wasn't anyone's fault but hers. Even if having Mackenzie leave made her feel trapped, again, not her friend's problem.

"Would you go to work somewhere else or start your own thing?" She sat up straighter. "You have money. From the postnup. It's probably a lot of money. Could you buy a winery? That would be great." She got up and collected butter and jam from the refrigerator.

"Maybe."

The toast popped and Mackenzie put the slices on a plate, then placed it in front of Stephanie.

"What does maybe mean?"

Mackenzie resumed her seat and picked up her coffee. "I don't know what to do. I don't like change. I want things to be how they've always been."

"Don't you ever think about having your own label, making all the decisions without my mother breathing down your neck?"

Mackenzie's mouth turned up. "I have fantasized about that."

"Well, sure. So make it happen."

"There's a lot more to running a winery than just growing grapes. I don't know the business end of things. Maybe it would be better to go work for someone."

"You'd hate that. It's the same as you have now. I'm encouraging you to think about buying something. You'd do great." Stephanie was proud of herself for meaning the words.

"Thanks. Your support means a lot. I've hated us fighting."

Stephanie nodded. "Me, too. I'm sorry. I won't be stupid again." She paused. "Okay, I'll probably be stupid, but I'll do it in a supportive way. You matter to me. I love you and I don't want to lose our friendship."

"I love you, too. And I want to stay friends, no matter what." She paused.

"You're thinking of my mom," Stephanie said as she finished buttering her toast.

"She's not going to be happy."

"It's not her life. She doesn't get a say."

Mackenzie nodded. "I wish things had been different. Rhys deserved better than he had."

"Didn't you?"

"Yes, but it's easier to worry about him. We both let go of what was important and we lost it." She set down her coffee. "Thinking about the future is terrifying. It's this void and I don't know what's going to happen. Since college, Bel Après has been my home. I don't know how to be anywhere else."

"Come live with me," Stephanie told her. "I have an extra bedroom on the first floor. There's a bathroom and everything. You'll have me and the kids and you can stay as long as you like."

Mackenzie's eyes filled with tears. "Thank you. That means a lot. I may take you up on that."

"You should. We'll have fun together and it will annoy my mother. A true win-win."

Mackenzie chuckled. "One day you're going to have to figure out how to get along with her."

"Oh, why start now?"

Mackenzie took a slice of toast. "I bought a Jeep. It's black and kind of cool looking. In high school, I drove my grandfather's car and then I married Rhys and I always had a company truck, so this is the first car I've owned."

"Congratulations. Good for you."

"I know. I had to get insurance and everything."

"Look at you, with the adulting."

Mackenzie smiled. "One step down, four thousand ninety-seven to go."

ten

Mackenzie drove east, past the small airport, then turned into a quiet industrial area. At the end of a dead-end road was a Mexican restaurant that had been at the same location for at least twenty-five years. The food was cheap and plentiful, making the place a favorite of high school kids, but it was far enough out of the way that no one she knew should be there at two o'clock on a Thursday. No one except the man she was meeting.

Nader English ran the biggest winery in the state of Washington. His production was measured in millions of gallons per year and the finished product had a worldwide distribution. She'd known him for years, and nearly every time they ran into each other at an industry event, he offered her a job. The offer was accompanied by a chuckle and a comment that Barbara would skin him alive if Mackenzie accepted, but it was always made. Now she wanted to know if it was real, or just cheap talk.

She parked next to the only other vehicle in the parking lot—a late-model full-size F-150 with the winery logo on the side. At least she hadn't had her Jeep long enough for people to associate it with her, she thought, turning off the engine and wiping her suddenly sweaty hands on her jeans.

This was a mistake, she thought, her stomach twisting. She didn't want to go to work for Nader or anyone. She wanted to stay right where she was. She loved Bel Après. Only staying might not be an option, not just because of the divorce, but also because the hope of having more—something she could build herself—had taken root deep inside. Maybe she was wishing for the moon, but right now she needed a little wishing in her life.

"In the meantime, there's no harm in having the conversation," she whispered to herself as she slid out of the Jeep.

She walked inside. Battered tables and chairs filled the space. There was a counter at one end and a broken jukebox at the other. Nader, a sunburned man in his late fifties, had already claimed a table by the window. He had a beer in one hand and a chip in the other.

"Mackenzie," he called, waving her over. "What can I get you to drink?"

She sat down and tried to ignore the continued writhing in her stomach. "Nothing for me."

He frowned. "We're not having lunch?"

"I wanted to talk but you go ahead."

"Damned straight, I will," he said with a grin. "I've been looking forward to eating here since you called. At home, Jody's practically gone vegan." He shuddered. "I'm here for carnitas tacos with extra cheese. You sure you don't want anything?"

Their server, an attractive dark-haired woman, appeared.

"Mackenzie," she said with a smile. "So nice to see you."

"Hello, Orla. Could I have a Sprite, please?"

"Of course." Orla looked at Nader. "I heard what you want. How about a couple of chicken taquitos on the side?"

Nader grinned. "You're my kind of woman. I'll take 'em."

Mackenzie and Nader talked about what was going on in the

area until her drink was delivered, then he leaned back in his chair and crossed his arms over his big belly.

"You called this meeting."

And here it was. She drew in a breath. "I'm thinking of making some changes in my career. I love Bel Après and everything I do there, but I'll never be more than an employee and I'm considering other options."

"Holy shit," he said, then gave her a wry smile. "Excuse my French. Are you serious? You'd leave Bel Après and come to work for me?"

"Maybe. I don't know. I'm at the exploring stage. You're always offering me a job and I didn't know if that was real or not."

"It's real. It's twenty times real." He glanced around and returned his attention to her before lowering his voice. "Mackenzie, I'd hire you in a hot second. Just tell me what you want. Your own label? Done. Complete control? You got it. I'll give you a percentage. Ten percent of the net. Hell, twenty. We could do great things together. We have vineyards all over. You could pick and choose the best grapes from Washington and Oregon and make something great. Just tell me what it would take. Your own offices, of course. You pick the staff. I can get you a travel budget, a house, a pony. Anything."

His words overwhelmed her, making it hard for her to catch her breath.

"Probably not a pony," she managed.

"How about Mackenzie Dienes Presents on the label?"

She looked at him. "That would be nice."

He reached for a chip. "So why are you doing this? You really gonna leave Bel Après? You've been there for years. What, twelve? Fifteen?"

"Sixteen," she said. "Since I graduated from college and Rhys and I got married."

"Uh-huh. That's a hell of a long time. So what does Rhys think about all this? You making a change."

She avoided his gaze. "He's very supportive."

He studied her for a long time. "Mackenzie, what's going on?"

"Nothing," she hedged. "Like I said, I'm considering options."

"You're getting a divorce."

"What? No. How did you know?" She pressed her lips together. "I mean we are, but that's not the reason I want to leave Bel Après. I mean it's not the only reason I'm thinking about…" Why was she so bad at this? It was just a conversation. "I'm doing this all wrong."

Orla walked up balancing three plates. She set the tacos and taquitos in front of Nader and put a cheese quesadilla in front of her.

"You look hungry," Orla told her. "I can tell you haven't been eating. You need food in your stomach, Mackenzie."

The act of kindness nearly made her cry. "Thank you," she whispered, inhaling the scent of cheese and tortilla and feeling her mouth water. "I am a little hungry."

"Good." Orla patted her shoulder, then left.

Nader picked up a taco. "When did this all happen?"

"In the last few weeks. It's not dramatic or anything. Rhys and I are friends and always will be. But it's made me think about other things. Like what to do about my career."

She picked up a slice of quesadilla and took a bite. The delicious combination of cheese and mild chilies reminded her she hadn't eaten in days. Suddenly she was starving.

While she gulped the first slice, Nader ate a couple of tacos, then wiped his hands on a paper napkin.

"I'm going to give you some advice," he said, picking up his beer. "Good advice, so you should listen. You helped me out a couple of years back when I was in a bad way."

She nodded, remembering how his crew of pickers had gotten waylaid by a bad bout of food poisoning in Oregon. He'd had acres of Syrah ready to be harvested and no way to do it with a limited team. Mackenzie had wanted to wait a couple of extra days on her own Syrah, so she'd sent her crew over to work for him. Barbara hadn't been pleased, but Mackenzie had felt taking care of a friend was more important than her mother-in-law's ire.

"I'm listening," she told him.

He leaned toward her. "Jesus H. You-know-what. You can't be telling everyone that you're thinking of leaving Bel Après. Word will get back to Barbara before you want her to know and then you're going to be in big trouble."

"How do you know I haven't told her already?"

"Because I didn't see a mushroom cloud anywhere. She's not going to take it well."

Something Mackenzie knew to be true. "Maybe I won't leave."

"You've already made up your mind, kid. Now you're just looking for what's next. While I would give up two of my kids to have it be with me, we both know that's not gonna happen. You don't want to work for someone. You want your own thing. Man, if I had a few million dollars, I'd go into business with you pronto." He grinned. "But the good Lord blessed me only with a pretty face."

She smiled. "That's sweet, but I really haven't decided what I want to do."

"Maybe you can lie to yourself, but you can't lie to me." He lowered his voice. "Here's the advice. No talking to people the way you did to me. You get an NDA first. A nondisclosure agreement. You protect yourself. Find a lawyer. Find two lawyers. One for the divorce and one for the business. Make people earn your trust. Once you leave, you're not going to be under the protection of the Barcellona family. It's a big, bad world out there, kid. You've got to take care of yourself."

He was making sense, she thought. "Thank you. You're being very sweet to me."

"I know. I'm a saint." He sighed, then pointed at her food. "Eat up. I'm buying, so you might as well take advantage of me.

Who knows—you might fall and hit your head, then wake up and think you want to come work for me."

She laughed. "I promise if I don't do my own thing, I will give your offer very serious consideration."

"You do that."

Mackenzie spent the rest of the afternoon driving around the area. She stopped in at a couple of small wineries and tasted their wines, walked through an open house for a condo by the golf course, and spent an hour walking around a park, trying to get her thoughts together. It was close to seven before she drove home.

She pulled into the garage, going slowly to make sure she didn't ding the Jeep. Parking something this big, rather than one of the golf carts, was still new to her. While she was used to driving trucks for the winery, parking those was more of a matter of pulling off a dirt road than maneuvering in a confined area.

As she climbed out, she saw two carts by the back door, which meant Rhys was home. She hurried inside.

"It's me," she called.

"In the kitchen."

She found him standing by the microwave, the scent of a heating frozen dinner filling the air.

"What are you doing?" she asked.

"Making dinner."

"Why didn't you take what the chef left us?"

He grimaced. "I didn't want to bother cooking anything."

"You are such a guy." She picked up the package and glanced at the picture of some kind of pasta. "You hate these dinners. I only buy them for myself."

"I know but I was hungry."

She walked to the refrigerator and checked on the meal that had been left earlier that day. There were two pork chops, twice-baked potatoes and salad.

"Give me five minutes and I'll have dinner on the table," she said as she walked to the sink and washed her hands.

"You don't have to cook for me," Rhys said.

"I'm cooking for both of us. And brace yourself, I have things I want to talk about."

Twenty minutes later, they were seated across from each other. Despite having had a quesadilla only a few hours before, she was hungry—probably because she hadn't been eating much lately.

Rhys had set the table in the dining room, as he always did. He'd also put a folder and a pad of paper next to his place setting.

She picked up her water glass and pointed to the folder. "So you have things to discuss, as well?"

"This is more related to your topic."

"But you don't know what I'm going to say."

He smiled. "I have an idea our conversation is work related. It's not as if we're going to be planning a trip to Europe."

Which was true, of course, but hearing him say it made her sad. Some because they'd never planned a trip anywhere and some because he was such a good guy and she was going to miss him.

How many more dinners would they share? How many more times around this table? How many more nights would she sleep in this house? There was no way to know and no point in speculating, she told herself. She was moving forward. Perhaps reluctantly, but as long as she got where she needed to go, did the motivation matter?

She passed him the salad. "I'm ready to get started with the divorce. I've done a little research, and if we agree on a settlement, then we just have to fill out some paperwork and wait ninety days."

His dark gaze was steady. "You need to get a lawyer."

"I will."

"I'm not going to be an asshole, Mackenzie, but you have to protect yourself."

"I will," she repeated before taking a bite of her salad. Nader had told her the same thing. She was going to get a few names and start doing phone interviews to find someone to help with the divorce.

He opened the folder. "I've scheduled a valuation of the house. We'll have that by the end of next week. Your share of my trust is a flat amount, so there's no work there. It is what it is."

He flipped to another page. "We've banked most of our salaries. Neither of us spends a lot of money on living expenses. We get paid about the same, so I suggest we simply split the accounts in half. Your wine royalties are in a separate account, so that's easy. Those are yours."

She nodded, trying not to think how, in the end, she would have a boatload of money and no family. Not exactly a fair exchange.

He passed her a piece of paper. She saw the totals of various accounts added up and divided by two. When that number was combined with her royalties...

"It's the two million dollars you mentioned before," she said, raising her head and staring at him. "Is that number right?"

"It should be. I've checked everything."

"I'm not sure what to say."

The amount shouldn't be a surprise, but seeing it in writing made it real. Two million dollars. She couldn't begin to grasp what that meant.

She stood and collected their empty salad plates, then went into the kitchen. After pulling the pork chops and potatoes out of the oven, she plated them and carried their entrée into the dining room.

"You'll have options," he said when she was seated. "Put the money away, buy a winery. You can do anything."

Which should have sounded amazing, but instead left her feeling lost and unsettled.

"I spoke to Nader today."

Rhys cut into his pork chop. "Did his head explode at the thought of you working for him?"

"He was excited by the idea but didn't think it was going to happen. He gave me a lot of good advice."

"Do you want to get a job there?"

"I don't know." She'd never seriously thought about having her own winery. Oh, sure, there had been times when she'd wished she could do things differently, but that wasn't the same as having her own place. But over the last few days, she'd started accepting the concept as more of a possibility rather than a far-fetched dream.

"I've never run a business," she admitted. "I manage my crews and I'm responsible for the wine, but that's not the same as handling the finances, marketing and everything else. I've only done the parts I like."

"So take on a business partner." He waved his fork. "You're the best winemaker in the state—anyone would be happy to go into business with you. The other person can provide the business expertise and you make the wine. Oh, and find someone with money—that way you can buy something good-sized and you won't need a loan."

Was it her imagination or was he pushing, ever so gently? She put down her fork and tested her theory with a teasing, "Plus if I go into business with someone else, you don't have to feel guilty anymore."

She expected (or hoped) for some denial. Instead Rhys looked away and shrugged.

"I'd feel better if you weren't going through everything alone."

And just like that, her appetite fled.

"I'm not. We're still friends and I have Stephanie."

"You two made up?"

"You knew we were fighting?"

He nodded. "She felt bad for what had happened and came

over to yell at me for not keeping my dick in my pants." He grinned. "My sister has a way with words."

"I hope you told her the divorce wasn't your fault. We're both to blame."

"I did, but she wasn't listening. Back to the partnership, Mackenzie. It's something you need to consider."

"Right, because I have so many people like that on my contact list. How would I even find someone?" She remembered Nader's advice. "I can't just ask around."

"You know one person with all those qualifications. Bruno."

Mackenzie picked up her wineglass. Rhys was right. Bruno had money and plenty of business experience. He'd even mentioned wanting to buy into a winery, but that was a long way from wanting her as a business partner.

"Talk to him," Rhys said. "If nothing else, get his take on things. He knows a lot of people and he knows what's happening in the industry. He could be a good resource."

And a way out for Rhys, she thought, trying not to feel bitter. "I'd need him to sign an NDA."

Rhys looked at her. "Someone's been doing her homework. You're right, you would want that."

"I can't take credit for the idea. Nader told me about it. He was very protective."

"Don't sound so surprised. You're well liked and respected."

"Thank you," she murmured. "Everything is happening so fast. I'm having trouble keeping up."

"Technically nothing has happened," he pointed out. "We're just talking."

"It's more than that. We're getting a divorce. That's real. And once that happens, I need to move on with the rest of my life."

"I'll say it again. You can stay at Bel Après for as long as you want. My mom won't care about our marriage."

She drew in a breath, bracing herself to speak the truth that she'd been avoiding. "I can't continue working here. Not just because of the divorce, but for a lot of other reasons. I need to do something else."

"Buy a winery?"

"I don't know. Maybe." Because going to work for someone else was just more of the same, and wasn't she tired of that?

Maybe Rhys *was* pushing her, but that didn't mean his advice wasn't sound. Especially about Bruno. She'd always respected him, and what she knew about him, she liked. If nothing else, she knew he would give her honest advice.

"You're right about talking to Bruno. I'll get that set up right away."

He smiled at her. "You're going to do great."

"I could fall on my butt."

"It's never going to happen. You're too good and you work too hard."

She hoped he was right about that. Since graduating college, she'd only ever had one job for one company and that was a family business. Did she even know what the real world was like?

Not that it mattered, she told herself, because she was about to find out.

eleven

Barbara reviewed the stack of checks in front of her. Lori handled the day-to-day bills, but every quarter, Barbara insisted on a review of all payments. There were also larger checks that she signed herself, such as the property tax payment and the royalty checks to Mackenzie.

"You're sure these are right?" she asked automatically, not bothering to look at Lori seated on the opposite side of the desk.

"Yes."

The review complete, Barbara signed the checks. She lingered over the one to Mackenzie, telling herself not to feel bitter about the money. For every dollar her daughter-in-law made, Bel Après made four, so that was a win. Still, she shouldn't have taken the bet, she thought, feeling mildly resentful.

"Knock!"

She looked up and saw Catherine standing in the doorway to her large office. As always, the sight of her youngest made her tense. Just the outfit alone—a hideous, shapeless dress with giant printed flowers—was enough to make her wince.

Catherine had so much promise. She was smart and creative. If she'd shown the slightest bit of interest, Barbara would have been thrilled to teach her about the business. She suspected that of all her children, Catherine was the one with the gift for wine-making. But like Stephanie, Catherine hadn't wanted anything to do with Bel Après. Instead she played with paints and clay, claiming art was her destiny.

"I wanted to let you two know I left baskets of blueberries in your kitchen."

Barbara took off her reading glasses. "There's a perfectly good farmer's market not three miles from the house. Why do you waste your time on that ridiculous garden?"

Catherine smiled. "Mom, given how much you love the vineyards, I would think you would be pleased that I want to grow something."

"The vineyards serve a purpose."

"So does my garden. It's important for my children to understand where things come from. There's magic in planting a seed and watching it become a carrot or a blueberry. Mother Earth is a great blessing to us, and we should respect that."

For the millionth time, Barbara wondered where she'd gone wrong with her youngest. She'd never been dropped on her head, so there wasn't an injury to blame.

Jaguar was far more grounded—he worked for a farm-equipment repair company. If it was big and had an engine, he could fix it. Barbara could respect his abilities and his work ethic. She might question his taste in women, but he was basically a good man. Honest and steady. But Catherine was another matter.

"I'll make some muffins," Lori said. "We can freeze them."

"How delightful," Barbara murmured. "Was there anything else?"

"That's all I have, Barbara. Enjoy the berries."

With that, Catherine left. Barbara shook her head. That girl.

But aside from her youngest, she had to admit everything else was going very well, especially with Bel Après.

"Your father would be proud of what we've accomplished," she said aloud.

Lori looked slightly startled, then nodded. "He would. The winery has grown so much. You've done a great job, Mom."

"Thank you. I believe you're right. Now, what's next?"

One quick trip to Seattle and a five-thousand-dollar retainer later, Mackenzie had a divorce lawyer. Ramona Spencer had walked her through the process and agreed that if she and Rhys could come to terms on the settlement, it would be easier for everyone. But, her lawyer had warned her, people got weird about money, so she shouldn't get her hopes up that there wasn't going to be a hiccup somewhere. The postnup agreement would help, but divorces could be tricky.

Mackenzie had tried to explain that Rhys was a really great guy and that they'd already talked everything through, but Ramona's pitying look had stopped her midsentence. She'd returned home with a stack of paperwork to fill out and a list of online articles about how the divorce would proceed. She'd left Ramona's contact info with Rhys so he could share his lawyer's information with her and they could get the divorce started.

If she thought about the divorce as if it were a project, she was fine. It was only when she allowed herself to realize that it was actually the death of her marriage that she had a difficult time. Adding to the stress was the fact that Barbara didn't know and Mackenzie didn't want to tell her. While she thought of Barbara as a surrogate mother, she wasn't sure their relationship was up to the strain of a divorce—especially if Mackenzie decided to also leave Bel Après.

And it was a big if. Her head told her staying wasn't an option, but her heart wasn't ready to walk away from her home, her family and her life. But staying meant surrendering to a paycheck every two weeks and nothing else. If she had the ability to make her dream come true, shouldn't she go for it?

Fortunately for her scattered mind, it was midsummer and there was less for her to do at work. She continued to monitor the vineyards. She'd completed a barrel tasting a couple of days ago and had reported her results to Barbara. Facing her mother-in-law wasn't easy, but Mackenzie had tried to act as normal as possible and Barbara hadn't seemed to sense anything was wrong.

Mackenzie drove to the house and went into her small office. After booting up her laptop, she created a file for the divorce, then downloaded the files her lawyer had sent her. After scanning them, she saved them, then opened a separate folder—this one on Bruno.

She'd started researching him after Rhys had mentioned him as a possible business partner. At this point she knew about as much as she could for $49.95. He was single, wealthy and successful. There weren't any bankruptcies, liens or pending lawsuits. He'd never been arrested. He owned several properties—some houses, some commercial. His private jet was leased.

On paper he seemed like someone she would be comfortable doing business with. But real life was different. Messier. Or maybe her hesitation was more about being scared.

She looked from the screen to her phone and back, then swore softly as she picked up her phone and searched her contact list, before pushing the button to call the number. He answered on the second ring.

"Hello?"

"Hi, Bruno. It's Mackenzie."

He was silent for a second. "How nice to hear from you. Surprising but nice."

She heard the smile in his voice and smiled in return. "Yes, I know. I don't usually call." Actually she never had before. She cleared her throat. "I was wondering if maybe the next time you're in town we could talk. Away from the winery. And if you could not say anything to anyone, well, that would be great."

She closed her eyes and thought that she should have really thought the conversation through before getting in touch with him.

"It's not bad," she added quickly. "It's a, um, business thing." She paused, not sure if she should mention an NDA or not. How exactly did people work that into the conversation? And speaking of an NDA, where on earth was she going to get one? Could she just find one online?

"I'm here right now," he said. "I can meet you in an hour."

"Oh. That's great. Thank you. I'm not sure where would be a good place. I don't want to be seen with you." She groaned. "Sorry. That came out wrong. It's not just you. I don't want us to be seen together." *Crap!* "I'm saying this all wrong."

He chuckled. "Now I'm intrigued. Let's meet at my hotel. We'll have privacy in my room. And before you start to freak out, I have a suite. We'll be in the living room. I'm not trying to lure you anywhere."

"I'm not worried about that," she told him. She so wasn't the "lure" type. "Where are you staying?"

She expected him to mention the Marcus Whitman Hotel or one of the upscale B and Bs, but instead he said, "I'm at the Marriott Courtyard."

"Really?"

"You sound surprised. I like the hotel. Summer is busy and sometimes it's hard to get a room, so I rent one for July and August. They take good care of me here." He gave her the room number.

"A man of surprises. I will see you at the Marriot Courtyard in an hour."

"Looking forward to it."

He hung up. Mackenzie did the same, then wondered what she'd gotten herself into. Maybe she was taking on too much.

Once the divorce was final, she could think about making other changes. Like in a year or two. If she left now, she would miss harvest. She loved harvest. Without her, what would happen to all her grapes? They needed her.

She rested her arms on the desk and her head on her arms and told herself to either grow a pair or accept she was stuck at Bel Après forever.

As soon as the thought formed, she straightened. *Stuck*, she thought in surprise. Was that how she felt? And if it was, then doing something about it was the only option.

Feeling like a third-rate actress in a high school production of a mystery play, Mackenzie drove to the hotel and parked. Nerves battled with fear and apprehension. She had no idea what she was doing and yet here she was—doing it. Whatever "it" was.

Talking, she told herself as she walked inside and headed for the elevators. They were going to be talking. She would ask for information and hopefully he would give it to her. Then she would know more than she had before.

After exiting on the top floor, she followed the room numbers to his, then knocked.

"Mackenzie," he said, as he opened the door.

"Hi."

He stepped back to let her in.

She had a brief impression of a sitting area, a small table and chairs, and a closed door leading to what she would guess was the bedroom.

This was so weird, she thought as she sat at the table. Bruno settled across from her, his expression curious, his posture relaxed. It was only then that she realized he was in suit pants and a dress shirt, while she had on jeans and a T-shirt. No doubt there was mud on her boots, and she wasn't sure she'd combed her hair even once since getting up that morning. Maybe she should start paying more attention to her wardrobe, she thought glumly. Dressing up for meetings. Only she hadn't known there was going to be a meeting and Bruno had met her dozens of times. She knew she was very—

"Mackenzie?"

She jerked her attention back to the room. "Sorry. I'm a little scattered."

He nodded politely.

She considered how to start, then remembered that she was supposed to have an NDA for him to sign. She really was going to have to get one of those.

"Can I have your word that what we're about to talk about remains confidential?"

One eyebrow rose. "Of course."

"Like NDA confidential?"

"You have my word, Mackenzie. Nothing you tell me will leave this room."

"Thank you." She hesitated. "I'm leaving Bel Après."

She spoke without thinking, then realized what she'd said. Her plan had been to tell him about the divorce, but apparently that was not what was most on her mind.

"You look shocked," he said mildly. "Did you just surprise yourself?"

"I did. What I meant to say was that Rhys and I are getting a divorce and that I was thinking about leaving, but maybe it's more than that." She pressed a hand to her chest and tried to relax. "Assuming I do leave, I don't know what to do with my career. I keep coming back to having my own place. I have all these ideas."

She paused. "Everyone has ideas, of course, but I think mine are pretty grounded. I know how to make good wine. I have some money, so buying a place is an option, only I don't want to do all the business stuff."

She met his steady gaze. "Bel Après is all I know, so the whole thing is scary, but it's exciting, too. You're the most successful person I know, so I thought maybe you could give me some advice." She stopped there, not sure how to mention the potential partnership thing. Asking him about that seemed presumptuous on her part.

"What do you want in a winery?" he asked.

"I haven't really thought about it."

"That's not true. You've been thinking about it your whole life. Tell me."

She closed her eyes and tried to imagine the perfect place. "Lots of land. More land than I would need at the beginning. Good vines. Healthy and strong. I want something established, but not so defined that there isn't room to play, you know? I have techniques I want to try. Wine can be trendy. At the same time, classic is wonderful and I wouldn't want to lose that. I want to make something great."

"So you're smart to think about buying an established vineyard. Building one from the ground up would take years and millions of dollars."

"I only have two million." Only. She tried not to laugh at the ridiculousness of the statement.

"Where have you looked?"

"I haven't. I don't know where to start and I haven't told Barbara anything, so there's that. Rhys knows. He's the one who said I should talk to you."

"Would you consider taking on a partner?"

Oh, so that was how it was done. He made it look easy. "I would. I'd want someone who would handle the business end of things, including marketing. I want to be left alone to do what I do."

"Would you consider going into business with me?"

She felt her eyes widen. "You'd want to do that with me?"

He smiled. "Mackenzie, you're the most talented winemaker I've ever met. You're smart, you're intuitive and you work hard.

You create magic. Yes, I'd very much like to go into business with you."

"That would be great. Sure. How would it happen?"

"First I'd want you to really think about it. This is a big deal. Everything would be different. We'd be fifty-fifty partners. You'd put in your two million and your talent, and I'd front the other money. I'm thinking about six million."

She held in a gasp. Eight million dollars in total? For that, couldn't they buy a small state?

"That would allow us to purchase something we could work with," he continued. "Something in the area, because you know the land here."

"Who would run the business?"

"I would."

"But you don't live here."

"I'm looking to settle somewhere," he told her. "If we did this, I'd stay here, in town."

"But we're so small."

The smile returned. "I'd adjust. Tell me what you're thinking. I'm not asking for a commitment, just if you can see yourself saying maybe."

"I'm very maybe."

"Good. Then I know a winery that might be coming up for sale. A winery that would meet all our criteria."

Did they have criteria? "Okay, which one?"

"Painted Moon."

She nearly came out of her seat. "Herman is going to sell Painted Moon?" She supposed it shouldn't be a surprise—he was in his eighties and his kids had never wanted anything to do with the business, but still.

"It's amazing land," she said. "Not just the acres on Red Mountain but the rest of it. Although the Red Mountain land is perfect. At the base, so it has centuries of runoff. All those nutrients. His cabs are incredible. I was sorry when he reduced wine production and started selling the grapes instead. I wonder what his library is like. It could be tens of thousands of bottles. He always cellared well. I'd want to know what's contracted from the harvest. We'd want to keep as many tons as possible because I can work with almost anything and—"

She realized she was doing all the talking. "Too enthusiastic?"

He laughed. "No. You're the perfect amount of enthused. He has wine in barrels, by the way. We'll have to sell that."

"Is it any good?"

"You'll have to tell me."

"He hasn't really been selling any retail and I don't think he has a wine club," she said. "It could be difficult to get distribution on finished wine." They would need to sell it regardless, she thought. Depending on the size of the barrels, they were talking thousands of gallons, which translated into hundreds of thousands of dollars.

"I already have that figured out," Bruno told her. "Give me a high-quality blend and I have a waiting customer."

"Who?"

"It's more a *where*. I know a distributor in China. They want great wine that's exclusive."

"Then I can make it great. We might have to buy from other wineries, but with the right blending, I can do it. Herman knows how to make wine."

Bruno nodded. "Want me to make a call and set up an appointment for us to talk to Herman?"

Her head was spinning, but she liked the sensation. "Yes, please."

"I'll also have my attorney draw up a preliminary agreement for you to consider. You're going to need to have your lawyer look at it. Run it by Rhys, as well."

Another lawyer? "I don't suppose it's something my divorce lawyer could handle."

"No. You need someone who understands contracts."

She nodded. "Why did Rhys give me your name as a potential partner?"

"I've talked to him about buying something. I wanted his advice." He rose. "We need to keep this quiet, Mackenzie. Rhys can know but no one else."

"I agree. I won't say anything. Not even to Stephanie."

He held out his hand. "Then we're moving forward with this?"

She, stood, shook his hand and smiled. "Is this like a gentleman's agreement?"

"It is."

She laughed. "Painted Moon. I can't tell you how excited I am. Let me know when we can go talk to Herman. I can't wait to taste what he has in the barrels and tour the vineyards."

"I'll get in touch with him today, then call you."

"Thanks."

She stepped out into the hallway and forced herself to walk normally to the elevator when what she wanted to do was dance and skip and spin. Painted Moon! There were so many possibilities. She knew the vineyards Herman owned and the quality of the grapes. There was so much potential, so much she could make happen. Between now and when she heard from Bruno, she was going to keep positive thoughts and try not to smile too much. Bruno was right—no one could know what they were considering. But she knew—and for now that was plenty.

twelve

Stephanie pulled into the parking lot of the restaurant. Even as she turned off her car engine, she thought about simply going home instead. She wasn't up for dinner out, but Kyle had caught her at a weak moment, and his claim that he was interested in dinner and not sex had reassured her. Not that she was worried about giving in to him. She was still dealing with the aftermath of her bad reaction to Mackenzie telling her about the divorce. While she'd made up with her sister-in-law, she was shocked about her behavior, and doing the wild thing was not on her radar.

She got out of the car. She'd put on makeup, she might as well have a nice meal. Maybe hanging out with Kyle would take her mind off things. He was easy company, she reminded herself.

She gave her name to the hostess and was shown back to a corner table. Kyle smiled and rose as she approached.

"Hey, beautiful."

The silly greeting made her smile in return. "Hardly," she said, leaning in and kissing his cheek. "Although you look good."

He did, as always. Well-groomed, classically handsome with blond hair and blue eyes. There was a reason he was successful on TV and it wasn't just his love of sports. Women adored him—they always had. Sadly for their marriage, he'd adored them right back.

"Just so we're clear," she said, "I meant what I said on the phone. There will be no seducing."

He pressed a hand to his chest. "You wound me. I said just dinner and I meant it."

She eyed him suspiciously. "Really? Because Seattle is about a six-hour drive."

"I was in Pullman," he told her. "I had an interview with one of the football coaches."

"So I'm a convenient stop on your way home." The news was reassuring.

She looked around the trendy bistro. "I haven't been here in forever. The food is really good, as is the wine list. Sadly I drove, so only a glass for me."

"We'll get a bottle. If you have too much to drink, you can text Avery to come get you. Your car will be safe in the parking lot."

"What about you?"

"I'm staying at a hotel nearby. Avery and I are having brunch in the morning."

"You are? She never said anything to me." Great. First she'd been a horrible friend and now she and her daughter weren't communicating at all.

"Stop," he said gently. "Whatever you're thinking, it's wrong. I texted her ten minutes ago and set up brunch. I waited until I knew I had a room in town."

"Oh. That's better."

He gave her best smile. "Why do you always go to the bad place?"

"You can't know that's what I was thinking."

He raised his eyebrows but didn't speak. She sighed.

"Fine. I was thinking she and I never communicate anymore, except when we fight. Did she tell you I'm keeping her from the love of her life?"

"She mentioned you were being difficult about all the summer parties she's been invited to."

"I'm worried about her sleeping with Alexander. She's too young and he's going to break her heart."

"You're a good mom."

"I wish."

Their server appeared and took their drink orders. Stephanie decided to take Kyle up on his suggestion about Avery picking her up and ordered a cocktail. He did the same.

When they were alone again, she said, "Carson's having a good time at baseball camp. His ERA is fantastic."

"Down a full point from last year. And his hitting is getting better."

"He gets his athletic ability from you," she admitted.

"I want to take credit, but I think our son is just a quirk of nature. No one on my side is as gifted as he is."

She smiled. "Maybe he'll get a multimillion-dollar contract and buy us each a house."

"We both already have a house."

"I wouldn't mind one a little farther from my mother."

"You could move back to Seattle."

She wrinkled her nose. "And do what? My skill set is very limited."

"Is that what you've been upset about?"

She stared at him. "How do you know I've been upset?"

"Avery told me there was something going on."

"I'm amazed she noticed. So that's why you wanted to have dinner? You're checking up on me?" She wasn't sure how she felt about that.

"Not checking up. I'm concerned. You're my kids' mother

ve always been friends." He leaned toward her. "Tell me what's going on, Steph. I want to help."

She debated whether or not she could trust him. "You have to keep it to yourself."

He made an X over his heart. "Scout's honor. Tell me."

She explained about Mackenzie and Rhys. "I was so shocked," she admitted. "I didn't handle it well, at all. I yelled at her for changing everything, because I didn't want my life upset." She covered her face with her hands. "I was a terrible friend and I'm so embarrassed and ashamed of how I behaved. I should have been supportive and I wasn't."

"You're being too hard on yourself."

"Oh, please. I completely let her down."

"Did you go back and apologize?"

"Yes."

"Then you're fine. You made a mistake and you corrected it. Of course it was a shock. Rhys and Mackenzie have been together since you were in college. Having them split up screws with the family dynamic."

Their server appeared with their drinks. He had a whiskey and soda while she'd chosen a margarita on the rocks.

"I'm still beating myself up about all of it," she told him.

"Is that your way of distracting yourself from what's actually happening? You have to be sad about the divorce."

She glared at him. "Where do you get off being so insightful? Stop it right now."

He grinned. "I can't help it, Steph. Sometimes I'm impressive. Admit it."

"Sometimes," she grumbled, then sighed. "Am I using guilt to protect myself from what's really going on with them? Maybe. I don't know. It makes me sad. Plus I had no idea they were unhappy."

"You're kidding. How could you not know? They never acted

like a couple. They didn't talk to each other or touch or even sit together at meals."

"Why didn't I see it?"

"You were too close. I came in every now and then so it was easier to figure out the pattern. I'm not saying they hate each other, but they weren't a couple."

"So you're not surprised about the divorce?"

He shook his head. "Not really. She should go out on her own." He sipped his drink. "Which leaves you screwed. You're trying to get up the courage to find another job and suddenly Mackenzie snaps up the only chance to leave."

All of which sounded sensible in her head, but ridiculous when he said it.

"There's not just one chance to get away," she said defensively. "It's not like the last seat on a plane. I could still leave if I wanted."

He raised his eyebrows. "You're saying it but I doubt you believe it."

She deflated. "I don't. As soon as she told me, I felt like my only chance to escape had been stolen from me. I'm so weak."

"You're not weak, you just don't know what you want. You have a sweet deal. You live in a great house that you own, your kids are happy, you have family nearby. Sure, a part of you wants more—a job you like that challenges you—but there's a price for that. Why rock the boat?"

She took a gulp of her margarita. "You're saying I'm spineless."

"I'm saying you're comfortable. That makes it hard to do the work that change requires."

He was telling the truth but she sure didn't like what it said about her.

"I need to be a better person," she grumbled.

"You need to decide what you really want."

"I went on an interview. Sort of." She told him about the meeting with the twins. By the end of the story, he was laughing.

"So are they having sex?"

"Yuck, they're brother and sister, so don't even think that. And why do you have to go right to the sex question?"

"I'm a guy. It's what we do."

"Well, stop it. Sex isn't the answer to everything. Look at us. We're doing much better now that we've stopped having sex."

"Speak for yourself."

She ignored the comment. No way she was stepping back into that mess. Sleeping with Kyle was nothing but a distraction. Sort of like her semi-great life. She was just comfortable enough to not be motivated to find something better.

"I need goals," she said firmly. "And a plan to achieve them."

He leaned close and smiled at her. "How about we start with a second round of drinks? Then we'll conquer the world."

She raised her glass. "I'm in."

Mackenzie felt like she was four and it was the night before Christmas. She was excited and happy and filled with anticipation and possibilities. In her head she knew there were about a thousand steps to be taken between where she and Bruno were and buying Painted Moon, but just thinking about what could happen made her so happy.

Over the next couple of days, she did her job at Bel Après, but all her downtime was spent thinking about what she would want to do differently if given the chance. She had so many ideas, so many things she wanted to try and change and expand.

Rather than talk to Rhys, she contacted her divorce lawyer for a recommendation for a business lawyer who could help with the partnership agreement. A two-hour phone call and yet another check for five thousand dollars later, she officially had her second lawyer on retainer. Along with the contract and the receipt for the check, the lawyer had sent her a list of articles to read on starting a partnership, including a couple on pitfalls and mistakes the novice could make. He'd included an NDA that she could print out as needed and get people to sign.

As she'd promised Bruno, she didn't say anything to anyone—not Rhys or Stephanie, although it was difficult to keep quiet. At times she thought she would burst from the gloriousness of the secret.

She drove back from inspecting the vineyards in Oregon. Midday, midweek meant the traffic wasn't bad and she got to her office in time for a late lunch. The chef had left quinoa salads with a peanut dressing, which sounded delicious. Mackenzie was starving—she'd skipped breakfast to get an early start on her day.

As she poured the small container of dressing over the vegetables, grains and chickpeas, she wondered if Rhys had slipped away for a fast-food lunch. He refused to eat quinoa on principle. Something about being a guy and standing in solidarity against grain oppression.

She was still smiling about that when he walked into the upstairs break room, a large envelope in his hand.

"I was just thinking about you," she said with a laugh and waved her salad. "Did you eat yours?"

Instead of grinning back at her, he half turned away. "I went out for lunch."

"Rhys? What's wrong?"

He tensed, then faced her again, his expression serious. "Nothing. Did you look at the Seven Hills vineyards?"

"Yes. The irrigation is working fine and I'm loving how the grapes are ripening. We're going to have a good year."

He made a motion toward the hallway with his hand. A man she didn't know walked in. "Mackenzie Dienes?"

She looked from the stranger to Rhys and back. "Yes."

"I didn't know how to do this," Rhys told her. "I didn't know the right time or—"

The other man took the envelope Rhys held and offered it to her. She instinctively took it.

"You've been served," the man said and walked out.

Mackenzie stared at Rhys. "I don't understand."

He hunched a little. "I know. It's the divorce papers."

She nearly dropped the envelope as the meaning of his words sunk in. Divorce papers? Yes, she'd seen a lawyer, and this was where they were headed, but she hadn't thought, hadn't expected...

All the happiness of the previous days evaporated, taking her upbeat mood with it. Her body seemed to deflate, as if she were getting smaller and smaller and would, in a very short time, disappear.

Slowly, carefully, she put the large envelope on the counter and fought against the need to scrub her hands until every trace of the paper had been erased.

"Mackenzie?"

"It's okay," she said, not looking at him and hoping she sounded less upset than she was. "We talked about this. It's the next step, right?" She faked a smile as she finally turned to him. "I'll look these over, then get a copy to Ramona to review."

His gaze searched her face. "Are you all right?"

"Perfectly fine. Don't worry." She drew in a breath and went for perky. "At some point we're going to have to come up with a plan on who we're telling and when. I guess that's on me, with Barbara and all. I'm thinking we could mention the divorce first and leave the other stuff until I know what I'm doing. Just not today. If it could not be today, that would be great. We have the family dinner tomorrow, but we can pretend for that, can't we? Unless you're going to bring someone, in which case—"

He put his hands on her upper arms. "Mackenzie, stop talking."

"All right."

"I'm sorry," he told her. "I thought you were ready."

"I am," she lied.

"I hope that's true. I'm not trying to rush you."

The words were just right, but his actions belied the truth of them. Or maybe he really wasn't rushing, but instead was going at his speed, which was a lot closer to "get this over *now*" than hers was.

"We don't have to say anything to my family until you're ready. We'll be fine at the dinner, just like our living arrangements are working out for us."

He was right about that. They were still in the same house, living the lives they'd had before. How sad was it that getting a divorce had changed so little? And if that was true, why did she feel so awful inside?

"Thank you." She stepped back and forced herself to pick up the envelope. "Thanks for getting me these."

He watched her cautiously. "There's a tentative settlement agreement in there. It's what we talked about. I want to be fair."

"I appreciate that. I'll talk to Ramona."

He hesitated a second, then opened the break room door and left. Mackenzie glanced from the envelope to her salad. She picked up the latter and dropped it into the trash. On the way to her office, she swung by the bathroom and threw up the meager contents of her stomach. After rinsing out her mouth, she leaned against the cool tiles and told herself she wasn't going to cry. She couldn't—not without everyone wondering what was wrong. So from now until she could go home, she would have to pretend that everything was going to be all right. Even if she knew it wasn't.

Mackenzie stood in her closet, not sure what to wear to dinner. Every few weeks, Barbara called for a family dinner. Attendance was mandatory. Normally Mackenzie looked forward to the get-togethers as a chance to catch up with everyone and hang out with the people she loved most in the world. But not tonight—not when she and Rhys were working their way through a divorce and she was considering leaving Bel Après. Pretending normalcy under those circumstances was going to require a level of acting ability she was fairly sure she didn't possess.

Still, not going wasn't an option, so she studied the dresses hanging in her closet and hoped one of them would provide a little courage.

She settled on a simple sheath with a square neckline. The dark green fabric brought out the red in her hair. She stepped into a pair of nude pumps and returned to the bathroom, where she checked that her minimal makeup was all right, then walked downstairs.

Rhys, already showered and changed into dress pants and a long-sleeved shirt, was at his computer. He was typing and smiling. She was about to ask what he was doing when he looked up and saw her. His smile faded and his gaze darted away from her to the screen and back. If she had to pick an emotion from the look on his face, she would say he was feeling guilty. Why on earth—

Her stomach clenched as she realized he was doing something online with a woman who wasn't her. Probably just sending an email, but still.

"You look nice," he said. "We're not expected for another twenty minutes."

"I know. I thought I'd go see Stephanie first. I'll meet you there?"

"Sure." He glanced at the screen, then back at her. "Anything else?"

She thought about asking who he was online with but didn't. Whatever was happening wasn't her business. And if knowing he'd already moved on still shocked her, then that was her problem.

She walked the short distance to Stephanie's house and let herself inside.

"It's me," she called.

"In my office," her sister-in-law yelled back.

Mackenzie walked down the short hallway and stepped into Stephanie's home office.

Stephanie had decorated her space with pale walls and brightly colored paintings. Open shelving displayed awards and certificates her children had earned, along with various art projects. A few drawings were framed—the primitive stick figures nestled up against professionally painted scenes.

Stephanie glanced up and smiled. "Hey, you. How's it going? I've stopped by to see you a few times, but you're never home these days."

"Sorry. I've been busy with different stuff." Mackenzie closed the door behind her and settled in a chair. "Rhys served me with divorce papers."

Stephanie's eyes filled with sympathy. "Are you okay with that or do I need to march over there and slap him really hard?"

"I'm okay. Sort of." She thought about the shock when he'd handed her the envelope. "I didn't know a person was actually served with the paperwork. I wasn't expecting it."

Stephanie closed her laptop. "You need to get mad at him. Anger gives you purpose."

"Four would tell you that's the wrong thing to say."

"Four lives in a world where woodland creatures help her dress every morning." Stephanie held up a hand. "That came out more bitchy than I mean, but you get my point. Divorce sucks, even if you both want it. I was crushed to end things with Kyle, and he'd been cheating on me for years. You commit yourself to someone when you get married and you assume it's going to last forever. Finding out that's not true isn't easy to deal with. There's a sense of failure, of loss. I was terrified, and I had a place to run to. You're going to be striking out on your own. It's got to be confusing and hard to think about and I'm sure you feel lost. Then my stupid brother serves you with papers. Want me to beat him up?"

Mackenzie managed a smile. "Thank you, but no."

"I could do it, mostly because he would never hit me back. You okay?"

"Sometimes. Other times, like you said, I feel lost." She sighed. "I've been thinking about all the last times. Is this the last family dinner? The last time I'll put out the cookie flag, the last time I'll visit you here?" She blinked against burning in her eyes.

"You'll visit me here lots of times. We're going to stay friends. If you try pulling back, I'll stalk you until you give in. We're friends. Forever friends. Don't you believe that?"

"I do, but I'm worried your mom will put you in a difficult situation. I don't want you to have to choose."

"She's a pain, but she's not totally unreasonable." Stephanie paused. "Well, she is, but not all the time. You and I are going to grow old together."

Mackenzie nodded. "I want that, but sometimes it's hard to see past what's happening right now. I'm losing everything I've felt anchored to. It's hard to just drift around."

"I'll be your anchor." Stephanie frowned. "Why does that sound like the title of a song?"

"I don't know. Maybe it is. Probably from the eighties. They had some great song titles back then."

"You were barely born in the eighties. How would you know?"

Mackenzie smiled. "I know things."

Stephanie laughed. "You're so weird." She glanced at the clock on the wall. "Okay, we need to leave now or we'll be late, and you know how my mom gets if someone is late."

They both rose and walked out together. When they reached the front door, Mackenzie paused. "Isn't Avery coming with us?"

"She went over before you got here. She likes hanging out with her grandmother, if you can believe it." Stephanie shuddered, then laughed.

Mackenzie didn't know what to say to that. She and Barbara had always gotten along, as well. Maybe because they weren't blood relatives. Mackenzie had been so grateful to have a mother figure in her life that she'd been able to overlook the other woman's, um, idiosyncrasies. They also had the winery in common. Each of them could talk about Bel Après for hours and still have more to say.

They crossed the courtyard together and went up the front stairs of the largest house. As Stephanie knocked once, then pushed open the door, Mackenzie couldn't help thinking again about the "lasts." Was this the last time she would walk through the big wooden door? The last time she would greet everyone with smiles and hugs? Had she already lived through the last Christmas, the last Easter, the last Summer Solstice Party?

Sadness gripped her, making it hard to breathe. Change was hard, but this was much more difficult than she'd thought it would be. Her fears weren't about the various holidays so much as wondering when she would experience the last time she could say this was her family. Because this was the only family she had in the world, and when she and Rhys were divorced, she would be completely on her own. And then who would she be?

thirteen

Stephanie spent a couple of days watching Avery without seeming to watch her. Not an easy trick, considering Avery was a sixteen-year-old and, by nature, suspicious of her mother. But at the family dinner, Avery had overheard her asking Mackenzie if she was doing all right and had wanted to know what was wrong. Stephanie wondered if she'd done the right thing in telling the girl. Was Avery mature enough to handle the information?

Things seemed to go fine until Sunday morning when Stephanie knocked on her daughter's bedroom door. Whatever else was going on in their lives, she always made a big breakfast with whatever the kids wanted.

"Avery, sweetie, I'm going to make breakfast. What do you want? Pancakes and bacon? An omelet?"

"Nothing. Go away."

Normally the rude response would have made Stephanie bristle, but there was something in her daughter's tone that made her open the door and step inside.

Summer sunlight spilled into the room, illuminating the unmade bed and clothes tossed everywhere. But what actually caught her attention was the sight of her daughter curled up on the floor, in a far corner of the room.

Stephanie rushed to her, sinking down to her knees and reaching for her.

"What happened? Are you sick? Did someone hurt you?"

Avery pushed her away and sat up on her own. "I'm fine. Leave me alone." Tears poured down her cheeks as she spoke. Her eyes were red, her face pale. "I don't want to talk about it. Go away."

Stephanie ignored all that and pulled her daughter close. Avery resisted for a second, then sagged against her. Tears turned into sobs, shaking her body with their intensity.

Stephanie hung on, rubbing her back, waiting out the storm. She was fairly sure her daughter wasn't sick, which left heartache or something much worse. Rape crossed her mind, but she pushed the thought aside. She would wait to find out what was wrong before she freaked out.

After a few minutes, Avery straightened. "Alexander slept with Bettina. He said he had to because I wouldn't sleep with him so I can't be upset because it's my fault. That made me mad so I broke up with him. Then he got mad at me and said I'm a stupid, immature little girl and he's done wasting his time with me."

Instead of screaming and then getting in her car to go beat up the boy in question, Stephanie forced herself to stay where she was.

"I'm sorry," she murmured. "Boys can be real jerks. You did the right thing. I'm so proud of you, sweetie. I know it hurts so much. I know you feel sick inside and you're questioning everything you said and did, but you are so strong."

Avery nodded, then grabbed a box of tissues from the desk. "I had to be, you know? I wasn't going to let him treat me the way you let Daddy treat you."

The statement was made so casually, in such a normal tone, that Stephanie didn't get it at first.

"What are you talking about?"

Avery wiped her face. "Dad's cheating. I've known, Mom, for a while now. About all the stuff he did."

She blew her nose. "I talked to him about it. He told me he'd been wrong and that I should never let a guy do to me what he did to you. That he made mistakes, but you suffered for them."

Stephanie was so incredibly grateful she was sitting on the floor—otherwise she would have collapsed in a heap. Shock and shame and horror swept through her.

"I never knew why you and Dad split up, but when I found out about the cheating, it made sense. I didn't tell Carson. He doesn't want to know about stuff like that." Avery's eyes filled with tears. "When Alexander told me what he did, I felt so awful. Like he'd betrayed everything we'd had, even as he tried to make it my fault. I knew then it was over, that I had to be strong. I wasn't going to do what you did and stick around."

The words were earnest and guileless, Stephanie thought, fighting the need to run as far and as fast as she could manage. Avery wasn't trying to hurt her—she was explaining the situation from her point of view. Just like Stephanie didn't want to be like Barbara, Avery didn't want to be like her. It was the circle of life when it came to mothers and daughters.

But that didn't stop her from feeling as if her daughter had ripped out her heart with her bare hands and then torn it up into tiny pieces.

Avery surprised her by leaning against her. "I just wish it didn't hurt so much to be strong."

"You did the right thing. When it gets really bad, keep telling yourself that. I'm proud of you and you should be proud of yourself."

"Thanks."

"Want some pancakes and bacon?"

"Okay."

Stephanie forced a smile, then got to her feet. She had to hang on to the wall to make it back to the kitchen, and when she was there, she looked down at the floor, expecting to see a pool of her own blood. There was only the hardwood and a few crumbs. Nothing that indicated she'd been emotionally flayed open by the casual comments of her teenage daughter.

Guilt trailed Mackenzie her entire drive to Painted Moon. Ever since Bruno's call two days before, she'd been torn between wild excitement at the possibilities and fear and worry about making such a big change. The "should she or shouldn't she" question had filled her waking hours, but the moment she drove through the big open gates, the feeling was replaced with one of anticipation.

The winery had been established for two generations. Not the first vineyard in the valley, but close.

She drove by a couple of acres of vineyard that had been planted for show on her way up to what had been the tasting room. That big building was closed now. Herman had stopped bottling wine a few years back. Now he sold grapes and directly from the barrel.

She'd met the old guy dozens of times at various events. He was knowledgeable and always friendly, but she'd sensed his heart hadn't been in the business for a while.

As she parked next to a new Mercedes she would guess belonged to Bruno, she tried to slow her breathing. Whatever the outcome, just asking the questions would be good for her. She was open to moving on. While buying Painted Moon would be an incredible opportunity, she shouldn't get her hopes up. A whole lot could go wrong.

All of which was true, but didn't stop the fluttering in her chest as she got out of her Jeep. In the distance was the old farmhouse, set up on a rise that would overlook much of the property. The morning was warm, the sun bright.

She found Bruno and Herman talking. She shook hands with both.

Herman, a small man with gray hair and weathered skin, grinned at her. "Your business partner there already had me sign an NDA. I like that you're protecting yourself. If we do this, Barbara is going to want to set us all on fire, so you want to cover your backside, for sure."

The combination of visuals had her struggling to keep up, although his point about Barbara was a good one.

"We're still just exploring," she said. "Thank you for signing the NDA."

"Did I have a choice?" he asked with a chuckle. "All right, let's get started." He started walking at a brisk pace. "My children have no interest in the wine business. They want me to sell, and to be honest, I'm getting old enough that I see their point. Painted Moon is producing about eighty-five thousand gallons a year." He winked at Mackenzie. "More than Bel Après, missy."

That many gallons? She'd had no idea. "You're right, it is." It was substantially less than the bigger, well-known wineries, such as Ste. Michelle, which produced over two million gallons a year, but it was plenty for her to work with.

He led them into the barrel room. The heavy barrels stretched out in rows, vertically and horizontally.

"Most of this is sold," he said. "There are about twenty thousand gallons I meant to do something with, but haven't yet." His humor faded. "I don't taste as well as I used to." He pointed at her. "You could make something happen here. You have the gift."

"Thank you."

They walked over to one of the barrels. Herman collected glasses and a pitcher, then they tasted a few different wines. Mackenzie swirled the liquid in her mouth before spitting it out. There was potential here, she thought. She could do something with this.

"I have contracts for about half of this year's crop," Herman told them. "But only for this year. I've been thinking of selling for a while now and didn't want to tie up my assets."

They tasted more wine. She wasn't happy with the whites, but all the reds had real potential.

"I had the business valued a couple of years ago," Herman said as they moved down the rows. "A couple of guys came from Seattle and walked around with clipboards. I'm in the nine-five range."

"Nine million, five hundred thousand," Mackenzie said, trying not to faint.

"Yup."

She looked at Bruno, who seemed unconcerned.

They spent the better part of the day looking at the facilities and a couple of the vineyards. By four, Mackenzie was exhausted and her head hurt from all she'd tried to absorb. She and Bruno thanked Herman, then they drove back to his hotel and went up to his room.

"What did you think?" he asked after getting them each a bottle of water and sitting across from her at the table.

"It was a lot to take in," she said. "The land is incredible. I'd want to see the rest of it and I'm guessing you'd need to look at his books and stuff. Nine-five seems like a lot."

"It is. I think we'd settle closer to eight. What did you think about the wines?"

"The white is crap. Honestly it was so bad, I'd want to dump it."

Bruno winced. "Seriously?"

She smiled. "Yes, I'd want to, but I'm sure we could sell it to someone to bottle and distribute. The reds are great. They have plenty of fruit and tannin. They could be blended a lot of different ways. They're money in the barrel."

She leaned back in her chair. "How do you even start with

something like that? We'd have to check all the deeds, look at the contracts, look at any liabilities. We have to confirm the water rights, because without them, we have nothing. All the equipment needs to be evaluated. The buildings themselves have to be inspected. What about liens and lawsuits and I don't know what else?"

Bruno smiled. "You've been doing your homework."

"It's all I can think about, when I'm not feeling guilty for considering leaving Bel Après."

"Is it still just a consideration?"

She thought about the divorce papers.

"No, it's not just a consideration," she said, reality hitting her in the gut. "But it makes me sad."

"You still want to move forward with this?"

"Is it possible?"

"Us buying a business together? Sure. I'm good with what we talked about. You put in your two million, I take care of the rest. We'll write up an agreement such that if we sell, I get a bigger cut of that. Until then, it's fifty-fifty. I run the business side and you run the winery. Painted Moon will be your vision." He finished his bottle of water. "You can have the house, if you want. It's not really my style. I'm thinking of buying a condo on the golf course."

"I'm interested," she said, "but it's a lot to take in. Plus I won't have my money until the divorce is final. That's three months from the day we file. What if we need the cash before then?"

"We'll work out a bridge loan."

"With a bank?"

His dark eyes glinted with amusement. "We'll keep it in the family."

Oh, sure, because he had an extra two million lying around. "How rich are you?" she asked before she could stop herself. "Sorry. Pretend I didn't ask that."

"There's something of a family fortune and I've done well on my own."

Must be nice, she thought. "So what happens now?"

"If you want to move forward, I'll draw up the partnership agreement with the terms we've agreed upon. You get your lawyer to look it over. Once that's signed, I'll get a team going on appraising Painted Moon. I'll have my finance people look over the books and you'll head the team that will be responsible for the vineyards and the winery. Once we know what we're talking about, we'll make an offer."

"Just like that?"

"Is there a reason to wait?"

"You're making it really easy," she said.

"I'm getting what I want. I have plenty of money, Mackenzie. What I don't have is your talent. You're the best and I want to work with you. Whatever I can do to make your decision easier is on my get-done list. Are you ready to move forward?"

He held out his hand. She thought about all that had happened in the past few weeks. Her life had changed in every way possible. If she wanted to keep her job at Bel Après, she could, but she wouldn't be part of the family anymore. Not after the divorce. Bruno was offering her the moon. She smiled. A painted moon, but a moon all the same.

"I'm in," she said, shaking his hand. "Let's do this."

Three days later, Mackenzie was drowning in paperwork. Her potential business partner hadn't wasted any time getting the process started. She already had a partnership agreement, a preliminary sales offer for Herman and the first of what she would guess were going to be dozens of survey reports.

She'd emailed a copy of the partnership and purchase agreements to her business lawyer but was determined to review them herself. To that end, she had a stack of sticky notes and a legal pad next to her so she could figure out her questions as she went.

To switch things up, she also had the divorce settlement to go through—oh, and in her spare time, a winery to run.

It was a lot to deal with, but also exciting. Lately she'd been waking up at four and reading for a couple of hours before starting her day job. After work, she rushed through dinner to spend several more hours in her office. At Bruno's suggestion, she'd purchased a small lockbox in which to keep all the paperwork—no doubt the smart thing to do, but it made her feel guilty every time she put all the various files away.

About seven, Rhys knocked on her half-open door. "Hi. I haven't seen you much in the past week or so. I thought I'd check in and find out how things are going."

He looked good, she thought with a twinge of sadness. Tall and strong. Steady. Rhys had always been steady. She didn't miss him romantically, but she regretted what had been lost.

She opened her desk drawer and pulled out a single sheet of paper. She slid a pen close and said, "Unless you want to talk weather and the divorce, you'll have to sign this first."

Her soon-to-be ex-husband stepped forward and scanned the NDA, then started to laugh. "Seriously?"

Her natural instinct was to tell him no, of course he didn't have to sign it. She trusted him—if he said he wouldn't tell anyone, he wouldn't. But her lawyer and Bruno had been very clear. Without an NDA, no one found out anything.

He grinned as he signed, then took the seat opposite her. "Someone's been giving you good advice."

"I hope so. Lawyers are expensive."

"But necessary. So what's going on?"

She drew in a breath. She and Rhys might be splitting up, but she respected his opinion. "We're looking at Painted Moon."

His eyebrows rose and he gave a low whistle. "Herman's property. That's a beauty. Great land. Quality, established vines. Make sure you confirm the water rights. No water, no business."

She smiled. "That's what I thought."

"Are you going to make an offer?"

"We're considering it." She held several papers. "My partnership agreement with Bruno. The lawyer's looking it over right now."

Rhys's humor faded. "I'd offer to read it, but that isn't my place anymore, is it?"

They looked at each other, then both turned away. She spoke first.

"Speaking of the divorce, I've gone over the settlement agreement and it seems okay. I'm waiting for a final approval from Ramona, but I don't anticipate any problems."

He shifted in his seat. "Once we file, it's ninety days until everything is final."

"Assuming we don't contest it."

He looked at her. "That would be like fighting. We never fight."

"I know." That was part of the problem. They hadn't had the energy to fight about anything. And without that energy, there wasn't any passion or drive.

Their marriage had been like the conversation they were currently having. At this point in a breakup, other couples would be casting blame and throwing accusations like knives. Not them. They were sensible and rational. Logical. They were both moving on and soon everything they'd had would be a memory.

Somehow that realization was the worst thing of all. Shouldn't sixteen years together have left a few visible scars?

"We need to tell my mom about the divorce, Mackenzie," he said. "You can keep the rest of it from her for as long as you'd like, but letting her know about us splitting up should happen soon."

"I agree."

"I can do it."

He was giving her an easy out—because he was the kind of man who did that sort of thing.

"I'll tell her," she said slowly. "I have a meeting with her to-morrow. I'll give her the news then, both about the divorce and about me leaving."

Rhys winced. "So soon? What if it doesn't work out with Painted Moon?"

"Then Bruno and I will buy something else. I can't stay here anymore. I'm hoping to take you up on your offer to live in the house for a month or so, just to give me time to settle every-thing, but then I need to be gone."

Saying the words made them real, she thought. So far there had been only bits and pieces of reality. Or maybe that wasn't true. Maybe it had become real the second Rhys had looked at her and asked if their marriage was over.

"Do you want me to come with you?"

"I'll be all right. It should be me, Rhys. You know that."

He nodded slowly. "I'll be around if you need me."

"Or protection?" she asked, mostly joking.

"You can always hide behind me."

A sweet offer, but not one she could take advantage of, she told herself. At least not anymore.

fourteen

Mackenzie tried to tell herself she wasn't nervous about her meeting with Barbara, only she knew she was lying. How could she not be? She'd been a part of Bel Après since college—basically her entire adult life. She didn't know anything else. Was she wrong to want more?

Trying to ignore the question, she prowled the barrel room, hoping to distract herself but unable to do anything but check the large clock on the wall and see if it was close enough to eight thirty for her to go into the main building and see Barbara in her office.

"I'm doing the right thing," she whispered to herself. "She'll understand."

Barbara, while occasionally difficult, had always been warm and affectionate toward Mackenzie. She remembered her first time on the property—when Barbara had invited her on a tour of the winery. They'd driven to the closest vineyards and Barbara had talked about her hopes and dreams for the business. They'd walked the barrel room and discussed the differences between a good wine and a great one. They had talked for so long that Rhys had finally come looking for them.

Over the next couple of years, Barbara had become like a second mother. She was the one Mackenzie turned to for advice. She'd been the one to give Mackenzie away when she'd married Rhys, joking that she was happy to perform the duty because she was getting Mackenzie right back. At social events, Barbara introduced her as her daughter of the heart—a title that had both embarrassed and warmed Mackenzie.

Now she looked around at the familiar room and wondered if she was making a mistake. Should she stay here instead of leaving? But she already knew the answer, and the truth was, she'd already decided what she wanted. As for Barbara and their closeness, perhaps that, too, had faded with time. Gone were the long walks in the vineyards and the late-afternoon talks that spilled into the evening. These days she saw her mother-in-law during their weekly meetings, at family dinners and in passing.

She walked to the office building, took the stairs two at a time and entered Barbara's office.

Her mother-in-law, dressed perfectly in a deep blue suit and pearls, smiled at her.

"You're right on time, as always." Barbara motioned to a chair. "I feel as if I haven't seen you in ages."

The warm tone and welcoming words made Mackenzie swallow hard. She closed the door and took a seat.

"I've been busy," she said. "There's a lot going on." She paused, not sure how to begin.

Barbara leaned toward her. "Oh, dear. Something's wrong. I can see it in your eyes. Tell me what it is. We don't have a pest problem anywhere, do we? I know the new fencing has made a difference with the deer. I hope it's not a bear getting into the grapes. Bears can do so much damage."

"It's not about the winery," Mackenzie told her, twisting her fingers together, trying to ignore the sense of foreboding. "It's about Rhys and me. We're getting a divorce."

Barbara's concerned expression didn't change. "Are you? I'm sorry to hear that. I thought you were happy together."

"We're not and we haven't been for a while. It's a mutual decision. It's sad for both of us."

"Of course it is." Barbara leaned back in her chair. "You must be disappointed. Do you want me to talk to Rhys for you?"

"What? No. We're actually getting along." She managed a slight smile. "We're being very sensible as we uncouple."

Barbara nodded but otherwise didn't seem to react. Was she not surprised or did the marriage not matter? Mackenzie wasn't sure which.

Barbara sighed. "However well you're getting along, the situation must be painful. I'm sorry, my dear. Let me know if I can help in any way. And to be clear, nothing between us changes. Your job isn't in jeopardy at all. I hope you know that already, but I want to say it anyway. You're a significant part of Bel Après. I'll miss having you as my daughter-in-law, but you'll always have a place here." She smiled. "We'd be lost without you."

"Thank you for saying that." Mackenzie's stomach flipped over and her chest got tight. "The thing is, I wanted to talk about that, too."

Barbara's body stiffened as her expression tightened. "I don't know what that means. Talk about what?"

"My future."

"Which is here, where you belong. I won't hear otherwise. You need to be here, Mackenzie. You and I are Bel Après. You're the winemaker. Together we create magic." She gave a high-pitched laugh. "Thinking of being anywhere else is madness."

"I can't stay," she murmured, wishing she could run and knowing she had to face whatever happened.

"Of course you can." Barbara's voice sharpened. "You must. This is your home. A divorce doesn't change that. Are you concerned about the house? We can have another one built. You can't walk away from this. We're part of your family, your history. Without us, what would you have?"

Her gaze narrowed. "Are you going to work for someone else? You can't. I forbid it."

"How can you forbid it? You don't own me." Irritation replaced worry.

"You have a noncompete contract with the winery."

"I don't have a contract with you at all. I never signed one."

Barbara rose to her feet. "You're wrong. Everyone signs one. I would have made sure of it. Don't you dare think about working for anyone else. If you try, I'll ruin you."

If the words were intended to intimidate, they weren't working. The madder Barbara got, the more determined Mackenzie felt.

"It doesn't have to be like this," she said, careful to keep her voice calm and reasonable. "I don't want to fight with you."

"Too late for that. You're leaving? Is that your point? Well, you can forget that. You're fired! Do you hear me? You're fired. I should never have trusted you. Never. I bought into that poor orphan-girl routine and the whole time you were planning to betray me."

Mackenzie stared at her, unable to believe what was happening. She'd always known the conversation was going to be difficult, but she hadn't expected anything like this. The ridiculous accusations bombarded her from all sides, making her want to find a way to protect herself.

"Barbara, please," she began.

Her mother-in-law cut her off. "Don't try changing your mind now. We're done."

"Barbara, I've been a part of this family for sixteen years. Surely we can talk about this." There had to be some middle ground where they could remember how much they meant to each other.

"Get out!"

Mackenzie realized there was no point in trying to reason with her. Maybe later they could have a real conversation. She walked out the door and down the hall, not sure what to do now.

She felt hollow and cold, and a little bit unsteady. She'd been fired. Should she empty her desk? Just leave? She had the thought that she should have let Rhys come with her. Even if he'd just waited in his office, she would have known he was close by.

Only he wasn't her husband anymore, she reminded herself, suddenly fighting tears.

"Bitch."

She turned and saw Lori glaring at her.

"I heard everything," Lori continued. "I'm glad she fired you."

The cold loathing in the other woman's voice was as shocking as a slap. Mackenzie took a step back.

"Lori, why are you acting like this? You *know* me."

"Better than you think. You're horrible and I hate you."

Mackenzie felt her stomach lurch and worried she was going to throw up. She ran downstairs and took a golf cart back to the house. When she was inside, she did something she'd never done in all the years she'd lived there—she locked the doors.

She texted Stephanie and Rhys to warn them what had happened. Stephanie didn't answer but Rhys texted he was on his way home.

Ten minutes later, she heard knocking at the back door. She ran through the kitchen and opened it, then threw herself into his arms. He held her tight.

"I'm sorry," he murmured, kissing the top of her head. "I knew it was going to be bad, but I didn't expect her to fire you."

"Me, either."

He urged her to sit at the kitchen table, then tell him what had happened.

"It was awful," Mackenzie said, wiping away tears. "She fired me and told me to get out. Just like that. I didn't know what to do. So much for being the daughter of the heart."

"She was in shock. She'll come around."

"You really believe that?"

He hesitated. "Maybe."

Despite everything, she managed to smile. "You are so lying."

"Just a little. I am sorry."

"I know. Me, too."

She told him what had happened with Lori.

"That almost shocks me more," he admitted. "I'll go talk to her."

"Don't. It's done now. I guess she and I weren't friends. I can handle it. If Stephanie turns on me, I'll have a big problem, but I can deal with Lori not being a fan."

Rhys took her hands. "How can I help?"

"Listening is big. Thank you. And it would be nice if you got my personal stuff from my desk at the office." She tried to smile. "At least I have more time to work on buying Painted Moon. Oh, and I need to find a place to live."

"No. You're staying here, just like we agreed."

"Rhys, no. It will make trouble with your mom."

He grinned. "All the more reason to stay. Look, you and Bruno are paying cash for the winery, so you can close in a couple of months. Stay here until then."

"I'll think about it."

Before she could say anything else, Stephanie raced into the kitchen.

"I just saw your text. Mom fired you? How could she?" she demanded, hurrying over to Mackenzie and hugging her. "Are you okay? How can I help? It's early to start drinking, but I'm all in if you want to go that route."

Mackenzie felt a little of her fear fading. "All I need to know is that we're still friends."

"Always." Stephanie sat next to her and grabbed her hand.

"Best friends. Come on, I'm not going to let my mother get between us. Who do you think I am? Lori?"

Mackenzie found herself laughing and crying. "Never that."

"I'm here," Stephanie told her. She waved at Rhys. "Go back to work, big brother. I've got this."

He nodded and stood. "Text if you need anything."

"I will."

When he had left, Stephanie leaned in. "So I'm thinking we find a witch and make a voodoo doll of my mom."

"I don't think witches do that sort of thing."

"Whatever. Come on. We'll go online and search for mystical revenge. That should bring up some really fun websites."

Mackenzie hugged her. "You're the best."

Barbara sat at her desk, trying to catch her breath. She felt as if the room had started spinning, and she couldn't make it stop. Fury welled up inside of her, making her want to throw something, but under that was a growing sense of betrayal and panic.

Mackenzie was leaving! How was that possible? They were a team, they'd always been a team. The two of them and the wine and everything they'd done together. Mackenzie was Bel Après. Without her, there was nothing.

The bitch had betrayed them all and, yes, that had to be dealt with, but first, what was she going to do now? If Mackenzie left—

"She can't," Barbara said aloud. "I won't let her. I'll take her to court. I'll have her arrested. I'll do something!"

She reached for her phone only to realize her hands were shaking. Two attempts later, she managed to pick it up and place the call.

Giorgio picked up on the second ring.

"I was just thinking about you, my love," he said, his voice full of affection. "But that's how I spend most of my time, so I doubt the news is a surprise."

At the sound of his voice, she started to cry. The action shocked her nearly as much as the news about Mackenzie—she never cried. Not once in twenty-six years. The last time she'd cried had been at James's funeral. Standing there as they'd lowered his coffin into the ground, she'd vowed to be strong, and she had been—until this.

"What is it?" he asked, his voice thick with concern. "What happened?"

"I need you. Can you come to my office?"

"I'll be there in fifteen minutes. Whatever it is, we'll take care of it together."

She nodded, even though he couldn't see her, and hung up. She was still shaking, and her heart was pounding so hard in her chest she thought she might throw up.

She had to focus, she told herself. Start thinking about what this all meant and how to make the situation workable. She had to figure out what she—

"Mom?"

She looked up and saw Lori standing in the doorway. The sight of her middle daughter with her too-tight suit and hangdog expression annoyed her more than usual.

"What?" she asked, her voice tense.

"I heard what happened with Mackenzie," Lori began.

"Of course you did. God forbid I have one second of privacy in this damn place. Fine. You heard. Now keep the information to yourself. No one needs to know until I decide what to do next."

"Maybe I can help."

"How, exactly? How could you possibly replace Mackenzie? She's a master winemaker. Your little foray into that side of the business was a disaster and cost me thousands of dollars. You have the taste buds of paint. So if not that, what other brilliant ideas do you have?"

Lori's lower lip began to tremble—a telltale sign that she was about to cry. Barbara deliberately turned away from her and opened her lower desk drawer. Behind a box of envelopes was a small bottle of tequila she kept for emergencies.

She unscrewed the top and took a long swallow. The liquor burned the entire way down her throat. When she set the bottle on her desk, she saw her daughter had left. Thank God. She couldn't take one more thing.

She sat there, sipping tequila, staring at the wall until Giorgio walked in.

"What happened?" he asked, holding open his arms.

She rose and ran into his embrace, letting his warmth and strength give her a false sense of security.

"It's Mackenzie," she said. "She's betrayed me. She's a horrible, lying, awful person and I never saw it until today."

The tears returned. Giorgio held her tight, murmuring soothingly until she had a little more control, then he led her over to the sofa in the corner.

"Tell me everything," he said.

She told him about the divorce and how she'd assured Mackenzie that it wouldn't affect her position at Bel Après. He listened attentively, holding her hands in his.

"It's just such a slap in the face," she concluded. "What is she going to do? Work somewhere else?" She stared at him. "What if she steals our secrets? What if she steals our customers? She's going to try to destroy us and I don't know why. We've been her family, her life. To act like this tells me there's something fundamentally wrong with her. Do you think I could get her committed somewhere?"

Giorgio smiled. "I love how you try to see the humor in such a difficult situation."

Barbara didn't bother pointing out that she hadn't been kidding. Getting Mackenzie into a mental institution was probably a little far-fetched, but it would certainly suit her purposes.

"I'm sorry about their divorce," he said. "It's always tragic when love is lost. Did you know they were unhappy?"

Why in God's name was he asking about that? She didn't care about their feelings or their marriage. Bel Après was at stake! But she understood that Giorgio was much kinder than she was, and while she might find that tedious at times, it was one of the reasons she'd fallen in love with him.

"Neither of them ever said anything," she told him. "She said it's a mutual decision and very amicable, so the winery is slightly more pressing. We don't have a winemaker. I always meant to get around to hiring a backup, but with Mackenzie here, it didn't seem necessary. None of the children can do it. I've stepped in before, but we were much smaller then. With how many gallons we bottle each year, I don't think I'm qualified. I need a plan."

"You need to talk to Mackenzie. Why is she leaving?"

"I don't know. She's a bitch. Isn't that a good enough reason?"

He squeezed her fingers. "My love, she's like a daughter to you. You've worked together so closely. But maybe her decision to leave is about being unhappy. You and yours are the only family she has. She wouldn't give that up easily, so there must be something else. Has she ever said anything to you about what she wanted from her life that she doesn't have?"

Barbara quickly tried to suppress the memories, but they were too strong. She recalled years ago when Mackenzie had asked if she would ever have a part of Bel Après. Barbara had explained about the will and how only blood relatives could inherit. Mackenzie had been desperate to somehow buy in or work hard so she could be one of the owners, but Barbara had told her that would never happen.

"What are you thinking?"

She pressed her lips together. "Oh, she talked about wanting to have a share of the winery. It couldn't possibly happen, and I told her to never ask again. It's not my fault," she added, knowing she sounded defensive. "James's will is very clear."

"There must be ways around that."

Possibly, but why would she want to look for them? Instead of saying that, she murmured, "I'm not sure it would help."

"Mackenzie's alone in the world. It makes sense she wants to feel connected to something as wonderful as Bel Après. Perhaps a tiny percentage of—"

"No."

"But my sweet—"

"Giorgio, no. She can't have any ownership in the winery. That's just how it is."

"But you love her."

"Not anymore."

He drew back. "You don't mean that. She's the daughter of your heart."

"She's a lying bitch who wants to leave us."

He studied her for a few seconds. "You're still upset. I'm sorry—I shouldn't have pushed you. Forgive me?"

"Of course. You're not the problem, you're never the problem. It's Bel Après. Everything could be ruined."

"Then focus all your incredible talents on finding a new winemaker. I would imagine there are dozens who would jump at the chance to work for such a prestigious label." He leaned close and kissed her. "How can I help?"

"Just being here makes me feel better."

"Good." He pulled her into his embrace. "Sweet, sweet Barbara. We'll get through this together."

She nodded, because it was the kind thing to do, but knew in her heart that there was no "we" when it came to this problem. There was only her and finding a solution to a horrible situation.

Damn Mackenzie, she thought grimly. Damn her straight to hell.

fifteen

Stephanie was not happy to be summoned to her mother's house, especially not on the day Mackenzie had told Barbara she was leaving. But the text had been specific enough that she couldn't figure out a way to get out of going.

Be at my house at 7 p.m. I will accept no excuses.

Stephanie stared at her phone, hoping for a reprieve, but sadly the screen stayed dark. In fifteen minutes she was going to have to walk the too-short distance between their homes and deal with whatever crap her mother wanted to send her way.

She debated getting drunk before heading over. A coward's way to deal, but she could live with that. Only there wasn't enough time, and in the name of self-preservation, she should probably keep her wits about herself—as much as she could, under the circumstances.

"Mom?"

She looked up from her place at the kitchen island and saw Avery standing in the doorway. Her daughter was still a little pale and there were shadows under her eyes, but she seemed to be on the road to recovery. Oh, to be young again, and bounce back quickly, she thought. Stephanie, on the other hand, kept flashing back to the conversation from a few days ago when her daughter had matter-of-factly mentioned she knew about Kyle's cheating and was doing her best not to be the fool her mother had been. Humbling, humiliating, but wise on Avery's part.

"Madison invited me over to her place," she said. "I'll be back by eleven."

Stephanie forced a smile. "I'm glad you're getting out."

"I heard from Alexander. He's sorry and wants me to meet him tomorrow."

"What are you going to do?" she asked, careful to keep her tone and expression neutral.

"I told him we were done and that I was blocking him on my phone."

Stephanie relaxed. "You're amazing. I'm so proud of you, sweetie."

Avery nodded without much enthusiasm. "I know it's the right thing to do, but it still hurts."

Stephanie risked rejection and wrath by hugging her daughter. "I know it's hard to believe now, but eventually you're going to feel better. Then you're going to find a great guy who treats you the way you deserve to be treated."

Avery returned the hug before stepping back. "Am I? You never have. You don't date or anything. Your whole life is here. You work for Bel Après, your best friend is your sister-in-law. Don't you ever want a bigger life?"

Stephanie did her best not to flinch. "I have a good job and I spend my days with the people I love best."

The words came automatically. It was only after she spoke that she remembered she hated her job and working for her mother, and that not saying that to her daughter was ignoring the truth and a chance to share an important life lesson.

"If you say so," Avery murmured before walking to the back door. "See you later."

"Wait!" Stephanie called, but it was too late. Her daughter was gone and she was left alone with her half-truths and regrets.

Ugh. Not the best frame of mind to go deal with her mother, she thought as she walked across the courtyard and into her mother's house.

Of the four homes clustered together, Barbara's was the most traditional. A two-story foyer opened into a formal living room. The dining room had a long table that could seat twenty when all the leaves were put in. High ceilings were decorated with elegant molding, and expensive rugs covered hardwood floors.

Stephanie walked into the family room at the rear of the house. Large sofas formed a U shape in front of a huge stone fireplace. There was no television—that was upstairs, in the media room. One did not visit Barbara Barcellona to be distracted by a cartoon or a football game.

She saw her mother and Lori already seated on one of the sofas.

"Hey, Mom," Stephanie said as she approached.

"You're here. Good." Her mother waved a crystal highball glass. "What would you like to drink?"

Stephanie eyed the liquid already in her mother's glass and had a bad feeling it was tequila. Wine was Barbara's usual drink, but when life got tough, she opted for the serious liquor and things generally went downhill from there.

Stephanie saw Lori had a glass of white wine in front of her. "I'll have what Lori's having."

She retreated to the kitchen and found an open bottle of chardonnay in the refrigerator. She poured herself a glass. She chugged half of it, then refilled it before putting the bottle back. She'd just settled across from her mother when Four walked in.

"Tell me you didn't start without me," Four said cheerfully. "I hate to miss anything."

Stephanie held in a groan. She'd texted Four earlier to warn her that Mackenzie had told Barbara she was leaving and had then been fired, so she couldn't say her sister didn't know she was stepping into a minefield. But that was Four's way—she often sailed unafraid into troubled waters.

"I can't believe you don't know what happened today," her mother snapped. "Stop acting so ridiculously happy and get yourself a drink."

"No thanks." Four sat next to Stephanie and tucked her feet under her. "I take it from your tone that you're upset about Mackenzie."

Barbara glared at her. "Why did I ever think you had a brain?"

"I must have a brain. I'm alive and fully functional. My nervous system and brain seem intact."

Stephanie couldn't decide if Four was the bravest person she knew or the dumbest.

"Besides," Four continued with a winning smile, "it's not a surprise that Mackenzie would want to leave. This was never her dream. She has to find where she'll be happy."

"She should be happy here," Barbara said, her tone a low growl. "I gave her everything and she betrayed us."

"She did," Lori echoed.

"Not everything," Stephanie said before she could stop herself. "She wanted to be a part of the winery and you wouldn't let that happen."

Her mother turned her cold, angry gaze on her. "You do realize how ridiculous you sound."

"Actually, I'm making sense. Everyone deserves to feel they belong to something. She wanted to be more than an employee. You made sure that wouldn't happen and now she's leaving. Do you think that makes any of us happy? She's my best friend, Mom. I see her all the time. We're in and out of each other's houses. We work in the same building and now all that is going to change. She was good for Bel Après and she was good for our family."

Four reached across the cushions and took Stephanie's hand in hers.

Barbara finished her tequila. After holding the glass out to Lori for a refill, she slid to the edge of the sofa, her gaze intense.

"You take that back."

"Take what back? It's the truth. She was devoted to you and the wines, she's a wonderful friend, and she loves us all."

"Not enough to stay."

"I go back to my original premise. What is she supposed to stay for? A paycheck? She can get that anywhere."

Lori got up and poured more tequila and handed the glass to her mother.

"She's a terrible person," Lori said. "I hate her. I always knew she was going to be trouble."

Stephanie rolled her eyes. "That is so much crap. You've always resented that Mom liked her best. There's a difference."

"Did not."

Four squeezed Stephanie's fingers, as if reminding her what was important.

"Barbara, what did you want to tell us?" Four asked.

Their mother swallowed a good portion of her drink. "She has to be punished."

"Flogged?" Stephanie asked, her tone snippy. "Are you going to take out a contract on her? You're being ridiculous, Mom. You made this happen and now you're having to deal with the consequences. She's going to leave and I don't blame her."

Her mother leaned back in the sofa. "You're very free with your opinion tonight."

Probably because she was trying to make up for not telling Avery the truth, Stephanie thought, still disappointed by her earlier behavior. Plus, she hadn't been supportive when Mackenzie had first told her about the divorce.

"I'm telling the truth."

"You're being disloyal. I would be careful about that if I were you." Her mother glanced at all three of them. "As of today, none of you will have any contact with Mackenzie. You're not to speak to her or text with her. As far as you're concerned, she's dead to all of us."

"Gladly," Lori said quickly.

"I don't think so," Four told her.

"Not happening," Stephanie added. "She's my best friend, Mom. That's not changing. I love her and I want her in my life. I want her in my kids' lives. Whatever she needs, I'm going to help her get."

Her mother stared at her, her expression stern. "You say the words so easily, but know this. There will come a time when you have to choose. Trust me when I tell you that you don't want to cross me, Stephanie."

Despite the shiver that rippled down her spine, Stephanie remained defiant. "Or what? I'll be punished, too? We're all adults, Mom. You can't ground us. Besides, you're wrong about how you're handling this."

Four leaned toward their mother. "We're a family, Barbara. No matter how angry you are, that doesn't change."

"And you two need to remember your places in my world. I can make things uncomfortable."

Stephanie stood. "I've had enough. I know you're upset, and yes, it's awful that she's leaving, but it's also your fault. You did this to yourself and to us. We're all going to suffer because of you. I don't care about your threats. I care about losing someone who matters to me. While Mackenzie and I will always be friends, everything is going to change. So threaten me all you want, but know that it's going to take me a long time to forgive you for this. For how you're acting. You're giving mothers everywhere a really bad name."

With that, she walked out of the house. Her defiance lasted until she was into her own place. Once there, she closed the door, then leaned against it, trying to ignore the trembling that started in her hands and worked its way down to her legs.

Unlike Four, she'd never gone out of her way to stand up to her mother. Mostly she simply ignored what Barbara said and went her own way. But not tonight. Tonight she'd overtly rebelled, and while she wasn't sorry, she couldn't help wondering if, one day very soon, she would be.

Mackenzie walked into the restaurant and moved toward the hostess station, but before she got there, she spotted Stephanie and Four already at a table and turned in their direction.

She was dealing with so many emotions—feeling both hopeful and adrift at the same time. She was still upset about her encounter with Barbara, sad about her divorce and scared about her future. Everything was different now, including the fact that she had to meet her sisters-in-law at a restaurant instead of just having lunch in one of their kitchens.

Mackenzie paused a few feet from the table, wondering what other changes there would be in her life. A few short weeks ago, she'd known exactly how each day was going to go. Her work and her days had been defined by the seasons. Now she wasn't sure about anything.

Stephanie looked up and saw her. Her immediate smile drew Mackenzie forward. Four followed her gaze and her mouth turned up in a huge grin. Their obvious pleasure at seeing her eased a tension she'd refused to acknowledge until that second.

Mackenzie walked into the three-way hug and hung on. "I was so scared you'd be mad at me for what happened with your mom," she admitted.

"Never," Stephanie promised.

"You've done nothing to make me mad," Four pointed out. "Besides, I'm not sure how you could upset my energy that much. I do my best to go with the flow. To observe rather than embrace negative emotions."

The very "Fourness" of that comment made Mackenzie laugh. She squeezed them both one last time, then released her sisters-in-law.

"Thanks for suggesting lunch," she said, taking her seat.

Stephanie sat across from her with Four between them.

"In a restaurant," Stephanie said with a laugh. "It feels very clandestine. Like we're in a spy novel and discussing an insurgency."

"With Mackenzie as our own insurgent."

Mackenzie shook her head. "That implies more strength and planning than I'm capable of at the moment. Right now I'm just getting by as best I can."

Stephanie and Four exchanged a look.

"At the risk of adding to your stress level, we wanted to talk to you about a few things." Stephanie sighed. "One thing."

Mackenzie tried not to let her apprehension show. "Barbara?"

"That's it," Four said cheerfully. "She totally went off on you last night. We're forbidden from having contact with you." Her smile turned impish. "Which is when I texted Stephanie and suggested we have lunch with you today."

"I should have thought of it myself," Stephanie said.

Mackenzie hated to think about what she'd done to the family. "I'm sorry," she began.

Stephanie shook her head. "No. You're not and you shouldn't be. This is my mom's doing, not yours. The work stuff. You and Rhys are responsible for your marriage."

"It was inevitable," Four added. "The change. You couldn't have stayed where you were forever. It wasn't right for you."

Mackenzie wondered if that was true. Until Rhys had mentioned getting a divorce, she'd been fairly content. Yes, there had been problems and disappointments, but she wasn't sure she would have ever thought to leave on her own.

"We don't expect you to do anything with the information about our mom," Stephanie said. "But we thought you should know she's gone a little cray-cray. Watch your back."

"I will."

"We're both going to let you know if we hear anything of real concern," Four told her. She smiled. "And that's all the grim news. How are things otherwise?"

"And how are you doing?" Stephanie asked.

"I'm trying to figure it all out. So much has changed so fast that it's hard to get my head around it all. I'm still recovering from my encounter with Barbara."

"She does love to leave a scar," Stephanie said.

The server appeared and took their drink orders. When she was gone, Four turned to Mackenzie.

"Barbara's just as lost and confused. I suspect she's not totally sure if you're really leaving or if you're playing her to get more money. She's also hoping she can figure out a way to make the winery work without you. She's angry, hurt and scared, not to mention furious that she doesn't have a backup plan. Every other winery has an assistant winemaker, an assistant to the assistant and so on. You and Barbara have always been so intertwined that you two never wanted to add a third person to the mix. You each resisted taking the sensible next step and now she's paying the price."

Mackenzie stared at her. "You are the most amazing person. Everyone assumes you're just a crystal-loving tree hugger, but you are emotionally deep."

"I observe," Four said modestly.

"I think she's secretly psychic," Stephanie teased.

They bantered for a few seconds, their familiar teasing helping Mackenzie feel as if there was a chance that one day things could be normal again. A new normal for her, but she was open to that. Just being around her friends was comforting. What Four would describe as grounding.

The server returned with their drinks. They ordered lunch. When they were alone again, Stephanie said, "How are you doing? Really? Are you sleeping? Eating right?"

Mackenzie smiled. "I'm taking care of myself. I'm not drinking and I'm also not sleeping that well, but I'm using the extra awake time to work on my business plan."

Which reminded her. She pulled out two pieces of paper from her handbag and handed them to her sisters-in-law. "If you want details, I'm afraid you're going to have to sign these."

Stephanie and Four glanced at each other, then at the NDA. Four finished reading first. She reached for Mackenzie's hand.

"I'm proud of you for taking care of yourself and for taking your future seriously. You have a true heart, you always have. That's what draws people to you."

Stephanie scrawled her name on the page, then handed the pen to her sister. "You're right. This is starting to feel like a spy novel. I like it."

"I'm going into business with Bruno," Mackenzie said, tucking the signed papers back into her bag. "We're looking at buying Painted Moon."

Both sisters stared at her with identical expressions of delight and shock. Stephanie recovered first.

"It's perfect. Big, and the land is excellent. Now that I think about it, I'm not too surprised Herman wants to sell. I'm so glad you'll be staying in the valley. I've been terrified that you'd leave me."

"Does Barbara know?" Four asked.

"No. I'm not telling her until we have an accepted offer. Or maybe not until we close."

"Keep it quiet as long as you can," Stephanie advised. "She'll only make trouble if she can."

"That was my thought," Mackenzie said.

"Where are you going to live?" Four asked. "I know Rhys will tell you to stay in the house for as long as you want, but eventually you'll have to go somewhere."

"If we buy Painted Moon, I'll move into the farmhouse there. If that doesn't work—"

"I have room," Stephanie said, interrupting.

"Us, too," Four added. "The kids would love having you around."

Their generosity made Mackenzie's throat a little tight.

"Thank you," she managed. "Let's see how this works out."

"Since Barbara fired you, you're eligible for unemployment," Four pointed out.

Mackenzie managed a chuckle. "I never thought about that. You're right."

She still hadn't processed her lack of a job. Currently she was telling herself that she was just taking a few days off. Her work with Bruno kept her plenty busy, so her hours weren't empty. But after working at Bel Après so long, it was going to be hard to let go.

"Enough," she said, holding up her hand. "How are you two doing? How's Carson enjoying camp?"

"He loves it. He texts me every day, mostly, I think because he knows if he doesn't, I'll fly down and humiliate him by hugging and kissing him in front of his friends. But I still miss him. Avery's dealing with her breakup with Alexander." She turned to Four.

"We're all fine," Four said. "I'm thinking of doing a mural in the dining room. I told the kids they could help."

The normalcy of the conversation comforted Mackenzie. This was what she'd been missing, she told herself. Hanging out with her friends in a fun, supportive environment. No drama, nothing but talking and laughing and being together.

She thought about how she'd felt after her grandfather had died. She remembered how alone and terrified she'd been.

This wasn't that. She was older, with more life experience, and she had family. Maybe not Barbara or Lori, but these two would stand by her. Of that she was sure.

Emotionally healed by her long lunch with friends, Mackenzie drove back home. She wanted to go through the house and decide if there was anything she wanted to take with her when she inevitably had to leave. There wouldn't be a lot—maybe a few mementos from her life, the odd piece of art. As she and Barbara had decorated the house together, she wasn't comfortable taking much with her. Too many memories, she thought.

She drove onto the property and turned toward her house, passing a sheriff's car on the way. The law enforcement vehicle was so unexpected, she didn't react at first, then slowed to stare at the car turning onto the main road. Someone from the sheriff's office had been here? But why?

She parked in the garage, next to Rhys's SUV, then hurried inside. She found him standing in the kitchen.

In the half second before he saw her, she studied the sharp lines in his brow. Lines that hadn't been there the last time she'd seen him. If she had to pick a word to describe his mood, she would say he was furious about something.

"Rhys? What's going on? Why are you home in the middle of the day and why did I see a sheriff's car leaving the property?"

He turned toward her. The fake smile made her chest tighten.

"Everything is fine," he said, his voice falsely hardy. "Nothing to worry about."

"These aren't the droids you're looking for?" she asked, quoting the original *Star Wars* movie line they often used on each other. "I think they probably are. What happened?"

He sighed heavily. "You couldn't have been five minutes later?"

"Rhys, please. If you're trying not to tell me something, it must be about your mother. She's already fired me. I'm not sure it can get worse than that."

The twist of his mouth told her she was wrong.

"My mother called the sheriff's office to have you evicted." His voice was flat.

"What? But we're married and this is my house." Except it wasn't, she thought bitterly. Only Rhys's name was on the deed—because he was family and she wasn't. "Can she do that?"

"No. That's what I told the sheriff. It's my house, and until the divorce is final, you're my wife and you can damn well live here as long as I let you."

"Thank you." Mackenzie still couldn't take in what had happened. Barbara wanted her gone that much? Mackenzie had known the other woman would be upset, but to try to evict her?

Rhys drew in a breath. "How can you think about moving on with everything if she's distracting you like this?" He crossed to her and pulled her close. "I'm sorry."

"I'm okay," she lied, trying to take comfort in his words and embrace and not question how much of his concern was about her getting out of his life.

"You're stronger than I would be under the circumstances." He released her. "I really am sorry about what my mother did."

But he wasn't sorry about the divorce, she thought sadly. He was ready to move on. She was, too, but she knew he was further along the path.

"I'm fine," she said, telling herself that with a little luck and time it would be true.

sixteen

Barbara tapped her fingers on her desk. The phone call from her contact at the sheriff's office had been disappointing. Apparently there were laws against evicting someone from their home, even when they deserved it. The best she'd been able to get was a visit by a deputy. She needed Mackenzie punished and broken so she would come crawling back. Perhaps not logical, but it was the truth.

She turned her attention back to her computer screen, but before she could start to make sense of the report, Rhys stalked into her office. He stood over her, glaring, as if he was trying to intimidate her.

"What the hell were you thinking?" he demanded.

She raised her eyebrows and pointed to the chair. "If you want to have a conversation, please do me the courtesy of speaking in a civil tone and refrain from swearing."

"You tried to have Mackenzie evicted."

"*Tried* being the operative word. I knew it wasn't going to work, but I had to do something. It's not as if you're helping, and this is all your fault." She pointed to the chair again.

As expected, he sat down. "How is it my fault?"

"You obviously didn't make her happy in the marriage and now we all have to pay the price for that. Why didn't you tell me there were problems in your relationship?" Actually the more important question was why he hadn't fixed them in the first place, but asking that would get her nowhere.

"My marriage isn't your business."

"If only that were true, but when your wife works in the family firm, it's all our business. Did you cheat?"

Rhys sighed. "I'm not discussing that with you."

She wasn't sure if that meant yes or no. Rhys didn't strike her as the kind of man who would do that sort of thing. He was a good man—honest and hardworking. He was also handsome and wealthy, which would make him irresistible to most women. So he would have had opportunity.

"So you're not going to fight for her?"

"Mom, this isn't your business. Mackenzie and I are getting a divorce. End of story."

"Perhaps for you, but not for me. Your divorce affects Bel Après and that means it affects us all."

She pressed her fingers to her temple, knowing that later she would have a headache.

Everything had been going along so well, she thought bitterly. The wines were excellent. Mackenzie was doing such good work and now it could all be lost.

"Why didn't you two have children? That would have kept you together."

"Now you want her pregnant? You were always happy Mackenzie didn't have any kids to distract her from her work."

"I never said that."

Rhys looked at her without speaking.

She waved the comment away. "Fine, I might have said it

once or twice, but I didn't mean it. Had I known you needed children to stay married, I would have encouraged it."

"I'm sorry to have missed that."

She ignored his sarcasm. "We have to fix this."

"No, we don't. Mackenzie and I are splitting up. That's on us. What happens with the winery is on you, Mom. You're the one who lost your temper and fired her."

"She told me she was leaving Bel Après. What was I supposed to do?"

"Ask her why she wanted to go. Maybe show a little compassion and understanding."

His idiocy shouldn't have surprised her and yet it did. "Perhaps have given her a parting gift? You do realize we don't have a backup winemaker. We'll be left with nothing. We could be ruined."

Rhys shook his head. "You'll find a solution, Mom. You always do. My point was you could have worked it out with Mackenzie. All she wanted was to feel like she belonged and was a part of things."

Barbara thought about her conversation with Giorgio. Rhys sounded exactly like him. Was there a conspiracy?

"The terms of the will are very clear. You know I can't violate them. Besides, what more does she want? I gave her everything. Free rein in all the winemaking." She felt her temper flaring and consciously suppressed it. "Someone's going to hire her. I wish I could stop that."

Rhys glanced away without saying anything. Barbara stared at him.

"What do you know that I don't?" she demanded.

He looked at her. "Mackenzie and I have a postnuptial agreement."

The edges of the room blurred a little as she struggled to comprehend what he was saying. A postnuptial agreement meant Mackenzie was going to get money from him.

"Why am I just hearing about this now?"

He looked away again. "It was between the two of us."

Anger rushed through her. "When did this happen?"

"Back when you told her she would never have a piece of the winery. She was devastated."

"So you gave her money?" she asked. "Dear God, you're an idiot. How much?"

He squared his shoulders. "Half the value of the house, some of my trust fund. I signed off on the royalties from her wines. In total, about two million."

"Dollars? You gave that bitch two million dollars?" She half rose, then collapsed back in her chair. No. It wasn't possible. With that kind of money, Mackenzie could buy something. Worse, she could use it as a down payment on a real winery and compete with Bel Après.

"It was right at the time," he said. "We were still happy together and I hated to see her so upset. She felt betrayed and dismissed by you."

Barbara ignored the rest of what he'd said and focused on what was important. "Right at the time? You're regretting the agreement?"

"Some. Maybe. It's unbreakable. I already asked my attorney. I'm going to live up to my part of the agreement. The point is, she's getting the money."

Maybe he wasn't as stupid as she'd feared, she thought, still enraged by what that kind of money would mean to Mackenzie.

"Ask your attorney again. There has to be a way to keep her from getting her hands on that much. It's ridiculous. What were you thinking?"

He stared at her for a long time. "I was thinking that I loved my wife. It's where we are. She's getting the money, Mom. You're going to have to deal."

"Oh, right. You create the problem and then leave me to fix it. How typical." She was back to wanting to slap him. "Why can't you comprehend what's happening? We're only a couple of months away from harvest. And then what? Who is going to take the grapes and make them into wonderful Bel Après wines? We all work hard, and yet without Mackenzie, what is there? Grapes. You have to make her stay."

"She offered to stay through harvest, Mom. You fired her."

"I didn't have a choice."

"You always have a choice." He stood. "No more evictions, no more anything like that. It's done. She's leaving. Let the rest of it go."

"I will not," she snapped. "Keeping her happy was up to you and you failed."

He walked out of her office. When she was alone, she stood and paced to the window, staring out at the view that usually delighted her.

Mackenzie had to stay, she thought grimly. That was all that mattered. Bel Après needed her, something her own son didn't seem to understand. Ironically Mackenzie would know what she meant. For Mackenzie, the winery had always come first. With her gone…

"I won't think about that," she said aloud. Except she couldn't think of anything else. Once people knew, they would—

She swore under her breath, then hurried back to her desk. She wrote a quick email to all her children, telling them to keep quiet about Mackenzie's threat to leave. No one else could know—not until Barbara had figured out a way to solve the problem. One way or another, she was going to get Mackenzie to see she couldn't leave.

Friday morning Mackenzie met Rhys in the kitchen while he was eating breakfast at the kitchen table by the window.

"Morning," he said.

"Morning. I need your help. I want to clean out my desk at the office and, well, I don't want to go there alone."

She half expected him to tease her about being a coward, but instead he nodded.

"Sure. I'll go with you. We can get it done before I head out to check the Seven Hills vines."

She poured herself a cup of coffee and sat across from him. "Is everything all right? I'm worried about the canopy on the south side. The weather has been so hot for the past couple of days and—"

She pressed her lips together. "Sorry. I forgot I was fired."

"I'll check the canopy for you." He gave her a slight smile. "I do know how to do my job."

"You're the best. I know that. It's just I'm a natural-born worrier."

"You're a great winemaker. It's how you're wired." He sipped his coffee. "If she'd offered you a piece of it, would you have stayed?"

She considered the question. "Yes. I never wanted to leave. This is all I know. You're my family and this is my life's work. But everything is different now. Bruno and I are business partners and we're moving forward with the purchase of Painted Moon." She smiled. "We have an office in town."

"No more working out of a hotel?" he asked, his voice teasing.

She smiled. "It was getting a little weird. The office is better. We have more space. I'm excited about the opportunity but sad that everything has changed." She paused. "I miss you," she admitted. "I miss us."

"The old us or the us we came to be?"

"Both. Mostly the old us. We were good together."

He nodded. "Just never that special."

Was that how he saw their relationship? She'd thought it was very special. Obviously she'd been wrong about that, too.

"Let me know when you want to go to the office," she said.

"We can go now," he told her, carrying his dishes over to the sink.

She'd already put a couple of tote bags by her purse. She collected them and followed him out to the garage. They each took a golf cart and drove the short distance to the office building, then climbed the stairs.

Mackenzie hurried into her office and glanced around. The only items she wanted were the personal ones. Rhys made himself comfortable in the visitor's chair while she collected photographs and put them in the first tote bag. There were a couple of knickknacks Rhys had given her, along with a few pictures Stephanie's and Four's kids had made for her.

She'd just sat behind her desk to check the drawers when Lori appeared in the doorway.

"You can't be here. Mom fired you."

Rhys turned to his sister. "Leave it alone."

"She's been fired. What if she steals proprietary information?" She turned to Mackenzie. "I'm going through your bags before you leave."

"No, you're not," Rhys told her. "She's getting what's hers and that's all. Jeez, Lori, give it a rest."

Mackenzie pulled open each of the drawers. She had some protein bars, hand lotion, a few Band-Aids, a charger for her phone. None of it significant, but all of it hers. She put everything into the second tote bag and tried not to think about how little she was taking. Shouldn't she have more to show for sixteen years of work?

But there wasn't anything else, she reminded herself. The rest of it belonged to the company. At least she had the memories. Those were hers to keep for as long as she liked. She thought about the late nights poring over reports, the times she'd stood at the window and watched a summer storm roll in as she eyed the sky and wondered about hail. Hail could ruin a crop in seconds. Here that rarely happened, but she still worried.

She stood and grabbed a couple of jackets she'd left on the coatrack in the corner. "This is everything," she said.

Rhys rose. "I'll walk you out."

"That won't be necessary."

They both turned and saw Barbara standing behind Lori. Mackenzie hoped she didn't flinch as she stared at the other woman. Their eyes met.

"Go back to work, Lori," Barbara said, her voice surprisingly pleasant. "You, too, Rhys. I want to have a word with Mackenzie." She smiled slightly. "I promise there will be no bloodshed."

Rhys glanced at Mackenzie. "You okay?"

She nodded.

He leaned close. "I'll stay in my office until you two are finished."

"It's okay. You need to get to Seven Hills."

He hesitated. "Are you sure?"

"I'm fine." She lowered her voice. "I'm pretty sure I could take her if I had to."

"Unless Lori joins in. Then it's two against one."

"Stop worrying. You need to check on the vines."

He nodded and left. Mackenzie followed him out of what had been her office and went into Barbara's.

"Close the door, would you please?"

Mackenzie did as she was asked. She left her totes by the door and took the visitor's chair.

Barbara sat with her hands folded on top of her desk. She looked as she always did—perfectly groomed, wearing a suit. There were no dark circles, no hint of worry. Mackenzie didn't know if the other woman was that unconcerned about what was happening or if she was just that good at makeup.

"We seem to have found ourselves in a pickle," Barbara said with a smile. "Maybe it's time to talk about getting ourselves out of it."

"I don't know what that means," Mackenzie admitted, wanting to believe they could work out some kind of compromise, but not willing to trust her soon-to-be-former mother-in-law.

"I want things to be right between us, Mackenzie. We've always been so close. I was just thinking about how long it took us to find the right sofas for your living room."

Despite everything, Mackenzie smiled. "I was thinking about the decorating, too. We did a good job."

"That's because we're a good team."

"We are. Barbara, you're so important to me. You've been like a second mother to me. I don't want us to fight."

"Good. I don't want that, either. So let's see if we can fix the problem. I'll double your salary. How does that sound?"

Mackenzie didn't know what to say. She'd been talking about their emotional connection while Barbara had obviously meant her job at Bel Après.

"So I'm not fired?"

"That depends on you, my dear. Do you want to not be fired?"

She thought about what she was doing with Bruno. The partnership and how generous he was being with everything. She thought about waking up every morning knowing she owned the land, the vines and everything in it. Or at least half of it.

"Would I own any part of Bel Après?"

"No, but you'd be very valued. Your work has always been the biggest part of your life. Why should that change?" Barbara leaned back in her chair. "I wish you wouldn't get in a snit about ownership. It comes with a lot of responsibility. Wouldn't you rather spend your time making beautiful wines?"

"And then what? Put money in my 401(k) every month and get a gold watch when I'm ready to retire?"

"No one gets a gold watch these days. Mackenzie, there's no need to be difficult."

"So I should just shut up and do my job."

Barbara's pleasant expression faded. "Expecting more is unreasonable. You're divorcing Rhys. You won't be one of us anymore. I'm willing to give you more money. You already have

control of the wines. Do you think you can do better somewhere else? On your own?"

Barbara raised her eyebrows. "I know about the postnuptial
agreement. Rhys mentioned how much he regrets it. What if he
fights you for the money? What if you end up with nothing?"

Mackenzie told herself not to react. Barbara was trying to
hurt her, to frighten her, and while she was doing a damned
good job, there was no reason to let her know it was working.

"I'll be fine," Mackenzie said as confidently as she could. "I
know what I'm doing."

Barbara laughed. "Do you really? Do you actually think you
can run a winery on your own? You can't manage the costs, the
marketing and keep it all going. You *are* good at what you do,
but that is all you can do. If you try to do more, you're going
to fail."

"Thanks for the pep talk."

Barbara's expression darkened. "I'm telling you the truth.
That isn't always kind, but that doesn't mean what I'm saying
isn't true."

Mackenzie told herself to ignore the sting of the words. She
would deal with the pain of them later.

"While we're talking truths," she said, "let me give you a
few of my own. I would have stayed for very little. I don't want
more money. I want to belong. But you've never been willing
to let that happen. You hold on so tight and I can't figure out
what you're afraid of losing. I suppose it doesn't matter, because
when you squeeze something that hard, you destroy it." She gave
her a bitter smile. "I was going to offer to help with harvest,
but I can see you're not interested in that." She rose. "I can't be
bought. Not for what you're offering."

"You ungrateful bitch." Barbara stood. "I should never have
trusted you. Well, don't try getting a job in this town. I'm going
to warn everyone about you. I'm going to tell them how you
betrayed me, betrayed all of us."

"Go ahead. Say what you'd like." Mackenzie walked to the door and picked up her bags. "One last truth. You can't say anything to hurt my career. Want to know why? Everyone likes me better than they like you, and they won't believe a word you say."

With that she walked out of Barbara's office for what she was sure was the last time. She made her way downstairs and into the golf cart. Minutes later she was at the house. It was only when she was inside that she gave in to tears. She sank onto the kitchen floor and cried until she was empty. The entire time she half expected Rhys to come in and check on her, knowing when he did, he would hold her and tell her everything was going to be all right. That of course he wanted her to have the money because he cared about her. Only he never did and, in the end, she was left completely on her own.

seventeen

Saturday morning, Stephanie drove into the parking garage behind Bellevue Square. The multistory shopping center was an upscale, busy place with lots of stores and restaurants, and was only a sky bridge away from not one but two movie theaters.

She'd brought Avery and her BFF, Madison, over the night before. The three of them had stayed in a cute Airbnb close by and would head back to Walla Walla on Sunday afternoon. In the meantime there would be plenty of shopping and hanging out. The teens had a list of three movies they wanted to see. Stephanie planned to do a little wardrobe update for herself, and maybe buy some things for Carson. Not that he cared about clothes, but she had a feeling he would need a few things when he got home from baseball camp.

Once she'd parked, she turned to her daughter.

"Are you two going to be all right on your own?" she asked, careful to keep her voice teasing rather than concerned. In the past week or so, she and Avery were getting along better and she didn't want to upset their tenuous détente.

"We'll be fine, Mom." Avery waved her phone. "We have movie tickets to the 2:10 showing. We're going to eat lunch at The Cheesecake Factory and meet you at five at the Starbucks on the second level."

Madison leaned forward from her place in the back seat. "The rest of the time, we're going to be shopping," she said in a sing-song voice.

The previous evening they'd had dinner at the Mexican place and had walked around, but there hadn't been time to do much more than stare at store windows.

"You two have fun," Stephanie said as she got out of the car.

"What are you going to do?" Avery asked.

"A little shopping. I'm meeting your dad for lunch." The real reason for the trip, although she hadn't shared that with her daughter when she'd suggested the outing.

They headed into the mall together, then split up by Nordstrom. While the girls went off in search of trendy boutiques, Stephanie browsed her favorite store.

Even as she tried on a few dresses and looked for a pair of new jeans, she was aware of the time. She was meeting Kyle at noon and didn't want to be late.

He'd been surprised when she'd told him she was coming over the pass to the Seattle side of the state for the weekend, but had quickly agreed to lunch. What she hadn't shared was the topic she wanted to discuss.

A little before noon, she stowed her purchases in her car, then walked through the mall and across the sky bridge to the restaurant. Kyle was already waiting by the host station, and he smiled when he saw her.

"How does it feel to be back in the big city?" he asked with a grin.

"I'm a simple country girl, trying not to get lost among you sophisticated people."

He laughed, then turned to the host and gave his name.

They were shown to a table by the window. They were over thirty stories up and the views were fantastic, but Stephanie was more concerned about their conversation than the view of the Sound and Mount Rainier. She fiddled with her menu, picking it up, then putting it down until Kyle took it from her.

"Talk," he said firmly. "You obviously have something on your mind. Let's get it out and then we can enjoy lunch."

She wasn't happy that he could read her so easily, but while that was interesting, it wasn't relevant to the moment.

"Avery and her boyfriend broke up a few weeks ago," she said, forcing herself to look at him. "She dumped him after he cheated on her, then said it was her fault, claiming he had to do it because she wouldn't have sex with him."

A muscle in Kyle's jaw tightened. "Alexander did that? She told me they weren't seeing each other anymore but didn't tell me why. That little bastard."

"Yes, it's awful, but not the point. I told Avery I was proud of her for being so strong." She squeezed her fingers into her palms, telling herself she wasn't going to cry.

"She said she had to end things because she wasn't going to be like me. She wasn't going to be weak and stay with a guy who cheated on her." She sharpened her gaze. "You told our sixteen-year-old daughter that you cheated on me and you didn't tell me she knew. You let me be blindsided, which is bad enough, but worse, you dropped the information on her without giving her any support, or letting me tell my side of things."

He flinched. "I'm sorry. I should have let you know what happened. She and I talked and I thought she was fine."

"When did this happen and why didn't you say something to me?"

"Over the holidays last year, when she and Carson were staying with me. A guy I know at the station came by to talk about what was going on in his marriage. He'd cheated and his wife found out and he didn't know what to do. It was late and I thought both kids were asleep."

Their server approached, but Kyle waved him away.

"I said that I'd been in his position and I'd handled it badly. That I'd been a fool and I'd lost something important to me because of that. I told him to own up to his mistake and make it right."

"Something you never did," she snapped.

"You're right. I didn't and I regret that more than you can know."

"Which sounds lovely and yay you, but why didn't you tell me? I should have known that Avery had been told."

"I know. I'm sorry." His mouth twisted. "When my friend left, Avery confronted me. She was mad and crying and she wanted to go home. I talked to her for a couple of hours. I told her I was wrong and a fool. I said you'd given me several chances to shape up and I'd been too immature to recognize what I was going to lose. By the time we were done, she said she was fine and I believed her."

He looked at her. "I didn't tell you because it's not behavior I'm proud of. I was ashamed and embarrassed. I really am sorry, Stephanie."

"Me, too."

"I should have said something."

"Yes, you should have. Is there anything else I don't know about my children?"

"No. That's the only secret I've kept from you. I know you're upset and I apologize for being responsible for that. I mean it, Steph."

She wanted to throw something heavy at his head but knew that wouldn't accomplish anything. "You were really stupid," she told him.

"I was."

"I'm getting the most expensive thing on the menu."

"I would encourage that. And we'll get a fancy bottle of champagne, if you'd like."

"It has to be over two hundred dollars."

"I'm sure they have that here. Are we okay?"

"I'm still upset. You pissed me off. We're their parents, Kyle. We have to be on the same team or it's not going to work."

"I know. You're right. I won't do it again."

She motioned to the server who was hovering outside of earshot, then pointed at her ex. "He's going to order a nice bottle of champagne."

Kyle quickly glanced through the wine list. "Dom Pérignon all right?"

"I guess," she said with a mock sigh.

When they were alone again, Kyle looked at her. "How are things with your mom?"

"A nightmare. She's ordered us all to not speak to Mackenzie."

"You doing all right?"

"No, but I'll figure it out. There's so much change. It's hard to take it all in."

"Did Carson text you about his no-hitter yesterday?"

She smiled. "He actually called me and gave me an inning-by-inning recap of the game."

"Our kids are pretty special."

"You're a good dad." She paused. "Most of the time."

He chuckled. "You're a better mom."

"That is true." She smiled.

He leaned toward her. "Friends?"

"Yes. I forgive you."

Instead of smiling, he nodded slowly. "You always were good that way, Steph. I should have appreciated it while I had it."

Mackenzie spent the next week or so burying herself in paperwork, which was not her favorite. Bruno had rented them an office in town. They each had a desk and there was a large filing cabinet with an impressive lock. Every document was carefully put away before they left and the cabinet locked. Just in case. She didn't think Barbara would send someone to break in and look at the paperwork, but why take the risk?

She'd already walked all the vineyards at Painted Moon. Most were in good shape. Parts of the irrigation system would have to be replaced in the next couple of years, but other than that, she was pleased with what she saw.

She still wasn't sure what to do about the wine in the barrels. Once they completed the purchase, she would have to take a few weeks to taste everything and then start making notes and, from there, decisions. It would be time-consuming but it was the only way to get high-quality wines. She had to find a few really good barrels to serve as the base, then pick directions.

"You're looking fierce," Bruno said.

She looked up and smiled. "I'm thinking about the blending. It's going to be a massive project. Until I know what's in every barrel, I can't start making decisions. Some of it will depend on what we want to do with the wine. We could just sell it as is and start over fresh."

There was a market for barrels of wine, and Painted Moon wines would bring decent prices.

"Wouldn't we make more if we got to the point of bottling it?" he asked. "I'm still working my contacts in China. They would like an exclusive vintage. We could move a few hundred cases there."

"I'm not comfortable making that decision," she said. "I don't know enough about the cost-benefit ratio."

"That's why you have a business partner."

Something she was still having trouble grasping. She and Bruno had come to terms and signed the paperwork. Barbara had taken care of any hesitation she might have had. Based on their last conversation, there was no going back to Bel Après. Not that she'd planned to. She couldn't keep doing what she'd always done. Not anymore.

She liked Bruno's calm nature. Whatever was happening, he listened, got all the facts and was reasonable in his decision making. There was no drama. Although the man still wore a tailored suit every day, she thought with a smile. He looked good in a suit, but still.

"What's so funny?" he asked.

"Are you going to wear a suit when we own Painted Moon?"

"What would you prefer?"

She rested her elbow on the desk and leaned her head on her hand. "Wineries aren't corporate America and you'll be going out into the vineyards with me, so it might be more practical to be a little more casual."

"Jeans?"

"Do you own any?"

"I do."

"Are they custom-made?"

He chuckled. "No. They're store-bought."

"Did you go to a mall yourself or did you send someone?"

He hesitated just long enough for her to start laughing. "You have staff that shops for you?"

"I might have sent an assistant out to buy some things for me."

"That still counts as staff. This is a small town, Bruno. I'm going to have to teach you to shop. We'll start at Walmart. You'll be impressed."

"I've been in a Walmart before."

She raised her eyebrows and waited. He laughed.

"Okay, maybe not, but I own shares."

"Are we going to have to hire you an assistant here?"

"I'm thinking an office manager is a better use of our funds." He glanced down at his desk, then back at her. "We have confirmation of the water rights."

"Do we? That's huge."

Water rights meant they were allowed to get their water directly from the source and weren't dependent on any municipalities. In times of drought, the winery would have priority over limited supply. Just as important, she would be able to control the amount going to her vines. Depending on the time of year, the amount of sun and the temperature, water meant the difference between success and everything dying.

"We're moving closer," she said. "I'm nearly finished with my five-year projection."

"Don't worry about formatting. Just get the information down. We can clean it up later."

He'd wanted her to develop a year-by-year projection of yields and the subsequent wines she would produce. They needed a master plan and targets along the way. She'd done similar work at Bel Après, but nothing this detailed. For every projection, Bruno estimated the profitability of each decision they made. Not every decision had to be made based on the bottom line, but some did.

"How's it going with Barbara?" he asked.

The question surprised her. For the most part she and Bruno didn't discuss anything personal.

"Not great," she admitted.

Instead of responding, he waited, as if expecting her to say more.

"She's not making it easy."

"Did you expect her to?"

"No, but I didn't think it would be this bad." She explained about the eviction. "Rhys says I can stay in the house for as long as I'd like, but that's only a temporary solution. Plus I'm right there on the property, so I need to avoid Barbara as much as possible." She gave him a faint smile. "I know what you're thinking."

"I doubt that."

"I shouldn't be surprised or even hurt. Of course Barbara isn't happy with me. I should have seen that coming."

"Do you think I'm judging you, Mackenzie? I'm not. In the past couple of months, you've made huge changes in your life. I'm impressed by your personal strength and character. You're exactly who I want to go into business with. We're going to be a very successful team."

His kind words made her eyes burn.

"Thank you," she said, then cleared her throat. "I like our partnership, too. You're very steady and you know a lot. I like the lack of drama."

"I'm not a screamer," he teased.

"Good to know." She smiled. "What does your family think of you settling here?"

"They're used to me being on the West Coast. My mother complains that it's all her fault." He smiled. "When my parents divorced, my mom moved to Napa for a couple of years. My sisters couldn't wait to leave, but I fell in love with the area. Eventually we returned to New York, but I came back as soon as I could." He raised a shoulder. "I went to UC Berkeley, much to the chagrin of both my parents."

"Your dad was in New York, too?"

"Yes, he was a hedge fund manager. He was killed on 9/11 when the towers came down."

"What? No. Bruno, I'm sorry."

"It was a long time ago."

"It's still not easy," she said, thinking of her grandfather and how much she missed him, even now.

"It's not," he agreed. "My sisters and I inherited a fair amount from him. I also had a trust fund from my paternal grandparents. I learned how to take care of money and to grow it. Eventually that got boring, so I decided to pursue my interests."

"Including wine?"

"Including that. My mother remarried and she's happy with her new husband. I see her and my sisters every couple of years."

She wanted to ask why he hadn't remarried. He was a good-looking guy who was easy to be around. The kid thing might bother some women, but not others. Did he not want to try to meet someone? Didn't he mind being alone?

Not that she would ask. It wasn't really her business, nor did she want him asking the same questions of her. She couldn't imagine going out with anyone ever. As for falling in love—she didn't see that happening, either. She was good at her job and she planned for that to be her focus for the next few years. She just wished she could figure out a way not to feel so alone all the time. While the future was exciting, the price was high— the only family she'd ever known.

She knew she and Stephanie and Four would remain friends, but it wasn't going to be the same. She wasn't just losing proximity—she was losing all the little moments that made up the rhythm of her days. The quick hugs, the impromptu hanging out, the everyday things she had, until now, taken for granted.

Bruno glanced at his watch. "We should head over to meet the inspector at the house." Bruno had insisted on having a home inspection on Herman's old place, not that it mattered what kind of shape it was in. They would buy the property regardless. But it would affect the price a little bit and Bruno wanted Mackenzie to know what kind of situation she was getting into.

The hundred-plus-year-old house had been remodeled a few times. The main floor consisted of a living room, dining room, half bath and kitchen. Upstairs were two full baths and three bedrooms. There was a big porch out front and an even larger deck out back. The house sat on a rise, overlooking the property.

"I still feel guilty about you giving me the house," she said.

"I told you, I don't want to live there. It's not my style. Besides, you'll like being close to the grapes."

She smiled. "That is my happy place. If you're sure."

"I am."

"Thank you. It's a little big for what I need."

"You'll want the space when your friends and family come to visit."

"I'm not going to have family after the divorce," she said, hoping she didn't sound pathetic. "But my friends will come over and that will be fun."

He looked at her. "Mackenzie, you have a lot of family. If you don't think that, you're underestimating yourself and them."

eighteen

Barbara found solace in the barrel room. There was something about the space that was soothing on those days when everyone seemed to be on a mission to annoy her. Lately, that was every minute of every day.

She rested her palm on a new French oak barrel and breathed in the glorious scent. The tag stapled to the barrel detailed what was inside—the vineyard, date and other notes. She recognized Mackenzie's handwriting. It was on every tag, on every barrel.

In the beginning, she and Mackenzie had tasted from each varietal, each vineyard every single year. Always together, walking through the barrel room, analyzing, discussing, keeping detailed notes. Later, when Mackenzie began blending, they did that together, as well, Mackenzie tasting everything and Barbara writing down her thoughts. Eventually, though, that had changed. Barbara had stopped going into the vineyards and Mackenzie had started managing the wine on her own. For the past few years, they'd had their defined areas of expertise—Mackenzie handled the winemaking, leaving the business end of things to Barbara.

When had everything changed, she wondered, still furious and at the same time incredibly sad. When had everything gotten out of hand? When had her trusted employee—someone she'd invited into her family—decided to stab her in the back?

She walked through the barrel room to where the wine was bottled. The equipment was silent now, but when it was ready, it would move the empty bottles along, applying labels and filling them, then pushing in the new corks and sealing the foil. The noise was incredible, the motors rumbling, the bottles clinking. And in the end…magic.

And it was all lost, she thought grimly. Destroyed by an ungrateful bitch who had decided to go out on her own. Barbara grimaced, again chastising herself for not taking care to have replacements waiting. There should have been two or three assistants ready to step in, but there weren't.

She was going to have to fix that. Hire someone, but as soon as she started asking around, word would get out about what had happened. She'd been so careful to keep it all quiet—some because it was good business practice and some out of shame.

"Damn her," she muttered, then pressed her lips together when she heard footsteps in the hallway.

Her level of irritation rose until she saw Giorgio walk into the bottling room. Instantly her breathing slowed and her anger faded as she rushed toward him.

"What are you doing here?" she asked. "Did I know you were coming?"

He smiled and drew her against him. "I've been thinking about you, my love. I can't think of anything else." He pulled back just enough to stare into her eyes. "How are you feeling?"

"Sad," she admitted. "Betrayed. Angry."

"Of course. You have lost a piece of your heart." He kissed her forehead. "I don't understand why Mackenzie is being so stubborn. You've offered her everything she wants, including a piece of the business. I was sure that would be enough to convince her to stay."

Barbara ignored the sliver of guilt that stabbed her. Giorgio had done his best to convince her that she should give Mackenzie a small share of Bel Après. Barbara had promised to "think about it." Obviously he'd assumed he'd changed her mind, which he hadn't. She would never give a single spoonful of soil to anyone who wasn't family, especially not her soon-to-be-former daughter-in-law.

"She's ungrateful," Barbara said, avoiding the truth.

"I'm surprised." He kissed her lips. "And disappointed. Perhaps I should go talk to her."

"I don't think that's a good idea," she said quickly, knowing she had to keep them apart. If Giorgio spoke with Mackenzie, he would find out Barbara hadn't offered her anything but more pay.

His dark gaze met hers. "Are you sure? I'm very good at negotiating."

She faked a smile. "Let's give her time."

"As always, you are right, my love. A few weeks away from all this will have her rethinking her stubbornness. I'm usually a good judge of character, but I was wrong about her. I thought she was reasonable."

"I don't think she ever was. We just didn't see it. At least not until now. She left without a word, without hinting." Real tears formed in her eyes.

He wrapped his arms around her, stroking her back. "You deserve better. Whatever happens with Mackenzie, we'll fix this."

She tried not to stiffen at his words. There was no "us" fixing the problem, she thought. She loved Giorgio more than she'd ever loved anyone in her life, but even he wasn't getting involved with Bel Après. That was for family only.

But then his mouth was on hers, and talking about the winery seemed less important. Later she would remind him about the prenup he'd signed and how she wanted him in her life, her heart and her bed, but not in Bel Après.

Mackenzie stared at the alert on her phone. The simple message, one she saw every single month, shouldn't have upset her. It was a gentle reminder, a way of saving herself difficulties. It wasn't supposed to make her stomach clench or her heart beat faster or her skin go cold. But it did.

Put on a pad. That was it. Four simple words. Put on a pad.

Depending on the time of year, much of her work was outdoors where she didn't have easy access to a bathroom. Getting her period when she was out walking a fence line wasn't convenient. So at six fifteen in the morning, once a month, her phone alerted her to put on a pad so that if her period started that day, she was ready.

She'd seen the alert last month, had followed the instructions but had never gotten her period. That happened from time to time, when she was stressed. But she'd never gone two months in a row without her period. And the alert had first appeared three days ago. She was three days late.

No. She was one month and three days late, a fact that wouldn't have concerned her if she and Rhys hadn't had sex about six weeks ago. Unprotected sex.

She closed her eyes and told herself it wasn't possible. It was just one time. No one got pregnant after just one time, did they?

She covered her face with her hands and told herself to breathe. There had to be another explanation. There was no way she was pregnant. She couldn't be. She was in the process of getting a divorce. She'd just signed a partnership agreement with Bruno, and they were buying a winery. Having a baby right now would be a big, fat mess.

She wasn't pregnant, she told herself. She was stressed. Her hormones were out of whack. Plus, she was thirty-eight. Maybe it was early menopause.

Unable to continue to worry without actually knowing, she left the office. At least Bruno was out of town for a couple of days. She didn't have to face him while she sweated this unexpected crisis.

She drove to the Walmart and bought three different pregnancy kits, using the self-checkout so she didn't have to talk to anyone. The whole way back to the office, she told herself she was fine. She wasn't pregnant—she wasn't. It was impossible.

Three bottles of water and a bunch of peeing later, the truth stared up at her. The information, while delivered in different forms, depending on the kit, was very clear. She was going to have a baby.

Mackenzie sat in her chair and tried to decide what to do now. Obviously she had to call her doctor and make an appointment, but that was the easy part. What about telling Rhys? And Bruno? What about the fact that being pregnant changed everything in her life?

A baby. She had no idea how she felt about that. The concept didn't make any sense. Children? Now? When they'd first been married, she and Rhys had assumed they were going to have children, but somehow it had never happened. Neither of them had pushed for it and eventually she'd decided she was okay with that. She had her nieces and nephews and they were enough. Plus, she had her work and she'd always secretly thought kids would take away from that.

Now it was even worse. A child would tie her to Rhys forever. A child meant they would be in each other's lives, despite the divorce. Worse, she didn't know how he was going to react to the news. While he'd been easy to deal with on the divorce front, he'd made it obvious he was ready to be done with her. A kid would get in the way of that. A kid would—

"Shit. Barbara's going to be my kid's grandmother."

She leaned back in her chair, not sure if she should laugh, cry or simply crawl under the desk and wish it all away. She was pregnant with her almost ex-husband's baby. She had to tell him and her new business partner, then she was going to have to decide how much this changed anything. Could she start a new business and be pregnant? What about after the baby was born? What about—

Mackenzie rose to her feet. "This is Barbara's grandchild," she said aloud. "It's a blood relation." She let the irony of the moment wash over her. "He or she is going to inherit a part of Bel Après."

And then she started to laugh.

"I don't know," Barbara said, with a sigh. "A DJ seems so tacky."

"We can have a live band," Stephanie murmured, trying to hang on to her patience as they entered hour two of wedding planning that afternoon. "It's up to you. However, they take up a lot more floor space and you don't have as much control over what they play or how they sound. It's your call, Mom."

Stephanie hadn't been sure her mother would want her to handle the event after their most recent encounter, but Barbara had sent her an email suggesting a date and time for them to "move things forward" regarding the wedding, so here she was, sitting in her mother's dining room, notebook in hand.

They'd agreed on the Saturday before Christmas as the date for the event and her mother had decided on the tasting room as the venue.

"Can I hear the bands play? Live?" Barbara asked.

"Live is more of a problem. We'll have to find out where they're going to be, then get permission to attend the event. It's going to take time. I know it seems like we have weeks and weeks, but bands book up early and the holidays are a popular party time."

Her mother glared at her. "Are you being deliberately difficult?"

"How am I being difficult? I'm doing my best to make sure you get exactly what you want. We can arrange to go listen to two or three bands if that's important to you, but I'm simply letting you know that by the time you decide, they will probably be booked, if they're not already."

"Surely they could change their plans."

"You mean blow off their other client for you?"

Barbara frowned. "That's very crude."

"But accurate."

They stared at each other. Barbara surprised her by looking away first.

"Fine. Get me the website links for samples and I'll make a decision in the next few days." She tapped the menus Stephanie had suggested. "These are awful. How would you even serve soup three ways? It's ridiculous."

Stephanie drew in a deep, slow breath, telling herself that she was proud of her menu suggestions, and if her mother didn't like them, she was a big old doo-doo head.

"The caterer uses small mugs that hold about four ounces each. Obviously they're not filled to the top, so each serving is between two and three ounces. The presentation is elegant, and the trio makes guests think they're being treated to something special without it being expensive."

Her mother pressed her lips together. "Well, I suppose that isn't a terrible idea."

"Gee, thanks."

Her mother's head snapped up. "Is that sarcasm? Don't try to sell me on one of your harebrained ideas. Just stick to what's traditional and we'll be fine."

"Harebrained ideas? What are you talking about?"

Her mother waved her hand. "You're forever coming up with ridiculous plans for the retail space. The café is a classic example. Why would we bother? Just do your job and don't try to be special."

Stephanie put down her pad of paper and stared at her mother. "Is that really how you see me?" she asked quietly. "When I took over the retail space, sales were stagnant. Now they're up over twenty percent every year."

"Of course they are. The wines are selling better and better. People come to taste them and buy whatever is in there." Her mother raised her eyebrows. "You didn't think you were making it happen, did you?" She smiled. "Oh, Stephanie. Really? It's not you. It has nothing to do with you."

The sentiment shouldn't have been a surprise or an emotional slap and yet it was both those things.

Barbara sighed heavily. "So now what? You're going to pout? I don't understand why you don't comprehend what's important. We are a winery. Everything else is simply there to support that. Why can't you learn that?"

"Just the wine, not the people?"

Her mother stared, her irritation obvious. "Oh, please, can we get emotional, because you know how I love that. Fine. Make me the bad guy in all this. After your divorce, was I too supportive? Poor you. Your evil mother had a house built for you and created a job for you. How do you stand the pain?" She patted the stack of magazines on the dining room table. "If you're done being ridiculous, can we please talk about the flowers?"

Stephanie felt as if she were observing herself from a distance. Her body was in the room, but the rest of her wasn't. She could see herself sitting there, hurt and sadness visible in her eyes.

She looked small, she thought in surprise. She looked small and weak and a little bit like a person who had never been brave. Perhaps because she hadn't been. Not once.

She'd left her husband, but instead of going out on her own, she'd run back to her mother, where, yes, a house had been built and a job arranged. Ten years later, she hadn't done anything to improve her skills, and her efforts to find a different job had been lackluster at best.

She complained plenty but did nothing. What kind of example was that for her children, and what did it say about how she respected—or didn't respect—herself?

"You're right, Mom," she said, looking at her mother. "It's not about me at all, is it? The work I do doesn't matter. The retail is just there to make the wine customers happy. The wine is what's important. You don't need me."

"Darling, I don't need any of my children. Don't take it personally."

If Stephanie had to guess, she would assume that her mother meant the words kindly. At least in her own way of being kind, which wasn't anyone else's definition of it.

She began collecting her notes. "I can't do this right now. I'm sorry. We'll have to reschedule."

"No, we won't. I want to get through this today. Don't you dare leave."

"Or what? I'm thirty-eight years old, Mom. What are you going to do? Tell me I can't go to a party?"

"Don't push me. I have too much going on right now to deal with one of your tantrums. Sit down and plan the damn wedding."

Stephanie could see the crossroads in front of her. She could stay where she'd been for too long, working a job she didn't like, feeling trapped and helpless. Or she could get off her butt and demand a little something of herself. She could, just this once, be brave.

"I quit."

She hadn't meant to say the words, but as soon as she did, she felt stronger, happier and empowered. Also frightened, but somehow that was okay.

"I quit," she repeated.

Her mother stared at her. "What are you talking about? You can't quit."

"I can. I just did." She picked up her papers and schedule.

"Mom, if you want me to plan the wedding, I'm happy to help. Just not today. As for working for Bel Après, I'm done. It's only the retail section that doesn't really matter, so you shouldn't miss me at all."

"You sit back down right now. If you walk out of this house, you'll regret it. You don't want to cross me."

Stephanie shoved her things into her tote bag and started out of the house. Her mother was still screaming when she closed the door behind her.

Once outside, she was surprised that it was still sunny, still warm and beautiful. There weren't any dark clouds, no threatening storm. The world went on.

"I quit," she whispered to herself, proud and terrified in equal measures. She knew she'd done the right thing. Her method might not have been the most mature, but the results were excellent. Or they would be once she figured out what on earth she was going to do next.

nineteen

Barbara's very bad week improved slightly as she read the list of potential winemakers Rhys had brought her. While none of them were Mackenzie, they all had possibility.

At least something was going right, she thought grimly, refusing to waste even a second of her workday thinking about her daughter's defection. What did she care if Stephanie didn't work for her anymore? A monkey could be trained to do her job.

Which might be true, but didn't take away the odd sense of loss she'd been feeling for the past few days. A ridiculous emptiness she couldn't explain and didn't like at all.

She glanced at Rhys over her reading glasses. "This is good," she said, waving the names of people he'd suggested they approach about a job at Bel Après. "You've been thorough."

"Just doing my job. We're going to find someone, Mom."

"Make sure they sign something saying they can't talk about what's happening here. I don't want word getting out."

"An NDA," he said with a smile. "Nondisclosure agreement."

There was something in his look, she thought. Some inside joke she didn't get, not that she cared.

"I'm still angry about the money you're giving Mackenzie."

"I'm not happy about it, either, but it's done. You have to let it go."

"Do I?" She tossed the papers onto her desk. "Her leaving is going to ruin us."

"It's not. Depending on the wine, we have anywhere from two to four years in the cellar. That buys us time. Most consumers don't know who the winemaker is for any given label. We'll get someone good and we'll get a backup person. We're going to get through this."

"You're thinking it's my fault we don't have someone to step into Mackenzie's job."

"You're the one who resisted adding the extra staff. She brought it up several times, Mom, and so did I."

He was right, which annoyed her. "I didn't think that tramp you married would do this to us."

"Mom." His tone warned her. "Don't bad-mouth her. She wasn't a tramp."

"You don't know that. She could have had lovers all over the valley."

"Stop it."

"You're getting a divorce. Why do you care if I say something bad about her?"

"Because it's not right. We're still friends."

How like him to disappoint her with that, as well. Friends. "Reasonable people dislike each other when they get a divorce."

"I've heard that." He nodded at the papers on her desk. "Once you approve the names, I'll get in touch with them individually. Set up a casual meeting without telling them why. I know most of them, so hearing from me won't raise any alarms."

"That makes sense."

She would rather do it herself, but she wasn't a casual-meeting kind of person, and while she knew most of the people on the list, they would be shocked if she called and suggested they get together to talk. Except for Lori, all her children were much more outgoing than she had ever been. Not that it—

Her office door burst open. Lori stared wide-eyed. "There's been an accident in the warehouse."

As one, they headed out the door and down the stairs. In the main building they raced toward the cellaring rooms. The smell of wine reached them long before they saw the disaster.

Barbara glanced around and saw that a pallet of cases of wine had somehow fallen. Hundreds of bottles lay smashed. Glass and ripped cardboard were everywhere and red wine pooled on the floor.

One of the warehouse guys stepped forward, his eyes wide, his hands twisting together. "I'm sorry. I was making a turn and one side of the pallet snapped and they went falling."

Barbara saw the broken pallet and knew he was probably telling the truth. Space was tight in here, so the pallets were moved high above the tops of the shelves, something Rhys had told her was a mistake.

"How much?" she asked.

"About a hundred and fifty cases."

Rhys picked up a broken bottle, showing her the label. "Not our most expensive, but pricey enough. Twelve bottles a case, at maybe forty dollars a bottle."

"We have insurance," Lori said quickly. "This will be covered."

Financially they would be, Barbara thought, feeling hollow and depressed at the sight. But the wine was gone forever.

She was aware of them all monitoring her, as if waiting for her to explode, despite the fact that it was an obvious accident. She watched the wine make its way toward the drain in the center of the warehouse. As the liquid swirled away, she knew that was how she felt. As if everything she'd worked for was slowly being sucked out of her.

"Handle it," she told Rhys and started back to her office. The symbolism, while not the least bit subtle, was painfully accurate. She could feel herself losing control and she had no idea how to get it back.

The land on Red Mountain was the most expensive in the state—for wine, that was. Mackenzie was sure a few blocks in downtown Seattle would go for a lot more—but on the agriculture front, this was Park Avenue, the Left Bank in Paris and the best part of pick-your-city pricey.

There were reasons. The soil, the sun, the wind, all of which combined to create perfect growing conditions for the fruity, full-bodied red wines the state was known for.

Once the deal went through for them to buy Painted Moon, this land would be hers, or at least half hers, which was plenty. She should be excited and giddy and overflowing with ideas. Her head was spinning but not from possibilities. All she could think about was the fact that she was pregnant.

She wanted to ask how it had happened, but she already knew the answer to that. A single night, a single event, had changed everything.

She glanced at Bruno, who was walking beside her. He'd traded in a suit and a white button-down dress shirt for jeans and a dark green polo shirt. He looked good. Tall, with broad shoulders. He was fit and had that air of easy confidence. Maybe he was one of those people who was comfortable anywhere. She wasn't like that. This was the one place where she felt at home, only she didn't today. She felt awkward and uncomfortable and scared and confused.

"What's wrong?" he asked, turning to look at her. "There's something on your mind. Usually when we walk a vineyard, you're studying every plant, hovering over them, practically communing with them."

His tone was light, but she saw the concern in his eyes. She had to tell him the truth—she knew that. What she didn't know was how he would react. Was the dream she'd barely allowed herself to believe could happen going to come to an end before it had begun?

"I'm pregnant."

She had to give him credit, he barely reacted. One eyebrow rose slightly, but that was it.

"Rhys?" he asked.

She nodded.

"Goodbye sex is very powerful," he said, watching her carefully.

"It was more like we haven't had sex in years and is this really the death of our marriage." She looked away. "I only found out yesterday. I still have to see my doctor and figure out what I'm going to do."

"You're keeping the baby."

Not a question, but she nodded anyway. "I have to. I want to," she amended. "It's just shocking. Did I spit?"

He tilted his head. "Just now?"

She managed a slight smile. "No. When we were tasting Herman's barrels. Did I spit? That's what I remember, but now I have to worry about the baby. You're not supposed to drink alcohol while you're pregnant and I'm a winemaker. How is that going to work?"

"You spit every time," he told her. "It was very elegant."

"I hope I did." She fingered a grape leaf. "I haven't told anyone yet. I barely believe it myself. I have to let Rhys know. I don't think he'll be happy."

Something else she was worried about. They'd never had kids. If they'd wanted to, they could have gotten pregnant a thousand times over. But they never had. Until now.

"Does the pregnancy change anything about the divorce?"

A reasonable question, she thought. "No. Neither of us is

going to change our mind." She looked at Bruno. "Does it change things with you?"

"Do you want it to?"

"That's not answering the question."

"I still want to go into business with you."

"But I'm pregnant. I'm excited about what we can do here, and I want to move forward with the deal. Having said that, a kid is going to change things and I don't know how. I don't see myself becoming a stay-at-home parent, but I could get weird with hormones. And I don't know how much I'll be able to do the last couple of months of the pregnancy." She waved her hand. "I'm guessing at all this. I don't know the first thing about being pregnant or having a baby."

He smiled. "I'm not worried that you'll suddenly want to spend your day knitting. I see you more as the strapping on the baby and heading into the fields type."

"I like that image a lot."

Thinking about carrying her baby with her as she worked made her feel good.

"We have a partnership agreement," he said. "I don't want to change that. You're the best, Mackenzie. You'll always be the best. Besides, I like kids."

His voice was a little wistful. She remembered him telling her he couldn't have children. Would her being pregnant be difficult for him?

Even as she thought the question, she shook it off. She was hardly the first pregnant woman he'd been around.

"You can bring the baby to work with you," he added. "We'll find someone to help with day care and move forward with our plan."

"Thank you. That's what I want, too." She hesitated. "I was afraid you'd back out of the deal."

He smiled. "It's going to take a whole lot more than a pregnancy to get rid of me."

* * *

Four's family room perfectly reflected the personality of the owners. The hardwood floors had been whitewashed. Sliding doors allowed sunlight to pour into the space, illuminating the floor-to-ceiling mural. The forest scene had a castle in the distance, trolls under bridges, sprites, unicorns, a very wild-looking bear and three children proudly marching together under a banner of what Four claimed was the family crest. Stephanie was less sure the small picture of a dragon holding a hamburger was historically accurate, but she wasn't in a position to say either way.

She curled up in the corner of a large sectional that faced the backyard. The square coffee table had been painted to represent a bouquet of summer flowers. The petals clustered together, while the legs were the green stems. In the corner, by the fireplace, a climbing wall was anchored to the wall and the ceiling. Brightly colored mats were scattered underneath, to protect the kids in case of a fall.

Painted baskets were filled with books and colored markers and building blocks and stickers. A nearly life-size rocking horse—Jaguar's fifth anniversary present to his wife—took the place of a table and chairs in the eat-in kitchen. Four's family ate in the dining room. Or outside. Or in the attic on nights when there was a thunderstorm.

The house smelled of flowers and herbs with an unexpected undernote of clean. The fabrics were things like organic cotton and bamboo. Splashes of color surprised from around every corner and the sound of a playful stream could be heard over the house's built-in sound system.

With the kids at summer camp and Jaguar at work, Four and Stephanie were alone in the house. Stephanie had shown up with no warning and immediately burst into tears. Her sister had settled her on the sofa, then retreated to the kitchen, where she quickly made chocolate martinis—heavy on both the chocolate and the vodka.

Stephanie took the finished drink and sniffed. "It's nine thirty in the morning," she said before taking a sip. "Not that this isn't delicious."

"Something happened," Four told her. "It felt more like an alcohol event. But if you'd like to go sit in the sauna and sweat out your pain, we can do that."

When the house was built, Jaguar and Four had insisted on a meditation space on one side. The quiet room led to an honest-to-God sauna, along with a Jacuzzi. Every December, during the winter solstice, Stephanie and her kids joined Four and her family, along with Mackenzie, for a meditation, followed by them all squeezing into the sauna.

After that they feasted on hamburgers, hot dogs and potato salad, as a reminder that summer was coming.

Stephanie smiled. "I think the martini will work just fine."

Four sat cross-legged on the chaise of the sofa, her long hair pulled back in a braid. She had on shorts and a T-shirt and, just for today, looked pretty much like any other stay-at-home mom her age.

"You took a while to come see me," her sister said.

Stephanie raised her eyebrows. "What are you talking about?"

"Whatever happened took place—" Four closed her eyes "—three days ago. I felt the disturbance, but I didn't know what it was."

Stephanie took a big sip of her drink. "Now you're scaring me."

"Why? My oneness with the universe should be a comfort. We all need to be connected with something larger than ourselves. That way we're reminded how we all fit together and should be working for the greater good."

Stephanie wanted to ask if Four had spoken to their mother but knew she didn't have to. If Four had heard about what had happened, she would have said so. Four said what was on her mind. She didn't believe in playing emotional games—it blocked her mental flow.

Stephanie set down her drink. "That's really good, by the way."

"I use dark chocolate syrup. It has a little bite to it."

"I quit my job."

Four's expression didn't change. "Go on."

"We were planning the wedding. I'd come up with several ideas I thought would make Mom happy. Somehow we ended up talking about my work at the winery and how I thought I made a difference. She called my ideas harebrained and said any increase in sales was about the wine and not anything I've done." Stephanie picked up her glass. "I'm saying this all wrong."

"You're saying it exactly right."

"I got mad, but I was hurt. It was like an out-of-body experience. I saw myself, sitting there. I looked small and then I decided I was done. So I quit."

Four smiled. "I'm really proud of you. Congratulations. You're free."

"Yeah? I mostly feel a little sick to my stomach. Avery took it fine when I told her." She raised a shoulder. "We went through a rough patch a few weeks ago, but things are good between us now. She actually told me that Grandma doesn't appreciate anyone who isn't Mackenzie and not to take her insults personally. Oh, and she wants to know if she can come work for me when I get settled somewhere."

"That has to make you feel good."

"It does." She and Avery had also talked a little more about Kyle's cheating and why Stephanie had stayed. Hopefully there would be no more surprises from Kyle and things could stay calm on the kid front.

Stephanie leaned forward. "I've been trying to figure out what to do now. There are financial considerations. I own the house, but I have to put food on the table and pay the bills. Not that I want to stay home. I like having a job. I like feeling as if I'm helping and I enjoy the challenge. But this is Walla Walla. Where am I going to find a decent job?"

Four tilted her head, her long braid hanging down and brushing against the sofa. "Really? That's the question?"

"You're going to say I should work for a winery, aren't you? There are dozens, maybe hundreds, in the area, and I know the business. Which sounds great, but I don't know if I can do it. Ignoring the guilt of working for what our mother would call 'the enemy.'" She made air quotes. "What if Mom is right? What if I didn't improve sales? What if I'm just a cog in a wheel?"

"What if you're not? What if you're creative and resourceful and you're finally able to be your best self? What if this is a new beginning and you can find the contentment that has always eluded you?"

"You're putting a lot of pressure on one little job."

"I'm asking the question."

"It's a scary question."

Four smiled. "All the good ones are." She finished her drink. "You can do this. You want to do this. Use your experience and your ideas to create something that will make you proud."

Stephanie nodded slowly. The pep talk was exactly why she'd come to see her baby sister.

"You are wise beyond your years."

"I think I was a shaman in a previous life."

Stephanie grinned. "I have no doubt about that."

twenty

Barbara sat in her usual seat at the table, with Giorgio at the opposite end. He was deep in conversation with Jaguar, perhaps discussing the farm equipment her son-in-law repaired. All her grandchildren were there, except for Carson, who was still at baseball camp. Avery, such a beauty with her long hair and big eyes, talked to Lori. Catherine and Stephanie were whispering and glancing in her direction.

Stephanie's appearance at the dinner surprised her. She had thought her daughter would boycott the event. But instead, she'd arrived on time, greeted everyone and acted as though nothing was wrong. Barbara couldn't decide if she was genuinely fine with what had happened, or if she was simply too stupid to recognize the danger she was in.

There was no going back, she thought grimly. Stephanie had betrayed her and she had to be punished. Should her daughter come crawling back for her job, Barbara was going to tell her no. To be honest, she quite looked forward to saying the words and reminding Stephanie that there was a price for her behavior. But so far, that hadn't happened.

Everyone was acting so normally, she wasn't sure if anyone even knew about Stephanie's little fit. Avery hadn't said anything, nor had Catherine. Perhaps Stephanie was keeping it a secret so she could simply ease back into what she'd done before. Or so she thought.

Barbara had no idea what she was going to do about the wedding. Stephanie couldn't plan it now and Lori was truly less than useless. Catherine would offer, but there was no way Barbara would let her youngest plan the purchase of a hamster, let alone a wedding. Just thinking about how hideous it would be made her shudder.

Regret tasted bitter on her tongue. It wasn't just the pieces of her family that had been lost, she thought grimly. Her enthusiasm at the thought of planning her big day had faded. Now a big wedding seemed like a chore—one more thing she had to get done. So what was she to do? Cancel the wedding? She and Giorgio could elope, she thought. Surely there had to be somewhere elegant they could go. She couldn't stand a tacky little plastic place where she waited in line with the other pathetic wedding couples.

Shaking off the image, she glanced around the table. The dinner was nearly finished, and while she should be happy to have her family around her, she wasn't. Despite the rearrangement of the chairs and place settings, in her mind there was still an empty seat and an equally large hole in her heart.

She missed her. There, she'd thought it, admitted it, if only to herself. She missed Mackenzie. Missed her helping with the meal. Mackenzie had always been the first to join her in the kitchen, eager to do whatever job Barbara assigned her. Mackenzie was the one who helped her pick out the linens and made sure the table was set the way Barbara liked it.

When the meal was served, Mackenzie sat close to her. They

talked wines and who was doing what in the valley. She enjoyed her time with the family and laughed often and now Barbara would never share that laugh with her again.

She caught sight of Rhys glancing at his watch.

"That's the third time you've checked your watch in the past half hour," she said. "Do you have somewhere you have to be?"

Rhys looked at her before nodding. "I'm meeting someone this evening."

Barbara tried to take in the words. "You have a date with a woman?"

The table went silent as everyone glanced between them.

Rhys smiled at her. "Yes, Mom. With a woman."

Not Mackenzie, she thought, feeling pain on her daughter-in-law's behalf.

"It seems a little soon," she snapped.

Giorgio watched her, as if prepared to rush to her side to comfort her, something she usually enjoyed. Just not today, she thought. Today she was sad and there was no solace to be found. A melodramatic thought, but still an accurate one.

"Jaguar and I have been looking at a new school for the kids," Catherine said in an obvious attempt to change the subject. "They'll be using a lot of new teaching techniques that are more nurturing than traditional teaching methods."

"Let me guess," Barbara said dryly. "No curriculum, no tests. In fact the children decide what they want to learn."

"You shouldn't dismiss something just because it's new," Catherine told her. "The old ways aren't always best."

"Explain that to my grandchildren when they discover how helpful reading and math would have been to get a decent job."

"Children need to be allowed to be themselves."

"So they can grow up and leave you without a second thought?" she asked, tossing her napkin onto her half-eaten lasagna. "Excuse me, I have a headache."

She walked out of the dining room and into the kitchen.

Once there, she didn't know where to go. Damn her! This was all Mackenzie's fault. The pain of missing her, how everything was different.

Familiar hands settled on her shoulders. She turned and let Giorgio pull her close.

"I miss her," she whispered into his shoulder. "I miss her so much. I hate her and I miss her."

"You love her," he corrected, stroking her hair. "It's a natural thing to be sad. To love her and want things back how they were."

She nodded. "You saw Rhys. He's already moved on. He doesn't care about their marriage. And Catherine with her ridiculous ideas. Where did I go wrong with my children?"

"They are beautiful children. You did a wonderful job."

She stepped back and looked at him. "Why do you always see the best in me?"

"I see what's real."

She wanted that to be true but knew it wasn't. He had an idealized vision of her that in no way matched reality. If he knew about the anger in her heart, how she wanted revenge and Mackenzie punished… But he didn't. He saw only what he wanted to see, which was probably for the best. Of course it meant that he never really saw her for who she was.

He pulled her close again. "We will be married soon and that will help. You won't have to be alone, as you have been all these years."

Alone? She wasn't alone. She had Bel Après, but he wouldn't understand that. Giorgio had created a business, but she'd been part of a legacy. There was a difference. Still, he loved her deeply and he tried. She really couldn't ask for more.

Mackenzie finished dressing. After picking up her purse, she walked the short distance to her doctor's office. Dr. Brighton was in her forties, with short hair and a confident air. She smiled when Mackenzie took a seat.

"I have some questions," Mackenzie said. "I'm a winemaker. It's my job to taste wine. I know alcohol is bad for the baby, so what do I do?" She tried to keep the panic out of her voice as she spoke. Telling her doctor about all the barrels waiting at Painted Moon wasn't going to help.

Dr. Brighton shook her head. "I know plenty of winemakers and they all spit rather than swallow when barrel tasting. I assume you do the same?"

Mackenzie nodded. "I can't get drunk first thing in the morning. It makes for a bad day."

"Then keep up the practice. Be more vigilant about it. The first three weeks after conception the fetus doesn't absorb alcohol. The first two trimesters are the most sensitive time. No drinking for pleasure. When you're going to be tasting, make sure you're completely hydrated so your body doesn't want to suck in the moisture. Keep the sessions short. Rinse out your mouth with water between sips. Spread out your tastings over days rather than hours. You don't have to give up your job, you just have to be careful."

"That makes sense." She could follow all those rules. She'd been doing a lot of reading online, and while there weren't a lot of articles about being a winemaker while pregnant, she'd been able to pick up a few tips. "And sampling at harvest is safe, right? They're just grapes at that point."

"Exactly. Sample away. Now, about the rest of your pregnancy." Dr. Brighton looked at her chart. "You're healthy. Your last bloodwork was excellent. Still, you're thirty-eight and this is a first pregnancy, so I'll want to watch you a little more closely until we see how things shake out. Do you have a personal support system?"

"I have friends."

"The baby's father?"

Mackenzie hesitated. "My husband. We're getting a divorce."

"How does he feel about the baby?"

"I haven't told him yet. I'm doing that tomorrow. I wanted to see you first."

"Pregnancy is a perfectly natural thing for a woman to experience, but that doesn't mean it's easy. Every system in your body will be affected. You'll be tired more, you'll have mood swings. At times your body is going to feel like an alien teenage creature, doing things out of spite." She smiled. "You need to eat right, get plenty of sleep and make sure the people around you are taking care of you. How does that sound?"

"Daunting, but doable."

At least she hoped it would be. Mackenzie knew she could count on Stephanie, for sure, and Four. She didn't know about Rhys—she hoped he would be happy and there for her, but with the divorce and all, she couldn't be sure. She also had Bruno. Something in her gut said he would be someone she could depend on. As for the rest of her world, she had no idea.

Dr. Brighton passed her several brochures. "Some reading material to get you started. You'll have to make some changes in your diet. Healthy eating is key. Lots of protein, fruits and vegetables. There's a list of foods to avoid."

Mackenzie took all the offered papers, thanked the doctor, then went and sat in her Jeep. Except for her head spinning, she didn't feel any differently than she had a week ago. So far she wasn't extra tired or experiencing morning sickness. But she would have to make changes to her routine. She was also going to have to start letting people know she was pregnant. She had a feeling she knew what Stephanie and Four were going to say. Barbara was going to have a fit, but the one reaction she couldn't anticipate was that of the man who no longer wanted to be married to her.

Stephanie had gone all out for her lunch date with Mackenzie. Sliced chicken breast, bacon and extra avocado. Easy on the mayo. A big bag of barbecue potato chips for them to share and, not one, not two, but four dark nut-filled brownies. In an effort to keep the calorie count down, she'd passed on the soda and had instead bought them each a bottle of water. Her meal in hand, she walked past several stores, a couple of tasting rooms, then turned at the corner and entered the small office building where Mackenzie and Bruno now worked.

She'd texted the previous evening, asking if they could hang out for lunch. With Bruno out of town, Mackenzie had suggested their office and Stephanie had offered to bring lunch. There was much to discuss.

Stephanie followed the suite numbers to the correct door, then knocked. Mackenzie let her in, smiling broadly as she pulled her close.

"I've missed you," Mackenzie said, taking the big lunch bag from her and setting it on a desk, then hugging her again. "It's been forever. I don't get home until late and I'm gone early and, wow, you look great."

Stephanie relaxed into the familiar embrace, thinking this was exactly what she needed in her life. More Mackenzie time.

As she drew back, she wrinkled her nose. "We've both been bad friends. We're letting circumstances get in the way of us hanging out. We're going to have to work harder to stay connected."

Mackenzie nodded. "I totally agree. Let's start texting every day. Just quick check-in texts, so we're in touch. And we'll have to plan more times to get together. It's not going to happen organically anymore. I really love you and I've missed you."

"I love you, too."

They smiled at each other. Stephanie felt a little of her worry fade away. She closed the door behind her, then took in the plain office. There were two desks that faced each other, a small round conference table, a couple of filing cabinets, some shelving and a door that led to what Stephanie would guess was a restroom.

"I would have thought this would be more fancy," she teased.

Mackenzie laughed. "We're saving the money for the winery. Actually this place works great. It's quiet and it's on the side of town closest to Painted Moon."

Stephanie watched as her friend set out the lunch. Mackenzie looked good. Maybe a little thinner, but she seemed fairly rested and there was a bounce to her actions that hadn't been there before.

"You're happy to be in business with Bruno?" she asked, taking a seat at the conference table.

"I am. He's great. Very knowledgeable and understanding. He's also calm. There's no screaming, no accusations."

"So the opposite of my mother."

Mackenzie grinned. "Yeah, there is that. I'll admit, I like it."

She passed Stephanie a sandwich and gave her one of the waters, then sat down. Stephanie opened the bag of chips and placed it between them.

"I keep thinking about your working there," Mackenzie added. "I feel guilty. I know she's making your life miserable, punishing you for what I did."

Stephanie opened her water. "Yeah, well, that's less of a problem. I quit my job."

Mackenzie paused with a sandwich partway to her mouth. Her eyes widened as she returned the food to the wrapper.

"You what?"

"Quit." Stephanie explained about helping Barbara with the wedding and how things had spiraled out of control.

"I felt ridiculous," she admitted. "She basically said my hard work didn't matter." She shook her head. "No. That's not right. I didn't matter. It was humiliating but ultimately freeing. Why was I torturing myself?"

"You quit?"

Stephanie laughed. "You have to stop saying that. Yes, it's done."

"I feel awful. It's all my fault."

"See, you always assume you have power that you don't have. I made the decision on my own."

"She wouldn't have been so difficult if I'd stayed."

"You're right and then I would have been stuck there another ten years, hating what I was doing and wishing I could be strong enough to leave. I finally did it. Maybe not in the most mature, thoughtful way possible, but it's done and I say yay me."

Mackenzie held up her water. "Yay you! If you're happy, I'm happy. What are you going to do about a job? Do you have to work?"

"If we're going to keep eating, then yes. Right now I'm considering my options. Four, like you, told me I have to get over the whole guilt thing about working for another winery. I've been putting together some ideas for marketing and retail. Once I do that, I'll set up some appointments."

Which sounded way more together than it was, but she was moving forward. She'd found several old campaigns she'd done for the retail space and had added those to her portfolio. After a couple of years of just phoning it in, she felt good being creative again.

"You sure you're all right?" Mackenzie asked.

"I have my dark moments, but I ignore them and do the work. I'm giving myself a few weeks to get a plan finalized. By then Carson will be home from camp and both kids will be ready to go back to school."

"You don't want to apply during harvest," Mackenzie told her. "Even though the marketing people and retail staff aren't part of it, there's still an air of frantic energy. They might not be able to give you the attention you need."

Stephanie knew that was true, but she wasn't waiting until mid-to-late October to start looking for a job.

"I'll make it work," she said. "So how's the sale coming?"

"Good. Fast." Mackenzie pressed a hand to her chest. "Some days I can barely catch my breath. I'm so grateful Bruno's handling all that. I just have to deal with the wines and plan for harvest."

"You love harvest."

"I do. It's the promise of what the wine is going to be. I just…" She drew in a breath. "I'm going to say something and you're going to react, but I need you to promise you won't say anything to anyone before I talk to Rhys. Really promise. I just have to figure—"

Stephanie threw a chip at her. "Stop stalling. Tell me!"

Stephanie half expected her friend to say she'd met someone or maybe kissed hunky Bruno, but instead Mackenzie looked at her and said, "I'm pregnant."

Stephanie heard the words clearly, but at first she had no idea what they meant. "Pregnant as in—" She stood up. "Holy crap! You're pregnant!"

She danced around the table and pulled Mackenzie to her feet, then hugged her. "You're having a baby? When did this happen? You had sex with someone? Who? When?"

There had to be a guy, because according to Rhys, he and Mackenzie hadn't done the deed in forever. So why hadn't she mentioned whoever it was she was sleeping with?

"It's Rhys," Mackenzie said with a shrug when they both settled back in their chairs.

"But I thought, I mean, you're getting a divorce. Are you still sleeping together?"

"We weren't. We're not now. It was a onetime thing." Mackenzie poked at her sandwich. "Actually that was the night we realized we were done. It was so sad."

Stephanie suddenly remembered Rhys telling her the same thing.

"As for birth control," Mackenzie continued, "I used to have an IUD, but I got it taken out."

"You did. A couple of summers ago. You were bleeding a lot. You never got it put back?"

Mackenzie shook her head. "No. We weren't exactly, you know, close. There didn't seem to be any reason, then I didn't think about it." She looked at Stephanie. "Just as an FYI, one time is all it takes."

"You're going to have a baby."

"I know. I'm scared and nervous and kind of excited, too. Not that I know what I'm doing."

That was a lot to take in, Stephanie thought. "Wow. Go you. Oh, wait. What about Bruno?"

"He knows and he says he's fine with it." She smiled. "He told me I'm going to be the kind of mom who straps on the baby and heads out into the fields."

"He's not wrong." Stephanie reached for her sandwich. "My head is spinning."

"Mine, too."

"Whatever you need, I'm here. I can go with you to appointments and be your labor coach. Four will want to help, especially with setting up the baby's room. You're not alone." She grinned. "I still have that spare room if you want to come live with me."

"Thanks, but I'm holding out for the farmhouse at Painted Moon."

"That will be a quieter option." Stephanie took a bite of her sandwich. "Pregnant. That's huge. Have you seen the doctor? There are things you can't eat and—" She stared at her friend. "You can't drink! You drink for a living."

"It's going to be a challenge." Mackenzie explained what the doctor had said.

"I've never liked the spitting," Stephanie admitted. "I get why it has to be done, but it's gross."

"You get used to it. I'm going to have to taste barrels and I'll be drinking tons of water before I do that. It's scary. I don't want to hurt the baby, but I still have a job."

An unexpected complication, Stephanie thought. "Let me know when you tell Rhys so I can be on the lookout for any behavior changes." She stared at her. "My mom. She's going to find out eventually. Oh, no! You're having Rhys's baby, so he or she will be part of the inheritance." Stephanie started to laugh.

"I've thought about that, too. She's going to freak and possibly firebomb my car."

"I think the firebomb is unlikely but she's going to lose it. I'm petty enough to be excited about that. Who says God doesn't have a sense of humor?"

Mackenzie held up her water. "Not me."

Stephanie bumped her bottle with her own. "Here's to beautiful babies and new jobs. May we always surprise each other in good ways."

"To my best friend."

"And to mine."

twenty-one

Barbara had no qualms about walking into her son's house in the middle of the day. If they wanted to keep people out, they should lock the doors. But of course they didn't. Everyone was forever running back and forth between the homes, putting up cookie flags and playing ridiculous games with the children.

Or at least they had been, she thought as she paused in the foyer. Lately there had been less of that. Probably because Mackenzie was never here anymore.

But there had been a time, she thought. When Mackenzie had arranged multigenerational hide-and-seek, or when she and Rhys had built a firepit and they'd stayed up past midnight to watch a meteor shower. Everyone had brought blankets and pillows and they'd all sprawled out together.

When had evenings like that stopped happening, Barbara wondered as she wandered through the downstairs of the house. When had Mackenzie and Rhys pulled back, retreating to their house rather than joining in? She supposed the change had been gradual enough that no one had noticed—not even them, she would guess.

She ignored Rhys's office, instead stepping into her daughter-in-law's. The colors were brighter, the desk smaller. There were photographs on the wall. A few of the wedding, some of the sisters, one of Mackenzie and Barbara, their arms wrapped around each other.

Barbara lingered over that one. Ten years ago, maybe twelve. They'd just finished harvest. They were dirty and exhausted, but happy. They'd both known it was going to be their best year yet and it had been.

She sat in front of the desk and began opening drawers. She wasn't looking for anything in particular. She shuffled through office supplies and an old bottle of aspirin. There was a half roll of mints and some hair ties. Nothing else—nothing significant.

She returned to the hallway and ran her hands along a table she and Mackenzie had bought on one of their shopping trips to Seattle. They'd also picked out the dining room set together, and the dishes.

She went upstairs and turned toward the master. The bedroom set was one that Barbara and James had inherited from his grandparents. A beautiful antique that she'd had refinished for the newlyweds. She wondered when the young couple had stopped being happy.

In the bathroom she found no trace of her son, nor did he have anything in the closet. There were only Mackenzie's clothes, neatly sorted. The shirts and jeans she wore for work were folded on a shelf. Her cocktail dresses were at one end, with more casual dresses next to them.

Barbara returned to the bedroom where she opened dresser drawers, not sure what she was looking for, then turned her attention to the jewelry box on the dresser.

In the top drawer sat the diamond stud earrings Mackenzie wore when she got dressed up. She wasn't really a jewelry type

235

of person, so she had only a few things. Gold hoops, a pair of ridiculous hippo earrings that Catherine had made for her. In the bottom drawer of the jewelry box, sitting alone, was her wedding set.

Barbara picked up the rings and put them in the palm of her hand. Rhys had asked her advice about the rings. He'd wanted to pick out something that Mackenzie would like.

"Simple but elegant," she'd advised him. "A round solitaire and a plain, platinum band."

He hadn't been sure, but in the end he'd listened, and Mackenzie had been thrilled with his choices. She rarely wore the engagement ring, but she used to wear the wedding band. When had she stopped?

Barbara put them back and closed the drawer, then looked around the room. She still had no idea what she was looking for, but it wasn't here. Not anymore. Everything she'd hoped for Rhys and Mackenzie had been lost or possibly destroyed. The broken pieces could never be made whole. There was nothing to do but pretend it didn't matter and keep moving forward.

She walked out of the bedroom, down the stairs and into the sunlight, blinking in the brightness of the early afternoon. Then she drove to the office and returned to her desk. At least there she controlled her world and those in it.

Mackenzie hesitated just inside the kitchen. She'd texted Rhys and asked him to meet her late Saturday afternoon, after work and before heading out for the evening.

She'd gone over what she was going to say a thousand times in her head but still found herself unsure of how much to get into when it came to things like custody and a joint-parenting plan. There was a fluttering in the pit of her stomach that had nothing to do with her pregnancy and everything to do with nerves.

She told herself she would be fine. This was Rhys. She knew him, loved him, had married him. He wasn't going to be mad or blame her. He might not be thrilled, but he was a rational human being. He would listen, deal and together they would come up with a plan.

They still lived in the same house, ate the food left by the family chef. He took her calls, answered her texts. In truth, very little about their lives together had changed. A reality that made her sad down to her bones.

When had that happened? When had they started living separate lives and why hadn't she noticed it happening? She supposed the changes had been small until they added up to something that mattered. Something that had ultimately broken their marriage.

"Why are you lurking?"

The teasing question came from behind her. She turned and saw Rhys walking toward her. She faked a smile.

"I was lost in thought."

"I don't know. It looked like a lurk to me." He crossed his arms and leaned against the island. "How are you? I haven't seen you in days. Bruno keeping you busy?"

"We're both scrambling to keep up with events," she said, sitting at the table and motioning for Rhys to join her. "Things are going very smoothly, which is both good and a little scary. I'm daunted by the paperwork."

"Herman's a motivated seller. He wants you to have Painted Moon because he knows you'll always care about it."

Rhys picked up a bottle of red wine and waved it toward her, as if offering a glass. She shook her head no. He sat across from her.

"So what's up? I know you don't want my advice on the business."

She managed a smile. "I already know what you think."

"It's a great opportunity for you. A chance to do your own thing. That would never happen here."

"I'm sorry about the trouble with your mom."

He shrugged. "You know how she gets. Eventually she'll move on to hating someone else."

Barbara hated her? Mackenzie tried not to react to the casual words, even though they cut down to her heart.

"Interesting about Stephanie," he added, as if he didn't know she was struggling to act normal. "Quitting like that. I guess she and Mom really went at it. Everything's changing."

She fought against a flood of guilt, knowing she had culpability in that breakup, as well. If she and Rhys hadn't split up, she wouldn't have left Bel Après. If she hadn't left, Stephanie wouldn't have had to defend her. And so on and so on.

He looked at her. "You called this meeting. What's up?"

Part of her wanted to say "Nothing" and bolt, putting off the confession, but she wouldn't do that. Hiding only made things worse. She looked directly at him and said, "I'm pregnant."

He stared at her blankly. "You can't be. You have an IUD. You're not pregnant."

"I had it taken out two years ago. Rhys, you knew that. You drove me to the procedure."

"No." He stood and moved until the island was between them, shaking his head the entire time. "No. You're not. You can't be. Not now. A kid?" He swore.

"You're upset," she whispered, mostly because she couldn't think of what else to say.

"Upset? I'm upset?" His voice rose. "I don't think that comes close to describing what I am. Pregnant? That's the last thing either of us needs." He turned and hit the wall with his fist, then spun back to her. "All I wanted was a life. Is that too much to ask? I've spent the past five years living like a goddamned monk in this house. No sex, no connection of any kind. All we ever talked about was work. I wanted something more. Anything that wasn't this and now you're pregnant?"

She hadn't expected him to be happy, but she hadn't expected this kind of reaction. Each of his words was a punch in the gut until she was mentally hunched over, trying to protect herself.

"I'm going to want you to have a DNA test when the baby's born."

She half rose, then sank down in the chair. "You really are a bastard. I wouldn't have known."

"What do you expect me to say?" he demanded.

"That you believe me. You know I wasn't having sex with anyone else. How exactly would that happen? I was on Bel Après property every second of every day. Do you think I was meeting some guy out in the vineyards? That's romantic."

"I know. I'm sorry. I just..." He braced himself against the island. "I don't want any of this. I just want to get a divorce." He looked at her. "You never thought to get on some kind of birth control?"

"Why would I bother?" she snapped, digging for the anger that would give her strength. "As you keep saying, we weren't having sex. For the second time in five minutes, I point out that you *drove* me to the doctor when I got out my IUD. You knew exactly as much as I did. We both forgot. If you remember, you're the one who started the whole let's-have-sex thing. I wasn't trying to get pregnant on purpose."

He drew in a breath and held up both hands. "You're right. I'm sorry." He glanced around, as if searching for an escape, then he slowly walked back to the table and sat down.

She thought about the early days of their marriage, when they'd still been talking about having kids. If only this had happened ten years ago, or even seven, she thought sadly. They would be so happy—excited about their child and the future. Something else that had been lost.

"What are we going to do?" he asked, sounding defeated. "Do you want this?"

"I'm having the baby." She'd never thought otherwise. Yes,

she was pro-choice, but she was a healthy woman with a good job and was perfectly capable of raising a child by herself.

"I wasn't asking you to have an abortion."

"No, but it would solve a lot of your problems."

"I'm not a jerk."

"You just play one on TV?"

He drew in a breath. "Let's start over. You're pregnant. Now what?"

"Now I have a kid and you have to decide what you want to do about it. Oh, and I get a DNA test because we need to make sure it's yours." She leaned back in the chair. "Don't worry. I'm not angling to stop the divorce. I'm telling you because it changes some things. Our simple property split isn't so simple anymore."

He rubbed his face with his hands. "I didn't even think about that. We have to do something legally, right?"

"It's called a parenting plan. I'll be the custodial parent, but you'll want to decide how much visitation you want. Or you can just sign away your rights."

She wasn't sure about the latter. Was it even legal? It happened all the time in movies and TV, but real life was often different.

He dropped his hands. "I'm not walking away from my kid. I don't know enough about this to have the conversation. Let me talk to my lawyer and get back to you. If we can come to some agreement, then we shouldn't have to hold up the divorce."

The all-important divorce, she thought bitterly. Because Rhys couldn't get away from her fast enough.

"Have your lawyer put together a proposal for a parenting plan and child support," she said, coming to her feet. "Once we agree on that, we can move forward with the divorce."

He stood and looked at her. "I'm not mad," he began. "I wasn't expecting a baby."

"Me, either, but here we are."

She searched for some trace of the guy she'd married, but he was nowhere to be found. Rhys might not be pounding his fist into the wall anymore, but he wasn't happy. Whatever fantasies she might have secretly held about them still being a team had just been flushed down the toilet.

After sixteen years of marriage, she was totally on her own. Single and pregnant. Hardly a new story, but certainly not one she'd expected to have to live through.

She went upstairs to her room and sat on the edge of the bed. Somehow she'd thought the conversation would take longer. It was funny what a couple could get through in fifteen minutes when they no longer cared about each other.

Stephanie hung on to Kyle's hand, not caring if she was digging her nails into his flesh. He was a tough sports guy—he could take it.

The last four hours had passed in a blur, starting with a call from Carson's coach saying her son had been in an accident. He and his friends had gone rock climbing at the sports center where they trained and Carson had fallen, breaking his arm and hitting his head on the mat.

"I'm going to throw up," she said, feeling her stomach writhing.

Kyle looked at her, his brows pulled together. "Do you mean that? Want me to find a bucket? I really don't think you should throw up on the seat. It's a crappy way to thank Bruno."

She stared at him, not quite able to understand what he was saying only to look around and remember that, yes, they were in a very well-appointed private jet.

As soon as Stephanie had gotten the call from the coach, she'd called Mackenzie to see if Avery could stay with her overnight while Stephanie went to be with Carson. Stephanie's second call had been to Kyle, who'd immediately started looking to get them a flight to Sacramento. The problem was Walla Walla was hours by car from Seattle and there were only a couple of flights a day between the two cities.

Mackenzie had interrupted that call to say Bruno was offering his private jet. The pilots would stay in Sacramento as long as needed, then fly the three of them back.

Less than an hour after she'd gotten the initial call from the coach, Stephanie found herself being flown to Seattle's Boeing Field, where Kyle got on board. The second she saw him, she'd let go of her self-control and fallen into his arms, sobbing.

"I'm not going to throw up," she said, trying to slow her breathing. "I have to hold it together."

"He's fine."

"He hit his head and they're keeping him overnight in the hospital."

"For observation."

She shook her head. "It's overnight, Kyle. There could be something wrong with his brain."

"He's going to be fine."

"You don't know any more than I do," she snapped.

Instead of pushing back, he wrapped his arm around her. "I know that imagining the worst won't make this trip go any faster. Now try to relax and enjoy our luxurious surroundings. You're probably never going to fly in a private jet again."

"I'll enjoy it on the trip home," she muttered, silently urging the pilots to fly faster.

Less than an hour later, they touched down. Kyle plugged the hospital address into the rental car's GPS and drove them directly there.

When they walked into the Emergency Department, Stephanie did her best not to start by screaming that she needed to see her son. Kyle headed directly to the information desk.

It took only a few minutes for them to be directed to Carson's room. They found their fourteen-year-old sitting up in bed, pale, a little wide-eyed, with his left forearm in a cast.

"Hey, Mom," he said weakly, waving his arm, then wincing. "So I kind of fell off the rock wall."

She rushed to him and wrapped her arms around him, determined to never let go. Thoughts crowded her head, mostly that he was never leaving the house again, and that she'd been wrong to let him go to baseball camp.

"I'm fine," Carson insisted. "It's no big deal."

She stepped back to allow Kyle to hug him, using the time to look for damage. Except for the broken arm and the pale skin, he seemed all right. Before she could start grilling him on other symptoms, a middle-aged woman in a white coat walked in.

"Hello," she said, holding out her hand. "I'm Dr. Leishman. You must be Carson's parents. The break was very clean and should heal quickly. We can't find any indication of head trauma or a concussion, but we're going to keep him overnight, just in case." She smiled.

"Can I go back to baseball camp?" Carson asked quickly. "We only have a week left. I won't be able to play, but I have to be there for my team."

Stephanie was about to tell him he was so coming home when she felt Kyle touch her shoulder. She glanced at him and saw he was slowly shaking his head.

"Let's see how you are in the morning," she said reluctantly.

"I'm fine now, Mom."

"And yet you're spending the night in the hospital."

Dr. Leishman looked between them. "Carson will be moved up to Pediatrics sometime in the next hour. We can have a cot brought in so one of you can spend the night with him. The doctor on duty will check in with you once he's settled."

"Thank you," Stephanie said, moving close to Carson and taking his hand. "Thank you for everything."

When the doctor left, Carson rolled his eyes. "It's not that bad, Mom. Look at me. Don't I sound normal? My head doesn't even hurt."

"Like you would tell me if it did."

He smiled. "I'm not that good at pretending I'm not in pain."

"Still, we'll talk about camp in the morning. First I want you to get a good night's sleep."

Once Carson was settled in his room in Pediatrics, Kyle pulled Stephanie out into the hallway.

"I'm going to go find a hotel. I'm sure there's one that's close. I know you need to stay here tonight, but you'll want to come over and use the shower in the morning. Once I'm checked in, I'll find out about takeout in the area, then come back for food orders. Carson isn't going to want hospital food for dinner."

"If they let him eat."

He smiled at her. "They're going to let him eat. Steph, I don't think there's anything wrong with his head. Let's assume the best until we have reason to think otherwise."

"Being that positive isn't in my nature."

"But you are feeling better about him."

She nodded slowly. "He seems completely normal and he's not in a lot of pain. He really doesn't fake that well. But he's still in the hospital. Doesn't that freak you out?"

"A little, but it's a short-term thing. You going to be okay by yourself?"

"Yes. Go find a hotel. While you're gone, I'll ask the nurse about what he can eat for dinner. Oh, and when you come back, can you bring my overnight bag? It's in the car."

"Sure." He leaned in and lightly brushed her mouth with his. "We'll get through this together."

"I know. You have many flaws, but you're a good dad."

"You're a good mom."

She managed a smile. "True, and I don't have any flaws."

He laughed. "If only that were true. See you soon."

She watched him walk to the elevator, then returned to her son's room. While she fussed over Carson and made sure he was comfortable, she thought about how grateful she was to have Kyle with her. There were times when he made her insane, but lately he'd been a really good guy. She knew he would take care of whatever needed doing. Funny how it had taken them ten years of being divorced to finally find a relationship that worked for them.

twenty-two

The farmhouse was at least a hundred years old, but it had obviously been loved. The outside paint was fresh, the big front porch sturdy. Mackenzie watched as Bruno walked toward the windows.

"Double pane," he said. "They've been replaced in the past five years. You won't have to worry about them."

"That's about the time Herman's wife got sick. She had cancer and only lasted a few months after diagnosis. I'm sure he had the windows replaced so she would be more comfortable in the house."

He opened the front door and motioned for her to go in first. There was a good-sized living room with a big fireplace on the left and a small guest bath off to the right. Stairs led to the second floor. She could see into the dining room and guessed the kitchen was to the right of that.

The ceilings were high, the floors refinished wood and probably the originals. The leaf-print wallpaper wasn't to her liking, but that was easily fixed.

It was a good house—solid and more than enough for her. She should be enthused, and she was trying to be. The problem was she couldn't shake her conversation with Rhys. While she hadn't expected him to dance for joy, she'd hoped for a slightly more positive reaction.

She forced her attention from that disastrous conversation to the house.

"It's nice," she said. "Are you sure you don't want to live here?"

Bruno looked at her. "We've discussed this. I'm in escrow for a large condo overlooking the golf course. That's much more my style. This is a perfect house for you and the baby."

"I guess." She wasn't sure what made a house perfect for a child. She supposed anywhere would work as long as it was safe, warm and filled with love.

They went into the kitchen. It was bigger than she'd been hoping, although fairly old-fashioned. The huge farm sink was a bit battered and the appliances had seen better days, but everything was clean and there were plenty of cabinets.

"You can gut this and have the kitchen of your dreams," he told her.

She laughed. "I don't usually dream about kitchens. I'm more into wine."

"Then get a designer to come up with a plan."

"Every penny I own is trapped until the divorce. The second that happens, it goes to you." She smiled. "I bring nothing to the table but my sparkling personality."

He chuckled. "You'll be making plenty within a year or two. Plus, you're getting paid a salary and you have your royalties from your Bel Après wine."

She nodded instead of admitting she was fully expecting Barbara to find a way to weasel out of paying her that. Bruno would tell her to stand strong and hire a lawyer, which was probably good advice, but everything was happening so quickly—the divorce, buying the winery, finding out she was pregnant. She wasn't sure she could take on one more thing.

They went upstairs. There was a large master with an attached bath and walk-in closet. Lavender rose wallpaper covered the walls and there was a faint scent of an old-fashioned soap, but nothing Mackenzie couldn't live with.

She made notes on the pad she'd brought. She needed to get a bed ordered, a couple of nightstands and a dresser. Downstairs she would need a sofa and maybe a TV. Everything else could wait.

When she was done writing, she and Bruno went into the first of the two secondary bedrooms. They shared a bathroom. Bruno stood in the center of the one with the big bay window.

"This one for the baby," he said. "There's lots of light. When she gets older, you can get her a curved sofa to put there so she can curl up on it and read."

"She?"

He gave her a sheepish smile. "I'm hoping for a girl."

"Are you? Then you're further along than I am. I can barely grasp the fact that I'm pregnant. Except for vitamins and the ridiculous amount of vegetables I have to eat every day, very little has changed for me."

A girl? "You have a fifty-fifty chance of getting what you want," she added.

"I'd be happy with either. Did you talk to Rhys?"

She nodded, hoping she didn't look as uncomfortable as she felt. Apparently she failed because Bruno exhaled.

"That bad?" he asked.

"He wasn't happy. There was swearing and he tried to put his fist through the wall. He was unsuccessful and the wall is very proud of the win." She kept her tone light, hoping to make Bruno think she was doing better than she was.

"When he blamed you, did you remind him it takes two?"

"Yeah, and I also pointed out that he'd driven me to the appointment to get my IUD out, so pretending he didn't know it was gone wasn't going to—"

She slapped her hand over her mouth and groaned. After lowering her arm to her side, she said, "I'm so sorry. I shouldn't have said that. It's way too personal and not anything you wanted to know."

"I've seen you spit, Mackenzie. This is nothing."

"Still. I'm humiliated."

"Don't be. Relationships are messy when they're ending. Anything you want to talk about, I can handle."

She appreciated his kindness and desperately wanted to change the subject. "Be careful what you offer, mister. I've been doing a little reading on the whole pregnancy thing, and there are facts that would put you off eating for a week."

"I don't scare that easily."

They went into the other bedroom.

"This would be a good home office," he said.

"Why wouldn't I just come into my regular office? It's like a fifteen-minute walk away."

"Because you're going to have a newborn, then a toddler, then a kid who might get sick and need you."

Oh, right. "A home office it is." She added a desk and chair to her list.

They walked back downstairs. Mackenzie paused to breathe in the feel of the house.

"I'm going to be happy here," she said. "Thank you."

"It's not just me. We're a team."

She and Rhys had been a team once, she thought wistfully. Not anymore. She looked at Bruno and thought maybe they would last a little longer together. They knew what they were getting into and there were no messy emotions to complicate things.

"What are you going to do about dating?" she asked. "Walla Walla's a pretty small town. I guess you could meet someone in Seattle. You have a private jet, so it's not like the distance is going to be an issue."

He raised his eyebrows. "Are you speculating about my love life?"

"Yes. It's so interesting to think about, mostly because I need a good distraction right about now."

"I'm focused on buying Painted Moon."

"You're saying I should mind my own business."

"I'm saying I'm not in a position to fulfill your speculation needs."

They walked outside and Bruno locked the door behind them, then handed her the key.

"Legally you can't move in until we close, but Herman said you were welcome to measure for furniture or rugs or whatever."

She hesitated before taking the single key from him.

"This is going to be the first home I've ever owned," she admitted. "My grandfather rented a small place by his work, and after he passed away, I went to college and lived in the dorms, and then I moved in with Rhys after college." She looked at him. "How ridiculous is it that I'm thirty-eight years old and I've never lived alone?"

"It's not ridiculous at all."

His brown eyes were kind, she thought. She had the strangest urge to ask him to hold her. Just for a minute, until she was feeling strong again.

But she didn't. Bruno was her business partner and he expected her to be tough enough to handle her own life. Speaking of which...

"Guess what I'm going to do now," she said.

"I have no idea."

She sucked in a breath and squared her shoulders. "I'm going to tell Barbara I'm pregnant."

Bruno stared at her. "Are you sure you want to do that?"

"Not in the least. I was going to wait, but based on how Rhys reacted, I need to get the word out on my terms."

"Do you want me to come with you? I can wait outside her office, or even in the car. I'm not trying to put myself in the middle of something personal, but you shouldn't do this alone. That woman is volatile."

"You're sweet, but I can handle her."

At least she hoped she could.

Bruno didn't look convinced, but he nodded anyway. "Text me when you're done."

"I will."

She would also text Stephanie and Four to warn them to stay clear because their mom wasn't going to take the news well. A sad statement, but a true one.

She made her way to her Jeep. Bruno held open the door.

"I'm sorry," he said. "Having a baby should be joyous news and she's going to make it anything but."

"Thank you for getting that. I was thinking the same thing. Wish me luck."

"You don't need luck, Mackenzie. You never have."

Mackenzie tried to hang on to Bruno's empowering words as she drove onto the Bel Après property. She slept at the house every night, but heading to the business side of the property wasn't something she did anymore.

Ignoring all the feelings swelling inside of her, she went into the building and up the stairs to Barbara's office. No one tried to stop her and she was careful not to look into any other offices as she walked to the end.

Barbara sat at her desk, her reading glasses on her nose. She was dressed in a suit, as always, her dark hair perfect, her makeup tasteful. Her engagement ring sparkled in the overhead lights.

That ring, Mackenzie thought. Funny how everything had started with the proposal. Sharing in the romantic moment had shown her the empty parts of her own life. She'd been restless for years, but that moment had brought everything into sharp relief.

Her mother-in-law looked up and saw her. After removing her glasses, she leaned back in her chair.

"I can't imagine what we have to say to each other."

Mackenzie closed the door and walked toward the desk. For a second she thought about blurting out the news and then running, but she knew that was wrong. Whatever might be happening between them now, at one time Barbara had been like a mother to her. If nothing else, Mackenzie owed her the respect of sitting down.

When she was seated, she got right to the point. "I'm pregnant."

Barbara stared at her unblinking. "Is it Rhys's?"

The question shouldn't have been surprising, but it was. "Yes, otherwise why would I bother telling you?" She held up her hand. "Before you ask, I'll have it confirmed via DNA when the baby is born. Rhys knows it's his." At least she was pretty sure he knew it, as much as he might wish it wasn't.

Barbara's eyes darkened with suppressed emotion. "Men believe what we want them to believe and nothing else."

Mackenzie told herself not to be distracted. "I don't want to fight with you. I told you because I thought you'd want to know you're going to have another grandchild. I'm hoping my pregnancy doesn't get wrapped up in your anger about me leaving."

Barbara leaned toward her. "Is that what you hope? That's sweet. So you think I should be happy that you've tricked Rhys into getting you pregnant. I should have seen this coming."

The outrageous statement wasn't even a surprise. Mackenzie shook her head. "I don't know how you maintain that level of fight. It's exhausting. I didn't trick Rhys and I didn't plan on getting pregnant, not that you'll believe me. And in the end, what you believe doesn't matter. I am genuinely heartbroken about how this has gone between us. I loved you so much. I thought we would always be close."

"Then you shouldn't have walked away. You started this, Mackenzie. Not me, not Rhys, not anyone but you."

"You don't care about the child at all, do you?"

"No. You're nothing to me. You were always a means to an end."

Mackenzie knew Barbara wanted to hurt her and she was doing a good job of it. What she didn't know was if she was telling the truth.

"Ironically that will you've always thrown in my face is about to bite you in the butt," Mackenzie said, rising to her feet. "Because the DNA evidence that proves my baby is a member of the family will entitle her to inherit just as much as your other grandchildren."

She started for the door, then turned back. "I wanted to make it about us having a familial connection, about you being my baby's grandmother. You want to make it about money and land. It's not a fight I went looking for, but if that's what you want, bring it on, because I'm going to win."

With that, she walked out. She was halfway down the stairs when she heard something heavy slam into the wall, followed by a high-pitched scream.

When she reached her car, she texted Stephanie and Four a quick **Brace yourself. She knows.** That done, she drove back to the offices she shared with Bruno. She had a stack of paperwork to read through. Escrow was very good at generating documents. Later, when she wasn't feeling quite so sick to her stomach, she would indulge in a big bowl of chocolate ice cream and daydream about everything she was going to do at Painted Moon. As long as she kept moving forward, she would be fine. Which turned out to be an okay thing because she'd never much liked standing still.

Barbara waited until just after six, then drove to the compound. She parked behind her son's house and walked in through the always open back door. As she'd expected, she found Rhys sitting at his desk in his office.

He was focused on his computer and jumped when she said his name.

"You about gave me a heart attack," he said, pressing a hand to his chest. "Don't you knock?"

"No, I don't." She walked over to the desk and clutched the back of the chair. "She told me about the baby."

Rhys leaned back in his chair. "She told me, as well."

"Is it yours?"

"Yes."

Barbara collapsed into a chair, the last of her hope fading away.

"You had to get her pregnant?"

"I don't like this, either, Mom. You think I want a kid now? I was finally going to be free of my marriage and start the life I wanted to have." He waved his hand at her. "It's done and I'm going to have to deal."

Her head shot up. "Not just you, Rhys. All of us. This is a nightmare on many levels." She leaned toward him. "I want you to sue for custody."

"What?" He stared at her. "No."

"Why not? You're the father. Society is different now. Lots of men raise children on their own. You'd have help. We'd all be here for you. We'd hire a nanny for the day-to-day work."

"Forget it. I have no interest in being the custodial parent. You want the baby so much, you sue for custody."

"Believe me, I've thought about it." And she would talk to her lawyer, if she couldn't convince Rhys to do the right thing.

"I'm shocked at how little interest you're showing in your own child," she said, wanting to gauge how much she could guilt him into doing what she wanted.

"Like you're the most maternal woman on the planet. Forget it, Mom. You're not going to get me to fight Mackenzie for the baby. My lawyer's working on a visitation plan. I'll show up because it's the right thing to do, but don't expect me to do more than what I have to."

She should have known he was going to be difficult.

"That doesn't work for me," she snapped. "She can't be allowed to keep it. What if it really is yours? Is my grandchild going to be raised by that woman?"

"As she's the mother, yes. That's exactly what's going to happen."

She knew yelling at him wouldn't help, although she desperately wanted to vent her frustration. "I just need you to cooperate on this," she said between clenched teeth. "I want to talk to your lawyer."

He stood up and put his hands on the desk. "Listen to me carefully, Mom. You're not going to screw with my life. Mackenzie and I will work out the parenting plan. When the baby's born, we'll confirm that I'm the father with a DNA test, and that's all you need to know. I'm not interested in any crazy plans you might come up with. It's done. Leave it alone. In a few months, we'll talk about how you can make things right with Mackenzie so you can have time with your new grandchild."

"Make things right with her?" she shouted, coming to her feet. "Did you really say that? She doesn't deserve that child. I wish she'd miscarry. She's the one who wants to destroy us. She's the one who—"

"Barbara!"

She turned and saw Giorgio standing in Rhys's office. He was pale with shock.

This was bad timing, she thought in annoyance. No doubt he'd seen her golf cart behind Rhys's house.

"What are you saying?" he demanded. "Tell me you don't mean it. Mackenzie's pregnant? That's something to celebrate."

She loved Giorgio's kind heart, but right now it was nothing but a pain in her ass. Of course he wouldn't understand because to him family was everything. He didn't share her connection to the land. He'd blithely walked away from his business, something she could never do. He wasn't ruthless and he didn't want her to be that way, either.

Funny how he thought he loved her when he didn't know her at all. She, on the other hand, was very clear about his strengths and weaknesses.

"You're right," she said quickly, pretending to sway on her feet before sinking back into the chair. "I'm overwhelmed by everything that's happening."

Given how on edge she was, she had no difficulty summoning a few tears. Giorgio was at her side in an instant, taking her hand in his and kissing her cheek.

"I'll take you home," he told her. "You need to rest."

"I do. Thank you, my love."

She let him help her out of the room and through the house. She had no idea what Rhys was thinking, but at this moment, she didn't care. One crisis at a time.

twenty-three

Stephanie saved the file on her computer and told herself she was doing great, all things considered. Carson had been released from the hospital and she'd been brave enough to allow him to stay the last week of camp. He would be home in a couple of days, right in time for school to start. She and Avery had maintained their friendly status, with her daughter announcing she was done with boys, at least for her junior year of high school. She was going to focus on academics and after-school activities.

Stephanie had agreed the plan had merit while secretly thinking it wouldn't last through the first two weeks of the semester, but at least Avery wasn't pining for Alexander anymore.

On the work front, she had an interview lined up with a local winery right after harvest, which was the most exciting news of all. She was working hard to get her portfolio in order so she could be dazzling. In the meantime, she'd signed on to help at Painted Moon during harvest. The temp work would keep her bank account healthy enough that she could sleep most nights. Things were looking up.

She was about to start paying bills when her phone buzzed with a text.

U around

She shook her head before replying. **What is it with you and abbreviations when you text? You're not 17. Write out the entire sentence. I know you can. And yes, I'm in my office. There are cookies in the kitchen.**

She pushed Send and began to shut down her laptop. A few minutes later Rhys walked into her study and threw himself on the sofa.

"You didn't want cookies?" she asked.

"I'm not hungry."

Her big brother's normal good humor was nowhere to be seen and there was a decidedly downward turn to his mouth.

She wondered if he was regretting the divorce. While his marriage hadn't been perfect, from the outside it seemed that he and Mackenzie got along. Okay, sure, the sex thing was a problem, but they could fix that maybe with some counseling or watching porn or something. If he was—

"Mackenzie's pregnant," he announced.

"I know. She told me."

Stephanie had been thrilled for her and secretly proud of herself for reacting the way a best friend should.

He leaned back in the sofa and stared at the ceiling. "I don't want a kid."

"But you used to talk about having a family."

He looked at her. "Years ago, right after we were married, but not now. I'm finally free to live my life, and instead of enjoying myself, I'm going to be stuck with some baby." He exhaled. "She had to have her IUD taken out. I guess I drove her to the appointment, although I sure don't remember it. So she wasn't on anything. It was just one time."

"That is all it takes. One time."

He glared at her. "How does that help?"

"I didn't know you wanted help. I thought you were just grumbling."

"I just don't want to deal with a baby."

"Rhys, this is your child. It's a part of you, a part of the family."

"I don't care. I wish I could sign my rights away."

Stephanie nearly fell off her chair. "Do you mean that?"

"Maybe. I don't know. I mean, I suppose there are legal ways to abandon a child, but I'm not sure I'm capable of doing that. Or if I should, you know. What if I have regrets later? Mom wants me to sue for custody, which is not happening."

She wasn't even surprised that her mother was looking for ways to make Mackenzie's life difficult. "Our mother is a horrible woman."

"She's never boring—I'll give her that."

"What are you going to do?"

He shook his head. "I've got my lawyer working on a parenting plan. There's a minimum amount of visitation that's considered acceptable. I'm going to ask for that. Plus I'll have to pay child support, but that's based only on my salary, not the trust or anything. I almost don't care about the money. It's everything else."

Stephanie knew that neither of them had expected a pregnancy, but she was still surprised at Rhys's resistance to being a father.

"Don't go into this with the idea of being half-hearted," she said. "Don't let your child grow up knowing he or she isn't wanted. That's a devastating thing to do to an innocent kid. You're not happy, but you're not a bad person, Rhys. Don't start acting like one now."

"Don't judge me. Your life isn't being twisted all around."

"You're right. I'm also not the one who knocked up his wife, so there's that."

He frowned at her. "You're not being very supportive."

"You're not being very human, so hey, we're even."

"We have to find a way to break the contracts with Mackenzie," Barbara said as she walked into Lori's office. "The ones for the wine royalties," she added when her fat daughter stared at her in obvious confusion.

"You can't break them," Lori said. "You went over them yourself and made sure Mackenzie could never get out of them. Remember how impressed the lawyer was?"

Barbara wondered why everyone had to be so stupid all the time.

"I'm not senile. Of course I remember. That's not the point. There's always a way out and I want you to call him and have him find it. Mackenzie is going to need the money to live on and I don't want her to get it from me."

Lori, frumpy as always in her ill-fitting suit, hunched over in her chair. "Money isn't a problem for her. She's going into business with Bruno Provencio. He's funding their purchase of Painted Moon. Mackenzie will pay him her share with the money she's getting from the divorce."

Barbara glared at her. "Are you sure? How do you know that? Who told you?"

"Herman told his foreman who told Jaguar when he was working on a tractor and Jaguar mentioned it to me. Bruno's already in escrow with a condo by the golf course. He's selling his wine distribution company and some other assets so he can focus on Painted Moon."

Barbara curled her fingers into her palms until her nails dug into her skin. "Why didn't someone tell me this? Does Rhys know?"

"I think so. She still lives with him so I'm sure they talk."

Outrage joined the fury. Everyone had turned their backs on her. Everyone wanted to hurt her and take what she had, even her own children. First Mackenzie left, then Stephanie quit and now Mackenzie was getting everything she wanted with the purchase of Painted Moon.

"This can't be allowed to happen. I was hoping she would go to a bank for a loan. I'd have leverage there, but if she's partnering with Bruno, there's nothing I can do." She sank into the visitor's chair and pressed her fingertips to her temples. "And to think I invited him to the Summer Solstice Party."

She looked at Lori. "We should have Mackenzie declared mentally unfit. She's obviously not well. Who would I talk to about that?"

"I don't like her, either, but there's nothing wrong with her brain."

"Oh, you don't like her. Well, isn't that nice." Barbara stood. "She's ruining us," she shouted. "Ruining. Why am I the only one who sees that?"

She stalked back to her office and slammed the door. The fury inside of her burned so hot, she thought she might set the building on fire. Something had to be done and everywhere she turned she was met with stonewalling and incompetence.

She paced the length of her office. Bruno. She knew she couldn't fight him—he played at a level she could only dream about. If he and Mackenzie went into business together, there was nothing to be done.

Tears burned, but she blinked them away. No, she told herself fiercely. She would not be defeated. She was Barbara Barcellona and she'd faced worse than this. She'd survived the loss of her husband. She'd built Bel Après into what it was today. She'd had four small children and little help and she'd worked day and night to make the winery a success.

She'd taught herself every aspect of the business. She'd stood against disbelievers, mostly men, who said she couldn't do it.

She hadn't just survived, she'd thrived, and she'd created an empire. By God, she was not going to let some no-name interloper ruin her.

Signing the bridge loan paperwork with Bruno took about fifteen minutes. The purchase documents to buy Painted Moon were more complicated and required the services of a notary, along with what felt like a couple of hundred signatures, but by eleven on Wednesday morning, it was done. Mackenzie walked out of the escrow office with Bruno, not sure how much the weird feeling in her stomach had to do with her being pregnant and how much of it was a combination of excitement, nerves and a real sense of wishing the moment felt bigger.

"Maybe I should have brought balloons or something," she said as they stood together on the sidewalk. "I thought there would be more."

Bruno, back in one of his expensive and well-tailored suits, smiled. "Normally I would suggest a fancy lunch with champagne, but under the circumstances, that doesn't feel appropriate."

She instinctively pressed a hand to her belly. "Yes, well, I would normally agree to the fancy lunch except I'm feeling a little queasy."

"Morning sickness?"

"I think it's more the fact that we bought a winery. How did it happen so fast? We made the offer six weeks ago."

"Having the cash helped."

She grinned. "Note to self—always go into business with a man with money."

"It makes life much easier." He led her toward the parking lot. "Are you going to pick up your things at Bel Après now? If so, I'll go with you to help you carry the boxes."

She tried not to roll her eyes. "I'm perfectly capable of lifting a few boxes. Seriously, Bruno, it's like five, maybe six. I'm only taking personal things. No box weighs over fifteen pounds. Besides, I took over most of my clothes yesterday, so there's very little left." She met his gaze. "Look at how determined I am. I'll be fine."

"All right. I'll accept that. I won't like it but I'll accept it. So you'll get settled today, and in the morning, we'll meet with the employees and talk about our plans for the winery."

"How many people do you think will want to stay on?"

"If we're lucky, eighty percent. If we're unlucky, about half will leave."

She winced. "We're only a week or so from harvest. I'd hate to go through that without a full team."

He looked at her, his brows raised. "We're going to use mechanical harvest for everything this year."

Something they'd talked about and she'd agreed to. Technological advances meant all the old concerns about mechanical harvesting—bruised fruit, too much MOG (material other than grapes) and damage to the vineyards—were no longer a problem. The winery already had contracts for machines that could pick over a hundred thousand tons, or the equivalent to nearly sixty-five thousand cases of wine in a couple of days. The machines were cheaper and more reliable than training hundreds of workers to pick grapes by hand. It was the logical solution. And yet…

"It makes me sad," she admitted. "I miss harvesting by hand."

"Next year, when you get the vineyards in shape, you can handpick the premium grapes." His tone gentled. "We have too many vineyards to harvest by hand. It would take too long and we'd lose acres of fruit."

"I know. You're right. I can't help it, I'm a traditionalist."

"And the best in the business." He unlocked his Mercedes. "I'll be at the house in a couple of hours to help you unpack."

She knew better than to tell him yet again that he didn't have to. She'd spent the weekend collecting her personal belongings

twenty-four

By three that afternoon, the last of the furniture delivery trucks had left. Pushed for time, Mackenzie had chosen the least amount of furniture she could get away with. She had a leather sectional and a TV in the living room, a bed, a nightstand and a dresser in the master, and a desk and chair in what was going to be her office. She'd decided to make the room with the big bay window the baby's room, as Bruno had suggested. She would fill in things like a dining room table and side tables as she had time.

It was only when she walked into the kitchen that she realized she had no dishes, no pots and pans, and nowhere to sit and eat her meals. She also hadn't thought to buy towels or linens for the bed or pillows. Or food. Or toilet paper.

Not her finest hour. She returned to the living room where she sat on the sofa and told herself she would be fine. This was a huge day for her, and she wasn't going to let it be ruined by the fact that she'd forgotten the basics of living on her own.

If only she didn't feel so alone, she thought, trying not to be sad that she hadn't heard from Stephanie or Four all day. They knew she was moving out. She would have thought at least one of them would have been in touch.

"I'm fine," she told herself, not caring that she was lying. "I'll make a list and go to Walmart."

At least Herman had left her a washer and dryer. Once she had enough supplies to get by, she would spend at least an hour a week doing things like taking care of the house and buying supplies. Make that two hours a week—she was going to have to start cleaning and paying bills and doing laundry. As for her friends, well, they had lives. If she'd wanted company, she should have told them. Expecting them to read her mind wasn't rational.

She dug a notepad out of her backpack. The list of everything she thought she needed was nearly a page long when she heard a truck rumbling outside the house.

She crossed to the front window and saw Stephanie's car parking next to hers. Four's SUV stopped behind her and a big pickup pulling a trailer circled around behind the cars.

"What on earth?" She walked out onto the front porch and smiled at her friends. "Are you lost?"

Stephanie and Four ran up to hug her. Their warm embrace chased away her sadness and made her feel loved again. She shouldn't have questioned them—they were her family and always would be.

"We came by last week," Stephanie told her. "After you told me how little furniture you'd bought. Herman gave us a quick tour of the house. I knew you wouldn't take anything from Rhys, because that would be weird, and I know you've been too busy buying the winery to think about things like getting milk and bread, so we're going to help with that."

Four squeezed her arm. "I'm also here to do a quick cleanse of the house. I brought sage and salt. It won't take long to have this beautiful house brimming with positive energy."

"So this is why you didn't come say goodbye earlier," Mackenzie said, fighting stupid tears. "I thought you were too busy."

"Never," Stephanie told her. "We were planning a surprise instead."

"It's a really good surprise. Thank you."

The three women hugged, then broke apart as Jaguar approached.

"I hear you're moving out," he said with a grin.

"I am."

"We have some stuff we don't need, so we brought it here."

"I love castoffs."

Four put her hands on her hips. "Castoffs? I don't think so."

Mackenzie followed them to the trailer and saw it was filled with furniture. There was a dining room set with a long table and six chairs. The old art deco piece had been stripped and painted pale green with beautiful flowers across the top. The chair cushions were a dark green velvet. There was a matching buffet with the flower motif on the drawer fronts.

"No," Mackenzie breathed, looking at Four. "You could sell this for thousands. I love it so much. Let me pay you for it."

Four smiled at her. "Or you could let me show you how much I love *you* and accept the gift graciously."

Stephanie put her arm around Mackenzie. "Gracious is not her thing. She's too bossy." She looked at Mackenzie. "Wait until you see the baby stuff. You're going to cry so hard, you'll embarrass yourself."

"There's baby stuff?"

There was a beautiful crib and changing table, a dresser and, most amazing of all, a wooden rocking chair.

Stephanie ran her hands over it. "I love this chair. I rocked both my kids in it. I've had it in storage for, what, twelve years now. I think it needs a new home."

Mackenzie shook her head. "You can't give this to me."

"I can, but if it makes you feel better, if I ever get pregnant again, you can give it back."

"Deal."

They carried the furniture inside. Her friends had thought of everything. There were lamps, throw rugs, an entry table, bookcases and waste baskets. Once the trailer was empty, Jaguar drove off, leaving the women to unload the two vehicles.

By the time the bags and boxes were empty, Mackenzie had linens, dishes, flatware, pots and pans, and her refrigerator was full. Cleaning supplies sat under the sink, laundry detergent was up by the washer and hand soap had been distributed to all the bathrooms. Stephanie had even bought her a copy of *What to Expect When You're Expecting*. It was every Christmas and birthday rolled into one. Mackenzie had never felt so cherished in her life.

A little after six, they collapsed on the new sofa. The scent of burning sage had faded, leaving behind the promise of something new and wonderful.

"This is amazing," Mackenzie said, fighting the tears Stephanie had promised she would shed. "You helped me make a home."

"You didn't need us for that," Four told her. "You bring home with you. We just took care of the details." She looked around. "You're going to be happy here. Of course without the resident chef, you're going to have to learn how to cook."

"And pay bills," Mackenzie admitted. "Rhys always did that. I was very fortunate in my previous life. But enough about me. How are the kids? Stephanie, when's your interview? Four, what's your latest art project? Tell me everything I've been missing."

Four motioned to Stephanie, who tucked her feet under her and smiled.

"I'm good. The kids like their classes. Carson will get his cast off in a few weeks. His coach is worried about Carson being recruited too early. It's a high-quality thing to worry about. Avery is still claiming she's not dating the entire school year, but we'll see how long that lasts, and I'm prepared for my interview, which will be right after harvest. So yay."

Four stretched. "We're doing well at our end of the compound. The kids are happy and Jaguar remains the love of my life. Barbara continues to be a problem, but now that you've moved, I'm hoping her negative energy will start to calm down."

She grabbed Mackenzie's hand. "Focus on being happy. You've made all the right decisions. You know your place in the universe. Believe in yourself."

Stephanie poked her in the ribs. "Stop with the spiritual sayings."

"I offer blessings."

"You need to spend more time on the internet. That will cure you from being so positive."

Four grinned. "I like being positive. It annoys people."

Mackenzie laughed. "I love you two so much."

"And we love you." Stephanie glanced at her watch. "Oh, look at the time. Any second now there's going to be a knock at the door."

She stood and pulled Four to her feet. Mackenzie rose, as well. "What are you talking about?"

The sisters grinned at each other, then at her.

"You're going to have a visitor," Four told her. "A very handsome man with impressive masculine energy is bringing over dinner."

Before she could ask what they were talking about, her doorbell rang. Stephanie reached it first and let in Bruno. He had a pizza box in one hand and a shopping bag in another.

"Am I early?" he asked.

"Right on time," Stephanie told him. She turned to Mackenzie. "We're heading home. I'll be by in a couple of days to hang out. Enjoy your new house."

They all hugged, then her friends left. Bruno had retreated to the kitchen, where he unpacked a container of salad, a small cake and a bottle of sparkling apple juice.

"Plates and glasses?" he asked.

Mackenzie nodded at the cabinets. "You planned this with them."

"I did. Once Stephanie told me what she and Four were

doing, I thought it would be nice to have a celebratory dinner together. Today was a big day." He glanced at her. "Unless you have something else going on?"

"I was going to fold the load of towels I have in the dryer and that's about it."

She helped him carry the food to the table. He poured them each a glass of the sparkling apple juice and took a seat across from her.

After running his hands along the table, he said, "Beautiful piece. Unusual."

"Four painted it."

"She's very talented." He raised his glass. "To our partnership, to Painted Moon and to your new home."

"Thank you."

They touched glasses. Mackenzie stared at her drink. "I miss wine."

"I'm sure you do, but it's for a greater good." He put a piece of pizza on her plate and took one for himself. "How are you feeling about the house?"

"I love it. With all the furniture, it's perfect for me. After dinner you'll have to come upstairs and see the baby furniture Stephanie and Four brought for me. I have Stephanie's old rocking chair and one of the cribs Four used." She pointed to the book lying on the counter. "Even reading material."

"So you're ready."

"Oh, I wouldn't go that far, but I feel slightly more prepared."

"Is the baby more real?"

"No, and I wish it was."

"You'll get there."

"If I don't, I'm in for a real shock when the labor pains start."

He chuckled. "But you're happier about the baby?"

"Yes. Despite everything, I'm excited about being a mom and having my own family."

"You and Rhys never wanted children?"

"I thought we did but we never made it happen. There are a lot of reasons. Timing, the business. I wonder if we subconsciously knew things weren't right between us."

"Barbara didn't pressure you?"

"I think she was afraid having a child would distract me from the business."

"That's a ridiculous fear. You can do more than one thing at a time."

"That's the plan." She took a bite of her pizza. "I'm really happy with the house and the winery."

"I'm glad. I have big plans for us. The contractor is getting started on the office remodel right away. It shouldn't take more than a few weeks. I'm less sure about the tasting room. Retail isn't my thing. I'm wondering if we should hire someone to help us plan that."

"It's probably a good idea. My taste is all in my mouth," she said with a laugh.

"Considering why I wanted you as my business partner, that's a good thing."

He'd changed into jeans and a shirt with the sleeves rolled up to his elbows. His hair was dark, his jaw strong. He was a good-looking man, she thought. Capable and smart, but kind. Not the type of man to be single.

"What are you thinking?" he asked.

"I'm speculating about your personal life again. You really weren't dating anyone back home?"

She asked the question as lightly as she could, trying not to be concerned about the answer.

"I'm moving here alone. I have been dating someone casually, but it's not going anywhere."

The unexpected admission produced a thousand questions. "You never said. Who is she? Where is she? What does she do? Does she know it's not going anywhere or is that your decision?" She pressed her lips together. "Sorry. I can't help being curious."

He laughed. "Her name is Gloria and she's a former model who is now a physical therapist who works with sick kids."

Mackenzie felt her eyes widen. "Please tell me you're kidding."

He picked up his glass. "It's all true."

"Great. So she's beautiful, altruistic and has a body five ways to Sunday. Why don't you want to go out with her anymore?"

"She doesn't make me laugh."

"Do you make her laugh?"

"Not often enough." His gaze met hers. "Sometimes laughter is important."

"Rhys and I didn't laugh that much, but I don't think of myself as funny. Stephanie has a good sense of humor. Better than me."

"You can be funny."

"Yes, but am I doing it on purpose?"

He chuckled.

"Gloria sounds very intimidating," she admitted. "Is she really beautiful?"

He hesitated just long enough to make her groan. "Ugh. I'm so never dating. I won't be good at it. I wasn't good at it before. Rhys and I just kind of happened." She served herself salad. "Plus I'm going to have a baby. Don't guys hate dealing with other men's children?"

"Are you looking to get involved with someone?"

"Not really. I mean maybe, at some point. I don't know. It's hard to think about. I get buried in my work. I'm not a brilliant conversationalist. Not like Gloria." She emphasized the name.

"Maybe she isn't, either."

"Oh, please. She's perfect. I hate her and I don't care if that makes me shallow." She ate more pizza. "Stephanie's single, and as we've discussed, she's funny. And pretty. And smart."

"I'm not interested in Stephanie."

There was something in the tone of his voice, although she couldn't begin to name it.

"Considering my lack of experience, I probably shouldn't get involved in your dating life," she said.

"I think that's for the best."

"Don't tell Gloria what I said, please. She'll think I'm mean."

"I thought you hated her."

"I do, but I don't want her to know."

He smiled at her. "It will be our secret."

Eight days after taking ownership of Painted Moon, Mackenzie woke at 3:29 in the morning, exactly one minute before her alarm was due to go off. She got up and turned on the small lamp by her bed, then walked to the window and opened the curtain.

The sky was clear, the air still and cool. Sunrise was more than two hours away, but by the time the first rays crept over the vineyard, she would be out there to greet it. Harvest would begin today.

She turned off her phone's alarm, dressed quickly, applied sunscreen and made her way downstairs. It took only a few minutes to mix up her smoothie and pack plenty of water. Normally she would go the whole day without eating, but being pregnant changed that. Stephanie would come find her and bring lunch, along with snacks and more water to keep her hydrated.

They would start in the southernmost vineyards. She'd been driving to them every day, checking the grapes visually, measuring the sugar, or Brix. They were ready.

She made sure she had a hat, sunglasses, a portable charger for her phone, her paperwork and her drinks, then headed for her Jeep. She was on the road by four, driving across the Columbia River to Oregon and Painted Moon's Seven Hills vineyards.

Anticipation fluttered in her stomach. All the hard work from early spring came down to this moment. Once the grapes were harvested, she would work with what she had, but until then, there was the promise of possibilities. The only dark cloud on her otherwise sunny day was that this harvest would be different. She didn't know the grapes or the vineyards—not the way she normally did. There would be no family dinner later to discuss how it had gone. Barbara wouldn't drive out to watch and give her a hug. She wouldn't see Rhys several rows away, pitching in where needed, waving at her when he caught her eye.

Change was hard, she reminded herself, and she'd been through a lot. Next year would be better. Next year the grapes would be hers and she would be more comfortable in her role. Next year she would have a baby.

That last thought shocked her more than any of the others. A baby. The pregnancy was still more intellectual exercise than reality, but in a year it would be a lot more than that.

"No distractions," she murmured to herself. "I'll deal with the baby when this part is done."

She pulled off the highway and onto the smaller road, then turned onto a dirt trail where she would park out of the way of the big equipment. Shortly after dawn the giant harvesters would rumble to life and start down the rows, picking fruit and sorting out the leaves and branches. Grapes would be carried across the row and dropped into waiting bins.

Once the first truck was full, Mackenzie would follow it back to the winery, where she would oversee the crushing process. She would monitor every delivery until sunset, and in the morning they would do it all again, with her staying with the harvested grapes and Bruno in charge of what happened in the vineyards.

She'd already set the order in which the various vineyards would be harvested but reserved the right to change her mind. Stephanie was spot-checking certain plants Mackenzie had marked, texting her the results of her testing. The Brix level would ultimately determine the order of harvest for the last three vineyards. When they were done, the big equipment would head off to another winery and start the work there.

Next year they would handpick some of the vineyards, she

told herself. Next year she would have time to plan better, but for now, they were going high-tech.

She'd barely finished half her disgusting smoothie when Bruno pulled up behind her, his sleek sports car out of place in the rural setting.

"Be careful you don't break an axel," she said as she got out of the Jeep.

"My car is tougher than it looks."

"I doubt that." She looked up at the stars twinkling overhead. "It's going to be a perfect day."

"You ready?" he asked.

"Yes. Nervous, but ready."

"Good nervous or bad nervous?"

"It's always good nervous." She pointed at the large harvesters. "And there are the dreaded machines that will do the work."

"You're going to be impressed."

"I hope so." She shook her head. "I'm interested to see how this all goes."

He motioned to the quiet vineyards. "Any last-minute testing or words of wisdom?"

"I trust Herman to have done the best he could. Now we blend science and magic to produce wine."

His dark gaze met hers. "Regrets?"

There was a bigger question in that single word, she thought. Did she regret the changes in her life? Her pregnancy, her divorce, leaving Bel Après. Did she regret leaving her home, her routine, her future, to step out into the unknown? Was she afraid? Did she want to go back to how things had been?

She looked past him to the vineyards that stretched for as far as the eye could see. In the east was the first hint of light at the top of the mountains. This was hers, she thought contentedly. She and Bruno owned every acre, every grape, every leaf. There was no one to tell her she couldn't, she shouldn't or that she was wrong. The mistakes were all on her, as were the rewards.

"No regrets," she told him. "Not a single one."

Barbara woke to the feel of a heavy arm around her waist. Giorgio had spent the night and, as usual, kept her awake pulling her close as he slept. It was a characteristic she usually found charming, just not this morning. Her eyes were gritty, and she felt as if she was operating on two hours of rest. Even the sex hadn't been as spectacular as usual. She'd been unable to shut off her thoughts and had failed to orgasm, despite Giorgio's efforts.

As she walked to the shower, she felt her ever-present irritation at the world in general and Mackenzie in particular crank up at least two levels. They were in the middle of harvest and there was no one overseeing the operation. Not the way Mackenzie usually did. Rhys was doing his best, but that was hardly enough. She tried to tell herself they would get through it, but she wasn't sure that was true.

With coffee and a few minutes alone in her office, she would get her feelings under control. She'd been on edge for weeks, something else she could blame Mackenzie for. She really hated that bitch.

Giorgio joined her in the shower. Before she could protest, he'd moved behind her. He slid his slick, soapy hands over her body, finding all the spots she liked. She was about to tell him not to bother, but before she could speak, his fingers were between her legs and the interest that had been lacking the night before sprang to life.

He made her climax in less than a minute, then dragged her laughing and dripping to the bed where he had his way with her again. When they were done, the sheets were drenched, conditioner was on everything and she just plain didn't care.

"You're so good for me," she said, lying on her side, staring into his eyes. "I've been horrible for the past couple of months and you've been there for me."

"I love you. Where else would I be?"

She kissed him, thinking that if she were him, she wouldn't have put up with her own behavior. Which was why she loved him—he was a better person than she was.

"You're a good man."

"Then come away with me. We're going to New York for my daughter's birthday. Let's add a week and fly to Bermuda first."

She sighed. "You know I can't be gone that long." At this point, she didn't think she could go to the birthday celebration, but she wasn't going to spoil the mood by saying that.

"Don't say no. I'll ask again in a week."

She touched his face. "How did I get so lucky?"

He smiled. "I'm the lucky one."

An hour later, Barbara made her way to her coffee. Her bad mood had vanished and she was no longer tired. Giorgio truly was magic.

She climbed the steps to her office, determined to get as much work done as possible in the next couple of days so that she could consider going to Bermuda with Giorgio. It was a silly idea, but if it made him happy, then it was worth considering.

But all her good intentions vanished the second she saw her son sitting in front of her desk. He didn't look happy.

"What?" she asked, dropping her purse into the bottom desk drawer and taking her seat. "Why aren't you out harvesting grapes?"

Mackenzie would have been there. When it was time, nothing could tear her away. Once she'd cut herself so badly she couldn't stop the bleeding, but she'd still stayed out until sunset, then had gone to the emergency room for stitches.

"Soon. I wanted to talk to you first." Rhys stared at her desk rather than her. "I'm having trouble finding a local winemaker willing to work here."

"What does that even mean? How many have you talked to?"

He raised his gaze to hers. "All of them. I'm expanding the search to California. We should be able to find someone there."

"No one will consider Bel Après? That's ridiculous. We're an award-winning company. Is it the salary?"

"No."

"Then what is…" She stared at him as an uncomfortable thought occurred to her. "Are you saying they won't work for me?"

He glanced away. "No one said that."

Which wasn't an answer. "Because I demand excellence," she grumbled. "That's fair. I work my ass off and I'm the bad guy. Did Mackenzie get to them first?"

"This has nothing to do with Mackenzie."

She could see he was waiting for her to explode, but she didn't feel angry. Instead her face was hot and her stomach hurt. All the glory from that morning faded, leaving her hollow inside.

"Fine. Find someone in California. We don't need anyone from around here. Better to start fresh anyway. All right. Get back to work."

He looked startled but rose. "I'll get interviews scheduled."

"You do that."

When he left, she tried to take a few deep breaths, but her chest was too tight. Her eyes burned, as well. As if she were going to cry, which she wasn't. What did she care if she had a reputation? She'd faced worse as she'd grown the company. She was a woman and not from around here—proving herself had taken years.

She wasn't a bitch, but let them think she was. Let them be afraid. They were all idiots and she would prove them wrong in the end.

She started to rise to get herself coffee only to realize she was actually crying. Frustrated with herself and her silly hurt feelings, she sat back down and waited for the emotional outburst to pass.

She was better than all of them, she reminded herself. Smarter, more determined, more willing to do what others wouldn't. That was why she always won. Tears were useless. What she needed instead was a plan.

twenty-five

Once harvest ended, the real work began for Mackenzie. She oversaw the beginning of fermentation, checking on the progress daily. When she wasn't prowling around the tanks, she was at her computer, transferring her notes to the files she kept on all the varietals.

The sound of saws, nail guns and compressors made it hard to concentrate. After trying to ignore the commotion, Mackenzie and Bruno had agreed that working in the offices was going to be impossible until the construction was done. They'd rerouted the phone lines and had sent the office staff to the space they'd rented in town, and the two of them had set up their computers on her new dining room table.

Bruno had insisted on buying a piece of glass to cover the surface, so their equipment wouldn't damage Four's exquisite painting. There were file cabinets in the corner and printers on two of the chairs. They were crowded, but Mackenzie didn't mind. This was going to push her and Bruno toward being a team.

There were a thousand things to get done. The office remodel, which was underway. Once fermentation and clarifying were finished and the wine was aging in the barrels, she had to make decisions about the vineyards. Did she want to keep everything as it was? Make changes? Grafting took time, although the rootstock was strong and healthy.

She'd never been an owner before, so had never had to deal with all the details. Despite finishing with harvest, she was having trouble relaxing enough to sleep. They really had to start making decisions.

"We have to talk about what to do with the library wines," she said, glancing across the table, her mind spinning with all they had to consider. "Some can stay where they are, but some need to be sold in the next year or so. And the tasting room needs serious work. You're right about hiring someone to manage that, along with the retail space, assuming we have some. Which I think we should. I mean, why just sell wine when people will buy knickknacks and kitchen stuff? Plus there's a wine club. Do we want to start one? It's probably too soon, but we should be collecting names. And what about selling our wines in restaurants? We could offer private brands for a few years while we're getting on our feet. Either exclusive or we provide the wine and they label as their house wine, although that might be a price-point problem."

She paused for breath.

Bruno looked up from his computer. "No."

"What do you mean, no?"

"We don't have to make any of those decisions today. Get settled into the new software and think about the wines. Breathe. We'll deal with the rest of it over the next few months."

"But we just paid eight million dollars for a winery. We need money coming in."

"It will happen. Trust me."

"But it seems like a good time to panic. Shouldn't we do that together?"

He smiled. "No panic. It's going to be fine."

"You said something about China. What's happening with that? Are we—"

She noticed that he was looking past her, out the front window. She turned in her seat and saw a familiar car parking behind hers. The driver's door opened and Barbara stepped out.

"Ugh," she said, coming to her feet. "That can't be good."

"Maybe she wants to be friends again."

She sighed. "Really? What are the odds?"

"Slim. I'll step out to give you some privacy, but I'll stay close. Scream if you need help." He paused. "Maybe I should go get my shotgun."

Despite the apprehension tightening her chest, she smiled. "Do you own a shotgun?"

"No, but getting one is now on my to-do list."

He opened the front door as Barbara stepped up to knock.

"Barbara."

"Bruno."

He flashed a smile. "That was meaningful. Enjoy your visit." He glanced over his shoulder. "Leave the front door open."

Mackenzie nodded as she faced her soon-to-be-former mother-in-law.

"This is unexpected."

"I can imagine. May I come in?"

Mackenzie thought briefly about searching the other woman's bag for explosive devices. She stepped back but left the front door open as Barbara entered.

Barbara glanced at the computers on the dining room table. "Can't afford an office?"

"We're in the middle of a remodel," Mackenzie told her. She waved to the sofa. "Have a seat."

Barbara shook her head. "I won't be here that long." She pulled a piece of paper from her purse, then passed it over.

The room went in and out of focus as Mackenzie absorbed the number on the check.

"Three million dollars?" She looked at Barbara, hoping she was doing a decent job of faking nonchalance. "I assume there's something you want in exchange?"

"Money must be tight," Barbara said. "Bruno's loaded, but you're not. I would guess every penny you're getting from your overly generous divorce settlement is tied up in the winery. This would help you sleep at night."

"I sleep just fine," she lied, handing back the check.

Barbara didn't take it. "You don't know what I want."

Because her soon-to-be-former mother-in-law wanted something. It was the only reason she would stop by.

Mackenzie looked at her, at the familiar features, at the cold expression that had once been so warm and welcoming. Had any of it been real? Had she been an actual person to Barbara? Had their relationship ever been more than a means to an end? Not that she would ask any of those questions—mostly because she didn't want to hear the answers.

Mackenzie held in a sigh. "Just go. We have nothing more to say to each other."

"Hear me out. What I want has nothing to do with you. There's nothing you have to give up. All I want is for you to sign away the baby's rights to Bel Après."

She knew she shouldn't be surprised, but the words still found her soft underbelly and dug in deep. "We're talking about your grandchild."

Barbara shrugged. "Sign away the baby's inheritance and the check is yours. It's a good deal. There are already five grandchildren. Yours makes six. The three million is a sure thing. Invest it and your child will be a multimillionaire. The winery divided seven ways is going to be worth less."

Mackenzie stared at the check. Barbara was right—until the settlement from her divorce, she wasn't just broke, she was broke with a two-million-dollar bridge loan. It would be easy to cash the check and have it all. Her kid would inherit Painted Moon—what did Bel Après matter?

Only her baby was family and that should matter. Her baby was going to have cousins and aunts and uncles. Her baby was going to belong—something Mackenzie had wanted her whole life, something she'd thought she had. Only she'd been wrong.

She carefully tore the check in half and handed the pieces to her mother-in-law.

Barbara's mouth tightened with anger. "You'll do anything to get back at me, won't you?"

Mackenzie sighed. "This isn't about you. It's about belonging and connection. I never wanted the money. I wanted to be a part of something."

"You will never be a part of Bel Après. Never!"

"Maybe not, but my child will be."

Barbara sat alone in her dining room, bridal magazines spread out all around her. It was the middle of a workday, but she'd had an appointment with Stephanie to discuss the wedding and, ridiculously, she'd come home to be there in case her daughter showed up. Which she hadn't.

"Not a surprise," Barbara murmured, thinking that her children always let her down. Of course if Stephanie had shown up, Barbara would have tossed her out on her butt, but still. She should have been here. Apparently quitting her job also meant not working on the wedding. Well, fine. Barbara could do it all herself.

She had a master list of what needed to be done. The entire process was choosing and ordering—hardly a mental challenge. She would take an hour or so, finalize her decisions and make a few phone calls. But even as she picked up the first checklist, she wondered what was the point of a big party. So she could show off her happiness to her friends and family? Right now she didn't feel the least bit happy.

The sense of being adrift wasn't like her. Whenever things got bad, she pulled herself together and managed the problem. She was strong. She was used to being the only one who did what had to be done. Only this time, she couldn't summon the will.

She couldn't believe Mackenzie had turned down the money. No, that wasn't true. Honestly, she'd expected no less. Mackenzie had always had courage and strength and a moral compass. In some ways, Barbara thought grimly, Mackenzie was the most like her. She saw what had to be done and waded in through the muck and did it.

She heard her front door open and the sound of footsteps in the foyer. For a second, her spirits lightened as she imagined Stephanie had come to apologize. Barbara told herself she would be stern but forgiving, telling her daughter that she had to—

"Hello, Barbara."

Not Stephanie, she thought, holding a sigh. Instead her youngest stood in front of her. As always, Catherine's choice of clothing was questionable, at best. Her blouse—a pretty sea-green color—was acceptable but her cropped pants were covered in quilted fish the size of dinner plates. The fish were three-dimensional with fins that stuck out and waved as Catherine moved. Her shoes continued the fish motif. They were covered in sequins that created a fish-scale pattern.

The outfit was nearly outrageous enough to distract Barbara from her disappointment.

"Why are you here?"

Catherine smiled. "To help with the wedding. Stephanie and I talked about it, and we agreed given what has happened, you wouldn't want to work with her, so I volunteered to come in her place."

"You decided amongst yourselves but no one thought to check with me?" she asked. "How incredibly typical."

Catherine pulled out a chair and sat across from her. "Do you want Stephanie planning your wedding?"

Yes, of course she did. Stephanie might not be the most talented person, but she had offered and Barbara had expected her to see her commitment through. Her sense of being abandoned was nothing more than an extension of her daughter's broken promise.

"I don't need anyone's help," Barbara snapped. "Certainly not yours."

Instead of bristling, Catherine smiled. "Oh, Barbara, how difficult you always make things. Where's the fun in planning your wedding alone? Let me take care of some of the little things." She held up her hand. "I know we don't have the same taste in anything."

"You have no taste. You want to dazzle everyone with your originality and end up looking ridiculous."

Catherine's smile never wavered. "I promise to be completely conventional. As the bride, your decisions are the ones that matter. I'm here to help, nothing more."

Perhaps all that was true, but she wasn't the daughter Barbara wanted. At least Stephanie had managed several parties, so she knew what she was doing. But she'd left. Like Mackenzie.

That was the real loss, Barbara thought, and the source of her emptiness.

"I miss her, too," Catherine said quietly.

"I have no idea what you're talking about."

"You were thinking about Mackenzie. You had to be. You got so sad. She is a huge part of this family and we—"

"She's nothing to this family and nothing to me. We're better off without her. She can't be trusted, and when she fails, we'll celebrate."

Catherine shook her head. "I'll never understand why, if you loved her best, you treated her the way you did. She might not have been born into this family, but she was the heart of us. We're never going to be the same—you most of all."

Catherine's mouth straightened into a flat line. "It must be hard to be you, Barbara. To be so unrelenting in your harshness, to always assume the worst. Living like that would crush my soul."

Barbara glared at her. "Get out."

"You're right." Catherine rose. "What was I thinking? You can't accept a gift, even one given freely. An act of kindness must be like an attack. Which makes your relationship with Giorgio so confusing. Why do you let him in and no one else? Is it because he's a man? Or is it that you know, in the end, it's never going to last?"

"You will leave here immediately," Barbara shrieked, coming to her feet and pointing to the door. "Get out right now!"

"You're going to drive him away. I'm sorry about that because he really seemed to make you happy. I wish you could be different." Catherine smiled. "But I'm sure you say the same thing about me."

With that, she left, her fish pants flapping as she went. Barbara waited until the door closed before sinking into the chair and covering her face with her hands. Her daughter's words echoed in the room, mocking her.

"It's not me," she yelled back. "It's everyone else. It's always been everyone else."

She swept the lists and magazines to the floor, then picked up her coffee mug and threw it against the wall. Even as the dark liquid stained the paint, she got up and walked out.

She would go to the office, she told herself. Things made sense there, and if that started to change, she would spend the rest of the day figuring out a way to make Mackenzie pay.

"I've had a lot of success with corporate events," Stephanie said, feeling her interview nerves calm down as she spoke.

"Weddings are an excellent source of revenue, but my main focus has been the retail store in the tasting room."

Elias, the general manager for a local winery, flipped through her portfolio. She'd included samples of her promotional material, pictures of displays and menus from events she'd pulled together.

Everything she'd read about interviews and getting a job said to always go in fully prepared but not to appear too eager. She was doing her best to show her capable side, while keeping the urge to beg with "Oh, please, oh, please, hire me!" tucked away. Her financial situation wasn't dire, and if this didn't work out, she would find another "opportunity," but it would be so great if Elias thought she was exactly what he was looking for.

Elias closed the large folder and looked at her. He was in his midfifties, with graying hair and glasses.

"I know your mom," he said.

Stephanie smiled. "Everyone does."

He didn't smile back. "The few times she's mentioned you, she hasn't been complimentary."

Stephanie told herself not to react to that. She kept her expression neutral and hands relaxed.

"I figured she was just being herself. Barbara rarely has anything nice to say about anyone. Except Mackenzie, of course."

Stephanie nodded. There was no need to panic. She'd known there was a very good chance that her mother had trashed her over the years. People understood that and would dismiss her words. Right?

"But this makes me wonder," he said, tapping the folder before opening it. "Maybe she's not wrong."

Stephanie felt her eyes widen. "I don't understand."

He pulled out a flyer for an end-of-season sale seven years ago. He drew out a second one that looked almost identical.

"This is from last year. You used the same flyer. Now, I don't have a problem with recycling work, but you put both of them in the material you wanted to show me. I'm assuming you consider this your best work. So why two of the same? A simple mistake maybe. I don't know."

She felt her cheeks start to burn. How could she have missed that?

"The work from when you first started is fresh and energetic," he continued. "But later, there's nothing original. What's the deal?"

She wasn't sure if the question was rhetorical or if she was supposed to answer. Fortunately, he kept talking.

"Every job has parts that are boring. I get that. But you weren't even trying. Worse, you brought me proof of that. You have a great plan for selling library wines, but we're not Bel Après. We're a high-volume, low-cost winery. If it's in a bottle, it's getting sold. Our customers don't care about things like library wines. They want a seasonal bottle with Santa on the label."

He pushed the folder toward her. "You should know that, Stephanie. You spent all your prep time thinking about what you wanted to say but very little thinking about what I wanted to hear."

"I researched the winery," she whispered, an amazing feat, considering she was barely able to breathe. Humiliation burned through her body. "I know how much you had in sales and where you're placed in retail."

"Those are just numbers. You don't know us." He shrugged. "I think you could probably do a decent job, if you gave us your full attention. But here's the thing. I don't want a maybe. I want to be sure, and with you, I'm not." He glanced at the door. "But I appreciate you coming in."

It took her a second to realize she'd just been dismissed. She reached for her folder and fumbled with it a couple of times before finally grabbing it. She collected her purse and her briefcase and stood.

"Thank you for your time," she managed, then bolted. Walking as quickly as her three-inch black pumps would let her, she made her way to her SUV.

She pulled into the parking lot of the nearest fast-food place, carefully turned off the engine, then clutched the steering wheel as tears filled her eyes. Mortification didn't begin to describe how horrible she felt. She hadn't just screwed up an interview, she'd exposed her lack of experience and talent to someone who knew her and her family. Elias was a big deal in the area. He could tell everyone what had happened and that her mother was right about her. The entire industry would be laughing at her.

She brushed away tears, only to have more take their place.

She'd been so sure, she thought, but she'd screwed up so badly. She'd done research on the presentation, she'd pulled the samples and laid them out on her desk. How hadn't she seen the duplicate? How had she not noticed that her work from the last couple of years was crappy? She'd thought she had talent but she was nothing. Nothing!

She managed to get the crying under control. She drove home and made her way to her bedroom. After stepping out of her shoes, she hurried to the bathroom and threw up the little she had in her stomach.

Lying there on the cold tile, she relived the interview while waiting for the nausea to pass. She saw herself walking in and proudly presenting Elias with her portfolio. She watched his expression tighten a little, probably because he was trying to conceal his shock at how bad she was. When he looked up, she saw the pity in his eyes.

She slowly got up, changed her clothes and went back downstairs, her portfolio tucked under her arm. In her study, she sat in her chair and wondered what she was going to do now.

If Elias spread the word, she would never find a job in Walla Walla. While she didn't think he was likely to do that, she couldn't be sure. Worse, she couldn't blame him. He'd been right about her not caring the last couple of years. Yes, her mother was a pain to work for, but so what? Compared to most people, she'd had it easy.

She fanned her samples out in front of her. The early work *was* exciting, she thought wistfully. Creative and eye-catching. After that, not so much, which was her own fault.

She wasn't surprised her mother had said awful things about her—she could live with that. But that she'd proved them to be true was unbearable.

She looked at the pages of research she'd done on Elias's winery. Knowing how many bottles sold a year was one thing, but not understanding the true nature of his customers was unforgiveable.

She picked up her marketing plan for the library wines. So what if she'd done a great campaign—he couldn't use it because he didn't have library wines. She should have known that. And because she hadn't, she'd lost a chance at a great job. Worse, she'd figured out she wasn't someone even she would want to hire.

twenty-six

At lunch Mackenzie did what women across the country did on a regular basis—she ran errands. After putting gas in her Jeep, she headed for the grocery store, a shopping list in her back pocket. She was still trying to figure out a routine, which was harder than she'd anticipated. She'd been so spoiled at Bel Après, what with a chef, a housecleaning service and Rhys handling things like bills and putting gas in her car. Now it was all on her— daunting, but worth it.

Two weeks after moving into the house, she was finally sleeping better and settling in. She liked how homey the place felt. Bruno was right—she would eventually want to remodel the kitchen and the two upstairs bathrooms, but for now it was enough that she had a place to call home.

The hardest adjustment was living by herself. She never had. She'd gone from living with her grandfather to rooming with Stephanie in college to moving in with Rhys. On the bright side, whatever leftovers she put in the refrigerator were always waiting for her. Sadly there was no one else to load the dish-washer when she was tired after a long day.

Last time she'd shopped, she'd wandered the aisles, forgetting half of what she needed. Last night she'd made a list, even plan-ning out a few dinners. On Sunday she was going to get out her new Crock-Pot and find a couple of recipes that looked good. She would make batches and freeze single-size meals for herself.

She got a cart and headed into the store. She had to backtrack a couple of times but finished her shopping in under twenty minutes. After paying, she carried the bags to her Jeep and felt a strong sense of accomplishment. She would quickly unload everything at home, then return to work. With the grapes busy fermenting, she could get caught up on paperwork. Later, after drinking two full glasses of water, she would sample from two more barrels and add to her growing file of notes.

She stopped at a traffic light. As she waited for it to turn green, she noticed a café taking advantage of the unseasonable warm October weather by setting out tables and chairs on the sidewalk.

The familiar silhouette of one customer caught her attention. Her whole body tensed as she saw Rhys sitting across from a pretty blonde. They were leaning toward each other, laughing at something one of them had said.

Behind her, a horn honked. She returned her attention to the road and pulled into the intersection, on her way back to the house.

"I'm fine," she told herself, ignoring her rapidly beating heart and the sudden dryness in her mouth. "We're getting a divorce. Of course he's seeing other people."

She wasn't surprised. She didn't mind. This was what hap-pened. People moved on. She'd moved on. She was perfectly all right with what she'd seen.

Only she wasn't all right, mostly because she'd always been one step behind Rhys on the divorce. He'd brought it up first, he'd had her served, and while she wanted all that, too, she couldn't help thinking that maybe they could have mourned what they'd had a little longer. She didn't miss him so much as what she'd always thought of as "them."

She got back to the house and put away her groceries. Bruno was sitting at the dining room table, two computer screens in front of him. She squinted as she stared at what looked like a very complicated spreadsheet, grateful she wasn't responsible for the finances.

"We have barn cats," he said, studying the screens as she took her seat. "I've counted four of them."

"Most wineries have cats. They're close to feral and help keep down the rodent population."

"I'm arranging for someone to come trap them and get them in to the vet. They need checkups. If they haven't been already, they need to be vaccinated, spayed and neutered before they're returned to us." He glanced up. "We don't want—" He swore under his breath. "What's wrong?"

She knew she should eat something, but right now she wasn't very hungry.

"Nothing. Why do you ask? I'm great."

He stared at her. "No, you're not. Something happened. You're pale and you look shaken." He swore. "Did Barbara come back? We can get a restraining order against her."

"I hardly think she's broken any laws and I doubt any judge would see her as a threat."

"She tried to buy your kid."

"No, she tried to buy my kid's inheritance. There's a difference." She managed a smile as she sat down. "I can handle her."

"Maybe. What happened?"

She had a feeling Bruno wasn't going to let it go and wished there was something dramatic she could share. Something that would justify her reaction. Unfortunately, all she had was the truth.

"I saw Rhys having lunch with a woman." She held up a hand.

"I'm not upset. It's more the shock of it. They were laughing and having a good time. She's very pretty."

He watched her cautiously.

"Bruno, I'm really okay. It's just everything has happened so fast, and even though I didn't want to stay married, divorce is hard. He was a part of my life for a long time and now he's gone. I thought Barbara was my second mom and obviously she's not. I still have Stephanie and Four, but sometimes it feels like my emotional life is slipping away from me. The day before the Summer Solstice Party, I knew what the rest of my life was going to look like. After that, everything changed and I'm still catching up. Being pregnant doesn't help."

She put her hands flat on the table. "Stephanie mentioned me needing maternity clothes the other day. I can't wear my regular stuff much longer, but I never thought about that myself, and to be honest, I'm resisting the thought. Isn't that bad? I don't feel connected to the baby. What if that never happens? What if I'm a terrible mother?"

He smiled at her. "Maternity clothes have nothing to do with being a mom. Bad parents don't worry about being bad parents."

"Logic? Really? This hardly seems like the appropriate time."

He chuckled. "It's always time for logic. Let's take these one at a time. The divorce. Of course it's hard. You were with him, what, sixteen years? You loved him. You don't just turn that off."

"He did," she grumbled.

"This isn't about him, it's about you. It's going to take time. The same with how you feel about Barbara. You're mourning that relationship, as well. You loved her and believed she loved you, too. You've been betrayed. That's a tough thing to get over. As for the baby, you'll get there."

"You're so rational. I must look like an idiot to you. You're seeing me at my worst."

"If this is you at your worst, then I have nothing to worry about."

She rested her elbow on the table and leaned her head against her hand. "You're nice. I knew you'd be a brilliant business-man and great partner in the winery, but I didn't know about the nice part."

"I'm not nice, but I do understand feeling badly about some-thing that's happened. We've all done things we regret."

"Tell me one."

He hesitated before leaning back in his chair. "I fell for a mar-ried woman."

Mackenzie felt her eyes widen. "For real? But you so don't seem the type."

"I'm not. I know better. Her name is Kristine. She lives on Blackberry Island." He gave her a faint smile. "We met because she was the caterer for my private jet."

She straightened and smiled. "So a Cinderella story."

"Not exactly. Her marriage was going through a rough patch and she had three boys she talked about all the time. I knew better but I began to imagine stepping into his place. Being a dad, being a husband. Not my finest hour."

She didn't know what to say. Bruno was always capable, so-phisticated and urbane. The vulnerable man in front of her was someone she'd never seen before.

"Were you in love with her?"

"No. I didn't know her well enough for that. We flirted and she immediately retreated. She didn't want someone else, she wanted the man in her life to step up."

"Did he?"

"Eventually. Last I heard, they're together and very happy."

"I'm sorry you got hurt."

"I wasn't involved enough to be hurt. However, the situation showed me that I needed to make some changes. That's when I decided I wanted a new career challenge."

She smiled. "We've certainly given you that, haven't we?"

"Painted Moon is going to become a name to be reckoned with in the wine industry."

"I hope you're right."

"I'm rarely wrong in business. It's my personal life that sucks."

"I don't understand why that is. Have you seen yourself? You're very dateable."

One eyebrow rose as he looked at her. Mackenzie immediately felt flustered and didn't know what to do with her hands. She wanted to call back the statement, only it was true and they were friends, so why couldn't she say it?

She supposed the problem was she was afraid he would see it as an invitation rather than an observation and she didn't want Bruno thinking she was interested in him that way. Mostly because, well, um…

He saved her from her spinning thoughts by smiling slightly and saying, "In my free time?"

She grabbed the gracious lifeline he threw her way.

"Yes, well, there is that. I know I wouldn't have time to date, either. Although the real difference between us is you're some good-looking rich guy and I'm a single, pregnant mom-to-be. I suspect you're the more desirable addition to the dating pool."

His dark gaze met hers. "You're not ready to start dating."

"You're right, but eventually I'd like to, I don't know, fall in love. Sometimes I wonder if I ever really loved Rhys." She shook her head. "That came out wrong. I loved him. I still do. What was missing was the 'in love' part. I think ours was a love built on shared interests and expediency."

"You'll do better next time."

"I trust your business track record. I'm less confident about your ability to see into my future."

"I know you, Mackenzie. You don't fail the same way twice." He stood. "Come on."

She looked at him. "Where are we going?"

"Nowhere. Stand up. I'm going to hug you. After what happened today, you need a hug from a friend."

Despite a sudden flush of awkwardness, she did as he requested. She rose and stepped toward him. Strong arms came around her and drew her close. She hugged him back, letting herself lean against him and absorb his strength and warmth.

She'd thought he would let go immediately, but he held on for several seconds, letting her step back first. As she looked at him, she realized she felt less tense and more like she was going to be all right.

"Thanks. You give really good hugs."

He smiled and lightly brushed her cheek with his thumb. "A perk of the partnership."

"I don't remember reading that in the paperwork."

"Some things are simply understood."

As she took her seat and opened her email program, she found herself thinking Bruno really was a good man. And a great hugger. Both characteristics she was pleased to find in her new business partner.

Barbara sat across from her lawyer and tried to keep her impatience to herself. They'd worked through nearly all of the things on the list she'd sent. But so far Dan hadn't said a single word about Mackenzie.

"I can't decide if you're being deliberately difficult or if you have a plan," she said when he'd brought up an annual review of the trust that had been set up for the investment accounts. "I don't want to discuss the trust. I want to know if you've gone over the contracts I have with Mackenzie."

Dan, a middle-aged man with brown hair and a fondness for three-piece suits, pressed his lips together.

"I told you in my email that the contracts were solid, Barbara. You insisted on that. For as long as you're selling those wines, Mackenzie gets her cut."

"That's ridiculous."

"That's the law."

"It's a stupid law. There's nothing you can do?"

"I've been over them myself, and I had one of my partners review them, as well."

"Can I sue her?"

"For what?"

She waved her hand. "You're the lawyer, you tell me. Anything. Walking away from her job. Buying Painted Moon. Divorcing my son."

"None of those are actionable. You didn't have an employment agreement with her or a do-not-compete contract. She was an at-will employee and she wanted to leave. The divorce is between her and Rhys."

"Well, it shouldn't be. It affects us all." She wasn't surprised by his assessment, but she didn't like it. "We'll have to stop producing the wines. That way she won't get anything."

"Aren't they profitable for the company?"

"Yes." Very profitable. All Mackenzie's wines were sought after and sold out within weeks of their release.

"Wouldn't it make more sense to simply pay her what she's owed?"

"I'm not interested in sensible. I want her punished. She's pregnant."

Dan's neutral expression didn't change. "I didn't know. Is Rhys the father?"

"So he tells me."

Dan shocked her by smiling. "Then congratulations."

She glared at him. "Is that you being funny?"

"What? No. I thought… She's having your grandchild."

"I already have grandchildren. I don't need any more and certainly not hers. Can I sue for custody?"

"Of what?"

Were all lawyers as stupid as him? "Can I sue Mackenzie for custody of her baby?"

Dan drew back in his chair, and his features tightened. "I don't handle family law. I'd need to refer you to someone else. Having said that, I don't see any grounds to sue her for custody of her unborn baby. The courts favor the biological parents. Now, Rhys would have a case."

"He's not interested in having much to do with the child. I'm insisting on a DNA test, but the way things are going, the baby probably is his."

She picked up the cup of coffee she'd been given when she first sat down. "It's the inheritance. I don't care how many children she has, but if Rhys is the father, then her child is going to inherit a part of Bel Après. I want to stop that from happening." She looked at him. "That would be where you come in."

"Once she has the DNA test and proves Rhys is the father, there's nothing you can do. The will is very clear on who inherits."

"Are you sure? Can you even pretend to find a solution?" Frustration bubbled inside of her.

Dan shook his head. "I'm sorry. No."

She sensed his disapproval. No doubt he thought she was cruel and heartless. Not that she cared about that. Protecting Bel Après was all that mattered, and to that end, she would do anything.

twenty-seven

Stephanie had trouble shaking her sense of shame and failure. She went through the motions of her life, telling herself that in a few days she would snap out of it and come up with a new direction. Or at least a plan to get a job. But nearly two weeks after the humiliating interview with Elias, she felt no more capable of putting herself out there again than she had the day it had happened.

She did her best to act normal in front of the kids. Carson was all about his friends and sports, and didn't notice anything was wrong. He'd recently started thinking about playing baseball in college rather than going from high school to the minor league, which meant he suddenly cared about his grades. That was only good news to her.

She was less sure if she was convincing Avery that all was well. She'd caught her daughter watching her a couple of times, but maybe that was just ordinary teenage wondering about how incredibly dumb parents were and why did it have to be that way.

When Kyle called and suggested they have dinner together

Friday night, she'd agreed because why not. He was a friendly face and she needed a distraction. He was heading east to Pullman for a WSU home game the next day.

She pulled herself together enough to shower and put on a little makeup, then lost interest when it came to finding something cute to wear. In the end, she pulled on leggings and a tunic top, and slipped her feet into ballet flats.

She was tired from not sleeping well and still getting flashbacks where she relived the horror of the interview. At some point she really was going to have to get her butt in gear and find a job. Her savings wouldn't last forever.

If only she could know if Elias was going to tell everyone what had happened. It wasn't as if she could call and ask if he planned to blab about what an idiot she was. But the thought of word spreading, of her mother finding out, haunted her.

Right on time, Kyle knocked on the door. Avery was babysitting for Four, and Carson was at a friend's house. Stephanie let him in while she grabbed her purse.

"Hi," she said, hoping she sounded more upbeat than she felt. "How was the drive?"

"Good." He leaned in and kissed her cheek. "It's raining in Seattle, but the skies cleared when I went over the pass." He frowned. "You okay?"

She started to say she was, then found herself blurting out, "No. I'm a mess." Tears filled her eyes. She tried to blink them away, but a couple escaped to slide down her cheeks.

Kyle surprised her by closing the front door, taking her purse from her and setting it on the entry table, then leading her into the living room.

"What's going on?" he asked when they were seated next to each other on the sofa. He angled toward her, his expression concerned.

"I'm such a disaster," she said, wiping her face. "I thought I was doing better, standing up to my mom and wanting to find a new job, but I've made so many mistakes. I've embarrassed myself and now I may not be able to find a job anywhere near here and then what?"

He frowned. "I have no idea what you're talking about. Start at the beginning."

She hesitated, not wanting to share the shame, but then reminded herself the man had seen her screaming in pain as she pushed out a baby, not to mention vomiting through the flu, so he could probably handle what she had to say.

"I had a job interview."

She told him how excited she'd been and how confident she'd felt about her answers and her material. Until Elias had started pointing out her failures.

"He was right about all of it," she admitted, fighting tears again. "I did a ton of research on the industry but none on his winery. I put so much effort into how to sell the library wines because Mackenzie was talking about the ones at Painted Moon. That's where I got the idea."

"So you had a good plan, but for the wrong business."

She nodded. "And the flyers. Why didn't I see how my work had gone downhill over the past few years? I'm mortified and I'm terrified Elias is going to tell everyone he knows that my mom was right about me and no one else will hire me and she'll get to *say* she was right."

Kyle pulled her close and held on to her. "He's not going to go around and talk about you like that."

"Maybe he will."

She felt him chuckle. "That's my little ray of sunshine."

"I'm so embarrassed. I don't know what to do now. I have to get a job, but I have no experience out of the wine industry and I'm afraid no one in the industry wants to hire me." She drew back and wiped away more tears. "I'm a failure."

He took her hand in his. "You're not. You had a setback.

That's all. You'll learn from the experience and do better next time."

"Easy for you to say. You're a famous TV sportscaster. What do you know about failure?"

"I lost you."

"Oh, please. That was a decade ago and you barely noticed I was gone."

"That's not true. I screwed up, Stephanie, and I have a lot of regrets."

While the words were nice to hear, she wasn't sure she believed him. "Thank you for saying that."

He squeezed her fingers. "Go work for Mackenzie. She and Bruno must need help with the retail space and other stuff. You already have a plan for their library wines."

She pulled her hand free of his. "No. I'm not going to ask my best friend to give me a job." She shuddered. "I want to be hired because I'll be the right person, not out of pity."

"You're not giving yourself enough credit. You're good at what you do."

She appreciated the words, even if once again she doubted the truth of them. "You want to see the best in me. That's really nice, but the last couple of years at Bel Après, I was phoning it in. I can see that now. I was bored and frustrated and I didn't do my best."

"So you learn from that, too. You have a lot to offer. You're honest and smart and you raised great kids." He smiled. "You put up with me longer than you should have."

She managed to smile back. "I did, but that was because I was crazy in love with you. I didn't want to walk away."

She'd kept hoping he would change so that she could stay, but in the end, she'd done the right thing. She supposed that was something to be proud of. Of course she'd continued to have sex with her ex for the next decade, which was so incredibly dumb.

"I'm a slow learner," she said with a groan. "I've got to get better at figuring out the problem and solving it."

"I have a thought," he said. "Give us another chance."

She stared at him, not sure she'd heard him correctly. "What did you say?"

"Give us another chance." He reached for her hand again. "I miss you, Steph. I miss us. I was so wrong before. I threw away the most important thing in my life and I didn't realize it. But I do now. I have so many regrets. I'm asking for a second chance. I know I have to earn your trust, but I'm up for the challenge. I've never stopped loving you."

She couldn't seem to form actual thoughts. There were a handful of words strung together, but they made no sense. In love with her? She couldn't grasp the concept.

"It's been ten years," she said, hoping she didn't look as confused as she felt.

"All that means is we've both had a chance to grow and change. I know I have." He gave her a rueful smile. "You were pretty perfect to begin with, so you had less of a journey. I mean it. I love you. I want us to try again."

He loved her? Since when? And how did she feel about what he was saying? Did she want to get back together with him? How would that work? Avery was a junior in high school. She wouldn't want to move and Carson had all his friends and—

Stephanie shook her head. No! This wasn't about her kids— this was about her and Kyle, and what she wanted.

"We could make it work," he continued. "I could move in here and commute to Seattle. You wouldn't have to worry about working unless you wanted to. I want to take care of you the way I should have before. I want to be everything you want me to be."

He sounded sincere, she thought, still having trouble grasping what was happening. He was offering her everything he thought she wanted. Everything she *had* wanted when she'd left him and run back home. They got along well, the sex had always been impressive and being around Kyle was fun. But was that enough? What about her hopes for her own future? Where would he fit in with those? Not that she had much of a future right now. Part of her was tempted—seriously tempted. After all, he was making it so very easy.

For a second time, she pulled her hand free of his as the truth smacked her in the face. It would be easy to say yes, to avoid all the problems in her life. Getting back with Kyle could solve them all. She wouldn't have to worry about money or what to do with her life.

But was that enough? Didn't she want—just once—to be brave? She'd been unhappy in her marriage for years before she'd gathered the courage to leave, and then all she'd done was run back to her mother. She'd taken even longer to try to find another job, and when the cheese place had been a disaster, she'd done nothing. She'd quit on impulse, which wasn't the least bit brave. And now she was facing the reality of a mediocre skill set and a bad reputation. Rather than get off her ass and deal, she'd been hiding and feeling sorry for herself. Worse, she was considering marrying Kyle because it was the easy solution.

"I'm a complete and total wuss," she said aloud.

"What?"

She looked at him. "I am. I've taken the easy way out my entire life. I wanted you, so I got pregnant to trap you. I left you and expected my mom to take care of me. I hated my job here, but I didn't do anything about it. I kept having sex with you so I wouldn't have to find someone I really wanted to be with. I've always taken the easy way out."

"You're being too hard on yourself."

"I'm not. Maybe for the first time in my life, I'm being honest." She sucked in a breath. "I don't love you, Kyle. I'm sorry, but I don't. I haven't for a long time. I think we're good as friends, but we can't get back together. It's been over between us for a long time. We both need to move toward the future, not retreat to the past."

He drew back, his mouth twisting. "You're not going to give us a chance?" His voice was laced with pain.

His obvious surprise, his emotional reaction, triggered guilt, but she ignored it.

"I care about you," she told him. "I always will. We're stuck with each other and I like that. But as friends. You need to find someone who can appreciate the man you've become."

He stood up and glared at her. "I could have gone national. I stayed with the Seattle station because I wanted to be close to you, and all this time, you didn't care what I did."

He was reacting out of anger, she told herself. Best if she didn't do the same. "I didn't know you'd had the chance to go national. Can you still? The kids would love visiting you in New York, and so would I."

As soon as the words came out, she knew they were wrong. He flinched.

"You don't even care if I'm around, do you?"

"Kyle, no! That's not what I meant. I want you to be happy. I want you to have whatever you want."

"Just not you."

There was nothing she could say to that. The awkward silence grew until he turned for the door. She went after him.

"I'm sorry," she said. "I don't want to hurt you."

He faced her. "We could have had it all, Steph."

He was right—they could have. But that chance had ended ten years ago. After all this time, there was no going back.

"I'm sorry," she repeated.

"Me, too."

He walked out into the evening. She watched him get into his car and drive away, then she closed the door and leaned against it.

She didn't feel good about what had happened, but at least she knew she'd done the right thing. For once, she hadn't taken the easy way out. Now the question was what was she going to do next.

Barbara drank wine because she loved it, but she drank tequila to get drunk. Sometimes she made a margarita and sometimes she drank it straight. On this particular afternoon, she was at least pretending, so had mixed it with fresh lime juice and Cointreau.

She sat in her family room, off the kitchen, staring out the window, wondering how her entire life had gone to shit so quickly. Everything was a disaster, and nothing made her feel better, not even gazing at her sparkly engagement ring. The idea of planning a wedding made her shudder—she hardly had time for what she had to do in a day, let alone plan a ridiculous celebration. What did her marriage matter—Bel Après had lost its winemaker and she didn't have a replacement. Even as she sat there, grapes were fermenting and then what? Who would decide what happened next, which were blended and in what ratios? You couldn't just ferment a bunch of grapes, pour the result into a bottle and expect to have something wonderful.

"No one in the area will work for me," she said, raising her glass toward her two daughters. She wasn't sure how they'd gotten there. Lori might have followed her from the office and Catherine had appeared a few minutes later. No doubt Lori had called her, wanting reinforcements.

Barbara had no idea for what. She was sitting by herself, drinking. She was hardly going to burn down the place, so why fuss. But she didn't say that, because it didn't matter, either.

"What do you mean?" Catherine asked, looking ridiculous as always in tie-dyed overalls. Dear God, tie-dye? Hadn't that gone out in the 1960s? "Who won't work for you?"

"Any decent winemaker in the area. We're looking in California. We're going to end up with some loser, but what choice is there?" She swallowed about half of her margarita. It was her third, she thought. Or maybe her fourth.

"Everything is ruined," Barbara continued. "First Mackenzie leaving, then Stephanie. I miss them both. They were so fun to talk to." She glared at her remaining daughters, wondering why they couldn't be more sparkling conversationalists.

"And the lawyer was a disaster. He refused to even consider suing Mackenzie for custody. Why not? I raised four children. She has no experience and she's an orphan."

Lori looked confused. "What does her being an orphan have to do with anything?"

"She has no family, no support system."

"But it's her baby, Mom," Lori said, her voice tentative. "You can't take it away from her."

"So people keep telling me," Barbara snapped, wondering why her middle daughter was so tiresome.

"Let's change the subject," Catherine suggested. "Talk about happy things. Lori, tell Barbara about Owen."

Barbara turned sharply to stare at Lori. "Who's Owen?"

Lori looked flustered, then blushed, which was always a disaster for her. She went blotchy. It was so unattractive.

"He's an assistant manager at a winery. We've been going out for a while now."

Lori dating? "Since when?"

"A few weeks." Her daughter looked past her. "I didn't think you'd want to talk about it, what with everything else going on."

While that was true, Barbara resented someone else deciding things for her. "You should have told me."

"I'm sorry. You're right."

"I am." Barbara finished her drink. "I'm glad he doesn't care that you're fat. That's something, I suppose."

Lori's eyes widened the way they always did before she burst into tears. Barbara held in a sigh and braced herself for the onslaught. Seconds later, her daughter raced from the room.

"Really?" Catherine shook her head. "Do you have to be mean all the time? Can't we limit it to odd-numbered days?"

"She's weak."

Catherine pressed her lips together. "You know, a lot of research says that overeating is the result of a bad childhood, so technically her weight issues are your fault."

Barbara raised her eyebrows. "Yes, it's very trendy to blame the mother, isn't it?"

Rather than respond, Catherine pulled out her cell phone and sent a quick text. She smiled at her mother.

"Are you happy?"

The unexpected question unsettled Barbara. She dropped her gaze to her glass, not wanting to respond.

"I am," Catherine added, her tone cheerful. "Every day. I have Jaguar and my children. My art fills my soul and I live in a beautiful house surrounded by my family. I'm blessed."

"You certainly don't require much from life," Barbara snapped.

Catherine's calm smile was annoying.

"I require what's important to me."

"Oh, please. Jaguar is a mechanic. He's never going to get into management. Your bits and pieces that you call art don't sell for very much."

"Happiness isn't about money or position. It's about feeling fulfilled by your life. Jaguar enjoys his job and doesn't want to move up in the company. He would rather have time with his family."

"What a shock. You married a man with no ambition."

Catherine, as per usual, ignored her. "We don't need much money, thanks to the family trust. I sell my art when it pleases me. The amount isn't important. I like knowing my pieces make people happy. I'm connected to the earth and creatures around me. My children thrive. What else could I possibly want?"

"A brain?"

Catherine laughed. "I know you're not trying to be funny, but sometimes you are." Her smile faded. "I wish you could be happy. You have so much and you never bother to appreciate it."

"What do I have? Betrayal? Abandonment? A failing company?"

"You have good health and family and a man who loves you."

As if on cue, Giorgio walked into the room. Barbara was surprised to see him, then he and Catherine exchanged a knowing look and she realized the text her daughter had sent earlier had been a request for him to come by. They were plotting against her, she thought grimly. She shouldn't even be surprised.

Giorgio sat next to her and took her hand in hers. "How are you, my sweet?"

"Angry. Depressed. Fearful about the future."

Old, she thought, but didn't say that. Why state the obvious?

"You should have a little faith," he told her, his tone chiding. "It will all work out."

"Will it? How wonderful. While you're prognosticating, when will the new winemaker show up? That would be helpful information."

Giorgio frowned. "Why are you angry with me?"

"Because you're making ridiculous statements. You don't know that everything is going to work out. In your mind, you say it's fine and it is, but that's not reality. If I don't stay on top of everything, then it will all fall apart."

He released her hand and moved to the sofa opposite. "If you hang on too tight, you'll strangle everyone."

"Am I hanging on too tight?" she asked, her voice stiff. "Do you want to tell me what else I'm doing wrong? How this is all my fault, from Mackenzie leaving to Lori's weight problem? I seem to be the villain of the day. Feel free to pile on."

She was both furious and close to tears. The former was fine, the latter only added to her anger. She was done with crying. It made her feel small and alone and accomplished nothing.

"Barbara, why are we fighting?"

"Because you're unreasonable." She glanced around and saw

that Catherine had slipped out of the room. "Stop telling me everything is going to work out. You don't know that it is."

"You don't know that it's not. Why do you have to look for the dark cloud?"

"Because it's raining trouble every single day."

They glared at each other. Barbara couldn't remember ever fighting with Giorgio before—not like this. He'd always been supportive and understanding, but lately, it felt like all he'd done was criticize her.

"Maybe we should change the subject," he said quietly. "Talk about something more pleasant."

She had a lot of energy and would have been fine yelling for another hour, but saw the sense in his suggestion. Although on second thought, she hoped he wasn't going to suggest they go upstairs. Right now sex was the last thing on her mind.

"We have to make our travel plans for Rosemary's birthday. I suspect you have no interest in going to Bermuda right now."

"That's perceptive," she said sarcastically, then wished she hadn't.

Giorgio leaned back in his seat and studied her. She felt herself flush and wanted to apologize, only she couldn't seem to get the words past the tightness in her throat.

He glanced away. "As I was saying, we're not going to Bermuda, so let's firm up our dates for New York."

"I'm not going."

"It's her fortieth birthday. She's having a big party with all her friends and family. You need to be there."

"She's not a child. She's a grown-up. She'll understand. It's just a birthday."

He tilted his head. "This isn't about her, Barbara. It's about us. This trip is important to me and I want you to go with me. Whatever is happening with the winery will still be happening when we return. It's one week. I don't think my request is unreasonable."

"It is to me. I don't want to go. Not now. My business needs me."

She wished she had another drink. She wished he would stop looking at her with a combination of surprise and disappointment that made her feel so small.

"Not everything in this relationship is about you," he said quietly.

"That's not fair. I'm in a crisis here. Why can't you understand that? I'm not making this about me, you're making it about you."

"Is that what you really think?"

"Of course. It's what's happening."

"I see." He rose. "Then there doesn't seem to be anything else to say."

She stood. "So you're going to leave? Just like that? No more discussion, no talking about it? Just throw your cape over your shoulder and walk out?"

His dark gaze was steady. "Is there anything I can say to change your mind about New York?"

"No."

"Then staying has no purpose. With Bel Après in crisis, you must be needed back at the office. Don't let me get in the way."

He walked out of the room. Seconds later, she heard the front door close. She collapsed back onto the sofa and covered her face with her hands. She'd gotten what she wanted from him, but somehow it didn't feel like a win at all. In fact, her stomach was churning as if she was going to be sick, and she honestly couldn't say why.

twenty-eight

Saturday afternoon Mackenzie let Stephanie into her bedroom. "Don't judge," she said, pausing in the hallway. "I did the best I could."

Stephanie laughed, then pushed past her. "It's shopping, not repairing the economy of a third-world nation. It's not supposed to be hard."

"And yet it is. But I have to do something." Mackenzie held up the front of her T-shirt to show that she'd been unable to zip her jeans. She had been forced to loop string through the buttonhole and then tie it to the button.

"Oh, honey, that's just sad."

"I know. I might not feel connected to my baby, but I'm getting bigger by the day."

Stephanie walked into the bedroom. "We'll deal with your emotional fragility later. Right now, clothes. What have you got?"

"Nothing that fits. It's all too big." She motioned to the open boxes she'd put on her bed.

As per Stephanie's advice, she'd ordered a bunch of stuff online, but none of it worked for her. She held up a T-shirt she'd tried on.

"It's huge. The shoulders fit, but I'm swimming in this. Why can't I find maternity clothes that fit? And don't get me started on pants. Mine don't fit but the ones I've bought online are too big."

Stephanie grinned. "You know that the baby is about the size of a lima bean, right? And in five months, it's going to be the size of a baby. You'll grow into the shirt."

Mackenzie didn't look convinced. "I can't picture that happening."

"You don't have to. It's going to happen all on its own."

Stephanie crossed over to the bed and pulled out a pair of jeans and a pair of leggings.

"The jeans will be less baggy right now because of how they're made and the fact that their tummy panel isn't as big as the ones on the leggings. You'll wear the leggings as the baby grows. Get four pairs of each, along with a couple of pairs of dressier pants for when you have a business event."

"How will I know if they're going to fit?"

"If they're your usual size and the legs fit, then just go with it. The same with the shirts. They should fit through the shoulders and arms. You wear T-shirts and sweatshirts for work. Buy those, along with a couple of nice blouses for when you have to dress up. That will get you started. In a couple of months, you and I will drive into Tri-Cities to do some more shopping."

"I'm not sure I can do this," Mackenzie said, staring at the clothes on the bed. "And I'm not sure about the whole baby thing."

Stephanie grinned. "Gee, I wonder why. Look at all you've been through. Having a baby has to be the last thing on your mind."

She crossed to the bed and quickly sorted through the clothes Mackenzie had ordered. She pulled out all the long-sleeved T-shirts, the sweatshirts and two sweaters and put them in a pile, then held up two blouses.

"These are hideous prints. What were you thinking?"

"I was feeling desperate and they were on sale."

"They go back. Find something you at least sort of like." She pointed to the pile. "Try those on, and if the shoulders and sleeves fit, keep them."

She crossed to the closet. It didn't take long to pull out every top that was fitted.

"These go into storage, making room for the maternity stuff." She pointed at the clear bins she'd brought with her. "You'll have to go through your bras and panties, as well. For a while you can make do with bikini underwear but eventually we all give in to the granny panties. Don't worry. We'll buy those when we go shopping. Are you still fitting in your bras?"

Mackenzie nodded. "I have a bunch of stretchy sports bras that will fit for a long time." She glanced at her chest. "I hate my boobs getting bigger. It's weird."

"It is so going to get worse."

Mackenzie sighed. "I couldn't get through this without you. I mean that. I'm totally lost, which isn't like me at all."

"I'm here for you and so is Four. Now let's go downstairs and have some of the muffins I brought over."

"I love your muffins. We're lucky it's Saturday and Bruno isn't here, otherwise he would have eaten them all. Four brought by cookies the other day and it turns out the man has a thing for homemade baked goods."

They went downstairs. Mackenzie knew she would have to deal with the clothes later, but for now she was grateful to hang out with her friend.

She poured them each a cup of coffee.

"Decaf," she said. "I don't have any real coffee here. Sorry."

"Decaf is fine." Stephanie pushed the plate of blueberry muffins across the table. "You have to save me from these. I already ate two this morning. Bruno isn't the only one with a fondness for homemade baked goods. The difference is he's a guy so it's harder for him to gain weight."

"He's a fairly healthy eater. He's always insisting we have salads for lunch. I want to say that's all about the baby, but I think some of it is him."

Stephanie raised her eyebrows. "You're having lunch together. Do tell."

"It's nothing." Mackenzie waved away the comment. "We're sharing very close quarters while the offices are being remodeled, so we eat lunch together."

"I'm not convinced. He's a good-looking guy, you're newly single. Are you saying there's not sparkage?"

"I've never heard you say sparkage before. I'm a little afraid."

"One of us should have a love life."

"Not me." Mackenzie thought about seeing Rhys having lunch with that woman. He'd been so quick to move on, but she wasn't the least bit ready. "It's too soon."

"Are you missing my brother?"

"Not exactly. I miss the us we could have been."

"Were you ever that us?"

She wanted to say of course they had been, but if she was honest, she knew the truth. "No, not even on our best day."

"Do you want that?"

"Do you?"

Stephanie reached for a muffin. "Eventually. I'd like to have a normal adult relationship with a man who isn't my ex-husband."

"You could meet someone online."

"Or I couldn't." She tore off a piece of the muffin and ate it. "What about you? How long do you think you're going to wait to find someone?"

"I have no idea. As you mentioned earlier, there's a lot going on. The last thing I need is a guy."

"What about a baby?"

"So we're circling back to that?"

"We don't have to." Stephanie smiled. "It's okay not to feel bonded to your kid. Right now it's a medical condition, not a person. You're doing all the right things. You're eating right, you're taking your vitamins, spitting after you drink wine. You have time to get used to the idea of being a mom."

"I don't know how to do that," she admitted. "Be a mom. I never had one."

"Love them with all your heart and don't let them drown in the tub. Four and I will be here for you. You know that."

"I do. Even with all the drama, you've been here. You're a good friend."

"If we ignore my initial screwup."

Mackenzie smiled. "I have no recollection of that event. So enough about me and my issues. What's new with you?"

Stephanie smiled brightly. "I'm moving forward with the job search. I have a few leads."

"What happened with Elias? You said he was going to get back to you."

Stephanie got up and poured more coffee. "He gave the job to someone else."

"Oh, no. You didn't tell me. I'm sorry."

"It's okay." Stephanie returned to the table. "I didn't do very well with the interview. But I did learn a lot. It turns out I wasn't a great employee at my last job."

"How can you say that? You were great. Retail sales were up every single year. Plus you had excellent ideas for expanding the retail base. And the café was brilliant. Barbara refused to see it, but it added a whole new element to what Bel Après offered. It was a chance to be a destination."

She held her hands palm up. "I hope you take this in the spirit I mean it, but I've been stealing your best ideas when I talk to Bruno about what we're going to do at Painted Moon. He's perfectly comfortable with our lack of income, but I hyperventilate on a regular basis."

"You're sweet. Thank you for stealing my ideas. Maybe I'll get some more and share them with you."

"I'll take anything." Mackenzie hesitated. "Bruno's in charge of hiring people, but I'm happy to talk to him if you want."

"No." Stephanie's voice was firm. "No and no. I want to get my next job on my own. I'm already doing a lot of research and coming up with a plan. Let me work it my own way."

Mackenzie knew all about wanting to prove herself. "I won't say anything."

"Thank you. Now I have gossip." Stephanie's eyes lit up. "Mom's been day drinking and by day drinking I mean tequila. Four was over there a couple of weeks ago and she was drunk at three in the afternoon."

Mackenzie smiled because she knew that was what Stephanie expected her to do, but there was no joy inside her. Despite everything, she felt badly for what Barbara was going through. Dumb on her part, but there it was.

"Is there a new winemaker?"

"Not yet, but I understand there will be interviews soon."

"I hope whoever she hires is careful with the Syrah. They can be tricky to work with."

Stephanie leaned toward her. "Mackenzie, not your rock."

"I know, but—"

"No buts. You have to let it go. You have Painted Moon now. Worry about those Syrah grapes."

"I do. It's just hard to let go."

Stephanie picked up her coffee. "Tell me about it."

The remodel of the Painted Moon workspace finished exactly on time—something Mackenzie had never experienced before. She supposed overseeing the construction was just another of Bruno's many talents. It took only a couple of trips to move her things into her new office. While the space was much nicer than what she'd had at Bel Après, it was nothing like the original plans.

Bruno had wanted to give her double the square footage, with a fancy attached bathroom. She'd explained she did most of her work much closer to grapes and wine, and that she didn't need anything other than a desk and a few files. He'd given her more than that, including lovely built-in bookcases and a small sofa against the far wall.

By nine thirty, she was settled, her computer hooked up to the new Wi-Fi. She had a fancy new phone with way too many buttons. Her cell she could handle, but a landline with two rows of buttons made her nervous. She was staring at it when Bruno appeared in her open doorway.

"Is someone going to explain all this to me?" she asked, waving to the phone.

"There's a hold button, a speaker button and one that has my name on it."

"What about the rest of them?"

"They're for when we start growing. I'm interviewing office managers in the morning. Any requests?"

"Don't make me participate."

He grinned as he walked into her office and settled on the sofa. "I promise. I'm taking care of all the office staffing. The bookkeeper is staying, as are both warehouse guys. The vineyard manager wants to retire."

"He told me yesterday. He's in his seventies and looks like he's a hundred and five, so he's earned it."

"He'll be hard to replace."

"I know."

"Know anyone who might be interested?"

"You mean poach from another winery?" she asked, trying not to sound scandalized.

The smile returned. He had a great smile, one that almost made her forget her train of thought. He wore a long-sleeved shirt tucked into dark jeans, and loafers. A little fancy, but still, he was an attractive package. She, on the other hand, had on the stretchiest yoga pants Target sold, and an oversize blouse she hated but that covered her stomach. Mackenzie didn't usually care about clothes, but dressed as she was, she felt frumpy.

"We make them a better offer," he told her, reminding her of their conversation. "It's just business. Let me put together a list of potential replacements."

"Is one of them going to be Rhys?"

His eyebrows rose. "Do you want it to be?"

"No." She hesitated. "He's very good at his job. Am I wrong to say I don't want to work with him?"

"No. You're handling the divorce better than most, but why make things awkward when they don't have to be?"

"Thank you."

"You're welcome. We need to figure out what to do with the bottled wine. I have some feelers out with distributors in the restaurant business. We put on a house label and, voilà, it's special."

"That would work." They had a lot of inventory and she would feel better knowing cash was coming in.

"We'll do the same with the barrels," he added. "Once you know what you want to do with all that, we can start making plans. We can sell some under the Painted Moon label here domestically, bottle some for house wines for restaurants and see if there's a market for the rest of it elsewhere."

While her first instinct was to dump the barrels and start over, that wasn't feasible—at least not financially. He was right—she had to let go of her quest for perfection. These weren't her wines and keeping the business making money was important.

"I'll be done tasting in the next couple of weeks," she told him. "I'm sticking to a schedule and it's slow going. I'm being careful like the doctor said to be."

"I wish I could do the tasting for you."

She smiled. "No offense, but I don't trust your palate."

"None taken, and you're right not to. Are you feeling all right?"

She nodded. "I've been really lucky to not have morning sickness. I feel fine. There are the physical changes, of course, but you don't want to know about them." She grinned. "Let's just say my jeans aren't fitting anymore and leave it at that."

"I appreciate the lack of detail."

She laughed. "I'm reading the pregnancy book Stephanie gave me, along with a couple of others my doctor recommended. They're kind of scary. Apparently having a baby is a whole thing."

"Are you overwhelmed?"

"Not if I don't think about it too much."

"I'm here if you need me. I can go with you to the doctor or get you pickles." He cleared his throat. "And when I say go with you to the doctor, I mean I'd wait outside. I think the exam part would be awkward for both of us."

She laughed. "It would be. Regardless, I appreciate the offer. I don't have any pickle cravings, but if that changes, I'll let you know."

"I'm looking forward to the baby. I like kids."

"If I bring him or her to the office, you're going to get to know this one really well."

"I think that's a plus."

He would be good with a child. He was patient and he understood people. There was something solid about him, but not in a boring way.

Her gaze drifted to his mouth and she had the craziest thought that she would like to know how he kissed. Did he just go for it or was he looking for a shared experience? He was powerful and used to getting his way and—

"I'm going to head back to my office," he said, coming to his feet. "I have calls to make and I know you'll want to spend some quality time getting to know your phone."

His statement drew her back to real life. Yikes, where had that weird kissing thought come from? Kiss Bruno? They were business partners. Sure, she liked him, but she liked lots of people and she never thought about kissing them.

Pregnancy hormones, she told herself as he left. Her body was becoming an alien being. She was going to have to ignore the weirdness and wait for things to return to normal in a few months. Kissing Bruno. As if!

Barbara waited for the ibuprofen to take effect. She'd awakened with a headache nearly every morning for the past week. She was tired of starting her day with painful throbbing in her head.

There were multiple causes—her nightly half bottle of tequila for starters, the stress of everything going on. She hadn't seen Giorgio since their fight about his daughter's stupid birthday party and Lori was keeping late hours, sometimes not coming home at all, no doubt staying with her loser boyfriend. Well, let her, Barbara thought, collecting her handbag and briefcase before stepping out into the morning.

She paused to take in the deep blue sky and the perfect fall temperature. Harvest was done, the wines were being transferred into barrels and the hard work for the year was finished. Or it would have been if Mackenzie hadn't left, ruining them all.

She drove over to work in her golf cart. After climbing the stairs, her head pounding in time with her footfalls, she made her way to her office. She clicked on lights and walked toward her desk, fighting a sense of dread and helplessness.

How would Bel Après survive? This was a critical time and they had no winemaker. Worse, no one would come to them now—at least no one decent. So what were they going to do?

There was no good answer, she thought grimly. She checked her email before heading into the break room. By now one of the staff would have started the coffee. The caffeine would make her feel better, she told herself. Once her head stopped hurting, she could think.

But when she returned, mug in hand, she found Rhys pacing in front of her desk.

"Oh dear God, either sit down or get out," she snapped. "This morning I have no patience for you or your moods."

He waited until she was seated, then slapped both hands on her desk and loomed over her. His eyes flashed with anger.

"How dare you?" he growled.

"You forget I've been dealing with your tantrums since you were two. You can't intimidate me. Sit down or get out."

Their gazes locked. She saw indecision in his, and the second before he settled in the chair, she knew that she had already won.

"You talked to a lawyer about suing Mackenzie for custody of the baby."

Catherine, Barbara thought, not even surprised that her youngest had been talking behind her back. There was no loyalty there.

"You won't do it, so one of us has to."

"I don't want custody. I'm still trying to figure out my obligations and I sure as hell don't need you getting in the way of that. Don't mess things up like you always do. For once, just act like a normal person."

"I'm the most normal of anyone in this family," she told him pointedly. "You're less than useless on this matter. If you'd just challenge her for the baby, I could stay out of it."

"That's not going to happen."

Because he didn't care, she thought grimly, surprised to feel a flicker of compassion on Mackenzie's behalf. James had been thrilled with each of her pregnancies. He'd been a wonderful, doting husband and a good father.

"Getting out of your marriage at any price?" she asked, her tone bitter. "You're going to let her get away with anything so long as you get your freedom?"

"If necessary, yes."

"How you disappoint me."

"The feeling is mutual, Mom."

They were at an impasse.

"I wish she wasn't pregnant," she said with a sigh.

"Me, too, but we are where we are. I'm tired of fighting."

"So you'll do whatever it takes to get along with me, as well?" she asked tartly.

"As long as it doesn't involve custody of the baby, yes."

How disheartening to realize he wasn't going to push back. He wasn't going to take the high ground and quit the way his sister had.

She and Stephanie had never gotten along very well, but Barbara had to admit at least her oldest daughter had principles and a spine. She was willing to walk away to prove her point, while Rhys was not.

She supposed his life was too comfortable. He had a lovely house, food delivered to his refrigerator, and even after paying off Mackenzie, he'd have plenty of money. No doubt he was very popular with all the single women in town. He was going to turn into a dilettante and throw away any opportunity for greatness. Why had she never seen it before?

Because of Mackenzie, she thought. He'd been swept along by her passion and work ethic. Mackenzie had been the driving force, loving her work and Bel Après with every fiber of her being. She'd brought a sense of purpose to them all and now she was gone.

Barbara's eyes burned and she knew the sensation had nothing to do with her hangover. Disillusionment, bitter and tinged with regret, flavored her tongue. She allowed herself a few seconds of emotional indulgence, then shook off the feelings.

"Are the barrels ready for the wine?" she asked, sitting straighter in her chair and picking up her mug of coffee. "Did you order enough?"

"I did. Everything is in place." He paused. "She would come back and help us for a few days. It would make things easier."

Barbara glared at him. "I'm not interested in easy, Rhys. I would have thought you would know that by now. Get it done and get it done right. What's happening with the winemakers in California?"

"I have interviews lined up with a couple. If I think they're all right, I'll send them along to you."

"Have you ever interviewed anyone for a job before?" she asked.

"Plenty of times." But he looked uncomfortable as he spoke.

"You might want to do a little research online. Otherwise you're likely to make a fool out of yourself."

He stood up. "Anything else?" he asked, his voice tight.

"No. Keep me informed about the interviews."

He nodded and walked out. She leaned back in her chair and wondered why he couldn't have been the one to leave instead of Mackenzie. Or any of her children, or all of them. Mackenzie was the only one worth anything. The rest of them were simply deadweight.

twenty-nine

Stephanie couldn't remember being this sick to her stomach since her pregnancies. Unlike Mackenzie, she'd spent most of the first three months unable to keep down anything but crackers. She could say for certain that her current state of nausea had nothing to do with hormones and everything to do with nerves. She was scared. No. Terrified.

Kyle's unexpected proposal and her realization that she was willing to take the easy way out had been what she'd needed to get off her butt and find the job of her dreams. Ignoring the top five producers in the area, she'd focused on the middle twenty or so who would appreciate her experience and skills. From there she'd done her best to figure out who might want to hire her and, of all of them, there was only one who was for sure looking for staff. Painted Moon.

Which presented a dilemma, she thought as she sipped coffee at the kitchen island. She wanted to be hired because of what she brought to the job and not because she was best friends with one of the two owners. To that end, she hadn't said anything to

Mackenzie, and when she'd phoned Bruno to set up the meeting, she'd asked him not to say anything, either.

"Oh, the lies we tell," she murmured to herself as she reviewed her notes for the thousandth time.

Carson ambled into the kitchen, pulling a Seahawks sweatshirt over a long-sleeved T-shirt. His cast was gone and he was back playing sports, as if his arm had never been broken.

"Hey, Mom."

He walked over and gave her a brief hug, followed by a kiss on the top of her head.

"Hey, I know you're a lot taller than me," she said in mock outrage. "Stop rubbing it in."

He flashed her a grin as he opened the refrigerator and pulled out the breakfast burrito she'd defrosted for him. She made them in batches and froze them individually so the kids could have them for breakfast.

After popping it in the microwave, he poured himself a glass of milk.

"You ready for your interview?" he asked.

"I hope so. I may have studied too much."

"You can never be too prepared. You ran the drills, Mom. You're going to do great."

"Thanks."

The microwave beeped. Carson collected his breakfast, then sat at the island where she'd put fresh fruit. He'd just started eating when Avery sailed into the kitchen.

"My hair wouldn't cooperate," she said, dumping her backpack on the floor, then crossing to Stephanie and hugging her. "Why does it have days like that?"

"It just does, sweetie."

"My hair always cooperates," Carson said.

Avery pulled out protein powder and almond milk. "Your hair is an inch long. You don't know if it cooperates or not."

"You should try it."

Avery drew in a breath. "Carson, you're not normal."

"I'm more normal than you."

The bantering had always been a part of their morning routine. Stephanie knew she was lucky when it came to her kids. She and Avery had gone through a rough patch in the summer, but now they were friends again. She was going to focus on the good in her life and let the rest of it take care of itself. As for her interview—she would do her best. This time she was prepared. If things didn't go well, she would come up with another plan, because no matter what, she wasn't taking the easy way out.

Stephanie had known Bruno Provencio for several years and always thought of him as impressive, but she'd never actually trembled in his presence before. Of course he'd never had any power over her life before, and that certainly made a difference.

"The remodel came out great," she said as she sat across from him in his large office. "There's lots of functional space."

"Mackenzie's office is smaller than the original plan," he said with a chuckle. "She refused the extra square footage and the private bathroom."

"She's not one for frills."

"I agree. She's not here right now. She's having lunch with your sister, I believe. Your doing?"

Stephanie nodded. She'd confided in Four, asking that she arrange lunch at the same time Stephanie had her interview.

"I didn't want her to know. She's a full partner in the business and her opinion would influence yours."

His gaze was unreadable. "Good to know. Tell me what you want to talk about."

Her stomach sank, her heart rate increased and her mouth went dry. At least she didn't feel like she was going to pass out. Fainting would not make her look capable.

"You're in a unique position. Painted Moon is well established and yet you're starting over. From my perspective, you need to remodel the tasting room, design and stock a retail space, re-vamp your digital presence, start a wine club, entice tourists, and sell your library wines."

"That's a big list."

"It is, so there need to be priorities. The digital aspect is out of my area of expertise." She smiled. "So that's on you."

One corner of his mouth lifted. "Passing the buck so soon?"

"Absolutely. As for the rest of it, the tasting room needs to be open by early spring for tourist season. The retail space falls in line with that. The other priority should be the library wines. From what I've calculated, you have over a million dollars' worth of wine tied up in that. Let's get it out there."

"You want to start a wine club?"

"Not yet. That should be a year-two endeavor. Right now you don't have wines to sell. The library wines are a separate project."

"How would we sell them without a wine club?"

And here it was, she thought, opening the folder she'd set on the conference table in his office.

"By letting the wines tell a story. Mackenzie had no part in them, so we can't use her. By the way, I have ideas on how to make her the star when it comes to the wines you're going to start producing. But for the library wines, I thought the focus should be on Herman and his family."

She opened the folder to show him the first of the labels she'd designed. "The oldest bottles are twelve years old."

"How do you know that?"

She felt herself relax. "You have very poor security. The last time I visited Mackenzie, I went into the production area and walked into the cellar. No one stopped me or asked me why I was there. I took a quick inventory."

"Interesting." He made a note on a pad. "Go on."

She explained how the new labels would feature pictures of

the winery dating back to when it had been a farm and how it had changed. Four had drawn the pictures in her whimsical style.

She flipped to another page. "See how we can do a boxed collection, featuring three years and five years? The presentation would be lovely and it's something we could offer in the retail space next year."

"How would we get customers?"

"Painted Moon used to have a wine club. You would have all those names and addresses. We do a mailing, talking about what's happened at the winery and what they can expect in the future. Herman said the list was nearly ten thousand people."

"Let me guess," Bruno said dryly. "You called him and asked."

"I did. He's so sweet. I've known him forever."

"Apparently."

She smiled. "Small-town living, Bruno. You need to get used to that."

"So Mackenzie tells me."

"Now, about the tasting room," she said, setting a second folder in front of him. "There are two stars of this particular show. The wines and the bar. Rumor has it, the bar started in a San Francisco brothel during the gold rush. Whether or not that's true doesn't matter—it's a great story and one that should be played up in all the materials."

She opened the folder to a picture of the bar.

"Let me guess," he said, looking from the picture to her. "You wandered around the old tasting room, as well."

"Of course I did."

An hour later, she'd gone through all her material. The last folder she handed him was about sales to China.

"Not my area of expertise," she admitted. "So these are just random thoughts. It's a huge market. There are already wine tours for Chinese tourists in California and Oregon. Why not do that here? There are plenty of wineries to tour, and if Painted Moon initiates the idea, you can be one of the star attractions."

"I've been thinking the same thing myself," he said, taking the folder. "You've done your research."

"I think you're in a unique position to grow over the next few years. I know how Mackenzie works, so having great wines is a given. I have retail experience from my time at Bel Après and I've learned a lot about the business simply by osmosis. I'd like to put those skills to use here."

He looked at her, his expression just as unreadable as it had been for the entire interview. But instead of being scared by that, she felt good. She'd worked hard and it showed. She'd studied Painted Moon and she'd had suggestions that were specific to them. Something she should have done the first time around, but at least she'd learned from her mistakes.

"I do the hiring here," he said, "but not without running the senior positions by Mackenzie."

Senior positions? Her heart fluttered in a very happy way. "Of course."

"Give me a few days to take all this in and I'll get back to you."

"Thank you."

She rose and they shook hands. Stephanie managed to get all the way to her car before pride made her pump her fist in the air. She'd done it. She'd worked hard and she'd had a great interview. That wasn't a guarantee of a job, but at least she knew she had it in herself. Whatever happened, she could tell herself she'd done everything right and that made today a very good day.

Mackenzie stood in the doorway to what would be the baby's room and stared at the furniture pushed together at one end. At some point, she was going to have to figure out what she wanted to do in here. The walls needed painting and she needed a rug for the hardwood floors, along with curtains for the windows.

Based on the books she was reading, she was going to need a bunch of supplies before the baby was born. Diapers and stuff.

Clothes maybe. Sheets. She wasn't sure about toys. Newborns mostly ate and slept, so she could wait on those. It was a lot to think about, and realizing that made her uncomfortable, which was why she tried not to think about the postpregnancy part of her life. At some point she was going to have to ask Stephanie and Four to talk her through the baby-prep thing, just not today.

She glanced at her watch and knew she had to get moving. She'd come home to shower and change after a day of walking the vineyards. But they had a meeting with a Chinese wine distributor at three and professional dress was required.

She'd chosen the least baggy pair of black maternity pants she could find and a floaty, sleeveless top. In honor of the meeting, she'd put on a little makeup and had replaced her work boots with cute flats.

Knowing she couldn't distract herself any longer, she went downstairs, then drove the short distance to the offices. She saw an unfamiliar rental car parked in front and realized their potential clients had arrived early.

"What happened to just being punctual?" She hurried to the conference room.

Bruno was there, along with three men Mackenzie had never seen before. Bruno saw her first. She mouthed a quick "Sorry" before turning to their guests.

"Hello, everyone."

All three men looked at her. Mackenzie gave a broad smile as she approached.

"I was out in the vineyards. Now that we're finished with harvest, I'm thinking about what changes I want to make. I know I could do that from my office, but I find it easier to think about the vines when I'm out among them."

For a second, no one said anything. Mackenzie had just enough time to wonder if she'd somehow put her foot in her mouth when the three men rushed toward her.

The tallest of the visitors reached for her hand. "Mackenzie Dienes. An honor. Your reputation precedes you."

The other two also praised her abilities, speaking in amazing English.

Mackenzie shook hands with them all, trying to put names with faces and willing herself not to say anything stupid. Around her grapes, she was absolutely in charge. It was the whole doing a business deal with people that she found intimidating.

Bruno saved her by taking charge of the meeting.

"Gentlemen," he said, directing them to the table. "Let me show you what we've been working on."

He passed around different label options. The three men spoke in Chinese before Mr. Lin pointed to the simple dark blue label with a plain font reading Painted Moon Presents.

"Next time we'll have your name on the wine," he said, looking at Mackenzie. "That will bring us top dollar."

Mackenzie smiled rather than speak. She didn't want to inadvertently make a commitment.

Once the labels were chosen, they went into the barrel room. Earlier Mackenzie had set up a tasting with a few wines from the library and the equipment necessary to taste directly from the barrel. She had a pad of paper and a pen, so she could keep track of their thoughts on the various options.

Mackenzie had already tasted everything, careful to spit the samples once she'd determined what she thought about them. For this tasting, she would talk about the wines without drinking. She and Bruno had decided that spitting in front of prospective clients wasn't a selling strategy.

"There are three wines from the Painted Moon library that I think are special enough for you to consider," she began. "All three are blends, combining the very best of what the vineyard had to offer that year. The wines are smooth, ready to drink and, if you bought the entire inventory, would be exclusive to you."

Bruno handed her a bottle. Mackenzie expertly cut through

the foil, then pulled out the cork. After pouring the liquid into five glasses, Mackenzie passed them out. She held up her glass.

"Let's start with the color. This one is a beautiful deep purple color. It looks as luscious as it drinks." She swirled the wine in the glass. "You can see there's a high alcohol content."

She inhaled the scent of the wine and smiled. "Very fruit forward, which I believe is your preference. You can smell the freshness, the health of the grapes, plus a hint of spice and choc-olate that's unique to our area."

Everyone else sniffed their glasses. Their guests smiled, then looked at her.

"Now we taste?" Mr. Meng asked.

She laughed. "Now we taste."

"How did you get the restaurant to deliver?" Mackenzie asked Bruno as she pulled out to-go boxes on her dining room table.

"They just made the food. I had someone else bring it here."

Her stomach rumbled as the delicious smells tempted her. After a long afternoon of entertaining their Chinese visitors, she was starving.

She'd already set out a wineglass for him. She had her lovely carafe of water to chug. Yum. But rather than think about what she couldn't have, she looked at the bounty spread out in front of her. Mushroom ravioli with a brown butter sauce, two different salads, a pork tenderloin and summer squash pancakes with feta.

"I love Whitehouse-Crawford," she said. "Rhys and I went there maybe once a month for dinner. Good food, a fun atmo-sphere. We preferred it off-season, but even dining with the tourists was fun."

"I enjoy their food, as well."

She looked at Bruno. "Should I not mention Rhys when I talk about my old life?"

"Why? He's a part of who you are. You're still friends."

"We are," she said automatically, although she wasn't sure that was actually true. They hadn't spoken since she'd told him she was pregnant. Their only contact had been through her lawyer, setting up a meeting to discuss a proposed parenting plan.

"Are you happy with how the meeting went?" she asked.

Bruno smiled as he served her ravioli. "I ordered this for us for dinner, didn't I? It's a celebration meal."

"You ordered this before the meeting. Our visitors only left a half hour ago."

His dark eyes brightened with amusement. "You're right. I ordered the dinner a couple of days ago. I had a feeling we were going to have something to party about. And if the meeting had gone badly, we would have used the food to get over our disappointment."

Instead they would be toasting the very large order Mr. Hsia and his coworkers had placed. They'd taken the entire inventory of all three of the library wines Mackenzie had suggested, along with a thousand cases of wine still in the barrel.

"We're going to have to make some decisions about the Chinese market," Bruno said. "They'll want to buy for as long as we want to sell to them. How much of what we harvest do we want to commit to the overseas market?"

"I don't know how to answer that. I did research a few years ago, but when I tried to talk about China as a potential market, Barbara was never interested. I know there's a huge profit margin."

"We could expand capacity by buying grapes from other vineyards."

Mackenzie stared at him, hoping she didn't look as horrified as she felt. "Grapes over which I don't have any control?"

He smiled. "I thought that would be your answer. If we want to keep selling into the Chinese market, then we might have to buy more land."

"That I could get behind."

"Stephanie is going to be disappointed about our meeting today."

Mackenzie looked at him. "I'm so confused. Why would she care?"

"Because she had big plans for the library wines. They're taking the oldest three years of inventory, which still leaves her with three to work with." He picked up his wineglass. "She came to see me last week. About a job."

"What? Why didn't I know about this? She never said a word. What happened? Are you hiring her?"

Emotions piled on top of one another. How could her best friend not have said anything to her about the job interview? Yet even as she asked the question, she knew the answer. Stephanie wanted to earn her place.

"She blew me away," Bruno admitted. "She understood the problems we're facing and had a lot of solutions. She has great ideas for the tasting room and retail space. She also came up with a unique plan to sell the library wines. A plan that will have to be modified now that we've sold three years of them out from under her."

"Does that mean you want to hire her?"

He smiled. "I do, if you have no objection."

"None at all. I like working with her. She's local, she knows the business and she's very creative."

"Then I'll call her in the morning and make her an offer."

"This day is getting better and better."

She ate a few of the ravioli and tried not to moan at the delicious flavor. The pork was just as good.

"There's going to be a ton of leftovers," she said. "You should take it home."

"You keep it. I want you to have food in the house."

"I have plenty."

"Still, it would make me feel better. I worry about you getting enough to eat."

Which was sweet, but unnecessary. "I'm pregnant, not infirm."

"I believe the phrase is 'in a delicate condition.'"

"Not in this century."

"When I care about someone, I worry. It's a thing. Deal with it."

His tone was so casual, she knew she would be foolish to read anything into his words, but she couldn't help wondering about the "when I care about someone" part. What did that mean? *Get a grip!* She sent the instruction to her brain. She was not going to get weird about her relationship with Bruno. He was the best thing to ever happen to her and he was a genuinely nice man. Nothing more. Although she had to admit, she kind of liked the idea of Bruno caring about her.

"How are you settling into condo life?" she asked.

"It's fine. The neighbors are quiet. When the business is running more smoothly, I'm going to take up golf again."

"You play golf?"

"Yes. I like it."

"Why? The sport has never made sense to me."

He laughed. "What about a Sunday afternoon watching football?"

"Oh, I like that."

"Football makes sense but golf doesn't?"

"Of course. I like team sports. There's lots of action. Plus the food is great."

"Football has food?" His voice was teasing.

"Of course. People eat all kinds of things watching football that they would never eat in real life."

"They also drink beer."

"I'm okay with that. Not every event has to be wine-centric."

He laughed. "You continue to surprise me."

"Only good surprises, though, right?"

"Only good ones. How are you feeling about the baby these days?"

The change in subject surprised her. "I'm slightly more accepting. Just before our meeting today, I was thinking I need to paint the baby's room."

"You're not painting it yourself. I'll do it."

Her eyes widened as she took in his elegant suit. "You know how to paint?"

"Yes. You can't breathe in the fumes." He pulled out his phone and typed something. "Once you pick out the color, I'll prime and paint the room while you're at the office. We'll keep the door closed until the space airs out."

"That's kind of bossy of you."

He raised his eyebrows. "I believe what you meant to say was thank you."

She smiled. "Thank you."

"Have you thought about colors? And themes for decorations?"

"You're not supposed to know all that."

"I've been reading and looking online. You should find out the sex of the baby in the next few weeks. Unless you don't want to know."

"I want them to tell me. I think knowing will help me feel that the baby is real." She shook her head. "I know it's real, but it's still, I don't know, complicated."

"You have time to figure it out."

She nodded because saying she would never be ready sounded weak and sad.

Their conversation returned to the wine business.

"There's a rumor that Bel Après is bringing in a couple of guys from Northern California for your position," he said.

Mackenzie flinched. "Really? They couldn't get anyone local? Although maybe that's a better idea. Fresh eyes and all that." Not that she wanted to picture anyone dealing with her grapes. What if they did it wrong?

"What are you thinking?" Bruno asked.

"That letting go is hard."

"Regrets?"

She looked at him. "None. This is an amazing opportunity and I'm grateful to be a part of what we're building."

"Me, too."

About nine thirty, she walked him to the door. He insisted she keep the leftovers.

"Have them for breakfast," he told her. "I know you're hating your protein drink."

"It's disgusting. I can't believe people drink those on purpose."

Bruno stared into her eyes. "Still missing Rhys?"

"What? No." She shook her head. "There's nothing to miss. I'm even letting go of the lifestyle, although I will admit the meal service was fantastic. There's nothing like coming home and finding a home-cooked meal in the refrigerator."

"We could make that happen here."

She laughed. "I keep forgetting how you love to solve a problem. And while I appreciate the offer, no thank you. I'm going to take care of my meals the way regular people do. With a little planning and a pressure cooker."

"If you're sure."

"I am."

He gave her a brief hug. "Then I'll see you tomorrow."

She smiled at him. "Yes, you will."

thirty

Stephanie listened intently as Bruno detailed the offer. She made notes, asked questions and was fairly sure she'd said all the right things, including a very calm, "I would be delighted to accept your offer." But when she hung up the phone, she spun in her kitchen and let out a little scream.

She had a job! A really good one that paid well, offered benefits. She came to a stop and waited for the room to settle back in place before glancing at her notes to make sure she was remembering correctly.

She would be in charge of the retail space and the tasting room. Bruno was going to be hiring someone to handle digital content and the PR aspect of the business but hoped she would be available to consult on those topics, as well. Oh, and she would be managing the people who worked for her!

She spun again, laughing out loud, and she held her arms wide. She'd done it! She'd—

She came to a stop and opened her eyes. "I have to call Mackenzie." Because she wasn't sure what her friend knew or even if she was upset about not being told what was happening.

She reached for her phone, but before she could dial, she heard a knock at the front door, then a familiar voice calling, "It's me."

Stephanie ran to the front of the house and met Mackenzie in the hallway. They stared at each other for a second before rushing into a big hug with them both jumping up and down.

"I have a new job!" Stephanie shouted.

"I know. I drove over when Bruno called, and I was waiting for him to say you'd accepted." Mackenzie grinned. "We're going to be working together. I'm so excited. This makes me so happy."

"You're not mad that I didn't tell you I'd applied?"

"No. Of course not. I know why you wanted to do this on your own. Bruno didn't say anything, by the way. Not until he'd decided to hire you."

They walked back to the kitchen. Mackenzie took her usual place at the island while Stephanie heated water for tea. While the bags were steeping, she drew in a breath and confessed the truth.

"I didn't tell you everything about my interview with Elias," she said, looking at Mackenzie. "I was too embarrassed to want to talk about it."

Her friend leaned toward her. "What does that even mean? What else is there to share?"

Stephanie busied herself putting the used tea bag on a small plate and then stared at her mug. "He wasn't impressed with my work," she began before explaining how she hadn't noticed the duplicate flyers and that her own mother had been saying she was basically a pity hire.

Mackenzie listened until she'd finished, then reached for Stephanie's hand. "None of that is true. He's wrong about you."

"I wish I could agree with you, but I can't. I didn't do the job I should have. I was mad at my mom for dismissing my ideas, and the last couple of years, I wasn't even trying. That's on me. I didn't even do a good job of researching the winery."

"Okay, sure, you had one stumble, but Bruno was very impressed with you and how you handled yourself. He loved your ideas."

"I'm glad. I worked really hard to be dazzling."

"It worked." Mackenzie smiled at her. "I love you. There's nothing you can say or do to make that change. Now what else don't I know?"

Stephanie felt herself warm with gratitude. "You're a better friend than I deserve, but I'm going to accept the gift of your love. As for other secrets, sorry, but I don't have any. You already know that I quit my job and that my ex-husband proposed and currently isn't talking to me. Mom's still a bitch, so hey, no news there. It's been nearly two years since I've had sex." She paused, as if considering, then laughed. "Those are the highlights."

"They're good ones. Have you heard from Kyle?"

"No. He's in touch with the kids, but he's avoiding me."

"Probably because you broke his heart."

"I'm less sure about that," Stephanie admitted. "We've been getting along better than ever lately, and while that's nice, it's not love." She held up a hand. "That's not to say I wasn't tempted, because I was. Getting back together with Kyle would have solved all my problems."

"Not if you don't love him."

"There is that." She picked up her mug. "You ever think about dating?"

"No." Mackenzie grimaced. "I was never very good at it when I was a teenager. I can't imagine meeting someone now and trying to make it work."

Stephanie understood the reluctance to make the effort, but if they didn't, they weren't ever going to find anyone.

"Do you want to be alone for the rest of your life?" she asked.

Mackenzie shrugged. "I don't know. Not really. I liked parts of being married. I just wasn't very good at it."

"Some of that is on Rhys."

"Yes, but a lot of it is on me." She bit her lower lip. "We didn't have much of a sex life. Or one at all." Color stained her cheeks. "I knew we'd grown apart, but I never much thought about the sex thing. Rhys did, though. He's mentioned it more than once, so I know I let him down."

"You didn't miss that part of things?" Stephanie asked, careful not to let on what her brother had told her.

"At first." She paused. "Okay, this is definitely TMI, but it wasn't ever that good. I never felt like your mother looked after a night with Giorgio."

"Ugh. You didn't just talk about sex with my brother and my mother doing it with Giorgio in the same sentence. No. Don't. It's too much."

Mackenzie grinned. "Sorry. I take it back."

"Too late." She paused. "I'm sorry things weren't great with Rhys."

"Me, too. Because I was a virgin when we met, so I have no way of knowing if it was because of me or because of him."

"Technically there *is* a way to find out."

Mackenzie looked at her. "I'm four and a half months pregnant. I'm not going to have sex with some guy just to figure out who was at fault."

"Fine. Wait until the baby's born."

"I'm going to have other things on my mind."

"Possibly. I, on the other hand, am going to start dating."

Mackenzie's eyes widened. "You are?"

"Yes. I'm giving myself six months to get settled into my new job and then I'm putting myself out there."

"I'm impressed."

"Let's wait on that to make sure I follow through."

Mackenzie smiled at her. "You will. Look at how far you've come."

Stephanie raised her mug of tea. "How far we've both come."

Barbara knew the man sitting in front of her was a third-rate winemaker at best. His resume was unimpressive, his appearance was run-down, and after tasting his wines, she wasn't the least bit excited about hiring him. Still, he was the best of the three she'd interviewed, and with fermentation finished and the wines about to go into the barrels, she was out of options. Beggars and all that, she thought, trying not to let herself fall into hopelessness.

The anger that had sustained her since Mackenzie's defection had faded—no doubt overcome by the enormity of trying to carry on without her former daughter-in-law.

"When can you start?" Barbara asked.

"I can stay until the wine's in the barrels, then head back to California for a week to get things settled."

This was not what she wanted for Bel Après, she reminded herself. She and the winery both deserved better. But there was no "better" to be had and it was this man or someone worse.

"Excellent," she said, holding out her hand. "Once you've moved here permanently, the first task we need to take on is getting an assistant winemaker in place."

"I agree. It's something you should have done years ago."

Barbara glared at him, fighting all the sarcastic responses that came to mind. Knowing they wouldn't help and might, in fact, scare him away, she forced out a tight smile and only said, "So let's fix that, shall we?"

When he was gone, she closed her eyes against the horror of it all. She turned her chair away from her desk and told herself to breathe. That they had a winemaker now and that was one problem solved. But when she opened her eyes, she found herself staring at a picture of her and Mackenzie, their arms around each other's waists, standing in the Red Mountain vineyard, laughing in the bright sunshine.

It had been a perfect day, she thought sadly. Everything had been as it should be. Unlike her life now.

"Damn you," she said quickly, then repeated the statement more loudly. When that didn't make her feel better, she took off one of her pumps and threw it at the picture. The heel hit the glass, shattering it. Shards fell onto the carpet. She saw a sharp gash over her own image.

But Mackenzie's half of the picture was untouched, and her smiling face seemed to turn mocking as Barbara looked away and let herself surrender to her tears.

Mackenzie tried to control her frustration. Taking time out of her own day was bad enough, but she'd also had to pay to have her attorney drive over from Seattle for a meeting with Rhys and *his* attorney. She had no idea why all this was required for what she had hoped would be a wrap-up meeting, finalizing the divorce settlement, child support agreement and parenting plan.

As per Rhys's recent request, she and Ramona had prepared a parenting plan for him to review. The amount of child support he had to pay was based on his salary, and she had no intention to ask for more, so there wasn't much to talk about there. Ramona had explained about the additional payments Mackenzie could request for things like private school or a college fund. Mackenzie had considered her options and had settled on asking him to set up a college fund such that he would put aside the equivalent of two years at WSU. She would do the same. If their kid wanted to go somewhere more expensive, she would figure that out herself.

Per Ramona's recommendation, there was also a clause about medical payments if their child be born with some kind of disability. Under those circumstances, Rhys would be expected to contribute more than the base amount. The rest of it—visitation and the like—had been pretty easy. She'd assumed Rhys would want every other weekend, alternating birthdays, Thanksgivings and Christmases. She'd offered him a month every summer, with a notation that deferring the month while the child was still young didn't take away his right to ask for it later.

Ramona had assured her that the parenting plan was fairly standard. There were mentions of who paid ordinary expenses. While the child support was meant to cover day-to-day costs, it was not unreasonable to ask Rhys to pay for an occasional haircut or new shoes.

As she pulled into Rhys's lawyer's parking lot, she told herself to breathe. That she would get through the meeting and then she and Rhys could be done with all this.

She met Ramona in the lobby of the small building. Her lawyer led the way to the receptionist, where she gave their names. They were immediately shown back to a large conference room with a table that easily seated thirty. Rhys and his lawyer were at one end. Ramona walked toward them and sat down, across from them. Mackenzie settled next to her.

As she greeted her soon-to-be ex-husband and his lawyer, she tried to remember the last time she'd seen Rhys. It had been several weeks ago, she thought, when she'd told him she was pregnant. Despite living in a small town, their paths rarely crossed.

She felt herself tense as she remembered she was wrong about the last time she'd seen him. It had been when she'd spotted him having lunch with a blonde woman.

Trying not to be obvious, she studied him. He was dressed in his usual jeans and a long-sleeved shirt. His hair was longer, and she thought maybe he'd lost weight. When his gaze met hers, he offered her a tight smile.

"How's it going?" he asked.

As she had no idea which "it" he meant—baby, winery, the divorce—she could only shrug and say, "Fine."

Mr. Norris, Rhys's attorney, slipped on his glasses. "Thank

you all for coming," he began. "We only have a few items left to wrap up to finalize the paperwork for the divorce. My client and I are hoping we can get through them all today."

My client? Mackenzie frowned at the odd phrasing. The formalness made her uncomfortable and gave her a bad feeling in the pit of her stomach.

Ramona pulled a stack of paperwork from her briefcase. "I have the copies of the settlement agreement you emailed me and I've looked them over. My client has agreed to the changes noted."

They'd all been minor and more procedural than anything else.

"Do you have your changes on the parenting plan?" Ramona asked.

Mr. Norris glanced at Rhys, who nodded. The older man passed over two sets of documents. Ramona took one and handed the other to Mackenzie.

"The modifications might be greater than what you were expecting," Mr. Norris said.

Mackenzie glanced at the pages in front of her. The first paragraph stated that Rhys claimed paternity of the unborn child and would not require a DNA test for the parenting plan to go into effect, although he did request one after birth, on behalf of a family member.

She looked at him. "You believe it's your baby?"

For the first time since she'd walked into the room, he seemed to relax. "I know it is. I was there when it happened, and I know you haven't been seeing anyone else. But it would make things easier with Mom if we could get confirmation."

"Sure. I'm happy to do that."

The tension she hadn't acknowledged eased a little bit. Everything was going to be fine. She'd been silly to worry about the meeting. It was what Mr. Norris had said—a chance to get everything finalized so the divorce could move forward. Rhys was the man he'd always been—she should trust him to do the right thing.

Mackenzie continued to read the document. Two paragraphs later, she realized that there weren't changes to the parenting plan so much as a complete rewrite of what she'd offered. She read the proposed visitation schedule twice before she could understand what it all meant.

He didn't want every other weekend, or holidays or summers. Rhys was proposing seeing his child one afternoon a month for the first year, two afternoons a month from ages one year to four years. From then until age eighteen, he would see his child two days a month.

She flipped to the second page, looking for some hint that he wanted more than a cursory relationship with his own kid, but she couldn't find one. Because it *wasn't* what he wanted.

She looked at him, trying to understand what was happening, but he wouldn't meet her gaze. He carefully stared down at the papers in front of him, his expression giving nothing away.

Disappointment joined shock. He'd meant what he'd said when she'd told him she was pregnant. He didn't want a baby in his life. He wanted to be free. He would do the very minimum required and nothing more.

"I thought you were better than this," she said into the quiet.

He flinched but still didn't look at her. Mr. Norris cleared his throat.

"We've increased the amount of child support, as you can see. It's a very generous amount."

She supposed it was but didn't bother looking at it. Instinctively, she put a hand on her belly, as if to protect her unborn child. By whatever circumstances, they had created this life together. It was a part of both of them and yet that didn't mean anything to him.

Oh, she didn't think he should have warm fuzzies about her, but his child should mean something to him, and it didn't.

That truth jolted her more than anything that had happened over the past six months. It made her wonder if she'd ever known him at all. She hadn't been foolish enough to think he would jump for joy at the thought of being a father, but she had thought he would suck it up and do what was right. And she'd been wrong.

Mackenzie squared her shoulders and turned to Ramona. "Once you look it over and make sure everything is legal, I'll sign it."

Her attorney raised her eyebrows. "You're willing to accept this parenting plan?"

"I am." She turned to Rhys. "I'm not going to force you to see your child when it's obvious you don't want to. I want to say I hope you'll have regrets about what you're doing later, but somehow I don't think that's going to happen."

If she'd expected shame or embarrassment, she didn't get it. Rhys looked at his attorney. "Has any of this gotten in the way of finalizing the divorce?"

The parenting plan proposal had been a blow to the heart, but that last statement was a kick in the gut.

Mr. Norris looked vaguely uncomfortable as he said, "I shouldn't think so. Ramona and I will go over the paperwork one last time. After that, all that's left is for you each to sign and then we file it with the court."

Mackenzie glanced at her attorney. "Anything else?"

"No. You can go."

Mackenzie nodded and rose. She walked out of the conference room and momentarily got turned around. She started to backtrack to find the reception area and the way out, only to come to a stop when she saw a familiar-looking blonde in one of the private offices. As Mackenzie passed, the woman looked up and her eyes widened with recognition and shock.

Mackenzie forced herself to keep moving, heading directly for the glass door she could see in front of her. She got into her Jeep and started the engine, then drove directly back to Painted Moon.

She managed to keep every thought, every emotion carefully locked away until she burst into Bruno's office. Her business partner took one look at her and came to his feet.

"What happened?"

"He doesn't want the baby. I don't care about me but how am I supposed to explain that his or her father doesn't want to know his own child?"

Strong arms drew her against a warm, wide chest. She let her purse drop onto the floor and wrapped both arms around Bruno's waist. The tears came after that, quickly morphing to sobs that shook her whole body.

"I don't love him," she said, her voice shaking. "I don't want to be with him. Whatever we had has been over for a long time. But he's not who I thought. He's not a good man. We're talking about a *baby*. Even people who don't like kids make an effort for their own."

Bruno didn't speak. Instead he continued to hold her tight. One hand moved up and down her back in a comforting, circular motion.

After what felt like hours but was probably ten or fifteen minutes, she managed to get control.

"I'm being very unprofessional."

He chuckled. "Pshaw."

She raised her head and sniffed. "What did you say? Pshaw? Are you like a hundred and twenty?"

He pulled a box of tissues off a bookshelf and guided her to the sofa in his office. He sat close to her, angled to face her.

"I'm sorry Rhys is being a dick."

"Me, too. And I'm surprised." She wiped her face and blew her nose. "I was so wrong about him. What else didn't I see? It's his own child. Possibly his only child. He's not some seventeen-year-old jock losing out on a college scholarship because he knocked up his girlfriend. He's a mature man. We were together sixteen years. This baby should matter and it doesn't."

"He's a fool, and years from now, he's going to have regrets."

She nodded. "You're right, and as you say that, I realize I don't care about his regrets. I don't want my child to suffer."

"She won't. You'll be a great mom, plus she'll have Stephanie and her family, Four and her family, and she'll have me."

She managed a smile. "Still hoping for a girl?"

"Yes, but I'll be equally thrilled with a boy. You have family, Mackenzie. Maybe not biological, but we're here all the same."

"You're very good to me."

His dark gaze was steady. "I care about you."

She nodded. "I care about you, too. And I got your shirt all wet."

"I'll wear it as a badge of honor."

She laughed and brushed at the soft cotton. "It will dry, but you'll be wrinkly. I'll try not to make a habit of crying on you, but you might want to keep a second shirt in the office, just the same."

"Tell me what else happened at the meeting."

She told him about the very pathetic visitation schedule. "Rhys is offering more in child support. Guilt money, I suppose. Ramona's going to go over everything one more time. Once it's finalized, I'll sign and he'll sign and then we get a divorce."

"How do you feel about that?"

"Sad. I was wrong about so much. Him, Barbara, my place at Bel Après. I feel as if I've been living a lie or something."

"You weren't the liar. They were."

He sat back on the sofa and pulled her with him so she was leaning against him. While the contact was unfamiliar, it felt nice. Comfortable and safe. Bruno always knew what to do and he was strong.

"You must work out," she said without thinking.

She felt his chest shake as he laughed. "Yes, I do. Most mornings."

She shifted so she was leaning against the sofa instead of him and drew her shirt tight across her belly. "I'm really starting to show."

"It's nice. Proof of life. Have you felt the baby move?"

"No. The books say it happens between sixteen and twenty weeks, with first-time mothers feeling it later. I'm almost at twenty weeks, so I'm kind of waiting, but so far, nothing. Oh, I have an ultrasound in a couple of weeks and we should find out the gender."

"I'm excited about that."

"Me, too." She sat up. "My breakdown is officially over. I married the wrong guy and I'll do better next time."

"Yes, you will." He smiled. "You know what would be great?"

"What?"

"If you picked out a paint color for the baby's room when you find out the gender."

She groaned at the thought of the little swatches he'd shown her. "Do I have to?"

"Yes. I insist."

"You're so bossy."

"Four needs the walls painted so she can get going on the mural. We're all trying to help and you're making that difficult. So in two weeks?"

She smiled at him. "How about if I don't even make you wait that long?"

She got up and walked over to his desk. She pulled out the second drawer on the right and removed the half-dozen swatches.

"This one," she said, pointing to the pale yellow. "It will be a good backdrop for the tropical jungle animals."

He smiled. "No unicorns?"

"I asked for toucans and monkeys, but knowing Four, she'll squeeze in a unicorn or a dragon somewhere."

"That's a good quality to have." He rose and moved toward her. "Come on. I'll buy you lunch. We'll go to that tacky Mexican place you like so much. Orla will fuss over you, bring you the healthy version of what you love, and you'll feel better afterward."

"That would be great. Just let me wash my face first. I'll meet you in the hall."

As she turned to leave, she had the thought that while Rhys was so much less than she'd thought he would be, Bruno was so much more. Nearly every day he showed her that he was a kind and honorable man, not to mention an excellent manager and a killer businessman. He also gave great hugs and didn't mind getting cried on. But she supposed the thing she liked about him best of all was the look in his eyes when he talked about her baby. Her girlfriends weren't the only ones on her side when it came to her pregnancy. Bruno was right there with them.

thirty-one

The big bar in the tasting area of Painted Moon had cleaned up better than Stephanie had hoped. Three weeks after starting her new job, she was knee-deep in the remodel, working long hours and loving every second.

She'd already designed a mailer to go to previous customers of Painted Moon, detailing the purchase and that Mackenzie was the new winemaker. Bruno and Mackenzie had approved the new labels for the remaining library wines, and they were getting started on that project. She felt energized by all she had to do in a day. Sometimes the work was hard, but a good kind of hard that challenged her.

She stood in the center of the construction zone, assessing what had been done for the week. Bruno liked her to do that on Fridays, then report back to him on the progress. She'd already gone over the plan for the coming week with the general contractor and was satisfied they were on time and on budget. A minor miracle.

Mackenzie walked through the layers of plastic around the construction site, Avery at her heels.

"Look who I found lurking around," Mackenzie said with a grin. "I like the looks of her. I think we should keep her."

Avery laughed. "You're stuck with me."

"Oh, good." Mackenzie glanced at Stephanie. "Homecoming's tomorrow night. I'll be at your place at, what, five? Is that too early?"

"Not if you want to be involved in the whole makeup ritual."

"I won't be involved," Mackenzie said, hugging Avery. "I'm nowhere near as good as your mom at the beauty stuff. But I do want to sit on the edge of the tub and tell you how pretty you are."

Mackenzie waved at them both before heading back to her office. Stephanie turned her attention to her daughter. Things were still good between them. Avery was going to Homecoming with a group of girlfriends. They'd rented a limo together and had an after-party planned at Stephanie's place. She and Avery had spent much of the week coming up with menu ideas and brainstorming movie possibilities. Carson would escape to Four's house, where he and Jaguar had a video game marathon planned once the younger kids went to bed.

"What can I do for you, girl child of mine?" Stephanie asked.

Avery looked around at the framed space. "It's going to look good in here, Mom."

"It is." Stephanie hesitated, not sure if she should point out that Avery had avoided the question. She sensed there was something on her daughter's mind and decided she would give her a little time to get it out.

"There's going to be a retail space, right?" Avery asked.

"Uh-huh. Similar to what you're used to at Bel Après, but with a slightly different vibe."

Avery sighed. "Vibe? Really?"

"I'm hip with the slang. Watch me get funky."

"Oh, Mom." Avery walked around the makeshift desk covered with floor plans. "When this is done, could I get a part-time job here instead of working at Bel Après?"

"Sure, sweetie, but why would you want to change jobs?"

"It's not fun anymore. Grandma's so intense. She keeps coming into the tasting room and yelling at the staff. She's even yelled at me a couple of times and all I was doing was stocking shelves. I need a job to pay for my gas, and I thought it might be more fun to be here. With you."

Stephanie tried not to let her pleasure show. "I'll be hiring people to staff the tasting room and the retail area in March. If you're interested, you're welcome to fill out an application."

Avery rolled her eyes. "Fine, but I'll point out I have experience and I can get a reference from Mackenzie."

"That would be helpful."

"You're not going to give me a break at all, are you?"

"Maybe a really small one."

But instead of smiling, Avery looked troubled. She looked at Stephanie, then away. Stephanie waited.

"Have you talked to Dad lately?" her daughter asked.

"Not really."

The more polite answer than the truth. She hadn't heard from Kyle since he'd proposed and she'd told him no. All their communication about visits and drop-offs had gone through the kids. Sometimes that happened, so as far as she knew, neither Avery nor Carson suspected anything was wrong.

She supposed at some point she was going to have to get in touch with him and force the issue. They had children together—they couldn't simply avoid each other forever.

"So he didn't say anything about Thanksgiving."

Ah, the holiday. It was his year to have the kids. Sometimes they were in Seattle, but as often as not, he spent the day in Walla Walla. It usually depended on whether or not he was covering the Apple Cup—the annual game between the cross-state rivals WSU and UW—and where it was being played.

"I'm going to Four's house," Stephanie said. "Does your dad want you in Seattle?" She would miss them both but was used to the occasional separations.

"Um, well, not exactly." Avery bit her lower lip. "You really haven't talked to him, have you? Dad's in New York. He's got an interview for a job there and he's going to be in New York for Thanksgiving."

She tried not to let her surprise show. "He's going national," she said, remembering how he'd thrown the possibility at her when they'd last spoken. "Good for him. He should have done it a long time ago."

"He said he didn't want to be that far from Carson and me, but we're older now."

An interesting twist on what he'd told her, Stephanie thought, then decided to be charitable and assume both could be true.

"I'm glad for him. So you'd like to go to New York for Thanksgiving?"

Avery avoided her gaze. "Kind of. I've never been and it's a cool city and Dad will know by then if he has the job, so if he does, we'll be apartment hunting with him. He's renting an Airbnb for us to stay in." She wrinkled her nose. "Carson and I have to share a room and a bathroom, which is so gross, but still, it's New York. What do you think?"

"That you're going to miss out on an amazing Thanksgiving here." Stephanie crossed to her daughter and hugged her. "But I want you to have a good time with your dad."

"You sure? You won't be too lonely?"

"I'll survive." Stephanie released her. "It's a big city, Avery. We're going to have to talk about staying safe."

"I know. And I'm responsible for Carson. He wants Dad to get the job, by the way, because then he can go to a Yankees game." She sighed. "Baseball. Why did it have to be baseball?"

357

They both laughed.

When Avery left, Stephanie pulled out her phone and sent a text to Kyle.

I hear you're in NYC. When were you going to tell me?

It took only a few seconds for his answer to appear.

I should have said something. Sorry. I was dealing with our last conversation. I'd had different plans, but then this opportunity came up, so here I am.

Will you get the job?

Probably. Which means a move. It will complicate things with the kids.

In more ways than one, Stephanie thought. Visiting their dad on the East Coast increased the chances that one or both of them would want to go to college there. She hated the thought of her children being so far away but knew she had to be brave about it. They deserved the chance to follow their dreams.

We'll make it work, she told him. **Avery told me about Thanksgiving. I would rather have heard it from you.**

I should have said something. Is it okay?

It's fine, although your daughter isn't thrilled about sharing both a bedroom and a bathroom with her brother.

We all have to make sacrifices. You sure you're fine with it?

Yes. You can buy their tickets. Oh, and Avery will want to go shopping. Don't let her spend too much.

There was a long pause before he replied.

I miss you.

Now it was her turn to hesitate.

To be honest, she really hadn't been thinking much about Kyle lately. She'd been focused on her new job and the kids. For her, the marriage was long over. But it would be cruel to say that.

This is the best thing for both of us. I know it is. I'll see you soon.

C U

Barbara could feel the heat of the flames as they rose higher and higher in the sky. They moved so fast, consuming row after row of vines, burning them down to nothing. The wall of fire roared past her, leaving nothing but dry, burnt earth behind.

She ran back and forth, not sure what to do. She couldn't find water, or anyone to help her. She screamed, but the wind swallowed up the sound. The temperature rose until she was afraid she would disintegrate into dust and blow away.

She ran closer to the vines only to realize that the fire was turning back, chasing her. She tried to escape but suddenly couldn't move and woke herself with her screams.

She sat up in the cool, dark bedroom, desperate to catch her breath as her heart raced and her body dripped with sweat. The nightmare was familiar—she'd had it often when she and James had first been married and things had been so tough—but it had been years since she'd had it.

Still shaking, she collapsed back on the bed. She went from hot to cold and quickly pulled up the covers. The bed seemed large and empty with no Giorgio to keep her company. He was back east for his daughter's birthday, she thought, then glanced at her clock.

Five o'clock. That meant it was, what, eight where he was?

She reached for her phone and pushed the button to call him. Three rings later she heard his voice.

"Yes?"

"Giorgio, thank goodness. I had the most horrible dream. I dreamed that Bel Après was on fire and there was nothing I could do." She shuddered at the memory. "It was awful. I used to have it all the time, when James and I were struggling. I'd forgotten what it was like. I'm still shaking."

Instead of comforting her or asking questions, he didn't say anything.

"Giorgio? Are you still there?"

"I'm here."

He sounded impatient or upset.

"What's wrong? I haven't talked to you in a few days. What have you been doing?"

"That's the question?" he asked, his voice low and cold. "What have I been doing?"

"Why are you angry with me?" She sat up again. "You're in a mood this morning."

"Last night was Rosemary's birthday party. You were supposed to be here with me. You didn't call, you didn't send a gift or flowers. In fact, you forgot completely."

"I didn't," she said, telling the lie automatically. "I couldn't call last night. By the time I got home, it was too late. I didn't want to wake up everyone."

"We both know that's not true. It's taken me a while to see the truth, Barbara, but now I have. You don't care about anyone but yourself. You put on a good act, but that's all it is. An act."

Her breath caught. "Giorgio, no! Don't say that. You don't mean it. I love you. I'm sorry about Rosemary, I am. Desperately

360

sorry. Let me make it up to you. When you get home, we'll go away together. Maybe to Portland. We'll stay at that hotel you like, just the two of us."

The long silence that followed frightened her more than his anger. Her heart sped up again.

"I won't be coming back."

"What does that mean?"

"I'm moving back here to be with my family."

She felt herself go cold as his words sank in.

"No! You can't. You're not leaving me. Darling, no. Please." Tears formed and fell. Her voice thickened. "Giorgio, I love you. You're the world to me."

"If that were true, we wouldn't be having this conversation. You were my princess, but I was never your prince. I don't know what you saw in me. I wasn't even a means to an end because I have nothing you want. I guess the problem is Bel Après is your one true love and I'll always come in second. Maybe that's enough for you, but not for me."

"Giorgio, stop." She found it difficult to talk but forced herself to keep trying. "Don't leave me. I love you."

"I don't think you're capable of love. You can keep the ring."

"Giorgio. Giorgio, don't. Please, I—"

The silence of her phone told her the call had been disconnected. He wasn't on the line anymore—he'd hung up on her.

She dropped the phone onto the bed and pulled a pillow over her face to muffle her screams. She screamed until her throat was raw and she couldn't make a sound, then she rolled on her side and cried.

With the wine in barrels, Mackenzie allowed herself to take a little breath. In theory there was nothing she could do but hover while science and nature did their thing. Still, when it came to wine, she was a worrier, so she preferred to stay close—as if her presence would make a difference.

"I'm crabby," she said, climbing into Bruno's elegant Mercedes. "I don't want to go."

He looked at her, amusement crinkling his eyes. "You sound like a two-year-old."

"Good. I feel like stomping my feet. I need to be here. It's not a good time to leave."

"The wine is in barrels. What are you going to do for it?"

"I provide an encouraging spirit."

"This is the first event for winemakers since harvest. You and I are the new owners of Painted Moon. We need to make an appearance."

She knew he was right, but she still resisted. "It's going to be weird."

"Are you nervous?"

"Yes. I won't know what to say to anyone. I've always been a part of Bel Après. Now I'm not."

He reached across the console and lightly squeezed her hand. "You'll do fine. Everyone will be excited to talk to you. Barbara isn't going to be there."

Her mood brightened. "Are you sure?"

"When I RSVP'd for us, I asked. The coordinator said Rhys and Lori would be representing Bel Après."

Mackenzie wasn't sure how she felt about seeing her ex so soon after their lawyer meeting. Not that it mattered. They lived in the same town and worked in the same industry. They were going to run into each other on a regular basis. Better to get that first awkward professional meeting out of the way.

"You all right facing Rhys?" Bruno asked.

"Why are you reading my mind?"

"I was guessing."

"I suppose it's the obvious question." She thought for a second. "I don't care about seeing him. I'm disappointed in him as a person and I'm questioning our relationship and I feel as if I wasted too much time on him, but I'm not angry. And my general dissatisfaction is more about the baby than him."

"Sounds reasonable. And on the Barbara front?"

She smiled. "Did you anticipate the emotional element of our partnership when you signed on to this?"

He grinned. "I knew there were would be baggage. At least yours is interesting."

"I hope it gets boring really, really soon. Okay, Barbara." She briefly closed her eyes. "It's not that I'm afraid to confront her, it's that I'd rather not. I'm not comfortable making a scene. Or screaming at someone."

"No scenes today," he promised. "We'll go in, say hello to everyone, stay a polite half hour or so, then duck out."

"You have a plan."

"Always."

"I like your ability to anticipate things. It makes me feel like I can relax."

He glanced at her. "Good. Some people find my planning annoying."

She smiled. "Not the ever-perfect Gloria."

He grinned at her. "She thought I was too much of a planner."

"She has a flaw! I'm so happy. I was worried your past was too perfect, which wouldn't be fair. You're dealing with mine nearly every day."

"You're worth it."

She told herself he meant that in a business-partner way and not personally, but that didn't stop a little happy warmth from filling her chest.

She leaned back in her seat and tried not to think about the upcoming event. "I'm wearing fake yoga pants," she grumbled. "It's horrible."

"How are they fake and why is it horrible?"

"They're weird looking. They're supposed to look like dress pants, but they're not. Soon I'm going to have to wear actual maternity pants and I don't want to. The whole having-a-baby thing is messy. What was nature thinking?"

"You would prefer children appear fully formed? Maybe left under a tree?"

"Not a tree. A bush. Or some kind of plant. Something pretty like a lily or an orchid."

"Climate-wise, that could be a problem. Orchids don't grow everywhere."

"That's true. Okay, so the current system is probably best, but still. Maternity pants suck. And I hate my shirt."

"You look nice. Stop fussing. I know you're nervous but in a couple of hours we'll be done and you can go back to hovering outside the barrel room."

"Promise?"

"Yes."

He pulled into the hotel parking lot. The meet and greet was in one of the large meeting rooms. The association put them on several times a year, allowing those in the industry to get together and catch up.

Mackenzie and Bruno walked inside. She was trying not to wonder if she looked pregnant or worry about what people would say. The last time she'd seen most of these people had been at the Summer Solstice Party when she'd been married to Rhys and working for Barbara. Five plus months later, everything was different.

They walked into the already crowded room. Mackenzie resisted the urge to cling to Bruno's arm or hide behind him. She would be fine, she told herself. She knew how to work a room and she was proud of what she'd accomplished.

She walked up to a group of men she knew and smiled.

"Hi, everyone."

"Mackenzie! Good to see you."

"Hey, Mackenzie. Who's the new guy?"

She introduced Bruno. They all knew he was her business partner and immediately started asking him questions.

Paul, a manager of a large winery at the other end of the valley, leaned close. "How was harvest? You went a hundred percent mechanical?"

"Because of the timing, we weren't able to hire anyone to handpick." She smiled. "I went in kicking and screaming, but it was actually a really smooth process. I was happy with how it turned out. Next year we'll handpick a little, but now that I've seen it in action, I'm going to stick with a lot of mechanical harvesting."

"I'm shocked."

"Me, too, but I can't argue with the results. It's going to be a good year."

"We got lucky," Paul said. "If the heat had stayed with us until the end, we would have been screwed."

"But it didn't."

Paul started to ask a question, then paused before shifting his weight. "Okay, this is uncomfortable. Rhys and Lori just walked in."

"Would you rather be talking to them?"

He relaxed. "You know I wouldn't. Rhys has no vision and Lori never has anything to say. It's just you two used to be married."

"I remember that." She did her best to look calm and relaxed. "It's fine, Paul. Rhys and I are working our way through the divorce. We're about to sign the final paperwork and then we'll be consciously uncoupled, as the young people like to say."

"And you're good with that?" He sounded worried.

She thought about all that had happened so quickly. How different things were these days, how different she was. The journey had been painful, but, she supposed, she'd taken the right path.

"I'm doing well and I'm very happy. Next spring come out

to Painted Moon and see what we're doing. It's pretty magical stuff."

Bruno and the winemakers he'd been talking to joined the conversation. Mackenzie tried to pay attention to what they were saying, all the while aware that Rhys was somewhere in the room.

Would he come over and speak to her? Should she try to speak to him? Was this ever going to be easy?

She shook off the questions and focused on the conversation. She and Bruno chatted for a few more minutes, then went to circulate. Mackenzie introduced him to people he didn't know and reacquainted herself with the winemakers and owners she'd known for years.

Jack, a grizzled old guy who had been growing grapes since the 1980s, pulled her aside.

"Good for you," he told her. "Leaving all that Bel Après crap behind. You're better off with Painted Moon. Put your mark on it. Barbara was always going to do her best to trim your wings. She didn't want anyone being the star and you can't help shining wherever you are."

The unexpected compliment surprised her. "That's so nice."

"It's true. We all knew you were talented. Lucky her, grabbing you first."

She smiled. "Rhys had a piece of that."

"True, but the rest of us wanted to make you a job offer. We'd heard about you from the folks at WSU. We all knew you had something. She got there first."

"I didn't know that," she admitted, surprised to find out anyone had even known who she was back then. How would everything have been different if she hadn't gone to work for Bel Après? There was no way to know.

She excused herself and got a glass of water. She glanced longingly at the various bottles of wine. Events like these were a chance to taste what everyone was doing. She had always enjoyed sampling, but not today.

"You came."

She turned and saw Lori standing behind her.

"I did." Mackenzie looked around. "Are you with Owen?"

Lori glared at her. "Who told you about that?"

"Stephanie mentioned you were dating him. I'm glad. He's a great guy."

She was going to say more, but Lori's expression tightened.

"Do you think I care what you think about him or anything? I don't. I can't believe you showed your face here, after what you did."

While Lori's vitriol was not as vicious as her mother's, there was a familiar theme. Mackenzie knew she had a choice—she could respond in kind or she could try to get through to the woman she'd always thought of as part of her family.

"Lori, please. I don't want to fight with you. I know things are different, but I never wanted to hurt anyone and I still care about you. Can't we please at least be friends?"

Lori stared at her for a long time. "We were never friends. I accepted you because I had to, but I always knew what you were. No matter what happens with the winery, I'm glad you're gone and I don't have to pretend anymore."

She walked away. Mackenzie stared after her, trying not to react. Her face heated and her legs felt a little shaky, but she refused to let herself be cowed.

Bruno appeared at her side. "What happened?"

"Nothing."

He looked at her. "I was watching both of you. It wasn't a friendly exchange."

"Oh. In that case, I thought Lori and I liked each other, and she made sure I knew that had never been true."

"You okay?"

"I will be."

"Want to leave?"

She smiled at him. "I don't retreat."

"Good. There are a couple more people I'd like to meet. In the meantime, let me say that I'm looking forward to seeing you in maternity pants."

The random comment was so startling, she couldn't help laughing. "You can't mean that, and if you do, you're just plain weird."

"I'll accept weird, if it's important to you."

"Thank you. So why are you looking forward to seeing me in maternity pants? I don't think they're an especially flattering look on anyone."

"You'll rock them."

She looked at him. "You're always nice to me."

"You're my business partner. What else would I be? Besides, you're not upset about Lori anymore, are you?"

She realized he was right. "You're trying to distract me."

"Not trying, Mackenzie. Doing. There's a difference."

"So there is. I'll have to remember that."

thirty-two

Stephanie arrived at her mother's house, a sweet potato casserole in hand. The family dinner tonight was a potluck, at least that was what Lori's text had said. An odd choice, Stephanie thought, letting herself inside. Her mother usually wouldn't trust anyone else to simply show up with food. What if the flavors didn't match or the colors were off? But she'd been asked to bring a potato dish that would go with pork, so she had.

She passed Four's kids playing a card game with Owen and Jaguar, then joined her sisters and mom in the kitchen.

"Hi, all," she said as she set the casserole dish on the counter. "This is just out of the oven, so it shouldn't need to be reheated."

Four hugged her. "You look so happy."

"I feel good."

"It shows."

Stephanie shrugged out of her coat and hung it on the rack just inside the mudroom. "Hi, Lori. Owen looks pretty comfortable out there with all the kids. You found a good one in him."

Lori gave her a suspicious look before offering a slight smile. "I think so."

Stephanie drew in a breath for courage before tentatively hugging her mother. "Hey, Mom. How are things?"

Her mother didn't return the hug, nor did she look the least bit pleased about anything.

"Hunky-dory. Now can we please get on with dinner? Did anyone check the table? Is it set correctly? Lori, that was your job. Let's go examine all the ways you failed."

She swept out of the room, Lori at her heels. Stephanie turned to Four.

"She's in a mood."

Four pulled a large pork roast out of the oven and set it on an unused portion of the stove, then grabbed Stephanie's hand and pulled her into the walk-in pantry.

"Giorgio dumped Barbara," Four said in a whisper. "I can't get more details than that. It happened a few days ago. I didn't know they were fighting, but I guess they were. Lori says it's been bad around here. The only thing I can figure is he got fed up with her selfishness. She wouldn't go back east with him for his daughter's birthday."

"Mom wouldn't think that was important. Not with everything going on."

"I know that and you know that, but I think it was a wake-up call for him." Four's mouth twisted. "It makes me sad. He was her one shot at happiness and now he's gone. She's going to get meaner and meaner until no one wants to be around her. It's very upsetting."

They heard talking in the kitchen and quickly moved out of the pantry. Their mother glared at them.

"If you two are done whispering like schoolgirls, we can work at getting dinner on the table."

Stephanie ignored the glower and the sharp words, crossing to her mom and taking one of her hands.

"I'm so sorry about what happened with Giorgio. I wish you'd told me. I could have come over to be with you."

Her mother snatched back her hand, her brown eyes cold and empty. "And do what? I'm perfectly fine. Giorgio was a ridiculous man who made impossible demands. He had no understanding of my responsibilities or expectations. He was a waste of my time. Good riddance."

Stephanie shook her head. "Mom, you don't mean that. You loved him. He made you happy. I'm sorry he's gone, and if there's anything I can do to—"

"What could you possibly do for me? You quit your job and walked out on my wedding planning. I don't need any more 'help.'" She made air quotes. "From you."

For a moment, time seemed to freeze. She saw Lori's look of relief at having someone else getting the brunt of Barbara's temper, and Four's genuine compassion for another human in pain. She saw the smallness of her mother's action and knew Barbara would rather die alone than ever admit to what she perceived as a weakness. She also saw herself—stronger now. Going in the right direction. There would be challenges, but she'd worked through the hardest part. She'd been brave, and as long as she kept being brave, then she was going to be just fine.

She thought of all the things she could say to her mother. All the cutting words, the sarcastic comments, and then she told herself it wasn't worth it. Barbara would be who she had always been. She wouldn't change until she wanted to.

"I'm here if you need me," Stephanie repeated. "Either way, I'm really sorry."

Her mother looked at the roast. "This is done. Get Jaguar in here to cut it and start putting the food on the table. Assuming you're all capable of those minor tasks."

With that, she walked into the dining room. Stephanie watched her go. "It must be hard to be her."

Four smiled. "And that, sister of mine, is the lesson to be learned."

★ ★ ★

Mackenzie stared at the blurry image that was, in theory, her daughter. According to the doctor, her weight was good, her blood pressure and blood sugar were perfect, and the baby was doing her baby-growing thing.

"Five months down, four to go," she told herself as she drove back to Painted Moon. And she was having a girl.

She let that information sink in. Bruno had teased her about wanting a girl, so the news would delight him. As for her feelings, she thought maybe a girl would be easier for her as a mom. She'd been a girl. She knew a few girl things.

"A girl," she whispered. "I'm going to have to come up with a name. Maybe Amy, after my mom."

She touched her belly. "Hi, Amy. I'm *your* mom." She grinned. "That is the strangest thing I've ever said, but it's true. I'm your mom."

She let the words settle on her, wondering when she would know they were true. She was pregnant and she was having a daughter.

She felt herself smile at the news and thought about everyone she wanted to tell. Bruno, for sure, and Stephanie. Four. She wondered about letting Rhys know. Would he care about the gender of the child? He'd never asked and she didn't know if she should offer.

"I'll deal with that next week," she told herself as she drove through the large gates at Painted Moon. Today was for her and the people she loved. She was having a girl!

She parked and hurried to the office. Before she got there, Bruno walked out of the building, as if he'd been waiting for her.

"You're back," he said, his voice tense.

"I am." She hadn't told him she had a doctor's appointment today, instead saying she was going to run errands. She'd known about the ultrasound and hadn't been sure she would want to discuss it when she got back. A silly thing, now that she'd been through it.

"We have to talk."

The edge to his voice brought her to a stop. Whatever he was going to say, it wasn't good. Had there been a fire? Was he calling the bridge loan? No, it couldn't be that. She was weeks away from the divorce being final and getting her payout. He wouldn't call the loan. Then what?

"I bought you something," he added, motioning for her to go with him to the production area. "It was supposed to be a surprise, but now that it's here, I'm not sure I did the right thing. If you're angry, I'll understand. I can always sell them somewhere else. I just thought for the Pepper Bridge vineyards you'd wanted to do something different and then this opportunity came up."

"This is about the winery?" she asked.

He came to a stop. "Yes. Why?"

"You scared me."

His expression softened. "Did I? I'm sorry. I didn't mean to. It's about—" He cleared his throat. "I bought some vines."

What did that mean? "You bought plants?"

Why would he do that? Ignoring the time it would take to have them grow from seedlings into mature vines, that just wasn't how they did things these days. Painted Moon had excellent rootstock. If she wanted to make changes, all she had to do was buy what she wanted and graft it in. That way she would lose only a year of production.

They stepped into the big, open building. There was a package about the size of a shoebox sitting on a workbench.

"No, not vines. I bought these." He pointed to the box. "Through a friend of a friend, I know a guy in the Bordeaux region of France. He's had some financial trouble and I helped him out. In return, he's going to send us these."

He lifted the lid. Inside was wet newspaper wrapped around what looked like fat sticks. Mackenzie felt the breath leave her body as she walked closer.

"Scions," she said, her voice a reverent whisper. "He sent you scions."

"Just a few. He'll send the bulk of them after the first of the year. It's better to cut them while the vines are dormant." He gave her a lopsided grin. "But you know that."

She carefully unwrapped the newspaper and stared at the beautiful thick sections of vine. They were healthy, about ten inches long. Grafted into rootstock, they would produce grapes within two seasons.

She looked at him. "What are they?"

"Cabernet sauvignon, merlot, petit verdot. He's sending enough for fifty acres. I have the particulars on the vineyards. His family has been making wine there for about six hundred years."

French grapes. He was offering her beautiful, vibrant, elegant French grapes.

"Do you know what I can do with these?" she asked, feeling as if she was close to touching the face of God. "Do you? We can go traditional. We can have estate-grown wines unlike any others in the state." She quickly put down the scion and held up her hands. "I'm shaking. Oh, Bruno, I don't know how you did this, but thank you so much."

"You're not mad?"

"Why would I be mad?"

"I'm kind of stepping on your toes here. You do wines, I do everything else. It's just when he made the offer, I thought you'd be happy."

"I am."

She was about to throw herself at him when she felt the oddest sensation in her belly. Sort of a fluttering, bumping, shifting that she'd never felt before. Almost as if—

"The baby," she breathed, instinctively grabbing his hand and pressing it to her stomach. "She's moving. Can you feel it?"

They both stood there for a second and then it happened again. His eyes widened until he looked as dazed and terrified as she felt.

"That's the baby?" he asked.

374

She nodded. "Or I have serious gas issues and will probably need a bathroom."

"You don't have gas." He smiled. "You said she."

"It's a girl. You got your wish."

"Are you happy?"

"Yes. I'm going to call her Amy, after my mom."

"That's a beautiful name."

They stood like that, close together, his hand on her stomach, for a few more minutes, but there wasn't any more movement. Slowly, Mackenzie became aware of their close proximity and the oddly intimate nature of their contact. She released his hand and took a step back.

"Sorry. I didn't mean to make you uncomfortable. I just thought you might like to feel her move."

"I did. Thank you."

She looked away. "Good. I won't make a habit of throwing myself at you like that or putting your hands on me because—" She told herself to be quiet because she definitely wasn't making the situation any more comfortable for either of them.

She cleared her throat. "What I meant was, um—"

Bruno stepped in front of her. "Stop talking."

"I really should."

"It wasn't awkward."

She raised her gaze to his. "It wasn't?"

"No. I liked it."

Feeling the baby move or touching her? Before she could figure out how to ask, he moved closer and slowly, carefully cupped her face in his hands.

His fingers were warm and held her gently. She supposed she could have pulled away if she wanted to, only she didn't. When he lowered his head, she knew exactly what he was going to do. Anticipation battled caution. Was she willing to take the risk of what a kiss could mean? What if everything changed and it was—

His mouth brushed against hers. The barely there contact made her breath catch and the world fall away. She felt heat and tingles and need and a thousand other wonderful things that she couldn't explain beyond the fact that she *knew* everything about this moment was right.

He drew back, still cupping her face, and stared into her eyes. She saw a matching desire, but also questions. He wanted her to be sure.

She smiled. "We should do that more."

"I like how you think."

He kissed her again, this time with more intensity. She wrapped her arms around his neck as she pulled him against her. They touched everywhere and she reveled in all of it. Her breasts nestling against his chest, their thighs pressing against each other, his lips on hers in a way that offered and took and made her want it all.

This, she thought happily. Unexpected and sexy and just plain right.

When he drew back a second time, they were both breathing a little hard.

"It's been a day," she said, her voice a little unsteady. "I find out I'm having a girl, we feel the baby move, you buy me grapes from France and now we're kissing. It's a lot to take in."

"Too much?"

"Just right."

One corner of his mouth turned up. "Dinner tonight?"

"Yes, please."

"I'll bring takeout."

She laughed. "One of us is going to have to learn how to cook."

He put his arm around her and they started back to the office. "Don't worry about it. I'll hire a chef."

"Of course you will." She was still laughing when they went inside.

★ ★ ★

Mackenzie carefully spit the wine into a pitcher, then rinsed her mouth with water. She was working her way through Herman's barrels on the schedule she'd created for herself, but it was slow going. Life would be much easier if she could just taste the wine like a regular person.

"Not that I'm complaining," she told Amy. "I want you to be healthy."

She made several notations on the pad on her clipboard. She wanted to start blending in the next few weeks. The response to Stephanie's first mailing to the Painted Moon customers had been overwhelmingly positive. If everyone who said they were interested in library wines and whatever blends Mackenzie created made a purchase, they would sell out in minutes.

She felt good, she thought happily. Physically, emotionally. She loved her work, she had finally wrapped her head around being pregnant and she was less than two weeks away from not owing Bruno two million dollars.

She had an appointment to sign the paperwork to finalize her divorce, and Rhys had put the payout into an escrow account. As soon as the courts did their thing, she would be single and momentarily flush with cash. Ten minutes later, she would wire the money to Bruno, but still. It was heady to think about.

She was still chuckling at the thought when she heard rapid footsteps on the concrete floor. She turned and saw Barbara rushing toward her. The other woman was pale and wide-eyed, her expression menacing and an odd contrast to her tailored suit and pearls.

"You have ruined me!" Barbara said, her voice tight as she approached.

Mackenzie wasn't afraid, exactly, but she was feeling cautious. She shifted to her right, putting a row of barrels between her and her former mother-in-law.

"Why are you here?" she asked, careful to keep her voice calm.

"To confront you once and for all. You stole everything from me and you're going to have to pay."

"I didn't take anything from you. You're the one who fired me and tried to get me thrown out of my house. You're the one who wanted me to sell off my child's inheritance."

"Why wouldn't I? You're nothing to me. Nothing!" She pressed a hand to her throat. "You took the China deal."

"What?" Mackenzie came out from behind the barrels and slapped her clipboard on a table. "You wait a minute. You never wanted to do anything with China. We talked about it and you said no every time. Just like you said no to buying land in Oregon so we could make great pinots and you said no to every other suggestion. The China thing is not on me."

They glared at each other. Mackenzie recovered first.

"Barbara, I'm sorry it's come to this. You were so much to me. I never wanted to hurt you. You were like a mother to me."

"I was never your mother. I wouldn't want a child like you. You came from nothing and you deserve nothing. I trusted you with Bel Après and you walked away." She narrowed her gaze. "I wish you were dead."

The words hurt but not as much as they would have three months ago. Mackenzie supposed that in addition to a bigger belly she was getting a thicker skin.

She took a second to collect herself. "You're going to leave now. If you come back again, I'll get a restraining order against you. As it is, I'm going to talk to Rhys about making sure you don't have any unsupervised time with the baby. I'll put it in the parenting plan. Unlike you, Barbara, I protect what's mine. Now get out."

She pointed to the open doorway for emphasis, only then noticing Bruno standing in the shadows. She was grateful for his presence and even more thankful that he was letting her handle the situation.

"I'll hate you forever," Barbara said in a low voice.

Mackenzie felt a rush of sadness. "I'm not going to say the same back to you. You're not worth the energy."

She picked up her clipboard and studied the notes, pretending she could read them, even with all the emotions pulsing through her. Several seconds later, she heard retreating footsteps, then silence. Barbara was gone.

Bruno walked over to her. "We're getting security."

"No, we're going to wait and see what happens. If she shows up again, we'll go talk to a judge."

"Did you mean what you said about making sure she can't be alone with Amy?"

"Every word. I'm not trusting her with my child, although she would probably tell me she would rather eat glass than spend time with my daughter." She gave him a humorless smile. "Regardless, I'm supposed to sign the final documents tomorrow. Do you think Rhys won't agree to the change? The man wants to be divorced. At this point he'll do anything to be free. I'm going to take advantage of that." She shrugged. "It's not as if I'm asking for anything outrageous. He'll agree."

"You have a ruthless streak," Bruno teased. "I like it."

"I'm kind of impressed myself."

thirty-three

Thanksgiving morning dawned cold and clear. Mackenzie woke at her usual time, a little after six. After pulling on yoga pants and a T-shirt, she drank an entire glass of water, then did her stupid pregnancy yoga video for twenty minutes before heading downstairs for her disgusting protein shake.

Technically she could have a real breakfast if she wanted, but it was too much trouble to cook. She needed to have protein and the right kind of carbs and fiber. A protein shake was easy.

Halfway down the stairs, she heard a noise in the kitchen, followed by the smell of bacon. She ran the rest of the way and found Bruno at the stove, bacon simmering and the table set.

He was intent on his task and didn't see her at first. A white "Kiss the Cook" apron covered his jeans and the front of his long-sleeved shirt.

The old fan above the stove was loud enough to cover the sound of her approaching. She walked up behind him and slid her arms around his waist.

"You're a surprise," she said, leaning against him. "Happy Thanksgiving."

He turned toward her and smiled. "Happy Thanksgiving. It's a holiday, so I thought I'd slip in early and save you from your protein drink."

"That's very thoughtful. Thank you."

"You're welcome. Now go sit down and I'll get going on the eggs."

She sipped the juice he'd poured while he finished cooking. When the toast popped in the toaster, she carried it over to the table. He put down the plates and they sat across from each other.

"You're okay with me using the key you gave me?" he asked. "I won't make a habit of it."

"I gave you the key so you could use it."

Not that he'd had reason to. It had been only a couple of weeks since their first kiss. They'd gone out to dinner a few times and continued with the kissing, but nothing more. She sensed he was taking things slow for her.

She took a bite of her eggs, moaned slightly at the deliciousness, then excused herself to go get her phone. When she was back at the table, she turned it so he could see the picture Lori had forwarded. It showed Rhys on a beach, the blonde from the café and the lawyer's office at his side.

"I'm sure Lori thought she was hurting me," Mackenzie said, picking up her fork. "But I'm fine with it. We've both moved on."

He set down her phone. "If you're sure."

"I am. Oh, and I sent you a wire transfer yesterday. You should have a notification first thing tomorrow."

One eyebrow rose. "You paid off the bridge loan."

"I did." She grinned. "It was freeing and yet painful."

"Want the money back?"

"No. Stop. Don't even kid about that. I owed you and I've paid you back. Thank you for the loan. And for buying Painted Moon with me."

"You're welcome." He put down his fork and met her gaze. "You're officially divorced."

"I am. Single. Pregnant, but single."

"I like the pregnant part. It's sexy."

"Hardly, but thank you for saying that."

As they stared at each other, she felt a familiar heat blossoming low in her belly. Her already sensitive breasts began to tingle. According to the books she'd read and the slightly embarrassing conversation with her doctor, sex was perfectly fine. She wasn't supposed to go in a hot tub, but if she wanted to do the wild thing, that was allowed. Wasn't pregnancy the funniest thing ever?

He glanced at the clock. "We're supposed to be at Four's house around one."

"That's what she said."

They would be spending Thanksgiving with her family. Rhys was in Mexico, Barbara had said she wouldn't be attending any celebration with anyone this year, and Lori was off with Owen's family, so it was just going to be the fun half of the Barcellona clan.

"Did you, ah, have any plans for the rest of the morning?" he asked, his voice thick, his gaze sharp with arousal. "After breakfast, I mean."

She walked around the table, then drew him to his feet. "Breakfast can wait."

epilogue

Three years later…

"You have completely blown me away," Mackenzie said, looking at the outdoor area by the tasting room at Painted Moon.

Massive awnings provided shade for fifty round tables, each seating ten people. To the east was the dance floor, and to the west was the huge buffet line. Servers would circulate with appetizers and several bars offered wines as well as mixed drinks to their guests. Twinkle lights were strung and the DJ was already setting up.

"The party's going to be epic," Stephanie said with a laugh.

"Don't let Avery hear you say that," Mackenzie teased. "You know how she feels about people our age trying to use slang."

They linked arms as they toured the area. Big fans, tucked in with plants, would provide a nice breeze. Thankfully, the weather had cooperated and it would only be in the low eighties when the evening began.

"I'm glad you and Bruno are doing this," Stephanie said. "It's a great tradition. It deserves to continue."

"I felt a little weird about it," Mackenzie admitted. "But you're right about the tradition."

For the past two years, Barbara had chosen not to have the Summer Solstice Party at Bel Après. Last January, Stephanie had come to Mackenzie and Bruno to discuss the possibility of starting up the parties at Painted Moon. They'd given her the go-ahead to start planning it.

"I was afraid no one would come," Mackenzie admitted.

Stephanie laughed. "Why? Everyone wants to be here. We sent out five hundred invitations and we had four hundred and ninety-eight people say yes."

"That still surprises me."

"You're so weird."

Mackenzie laughed. "That is probably true." She looked around at what they'd all created together. "This is really good. I'm happy."

"Me, too."

Mackenzie stepped back and pointed at her. "That's because you have a shiny new boyfriend."

Stephanie blushed. "Liam does make the day more sparkly."

Liam was a professor at the local college. Handsome as a movie star and five years younger, he'd swept Stephanie off her feet last fall. Things were getting serious and Mackenzie had a feeling there would be an announcement in a few months.

"All right, you," Stephanie said with mock sternness. "I have last-minute details to check on and you have to get changed. Don't you dare be late to your own party."

"I'll be on time," Mackenzie promised.

She made her way to the farmhouse, thinking about how far they'd all come since the last Solstice Party. Avery was in college, studying at Georgetown. Carson was a senior in high school and still trying to decide between college and going pro. Four, Jaguar and their children were who they always had been—loving, content and unique. Rhys had yet another woman in his life. His relationship with Amy was distant at best. He rarely saw her, and while that made Mackenzie sad, she wasn't going to push him. Amy was surrounded by people who loved her and Bruno was father enough for ten children.

Lori had married Owen and gotten pregnant right away. Mackenzie had reached out a few times, but Lori really wasn't interested in being friends. Even more disappointing, Barbara had become something of a recluse. She was rarely seen in public, and from what Stephanie occasionally mentioned, the other woman was more bitter and mean-spirited by the day.

As for herself, Mackenzie was happy—happier than she'd ever been. She had work she loved, a winery that filled her with joy and a husband who made her feel like the most cherished woman alive.

She paused in the driveway to admire the new addition to the farmhouse. Last year they'd added a big family room, along with a larger office for her and Bruno to share. The one upstairs had been turned into a playroom for Amy. They'd also remodeled the kitchen and bathrooms but hadn't added any bedrooms. Mackenzie had learned her lesson—this house wasn't big enough for her and Bruno to live separate lives. Their daily routines were completely intertwined and that was how they both wanted it.

Once inside, she called out that she was back.

"We're upstairs."

She hurried to join Bruno and found him putting flower clips in their daughter's bright red hair.

"Mommy," her two-year-old said, smiling and holding out her arms. "I'm wearing pink."

Mackenzie took in the frilly dress and matching shoes. "I can see that. You're beautiful."

"You are, too."

"Thank you. Now I'm going to put on my own party dress."

Bruno, handsome as ever in black pants and a dark gray shirt, raised his eyebrows. "Need some help?"

"I know exactly where your 'help' would lead and we don't have time."

Although the thought of what he wanted to do made her a little weak at the knees. Even after nearly three years together, they couldn't get enough of each other. Just last week, while walking the Pepper Bridge vineyard, things had gotten a little out of hand and they'd ended up making love in the truck. A memory that still made her smile.

"Give me fifteen minutes," she said as she hurried toward the master bedroom.

"Don't rush," Bruno called after her. "We have plenty of time. It's our party—we get to arrive when we want."

Mackenzie showered and then blew out her hair. After putting on mascara, she pulled on the dress she'd picked out earlier. Given that she would be on her feet for hours, she chose flats rather than heels, then opened her jewelry box to choose something to wear that night.

One of the things she'd learned in the past couple of years was that Bruno liked to buy her jewelry. Just as surprising, she liked to wear it. She put on an emerald choker and slid on several gold bangles. She always wore her wedding ring and added a pretty diamond cocktail ring to her right hand.

"Donna's here," Bruno said, walking into the closet and pulling her close.

Donna, their full-time nanny-slash-housekeeper, was a godsend. She loved Amy nearly as much as they did and helped keep their busy lives running smoothly.

"She's coming to the party, isn't she?" Mackenzie asked, gazing up into his eyes.

"Yes. She'll stay until Amy's ready to come home."

They went downstairs and collected Donna and Amy before heading to the party. People had already started to arrive. The

386

valet service they'd hired was parking cars and music spilled into the night.

Bruno walked with her, Amy in his arms. The little girl leaned against her father, her soft pink dress a contrast to his darker shirt. A couple of years ago, Mackenzie would have said owning Painted Moon was the best thing that had ever happened to her, but now she knew that was wrong. It was the love that was the true gift in her life. The family she'd built over the years, the daughter she'd given birth to, and the wonderful man who loved her with all his heart. That was what mattered, and tonight was a celebration of all of that. On the best day of the year.

★ ★ ★ ★ ★

Read on for Susan Mallery's own guide to wine

SAUVIGNON BLANC

This is a lighter, fruitier white wine. It's best served chilled and is very drinkable. Try it with goat cheese, either plain or lightly flavored. It pairs well with salads made with a light vinaigrette and summer fruits. Honestly, a glass of sauvignon blanc and a ripe nectarine is pretty amazing.

CHARDONNAY

Chardonnay has changed over the years. Most winemakers are aging chardonnay in stainless-steel barrels rather than in oak, so the flavor is brighter, without the butteriness. I personally love an oaky, buttery chardonnay, but they aren't everyone's taste. Either chardonnay is great with a light-flavored fish, especially if there is a delicious cream or butter sauce. Shrimp scampi is a classic. For a good cheese pairing, try Brie on a piece of French baguette with a glass of chardonnay. And you're welcome!

PINOT NOIR

Try to find one from Oregon. They have the best climate for growing pinot. There are a few good ones in Northern California, but if you see one from Oregon, give it a taste. Pinot noir is a lighter red wine, but often with a hint of sweetness. Nothing overpowering, but that sweet edge gives it the ability to pair with some unexpected foods. What you want is a sweet/savory combination. Pork is perfect, but one of the best pairings is Thai food. Seriously. Try it. For a cheese pairing, either burrata or mozzarella would be great. Add basil, a little tomato and olive oil, and you have something magical.

CABERNET SAUVIGNON

I'll admit, this is a personal favorite for me. I love a wine with a lot of body and flavor. Cabs and cab blends often make their way to the dinner table at my house. Pair your cabernet sauvignon with beef, salmon and heavier chicken dishes. Also tomato-based pasta dishes. I speak from experience when I say cab and a burger are delightful. For a cheese pairing, try Gouda or blue cheese. Last but not least…dark chocolate and cabernet sauvignon. So good and the perfect way to end a meal.

SYRAH

If you can find a Washington State Syrah, please try it. They're really good here. Syrah is a heavier red wine, so it goes well with heavily spiced and braised meats. If you're not sure if you like red wines, don't start here. There's a lot of flavor. For a cheese pairing, try a nice sharp cheddar or a blue or Stilton cheese.

CHAMPAGNE

I know you already know this, but a sparkling wine can be called champagne only if it comes from the Champagne region of France. Otherwise it's sparkling wine. To open a bottle without "popping" the cork, hold the cork in one hand and the base of the bottle in the other. Rotate the base rather than the cork. I know the pop sounds fun, but the flying cork is dangerous. Plus, you lose a lot of champagne and about half the carbonation! Champagne is a magical wine that literally goes with everything. Really! Having something greasy? The champagne will cut through the grease and bring out the best flavors. Fast food? Tacos? Crab puffs? Champagne works. Brunch—well, we already know that one. Birthday cake? Best with champagne.

So those are my suggestions for pairing food and wine. It all comes down to what you like. Don't be afraid to experiment. If you want to know more, see if there's a wine store nearby. They often have tastings on the weekends. Once you've explored the basic wines, you can branch out to other wines and different countries. Cheers!

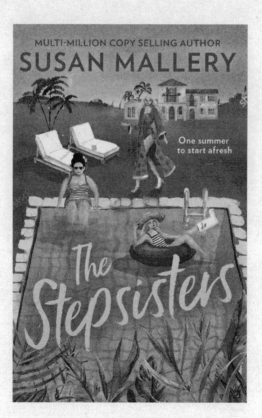

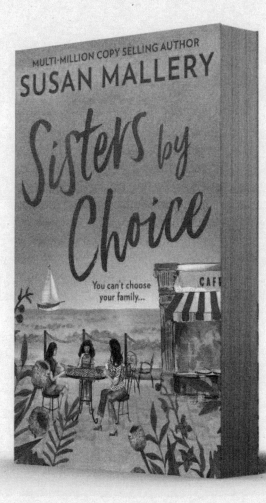

"You know as well [...] of us can't be toge[...] was Geraldine thin[...]

Her blood simmering, Mercedes tossed her head, sending her thick hair rippling down her back. "She was thinking that we're two adults with a job to do. Not to claw and hiss at each other."

Gabe's eyelids lowered as his gaze settled on her lips. "Or to make love," he whispered hoarsely.

Make love.

She didn't know whether it was those two words or the low growl of his voice that sent a sultry shiver down her spine. Either way, she couldn't stop her body from gravitating toward his. "That—won't be on the agenda."

"Unless you want it to be."

Dear Reader,

Have you ever been betrayed by a friend, a loved one? I figure most all of us have at one time or another. It's a crushing, humiliating experience. One that's very hard to move past and forget.

When Mercedes Saddler comes home to the Sandbur after a long stint in the military, she's dealing with past betrayals that have made her sidestep the desire for love and family. But then she meets Gabe Trevino, the Sandbur's new horse trainer, and soon learns that he's not only hiding physical scars, but also scars hidden deep in his heart.

Sounds impossible for this pair to get together, doesn't it? But love is a powerful thing. Once it blooms, it gives us the strength and courage to trust again, to push aside our fears and reach for happiness.

I hope you enjoy reading how Mercedes and Gabe finally learn to open their hearts to each other!

God bless each trail you ride,

Stella

HITCHED TO
THE HORSEMAN

STELLA BAGWELL

Silhouette®

SPECIAL EDITION®

Published by Silhouette Books

America's Publisher of Contemporary Romance

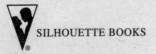

SILHOUETTE BOOKS

ISBN-13: 978-0-373-24923-7
ISBN-10:   0-373-24923-3

HITCHED TO THE HORSEMAN

Printed in U.S.A.

STELLA BAGWELL

sold her first book to Silhouette in November 1985. Now, she still loves her job and says she isn't completely content unless she's writing. She and her husband live in Seadrift, Texas, a sleepy little fishing town located on the coastal bend. Stella says the water, the tropical climate and the seabirds make it a lovely place to let her imagination soar and to put the stories in her head down on paper.

She and her husband have one son, Jason, who lives and teaches high school math in nearby Port Lavaca.

To my husband, Harrell,
my very own horse trainer.
All my love.

Chapter One

What the hell was he doing here?

Gabriel Trevino tilted the bottle of beer to his lips to hide his frown as his eyes cut across the sweeping lawn filled with people. Normally his social events consisted of sharing a beer with his buddies behind the bucking chutes at a local rodeo. This gathering at the Sandbur Ranch could hardly be compared to that sort of tobacco-spitting, curse-laden entertainment. Even the boring parties Sherleen had dragged him to during their ill-fated union paled in comparison to tonight's lavish celebration.

The best that money could buy.

The food, the drinks, the five-piece band, the women with hunks of diamonds glittering at their necks and wrists. Only in Texas, he thought wryly, could a woman justify wearing her best to an outdoor barbecue.

Leaning against the massive trunk of a live oak, he turned

his attention to the portable dance floor that had been erected several yards away from the house. Presently, it was crowded with couples. Some of them old, some young, all of them having a high old time kicking up their heels to the Cotton Eyed Joe.

"What's the matter, Gabe? Don't you like to dance?"

Glancing around, he saw Geraldine Saddler, the matriarch of the Sandbur, approaching him. The tall, elegant woman with silver hair hardly looked like a woman who knew how to burn a brand into a cowhide, but since he'd come to work here at the ranch two months ago, he'd seen her do things that would make even some cowhands squeamish.

"Sometimes," he replied.

Eyeing him keenly, she smiled. "Just not now?"

Embarrassed that his discomfort was showing, Gabe straightened away from the tree and turned to face her.

"It's enough for me just to watch, ma'am."

Kindness and grace emanated from Geraldine and for one brief moment, Gabe wondered what his mother's life would have been like if she'd been exposed to this sort of wealth, if she'd had a nice home, plenty of food and enough money to pay the bills with plenty left over for luxuries.

"This is the first party we've had since you arrived here on the ranch," Geraldine remarked. "I'd like to think you're enjoying yourself."

"Oh. Well, it's a real nice affair, Ms. Saddler. Real nice."

Looping her arm through his, she chuckled. "Come along, Gabe. I want to introduce you to someone."

Not about to offend her by protesting, Gabe allowed the woman to guide him through the milling throng of merrymakers until they reached the patio where several people were standing around in a circle.

Lex Saddler, Geraldine's son and the man who regulated

the cattle sales here at the Sandbur, was one of them. Apparently he'd just said something funny, because a tall, blond woman was laughing rowdily. She was wearing a skimpy white sundress with vivid tropical flowers splashed along the hem. The garment struck her long legs somewhere in the middle of her tanned thighs while the top was held up by tiny straps that could easily be snapped beneath the pressure of his fingers. Unlike most of the other young women present tonight, she wasn't stick-thin. She had enough flesh to fill out the sundress with delicious curves.

As Gabe and the boss lady drew nearer to the group, the blonde turned slowly toward them. Almost instantly, a faint look of unease crossed her features, as though seeing him with Geraldine was like spotting a wolf in a pen full of sheep.

"Mercedes, come here," Geraldine called to her. "I'd like for you to meet someone."

Mercedes. This was Geraldine's daughter, he realized. Lex and Nicci's sister. She was the reason hordes of guests had swarmed upon the Sandbur Ranch tonight. She was the reason he was standing here wishing like hell he was somewhere else.

Excusing herself from the intimate circle, the woman walked over to where they stood. Soft, expensive perfume drifted to his nostrils as he struggled to keep his eyes on her face, rather than the sensual curves of her body.

He sensed Geraldine releasing his arm as she quickly made introductions. "Gabe, this is my daughter, Mercedes. And this is Gabriel Trevino. He's our new head horse trainer here on the ranch."

The woman was young. Much younger than Gabe's thirty-five years, he decided. But her dark blue eyes were eyeing him with a shrewd perception that implied she was mature beyond her years. Pure attraction for the sultry beauty standing before him twisted in his gut.

Tilting the brim of his straw cowboy hat, he inclined his head toward her and she responded by thrusting her hand out to him.

"Nice to meet you, Mr. Trevino."

Closing his hand around hers, he was surprised by her firm shake, the warmth of her fingers.

"My pleasure, Ms. Saddler."

Sure. He was feeling as pleased as a bull in a squeeze chute, Mercedes thought. The man was bored. She could see it all over his face. But oh, my, what a face. Strong square jaw, dimpled chin and a Roman nose that had arrogance written all over it. Storm cloud-gray eyes peered at her from beneath heavy black brows. And his mouth—well, it would have looked delicious if a smile had been curving the corners. Instead, the firm slash was bracketed with faint lines of disdain.

Much to her dismay, her curiosity was instantly aroused by his reaction and she continued to hold on to his hand. Partly because she found touching him pleasant, and partly because she knew it was making him even more uncomfortable.

"So you've taken over Cousin Cordero's job," she mused aloud. "How do you like it here on the Sandbur?"

His dark gray gaze momentarily slanted over to Geraldine, and Mercedes watched a genuine smile cross her mother's face. Apparently she considered this man more than just a hired horse trainer. But then Geraldine was the sort of person who'd always gotten close to her employees, who always focused on the good in people rather than their faults.

"I like it," he answered quietly. "Your family has been very generous and gracious to me."

There wasn't anything particularly distinctive about his voice, yet something about the gravelly tones left her feeling a bit breathless. Silly, she told herself. She wasn't about to give in to the sensation. The feeling would pass. Just like this man would no doubt eventually move on from the Sandbur. He sure didn't look like the establishing-roots kind.

"The Sandbur has always had an excellent *remuda*," Mercedes remarked. "I'm sure you'll enjoy working with them. And Uncle Mingo is a legend in the cutting-horse business."

"Your uncle is a very special man," he agreed.

Her fingers were beginning to sweat against his, forcing Mercedes to drop his hand. As Mercedes shifted her weight on high-heeled sandals, Geraldine began to speak.

"Gabe has worked for years with problematic horses," she proudly explained. "He gets them over difficult issues and teaches them to bond with man rather than fight him. We're very lucky to have Gabe with us."

So the man could tame a wounded beast. Wonder what he did for women, Mercedes asked herself as her gaze slid to his ring finger. Empty. No surprise there. Obviously there wasn't a woman in the background to smooth out his rough edges. He looked as tough as nails and as wild as a rangy mustang.

"That must be challenging," she said to Gabe.

A faint smile curved the corners of his rough-hewn lips, and Mercedes was both ashamed and shocked at the little thrill of attraction that suddenly zipped through her. He was pure male animal. Any woman would be attracted, she tried to reason with herself. But it had been years since any man had stirred her with a prickle of sexual interest. So why was this one stirring up cold ashes?

"That's why I do it," he told her.

Mercedes was studying his face, trying to read beneath the surface of his words when Lex suddenly called to her from across the lawn.

"Hey, Mercedes, come here! A long lost stranger has arrived!"

Glancing over her shoulder, she saw Lex standing with an old classmate of hers. Vernon Sweeney, the nerd of St. Mary's High School. He was sweet and not nearly as exciting as the man standing in front of her. But he was safe. And right now safe was far easier to handle.

Turning back to Gabe, she swiftly explained, "An old friend calls. Will you excuse me?"

His stoic expression didn't falter. "Certainly, Ms. Saddler."

For the next hour, Mercedes mingled, talked, laughed and danced with the endless guests that spilled across the two hundred feet of lawn separating the big house from the old bunkhouse.

She'd been home for just a little over a week and truthfully hadn't had time to get her feet firmly planted back on Sandbur soil when her mother had started planning tonight's event. Mercedes hadn't really been up to this much socializing so soon. She would have preferred to get back in the groove of civilian life before being tossed into a crowd. But this homecoming was important to her mother and she'd not wanted to hurt her feelings for any reason. And these were her friends, she reminded herself. All of them except Gabe Trevino.

In spite of the evening's distractions of dancing, eating and reacquainting herself with old friends, she'd not been able to get the dark horseman off her mind. Which was really very foolish of her. They'd not exchanged more than a handful of sentences, and the few words he'd directed at her had been polite— nothing out of line. Yet she thought there had been an underlying condescension in his attitude, as though he found her boring or, even worse, a spoiled brat. She continued to bristle at the idea as her brother whirled her around the dance floor.

"Still as light on your feet as ever," Lex said with a grin. "Guess all those ballet lessons you took as a child are still paying off."

She laughed. "Poor Mother. I don't think I ever quit fighting her about those."

"You wanted to wear chaps instead of a frilly tutu."

Mercedes sighed. It seemed so long ago since she'd been that innocent age. If only her life had remained that simple and sheltered. "I was a tomboy. She wanted me to be more refined, like Nicci. So did Daddy."

"Nah. Dad loved you any way you wanted to be," he said.

She couldn't help but notice a tiny shadow crossing her brother's handsome face. He still missed their father desperately. Mercedes missed him, too. She'd give anything to have him here with them. But back in 1996, Paul Saddler had died in what the police had called a boating accident. To this day, Lex didn't like to discuss the tragedy or say one way or the other what he believed happened that fateful day on the Gulf. All Mercedes knew was that her father was gone and their lives were far lesser because of it.

"Enjoying yourself, sis?"

She smiled up at him. "Certainly. It's a very nice party. Mother has outdone herself. And Cook still has her special touch, doesn't she? The brisket melted in my mouth."

"Bet you didn't have anything like that over on Diego Garcia."

No. The military air base located on the tiny island in the Indian Ocean didn't cater to parties or home-cooked Texas meals. She'd spent the last two years of her eight-year stint in the Air Force on the isolated island and had to admit that she'd forgotten just what a spoiled, luxurious life she'd once had here on the Sandbur.

"We had turkey and pecan pie on Thanksgiving," she said,

then laughed. "'Course, it had to be flown in—just like everything else."

Lex's smile was full of affection. "We've missed you, honey. Everyone is so glad to have you back home. We're all going to give you hell if you try to leave again. Just keep that in mind if you get the urge to travel."

Her brother's words made her feel wanted, yet at the same time uncomfortable. He and the rest of the family had simply taken it for granted that she was home to stay. But Mercedes wasn't at all sure that her life was meant to be spent on the ranch. Not when old memories and past mistakes continued to haunt her at every turn.

She was trying to push the unsettling issue of her future out of her mind when her gaze slipped past Lex's shoulder to another couple circling the dance floor. So far this evening, she'd not spotted the horse trainer taking a turn to the music. She'd already decided the man wasn't into dancing, but it looked as if she was wrong.

Alice Woodson, an old classmate of Mercedes's, was snuggled up to him, looking as though she was enjoying every second of being in his arms. She would, Mercedes thought with a measure of sarcasm. The woman was man-crazy and had been since junior high.

"Yoo-hoo, sis! The song is over. Want to go another round?"

Realizing the music and her brother's feet had both stopped, Mercedes looked up at him and hoped her wandering thoughts didn't show. "I think I'll sit this one out, Lex. I'm ready to get something to drink."

Looping his arm around her waist, Lex ushered Mercedes off the dance floor. As the two of them walked to the nearest galvanized tub of iced drinks, Mercedes couldn't help but ask, "Do you know why Mother invited Alice?"

Lex frowned. "She's one of your old classmates, isn't she?"

"Yes. But I never cared for her," Mercedes muttered. "Although it seems that someone around here does."

Lex followed Mercedes's gaze as she watched Gabe escort Alice off the dance floor and over to a nearby table.

"Gabe and Alice?" Lex laughed. "He's just being gentlemanly. I don't think Gabe is much into women."

Mercedes frowned as she reached down and plucked a diet soda from among the assortment of drinks. "What do you mean?"

Lex shrugged as though he didn't much want to elaborate, which only made Mercedes even more curious.

Lex finally said, "I think he's had a bad experience and doesn't care to repeat it."

Mercedes could certainly understand that. She'd spent the past eight years dodging men, telling herself that being alone was much better than having her heart ripped out, her trust shattered again.

Popping open the can, she took a sip as she covertly studied the horseman out of the corner of her eye. He was a tall devil, shaped like a wedge with strong broad shoulders and narrow hips. His jeans and Western shirt were probably pieces of clothing that he wore to work every day. Yet he wore the casual garments with so much class that he made all the other men seem ridiculously overdressed.

Mercedes's lips pressed together as she watched Alice place a hand on Gabe's arm. "Then he'd better stay away from Alice. She'll try to devour him."

Lex chuckled. "If you're so worried about the man, why don't you go to the rescue and ask him for a dance?"

Mercedes stared in thoughtful surprise at her brother. Back in high school, she'd been bold enough to ask a guy for a dance, or even a date. But once she'd grown older, once she'd loved and lost, her courage with men had faltered. Then later, when she'd learned the hard way that trusting a man was equal to rolling a dice, her desire to be close to one in any circumstance had dwindled down to nothing.

"Me?" she asked. "No. I'm not the type to ask a man to do anything."

"Getting a little haughty, are we?"

Haughty? If she told her brother how insecure she really felt, he'd be shocked. But she didn't want him to know that his once fearless sister had changed to a cautious soul, that she saw men as things that could hurt her rather than give her pleasure and companionship. "No," she said curtly. "More like getting smart."

With a roll of his eyes, Lex shook his head at her. "Coward."

Why was it that her brother had always known exactly how to push her buttons? He could have said anything else and it would have rolled off her back. But being home on the ranch reminded her that being a Saddler meant facing a challenge head on. Mercedes wanted her brother to see she was still worthy of the family name.

With a toss of her head, she gave Lex a cunning smile and then started off in Gabriel Trevino's direction. After all, the worst the man could do was turn her down. And even if he did, it was only a little dance. She wouldn't let it bother her.

Alice saw her coming first and Mercedes watched a plastic smile form on the other woman's face.

"Mercedes, have I told you tonight how fabulous you look?" Alice asked as Mercedes edged up to the table where the pair were sitting in folding metal chairs. "The Air Force must be getting lax, 'cause you look as if you've spent the past month in a spa. 'Course, it wasn't as if you were toting a gun through the jungle or anything."

Mercedes merely looked at the woman, and Alice, sensing she'd just chewed on her own foot, began to giggle nervously.

"It's great to see you, Alice. I'm glad you could make it tonight," Mercedes said politely, then turned a questioning gaze on Gabe. "Would you care to dance with me, Mr. Trevino? When the band starts playing Bob Wills, I can't keep my feet still and Lex is all tuckered out."

"Yeah, Lex looks plumb beat," Alice said mockingly.

Ignoring the other woman's jab, Mercedes watched Gabe's gray eyes flicker with surprise, but then slowly he rose to his feet and reached for her arm.

He said, "Excuse me," to Alice, and the woman made some sort of reply, but Mercedes didn't hear it. Her ears were roaring with her own heartbeat as the two of them walked toward the elevated dance floor.

"What was that all about?" he asked once they were a few steps away from Alice. "You have a grudge against that woman?"

"Not really. I just thought you ought to know she's a man-eater. She's already been through two husbands and she hasn't celebrated her thirtieth birthday yet."

To her surprise, he chuckled.

"Do I look like a man who can't take care of himself?"

He looked like a man who could take care of anything. But she'd only just met the man; she was hardly ready to give him a gushing compliment.

"I don't know. Can you?"

"I've survived thirty-five years," he said curtly. "I'm doing okay."

By the time they reached the dance floor, the western swing number had finished and the lead singer began to sing a slow ballad about lost love. It wasn't the sort of dance she'd intended to have with Gabe Trevino, but there wasn't much she could do about it now except step into his arms and move to the music.

"Why did you ask me to dance?" he asked bluntly as his hand settled at the back of her waist.

His arms were rock-hard and though she tried to keep space between the front of her body and his, her breasts brushed against his chest and her thigh slid between his. In spite of their slow pace, she felt a desperate need for oxygen as her body began to hum with excitement.

"Actually, Lex challenged me to ask you," she said honestly. "You see, I was worried about you and Alice. He thought I ought to rescue you. So did I."

"I don't know whether to feel flattered or insulted."

And she didn't know why, after several years of celibacy, this stranger had woken her sleeping libido. "I wouldn't bother with either," she said as casually as she could. "It's just a dance."

Even though her head was turned to one side, she knew he was looking down at her. She could feel his gaze examining the side of her face, then dropping to the V neckline of her dress. At the same time, the hand at the back of her waist slid upward until his fingers splayed against her bare back.

From somewhere deep inside her, a flame unexpectedly flickered, then burst into an all-out inferno. Dismayed that she was reacting to him so strongly, she could only thank God that it was dark and he couldn't see the droplets of sweat collecting on her upper lip.

"I thought maybe you were just feeling generous," he said close to her ear. "Wanting to give the hired help a dance with royalty."

Easing her head back, she glowered at him. "Look, just so you know, I don't think of myself as a princess or you as hired help. You have a chip on your shoulder or something?"

Gabe had never felt sorry for himself or his position in life. He was proud of who and what he was. Maybe he needed to make that clear to her. "I just don't need for you to feel sorry for me, Ms. Saddler. I like myself."

She surprised him by laughing. Not just one short sound of amusement, but a long laugh filled with joy. Yet instead of feeling annoyed with her, the infectious sound put a grin on his face.

"Please, call me Mercedes. And just to set your mind at ease, Gabe, you're the last person I would think needs sympathy."

She felt like a dream in his arms, he thought. A soft warm dream where one pleasure seeped into another and every spot he touched thrilled him just that much more.

He struggled to control himself. Hell, just because it had been a long time since he'd had a woman didn't mean this one was supposed to turn him into a randy buck, he thought with self-disgust. So what if she was as sexy as sin? That didn't mean he needed her any closer than she already was. No, sir, he'd already learned the hard way the price he'd have to pay for a woman like her.

"I heard Alice say something about the Air Force. Is that why you've been away from the ranch? Because you were in the Air Force?"

"Eight years," she answered. "My job was intelligence gathering."

It just didn't fit, Gabe pondered. A woman like her didn't need to work, much less go into the strict, disciplined life of the military. He had to admit that he admired her ambition. Even more, he had to admit that he wanted to know what was really behind those deep blue eyes staring back at him.

"What made you decide to enter the military?"

One of her shoulders lifted and fell with nonchalance, but he noticed that her gaze deliberately swung away from his.

"You and I are more alike than you think, Gabe. I like a challenge, too."

He didn't figure she was giving him the complete reason. But then he hadn't expected her to spill her life's story through one slow dance.

"What about you?" she asked. "How did you come to be here on the Sandbur?"

"I met Cordero at a horse seminar over in Louisiana. He liked my work and asked me if I'd be interested in settling here."

"And you were," she stated the obvious.

"Here I am."

She seemed on the verge of asking him more when the song suddenly ended.

"Want to go another round?" he asked.

She smiled. "I really shouldn't ignore the other guests who've come to see me tonight."

"Then thank you very much for the dance." He lifted the back of her hand to his lips and pressed a kiss on the soft skin.

Wide-eyed, she asked, "Did you give one of those to Alice, too?"

A faint grin curved the corner of his mouth. "No. She didn't dance nearly as well as you."

She studied him for several long, awkward moments and then smiled impishly. "Oh. Well, I won't wipe it off, then," she said brightly. Before he could make any sort of reply, she pulled out of his embrace and hurried off the dance floor.

Gabe stared after her and wondered why he felt as though he'd just taken a hard tumble from the saddle.

Chapter Two

Once the party finally ended, Mercedes didn't get into bed until the wee hours of the morning. Though she was exhausted, her sleep ended abruptly when she woke up long before daylight, her body drenched in sweat, her senses disoriented.

Swinging her legs over the side of the bed, she pressed a hand to her damp face.

You're okay, Mercedes. You're in your old bedroom on the Sandbur. The bedroom where you played as a child, had sleepovers with friends.

Dropping her hand from her bleary eyes, she gazed around at the shadows shrouding the walls and furniture while she waited for the axis of her brain to spin in the right direction.

She'd been dreaming, she realized, but not of something pleasant or peaceful. The dream had involved a man and a horse inside a corral. She'd been watching from the fence, calling out to him, trying to warn him that he was about to be hurt. The horse had charged, knocked the man down, then reared and viciously brought his front hoofs down on the man's back.

Gabe! She'd been dreaming about Gabe Trevino. The realization stunned her almost as much as the vivid dream had shocked her senses. She'd not gone to bed thinking of the man much. Well, maybe that tiny kiss on the back of her hand *had* fluttered through her thoughts right before she'd gone to sleep, she corrected herself. But her mind certainly hadn't been consumed by the man.

With a rough sigh, she rose from the bed and stumbled into the bathroom. She might as well shower and start the day, because there was no way she could go back to sleep now.

A few minutes later, Mercedes, dressed in jeans, boots and a cool summer shirt, walked through the quiet house. In the kitchen, she realized that she'd even beaten Cook out of bed. The room was still dark.

For a brief moment, she considered making a pot of coffee, then decided she'd wait until the rest of the family was up to enjoy it with her.

Instead, she let herself out of the house through a back exit and made her way through the dark early morning to the horse barn. Across the way, she could see a faint light glowing in the bunkhouse. The wranglers would be stirring soon, catching their mounts and saddling them up for the day's work ahead.

Mourning doves were cooing and mockingbirds were beginning to flitter to life among the live oaks. There was a peaceful beauty to the ranch that Mercedes had always loved. Even when the ranch yard bustled with life, it was a poetry of sights and sounds. The hammer of the farrier, the bawl of a calf, the nicker of a horse, the sun coming up and the moon going down.

From generation to generation and year after year, her family had worked and carved this ranch from prickly pear patches and endless stretches of mesquite trees. As for Mercedes, she'd been born here in her parents' bedroom.

Yes, she'd been rooted here. But eight long years ago, she'd pulled up those roots and run as fast and hard as she could. Now she wondered if she'd made a mistake by coming back, trying to make this her home once again, trying to pretend that she could fall back into the life she'd led before her college life and John's big deception, before her stint at Peterson AFB and the humiliating mistake she carried from there.

Trying to shake away the nagging questions, she walked on to the barn and climbed up on a board fence that corralled a small herd of yearling horses. From a lofty seat on the top rail, she watched the colts and fillies play in the cool morning air until she heard a footfall behind her.

Glancing over her shoulder, she was more than surprised to see the man of her disturbing dream propping his shoulder against the board fence. He was dressed in a dark blue denim shirt with pearl snaps, the standard fare that cowboys had worn for decades. Funny how the shirt looked tailored just for him. Some men tried to play the part, while others were naturals. She realized that Gabe was one of those naturals, the epitome of all things Western right down to the square toes of his brown cowboy boots.

"You're up very early," he remarked.

"So are you. Today is Saturday," she pointed out. "Don't tell me that you start your workday this early on a Saturday."

Even though he had no way of knowing that she'd dreamed about him, the fact that he'd shouldered his way into her subconscious thoughts was enough to put a sting of embarrassment on her cheeks.

He jerked his head toward the pen full of horses. "They don't know it's a weekend."

He was right. Nothing stopped on the ranch. At the least, livestock had to be fed and cared for every day of the week.

She drew in a long breath and let it out as she guided her gaze back to the pen of horses. "Are all of these broken to the halter?" she asked.

"Yes."

"What are you doing with them now?"

"Getting them used to blankets and saddles on their backs. When they get closer to two, I'll put someone lightweight like you on them. Ever ride a green horse?"

Even though he was standing on the ground and a good foot away from her, his presence was a huge thing, crowding toward her, making her completely aware of her femininity.

She answered, "I've ridden a few outlaws before. But as for green horses, only once. Daddy forbade us to climb on anything that wasn't completely broken to ride, but I didn't always do what I was told."

"Imagine that."

Even though she didn't glance at him, she could hear a smile in his voice, and the sound warmed her, drew her to him.

"Yeah. I got bucked off and broke my arm. I missed the whole softball season at school that year. I learned about green horses the hard way."

Apparently she'd always been an outdoors person, Gabe thought. The notion surprised him, although it shouldn't have. She'd been in the military, after all. She'd had to go through rigorous physical preparation to graduate basic training. Still, she seemed so womanly, so soft, that he couldn't imagine her in camouflaged fatigues or wearing a pair of spurs and chaps.

"Don't feel badly, we've all been dumped," he told her.

She remained quiet and after a few moments, Gabe glanced up to see her wiping her hands down her thighs as she rose from her seat on the fence. She was wearing a blue and white patterned shirt with short sleeves. A white scarf was twisted and tied around her thick hair. Once she was standing on the ground, he could see her face was void of makeup, yet it held as much color and beauty as the sun breaking over the treetops.

Smiling faintly, she said, "I'd better get back to the house. I haven't had any coffee yet, or breakfast."

"I can't do anything about the breakfast, but I've just made a pot of fresh coffee. Would you care to join me for a cup?"

She glanced questioningly around her. "Here?"

He jerked his head toward the barn. "I've got an office inside the barn."

Surprise arched her brows. "I thought Cordero's office was over by the cattle barn."

"It's still there. But I like it here—keeps me closer to the foaling mares. And your mother kindly supplied me with a few things to make it comfortable."

She gestured toward the building situated several yards behind him. "I'd like to see this new office of yours," she agreed. "And I'd especially like the coffee."

Built when the Sandbur had first become a full-fledged ranch in 1900, the barn was one of the few original structures that had weathered more than a century of the extreme climate of South Texas. Because the building was made of heavy lumber, it stayed cooler in the summer and warmer in the winter than some of the newer barns that were built from corrugated iron. It had always been one of Mercedes's favorite spots on the ranch.

As the two of them stepped inside the cavernous building, Gabe took Mercedes by the arm and guided her down a long, wide alleyway to a closed door. Gabe opened it and gestured for her to enter.

The moment she stepped into the room, she was immediately impressed with the large teacher's desk and office chair, the computer, fax and copier, telephone, refrigerator and small cooking element. "Why, this used to be a tack room," she said with amazement. "How did you make such a transformation?"

"Me and some of the hands partitioned off part of the feed room and moved all the riding equipment in there." He gestured for her to take a seat on the long couch running against one wood-paneled wall. "Sit down. You might recognize that couch. It came from the den in the big house. Your mother said she needed a new one anyway. I think she was just being generous. During foaling season, I need a place to stretch out from time to time."

While she made herself comfortable on the couch, Gabe poured coffee into two foam cups.

"Cream or sugar? Or both?" he asked.

"Cream. Just a splash. But I can do it."

She started to rise from her seat, but he motioned her back down. "I can manage."

Back at the couch, Gabe handed her the steaming coffee and then took a seat on the cushion next to her. Other than Geraldine Saddler, no woman had set foot in his private domain until now. It seemed strange and even more distracting for Mercedes to be sitting only inches away from him.

"Mmm. Thank you," she murmured as she lifted the steaming drink to her lips.

As he sipped from his own cup, he realized he shouldn't have invited her in here. In fact, he shouldn't have danced with her last night. Because even now he was assaulted with the memories of her curvy body brushing temptingly against his, the scent of her skin, the softness of her sigh as it skittered against the side of his neck. He couldn't remember a time that any woman had left such an indelible impression on him, and that could only mean trouble. Mercedes was rich, strong and independent—just like the woman who'd married him, then smashed him into useless pieces.

"So you're home now," he said. "What do you plan to do with your time?"

She stared into her cup rather than at him. "I—I'm not sure yet. For starters, I'm going to give myself a few days to adjust to civilian life."

She could afford to do that, Gabe thought. In fact, she could afford to do anything she wanted to do. He couldn't imagine having *that* much financial security. Sherleen had been rich, before and after they'd married. Not nearly as rich as Mercedes or her family, but wealthy enough. As her husband, Gabe had never considered his wife's money as his, too. In fact, he'd never wanted it and had done his best to pay his own way throughout their short years together. A man of any stock didn't want to be labeled as being kept by his wife. And to Gabe, riches weren't measured by the balance in a bank account. Unfortunately, his ex-wife had thought differently. Now he found himself attracted to another rich woman. What the hell was the matter with him, anyway? He'd learned the hard way that he and wealthy women didn't mix.

He said, "I guess that was a stupid question on my part, anyway."

Her eyes were full of questions as they roamed his face and Gabe realized he needed to be more careful or his personal feelings would show.

"Why do you say that?"

What the hell, he thought. He wasn't going to tiptoe around

this woman as though she were royalty. "Nothing. Just that— well, it's not like you have to go out and find a job."

Disgust turned the corners of her lips downward as she rose from her seat to amble around the tiny room. "I can't read your mind, Gabe. So I don't have any idea what sort of impressions you have about me. But I can assure you that I don't plan to sit on my hands."

"I wouldn't think so," he drawled with a bit of sarcasm. "It might flatten them."

She shot him a droll look and then chuckled. "Smart mouth. I'll bet as a teenager you gave your mother fits."

A dark cloud suddenly shadowed his thoughts. Though he reminded himself that this woman was teasing, that she couldn't know about Jenna Trevino's death, it still hurt to think of growing up without his mother and the horrible way she'd left this world.

"No. I didn't give her fits," he said curtly. "She was in her grave."

Mercedes couldn't have felt more awful. She wanted to walk behind the desk and crawl inside the knee hole, but hiding would hardly help her now. "Oh, boy, I messed up there, didn't I?" she murmured more to herself than to him. Glancing regretfully at the man, she tried again, "Gabe, I— You're a young man. I just assumed that your mother was still alive. Forgive me."

She watched him draw in a long breath, then release it, and from the strained expression on his face, she got the notion that he felt more awkward than even she did.

"Forget it, Mercedes. You didn't know."

Afraid she'd worsen her foot-in-mouth disease with any sort of reply, she waited for him to say more, anything that would explain how his mother died. But after several more clumsy moments passed in silence, she decided it best to change the subject completely.

Resting a hip on the corner of the desk, she said, "So. What do you use the computer for? Keeping track of sales?"

"Yes. And I also keep a file for every horse on the Sandbur. It's a big help in keeping track of their breeding, farrier visits, vaccinations, injuries, progress in their training. You get the picture."

Mercedes was very impressed. Her cousin Cordero was a good horse trainer, but he'd never been that meticulous about keeping data. "You sound like a doctor keeping updates on his patients' charts."

"Exactly. I'll show you."

Leaving the couch, he walked past her and went to stand behind the desk. Mercedes swiveled around to see him switching on the computer. While the machine whirred to life, she used the time to study him from beneath a pair of lowered lashes.

Apparently he'd not taken the time to shave this morning. A black stubble of beard covered his jaws, upper lip and chin. His hair, what she could see of it beneath the brim of his hat, curled damply against the back of his neck, as though it hadn't been long since he'd stepped out of the shower. The scent of soap and musk and man all swirled together and drifted across the small space between them.

Stirred in spite of herself, she looked away and made a steeple of her hands. For the past eight years, she'd worked around men on a daily basis. Some of them had been good-looking, even sexy. A few had become buddies. And one— Well, she'd thought Drew was a very special friend until he'd proved not to be a friend at all. But even before his betrayal, she'd never found his flirtatious smile and rumbling laugh this distracting. He'd never had her thinking of hot nights, sweaty sheets or even a slow, wet kiss the way this man was doing now.

Mercedes believed the sexual side of her had died along with her dreams of finding love. Yet for some reason she couldn't understand, Gabe Trevino seemed to be shaking her back to life.

"Okay," he said, breaking into her thoughts. "Here's a chart on He's A Peppy Charge. Take a look."

Attempting to shake away the sensual fog settling over her, Mercedes placed her coffee mug on the desk then walked around to stand next to him. With every ounce of strength in her, she forced herself to focus on the monitor screen rather than him.

"Everything is here," she observed. "His birthday, family tree, color and markings, vet visits, blood tests." She scanned the data until she reached Gabe's personal comments and then she read aloud, "Deceptive charmer. Tries to buck if not completely warmed up. Great speed and athleticism. Needs experienced cowboy on his back."

A provocative smile curved her lips as she turned her head to look at him. "Does that mean you?"

The moment she saw his eyes narrow, Mercedes knew she'd struck a nerve and nudged him over the invisible line that had been acting as a polite barrier between them.

As he moved closer, she sucked in a bracing breath.

"Just what are you doing here, anyway, Ms. Saddler?"

Gabe had never intended to let this woman provoke him. From the moment he'd spotted her on the fence, he'd planned to appear cool and collected, even if his insides felt like a boiler on the verge of exploding. But now the teasing glint in her sexy blue eyes made him forget all about his earlier determination. Now his focus refused to go beyond the moist pout of her lips, the idea of how she would taste and feel.

"Uh—what do you mean?" she asked hoarsely.

Before Gabe could stop himself, he wrapped his hand around her forearm and tugged her against him. As her breast flattened against his chest, he could feel her heart flutter, and his own begin to pound.

"I mean, here," he clipped out. "At the horse barn. Where you knew you would find me."

Gabe hated the way her soft curves aroused him, yet at the same time, he couldn't deny the excitement rushing through his veins.

Scowling at him, she said, "I walked down to the horse pen because it's a nice, cool morning and I wanted to get out of the house. This is the last place I thought you would be."

Her lame excuse filled his snort with a mix of humor and sarcasm. "Really? This is where I work. Where did you think I'd be?"

"In bed. Where everyone else is right now!"

Her nostrils flared like a filly being circled by a stallion, and Gabe felt a hot, feral flame flicker deep inside him.

"Everyone is in bed—but you and me," he pointed out lowly.

Her tongue darted out to moisten her lips and it was all Gabe could do to keep from closing the last bit of space between their faces. "If you think—"

"I think a whole lot of things," he bluntly interrupted, "but I know we're both thinking about this."

Mercedes wasn't sure if he tugged her forward or if she simply wilted against him, but the next thing she knew his mouth was hot and heavy on hers, his arms were wrapped around her shoulders, anchoring her upper body against his.

The intimate connection was such a shock to Mercedes's senses that the thought of resisting didn't have time to enter her mind. And then as his lips began to search and plunder her mouth, she realized that she didn't want to resist. She didn't want to do anything but stand in the circle of his arms and drink in the heady taste of him.

Somewhere outside, she heard a rooster crow, a horse snort, another squeal. Inside the room a clock was *tick, tick, ticking.* Or was that the sound of her heart beating in her ears? She couldn't tell anymore. Her senses were beginning to melt into a useless puddle.

A keening moan gurgled in the back of her throat as her hands searched for some sort of support. It came in the way of his hard shoulders, and her fingers were about to latch over them when he suddenly jerked back from her.

The abrupt separation of their bodies tilted Mercedes's footing and left her snatching a steadying hold on the edge of the desk. As she stared at him in stunned fascination, she felt her lips burning, her lungs dragging in long ragged breaths.

After several hard swallows, she finally managed to ask, "What—what was that all about?"

His jaw hardened as his gray gaze swept over her flushed face. "To let you know that I don't play games, Mercedes. Not with you. Not with any woman. Try it again and I promise you—you'll get burned."

Straightening her shoulders, she lifted her chin. "Pompous ass," she snarled at him. "Do you think every woman that gets within speaking distance of you wants to crawl into your bed?"

Without warning, his hand shot out and cuffed around her upper arm. Mercedes glanced down at his fingers biting into her flesh and then she saw them—tough welts of jagged scars on top of his wrist and disappearing beneath the cuff of his shirt.

Somewhere, somehow he'd been terribly injured. The visual evidence, even the mere thought, shocked Mercedes almost as much as his kiss had, and for long moments she couldn't tear her eyes away from his brown skin.

"Gabe, your—"

Before she could say more, he jerked his hand away and quickly stepped back from her.

"Get out of here, Mercedes," he gritted. "Go find some other man to amuse you."

She couldn't believe that only seconds before sympathy for the man had swept through her. Right now, she'd love to slap his jaw.

"In case you've forgotten, the Sandbur is my home. I'm not going to tiptoe around you as though you're something special. If I want to come here to the horse barn or anywhere else on the ranch where you just happened to be, I will! And if you don't like it, you can just—go!"

Not about to wait for any sort of reply from the man, Mercedes stomped out of the little office and marched down the alleyway of the barn. By now, sunlight was slanting through the door of the cavernous building, shedding light on the stalls lined against both walls. Several horses were sticking their heads over gates, watching her movements. Under normal circumstances, she would have stopped and greeted every animal. As it was, her lips were on fire, her eyes stinging with tears, and she couldn't get out of the barn fast enough.

Back in the tiny office, Gabe switched off the computer and slumped into the desk chair, then immediately jumped back up and grabbed his coffee cup. As he splashed more hot liquid over the portion that had cooled, he muttered several choice curse words at himself. He didn't know what in hell had come over him or possessed him to grab the woman, much less kiss her.

She'd done nothing more than tease him. And she'd done it gently, at that. Nothing she'd said or done had warranted his behavior. Even if she had come down to the barn purposely to see him, even if she *was* using him to amuse herself, that didn't mean he should have taken the bait. He liked to think he was older and wiser than to let his head be turned by a pretty face.

But the moment she'd stood next to him, her face only inches away, her scent drifting over him, tantalizing every cell in his body, his common sense had crawled out the door. Now just the memory of her lips beneath his, the feel of her hands moving against his chest was enough to leave him hard and frustrated.

So what are you going to do now, Gabe?

Remind himself that he was nothing more than a hired hand and get to work.

Chapter Three

Later that morning, Mercedes was in her bedroom, trying to motivate herself to finish unpacking the boxes that were stacked in one corner. So far, she'd done little more than hang a few garments in the armoire.

What was she really doing here on the ranch, anyway? she asked herself for the umpteenth time. Was she really home to stay, or was she simply using the ranch as a launching pad to some other job at some other place?

Sighing wistfully, she dropped the slinky blouse back to the open box lying upon the bed and walked over to a huge arched window. Since her upstairs bedroom was on the west end of the house, the window was partially shaded by the enormous limbs of a live oak, yet through the break in the leaves she could see a part of the ranch yard and a small portion of the horse barn. Just looking at the old barn and recalling her encounter with Gabe Trevino was enough to make her blush.

Unwittingly, her fingertips lifted to her lips. She'd never been kissed like that before, as though she were a piece of meat and he a starving animal. It was embarrassing to think how much the kiss had excited her, had shaken the very core of her womanhood.

She'd thought John had been an adept lover. She'd believed that she would never meet another man whose touch would sweep her senses into such a mushy state of bliss. But Gabe had done that and more. Those few moments in his arms had left her feeling like a hungry tigress. She'd wanted to tear at his clothes and her own. She'd wanted to surrender to him completely. It was frightening to think how he'd woken her sleeping sexuality and turned it into a sizzling libido.

"Darling, you haven't even gotten started with these boxes. Would you like for Alida to come up and help you?"

At the sound of her mother's voice, Mercedes turned away from the window to see that Geraldine had walked into the room. Concern was on her face as her gaze flicked from her daughter to the still packed boxes.

"Mother, I didn't have a maid in the Air Force. I hardly need one now."

Geraldine scowled. "No need to get huffy. I was just offering. Or would you rather I help you?"

"No. I can manage," she insisted. Spotting the faint look of hurt on her mother's face, she crossed the space between them and pecked a kiss on her smooth cheek. "I don't mean to sound sharp, Mother. I'm tired, that's all. This past week has been a little hectic. I don't think I've caught up from the jet lag yet."

Mercedes didn't go on to say that having a maid in the house made her feel guilty and overly pampered, especially after some of the pitiful sights she'd endured while on rescue missions in America and abroad. Floods, fires, earthquakes. The U.S. military stepped in to help when natural catastrophes shredded people's lives and left them homeless and frightened. In those cases, having necessities was the difference between living or dying. The word *maid* didn't exist in that reality.

Geraldine turned a sympathetic smile on her daughter. "And the party last night went on forever," she conceded. "I guess I should have waited to throw it. But everyone has been so excited about you coming home. I didn't want to wait."

Nodding that she understood, Mercedes went over to the queen-size bed and sat on the edge of the mattress. "I'm glad you didn't wait. I enjoyed seeing everyone again."

Geraldine walked over to a nearby armchair and sank into it. As she crossed her long legs, Mercedes couldn't help thinking that her mother had hardly aged the past eight years. She was quite slim and shapely for a woman of sixty-four. Her complexion was tanned and smooth, while her silver hair sparkled with life. This past year, she'd started to date again, a widowed Texas senator. Mercedes admired her courage and was especially glad that she'd never given up on life after her husband had died.

The way you've given up on men? Maybe she had given up on men, she told herself, but she had good reason—they weren't to be trusted.

"Darling, we've not done anything to this room since you left for the Air Force," Geraldine commented as she looked around the room. "Maybe you'd like a change. New paint? Drapes? Furniture?"

The walls of the room were a soft, textured pink and the furniture was antique heavy oak that had been here since her grandparents' heyday. She didn't want to change a thing about the room. It was *herself* that Mercedes needed to change. But she didn't have a clue how to start. How did a person forget pain and betrayal? How could she ever have a family of her own if she couldn't trust a man to take out the garbage on time, much less take care of her heart?

Mercedes's gaze joined her mother's as it traveled around the walls that were crowded with photos and paintings, then down to the Spanish tile scattered with thick looped throw rugs. "There's nothing wrong with this room, Mother. I don't want it changed."

Seeming not to hear her, Geraldine went on, "Well, since Nicci's moved out, you could take over her room if you like it better."

Now that Nicci had married Ridge and given birth to a new daughter, Sara Rose, her sister's bedroom was empty. As empty as Mercedes's heart.

"No," Mercedes said flatly. "I'm happy here."

Geraldine's lips pursed together. "You hardly look as if you're happy, Mercedes. And I don't mean to push you, but frankly, I'm worried about you, honey. I thought—" She paused and shook her head with frustration. "Well, let's just say that I hoped coming home would make you feel differently about things."

Mercedes plucked at the knobby bedspread. "What things?"

"Well, dammit, I'm not going to beat around the bush with you. I never have, so I don't guess I should start now. I'm talking about that bastard—John. And don't tell me that you're still not moping about him. I would have thought that after eight years, you would have gotten the man out of your system. But no, I still catch you staring off into space with that my-world-has-ended look. Frankly, Mercedes, I'm sick of seeing it."

Geraldine's angry words snapped Mercedes's head up.

"That's not true! I'm not moping about John Layton. Good Lord, Mother, it's like you just said, that was more than eight years ago!"

"But you haven't forgotten."

How could she forget the most humiliating, heartbreaking experience of her life? John had been her history professor at the University of Texas. He'd been a quiet, serious man, highly intellectual and handsome to boot. When he'd first shown a romantic interest in Mercedes, she'd been completely bowled over by his charm. Later, as their relationship had progressed into a full-blown affair, she'd truly believed that he loved her and wanted to marry her. She'd thought that the two of them together could conquer the world. God, she'd looked at him and the world through rose-colored glasses.

Sighing, she tried to explain. "Look, Mother, I believed John was the love of my life. I thought he was going to be my husband. The father of my children!"

"Instead, you learned in an offhanded way that he already had a wife with a child on the way. Believe me, Mercedes, that would have been enough to wipe all memories of love or anything else from my mind. Apparently, you're different from me. I guess I'm just too hard-hearted to let some no-account, playboy college professor ruin my life."

It was just like her mother to lay the whole affair out in such blunt terms. She didn't play favorites with her children. She treated them all with the same tough love.

"I don't still care for the man, if that's what you're thinking, Mother. In fact, I couldn't care less what has happened to him. It's just that the whole thing with John made me see how easy it is to be duped by a man. I'm not sure that I'll ever be able to trust another one."

Mercedes didn't go on to explain to her mother that John's deception was only a part of her reluctance to enter another relationship with a man. Three years ago, she'd been terribly betrayed by Airman Drew Downy. Because of him, her security status had been lowered and she'd been reprimanded severely for her lapse in judgment. It had taken months of hard work for her to regain the trust of her superior officers. All because she'd trusted a man. Because she'd believed he was a good friend and had truly cared for her. But instead of being loyal, Drew had blown the whistle on her for sharing classified secrets that *he* had prompted her to disclose. The memory still made her cringe with humiliation and hurt.

Even though Drew hadn't been her lover, Mercedes had believed their relationship might grow and blossom into something lasting. When she finally figured out that he was only using her to show himself in a positive light, she'd been crushed and shocked that she'd once again so misjudged a man. After that, she'd gone numb and so guarded that she was reluctant to even share the time of day with a male counterpart in a social context.

"God help you," Geraldine murmured.

Trying to swallow away the ball of bitterness in her throat, Mercedes thrust a hand through her thick hair. "Mother, I have other things on my mind. And they hardly revolve around finding a man."

Looking extremely disgusted now, Geraldine tapped her fingers against the arm of the chair. "Okay. So you want to put sex and love and marriage last on your to-do list. What's first?"

Mercedes quickly glanced away from her mother as this morning's encounter with Gabe danced through her thoughts. Sex had hardly been the last thing on her mind when he'd planted that sizzling lock on her lips. But pure sex was all it had been, she told herself. And she wasn't planning on letting it happen again. Not if she could help it.

Trying to shake the memory away, she said firmly, "I want to be productive, Mother. Useful. I want to feel as though I'm where I'm supposed to be."

Clearly concerned with her daughter's attitude, Geraldine left the chair and came to stand in front of Mercedes. "Honey, I know with your training in intelligence you could easily get a job most anywhere you wanted. You'd be making good money—not that you need it, but you'd have it to fall back on if, God forbid, the ranch ever slid into a losing hole. But I'm not all that sure that throwing yourself into a government job is what you really need at this time in your life."

Not bothering to hide her unsettled thoughts, Mercedes held her palms up in a helpless gesture. "I'm not sure it's what I need, either. But what am I supposed to do, Mother? I'm not the idle type. And I can't simply chase cows from morning 'til night."

And she sure as heck wasn't going to work with the horses and face Gabe Trevino every day, Mercedes thought. Her peace of mind would be torn to shreds.

"There's more to do around here than chase cows! Ask your brother. Ask your cousin Matt. They work themselves to the ground every day to keep this place in the black. Maybe it's time someone else in the family offered to step up to the plate and do their part!"

Mercedes was cut to the quick by her mother's retort, and she couldn't utter one word in reply. Instead, she rose from the bed and brushed past Geraldine. At one end of the room, rows of wide wooden shelves held souvenirs and mementos from her past. A 4-H trophy for best heifer at the state fair.

Another for horsemanship. A rhinestone tiara from when she'd won Miss Junior Rodeo for Goliad County. A pair of scarred ballet slippers. A sheet of music she'd played in a piano recital. A dried rose taken from her father's coffin.

There were many more bits and pieces of her life scattered across the shelves and as she gazed at them, she tried to rein in her exploding emotions. Her parents had given her a wonderful childhood and opened doors to any path she'd wanted to take. These years she'd been away, she'd not stopped to think that her family might be expecting her to eventually give back to the ranch. Instead, she'd been selfishly focused on her own career.

"If you're trying to make me feel guilty, Mother, then you've certainly succeeded," she murmured hoarsely.

Mercedes had hardly gotten the words out when she felt her mother's hands on her shoulders, gently pulling her around.

"Mercedes!" she scolded softly. "I'm not trying to make you feel guilty. I'm sorry if I did. But I *am* trying to jar you. To wake you up out of this foggy sleep you've been in ever since you left the Sandbur."

Pressing her lips to a firm line, Mercedes swung her head back and forth. Eight years ago, shortly after she'd learned the truth about John, she'd met an Air Force recruiter on campus. He'd made the idea of serving her country and acquiring a new career sound exciting and challenging, just what she'd needed to take her mind off the miserable mistakes she'd made. Initially, she supposed she had used the military as a way to get away from campus and the Sandbur. She'd had her fill of her family watching her with sympathy and treating her as though she had an illness instead of a broken heart. But once she'd gotten through basic training at Lackland Air Force Base, her whole attitude toward her enlistment had taken on a different meaning. Now, her service as an airman was important to her and was something she was definitely proud of. The past eight years had shaped and strengthened her. She wanted her mother and the rest of her family to see that she could bear up under any pressure.

"I've hardly been living in a coma," she muttered.

Geraldine rolled her eyes. "Okay, maybe I should have said you've been hiding in your job. You loved being on Diego Garcia because the tiny island was totally away from the rest of the world. Away from the rest of us regular folks doing the mundane task of living. I actually think if you'd been given the choice, you would have stayed there forever."

Her mother's mistaken assumptions fueled Mercedes's temper. If she'd wanted to stay, as her mother had so bluntly suggested, she could have reenlisted. More than that, she could have easily continued to make the Air Force her career. But her heart had been crying out to come home. It had been longing for more than simply going through each day carrying out her duties as an airman. She'd thought her mother understood, but apparently she didn't. Mercedes couldn't stop herself from raising her voice, "And what the hell do you think I was doing there? Drinking margaritas and strumming a guitar beneath a palm tree?"

Temper sparked in Geraldine's eyes. "Your job. While conveniently forgetting the rest of your life."

Mercedes stared at her, aghast that their conversation had escalated into such a verbal war. Over the years, the two of them had argued before, but this time Geraldine's barbed words stung her worse than ever.

Mercedes was wondering what to say, or if she should even make any sort of retort, when her mother solved the problem by turning and walking out of the room.

Her eyes stinging with tears, Mercedes went over to the closet and pulled out her favorite pair of old cowboy boots. She had to get out of the house. She needed to see the ranch and remember why it had pulled her back to Texas in the first place.

Later that afternoon, Gabe stepped out of the horse barn carrying a saddle on his shoulder when the sound of cantering hoofbeats caught his attention. He looked around to see Mercedes and her mount flying toward the ranch yard. Dust boiled behind the blue roan as she steered him toward a nearby corral, then skidded the animal to a stop a nose-length away from the board fence.

His jaw slack, Gabe watched her leap from the saddle and land on the ground like an agile cat. Coming from a ranching background, he'd expected Mercedes to be able to ride, but not like Annie Oakley! Was there anything the woman couldn't do?

He walked over to one of the wranglers working in the yearling pen. "Hey, James, is that Mouse that Ms. Saddler is riding?" he asked.

The young cowboy glanced up from the rope halter he was trying to untangle and stared across the pen to where Mercedes was now slowly leading the horse around in a large circle.

"Yep, that's him. She took off on him this mornin' sometime before lunch."

Gabe silently cursed. The horse was definitely a beauty, with a blue roan coat and flax mane and tail. Part Thoroughbred, he was long and tall, as well as fast, nervous and totally unpredictable. Mouse still needed hours more training to be trustworthy for any rider, including himself.

"Did you catch him for her?"

"Nope." Glancing around at Gabe, the cowboy shook his head with a bit of admiration. "She picked him out of the *remuda* we'd rounded up for today's work and roped him herself."

Gabe stared at the ranch hand. Plenty of Texas women knew their way around a horse, but not many he knew could handle a rope, especially a loop that was tossed backward to keep the line from tightening and choking the animal. "She roped Mouse?"

"That's what I said. She threw one of the prettiest houli-hans I'd ever seen before. Surprised the heck out of me. I mean, she's the boss's daughter, but she looks so delicate. I figured she'd always had her mounts saddled for her. And I dang sure never seen a girl throw a houlihan before. But she did. Then saddled him herself and took off toward the river. After that, I didn't worry about Mouse being too much horse for her. She handled him better than I could."

Gabe's gaze left the cowboy to settle on Mercedes, who was continuing to carefully cool down the horse. Since the moment he'd met her, she'd surprised him, amazed him, even worried him and now he had to admit that she wasn't the spoiled princess he'd expected her to be. Yet she *was* trouble. He could feel it stirring in his gut, whispering in his ear.

"I guess I could have tried to stop her from riding Mouse," James went on. "But she didn't look like she was in any mood to take advice from me. I warned her that he was high-strung. That's about all I could do."

Gabe dropped an understanding hand on James's shoulder. "Don't worry about it," he told the cowboy, then walked over to the fence. After he unloaded the saddle on the top rail, he headed straight to Mercedes.

By the time he reached her, she had tied Mouse to a hitching post and was working loose the back cinch from beneath the animal's underbelly. As Gabe came to a stop a few feet from where she was standing, she tossed him a stoic glance.

"Good evening," she greeted.

He inclined his head politely toward her. "Evenin'," he replied as his eyes slid over the curves hidden behind her white shirt and dark blue jeans. It was hard to believe that he'd had that perfect body crushed against his, that he'd tasted the sweet wine of her lips.

Not bothering to say more, she continued to unsaddle the horse. Gabe studied her for long moments and wondered why he couldn't stay away from her. He didn't like to think of himself as weak willed, but she definitely made him feel out of control.

After a bit, he stated the obvious. "I see you've been riding Mouse."

"Is that his name?"

"Nickname."

"Not a very good one," she said. "Because he's not afraid of anything."

Apparently she wasn't, either, Gabe thought. Stepping closer, he said, "Did he give you any problems?"

She glanced at him as though she found his question surprising. "None at all. He's a honey horse. I really like him."

As though to emphasize her words, she stroked the animal's sweaty neck. As Gabe's gaze followed the movement of her small hand, he couldn't help but remember the way it had touched him, the way it had tasted when he'd kissed the back of it.

"Then Mouse must like you better than he likes the cowboys here on the ranch. He's usually a devil. A few weeks ago, he tossed one of the hands and broke the guy's collarbone."

She hefted the saddle from the horse's back and lifted it

onto the top rail of the fence. It wasn't like Gabe to stand still and allow a woman to do such manual labor, but he instinctively understood that she didn't want or require his help. She was just the sort of independent woman that enjoyed showing a man she didn't need him. The same way Sherleen had taken pleasure in reminding him how easily she could get along without him, he thought sourly.

"Mouse knew that I trusted him," Mercedes said. "And that's all he needed to trust me back."

Gabe would have never expected this woman to understand a horse's psyche. The fact that she did impressed him, in spite of himself.

Clearing his throat, he said, "Uh, Mercedes, I'm glad I saw you ride up. I think— I want to apologize to you."

Twisting her head, she peered skeptically at him. "You *think* you want to apologize? Or you *know* that you want to apologize?"

He moved closer, until the scent of horse and woman mingled and swirled beneath his nostrils.

With a rueful grimace, he said, "I want to apologize. I was out of line this morning. I had no right or reason to—uh—grab you the way I did in the office. You were only teasing and I should have took it as such."

He watched her blue eyes widen with surprise. Her whole body turned to face him.

"Do you really mean that?" she asked softly.

Gabe could feel his heart jerk, then take off in a hard gallop. God, but this was crazy. No woman, including his ex-wife, had ever affected him this much. He'd thought about her all day. All day.

"I really mean it," he said.

She let out a long breath, smiled briefly, then quickly

dropped her head. A few moments passed before Gabe realized she was crying. Seeing her in such a vulnerable state stunned him, tore him like the tip of a lashing whip.

"Mercedes?" he asked softly, then carefully placed a hand on her shoulder. "What's wrong?"

Blinking back her tears, she lifted her eyes to his face. "Forgive me, Gabe. I—I don't normally behave as though I'm having an emotional breakdown."

His fingers tightened and unconsciously began kneading her shoulder. "I didn't mean to hurt you. Forget what I said this morning."

She sucked in a deep breath. "It's not you. Although I'm glad we're not at war with each other. It would be pretty awful for the two of us to circle each other like mad dogs every time we crossed paths."

"Yeah. Someone might have wanted to shoot the both of us," he teased.

She tried to smile, but fresh tears spilled from her eyes. The urge to pull her into his arms and kiss those tears away rushed over him like a sudden, unexpected rainstorm. The strange reaction dazed him, making him feel worse than gullible. Hell, he'd never felt the urge to console anybody. Except maybe as a very young boy when he'd found his mother crying over the empty cupboards and unpaid bills. Yeah, he'd hugged his mother tightly and told her how much he loved her. *As if love would fix anything,* he thought bitterly. He'd tried to comfort Sherleen when she'd been upset, but she'd never been the tearful sort. She'd been a screamer and his attempts to placate her had been shunned.

Shoving that unwanted thought aside, Gabe watched Mercedes dash the tears away with the back of her hand. "I got into a quarrel of sorts with Mother this morning. I've been riding out over the range this afternoon thinking about her and the ranch and—a lot of things."

His gaze touched the sweet lines of her face. "Coming home isn't as easy as it sounds."

Mercedes realized his simple statement completely summed up the emotional turmoil inside her, and she looked at him with new regard. "Sometimes I think I've been gone too long, Gabe. Maybe I've forgotten how to be a part of this ranch."

"You haven't forgotten."

His gaze was piercing, unsettling, forcing her to look away from him and swallow.

"Mother expects me to make my home—my life—here now."

"And what do you want, Mercedes?"

She could feel his fingers cease their movement on her shoulder, as though every part of him was waiting for her answer. Could it really matter to him whether she stayed on the ranch or left for parts unknown?

"I rode Mouse all the way to the river," she said quietly. "And by the time I got back here to the ranch yard, I realized how much I still love this place."

"Enough to stay?"

A wry smile touched her lips. She'd already made up her mind that the Sandbur was her home now, but she wasn't comfortable sharing that information with Gabe just yet. It was hard enough for her to have a simple conversation with him. "You'll have to ask me that later, Gabe. Right now I'd better go make peace with my mother."

She turned to untie the reins from the hitching post, but Gabe's hand suddenly swept hers away.

"You go find Geraldine. Let me take care of Mouse for you."

She hesitated, feeling both awkward and touched that he was being so thoughtful. Maybe he had truly put their cross words of this morning behind him. She hoped so. The sexual tension between them was more than enough to handle without adding hostility to it.

"He needs a bath," she said of the horse.

His grin was droll. "I know how to give him one."

The playful look on his face filled Mercedes with relief and a lightheartedness she'd not felt in a long, long time.

Laughing, she rose on her tiptoes and planted a kiss on his cheek. "Yes, I guess you do. Thanks, Gabe!"

As she turned and hurried away, Gabe stared after her and, like a fool, wondered how long it would be before he watched her walk away from the Sandbur. From him.

Chapter Four

An hour later, freshly showered and dressed in shorts and a tank top, Mercedes came downstairs to find her mother sitting on the front porch, talking on a cell phone. Near her armchair, on a low wicker table, sat a small pitcher filled with what looked to be margaritas. Next to it was an insulated ice bucket, along with empty glasses.

Mercedes helped herself to one of the drinks, then eased down in a rocker angled to her mother's right. By the time she'd swallowed the first sip of the icy lime and tequila concoction, Geraldine had folded the phone shut and tossed it onto the table.

"That was Mrs. Richman, scolding me for not being present for the library fund-raiser last week," she said. "I was trying to explain that my daughter had just come home from a job that has kept her halfway around the world for two years, but that didn't faze the woman. I guess the five thousand dollars I contributed wasn't enough to suit her."

Geraldine sighed with frustration and Mercedes tossed her an understanding smile.

"Sounds as if things haven't changed a bit around here. Everyone is always wanting more and more from you. If not your money, then your time. I honestly don't know how you do it, Mother."

Geraldine reached up to push a hand through her hair and, not for the first time since she'd been home, Mercedes noticed that her mother no longer wore the wide gold wedding band on her left hand. Her father had been dead for eleven years and Mercedes was glad to see that her mother had moved on, but it still affected Mercedes to see the empty ring finger. To her, it signified the end of a beautiful union that had produced her and her two siblings. It also said that relationships, even the best of them, sometimes ended in tragedy. Something she was definitely acquainted with.

"You just deal with things one at a time, honey. Otherwise, I would have been be carted off to the psychiatric ward a long time ago." Turning her head, she leveled a look on Mercedes. "I'm glad to see you're in a better frame of mind than you were this morning."

Shamefaced, Mercedes dropped her gaze to the drink in her hand. As she swirled around the milky green liquid, she said, "I want to apologize for my behavior this morning, Mother. I was acting like a shrew—or a spoiled brat—or something that I shouldn't have been. I hope you'll forgive me."

Geraldine's soft laugh drifted on the muggy breeze and Mercedes lifted her head to look at her.

"You never have to ask for my forgiveness, kitten. You know that. Besides, I said some pretty harsh things to you."

"You were only trying to shake me up," Mercedes reasoned.

The faint grin on Geraldine's face faded. "Did I succeed?"

Mercedes absently plucked at the hem of her shorts. "Well, it made me realize how much I love this place and still think of it as home."

Her mother reached across the space separating their chairs to pat Mercedes's forearm.

"I always knew that, darling. But it's very nice to hear you say it." She studied her daughter's serious face. "Does this mean you've definitely decided to stay on the ranch?"

Mercedes gave her a brief nod. "It does. But only if I can be useful. I'm not a hanger-on, Mother. You know that. I never was, and I don't intend to start now. I guess—well, I've done a lot of growing up since I've been away from the ranch and this morning—I'm ashamed that you had to remind me of my responsibility as a Saddler."

Geraldine's slender fingers gently rubbed the top of Mercedes's hand. "Mercedes, if you think I was implying that you've neglected your family while you were away— well, I couldn't be sorrier. I'm proud of all that you've accomplished. The whole family is proud of you. I was only—"

"Being your blunt self," Mercedes said with a soft chuckle. "Forget it, Mother. I have. The only thing I want to hear is what I can do around here to be truly helpful—other than get in Lex's way," she added teasingly.

Leaning back in her chair, Geraldine took a long sip of her drink before she gave Mercedes a smug smile. "I have the perfect job for you, dear. We need someone to help with the marketing for the ranch. Cordero used to do some of it, but as you know, he's over in Louisiana now getting the horse farm going. And Lex doesn't have time for it. Now with us using the Internet and television to reach buyers, it's a huge job to take care of these issues. Matt is already getting ready for the second annual televised cattle auction in September and now he and Lex are making noises about doing another one with the horses. I don't know when they'll find the time, but if you pitch in, maybe they can swing it."

Mercedes's interest was more than piqued and she scooted excitedly to the edge of her seat. "That sounds great, Mother! And I'm surprised. I didn't have any idea the ranch was getting that deeply into advertising and marketing. I thought it was still just ring up a buyer on the phone and they'd show up sooner or later with a few cattle trucks to haul off what they bought."

Geraldine chuckled. "Sorry, Mercedes, but the U.S. military aren't the only ones to use high-tech devices. Your grandparents wouldn't believe how far the Sandbur has come since their heyday."

"Hmm. It sounds interesting and challenging and it's something I would love to do." But would it mean she'd have to deal with Gabe on a fairly regular basis? That might be tricky. Still, she wasn't a coward. If she had to deal with Gabe, she would.

Geraldine's grin was a bit wry. "Well, it wouldn't be like gathering information for the military. But it would be a challenge, I grant you that. Think you want to tackle it?"

Mercedes left her chair and sat on the floor next to her mother's knees. "Of course I want to tackle it." She reached for Geraldine's hands and squeezed them tightly. "And I want to thank you for not trying to manufacture some sort of job for me just as a way to make me feel needed or useful. I—I couldn't stand that."

Geraldine made a noise of disapproval. "Mercedes, you know I'm too direct to try to dance around or spin the issue. Lay things out as they really are—that's the best way to handle a problem."

Her mother's frankness when dealing with people had always been something Mercedes counted on and respected.

Sometimes her brutal honesty hurt, but painful or not, it was usually right. Geraldine hadn't been exactly on the mark when she'd accused Mercedes of wanting to stay in Diego Garcia as a way to avoid civilian life, but she'd been right that Mercedes had used her job to help push away personal disappointments.

Sighing, she rested her cheek on her mother's knee and gazed out at the front lawn of the ranch house. For the first time since she'd arrived home, she felt a sense of peace, of belonging.

Was that because of the job her mother had just offered her, a job that would truly be beneficial to the ranch and her family? Or was she feeling this spurt of happiness because of Gabe?

Even asking herself that last question seemed ridiculous. Gabe Trevino didn't have anything to do with her coming home to the Sandbur or putting a smile on her face, Mercedes told herself firmly. Even so, she still couldn't forget the wicked way he'd kissed her or the way she'd wanted to melt against him. The fact that he was here on the ranch, that she'd likely be dealing with him through her work, filled her with an excitement she'd never expected to feel again.

"Mother, do you know much about Gabe Trevino?"

Geraldine stroked a hand over her daughter's thick hair. "You mean, other than the fact that he's a wizard with horses?"

"Hmm. Where did he come from?"

"Well, from what Cordero said, the man has been traveling from coast to coast for the past few years, working mainly for wealthy horse owners. But I believe he grew up here in Texas, down south in the valley."

Coming home isn't as easy as it sounds. Where she was concerned, Gabe's comment had hit the mark. But now she wondered if he'd said it out of his own personal experience.

"Then settling here must be like coming home for him," Mercedes said thoughtfully.

"Guess you might say that," Geraldine replied. "Although I've not ever heard him mention having relatives anywhere close. But he did tell Lex and Matt that he was single. I suppose you're the teeniest bit interested in that detail about the man?"

Lifting her head, Mercedes countered her mother's question with a low chuckle. "Why, Mother, I wasn't asking anything of the sort. I just— Well, I was just curious about him. That's all."

With a shrewd smile, Geraldine tapped a finger on the tip of Mercedes's nose. "Okay. I admire Gabe. As an employee of the ranch and as a person. Does that tell you anything?"

Mercedes chuckled again, but deep inside she sadly wondered why she couldn't be more like her mother. "Yeah. It tells me that you're a very trusting woman."

A week later, Mercedes stood in the middle of her new workplace and surveyed the stark contrast. When she first entered it, the office that had once been Cordero's had resembled a storage room more than anything. Among the old furniture coated with an inch of sandy dirt, there'd been piles of papers and magazines intermingled with sales receipts, horse registrations and junk mail strewn around the room. Not to mention spurs, bits and leather tack that had been carried in from the horse pens and never returned to their proper places in the barn.

With her mother's help, all of the clutter had been cleared away, the dirt and grime cleaned from the windows and furniture and a new tiled floor installed, along with fluorescent overhead lights. Potted plants filled the corners and the space beneath the windows while a row of filing cabinets lined one wall and a new computer system took up most of the desktop.

Since she would be spending most of the hours of her days

here, Mercedes was very pleased with the room. It was now clean and comfortable and had everything she needed. The only thing she wasn't sure about was the wide-paned window overlooking the training pen.

The huge corral was where most of the yearlings were taught to lead, where the two-year-olds were broken to ride, and later trained to gait and neck rein. Simply put, it was where Gabe spent most of his time and where she'd caught herself gazing out to see him at work, or to see if he was anywhere near. The idea that she could glance up from her desk and most likely get a glimpse of the man was more than distracting.

In fact, she'd tried to maneuver her desk to a position where the window wouldn't be in the line of her vision, but her mother had considered her decision more than a bit odd. No normal person wanted to stare at a wall when he or she could gaze out at a crop of beautiful horses, Geraldine had told her. It had been impossible for Mercedes to explain that the wall would be easier for her peace of mind than gazing out at the sexy horseman.

Yesterday, her first official day on the job, he'd called to inform her that he needed a whole folder of information typed and sent to an auction company in North Texas. When he'd offered to bring the papers to her new office, she'd quickly put him off and offered to pick them up at his office, instead. For some ridiculous reason, she'd wanted to avoid having the man inside her small working space. She'd been afraid that his presence would be too big to ever leave and then she'd have even more trouble concentrating on her work.

Yet going to his office hadn't been a bit easier. She'd been stupid to think she could return to the scene of the crash and not be jolted all over again. She'd gotten out of there so fast, he'd still been talking as she'd backed out the door. She suspected that he knew exactly why she'd scampered like a scalded cat.

Sighing, Mercedes walked over to the desk and was about to take a seat in the wide leather chair when she noticed the papers she'd bundled together with a rubber band. The horse registrations belonged in Gabe's files, and since he had no idea they were here, it was her responsibility to deliver them.

Seeing the man again was not something she was looking forward to, but she was going to have to get accustomed to it. Horses were big business on the Sandbur, and Gabe was the boss over all things equine. Like it or not, she was going to have to deal with him and this strange attraction that came over her whenever he was near.

And with that in mind, Mercedes snatched up the papers and headed out the door.

Even though it wasn't yet nine o'clock, the morning was already hot, the air heavy with humidity. During the past few years, Gabe had worked in several different states, most of which had a much drier and more pleasant climate than South Texas. Five minutes of this weather had sweat rolling down his face and soaking his shirt. After an hour of the oppressive heat, his legs felt as though lead balls were fastened to his boots.

A smart person would never purposely choose to live here, Gabe thought, but he'd never been accused of being smart. He could have stayed in Colorado or the cool northern mountains of California, where jogging five miles never made him break a sweat. Instead, he'd chosen to come back to Texas, back to the prickly pear and thorny mesquite, where alligators ruled the rivers and rattlesnakes almost outnumbered the fire ants. Where old memories haunted him at every turn. Yeah, he'd been crazy for coming back here, but it was home—a fact that he couldn't change. Nor did he want to. And maybe, just maybe, he'd come back to Texas as a way to punish himself. After all, his parents had never gotten out of Grulla, so why should he?

Shoving that dismal question out of his head, Gabe slipped a bright green halter over the ears of a red roan filly. She was thirteen-months-old and as pretty as a calm lake beneath a full moon.

"It's all right, little darlin'," he crooned to the yearling. "We're gonna get along fine. As fine as rain in the desert."

"Good morning, Gabe."

The sudden sound of a female voice came from somewhere behind him. He glanced over his shoulder to see Mercedes sitting atop the board fence of the corral, a cupped hand shielding her eyes.

Since the day she'd ridden Mouse, he'd only seen her once and that had been yesterday, when she'd come to his office to pick up a stack of auction data. For the most part she'd been friendly and had seemed eager to do the work he asked of her. Yet he'd sensed that she was doing her best to keep plenty of distance between them. He could only guess that she'd had time to think about the kiss they'd shared and was now regretting that she'd allowed it to happen. Well, he was regretting it, too. Mainly because the memory only made him want to repeat the act.

As for her taking on the marketing job for the ranch, Gabe had been totally surprised when Lex had given him the news. Gabe had been expecting to hear she'd headed off to some high-powered job with the CIA or FBI. Instead, he'd watched building contractors move in to the old cattle barn to erect the woman a fancy office.

With the filly obediently following him, Gabe decided he didn't have much choice other than to stroll in Mercedes's direction. "Good morning," he greeted as he drew near the spot where she was sitting. "You're out early this morning."

Squinting, she lifted her eyes toward the east where the morning sun was already bearing down on the spreading live oaks. "This is late for me. I've been up for hours."

"Guess it's hard to change military habits."

She nodded, then gave him a brief smile and Gabe realized he was staring at her, his gaze eating up her fresh face with its full soft lips and dark blue eyes. Dammit, why did she have to be so beautiful, so tempting?

"Uh, I didn't want to interrupt your work. I was on my way over to your office and I spotted you here." She held up a packet of folded papers. "I wanted to give you these American Quarter Horse Association horse registrations. Cordero wasn't too good about keeping things filed. I'm not sure if we still own the horses or not. Maybe you can figure it out."

He took the papers from her, then immediately stuffed them in the back pocket of his jeans. "Thanks. I'll go through them later. Could be the buyers never picked up the papers or Cordero never mailed them out."

Gabe watched her hands slide nervously down her thighs. Today she was wearing faded jeans and a white shirt with the tails knotted in the front at her waist. Her hair was hanging loose, and he figured if he slid his hand beneath its weight and touched the back of her neck, he'd find it damp and hot. Like a few other places on her body.

She laughed softly, and Gabe felt a rush of pleasure pass through him. The sound was happy and sensual at the same time, and he found himself wondering if she would be the sort of woman who'd smile as he made love to her.

Hell, Gabe, get your mind on your own business and off this blond siren. Her last name is Saddler, remember? She's the boss lady's daughter and that makes her a rich ranching heiress. You'd better never touch her again. Not that way.

He said, "From what I know about Cordero, he doesn't like working under a roof, much less filing papers."

She leveled her eyes on his face, and for the first time in his life, he wondered how women—particularly this woman—saw him. The idea that she was scrutinizing him for any reason left him uncomfortable and he deliberately looked away from her and back to the roan who was standing quietly behind him. The filly's ears were perked forward, her brown eyes soft and trusting.

Warmed by the animal's faith in him, he gently stroked her slender neck while he struggled to minimize the effect Mercedes's presence had on him.

"You don't look as if you particularly enjoy being under a roof, either," she remarked.

"You're right. I've always been an outdoorsman. But I do force myself to keep up with paperwork. It's an important part of the job."

"From what my family tells me, you're filling Cordero's boots and then some. All of them are very pleased with your work."

There was a white jagged streak down the filly's nose and Gabe traced the marking with his forefinger as he carefully digested Mercedes's comment. It would be stupid as hell to let her compliments go to his head. Still, he couldn't help but ask, "What about you? Do I measure up to your standards?"

Silence stretched for long moments until it seemed that even the birds had stopped chirping. Finally she said, "I haven't been here long enough to make that judgment. But I trust my family's opinion."

Hearing a smile in her voice, he glanced over his shoulder

to see a half grin curving one side of her lips. It was a sexy expression. One that said she could be very playful if she was with the right person. And he was a damn fool for wishing that person could be him.

Without warning, she suddenly jumped into the pen and walked over to where he was standing. Her nearness surprised him. Especially after yesterday, when she'd gone overboard to keep a professional distance between them.

"What are you doing with the little filly?" she asked.

Did she really care or was she simply making conversation, trying to alleviate the obvious tension between them? *What the hell does it matter, Gabe? She's here by your side. Quit trying to figure her out and simply enjoy having her close.*

He glanced at her. "Just seeing if she'll give me her head. And yield to my pressure."

She leveled those blue eyes on him again, and this time Gabe was acutely aware that she was only a step away, close enough to pick up her scent and see the faint spatter of freckles across her cheekbones. He could feel the heat of her gaze sliding over his face, down his shoulder and onto his hands.

He could never remember a woman looking at him in such a sensual way. Or if they had, he hadn't noticed. Mercedes's slanting glances were causing fire to lick at his insides and he silently cursed the strong reaction.

She was everything in a woman he'd promised himself to avoid. Strong-minded. Independent. Wealthy. She didn't need a man on a permanent basis. And after one failed marriage, he wasn't looking to enter into another relationship that was doomed from the start.

"Does she have a name yet?"

"I call her Penny." In spite of the mental argument he'd just made with himself, every cell inside Gabe was urging him to step closer, to enjoy the heat she was throwing at him. But he stopped himself short.

She glanced beyond him and the filly to an adjoining pen where ten more yearlings were waiting to go through a morning of schooling.

"How do you keep them all straight? And where do you find enough time to give them all the handling they need?"

Instead of following her gaze to the other young horses, he allowed his eyes to travel over the graceful line of her profile, the curve of her throat and the thick waves of her long hair. Even though she was everything he didn't need, she had everything he wanted.

"I have several wranglers that I trust to deal with the young horses in the way I insist upon. As for the horses themselves, they're just like humans—they all have different personalities that make them unique. Like Penny here, who's sweet and docile and is willing to do anything I ask of her."

Mercedes smiled perceptively. "Hmm. She must be a favorite of yours."

"She is. But I'd say a bit of fire added to all that sweetness isn't a bad thing."

Mercedes cleared her throat as the subtle undercurrent of his words splashed heat across her cheeks. She'd not stopped to flirt with the man. She'd simply wanted to deliver the papers, pause long enough to appear friendly, then head back to work. Yet it seemed that whenever she got near him, her brain seemed to lose control of her body. As for him, Mercedes wasn't sure how to take anything he said. But then, she'd stopped believing in men a long time ago.

"If that's the case, you should have supper with us tonight," she impulsively blurted out before she could stop herself.

"Cook is grilling steaks. I'm sure she'd supply you with all the Tabasco you need."

Dear God, where had that come from and what had she been thinking? Being around this man was like striking matches near a puddle of gasoline. For the past few days, she'd been convincing herself that the safe thing to do would be to forget his kiss and keep everything friendly and professional between them. But for some reason she couldn't fathom, the risk, the pure excitement of being in his company was too much to resist.

Mercedes could see he was carefully weighing her invitation, as though he didn't trust her nearly as much as he did the little roan filly nuzzling his shoulder. She didn't understand why he would be skeptical about her sincerity, but after years of information gathering for the military, she'd learned that outright questions rarely provided as many answers as sitting back and observing. Sooner or later, she'd figure out what lay beneath Gabe Trevino's dark eyes and why he thought she had a hidden agenda where he was concerned.

"I'm not sure that's a good idea," he said finally.

Disappointment speared through her...which was a ridiculous reaction on her part. Her happiness didn't depend on this man liking her or her company. In fact, she'd most likely be better off if he did decline her invitation. Still, her heart was beating with an eagerness that frightened her.

"Why? Don't you eat in the evening?"

"Yes. But—"

"Then there are no buts," she quickly interrupted with a smile. "I'll tell Cook to set another plate. We eat around seven."

Before he could issue another objection, she turned on her heel and hurried to climb out of the horse pen. Once she'd reached the top rail, she looked back at him and waved. "Oh, and don't dress up," she called out. "This is just a family affair."

* * *

Later that evening, Gabe stood on his front porch and stared out at the rough ground dotted with scrubby oak and mesquite. The house where he'd settled on the Sandbur had once been little more than a line shack. A three-room building with a rusted iron roof and a separate outhouse for bathroom facilities. Just a spot for line riders to rest and find shelter from the weather.

Over the years, it had been updated and expanded. A well had been dug, electricity added and the house modernized with indoor plumbing. Even so, the place felt isolated and hidden from the rest of the world.

Almost five miles away from the main ranch yard, the homestead sat on a brushy knoll that angled down to the banks of the San Antonio River. Sometimes a few cows would appear in the yard to graze around the patches of prickly pear, or deer and wild turkey would stroll by to feed at the dry corn he tossed beneath the lone pine tree standing in front of the house. But other than the wildlife, he didn't hear or see anyone. It was just him and the wind. And he liked it like that.

At first, Geraldine and Matt had thought he was kidding when he'd told him he wanted to move his things into this empty house. No one had used it in several years and the ranch had much better places to offer as living quarters.

Gabe had finally convinced them that he was serious about making the old house his home. But before he could move his things in, Geraldine had set a contractor to work installing wood parquet on the floors and exchanging the old appliances in the kitchen with new ones. Thankfully, she'd left everything else as it had been and Gabe could truthfully say that this was the first place, since his childhood home in Grulla, where he felt comfortable.

At least, he'd felt comfortable until Mercedes had made an appearance on the ranch, he thought soberly. Now thoughts and images of the woman were invading his private space and that unsettled him more than anything had in a long time.

A family affair. Those three words were enough to tell Gabe he didn't belong at the Saddler supper table. But he could hardly call the house with some feeble excuse and tell them he didn't want to be there. Dammit, why had she asked him, anyway?

The question had rolled through Gabe's head all afternoon, but now it was too late to be asking himself anything. He had no choice but to get ready and go. And later, before the evening was through, he had to get the message across to Mercedes Saddler that he wasn't interested in socializing, or anything else, with her.

Chapter Five

At the same time in the Saddler house, Mercedes had gone to the kitchen to remind Cook to set another plate for supper and had just received a shock from the older woman.

"Honey, there's no need to be adding another plate. One ought to do it. Your mother is already gone for the evenin'. She had some sort of dinner thing with the volunteer firefighters going on. I thought you knew that. And Lex has gallivanted off to some Cattle Association meetin' up at Fort Worth. He won't be back home for three days."

Mercedes stared blankly at Cook, a tall slender woman in her midseventies, who'd worked at the Sandbur for longer than Mercedes had been alive. Her long hair, which was still more black than gray, was oftentimes pulled into a tight ponytail, a style that Cook called her instant face-lift. But it was her red lips and fingernails that were her signature fashion statement, telling the world that the woman had been a glamor gal in her prime.

"I just talked to Mother this morning—before I went to work," Mercedes explained with frustration. "She didn't mention the firefighter thing. If she did, I didn't remember. And when did Lex decide to go to Fort Worth? It's funny that you know all about these things and I don't."

"That's what you get for puttin' your office way out there in the cattle barn. If you'd stayed here in the house, you might know what was going on."

That was true. But that still wouldn't have prevented her from seeing Gabe, she thought with a prickle of nerves. She'd had to deliver those damn papers.

But that didn't mean you had to invite him to dinner, Mercedes. So why did you? So you might have the chance to spend time exclusively with the man?

Purposely shoving that question aside, Mercedes rolled her eyes at Cook. "I put my office in the cattle barn so that I'd have enough peace to concentrate. Besides, I know I didn't misunderstand you this morning when you said that you were going to be grilling steaks for supper."

"I did say that. Before I knew that more than half the family was going to be gone."

Mercedes groaned. "Cook! I've invited Gabe to eat with us tonight! I told him we'd be having steaks!"

Cook took a step back and surveyed Mercedes with new interest. "Gabe, is it? You settin' your eye on the ranch's new horseman?"

Mercedes was astonished to feel a blush creeping up her throat and onto her cheeks. She was a grown woman who'd lived halfway around the world. For the past eight years, she'd worked in situations which could be described as stressful or worse. Nothing, other than Drew Downy's betrayal, had fazed her. Now Gabe, or the mere mention of the man, was enough to shake her nerves and color her face.

"No! I…just happened to be talking to him this morning and wanted to be sociable and invite him to supper, that's all. He's…well, he's all alone and I figured he might like a bit of company."

Cook's dark eyes glinted mischievously. "Hmmph. There's a whole bunkhouse full of beer-drinkin', poker-playin' cowboys out back. The man can find all the company he needs right there."

Mercedes frowned. "Gabe is more…refined than that."

Cook laughed. "Honey, there ain't no man on this ranch more refined than that," she said. Then, her expression more serious, she reached over and patted Mercedes's shoulder. "Don't look so glum. I'm only teasing. I think it's nice that you asked Gabe to supper. He don't have any family around here and he lives alone, way out there in the line shack. Did your mother tell you that?"

Surprised by this news, she looked at the older woman. "No one told me. I took it for granted that he probably lived in one of the newer houses here near the ranch yard."

Cook shook her head. "He's independent, I'll say that." She narrowed a shrewd gaze at Mercedes. "Sorta like you."

Mercedes straightened her spine. "I'll take that as a compliment. Now what about supper? Can you still prepare the steaks?"

Cook batted a hand through the air. "Sure. No problem. I'll make something hearty to go with them. You wanna eat in the dining room?"

Mercedes thought about that for a moment. "No. That's too stuffy for just the two of us. I'll fix a table out on the patio. What do you think?"

Cook's laugh was suggestive. "I think you're wantin' to be more than sociable."

Groaning, Mercedes hurried out of the kitchen before Cook could say more.

An hour later, she'd changed into a short denim skirt and a sheer pink blouse with a lacy camisole beneath it. After twisting up her hair in a knot at the back of her head and swiping on a bit of pink lipstick, she hurried downstairs to locate a table to use on the patio.

She found a card table in the den and covered it with a checked tablecloth from the kitchen pantry. By the time she'd added dishes, cutlery and candles, she heard a vehicle pulling up to the parking area at the west end of the house.

It had to be Gabe. She walked across the yard to the end of the two-story hacienda-style house, and as she rounded the corner, she spotted him climbing down from the cab of a black pickup truck.

He was dressed basically the way he'd been dressed this morning, only minus the spurs. Even his black hat was still wearing dust from the horse lot, yet as she came nearer, she could see that he'd shaved and his dark hair was damp and shiny.

Her gaze slid over his hard, trim body, and she felt desire gurgle in the pit of her stomach, like fire being stoked beneath an already simmering cauldron. The idea that she could feel like a whole woman again was both exhilarating and frightening.

"Hello," she called out to him.

Spotting her, he paused long enough for her to join him.

"I wasn't expecting you to meet me outside," he said.

She laughed. "I was already out back," she explained. "I heard you drive up."

Forgetting her plan to keep distance between them, she

threaded her arm around his and began to lead him toward the backyard. "I hope you don't mind, I've set a table on the patio for our supper. But if you'd rather, we can move inside to the dining room."

Gabe tried not to notice the way she was holding his arm or the way her curvy body brushed against his side as they walked. He tried to ignore the scent of her perfume and the fact that he could see through her blouse to the intimate garment beneath. But his attempts were so feeble that his senses were instantly overcome with her presence.

"I think you should be worrying about where your family would prefer to eat instead of asking me. I can eat anywhere. Standing up, or in the saddle, if necessary."

She looked at him and smiled. "That won't be necessary tonight. And as for my family, I'm afraid it's going to be only you and me. Mother had to go out this evening and Lex has gone to Fort Worth on business."

He felt as though someone had struck him over the head and it took him a moment to recover from her announcement. "Oh. You should have called me."

"Why? So you could have backed out and left me to eat all by myself?" Dimples curved the sides of her lush lips. "No. I wasn't going to give you that chance." She urged him forward. "Come on. I'll let Cook know you're here and then we'll have a drink."

Once they reached the patio, she invited him to take a seat. While she hurried into the house, Gabe walked under the vine-covered roof and stood looking at the cozy little table set for two. The fact that she'd gone to this much trouble for him was both puzzling and touching. Moreover, he couldn't figure this sudden change in her attitude or why she was bothering with him in the first place.

She was a Sandbur heiress. She could have any man she wanted.

She doesn't want you, Gabe. Not the way you're thinking. She's only being sociable. Like her mother. Or else she's only playing with you.

Trying to forget about Mercedes's motives, Gabe turned and strolled away from the patio to where the short-cropped lawn grew beneath the arms of a spreading live oak. A wrought iron bench sat near the massive trunk and Gabe sat on it while he waited for his hostess to reappear.

He was watching a couple of fox squirrels battle with a group of mockingbirds over a feeder full of seeds when Mercedes finally reappeared from the house, carrying a tray.

As soon as he spotted her walking toward him, he found himself wondering what he was doing here. Dreaming? Pretending that the long-legged beauty smiling at him could actually be more than a friend to him? *Get real, Gabe. Sherleen already taught you a good, hard-learned lesson about high-maintenance women and trying to keep them satisfied. Even if you could have her, you know you'd never be able to keep her contented.*

Rising to his feet, he walked across the lawn to meet her.

"I brought ice-cold beer and wine so you can take your pick. Or if you don't want spirits, I'll go back for fruit juice." She grinned impishly at him. "I'm saving the sweet tea to go with our supper."

He plucked a long-necked bottle of beer from the tray. "This will be fine. Thanks."

"Let me put this down and we can go back under the tree if you'd like," she said. "I think it's cooler there. There's not much air stirring tonight."

He waited while she put the tray on a small table on the

patio. When she returned to his side, she was carrying a beer for herself. That surprised him. He'd figured her for light wine or a fruity cocktail. But he was quickly learning that Mercedes was not a predictable woman.

They walked over to the wrought iron bench and he waited for her to take a seat before he sat down next to her. Since the piece of furniture was small, he couldn't put much space between them and he wondered if she was as intensely aware of his body as he was of hers.

"I hope you're not completely starving. Once Cook learned that I was the only one who'd be home this evening, she let the help off with plans to give me a salad. I had to remind her that I don't eat like my sister, Nicci. I want something I can really bite into. And it shows," she added with a laugh. "But I don't care. I like having healthy, strong muscles."

And he liked all the curves, Gabe could have told her. Instead he stuck to the point. "I'm not starving. And I'm sorry that Cook had to go to extra trouble for me."

She waved dismissively. "It's no trouble. She loves what she does. Besides, I've promised to clean up the kitchen for her."

Gabe's gaze slid to her hands, lightly cupped around the glass bottle balanced on her knee. Like her legs, her fingers were long, but not skinny. The bare nails were short and squared at the corners. He couldn't imagine them dipping into dirty dishwater, but he could surely imagine them sliding over his chest, down his back and onto his hips.

He let out a long breath. "You mentioned your sister, Nicci. I met her right after I came to work for the ranch and spoke to her at the party the other night. She's the PA, isn't she?"

Smiling, Mercedes nodded. "That's right. She's the brains of the family. Lex and I always had to work to keep up with the grades she made in school. It came easy to her."

"You never had the desire to follow her into the medical field?"

She laughed lowly. "Gosh, no. I don't have the patience. When I was growing up, I was too much of a tomboy, I suppose, to think of becoming a doctor. That would have required me to stay indoors and study, something I've learned to like after getting in the military. But back then I was the cowgirl and Nicci was the student." She paused and let out a sigh so soft he barely picked up the sound. "Now she has a doctor husband and a beautiful baby daughter. Have you seen Sara Rose?"

"No, but I've seen Matt's little boy. And Cordero's son."

She smiled briefly, then went very quiet for a few long moments. Gabe wondered what she was contemplating and why the mention of the children had put such a pensive look on her face. But he didn't ask. Something that personal was none of his business.

Glancing out to the feeder, he noticed the shadows had lengthened, sending the birds and the squirrels to their nightly resting places. Beyond the yard and the graceful arms of the spreading oaks, he could hear the distant sounds of male voices and the intermittent clang and thumps of a horseshoe game down at the bunkhouse.

Eventually, she turned her head slightly to look at him. "Do you have siblings, Gabe?"

Nodding, he swirled the remaining beer in the bottle he was holding. "Three. Two sisters and a brother."

Clearly curious, she squared her knees around so that she was facing him. "Really? I'm surprised. I thought—for some reason I pictured you being an only child."

"I'm the youngest." His lips twisted to a wry line. "If you can still call thirty-five young."

"I call it that," she said. Then, after swallowing a sip of her drink, she spoke again. "Tell me about them. Do they live around here?"

"No. My sisters are the oldest and after they married, they both moved away. Nita lives in Colorado now, near Cortez. Carla lives in Nevada. They both have children."

"What about your brother?"

"Joseph is three years older than me and divorced. He owns a ranch in California now—just north of Lone Pine."

"So they all live away," she mused aloud. "Do you ever see them?"

"Sometimes. Not too often." He shrugged. "When we were all children, we were very close. But then we all became adults and life took us on different paths. I think—well, if our parents had lived, we would have all remained closer."

He could feel her going very quiet again and he glanced up to see her studying him with a solemn expression.

"Your father is dead, too?"

An old, familiar pain drifted through his chest and he wondered how many years it would take for that hollow ache inside him to leave. Twenty-four had already passed and yet the time hadn't extinguished the agony of losing them. The pain was still there, haunting and hurting him anytime he thought of his loving parents.

"Yes. They both died when I was eleven."

"Oh. That's tough. Real tough," she murmured. "I guess someone has probably already told you that my father died about twelve years ago. I still miss him terribly. But I think it's worse for Lex. A man needs his father for so many reasons—that's something you know about far more than me. And it doesn't help Lex or any of the family to think Daddy might have been murdered."

Gabe's eyes narrowed on her face. "Murdered? I haven't heard anyone say anything like that about your father."

She swallowed down more of the beer. "That's because none of the family goes around saying such things to anyone. But I think—well, Mother never was convinced that the investigators did a thorough job on the case. You see, Daddy was out on a fishing trip with his friends down near Corpus. Apparently, he fell overboard with a heart attack and drowned before they could pull him back into the boat. Trouble is, Daddy didn't have an ounce of heart trouble. He'd just had a thorough checkup only weeks before the accident."

So this woman had tragically lost a parent, too, Gabe thought. He would have never guessed. For some reason, he'd always thought of families like the Saddlers and Sanchezes as never having problems or suffering losses. Which was foolish on his part. He knew firsthand that wealth didn't fix everything. It didn't necessarily bring happiness, either.

"Sometimes doctors miss problems."

"Yeah. Sometimes," she murmured, then suddenly rose to her feet. "I think I'll go check with Cook and see if our meal is ready."

"Sure. Take your time."

Fifteen minutes later, Mercedes and Gabe were sitting at the little table on the patio. Above their heads, honeysuckle vines were dripping with blossoms and filling the heavy evening air with their pungent scent. Nearby, torches burned to ward away mosquitoes.

On the table, wedged around the flickering candles, there was a platter of thick beef steaks that had been marinated, then coated with coarse black pepper and grilled to perfection. There was a bowl of pan-fried potatoes and onions, along with another bowl filled with baked beans heavily spiced with chili powder. Beneath a cloth-covered basket, sourdough biscuits were hot from the oven.

Gabe couldn't remember ever eating food that tasted so good—yet he was distracted from each delicious bite by the sight of Mercedes sitting across from him.

Except for the flickering candlelight and nearby torches, black shadows cloaked them in darkness, reminding Gabe that the two of them were entirely alone. Even the faint lights from the back of the hacienda had gone out and the muted sounds from the distant bunkhouse were now quiet.

Before Gabe had driven to the ranch yard, this was not the sort of meal he'd envisioned having with Mercedes. He'd expected to be eating in the Saddlers' elegant dining room with the whole family present. The last thing he'd anticipated was this intimate tête-à-tête.

He was washing a piece of steak down with a swig of tea and asking himself if he would have accepted her invitation if he'd known how the evening was going to turn out, when her voice broke softly into his rambling thoughts.

"I guess you're probably thinking I put these candles out here to make the dinner a romantic affair."

He looked across the short space at her and felt his gut twist with desire. The glow of the candlelight gave her skin a pearly sheen and her lips, which had been covered in pink lipstick, were now bare and moist. The memory of kissing them was still fresh in his mind. So fresh that the taste of her lips overpowered the flavor of the food on his plate.

"Did you?" he asked.

Her gaze met his in a subtle, but challenging way. "Not really. They're citronella—I didn't want us to become supper for the mosquitoes."

Her response was so unexpected that he had to laugh. "You've put me at ease."

A broad smile spread her lips. "Good. Because—well, this morning, when I first invited you to have supper with us, I hadn't planned on this." She waved her hand to encompass the table and patio. "But then, when I learned it was going to be just you and me I decided I wanted to make it a little special. Can I say that?"

He gave her a wry grin. "You just did."

She shot him a playful frown. "I mean, can I say that without making you angry?"

He shrugged. "I'm not a bit angry. Do I look like I am?"

"No. You look…skeptical. And that doesn't make me feel very good."

He forked a morsel of steak to his mouth. "I didn't know I was supposed to be making you feel good."

She let out a long breath. "All right. I'll just come out and say what I was trying to say in the first place—I wanted to show you that I like you, but I'm not trying to seduce you."

He slowly chewed the steak, then swallowed before he finally replied, "Even if you're not *trying* to seduce me—you are."

She let out a small gasp, and even in the dim light he could see her cheeks were turning dark with color. The fact that she was capable of blushing charmed him even more.

"Lord, Gabe, I never expected you to say something like that to me," she said in a low, hoarse voice.

"I don't know why," he pointed out. "You say what's on your mind to me."

She leaned back in her chair and folded her arms protectively against her breasts. For the first time since he'd met this beauty, Gabe wondered if she was really more innocent than she pretended to be.

"Well, that's because it seems like the only way I can deal with you," she reasoned.

He smiled as his eyes slid over her flustered face. "Tell me, Mercedes, have you ever had a lover?"

Surprise parted her lips and then she purposely looked away from him. "Is that question really necessary between us? I thought we were going to try to be friends."

"I don't believe we'll ever get that done."

Her gaze jerked back to his and she opened her mouth to speak, but caught herself at the last moment. Finally, she said, "Okay, since you asked, I'll tell you. I have had a lover. One. And he—well, after him I haven't wanted another."

Something about the way she spoke, the tremor in her voice, made Gabe wish he'd not asked about her past. Yet this woman consumed his thoughts and he wanted to know her. Inside and out. "Was this guy recently in your life or did it happen a long time ago?"

She looked down at her plate. "A long time ago."

"And you haven't wanted another man in your life because you still love him? Or because he twisted you?"

Twisted. Oh, yes, John had done that and much more, Mercedes thought ruefully. He'd shaken her self-esteem and made her doubt her own judgment. He'd blackened everything she'd believed love would or could be. And then, just when she'd begun to get over him, she'd met Drew and started to believe once again that men could be trusted. What a hell of a mistake that had been.

"I certainly don't love him anymore. So I guess you could say he sorta ruined my image of men in general."

"Well, don't feel alone," he said. "I think we all have our images of the opposite sex ruined at one time or another. Mine was when my wife and I divorced."

Stunned, Mercedes leaned toward him. "You were—married?"

The incredulous sound of her voice put another wry twist to his lips. "For three years."

Three years! She couldn't imagine this man being tied down for three days, much less that length of time. Apparently he'd changed since then, or he'd been wildly in love with the woman. A thought that she didn't want to contemplate.

It was silly, she knew, but after kissing the man, she was beginning to get the faintest twinges of possessiveness where he was concerned. No doubt that would give him a laugh, she thought grimly.

"What happened?"

His steak finished, he laid his fork to the side of his plate. "We had different aims in life. She couldn't live the way I wanted. And I couldn't live the way she needed. We were doomed from the start. It just took me a while to realize it."

She studied his smooth expression and wondered what was hidden behind it. Outwardly, he seemed indifferent to his failed marriage, but who knew? Maybe the man was still in love with his ex-wife. It was a notion she refused to think about.

"Uh, did you—have children?"

He shook his head. "No. Thank goodness there was no one else to be hurt by our parting."

He went quiet after that, and so did Mercedes. He'd given her much to think about. Too much.

After a while she put down her fork and settled back in her chair. "Cook tells me that you're living out at the line shack. Well, that's what we've always called it even after it was turned into a house." A tentative smile tilted the corners of her lips. "When are you going to invite me out to see it?"

She watched as his thumb and forefinger bracketed his

chin in a thoughtful pose. He was probably thinking her question was forward. It probably was. But something about this man made things tumble from her mouth that she normally wouldn't dream of saying.

"Now how am I supposed to answer that question?" he asked.

A low chuckle rumbled in her throat and she realized he was the first man other than a relative in a long, long time to make her laugh. "You're suppose to say, 'Mercedes, I'd be glad for you to come out and see the house anytime you like.'"

His eyes narrowed but not enough to hide the gleam in their gray depths. The glimmer stirred her pulse.

"Oh. Okay. Mercedes, I'd be glad for you to come out and see the house anytime you like."

"Really?"

"I said it, didn't I?"

"You were prompted."

"I said it anyway."

God, but he was stoic and frustrating, she thought. He was also too sexy to be legal. Just looking at him left her simmering and picturing the two of them in the most erotic situations. In all of her imaginings, she'd never dreamed that coming home to the Sandbur would be like this.

"All right," she told him with far more confidence than she felt. "I just might surprise you one evening with a visit."

He picked up his fork and began to draw absent lines through the crumbs on his plate. "You might be disappointed. I haven't done anything to the house, except move my things into it. I'm not one for frills and curtains and that sort of thing."

"I'd be disappointed if you were," she replied with a grin, then added, "The line shack has always been one of my favorite places on the ranch. I went out there and stayed a few days before I left for basic training."

Surprise flickered across his face. "By yourself?"

"Yes. By myself. That's the whole point of the line shack. It's away from everything and everybody. Is that why you like it?"

"Maybe."

There was no maybe about it, Mercedes thought. The man was a loner. But why, she wondered. Had losing his wife made him want to retreat from society? Or was it simply his nature to prefer his own company to others?

One way or another, Mercedes planned to find out.

Chapter Six

As moments passed, Mercedes began to sense that he didn't appreciate her throwing questions at him, so as they finished the last of their meal, she decided to move on to other things.

"Cook made blueberry pie for dessert. Would you like to go inside and have a piece? I'll make coffee to go with it."

He rested a hand against his midsection. "I'm not sure I can hold another bite."

Rising to her feet, she began to gather up the dirty dishes. She should probably let the evening end. But this time with Gabe had been far more pleasant than she'd expected, and to be honest with herself, she didn't want to say good-night. "Cook will be very hurt if she shows up in the morning and finds the pie uncut," she told him.

"Put that way, I can't turn it down," he conceded. "Let me help you carry these into the house."

Fifteen minutes later, the dishes were piled in the sink, the coffee was made and they were sitting at the kitchen table, eating the first few bites of pie, when the swinging doors pushed open and Geraldine walked in.

"Why, Gabe! How nice to find you here!" she exclaimed as she hurried toward them. "I thought I was going to find Mercedes in here going through the refrigerator. She's a night raider."

Gabe stood up to greet Geraldine, but when he stuck out his hand toward her, she pushed it away and laughed. "I don't want a handshake from you, I want a hug."

As her mother pulled Gabe against her, Mercedes could see that the physical affection left him both awkward and surprised. Suddenly, she started thinking about the loss of his parents at a time when he'd needed hugs, encouragements and love. Maybe he'd never received that from anyone, she thought. Maybe he didn't know what it was like to be loved. Really loved. The notion saddened her greatly.

"I invited Gabe for supper tonight," Mercedes explained to her mother. "I didn't know you and Lex were going to be gone."

Stepping away from Gabe, Geraldine went over to the cabinet counter and poured herself a mug of coffee.

"Sorry. I should have called your office and told you," she said. "The county firefighters need new equipment and we're trying to come up with ideas on how to pay for them. We ranchers decided to each donate a steer, but that won't be enough. Anyway, the talking went on far too long. I'm bushed." She returned to the table and took a seat at the end of one of the long benches. "But I'm glad you and Gabe had a nice supper together. My being home would have just spoiled it."

Mercedes exchanged an awkward glance with Gabe, then cleared her throat.

"Uh, Mother, Cook made blueberry pie. Why don't you have a piece with us?"

"It's tempting. But they had donuts at the meeting. The filled kind. I ate three."

"Mother! What do you think that's done to your cholesterol?"

"Shhh! Don't tell Nicci. She'll scold me for days. Besides," she added with a pointed glance at Mercedes, "I doubt you ate rabbit food for supper."

"No," Mercedes agreed with a smile. "We had steak. And just tell Nicci what I always do. It's not the quantity of life that counts, it's the quality."

Geraldine chuckled. "See, Gabe? My daughters are nothing alike. Nicci is careful and cautious. Mercedes has always been my little daredevil."

Amused, his gaze settled on Mercedes's face. "That doesn't surprise me."

Mercedes grimaced. "I don't know why you call me a daredevil," she said to her mother. "Lex is the one who rode saddle broncs on the rodeo circuit."

"Yes," Geraldine said with a weary sigh. "And that took far more years off my heart than the damned cholesterol I eat."

From the corner of her eye, Mercedes watched Gabe glance at his watch, then push his empty pie plate to one side.

"I hate to leave good company, but it's getting late. I'd better be going," he said as he rose to his feet. "It was nice seeing you again, Geraldine."

The older woman smiled warmly at him. "I hope everything has been going okay for you here on the ranch. If you have any problems with the house, the horses, anything, just tell me. I'll fix it."

He nodded with appreciation. "Thank you. But everything is fine. No problems."

"Good." She motioned for Mercedes to get to her feet. "Where are your manners, young lady? Aren't you going to walk Gabe to his truck?"

Manners were something Geraldine had always insisted upon with her children and her employees. Short of making a scene, Mercedes had no choice but to rise to her feet. But for some reason she couldn't understand, the notion of being alone again with the man made her very nervous.

"Of course. I'll take him on the lighted path. Matt said they found two rattlesnakes on their back steps yesterday. Now he's afraid to let Juliet and the kids walk outside."

"Matt is a worrier," Geraldine said. "But it might not hurt to take a flashlight with you. There aren't any footlights on the west side of the house."

Mercedes could see very well in the darkness, but she knew better than to argue with her mother. She fetched a light from the pantry, and after Gabe wished Geraldine a good night, the two of them left the house.

Outside, Mercedes handed him the flashlight, then looped her arm around his as they followed the illuminated graveled path. But once they reached the west end, the lights faded, leaving them in total darkness.

Gabe switched on the flashlight and started to hand it back to Mercedes. "Here. I can make it the rest of the way to the truck."

"No," she told him. "We're still a good thirty feet away. A rattler might be stretched out to cool under the driver's door. I'd hate to think I was the one who caused you to get bitten."

With the orb of the flashlight pointed to the ground, the outline of his face was shrouded with shadows, but she could hear him sigh wearily. The sound bothered her. This past week, she'd come to realize that the physical attraction she felt for Gabe was only a part of what drew her to the man. For some reason she couldn't explain, she wanted him to like her as a person. She wanted to think that he savored her company rather than tolerated it. And for a while tonight, she'd believed he was enjoying spending time with her. But he was a hard man to figure.

"All right," he told her. "We'll go together."

Once they reached his truck, he paused at the door and handed the light back to her. "Thank you for the meal, Mercedes. And your company."

Strange, Mercedes thought, how just a few little words from this man had the power to lift her spirits, to make her heart trip over itself. She realized she was plunging head-first into these new feelings, but no matter how many danger signals were clanging in her head, she couldn't seem to stop them.

"Gabe, I'm sorry about Mother being so—suggestive. I don't think she realizes how transparent she is at times."

"I call it being frank."

She laughed in spite of the awkwardness between them. "Well, she does speak her mind without thinking how it sounds. And you see, for a long time now, she's been pressing me to think about marriage."

His snort was a sound of pure cynicism. "With me? You actually think your mother sees me as a potential son-in-law?"

Anger spurted through her, but she tried her best to tamp it down. So far tonight, they'd gotten along. She didn't want him to leave on a sour note. "Yes. Why? What's wrong with you?"

As the silence increased, she began to dwell on the fact that he stood only inches from her and that his warm, musky scent was filling her nostrils. Everything about the man was pulling her toward him; all she wanted to do was touch him, feel the hardness of his body beneath her hands and taste the wild passion on his lips.

"I'm not the marrying kind, Mercedes."

The sound of his voice jerked her back to their conversation. "Neither am I," she admitted. "So where I'm concerned, you don't have anything to worry about."

"Don't I?"

She sucked in a breath. It had been so long since she'd had any sort of intimate conversation with a man that maybe she was coming across in all the wrong ways. He certainly seemed to misunderstand her. "I'm not a Daisy Mae, chasing you around the hills, Gabe. And even if I were, you have two able legs. You can surely run."

She wasn't sure if he stepped closer or if she imagined it. Either way, her heart jerked with anticipation.

"You may not be Daisy Mae," he muttered wryly, "but you certainly have her…charms."

His gaze dropped from her face to slide ever so slowly down the thrust of her breasts, the curve of her waist and onto her legs, or what he could see of them in the limited light. All night he'd kept telling himself he didn't want anything from this woman. But his body was screaming it wanted to make love to her.

Mercedes's breathing sped up to such a point that she felt herself growing lightheaded.

"And that gives you a problem?" she asked.

"It does when I spend most of my waking hours imagining myself making love to you." His hand touched her hair, then settled onto her shoulder. "But then, that's what you want, isn't it? To tempt me."

Her head jerked back and forth as heat from his hand spread from her shoulder all the way to the tips of her fingers. "That's not true," she whispered hoarsely.

Suddenly his face was a breath away, his lips poised over hers. Mercedes's heart was thumping madly.

"You want me to want you," he murmured. "Don't try to deny that."

Her breaths had turned to tiny gasps, doing little to feed her oxygen-starved brain. "I'm not denying it. But I...want you to want me—like me—for...different reasons. Not the ones you're thinking."

"You just said you're not the marrying sort," he pointed out. "What other reasons could there be? Other than sex?"

Completely frustrated with him and herself, she stepped back and was about to turn in the direction of the house when he caught her upper arm and tugged her back to him.

"You didn't answer my question, Mercedes."

Her lips compressed to a thin line before she finally blurted out, "You're trying to twist everything I say and do. I'm not going to answer, or even try. You wouldn't understand."

The last three words were said with a tremor in her voice and Mercedes hated herself for showing him just how much he affected her. It wasn't right that he could twist her into knots while he appeared to be as cold as a piece of steel.

"Understand this, Mercedes. I'm a man. Not a plaything."

She struggled to keep her temper from rising and to ignore the hurt spiraling through her. But her low voice quivered with emotion when she was finally able to reply.

"Is that what you think this is all about? That I invited you here to my home because I—I want you for a sex partner? Do I look that desperate?"

No. She didn't look desperate at all, Gabe thought. Hell, she could have most any man she wanted. And that only confused him more. He couldn't understand her motives, or believe that she simply wanted his company and friendship, and it had him behaving like an ass. Yet when he looked at this woman, all he could think of was how much he wanted her and how easy it would be for him to become her fool.

"I'm sorry, Mercedes. I shouldn't have said any of that. You've been very gracious tonight. And—well, something about you brings out the worst in me." He released his hold on her arm and turned back to his truck. "I'd better go."

"Gabe."

She said his name with such soft yearning that he had to pause, had to look back.

"It's all right for me to like you, isn't it?"

"I can't think why you would."

He opened the door of the truck and climbed in. As he started the engine, he glanced out the open window to see her hovering a couple of steps away.

Lifting her hand in farewell, she called out to him, "Don't forget that I'm coming out to the line shack."

"I won't," he replied, then before he could let himself slide back to the ground and kiss her, he quickly put the truck in gear and drove away.

Three days later, Mercedes was at work in her office, downloading a series of photos she'd taken of Sandbur horses to use in a sales flier, when the door opened and her sister's head appeared.

"Nicci! Come in!"

"Are you busy? If you are, we can come back later."

"We?" Mercedes rose from behind the desk at the same time Nicci opened the door and pushed in a baby stroller.

Mercedes clapped her hands together with glee. "You've brought Sara Rose with you! How wonderful!"

Without asking permission, Mercedes immediately rushed

over to the eight-month-old child and lifted her from the stroller. "What a doll! Let me see those curls," she told the baby as she pulled a floppy pink hat from her head.

Chewing on a finger and drooling down the front of her T-shirt, Sara Rose studied her aunt with an indifferent expression, making Mercedes laugh.

"She's really impressed with me, isn't she?"

Nicci laughed. "Don't feel badly. She doesn't like just anybody. She'll hardly let Lex hold her at all. But she loves Matt."

"That's because Matt knows how to hold a real baby. Lex only knows about the grown-up females." Mercedes gestured toward the couch. "Have a seat. There are homemade cookies over by the coffee machine."

"I'll leave them alone," Nicci said, "but you might let Sara Rose chew on a half of one. It's still a while before supper."

Mercedes carried the baby over to a small table where she stored drinks and snacks and gave her half of an oatmeal cookie. Sara Rose gave the food item a hard shake, laid it on top of her head, then finally shoved it into her mouth.

"I saw another tooth!" Mercedes exclaimed. "Has she gotten another tooth?"

Nicci smiled as she settled herself on the couch. "A few days ago. I think another one on the top is coming in, too."

"Wow! The next thing I know, it'll be time for her to start nursery school."

"Please, let her start walking first," Nicci said with a good-natured groan.

Mercedes went over to the couch and sat down by her sister. After a short minute, Sara Rose began squirming and sliding off her knees, so she set the girl on the floor.

"Don't worry. It's fairly clean," Mercedes assured her sister. "No nasty boots have been in here for a while."

Nicci glanced around the neat office. "This is very nice. How do you like working for the ranch? Getting adjusted?"

"I've got to admit that it's much busier than I ever expected. In fact, I never get caught up." She gestured toward the desk where she'd been working before Nicci arrived. "I was just downloading some horse photos that have to be turned in to the auction company before noon tomorrow. I took them myself and I'm not sure if the poses show off their best points or not. I've got to show them to Gabe this afternoon so he can make the final decision about them."

Nicci's expression turned thoughtful. "Mother said you invited Gabe to supper the other night. Does that mean you're getting interested in the man?"

Leaning forward, Mercedes brushed her fingers over Sara Rose's light brown curls. "We have to work with each other and I want us to be friends. But that gets sort of complicated whenever I get around him. He's so sexy that I can hardly breathe—" She broke off as embarrassed heat colored her cheeks. "Nicci, I don't know what it is about the man. I never expected him, or any man, to make me—feel like I'm on fire."

Nicci leveled a puzzled look at her. "You used to swoon at the mention of John's name. Are you telling me this is more serious?"

Rising to her feet, Mercedes walked across the room to stare out the window overlooking the training pen. For some reason, today the wranglers had been handling the horses without Gabe overseeing them. He'd not informed her that he'd be gone. And she'd found herself glancing out the window all day for the sight of him. Her behavior made her realize she was becoming obsessed with the man. To Mercedes, that was the scariest notion of all.

"I don't know." Turning, she looked worriedly at her sister.

"Nicci, how long did it take for you to realize you—" She stopped short of using the word *love*. To imply that she was falling in love with Gabe Trevino would sound ridiculous, even to herself. "That you really cared about Ridge?"

The question caused Nicci to pause thoughtfully. "That's hard to answer. One day, it just suddenly seemed like he was all I could think about." She chuckled softly. "And that hasn't changed. He and Sara Rose are still pretty much all I think about."

Envy stabbed Mercedes as she watch Nicci's loving gaze settle on her daughter. During the past three years since Drew's betrayal, Mercedes had told herself that being a career woman was enough for her. That she could be happy without a husband or children. Yet seeing Nicci with her daughter made her hunger for a family of her own and the courage to go after her long-buried wishes.

"After all you went through with Bill, I'm surprised you were brave enough to look at another man," she commented.

Nicci shook her head. "It wasn't a matter of being brave, Mercedes. I didn't have a choice. After I met Ridge, I discovered that love wasn't something I could control. It leads you around by the nose, whether you want to be led or not."

Yes. Mercedes could believe that. The things she felt when she thought of Gabe, whenever she was near him, were beyond her control. "So what does that mean?"

Smiling impishly, Nicci answered, "It means that your heart will start overpowering your brain."

"That's a scary notion," Mercedes muttered, then walked back over to the couch and eased down next to her sister. "I can't understand it, Nicci. The man is stoic, guarded, skeptical of everything I do and say. He seems to prefer the company of horses to that of people. So why does he make my heart kick into high gear every time I see him? I really think civilian life is causing me to lose my mind."

With the cookie now little more than soggy crumbs around her mouth, Sara Rose began to crawl across the office floor straight toward a small wastebasket. Nicci jumped to her feet to go after the baby.

"Maybe it's good old-fashioned chemistry, sis," Nicci said. "My suggestion is to spend some quiet time with the man. If it's nothing more than lust, then it will burn itself out."

How could her feelings burn themselves out when Gabe wouldn't allow a flame to ever start? Mercedes tossed Nicci a dry look. "I can't even make a spark with Gabe, much less make flames. You know, sis, I'm beginning to wonder if I stayed in the Air Force too long."

Nicci chuckled as she stood Sara Rose on her feet and helped the baby balance. "What does that have to do with romance?"

Mercedes sighed. For eight years, she'd been one of the guys, a part of a team. And after Drew had cruelly used their friendship, she'd found it easy to forget she was a flesh and blood woman with needs for any sort of companionship. "Maybe I've lost my ability to attract a man."

Nicci burst out laughing. "Mercedes! You're one of the sexiest, most sensual human beings I know. Where is this self-doubt coming from? It's not like you!"

Rising to her feet, Mercedes began to wander restlessly around the small room. "I guess it's because I…haven't really had any sort of physical relations with a man since John."

Nicci's mouth fell open. "Oh, sis. That's been such a long time. Why? Don't you get lonely for a man's company?"

Her eyes full of sad shadows, Mercedes swallowed at the emotions thickening her throat. "I wouldn't let myself think about it. But when I met Gabe, everything just seemed to burst to life. And now I'm not even sure I know how to be a woman around him."

Picking Sara Rose up in her arms, Nicci walked over to Mercedes and cupped a gentle hand against the side of her face.

"You know how. Just be your beautiful self."

Be herself? She'd been an airman for so long that she'd almost forgotten that she was also a part of a family, a woman with basic desires and a heart that needed nurturing. It had been easier to focus on her job, where she could forget the shame and heartache she'd felt over John, push aside the second devastating mistake she'd made by trusting Drew. It had been convenient to let herself think that serving her country was all that she would ever need.

But now she was beginning to see that she wanted more. She wanted a family. Someone to love who would love her back. If that person was Gabe Trevino, she had to find the courage to show him. Even more, to trust him with her heart.

Chapter Seven

The ratchet slipped, causing hunks of grease and dirt to fall on Gabe's face and join the sweat that was already there.

Muttering a curse under his breath, he refastened the tool to the oil plug, then grunted with relief as the threads gave way to his shove.

Dammit, he didn't have time to change the oil in his truck. Neither did he have time to wait around town for a mechanic, so he'd chosen the lesser of two evils.

With the plug finally out, the dirty crude began to drain into the flat plastic pan he'd positioned beneath the motor. While he waited for the motor to empty, he climbed from beneath the truck and unscrewed the cover on the brake fluid well.

Satisfied with the measurement, he was returning the cover when he heard a vehicle approaching behind him. Since he could count on one hand the number of visitors he'd had since he'd moved here three months ago, the sound was both totally unexpected and a tad irritating. He'd had a hell of a day already, and there wasn't much sunlight left. He didn't want to have to round up a drop light just to finish servicing the truck.

Reaching for the straw hat that he'd laid on the front fender, Gabe screwed it down on his head, then peered beneath the shade of the brim at the approaching truck. It was several years old and white. At first glance the driver was obscure, but as the vehicle grew nearer, he could see it was a woman.

Mercedes.

She'd warned him that she might show up at the line shack sometime, but a part of him believed she never would. Or maybe he'd hoped, more than believed. Either way, she was here. And now, in spite of his exhaustion, he was going to have to find the strength to keep her at arm's length.

Using the sleeve covering his forearm, he reached up and wiped at the grime covering his face. A few feet away, she parked her mother's old work truck and hopped to the ground with energy to spare.

Gabe walked over to greet her.

"I see you found your way out here," he said.

She smiled. "I've never forgotten it," she informed him, then glanced toward the raised hood of his truck. "Having problems?"

"No. Just servicing the engine."

She looked back to him. "You should have gotten one of the hands to do it for you."

"I like doing things for myself." Besides, he wanted the other ranch hands to think of him as an equal. Not as a higher-up who got special favors from the family. He'd rather be one of them than above them.

"I don't blame you for that."

She stepped closer and beneath his lowered lashes, Gabe allowed his gaze to travel over her long legs encased in faded blue jeans, the yellow shirt that clung to her midriff and made a low V between her breasts. It didn't matter that the clothes appeared to be well-worn work clothes or that her feet were covered in old cowboy boots with scuffed and scarred toes. She looked as sexy as hell.

"So this is the evening you decided to surprise me with a visit? Or are you here on business?" he asked.

She shook back her heavy hair, which was tied away from her face with a silk scarf a shade lighter than the pale yellow tresses.

"A little of both. I have some last-minute photos to show you. I couldn't find you at the ranch, so I decided to look for you here. But don't let me interrupt. I'm in no hurry and, besides, I'm pretty handy with a wrench—I can help."

She walked over and began poking and prodding at the engine, testing the belts and opening the radiator cap. "Have you checked the brake fluid and air filter? The transmission fluid?"

"I haven't gotten to all of those yet. But I can—"

She waved a dismissive hand at him. "Of course you can. But two can do it faster. You deal with the oil and I'll take care of everything up here," she told him.

Knowing it would be futile to keep arguing with her, Gabe slid under the truck and got back to work while Mercedes started removing the old air filter.

"Yeew. This thing looks awful," she exclaimed. "Got a new one anywhere?"

"In the tool box on the truck."

She went around to the back of the truck and Gabe tried to refocus his attention to the task at hand. It was difficult when he knew she would be back at any moment to stand near his head. She'd be stretching that long, curvy body under the hood to replace the filter and he'd have to imagine while his body grew harder and harder. Dammit.

"I didn't see you around the barn today," she said as she worked. "Did you take the day off?"

Gabe realized he should have called and told her that he'd be away from the ranch for the better part of the day. But he'd conveniently ignored the task. Interacting with her, in even the smallest way, unsettled him no end. Because he was beginning to like her. And that could only lead to problems.

"Sorry. I should have let you know. I've been riding all day with your brother and a couple more wranglers. One of the ranch's foundation stallions and a mare got out of a holding pen last night and took off for parts unknown. We finally found them this evening about four miles from the ranch yard."

"Oh, my. Did you get them corralled?"

He tossed the empty plastic jug into the back of the truck. "About a couple of hours ago."

"That's good. How did they get out? Someone left the gate open?"

He chuckled wryly. "No. It appears the stallion tore down a part of the fence. Or could be the mare wanted to get away from him and tore it down. It would be hard to say which one to pin the blame on."

"Maybe they both wanted out," Mercedes suggested with a grin. "Just to run and have fun."

That was probably right, Gabe thought ruefully. Whenever a male ran after a female, she always led him on quite a chase.

"No matter," he said. "We had a hell of time getting them captured again. Lex was saddle-weary. You didn't see him come in before you left the ranch?"

"No. Nicci came by my office and I was late getting away. I thought about waiting until morning to show you photos, but

I need to make the mail pickup before noon. If you decide I need to take different shots, I knew I'd need more time."

So she did really need to see him on business. He should have known she hadn't raced all the way out here just to see him. What in hell ever made him think she would? She could have her pick of wealthy, well-educated men. Men who mixed well with her social set. She'd never be seriously interested in a cowboy with horse manure on his boots. Besides, he didn't want her to be, he flatly reminded himself.

"Let me finish up here and I'll take a look," he said to her.

After motioning her out of the way, he started the engine to circulate the new oil, then after a couple of minutes shut it off and slammed the hood.

Mercedes looked at him with arched brows. "What about checking the transmission fluid? The engine has to be running for that. And have you greased all the sockets?"

She obviously understood mechanical workings and he admired her knowledge. Still, it irked him that she thought he needed instructions. Sherleen had always been quick to tell him how to do everything, as though he were ignorant or incapable of handling anything. After their divorce, he'd sworn to never get involved with another woman who told him what to do or how to do it.

"Don't worry. I'll take care of that later." Gabe gestured toward the house and the two of them began to walk in that direction. "Where did you learn about machinery?"

"From Dan, an old wrangler who worked on the ranch for probably sixty years or more. He was a hell of a cowboy, but he also knew how to keep things running. He maintained all the tractors and trucks, hay equipment, anything with wheels. I adored the old man and liked to hang around the ranch yard and help him. Mom and Dad never knew it, but he'd tell me shady stories about when he was young and all the escapades he'd had with the, uh, ladies. Anyway, he taught me a lot about motors and things. And maybe a little bit about fast women," she added with a laugh.

Amused, Gabe glanced at her. "What ever happened to this Dan? Is he still around?"

"He's in his nineties now and Nicci and Ridge keep a close watch on his health. Not to mention Cook. Dan's had a crush on her for years, but the most she'll give him is a pie or a box of homemade cookies."

"Poor man," he replied. "Sounds as if he only gets the crumbs."

"I wouldn't say that. That's more than Cook will give any other man."

"Oh? Is she a man hater or something?"

"No!" she said in a half-scolding tone. "Cook doesn't hate anyone. Her heart is too big for that. But she—well, she was widowed way back in the sixties. She'd only been married to her husband a short time when he went to Vietnam. I guess it's as if her love is still frozen in that time—still there with him."

"That's tragic."

"Yes. But on the other hand, she had something with him that some will never have in a lifetime. I think old Dan is wise enough to know that and accept it."

Even though she was talking about Cook, he could hear a dreamy bit of romance in her voice. After the other night at supper and the bitter story she'd told him about her broken relationship, he was surprised to hear the soft wistfulness in her words.

Not wanting to dwell on anything to do with hearts and flowers, Gabe said, "It sounds like the ranch has had some lifetime workers."

"Most people that come to work for us stay." Her glance at him was surreptitious. "Are you going to join the ranks of the stayers?"

Was she feeling him out for personal reasons or did she truly want to know how he felt about working and living on the ranch? Gabe told himself that, either way, he couldn't let it matter to him.

"So far, living here on the Sandbur is much better than going from town to town, place to place. I can see myself growing old here. But nothing in life is ever certain."

"Except death and taxes," she added, completing the old saying.

By now they'd reached the porch of the little house. Stepping onto the planks, Mercedes wrapped her arms around one of the fat cedar posts that supported the porch's roof and looked wistfully out at the lone pine shading the yard. In the years since she'd been gone, the tree had grown tremendously. Some of the branches now reached the roof of the house and each time the wind blew she could hear it whispering through the needles as they scratched against the corrugated iron. The sound was a part of nature's music, added to the bawl of a nearby calf, a horse's nicker, the high-pitched buzz of cicadas. She hadn't realized how much she'd missed those sounds until she'd returned to the Sandbur.

"My family expects me to stay here."

"But is that what you expect to do?" he asked.

Mercedes looked over her shoulder at him, wondering if any of that actually mattered to him. He'd made a decision to make his home here long before he'd ever met her. And she figured his decision to stay through the years ahead would not depend on the direction her own life took.

"That's my plan." She released her hold on the post and

looked around her. "The porch is longer than what I remembered. I guess Mother's had contractors out here building on. She can't leave anything simple," she added with a short laugh.

"She will now. I've told her I don't want anything else changed." Realizing he had little choice but to invite her inside, he gestured toward the door. "Would you like to come in?"

"Thanks. I'm dying to see the inside."

He opened the wooden screen door, then another oak door behind it. As they stepped into the cool living room, Mercedes said, "When I stayed out here, the only heating and cooling system was opening or closing the windows and doors. This is very modern. And the wood floor is beautiful."

"Geraldine insisted on putting in new flooring and appliances. But everything else is the same." He gestured toward an opening that led to the back part of the house. "The bathroom is still in the same place if you'd like to wash up before you look around."

She held up her greasy hands and laughed. "I'd better. Thanks."

Mercedes found her own way to the bathroom and shut the door behind her. As she scrubbed at the grease on her hands, she glanced around the small, but efficient space. There were no frilly decorations to play up the beige tiled walls, just white towels and washcloths, a blue plastic shower curtain and a blue rug on the floor. In front of her, below a small oval mirror, a single shelf held a razor, a shaving cup with soap and brush and a flat hairbrush. It was all neat, utilitarian and very masculine, like Gabe.

Moments later, she retraced her steps to the kitchen and found him washing his hands at a double, stainless steel sink.

Being alone with him was beginning to make her nerves

jump and jitter. How could she want the man, yet at the same time be frightened of wanting him? It was crazy.

At the sound of her footfalls, he glanced up. "Go ahead and look through the house, if you'd like. I'm going to change out of this dirty shirt."

"I'll wait for you to show me through it." Her smile was hesitant. "That way you can't accuse me of being snoopy like Lex always did back when we were kids and he'd let me come into his room. I'd pick up one thing and he'd start yelling. He always guarded his mementos with his very life."

He ripped off a length of paper towels and dried his hands. "Well, you don't have to worry about putting your hands on the wrong thing. I don't keep mementos."

"Why not?"

He darted an impatient glance her way. "I guess I'm just not the sentimental type, Mercedes."

She'd not thought of herself as being overly sentimental, either. But she supposed the memories lining her bedroom shelves said otherwise. "Hmm. I thought everybody kept little things from important moments in their lives."

"What I've kept, I wouldn't want anyone to see," he said brusquely, then stepped away from the sink and motioned for her to follow him.

Trying not to let his curtness get to her, she followed him into the living room. "You've already had a quick view of this area. There's not much here. I kept some pieces of the furniture that were already in the house and added a few of my own."

A couch and armchair done in navy leather faced the two long windows that looked over the front yard, which in all rights, couldn't be called a yard. The uneven ground was actually just pasture grass cropped short by cows.

"You don't have a television?"

He shook his head. "Don't have time for it. I keep a radio. And I read a bit at night. But most times I'm too tired for even that."

"I'm sure," she agreed knowingly. "Wrestling young horses around all day must physically wear on a person. But—well, Mother has made several comments lately that she thinks you do too much. She wants to hire more help for you."

He grimaced. "She needs to get that off her mind. I do things at my own pace. And the wranglers that help me are plenty enough. Your mother is sometimes too generous for her own good."

Mercedes walked over to where he stood near a small farm table with one chair pushed beneath it. Scattered across the top were several notebooks neatly stacked and an open accordion folder jammed with envelopes and other papers.

"Sometimes Mother can go overboard. But that's because she truly cares about people."

"Yeah," he agreed. "She's genuine."

He moved away from the table and she followed a step behind him as he headed down a tiny hallway where the bedrooms were located.

Bedrooms. Oh, dear, maybe she'd made a mistake in wanting to see the house, she thought. But it was a bit too late to be concerned about it now.

Hoping to talk away her nervousness, she said, "Yes, Mother is exactly the woman you see. She's also going on vacation. Her beau, Senator Wolfe Maddson, is taking her next week to his cabin up on the river at Concan. I think she already has four bags packed," she added with a little laugh. "No telling how many she'll have by the time she leaves."

He paused at the open doorway of the larger bedroom and Mercedes tried not to notice the broad expanse of his shoulders, the way his black hair curled against the back of his neck. He was the most sexual creature she'd ever seen in her life and the funny part of it was, he wasn't even trying to be.

She stifled a sigh.

He said, "You don't sound as if you resent her going."

"Why no," she said with a bit of dismay. "Why would I?"

He shrugged. "Because she has affections for a man other than your father."

Shaking her head, Mercedes said, "Mother has lived for a long time without companionship. More than anything, I want her to be happy." Her gaze settled on his face. "Wouldn't you want the same for your mother?"

His eyelids dropped to cover any feelings she might have spotted there.

"I can't answer that, Mercedes. I always saw my parents together and that's the only way I can imagine them."

Sensing that her question had called up bad memories for him, she tried to make amends. "If I could bring them back for you, Gabe, I would. But since I can't, I'll share my mother with you. She'd like that idea."

His gaze flickered to her face. "What makes you think I need a stand-in mom?"

The sudden need to reassure him had her placing a hand on his arm. "Everybody needs somebody."

He glanced down to where her hand rested on his arm and suddenly the air around them seemed to disappear, leaving Mercedes feeling so smothered that she was dizzy from lack of oxygen. Beads of sweat started trickling down her rib cage and between her breasts. The man affected her in ways he couldn't imagine. Or could he? Was he reading the wicked thoughts darting through her mind? Dear God, she prayed not.

"Uh, this is where I sleep," he said after a moment.

The quietly spoken words seemed to break the sparked atmosphere between them. Mercedes quickly jerked her hand from his arm and followed him across the threshold.

Like the rest of the house, it was sparsely furnished, yet she could see signs of him in the row of cowboy hats hanging from pegs along one wall. Most were battered and sweat-stained, telling Mercedes that he'd owned them for a long time.

The bed itself was a standard size with a scrolled iron head- and footboard. Presently the covers were tumbled to expose a set of white sheets. Mercedes tried her best not to imagine him lying there, his bare brown skin in stark contrast to the pristine cotton. Yet her imagination went on without her permission, and the sweat that had so far remained beneath her blouse began to bead across her upper lip.

Drawing in a deep breath, she forced her gaze away from the bed and over to a cane-bottom chair. Thrown over the back was a pair of fancy tooled chaps, the flashy, fringed sort that rough stock riders used on the rodeo circuit.

Walking over to them, she lightly fingered the oak leaf pattern decorating the belt. "Are these yours?"

"Yes," he said quietly. "I've not worn them in years, though."

She glanced curiously over her shoulder at him. "You used to ride broncs?"

He nodded. "Saddle broncs. For a while, when I was very young."

"Really? So did Lex," she told him. "But he got tired of the aches and pains that went with it."

His expression turned wry. "I got tired of being broke. And I decided I'd rather be training a horse not to buck than trying to ride one that did."

Turning away from the chaps, she leveled a teasing little

smile at him. "You fibbed to me a while ago, Gabe Trevino. You told me that you didn't keep mementos."

He frowned. "Those aren't a memento, they're a reminder."

"Of what?"

"Not to ever be that man again."

She simply stared at him and hoped he would elaborate. After several silent moments, she was about to decide he didn't want to share his personal past with her when he leaned a shoulder against the doorjamb and said, "After my parents died, my uncle raised me. A year before, his wife had left with their two boys and he was a bitter guy that liked to drown that bitterness in beer. But he was family and I needed a place to stay. And for the most part, he was good to me."

Something in his words pulled her toward him. "What about your other siblings? They didn't go to live with this same uncle?"

"At that time, my sisters were already married. My brother went to live with one of them. I stayed with Uncle Tony because I didn't want to leave Texas. Just to think of that prospect scared the hell out of me."

Empathy softened her voice. "Oh, Gabe."

Sardonic grooves marked his cheeks. "I was only eleven years old, but already strong-minded. Anyway, Tony wasn't too much on discipline or parenting. He pretty much let me run wild. After a while, I figured his indifference was because he didn't care about me. By the time I graduated high school, I wanted to get away. Any way. Anyhow. Riding broncs let me do that. And for a year or so, I traveled from one end of the country to the other, drinking, carousing, not ever thinking about tomorrow or the risks I was taking. Breaking my neck didn't worry me. I'd already lost everything anyway. Or so I believed."

"Something must have happened to change you," she stated.

"I got word that Tony was very ill. I raced straight back to Texas to help him—or at least try."

Mercedes was puzzled. "But I thought you left because you were at outs with your uncle?"

He shrugged. "He was my father's brother. To think of losing him, too, shook the ground right under me. It shook me even more when I got to the hospital. His kidneys and heart were barely functioning. Drinking doesn't mix with diabetes. Tony learned that the hard way."

"Did he recover?"

"After a long recuperation. I stuck around to help him and—"

Mercedes interrupted. "You mentioned that he had sons. Didn't they show up to help their father?"

Gabe snorted. "Belinda pretty much brainwashed the sons into thinking their father was the cause of their divorce. They abandoned him. After that, I became his son."

"At least you were there for him," Mercedes said, then looked at him thoughtfully. "How did you two make it financially? If he was ill and you'd given up your riding career to be with him, you must have had a struggle on your hands."

Straightening away from the doorjamb, he ran a hand around the back of his neck. "I put in long hours nailing shingles for a local roofing contractor. And when Tony's health began to return, he took in a few horses to train."

"You learned about horses from him?"

Even at a distance, she could see his eyes soften in a way she'd not seen before.

"Everything I know I owe to him."

The fact that he was so humble about his skills, so quick to give credit to others rather than himself, was one more thing Mercedes liked about the man.

"So how is your uncle now?"

A faint smile touched his lips. "He's healthy and sober, thank God. A few years ago, he moved away from Grulla and took a job up on the Four Sixes." His eyes met hers. "I don't get to see him as often as I'd like anymore. But time or distance could never change our relationship. We needed each other back then. We still do."

She glanced over her shoulder at the chaps lying across the back of the straight-back chair. He'd come a long way since those days, she thought. Financially and emotionally.

Suddenly moving past her, he walked over to the closet. "If you'll excuse me, I'll change out of these dirty clothes. Make yourself at home and help yourself to anything in the kitchen."

She thanked him, then shut the bedroom door behind her as she left the room. As she passed the open doorway of a second bedroom, she peeped inside to see that the room had been more or less turned into storage space.

The pine bed and dresser she remembered from years back were nowhere to be seen. Instead, there were several cardboard boxes filled with odds and ends and a couple of shelves lined with paperback books. A corner was piled with old cowboy boots and another with a fancy tooled trophy saddle resting on a wooden stand.

Intrigued by the saddle, Mercedes stepped into the room and over to the stand. The saddle's leather was still shiny from its coat of lacquer, telling her that it had never been ridden. The tooling was deep and done by hand, which would have made the cost of building the item skyrocket.

On both stirrup fenders, raised letters were stenciled. *San Antonio Cutting Championship 1996.* Had Gabe won the saddle? He'd said he didn't keep mementos, but she was discovering that wasn't entirely true. The chaps in his bedroom had proven that. They had also proven that in spite of the image he wanted to project, he was a family man at heart. He loved and needed as much as the next man. Maybe even more than the next man.

Touching the seat of the saddle, she wondered what had happened to end his marriage and wondered, too, if he would ever have the heart to try again.

Chapter Eight

First minutes later, when Gabe entered the kitchen, Mercedes was sitting at the kitchen table, sipping from a foam cup.

She smiled brightly at him.

"I made coffee. Would you like some?"

Before he could answer, she rose to her feet and poured it for him.

"Thank you," he said as he took the cup from her hand.

Her breathing shallow, her gaze quickly flicked over him. He'd changed into jeans and a long-sleeved blue checked shirt that was, in spite of the heat, buttoned at the wrist. Remembering the scars she'd spotted on his wrist that day at the horse barn, she began to wonder if the long sleeves were more than just a barrier to the hot, tropical sun. Perhaps the sleeves were hiding more scars than those she'd glimpsed.

Mercedes hated the idea that he might have endured that much physical trauma, especially when he'd had more than

If offer card is missing write to: Silhouette Reader Service, 3010 Walden Ave., P.O. Box 1867, Buffalo NY 14240-1867

NO POSTAGE
NECESSARY
IF MAILED
IN THE
UNITED STATES

BUSINESS REPLY MAIL
FIRST-CLASS MAIL   PERMIT NO. 717   BUFFALO, NY

POSTAGE WILL BE PAID BY ADDRESSEE

SILHOUETTE READER SERVICE
3010 WALDEN AVE
PO BOX 1867
BUFFALO NY 14240-9952

Get FREE BOOKS and FREE GIFTS when you play the...

LAS VEGAS
GAME

7

Just scratch off the gold box with a coin. Then check below to see the gifts you get! →

YES! I have scratched off the gold box. Please send me my **2 FREE BOOKS** and **2 FREE GIFTS** for which I qualify. I understand that I am under no obligation to purchase any books as explained on the back of this card.

335 SDL ESS2	235 SDL ESWE

FIRST NAME	LAST NAME

ADDRESS

APT.#	CITY

STATE/PROV.	ZIP/POSTAL CODE

(S-SE-09/08)

7	7	7	Worth TWO FREE BOOKS plus TWO FREE GIFTS!
🍒	🍒	🍒	Worth TWO FREE BOOKS!
♣	♣	♣	TRY AGAIN!

www.eHarlequin.com

Offer limited to one per household and not valid to current subscribers of Silhouette Special Edition® books. All orders subject to approval.

his share of emotional injuries in his life. But she wouldn't ask. Not this evening. He'd already opened up about his past much more than she'd ever expected, and for now that was enough to make her happy.

He looked at her over the rim of his cup. "So—where are the photos you needed for me to see?"

Was he that anxious for her to leave? Even though she told herself not to let it bother her, the idea hurt.

"I left them in the truck." She cast him an apologetic smile. "I'm sorry I'm disturbing your evening. It's just that it's been a long time since I've been out here. And I was thinking—before it gets completely dark, would you mind if I walked down to the river? Maybe you'd like to come with me?" she added, hoping she didn't sound overly eager for his company.

He scowled toward the window over the kitchen sink where one could catch a glimpse of the San Antonio as it meandered through a pair of steep banks.

"I don't have any business down at the river."

She rolled her eyes. "I don't, either. Don't you ever just do something for pure pleasure?"

Her question caused his gray gaze to slide slowly down her body, and Mercedes felt the small kitchen suddenly grow even smaller.

"I have my moments," he clipped, then gestured toward a back door. "Let's go. It'll be dark soon."

He was going, but he obviously didn't want to. Mercedes wanted to tell him he didn't have to do her any favors, but she kept the remark to herself as they stepped onto a screened-in back porch furnished with cushioned wicker furniture and several huge potted plants.

Seeing the surprise on her face, he explained, "Your mother

did this. Even though I told her I didn't have time to sit out here. Not working sixteen-hour days."

"No one expects you to put in that many hours."

"I do it because I want to. Isn't that why you went into the military? Because you wanted to?"

She'd gone into the military for a myriad of reasons, some of which she wasn't ready to share with him. She said, "I understand what you're saying."

The porch was built on the side of a hill, making the wooden steps descend steeply. Mercedes was surprised when his hand came around her upper arm to offer her a steadying brace.

Once they reached the sandy ground, there was a trail that led beneath a hackberry tree.

Thankfully, the setting sun had dropped the temperature to a bearable point. Above their heads, a brisk wind began to rattle the leaves.

Mercedes glanced up at the patch of sky visible between the tree branches. "Are we in for a rain shower?"

"I don't know, but it would sure be welcome."

Shaking back her hair, Mercedes sighed with a bit of pleasure. "The wind is nice."

Gabe realized he could now let loose her arm, but he didn't want to. It felt good to touch her, to feel the warmth of her flesh beneath his fingers.

Since the path was too narrow for them to walk comfortably abreast, he allowed Mercedes to walk on the smooth trail while he remained on the outer edge, where tufts of sage and nut grass forced him to watch his step. The fact that he was strolling along with her, for no real purpose except pleasure, felt odd, although he wasn't sure why. This wasn't the first time he'd been outdoors with a woman. He and Mercedes had shared that outdoor supper only a few days ago. Yet this felt entirely different. It was as if the two of them were setting off on an adventure together, and he was letting her lead him to new and secret places that he'd never seen or dreamed about. For the first time since he'd been a youngster, he felt the fun of the moment.

"What was the weather like over in Diego Garcia?" he asked as they carefully stepped their way forward.

"Tropical," she answered. "Hot and humid with lots of rain."

The trail suddenly reached the edge of the steep bank, where it spilled down the side, then wound through a stand of willows. Near the bottom, they stopped on a sandy bar and stared out at the sluggish water slowly working its way to the Gulf some thirty miles away.

"I don't know much about the military, but I thought Diego Garcia was a naval base. Weren't you in the Air Force?"

"I was and it is," she answered. "But a few Air Force people are there working in different capacities."

"Are military people the only ones living on the island?" he asked. She seemed so independent and strong-minded that it was hard for Gabe to imagine her in such a structured day-to-day routine, taking orders from superiors.

"Civilian contract workers are there."

She didn't offer more, and that surprised Gabe. Normally, she was eager to talk. Was there something about the place she wanted to forget?

In spite of his plans to keep an emotional distance from her, he wanted to know about her past, about the things that had affected her and eventually sent her back here to the Sandbur.

"So what was it like there?"

A heavy sigh slipped from her. "It wasn't any different than any other military base. I did my job and relaxed on my time off."

"You didn't have a boyfriend?"

Her features took on a bitter cast. "I didn't want one."

"Why not?"

From beneath her long dark lashes, she darted him an impatient glance. "Because I was more interested in my work. And since I worked with men, I learned it was best to keep things professional."

Gabe couldn't imagine any man in his right faculties standing next to this woman and not feeling some sort of spark. Just looking at her from a distance heated his blood. And somewhere in the undercurrent of her voice, he suspected she'd dealt with something or someone that she wanted to forget.

Secrets. It was obvious she had them and that she didn't want to share any of them with him. But that hardly surprised Gabe. He'd been married to a woman who'd made a profession out of keeping secrets from him. Sherleen had hidden everything from money to relationships from him. Then when he discovered them, she expected him to forgive and understand.

Dear God, he didn't want to dwell on that part of his life now. He didn't want to think that Mercedes could ever be on Sherleen's level. But how could he ever know without letting himself get close to her? And once that happened, it would be too late to protect himself if he was wrong about her.

"So where were you stationed before you went to the island?"

"After basic I was sent to Edwards in California, then on to Peterson in Colorado. That's where I furthered my training in intelligence. I didn't care for the cold and the snow, though, and asked to be transferred."

Before he could ask her anything about those places, her expression became totally shuttered. She moved away and began walking close to the river's edge. For a few moments, Gabe stared thoughtfully after her, then forced himself to rise and follow. A few feet beyond, an oak tree had grown at a severe slant out over the water. With the balance of a cat, Mercedes walked out on the huge trunk and sat down.

Gabe felt like an idiot as he carefully tread onto the tree to join her. He'd not behaved like this since he'd been a small kid. What was he doing following her around like this? He'd had a hell of a day. This was the last thing he needed. But once he sat down next to her, he had to admit it was a cozy seat with the twilight settling around them and the water running lazily beneath their dangling boots.

Mercedes's sigh was audible as she looked around her. "Now this is nice. Very nice."

She tossed him an impish grin and Gabe decided she must have pushed away whatever dark thoughts had been on her mind. He was glad. Dealing with her in a happy mood was much easier than imagining her brooding over a military man.

"I have to confess that this place caused me and my cousin Cordero a lot of problems. Instead of doing our chores, we'd sneak down here and go swimming. The last time we were caught, we were both grounded for a month. Because of that, I missed a party that my best friend was having. At the ripe old age of fourteen, I thought the world was coming to an end and I'd never survive."

"Obviously the grounding taught you a lesson," he said.

"No. A few weeks later, Cordero persuaded me to come out here and go for another dip. He was good at that. He could charm a snake if he tried."

"Sounds as if he was your partner in crime."

She laughed softly. "Yes, he was. I really miss him, you know. But if he's happy living over in Louisiana, that's what matters the most." She looked at him from the corner of her eye. "And if he were still here, then you probably wouldn't be."

Was she trying to say his coming here had affected her in

an important way? No. He couldn't start thinking that he could ever be important to this woman. She might want him, but she would never need him. Not the way a man wanted to be needed.

Shoving his straw hat back on his forehead, he wiped at the sweat with the back of his sleeve. "Everything happens for a reason."

She didn't say anything to that and after several long moments of silence passed, she gestured toward the river.

"See what you've been missing by not coming down here? It's beautiful."

It wasn't the river that made this place special, he thought. It was her. She made walking, talking, even breathing, extraordinary and that realization was beginning to nag him with worry. He didn't want anything becoming special to him. Even the horses that he trained, he tried to keep at an emotional distance. Attachments only caused heartaches. But his heart often got in the way of his plans to remain indifferent.

After more silence passed, she said, "I saw the trophy saddle in the spare bedroom. Did you win it?"

"Ten years ago."

"You don't ever ride it?"

"I want to keep it preserved. Uncle Tony talked me into entering a mare I'd been training in that particular cutting competition. I'd not expected to win, though, and it shocked me when I did. Needless to say, the saddle is significant to me."

Placing one hand on the small space of bark between them, she turned slightly to face him. "Why did winning surprise you? Didn't you think the mare was good enough?"

He chuckled with fond memory. "It wasn't her I was worried about, it was me."

Dimples marked the corners of her mouth and it was all Gabe could do to keep from leaning forward and pressing his lips to her cheeks, her lips. During the past days, he'd ordered himself to forget her. But their work threw them together, and every time they met, he was struck with proof that she wasn't a woman he could easily forget.

"All of us lack self-confidence at some time or another," she said lowly. "There were many times while I was going through basic training that I thought I couldn't make it. But somewhere, deep down, I found something to push me onward. Mainly, I didn't want to fail. And I didn't want to have to come home and tell Mother that I couldn't stand up to the pressure. She doesn't understand failure. She thinks her children, her niece and nephews should all be like this." She held up a tight, warrior-like fist. "But sometimes that's hard to do."

Each time the wind blew he caught the faint scent of jasmine coming from her skin and clothes. The fragrance stirred him almost as much as her nearness.

Gabe drew in a long breath and blew it out. "Yeah. We want to impress the people we love. And sometimes that's good. But sometimes it's the very wrong thing to do. I ought to know. I spent three years trying to impress Sherleen. But in the end, those were three years wasted. Three years that I should have spent being true to myself instead of trying to be something she wanted me to be. Hell, you can't expect to make anyone happy if you're not happy yourself."

Her blue eyes studied him for long, thoughtful moments. "Are you happy now?"

Was he? At times he could say he was content. He had a home that perfectly suited him. He had a job that was everything he'd ever wanted and more. Yet in the dark of night there were moments when he felt so completely and overwhelmingly alone. There were times he imagined children, his children, smiling up at him, holding their arms out to be hugged and loved by him. He thought of a woman in his arms, by his side. Supporting him. Growing old with him. But those were fleeting dreams. Mostly, he pushed them away and assured himself that he already had enough blessings to be a happy man.

"Why shouldn't I be?" he murmured the question. "I'm doing exactly what I want to do."

She shrugged and he could see she'd expected something more from him.

"That's about all anybody can ask for, isn't it?" she said softly.

The wistful note in her voice wound around his heart and spread a cold fog through his chest. He didn't like the feeling. It made him want to reach for her. To feel her warmth, to draw from it and then give the same pleasure back to her.

Suddenly a ball of emotion was choking him, forcing him to swallow. Next to him, Mercedes was nervously wiping her hands down the thighs of her jeans.

"Well, we'd better get to those photos," she suggested.

She was definitely right about that. They needed to leave this spot before he succumbed to the strange urges that were stirring inside of him.

Night was quickly closing in, intensifying the long shadows made by the tree limbs and other scrubby brush growing along the path. As they made their way back to the house, Gabe once again put a steadying hold around Mercedes's elbow.

As they reached the porch, Gabe blurted, "Have you eaten this evening?"

Surprise flickered across her face, yet Gabe figured she wasn't nearly as taken aback by his invitation as he was. The words had burst from him before he could even think of stopping them.

"Uh, no," she answered. "I came straight here after I left the office."

"Why don't you get the photos and I'll see what I can find for us to eat?" he suggested. "Do you need a flashlight to make it out to your truck, or can you see well enough without one?"

"I can see like a cat in the dark," she assured him. "I'll be back in two minutes."

Inside the kitchen, Gabe went to work pulling out an assortment of cold cuts, bread and condiments, and placing them on the small Formica table in one corner of the small room.

He was adding a bag of potato chips and two chilled soda cans to the rest of the food items when Mercedes returned, carrying a manila envelope.

She looked at the table and the things he'd laid out and her expression softened. "Gabe, I really should apologize for causing you this much trouble. But I won't. I love sandwiches!"

He gestured to the table. "Everything is ready."

She flashed him a smile. "Just let me wash up and I will be, too."

Minutes later, as Mercedes popped the last bite of a salami sandwich into her mouth, she couldn't think of a time that food had tasted any better than this. There was something very pleasurable about eating simple food with your hands and sharing a meal with the right person.

And slowly but surely, Mercedes was beginning to believe that Gabe was the right person. Being with him made her feel happy and alive. She didn't know where those feelings were going to lead her. If her past experiences with men were anything to go by, she was in for a brutal fall, yet she had no choice but to follow the whispers in her heart.

Once they'd eaten, Gabe cleared everything from the table

and Mercedes used the clean area to spread out the printouts of photos she'd taken.

As the two of them sat closely side by side, examining the snapshots, she tried to keep her mind on her business and off him.

"I tried to use the sunlight to emphasize favorable lines like long necks and high withers, but I'm not certain if I got the job done," she said with a hint of uncertainty. "When I told Mother I'd take on this job, she didn't tell me it would involve so much photography. I'm not a professional by any stretch of the imagination."

"I think all the photos are good, Mercedes. Very good."

She looked at him with relief. "Thanks. I was a bit worried you wouldn't like them."

"I'm not exactly in a position to fire you if I don't like them."

She frowned. "That's what you think. Mother would fire me in a minute if she thought you were disappointed with my work. Blood might be thicker than water, but not when it comes to the ranch work. But—" her gaze skittered shyly away from his face to settle on the photos "—that's not the point. I admire your work. And I want—well, I'd like for you to think I'm doing a good job, too."

"I do," he said simply.

She dared to look at his dark profile. "That makes me happy."

His gaze suddenly met hers and the dark fire Mercedes saw in his gray eyes shoved her pulse into overdrive.

"Mercedes, I've tried to tell you before that there's not much to like about me."

She tried to breathe, but her lungs felt smothered. The air around them was as charged and heavy as the atmosphere before a tornado. "Why don't you let me be my own judge?"

Disgust twisted his lips. "Because you're not seeing things—me—clearly."

Impulsively, she reached over and covered his hand with hers. "And I could be seeing more about you than even you can see about yourself. Did you ever think about that?"

The muscles in his throat worked as he swallowed, and in his eyes she could see dark doubts flicker. But those fleeting shadows were hardly enough to mask the simmering desire staring back at her, turning her insides into a bubbling cauldron.

"I think you're a stubborn little fool," he murmured.

Her head leaned a fraction closer to his. Close enough to see the pores in his brown skin, the creases at the corner of his eyes, the faint lines in the hard curve of his lips.

Oh, how she wanted to feel, to taste those lips again. The need burned so hotly inside her that it robbed her of breath. She could feel her heart thudding so madly against her ribs that it was causing her whole upper body to tremble.

"Why?" she whispered.

"For wanting to be next to me."

His hand lifted and his fingers threaded into the hair at her temple. The vein in her forehead throbbed beneath his touch and for once in her life, Mercedes was light-headed. If she didn't breathe or move soon, she was going to faint.

"And you won't be satisfied," he went on in a low, guttural tone, "until I want to be next to you."

Even if she was in any condition to speak, to try to deny his words would be futile. Since she'd met him at her coming home party, she'd made it clear in a thousand little ways that she was attracted to him. Now if she tried to turn away and pretend otherwise, it would be the same as lying to him and herself.

"What could be bad about that?" she finally managed to whisper.

"Just about every damned thing," he mouthed under his breath. "You sit there with your eyes full of sultry smiles, your lips calling to me. Yet you have no thoughts about tomorrow. Or what your game might do to us if—"

Mercedes wasn't about to let him go on. She didn't want him to rationalize, analyze or warn. Love couldn't flourish under those terms. It was as Nicci had said. Love couldn't be controlled.

Not wanting to give him the chance to protest more, she closed the tiny space between their faces and captured his lips with hers.

For the first few seconds, his mouth was frozen motionless, his body rigid and withdrawn. She was wondering if he was going to end the kiss as quickly as she'd started it, when he suddenly burst to life. His lips opened and the crush of his mouth upon hers swamped her with such overwhelming pleasure that all she could do was moan.

In a matter of moments, Gabe's arms were circling her shoulders, his lips deepening the kiss. The ability to think was lost for Mercedes. Behind her closed eyes, she gave herself up to the sensations erupting inside her head, the pleasurable ache that was building deep, deep inside her.

The moment Gabe's lips touched hers, he'd forgot all about the consequences of kissing the firebrand in his arms. At the moment, he didn't care what he'd find at the end of the road. All that mattered was the incredible sweetness of Mercedes's lips, the warmth of her body next to his, the need in her hands as they clenched the muscles of his shoulders.

He wanted her desperately. And right now he couldn't think of a good reason to stop.

Slowly, without breaking the contact of their lips, Gabe eased himself up from the chair while drawing her up with him. Once they were standing, he tugged her body forward until her breasts, hips, legs were all aligned with his.

The contact was like kerosene splashed on flame. Fire roared, then a slow, steady burn inched its way through his body until it finally settled in his loins. Instantly, his manhood hardened and in response, his hands slipped to her buttocks to pull her hips tight against the fiery ache bulging behind the fly of his jeans.

Breathless, he lifted his mouth away from hers to suck in long, ragged breaths.

While he restored his lungs, Mercedes's head fell limply back to expose the long, lovely line of her throat. Bending his head, he allowed his lips to glide down the soft skin until he reached the hollow near her collarbone. There he paused to draw in her jasmine scent, to collect on his tongue the sweat that had gathered in the shallow valley.

Goose bumps erupted along her skin, telling Gabe that his touch was affecting her in a way that thrilled him and urged him onward. Dropping his head even more, he looked for and found the point of one breast, then opened his mouth to bite softly through the layers of her blouse and bra.

Immediately her hips began to move against his in an age-old invitation that left no doubt to what she wanted.

"Oh. Oh, Gabe. Make—love to me," she pleaded breathlessly. "Please…make love—to me."

Whether it was the word she'd used or the fear of his own raging need that suddenly chilled him, Gabe didn't know. Either way, he released his hold on her and quickly stepped away, turning his back to her.

Behind him, Mercedes stared in dazed confusion at the rigid line of his shoulders. What had happened? One minute he'd been touching her as though there were no tomorrow and then he'd turn to a chunk of ice. "Gabe? What's wrong?" she whispered hoarsely. .

"You."

The one word rattled around the room before he finally turned to look at her. She winced at the accusation in his gray eyes. How could he seem to want her and hate her at the same time? she wondered achingly.

"I want you to leave. Get out of here," he went on sharply. "Before both of us do something crazy. Something we could never fix."

Crazy? He thought it would be crazy to make love to her? The notion cut her so deeply that she couldn't have made any sort of reply even if she'd wanted to.

Instead of trying, she raced out of the kitchen and didn't stop until she'd reached her truck.

Back inside the house, Gabe glanced at the photos scattered across the table. But he didn't make a move to gather them up and intercept her before she drove away. He couldn't trust himself to face her again. Not tonight. Not when all he wanted to do was take her to his bed and forget there would ever be a tomorrow.

But tomorrow would come, he thought ruefully. He'd have to see her and the wanting would start all over again. And once again, he'd have to remind himself of all the reasons he couldn't let himself love her.

With a self-deprecating groan, he walked over to the table and began to stack the photos. Before he finished the task, he realized that rain was drumming loudly on the tin roof. Even so, the sound couldn't drown out the lonely beating of his heart.

Chapter Nine

The next evening in Geraldine's bedroom, Mercedes stared at her mother in dismay. "Mother, you are kidding, aren't you?"

Geraldine didn't pause a beat as she placed a folded blouse in the suitcase lying open on the bed. Early in the morning, she was driving up to San Antonio to meet her beau, and from there the couple were driving to West Texas for a week. Mercedes had been aware of her mother's plans for days now. But she'd not been aware that Geraldine had also been making plans for Mercedes to accompany Gabe on a horse-auction trip that weekend.

"Mercedes, the Western Heritage Auction is not anything to kid about. It's not like going to the county sale barn where a few grade horses are run in the ring behind the cattle and the hogs. There will be buyers dressed in designer suits and handmade boots, horses that will sell for six figures. It's an important auction for buyers and sellers across the Southwest and beyond. You need to be there to get a sense of the sort of marketing ideas the Sandbur needs to focus on. And as a member of the Sandbur family, you should also be there to help Gabe represent our horses. It's that simple."

It was all Mercedes could do to keep from telling her mother in no uncertain terms that Gabe didn't want or need her help. But that would only arouse Geraldine's suspicions. Besides that, only three weeks had passed since Mercedes had agreed to take on the marketing job for the ranch. To start whining about her responsibilities now would make her look worse than difficult and ungrateful.

"I see," Mercedes said in a low, thoughtful voice. "I didn't realize the Western Heritage Auction was such a big deal."

"Very big," Geraldine replied matter-of-factly. She straightened from her bent position over the suitcase and leveled a direct gaze on her daughter. "Are you having a problem with this plan, Mercedes?"

Problem? Gabe had been so upset with her that he'd ordered her out of his house. And this morning, when she'd entered her office, she'd found the photos on her desk. He'd obviously placed them there early, so he wouldn't have to face her. Yeah, there was a huge problem, she thought dismally.

"No. I—um—I'm just—surprised to hear I'll be making the trip. I figured Lex would be a much better person than me to tag along with Gabe. They get on well together, and he's got more experience representing the Sandbur."

Shaking her head, Geraldine walked over to a long oak dresser and picked up a bag full of toiletries. "Lex is a cattleman. And that's where his expertise is needed most. Anyway, he's going to Florida this weekend—on business."

Fighting off a groan, Mercedes stepped to the foot of the bed and wrapped her hands around the carved oak post.

"Yes, I've heard about Lex's little trips to Florida. He says they're business, but who calls fishing and swimming and lounging around on the beach, business?"

Geraldine created a spot for the toiletries among the other things in the travel bag, then zipped the whole thing closed. "Lex has latched on to one of the best cattle buyers we have," Geraldine told her, "and if keeping the man happy includes beach recreation, then more power to your brother."

Mercedes frowned. "I wasn't complaining, Mother. I just think it's amusing that you call these trips of his to Florida business trips."

"But they are business trips," Geraldine countered. "It's not always pleasant cozying up to someone you don't know all that well." She placed the bag on the floor, then glanced skeptically at her daughter. "Are you having problems with Gabe? You don't sound exactly thrilled about this trip. If something is going on between you two that I need to know about, then you'd better let me in on it now. I'll be leaving the house at five in the morning."

This was the first time in years that Geraldine was going on a vacation and Mercedes wanted her mother's time with Wolfe to be quiet and special, without her having any nagging worries about her children or the ranch. Besides that, Mercedes would bite off her tongue before she'd admit to her mother that she'd thrown herself at Gabe and he'd rejected her. The whole thing was simply too humiliating.

"There's no problem. Don't worry." Mercedes straightened away from the footboard. "Does Gabe know that I'm going with him?"

Geraldine smiled, and if Mercedes hadn't known better, she would have sworn she saw a mischievous twinkle in her mother's eyes.

"I thought I'd let you tell him," she said.

Mercedes exhaled slowly. After last night, she was embarrassed to even face the man, much less inform him that the two of them would be making a five-hundred-mile trip together, and spend two nights sharing cramped quarters.

How was he going to take this news? *How do you think, Mercedes?* a sarcastic voice inside her answered. *The man literally ordered you to get away from him.*

Okay. So Gabe had ordered her out, she mentally argued with herself. But not before he'd ravished her with his lips, heated her body to the bursting point. He'd wanted her. Oh, yes, in spite of his sharp demand for her to leave, Mercedes had felt his desire. He couldn't be as indifferent as he wanted her to believe.

"I'll discuss the trip with him in the morning," Mercedes told her mother. Before Geraldine could say more on the subject, Mercedes quickly switched gears. "Are you sure you have everything ready for your own trip?"

Laughing, Geraldine looked over at the group of leather bags waiting to be loaded in her car. "Doesn't it look like I have everything?" Concern suddenly marked her face. "I hope you and Lex and Nicci don't resent me going with Wolfe for the next week or so to his summer cabin. Do you?"

"Not in the least. We want you to be happy, Mother. And you deserve this time away from the ranch. God knows how hard you work to keep this place going."

"I don't do any more than anyone else," she said dismissively. Then, in an uncharacteristic display of uncertainty, Geraldine's gaze dropped to the floor. "But the ranch isn't what I'm thinking of now, honey. It's you and Lex and the memory of your father that worries me. I know how much you both loved him."

Sensing that words weren't enough to ease her mother's mind, Mercedes walked over to Geraldine and wrapped her arms around her slender shoulders.

"We did love Daddy. But we also want you to be happy, Mother. And if Wolfe makes you happy, we're not about to stand in your way."

A wan smile touched Geraldine's lips. "I would expect that from you, Mercedes. But Lex—I'm not so sure. He was so very close to Paul. And being a man, I'm not sure he understands the loneliness a woman can feel when her spouse is gone."

Frowning, Mercedes asked, "Lex hasn't voiced any sort of disapproval about you dating Wolfe, has he?"

"No. But you know your brother. He's all jokes and laughs. Who knows what's really going on in that head of his."

Mercedes smoothed a hand over her mother's silver hair. "Trust me, Mother. You needn't be worrying about Lex. When it comes down to the bottom line, he loves you and wants you to be happy."

Sighing, the older woman turned away and crossed to the closet. "All right. I'll put that out of my mind. Now what about you? Can you handle this trip with Gabe?"

Mercedes couldn't handle Gabe in any way. He was a man with his own ideas about himself, her and life in general. If last night was any indication, he wasn't about to let her seduce him. And as for him seducing her, well, he'd already done that without even trying.

"I'll be fine, Mother. For the past eight years I've worked with men. Gabe isn't any different."

The words were hardly out of Mercedes's mouth, when that sarcastic voice inside her head was sounding off again.

Liar, liar, pants on fire. Everything about Gabe is different. Everything you feel about Gabe is different.

* * *

The next morning, Mercedes rose early enough to wave her mother off and make a pot of coffee before Cook arrived to make breakfast.

While she was eating an omelet and toast, Lex, dressed in starched jeans and shirt and brown ostrich boots, entered the kitchen. His streaked blond hair was slicked back from his face and he whistled beneath his breath as he headed straight to the coffeepot on the cabinet counter.

"Oh, what a lovely mornin' it is when I wake up to see two roses like this," he said, encompassing both Cook and Mercedes with his compliment.

From her position in front of the gas range, Cook snorted cynically as Lex kissed her cheek.

"What are you wantin' this mornin'? Hotcakes? Well, I'm not fixin' them, so don't bother askin'," she told him. "You can eat what your sister is eatin' and be thankful for it."

"My Lord, but you're crabby this mornin'. Why are you sticking your claws out at me? All I've ever done is love you," he told the older woman.

She looked at him with pursed red lips. "Well, to put it plainly, I'm feelin' pretty useless around here. First your mama leaves, now you and then Mercedes. I don't guess I need to even show up for the next few days, unless I want to help Jorge cook for the boys down at the bunkhouse. And he don't really need me."

Looking over her shoulder, Mercedes suggested, "Why don't you just enjoy the next few days? Relax. Go shopping."

Muttering under her breath, Cook began to break eggs into a glass bowl. "Why would I want to go shopping? I already have everything I need right here."

"Well, you could buy a new dress and surprise old Dan with a visit."

Cook let out a comical wail. "Me showing up would surprise the old codger, all right. Probably give him a heart attack."

Laughing, Lex curled his arm around the back of Cook's waist. "Are you telling me that your legs still look that good?"

Lifting the metal spatula from the stove top, she threatened to swat him. "Get away from here. Now! Or you're gonna be cookin' your own breakfast," she warned.

To show the old woman how worried he was, he kissed her on the cheek again, then sauntered over to his sister and eased down on the long bench across from her.

"So what's this about you leaving?" he asked as he sipped from his coffee mug.

"I'm going to be accompanying Gabe up to the Western Heritage Auction in Oklahoma City."

"Oh. That sounds like fun. Buying or selling?"

Mercedes's brows lifted in surprise. "I'm not sure about the buying. I know we're selling five."

Lex chuckled. "Just wait 'til you get up there, sis. You'll be buying, that's for sure."

She dropped her gaze from his face and refocused it on her plate. "It's not my place to be spending the ranch's money."

"Why not? You're just as much a part of this ranch as anyone else."

She gave her brother a halfhearted grin. "I've been gone for a long time. Let me pay some dues before I start buying livestock."

He patted her cheek, then glanced toward the swinging doors that led in and out of the kitchen. "Mom already gone?"

"She drove away before five o'clock."

"I haven't seen her this excited about anything in a long time." He turned a thoughtful look at Mercedes. "Do you think she plans to marry the senator?"

Mercedes shrugged. "I don't know. She's not mentioned that word around me. But it wouldn't surprise me. She wouldn't just go off with a man unless she really felt deeply for him."

Lex blew out a breath. "Yeah. That's what I was thinking."

Mercedes studied him for a moment. "Mother worries that you disapprove of her relationship with Wolfe. I told her you weren't that selfish."

Lex looked surprised. "Why would she think I'd disapprove?"

"Because you were so close to Daddy."

Rarely did Mercedes ever spot a serious look on her brother's face, but she was seeing one now.

"I'd give both my arms, anything, to have him back," Lex said. "But that has nothing to do with Mom finding happiness. She can't live in the past forever."

"Then you don't resent her relationship with Wolfe?"

"Hell no." He tapped a finger against the middle of his chest. "But if he or any man ever hurts her, he'll have me to answer to."

A knight in shining armor, she thought wryly. If only her gallant brother had been around to save her when John had broken her heart. But she'd been far away in Austin and he'd been here on the ranch, throwing his shoulders into being a cattleman with a mission. And she'd not wanted to share with Lex the humiliating mistakes she'd made with Drew. She'd always wanted her brother's admiration. She couldn't let him know, even to this day, that she'd let a playboy professor and a deceitful airman turn her head.

Lex's eyes sparked with sudden mischief. "So you're going with Gabe this weekend. How's he taking the news?"

A smirk twisted her lips. "He doesn't know about it—yet. I plan to tell him right after I finish breakfast."

"Hmm. I wouldn't want to be around when he hears you're tagging along."

The smirk on Mercedes's face shifted to a frown. "Why? You make it sound as if I'm a case of the measles, or worse."

"I figure Gabe considers women worse than measles."

That's what you think, Mercedes silently retorted. When his lips had fastened over hers, when his hands had cupped her breasts and his hips had ground into hers, it sure as heck hadn't felt as if he was treating her as though she had the measles. But that had been pure sex on his part, she reminded herself. Those moments she'd been crushed up against him had nothing to do with liking or loving. That part had come when the kiss had ended and he'd ordered her to get away from him.

"Well, he's gonna have to either like my company or ignore it," Mercedes said with far more confidence than she felt. "Because one way or the other, I'm going to go and do my job."

Some thirty minutes later, fingers of sunlight had already spread their hold across the ranch and crept up the sides of the barn. As Mercedes made her way to Gabe's office, the blustery words she mouthed to her brother cowered somewhere behind the nervous beat of her heart. So much for Nicci's sage advice, she thought ruefully. She'd tried her rusty sexuality on the man and he'd found it lacking. So where did that leave her plan to impress him?

At Gabe's office, she caught the sound of male conversation drifting from the open door. Deciding it would be best to leave and come back later, she turned to walk away.

"Mercedes," Gabe called out, "come in."

Realizing he must have spotted her, she stepped inside the small room with plans to tell him she'd come back later. But before she could acknowledge Gabe, her gaze caught sight of her uncle Mingo relaxing on the couch.

With a little cry of pleasure, she raced over to the older man and hugged him close. Mingo was more like a father to Mercedes than an uncle, and seeing him this morning was just the thing she needed to give her the courage to deal with Gabe.

"My, my, don't you look as fresh as a spring bluebonnet," Mingo declared as he gave his niece a tight hug.

"And you look like an old teddy bear," she teased, then tugged on the short bristle of white and black whiskers sprouting from his chin and upper lip. "When did you decide to grow this? Don't you know that facial hair makes a man look older?"

Clearly amused, he said, "If that's the case, then why do all the women I know seem to like it?"

Laughing with delight, she leaned close and rubbed her cheek against his chin in a testing way. "Aww, well, I guess it does feel nice. But it makes you look too autocratic."

Mingo laughed. "If I knew what that meant, I might do something about it."

Laughing with him, Mercedes explained, "It means you look as if you should be sitting on a throne with a scepter in your hand."

Mingo glanced over at Gabe and winked. "Just give me a bullwhip. That'll do me."

Mercedes kissed her uncle's cheek, then forced herself to face Gabe. He was watching her through narrowed eyes, as though her unexpected presence in his office was annoying. She tried not to let him get to her, but it was hard to do when just looking at the man sent odd little thrills straight through her. Had she really kissed those stern lips? In the light of day, it seemed impossible.

"Sorry to interrupt," she said to him, then glanced adoringly at Mingo. "But I don't often get the chance to see my uncle."

Mingo gave her an affectionate grin. "A beautiful young

thing like you shouldn't be wasting time with an old man like me anyway."

She frowned at him. "You're not old, Uncle," she scolded gently. "You're just reaching your prime." She looked pointedly at Gabe. "Did you know that my uncle is a living miracle? Three years ago, he couldn't walk or talk. He was in a nursing home—and sitting in a wheelchair instead of a saddle. Now look at him. He has to carry around a stick to knock the women away."

Close to her side, Mingo chuckled. "You're stretching that last bit about the women, aren't you, girl?"

She gave her uncle a sidelong glance. "Not from the stories Cordero tells me. He said Juan quit answering the phone because it was always some lady wanting to speak with you."

Mingo only slapped his knee and shook his head. Across from them, Gabe said, "I knew that Mingo had been disabled sometime back. I didn't know it was to that extent."

Mercedes nodded. "That's why I call him a living miracle. He was in Goliad late one evening when two thugs jumped him with a baseball bat and left him with a brain injury. Thankfully, a wonderful neurosurgeon over in Houston fixed everything back the way it should be, but Uncle Mingo still went through months of difficult therapy."

"Yeah," Mingo echoed. "Now the only thing left is to find the two hoodlums and put them behind bars."

Clearly surprised, Gabe's gaze vacillated between Mingo and Mercedes. "You mean, the persons that did this haven't been caught or prosecuted?"

Mercedes shook her head while Mingo said, "Sheriff Travers and the whole department are still working on the case. And I have faith, Gabe. I'll have my justice in due time."

The older man rose to his feet and announced he had to be going. "Gracia has her eye on a new horse up at San Marcos.

Matt says he'll buy the animal for her if I go have a look at him first." He chuckled fondly. "She's probably already sitting in the truck, waiting for her grandfather to show up."

"Have a safe trip, Uncle," Mercedes called after him. Once he was out of sight, she turned to Gabe. "I didn't expect you to have company this early in the morning."

His gaze was like a gray laser cutting hot streaks across her face and down the length of her body. "Mingo comes by fairly often," he drawled. "He likes to get updates on the horses. And I like to get his advice. He's already forgotten more things about horses than I've ever learned."

In spite of her nervousness, she warmed to him. How could she not, when he had nothing but kind words for her family? "I'm glad you don't resent him."

"Resent him, hell," he mouthed under his breath. "I don't have an ego problem, Mercedes. I'm not some jerk who thinks he's the only man alive that knows how to handle a horse."

Her pulse fluttered. "I never thought you were. And actually—I'm not here to discuss my uncle. I—"

"Mercedes, if you're here to discuss last night, then forget it," he said sharply. "I have."

Had he? That wasn't what the slumbering shadows in his eyes told her. But now wasn't the time to discuss their hot embrace in his kitchen. She had to get through this coming weekend without making a fool of herself.

"I assure you," she said stiffly, "that I have no intention of discussing that—lapse between us. I'm here about the upcoming auction."

His brows drew together to form a black streak above his gray eyes. "The Western Heritage Auction? What's that got to do with you? I thought all the pertinent information had already been sent. If not, it's far too late to be in the sale catalog."

Drawing in a bracing breath, Mercedes shook her head. "It's not about catalog information. I— Mother discussed the whole thing with me last night. She insists that I make the trip with you."

Silence ensued as Gabe stared at her. "No. I'm not about to take you on this trip."

His blunt refusal should have angered her. After all, she was a part of this ranch, too. She had as much right and reason to make the trip as he did. But as she studied his narrowed eyes and rock-hard jaw, all she could feel was hurt. Hurt that he obviously couldn't bear to think of spending that much time in her company.

Oh, Mercedes, you've learned that things are bad when a man has the power to hurt you.

"I'm sorry you feel that way, because Mother didn't leave either one of us a choice," she told him. "She wants me there to observe, to represent the Sandbur and to help you in any way you might need."

Rising to his feet, he walked over to a small table holding a coffee machine. "Then I'll talk to her," he said brusquely. "I'll tell her that I can handle things by myself."

"Too late. She left this morning to meet Senator Maddson in San Antonio. I have her cell-phone number if you'd like to call her. But I can tell you right now that arguing with her about this isn't going to make her happy. And I wouldn't like that at all. This is the first time in years that my mother's actually taken a vacation. I don't want her fretting—about anything."

Glancing over his shoulder, he stabbed her with an accusing gaze. "You're getting pleasure out of this, aren't you?"

Unable to remain still, Mercedes left the couch and walked over to the front of his desk.

"If you think I could possibly get pleasure from having someone tell me they don't want me around, then you've got to be crazy." She folded her arms against her breasts as she tried to hang on to her temper. "I argued with Mother about me making the trip. I told her that I didn't want to go because I knew you were going to react this way!"

Plopping his coffee back down on the table, he stalked over to where she was standing. "Of course you knew I would react this way, because you know as well as I do that the two of us can't be together! When we're together, we both act like fools!"

She drew in a long, shuddering breath. "Thank you, Gabe," she said with sarcasm. "I've always wanted a man to call me a fool."

He inched close enough for her to catch a whiff of the scents of soap and horses emanating from his denim shirt, to see the dark glint in his gray eyes and the moist sheen on his bottom lip. Even in anger, she was astonished at how much she wanted him.

"I included myself under that description." Shaking his head, he muttered a curse under his breath. "What in hell was Geraldine thinking?"

Her blood simmering, Mercedes tossed her head, sending her thick blond hair rippling down her back. "She was thinking that we're two adults with a job to do. She was thinking we're going to Oklahoma to do those jobs. Not to claw and hiss at each other."

His eyelids lowered as his gaze settled on her lips. "Or to make love," he whispered hoarsely.

Make love.

She didn't know whether it was those two words or the low growl in his voice that sent a sultry shiver down her spine. Either way, she couldn't stop her body from gravitating toward his. It was crazy, she thought. How could she still want this man so much even when he was making it clear he didn't want her around. "That—won't be on the agenda. Unless you want it to be."

His nostrils flared with disdain. "That won't be an option. Ever."

The sharpness of his voice brought a stinging ache to her throat. "Then that's the way it will be," she murmured.

Mercedes blinked hot moisture from her eyes and quickly turned to leave the office. She'd taken one step when his hand wrapped around her upper arm. Her heart racing from his unexpected touch, she dared to glance back at him.

"Was there something else?" she asked coldly.

His gaze flicked over her face in a dismissive way. "I'll be leaving the ranch yard at five in the morning. If you're not there on time, I'll leave without you. Got it?"

He knew that she was an early riser. For him to imply that she was some spoiled princess that didn't rise from bed until midmorning made her want to slap his face.

"Don't think for one minute I'll let you off that easily, Mr. Trevino. I'll see you in the morning," she muttered furiously. Jerking her arm free from his grasp, she rushed out of the office and didn't stop until she was halfway across the huge ranch yard.

By then, tears were on her face and she dashed them back with an angry hand. Eight years ago, she'd cried a bucket of tears over John. She'd learned a painful lesson about lying men, but apparently the lesson hadn't been enough. Drew had come along and once again she'd fallen into the trap. Now she was making that same mistake all over again with Gabe Trevino. But this time, she'd stay strong. She would stiffen her spine and show him that she wasn't going to let him walk all over her heart.

Chapter Ten

Dark gray shadows still shrouded the ranch yard the next morning when Mercedes walked to the waiting truck and trailer parked near the horse barn.

Even though it was several minutes before five o'clock, the diesel motor was already idling and the cargo lights were on, along with the rows of lights illuminating the outline of the thirty-foot horse van. Five heads, their eyes goggled with safety screens, hung out the open windows, telling Mercedes the horses were all loaded and ready to travel.

She quickly stowed her bags in the living quarters of the trailer, then stepped out to see Gabe standing near the back of the big rig, apparently checking the van one last time to ensure the horses' care and well-being during the trip.

Mercedes didn't bother announcing her presence. Instead, she simply climbed into the cab of the freighter and waited for Gabe to join her.

Five minutes passed before the cab door finally opened and he climbed in the seat behind the wheel. By then, she'd already fastened her safety belt and tuned the radio to a station that played only Elvis. After all, she didn't intend to let Gabe dictate everything about this trip.

"Good morning," she greeted, forcing a normalcy to her voice that she was far from feeling.

He nodded slightly in her direction. "Good morning."

"Are we ready to go?" she asked.

He reached for the gearshift in the middle of the floor. "We're off."

In spite of their sharp exchange yesterday morning, Mercedes couldn't help but feel a spurt of adventure and excitement as the big truck began to lumber across the ranch yard, then on past the ranch's entrance.

The last time Mercedes had taken a major driving trip was back as a teenager. She'd gone with her uncle Mingo to Clovis, New Mexico, for a three-day horse sale. If this trip gave her only a fraction of the fun she'd had on that one, then it was something to look forward to. And maybe she could enjoy these days ahead, she thought hopefully. All she had to do was stay out of Gabe's way.

But how could she do that, when everything inside her wanted to be near the man?

After an hour's travel, the sun had risen high in the morning sky, and Gabe had directed the big rig onto a major interstate directly north through the heart of Texas. For the most part, his passenger had spoken very little. Whenever she did, it was only to make a comment about things she spotted along the highway.

Gabe had to admit he didn't know what to make of her quietness. Up to this morning, the Mercedes he knew normally chattered. But for the past hundred miles, she hadn't appeared interested in conversation or in him. Which was well and good, he thought sourly. He'd not wanted her on this trip in the first place. A man could take just so much temptation before he succumbed.

Still, he couldn't ignore the beautiful picture she made sitting only inches away from him, her face quiet and thoughtful as she gazed out at the passing landscape.

She'd dressed totally western for the trip in a red flowered shirt with white piping and wide cuffs buttoned at her wrist. The hems of her blue jeans were tucked into a pair of tall, black, cowboy boots, while the waist was cinched with a matching black belt. Her long hair was brushed in loose waves and pinned behind one ear with a silver tooled barrette.

She managed to look cute and classy at the same time and he wondered what her fellow airmen would think if they could see her like this. Had any of them known there'd been a cowgirl inside the military woman?

Or was she still a military woman inside that cowgirl outfit? It was a question that nagged Gabe daily. From the first moment he'd met her at the homecoming party, he'd formed the impression that she was a violet among a bunch of tough weeds. She didn't fit with the life of an isolated ranch, even one as big and wealthy as the Sandbur. He feared she was going through the motions of this marketing job just to appease her mother and the rest of the family until she found a job that would take her away again.

Either way, it couldn't matter to him, he told himself. Mercedes was off-limits.

Yeah, off-limits. In spite of all the times he'd told himself just that, in spite of the fuss he'd made yesterday about her coming on this trip, he couldn't stop the thrill he felt at having her near. It was stupid and dangerous. It went against every vow he'd made about letting a woman make him vulnerable again. But he couldn't help himself.

She began to shift in the seat and he glanced over in time to see her crossing her long legs and smoothing a hand down her shapely thigh.

"Are you getting tired?" he asked.

Faint surprise marked her face as she darted a glance at him. "No."

"Well, if you need to stop for the restroom or anything, just tell me. I'm not like those drivers who think they have to keep barreling on until they reach their destination."

Her brows piqued with interest. "That's hard to believe. To me, you've always come across as a man on a mission."

Why did he want to reach over and touch her? he wondered. Why did he want to drag his fingers down her honey-brown cheek, along the tender curve of her throat? Why did he want to believe the kisses she'd given him at the line shack had been more than fun and games?

"We're on a trip, Mercedes," he pointed out dryly. "Not a death march."

She straightened upright in the wide leather seat and stared at the windshield in front of her. "That's good to know," she said with a hint of sarcasm. "Especially after you so *kindly* accepted my part in this jaunt."

He groaned. "We're not going to go over that again, Mercedes. You're here. I'm here. We don't need to spend the next few days being hostile to each other."

Her head twisted toward him and as he watched her features soften into a beautiful smile, he felt his heart jerk, then begin to melt like a roasting marshmallow.

"That's the way I see it, too," she agreed. "And since you're being so agreeable for the moment, I should mention that Cook packed us a picnic basket. I thought we might stop at a roadside park for lunch."

She'd planned a picnic? That kind of lighthearted meal wasn't the sort of thing he normally shared with a woman. Partly because it had a family feel to it, and partly because the majority of his lady friends expected to be fed in nice restaurants. "Are you sure you'd rather not eat in a restaurant?"

Over the crooning voice of the King coming from the radio, he could hear her soft, impatient sigh. "It's always nicer to eat outside in the peace and quiet. Besides that, you could stop at every food joint from here to the Oklahoma border and not find anything as good as what Cook sent."

He might as well face it, Gabe thought, the woman was never going to be predictable. And he could only wonder what to expect from her next.

Three hours later, just outside the busy outskirts of Fort Worth, Mercedes spotted a roadside park with a wide, circular pull-off, plenty of grassy grounds and cement tables shaded by massive oak trees. Both agreed it would be a good place for lunch before they reached the hectic city traffic.

Gabe parked the rig in a far, out-of-the-way space, and Mercedes fetched the picnic basket from the front of the trailer. While she spread the food on a table located at one end of the little park, Gabe went to check on the horses and offer them a drink of water.

The day was hot and windy enough to toss Mercedes's blond hair all about her head. She was tying it back with a scarf when Gabe finally joined her. Thankfully, after their fragile truce this morning, he'd actually been easy to travel with and the past few hours had passed quickly as they'd talked about an array of subjects.

She'd been surprised to learn that he was very knowledgeable about current world events, which he kept up with by reading the newspaper rather than watching television, a device he didn't own. Up until today, she'd considered him an indifferent man. One that didn't care about the outside world, only about the small area around him. She'd been wrong, and that had pleased her. A man had to care before he could love. Not that she could ever expect him to ever love her. But at least she knew he had the capability and that was a teeny start.

"How are the horses making it?" she asked. "Do we need to get them out and let them walk around?"

He lifted his hat and raked a hand through his hair. "No. They're resting just fine as they are. Getting them out in a strange place, especially this close to a large interstate with all the loud traffic, might upset them. They feel safe and happy together inside their little cubbyholes. And they all drank, so I'm not worried about them getting dehydrated."

"That's good," she said with a relieved smile. "So that means we can enjoy our meal."

Gabe glanced behind her at the table. "My word, there's enough food there to feed the whole ranch," he declared.

Mercedes laughed. "Cook never lets anyone go hungry. And what's left over, I'll put in the refrigerator and we can have it later." She motioned for him to take a seat, then slipped onto the bench opposite him. "C'mon, let's eat."

Besides containers of fried chicken and coleslaw, there were also thick sandwiches made of pork loin and kosher pickles, along with all sorts of condiments, chips, drinks and homemade cookies. Mercedes dipped into the chicken first while Gabe chose a sandwich.

"I guess you've traveled a lot in the past few years," she said as she spooned slaw onto a paper plate. "What was that like?"

He shrugged. "Seeing different places was nice—for a while. But I like having my own home—knowing where I'm going to be sleeping at the end of the day."

Roots. Most everyone needed them at some point in their life, Mercedes thought. The Sandbur was her roots and she'd come back to let them nourish and direct her. But what about Gabe? He'd lost his parents at a tragically young age. Then his marriage had ended, tearing away what few roots he'd tried to sink with his wife. Maybe after all that, he'd come to the Sandbur for the same reasons she had. To be home. Really home.

"The people you worked for, what sort of people were they?" she asked thoughtfully.

A smirk tugged at one corner of his lips. "Rich, indulged, used to getting anything and everything they wanted."

Like her? Was that really what he thought? She didn't ask. The cease-fire between them was too tenuous to survive such a question. "If that's the case, why didn't they simply buy other horses rather than have you fix the ones they had? Wouldn't that have been easier?"

He chuckled as he reached for a handful of corn chips. "Sure, that would be the reasonable option. But people like that aren't used to having anyone tell them no—even a horse. They can't let anyone, particularly an animal, outdo them. So they try to bend the horse to do their will and then the fight is on."

"Dear God, but that's twisted," she murmured.

He nodded soberly. "Yes, but true."

With a slight shake of her head, Mercedes looked at him with dismay. "How could you tolerate working for folks like that?"

To her surprise, he grinned.

"Because I knew that in the process of healing the horse,

the owner could be healed, too. When a person learns to focus their interest and affection on an animal, rather than himself, it changes him for the better. In the end, that gave my job some meaning. And isn't that what we all want—for what we do to have meaning?"

Mercedes absently stirred her plastic fork through the shredded cabbage. "Mmm. Yes. That's why I didn't want Mother fabricating a job for me. I couldn't stand that. It would be like living a waste."

Feeling his eyes upon her, she glanced up to see he was studying her with a skeptical expression.

"Lex has told me that you were very good at your job in the Air Force. He says you could easily get a nice position with the CIA, FBI or other government agencies. Do you ever think about that?"

She sighed. "It's an option. But I've spent years serving my country. After I was home at the Sandbur for a few days, I realized the ranch was my calling."

"Isn't that too convenient?"

Any other time, his question would probably have angered her, but something on his face told her that he wasn't being sarcastic; he actually wanted to know how she felt. That idea was enough to send a warm feeling spilling through her.

"It probably looks that way," she agreed. "But you see, my roots are important to me, too. The Sandbur isn't just a ranch that raises cattle and horses. It's a history. It's a family legacy—my family. My great-grandparents struggled through the Depression to hold on to the land. Their descendants before them carved the place out of the wilds, fought with outlaws and comancheros, only to have the homestead burned to the ground and their stock scattered by Santa Anna's army. But they never gave up on the ranch." She paused long enough to shake her head. "They all, including my own parents, have sacrificed so much to make the Sandbur what it is today. Surely you can see it's important for me to contribute my part?"

But why? Gabe wondered. Out of love for what she was doing or guilt that she'd spent the past years away from the ranch? If she'd only taken the job out of a sense of obligation, then would that be enough to make her stay?

"You knew all of this before you joined the Air Force. If you felt that passionately about the ranch, why did you leave in the first place?"

Her head dipped and hid the expression in her eyes as though his question made her ashamed. Gabe found himself wanting to reach across the table, to lift her chin and assure her that washing her with guilt had never been his intention. All he wanted was to dig inside her, to take out her feelings and see if they were actually coming from her heart.

"You're right. Eight years ago, I wasn't blind to the sacrifices my family had made for the ranch. But I—" Sighing heavily, she looked up, regret written on her face. "I had other issues going on at that time. I needed to get away—to get my life back in order before I could ever make a worthwhile contribution to anyone—especially my family."

Those other "issues" could only refer to the man who'd broken her heart, Gabe thought grimly. She'd said she was long over the guy, but that didn't ring true with him. If her heart was truly mended, she would've already found another man to love and marry. Yet she'd told Gabe with her own lips that she wasn't looking for marriage. The whole thing made him wonder if there was more to her reluctance to become a wife.

Hell, it doesn't matter why she's chosen to stay single, he told himself. He wasn't looking for a wife. And even if he were, Mercedes wouldn't be on his shopping list.

Back when he'd been married to Sherleen, his caring and his efforts to lay everything at his lady love's feet had gone unappreciated. He figured it would be the same for any man who tried to keep Mercedes happy. What could a man give a woman who already had everything, a woman who could easily take care of herself? Nothing. And he needed to remember that.

Brushing cookie crumbs from his hands, he rose to his feet. "We'd better hit the road. I want to get the horses stabled and settled before dark. And I'm sure you need to register at your hotel."

Rising to her feet, Mercedes stared at him as though she could see his lips moving but couldn't hear his words.

"What did you say? A hotel?"

He picked up the plastic wrap that had covered his sandwich, along with his empty soda can. "That's right. We will be staying in the city for the next two nights. You were aware of that, weren't you?"

Frowning, she quickly began to gather up containers of food and shove them inside the picnic basket. "Of course. But I have no intentions of staying in a hotel, motel, bed-and-breakfast or any other place of lodging." She pointed directly at the horse trailer. "We're hauling our living quarters with us. There's no need for me to spend an exorbitant amount of money on a room that would only be used for sleeping."

His jaw dropped. "But I'll be bunking in the trailer."

She shrugged as if his presence was no concern at all to her. And maybe it wasn't, he thought grimly. Maybe those kisses she'd given him at the line shack had been just a game to her.

"So?" she asked. "If I recall correctly, there are three beds. One double and two bunk beds. That's more than enough sleeping area for the both of us."

Sleeping was hardly what Gabe was worried about. If she stayed in the trailer's living quarters with him, he wouldn't just be fighting for sleep, he'd be in a hell of a war to keep his hands off her.

"I seriously doubt Geraldine expects you to be housed in a horse trailer for the next two nights," he began to argue.

Smiling smugly, she placed the last container of food in the basket, then shut the wooden lid over the top. "Apparently you don't know my mother as well as I thought you did. When roundup is going on in the spring and fall, she sleeps on the ground in a bedroll. As far as she's concerned, the trailer is a luxury. And as her daughter, I don't expect more. Understand?"

No. Gabe didn't understand. All this woman had to do was pull out a credit card and she could pay for as many nights as she wanted in the most luxurious hotel in Oklahoma City. But deep down he knew that wasn't her style.

Desperate now, he walked around the table and peered down at her. "Dammit, Mercedes, you know this is different. Why the hell are you trying to be difficult?"

Her little chin pointed up at him in a challenging way. "How is it different?" she demanded. "We're on a job together. Nothing more. Nothing less. That's the way you want it—isn't it?"

"Yes! But—" He paused, then a look of relief washed over his face. "I don't know what the hell I'm arguing with you for. You can have the trailer and *I'll* rent a hotel room."

Her soft lips suddenly doubled together to form a grim line. "No. You can't do that. You need to be near the horses. Their welfare is your responsibility."

Dammit, she was right. He couldn't go off to another part of town and leave her there alone to contend with the horses by herself. If anything should happen to one of them and he wasn't around to deal with the problem, he'd look like an ass or worse.

"You're getting pleasure out of this, aren't you?" he asked tightly.

Biting down on her bottom lip, she glanced away from him. "Pleasure?" she echoed hoarsely. Twisting her head back to him, she stabbed him with an accusing look. "If you'd actually like to know, I can tell you what would give me pleasure. To hear you say that you're glad I'm making this trip with you. That you look forward to having my company for the next couple of nights instead of spending them alone. But admitting to anything close to that would be too much for you, wouldn't it? You couldn't bear to have me thinking that you might actually like me. No, you're scared that might give me the wrong ideas. God forbid, it might even make me grab you and kiss you. Like this."

Before Gabe realized her intentions, she had curled her arms around his neck and plastered her mouth over his. The shock of her actions very nearly caused him to stagger backward, but he managed to catch himself, and soon her lips were working magic on his senses.

For a few reckless moments, he let himself forget that they were standing out in the open at a public place. He forgot that he wasn't supposed to be touching, tasting, giving in to her delicious charms.

He could hear the hot wind whistling past their bodies, the birds above their heads, the speeding traffic somewhere far behind them. But none of those distractions were enough to break the spell of her kiss. It was the sudden hardening of his body that shocked him back to his senses and gave him the will to finally break the contact between them.

Still facing her, he sucked in several long breaths and tried to collect himself while Mercedes's eyelids slowly lifted. Her blue eyes had a smoky sultriness to them as she gazed up at him. The sight made his gut clench, his teeth snap together. He wanted to wring her neck, yet at the same time, he wanted her back in his arms. The war of contrasts waging inside of him was so violent that it made it impossible for him to form words of any kind.

All he could do was turn on his heel and stalk back to the truck.

As for Mercedes, she tried to tell herself that his walking away didn't matter. But it was very hard to ignore the rejection slicing through her with double-edged blades. Still, she wasn't going to let humiliation or tears take her over. No. She wouldn't give the man that much satisfaction.

Slowly, she ambled to the restroom. She took more than enough time to use the facilities, then strolled back out to the picnic table to pick up the basket of remaining food.

After she'd carefully stowed the perishable items in the refrigerator in the living quarters, she secured the door, then climbed back into the cab of the truck.

Once she'd secured her seat belt and settled back for the ride, Gabe flicked her a sardonic look.

"Are you ready now?"

The cutting tone of his voice brought her temper to a low boil, but she refused to let him see it.

"Yes, thank you," she said with prim sweetness.

"Good," he growled as he thrust the transmission into low gear. "Maybe we'll get there before midnight."

Not bothering to make any sort of retort to his barb, Mercedes waited until he'd gotten back onto the highway and was speeding toward Fort Worth before she spoke again, struggling to keep her voice from trembling with anger and hurt.

Staring straight ahead, she muttered forcefully, "If you think I'm going to apologize for that—for kissing you back there—then forget it! At least I'm not trying to hide my feelings—like you!"

From the corner of her eye, she could see his head whip around, his hard gaze fix itself upon the side of her face. Mercedes could only sit there and wonder why he held such magnified importance to her heart. It was as if her happiness, her very life hinged on his every glance, every word, every touch. *Oh, God, don't let me be hurt all over again,* she silently prayed.

"What is that suppose to mean?" he asked sharply.

Making her face as stoic as possible, she turned her head slightly to look at him. "Think about it, Gabe. You might just figure it out on your own!"

Chapter Eleven

The remaining miles to Oklahoma City passed for the most part in silence. With Gabe doing little more than glaring at the highway ahead of them, Mercedes used the time to read a paperback book she'd brought with her.

Mercedes was greatly relieved when they reached the sale barn where the auction would be taking place. The stress of being cooped up with a reluctant traveling companion, along with sitting in one spot for hours on end, had utterly drained her.

Across from the massive building, several acres of manicured lawn were equipped with RV and trailer hook-ups. Gabe chose an out-of-the-way spot that was shaded with a huge sycamore tree, and after he'd parked and hooked up the utilities to the living quarters, Mercedes helped him unload the horses and remove their goggles.

Since they were already privy to the stall numbers that their horses had been assigned, they took them directly to the barn, Gabe leading three and Mercedes the other two.

Without him saying anything, she understood that he didn't want her help with any of the actual hands-on care of the horses. But she didn't let that prevent her from hanging around until each animal was groomed, fed, watered and settled down for the night.

"I'm going over to the sales office and check in," Mercedes told him after the last horse was fed. "Would you like to come with me?"

Without looking at her, he bent down and picked up two black feed buckets. "No. That's your department."

Growing more aggravated by the minute, Mercedes closed her eyes and pinched the bridge of her nose. "If I'd stayed home like you wanted me to, it would have been *your* department," she couldn't stop herself from reminding him.

Rising to his full height, he glared at her. "Look, if you don't want to go to the office and let someone know that we've arrived with our horses, then I'll do it."

Her eyes popped open. "That's not what I said! I was inviting you to go with me. I don't know my way around this place any more than you do. I thought it would be nice if we could search for the office together. But I guess that's asking too much of you." She gritted her teeth. Before he could utter a word, she turned on her heel and headed toward the exit of the barn.

Along the way, sellers were tending to their horses, while potential buyers were strolling, catalog in hand, from one stall to the next. When a hand caught her from behind and prevented her forward progress, she expected to turn around and see an old acquaintance, someone who had spotted her and wanted to say hello. Instead, Gabe was standing a step behind her, a faintly sheepish expression on his face.

"What's wrong?" she demanded, knowing he wouldn't have come after her unless there was a problem.

His gaze dropped from hers to the dirt beneath their boots. "Nothing is wrong," he said gruffly. "I changed my mind. We'll go to the office together."

Not feeling the least bit appeased, especially when he sounded as if he were coughing up nails instead of complying with her wishes, she pulled her arm from his grasp. "I wouldn't knock myself out, if I were you."

That brought his head up, and he stared at her for such a long time that Mercedes began to tremble inside, to warm with the need to get close to him.

"Okay, Mercedes, I'm sorry if you think I'm being difficult. This tension between us is not what I want. We have two more long days together ahead of us. We can't spend it fighting and snarling."

"I'm glad you see it that way," she said softly. "There was no reason to let one little kiss make you so angry."

His jaw grew rigid. "I suppose you've forgotten it?"

As she looked into his eyes, she felt her upper body gravitating toward his, but she quickly snapped herself to a ramrod-straight posture.

"No. And I hope you haven't, either."

He sucked in a long breath, then fastened a tight hold on her upper arm. "C'mon. Let's get this over with. I'm hungry and tired and I want this day to be over with."

Mercedes wanted to tell him that he certainly knew how to stroke a girl's ego, but she didn't. For now, he was by her side—she didn't want to say or do anything to change that.

Thirty minutes later, they left the office and stepped back outside. Gabe suddenly realized there was no way he could go to a restaurant without inviting her to join him. Sitting across the dinner table from her wasn't something he relished. After that kiss she'd whammed him with that afternoon, he didn't know what to expect from her. And he'd just as soon eat in peace than to constantly be on guard. But he wasn't a complete heel, no matter how much her company disturbed him.

As they walked away from the sale barn, he said, "There are several restaurants across the highway. Are you ready for dinner?"

Fully expecting her to latch on to his arm and give him a bright smile, she surprised him by shaking her head. "No thank you, Gabe. You go ahead. I'm tired. I'll just grab a bite from the leftovers I put in the fridge."

Instead of the happy relief he should have been feeling, Gabe was deflated. "Oh. Well, I guess I'll see you later—back at the trailer."

Nodding, she turned to leave. "Yes. Have a nice dinner."

Gabe watched her walk off and wondered why he felt as though half of him had been whacked away. Then, muttering a self-deprecating curse under his breath, he headed in the opposite direction.

Five minutes later, he was inside a large steak house, seated in a red-cushioned booth, waiting for a waitress to arrive. When a tall woman with dark auburn hair, carrying a glass of ice water and a menu, approached his table, he glanced at her face, then cast a second, closer glance.

"Caroline, is that you?"

The waitress paused, carefully studying him as she placed the water and menu on the table. "Gabe," she said finally, smiling with fond recognition. "Gabe Trevino! My word, I never expected to see you walk in this place. How are you?"

Caroline Myers had grown up in Grulla. The two of them had attended the same school, and she and her family had lived only two blocks away from Gabe and his uncle. They'd been acquaintances for years, but shortly after he and Sherleen had divorced, he'd heard that Caroline had left town. Until now, he'd not seen her and had thought of her only in passing.

"I'm fine. I'm up here for the horse auction," he told her. "What about you? You live around here?"

She gave a negligent shrug. "Yeah. Guess here is as good as anywhere."

The woman looked much older than her thirty-five years. There were lines around her mouth and eyes that bespoke of fatigue and worries. Like him, Caroline had grown up poor. He'd managed to pull himself up the rungs to a more comfortable life, but it appeared that his old friend was still stuck. That saddened him.

"You must be doin' great," she said as she grabbed a pad from a pocket on her uniform and pulled out the pencil resting above her ear. "I hear some of those horses are worth a small fortune. You know, the kind that rich folks buy. What are you doin'? Buyin' or sellin'?"

"Selling. For a ranch that I work for."

She rested her hip against the edge of the table as she studied him with open curiosity. "Oh. You still down in Texas?"

"Not at Grulla. A little north of there. You still with Gilbert?"

The corners of her mouth turned downward. "No. I finally wised up and divorced him. He wasn't like you, Gabe. He was no good through and through." She let out a long breath, then gave him a halfhearted smile. "I'd better take your order, or you'll never get to eat."

He picked up the menu and, after quickly scanning the dinner options, ordered a rare ribeye steak with fries, tossed salad and coffee. After she'd jotted it all down on a small pad and walked away, he wondered what Mercedes would think of his old friend. That she was coarse and uneducated? That Caroline was far beneath her? No. One thing he'd learned about Mercedes was that she treated everyone the same. From the dirtiest cowhand to her mother's senator beau, they were all simply people who deserved equal respect.

So why do you think she's playing with you, Gabe? Why do you think her kisses couldn't be the real thing? She doesn't think she's better than you.

Pestered by the little voice prodding him with questions he didn't want to consider, he purposely turned his mind back to Caroline. He was glad she'd ditched her husband. It had been no secret in Grulla that the man abused her and, frankly, Gabe had never understood why she'd stayed with him. But he knew that love made people toss away their pride and common sense. He was a prime example. For three years, he'd acted like a trained seal, jumping through hoops just to make Sherleen happy, and all the while she'd controlled their finances and made important decisions behind his back. She'd excluded him from all the things a husband and wife should have decided together. Because she hadn't needed him. Nor loved him. Hell, she'd not known what love meant.

He was trying to wipe that dark thought from his mind when he looked up to see Caroline returning with his coffee. After she'd placed it on the table, she gestured to the empty seat across from him. "Mind if I sit down a minute? There's no one else eating in my area right now."

He motioned for her to take a seat. "I'd be glad for your company," he said.

With a wan smile, she brushed off the front of her black uniform, then settled herself in the cushioned seat.

As she folded her work-roughened hands upon the table-top, Gabe said, "It's been a long time since we were in high school. I always thought you'd wind up working as a graphic artist for some big company. I remember you were always good at art."

She laughed as though his suggestion was as absurd as reaching up and plucking a star from the sky. "Oh, Gabe, there wasn't any way that I could have ever gone to college. That kind of life wasn't meant for me."

Caroline's mother had sold tacos and tamales for extra money for the family. Her father had worked as a mechanic for a car dealership in town. They'd been good, hardworking people, but paying for their daughter to attend college had never been in their plans.

"You're still young," he suggested. "It's not too late."

She smiled wanly, then quickly changed subject. "I was sorry to hear about you and Sherleen. But I honestly never did think she suited you, Gabe. Too snooty, in my opinion."

Gabe chuckled. "I wished you'd been around to tell me that sooner." He looked at her. "So are you married now, Caroline?"

She shook her head in a resigned way. "No," she said with a wistful sigh, then her eyes suddenly lit up with joy. "But I have a son now. And you know, he makes everything worthwhile. You got any kids, Gabe?"

He reached for his coffee and wondered why her question left an empty feeling inside him. "No," he answered. "I'm on my own."

Thirty minutes later, Mercedes was sitting at the tiny table inside the trailer when Gabe opened the door and stepped inside. As he looked her way, she unconsciously wrapped her fingers tightly around the mug of coffee she'd been drinking.

"Find something good to eat?" she asked.

He nodded. "Steak. What about you?"

"I dug into the cold fried chicken." She watched as he took off his hat and placed it on the top bunk bed. "I'm sorry you had to eat alone. I guess the trip tired me more than I thought."

He moved over to join her at the table and she suddenly realized how tiny the trailer space seemed now that he was inside it. His presence was so huge she felt as if she were squashed against the walls and struggling for breath. Had she been crazy to insist on sleeping here with him? She'd wanted him to see that she wasn't a pampered princess, but maybe she could have proven it another way. Like this, she probably wouldn't be able to shut her eyes all night.

"Don't worry about it," he said. "I ended up having company anyway."

She darted a glance at his face. It wasn't often that she saw him without his cowboy hat and her gaze glided with appreciation over the thick black waves dipping over his forehead.

"Oh? You ran into a rancher or horseman that you're acquainted with?"

"No." He eased down on the small bench seat facing hers. "Actually, it was a woman. An old friend from Grulla. We grew up on the same street, a couple of blocks from each other."

Her brows arched with curiosity. "What a small world."

"Yeah. She's a waitress in the steak house where I had dinner. She says she lives somewhere around here now."

"Does she have a family?"

"A son. But she told me she was divorced now. I was relieved to hear it. Her ex used to abuse her."

"You don't look all that relieved," Mercedes commented. In fact, she couldn't remember ever seeing such a defeated expression on his face before and it troubled her greatly. No matter how cutting or indifferent his behavior, she still wanted

Gabe to be happy. Was that the way it felt when you really loved someone? she wondered.

He sighed. "I guess seeing Caroline reminded me of times I'd sooner forget. She's been poor all her life, Mercedes. And the hell of it is, she always will be, unless she plucks up enough courage to make a change in her life."

Reaching across the tiny table, she covered his hand with hers. "If she needs help, Gabe, I'm sure we can find a spot for her at the ranch. If you'd like, I could go talk with her."

Surprise flickered in his eyes. "You'd do that?"

"Of course. We could help her with housing and child care, too. That might be enough to allow her to work on her education, or whatever she might need."

His gaze dropped to her hand and her heart began to thud with awareness. The two of them were so alone, cocooned together for the night. How could she not touch him? Show him how very much she wanted him?

"That's very kind of you, Mercedes."

"I'd like to think someone would reach out to me if I was in her position," she said quietly.

His gray eyes met hers. "Why do you have to be so nice? Why can't you go around with your nose stuck in the air and your mind on yourself?"

She laughed softly. "Would you really like for me to be that way?"

He grimaced. "It would make it a hell of a lot easier for me not to like you."

The corners of her pink lips turned upward. "Does that mean you *do* like me? A little?"

A wry expression twisted his features. "I have my weak moments, Mercedes. You know that."

Moments. Yes, there had been moments when he'd held her

in his arms, kissed her as though there were nothing in the world he wanted more. But those times were too few and far between for Mercedes's liking.

"I'm not sure I like being called a weakness," she said.

Sighing roughly, he started to pull his hand from beneath hers. As his arm moved, so did the cuff of his shirt, and Mercedes's gaze zeroed in on the thick welt of scars wrapping around his wrist and running beneath the fabric of his shirtsleeve.

At the last moment, before he could pull completely away from her, she caught his fingers and held on tightly. "Where did you get these, Gabe?"

He outwardly winced as she ran the tip of her forefinger over one of the thick scars.

"It doesn't matter where I got them," he said flatly.

Not to be deterred, she asked, "Do you have more of them?"

He shot her with a pointed glare. "Do you really think that's any of your business?"

Her chin thrust forward. "Yes. I want to know."

Without warning, he abruptly rose to his feet and began to unbutton his shirt with short, angry jerks.

Stunned, Mercedes stared in silence as he pulled the fabric apart, then slipped it over his broad shoulders. The dim, overhead light gleamed across his bronze skin and lathed the mounds and valleys of his hard muscles with gray shadows.

Slowly, slowly, her gaze traveled from his neck down his chest to the flat male nipples decorating the heavy muscles, to the patch of dark hair growing between, the corded abs and the lean waist circled by the waistband of his jeans.

Perfect. Utterly perfect, she thought. And then her breath caught in her throat as she moved her attention to his arms. The biceps were the image of pure strength, his forearms long, sinewy cords—striped with a web of jagged scars.

"If that's not enough to sicken you, there's more," he said curtly, then turned his back toward her.

As she noted the same similar scars on his shoulders, she swallowed at the thickness building in her throat. "Oh." She breathed the one word of dismay. "Oh, Gabe. How did that happen?"

Turning back, he eased down on the seat. "I don't talk to anyone about this, Mercedes. Why do you think I should tell you?"

She swallowed again. "Because I care. Because you matter to me."

"Yeah," he said dryly. "I've heard that before."

Mercedes didn't say anything more. After all, if he couldn't accept her simple words for what they were, arguing with him would be pointless.

Long moments passed as she waited. Then, with a heavy groan, he thrust his arms out toward her as though he dared her to take a closer look.

Not about to shy away, Mercedes leaned forward and placed her fingers gently upon one marked wrist.

"Mercedes," he said thickly, "those scars don't just remind me of an accident, of pain and months of healing. When I look at them, I see a fire. The fire that took my parents' lives."

Horrified, she stared at him. "And you were in the fire, too?"

Resigned to telling her the whole story, he nodded. "I was ten, almost eleven years old at the time. By then, my sisters were married and gone. It was only me and my older brother, Joseph, living at home with our parents, but the night of the fire, Joe was staying over at a friend's house.

"I woke up coughing and it took me a minute to realize the room was full of smoke. I jumped out of bed and jerked open the door to run to my parents' room, but the flames were already eating through the walls and the ceiling."

The image sent chills down Mercedes's spine. "How far were you from your parents' room?"

His jaw rigid, he shook his head. "The house was very small, Mercedes. I couldn't have been more than ten steps from their bedroom door. But a wall of flames stood between me and them."

Her fingers tightened on his wrist. "What did you do? How did you get out?"

"I retraced my steps to the opposite side of the house where the flames hadn't yet reached and went out a window. I was hoping by some miracle that my parents had made it out and I'd find them standing in the yard. But on the other hand, I knew that neither of them would have left the house without me." He paused long enough to wipe a hand across his face. "When I didn't find them there, I began to yell to wake the neighbors, then grabbed a ladder and climbed through a window to my parents' bedroom."

Mercedes gasped. "You could have been killed!"

His gray eyes were stark as they settled on her face. "Could you stand by and watch your parents die without trying to do something to save them?"

The desperation of what he must have been feeling struck her hard, and all she could do was shake her head.

He went on. "Neither could I. So I had to try. But the room was black with smoke and the heat of the flames felt like my whole body was being seared. I couldn't see any sign of my dad, but I finally managed to spot my mother. She was lying near the door that led to the hallway. I was trying to reach her to drag her out when part of the ceiling fell between us. Much of it landed on my back and crashed me to the floor. That's the last thing I remember until I woke up a few minutes later on the lawn."

"How did you get out?" Mercedes asked in amazement. "The smoke inhalation would have been more than enough to kill you, much less the burning debris."

"Apparently our next-door neighbor had heard the commotion and came out just in time to see me crawl through the window. If he hadn't come after me, I would have perished with my parents."

Gabe had gone through a living nightmare, Mercedes thought sickly. He'd only been a child, yet he'd risked his own life to save his parents. It was no wonder he hid his scars from the world. He probably wanted to hide them from himself, too, so he wouldn't have to relive the loss of his parents over and over.

After a stretch of silence, she asked, "Did the authorities ever figure out what started the fire?"

He nodded. "Wiring in the attic. It was old and needed to be replaced. Something, probably a mouse, caused it to short out and shower sparks over the rafters. The whole thing originated over my parents' bedroom."

Tears suddenly burned her throat. "I don't have to ask about your folks to know that they were good people. I'm so sorry you lost them, Gabe."

He glanced away from her. "My father's name was Franco. He worked all his life as a carpenter, building fine houses for the well-to-do, but never earned enough to build one for himself and his family."

"Tell me about your mother," she urged softly.

He rose from the seat and moved the few steps to the door. A tiny window was framed in the upper part of the aluminum panel and though he was gazing beyond the glass pane, she knew that he wasn't really seeing the things outside the trailer.

From where she sat, his eyelids appeared to be closed and she could see the muscles work in his throat as he swallowed with obvious difficulty.

The fact that he still felt such loss for his loved ones didn't surprise her. She'd sensed, from the very first moment he'd whirled her around the dance floor, that he was a man of complex layers and deep passions. She was seeing that part of him now, and the hurt he was feeling was arcing into her, filling her with an ache to ease his heart.

"Her name was Jenna," he said huskily. "She was Irish with chestnut hair and gray eyes. Dad always called her his cactus rose. She had a sweet singing voice, but that never earned her a paycheck, just a spot on the church choir. She took in ironing and sewing to help support the family. And most all of that went to us kids for our needs. When our house burned, she probably had five changes of clothes hanging in the closet. But she never complained, Mercedes."

He turned his head to look at her, and Mercedes was struck by the bleakness on his face.

"I caught her crying in the kitchen one time. I guess she thought no one was around to see her. She was standing in front of the refrigerator, staring at the empty shelves. Can you imagine crying over an empty refrigerator?"

She felt sick for him. "I'd be lying if I said yes. I've never had to worry about my next meal. Or how I was going to feed my children."

He let out a heavy breath of air. "I vowed then that I was going to grow up and change things for her. I was going to make enough money to make her life easy. I didn't get that chance." Regret shadowed his eyes and twisted his lips. "Hell, I couldn't make anything better for her. I couldn't even drag her from that burning bedroom. She lived and died with nothing."

Rising from her seat, Mercedes picked up his shirt. She moved over to where he stood and draped the garment over his bare shoulders.

"You're wrong, Gabe," she whispered gently. "She had the things that matter the most. She had a family that loved her. She had you."

Chapter Twelve

When Gabe woke the next morning, Mercedes was not in the trailer.

He glanced at the wristwatch he'd not bothered to remove last night and let out a groan. He'd not expected to sleep at all last night, much less sleep later than usual.

Slipping a hand through his tousled hair, he glanced at the bed where Mercedes had slept. She'd been so close that if he'd stretched his arm in her direction, he could have touched her. But he hadn't. Instead, he'd lain there, listening to her breathing and thinking about her reaction to his parents' tragedy.

Sharing that part of his life with her had ripped him open, past the scars on his skin, down to the raw wounds that had never healed. Showing her that vulnerable part of him had changed him, drawn him to her in a way he'd never expected.

Suddenly the physical attraction he felt for her had been overridden by something deeper, something stronger than the sexual urge to touch her, make love to her. He'd felt incredibly close to her, happy that he had her company, and solaced by the fact that she understood the loss of his parents.

Watch it, Gabe, or your heart is going to start leading you around instead of your head. And that's when you're going to get it broken in so many pieces you'll never get it put back together.

Trying to push that unsettling thought from his mind, Gabe rose from the bed and reached for his boots. He didn't have time to think about anything except getting the horses ready for the sale ring.

Five minutes later, he was washed, dressed and stepping outside when he glanced around to see Mercedes, a white paper sack in her hand, walking toward him.

"Good morning," she said cheerfully when she got within hearing distance. "I'm glad I got back before you headed to the barn. I've got hot coffee and breakfast."

Even before she opened the sack, he could smell the delicious aroma of hot biscuits and coffee. His stomach growled, insisting he had to take five minutes to fill it before he went to work.

He inclined his head toward the sack. "Where did you get that?"

"Over at the steak house. Let's get a pair of lawn chairs and eat out here," she suggested. "The morning is beautiful."

Yes, the sky was clear and blue, the air dry and pleasant. A warm smile was on her face, and Gabe's heart did an odd little dance every time he looked at her. Dammit.

He grabbed chairs from the bed of the truck and quickly set them up beneath the sycamore tree. Once they were both seated, Mercedes began to pull out the food.

As she handed him a biscuit and sausage sandwich, she said, "While I was at the restaurant, I talked to your friend, Caroline."

He bit into the bread and meat. "If she's working this early, she must have very long shifts."

"She was filling in for someone who had called in sick," Mercedes explained.

He took the foam cup she offered him and pulled off the plastic lid. "I didn't tell you her name. How did you figure out who she was?"

"Intuition, I suppose. I asked her if she knew you and that was all it took." Her blue eyes studied him thoughtfully as she chewed her food. "Before I left the restaurant, I gave her the Sandbur's number and instructions to speak to Cook."

Even though she'd mentioned helping Caroline, the fact that she'd already put things into motion surprised him. "For a job?"

"What else?" she asked with an indulgent smile. "You implied that she needed help."

"Yes," he reasoned. "But that isn't your problem."

"I don't see it as a problem. The ranch can always use good help. And if she's your friend, that's enough reference for me."

Gabe didn't know what to think or say. Had she done this to actually help Caroline or just to impress him?

Hell, Gabe, for once in your life can you quit viewing everything with a cynical eye? No matter what Mercedes's motives, she's done a good thing. Accept it for that.

"Thank you, Mercedes."

She smiled. "My pleasure."

Once their simple breakfast was over, Gabe left to care for the horses while Mercedes spent the remainder of the day schmoozing with rich buyers and taking note of how the auction was run. Her mother had understated the grandeur of the event, and she'd been greatly surprised when she'd entered the sale barn to see huge baskets of cut roses and other fresh flowers lining the area where the horses would be shown.

The men working the auction were all dressed in dark suits and ties and the registry catalogs handed out to potential buyers were more like glossy magazines rather than facts printed on rough paper.

As for herself, she was glad she'd thought to bring a Western-cut pantsuit that she sometimes wore on dressy occasions. She'd also taken pains with her makeup and hair. She wanted to look her best when she represented the Sandbur.

Yet as she milled among the privileged crowd and introduced herself to both buyers and sellers, she realized she'd much rather be in the horse barn with Gabe, wearing her old jeans and boots and getting her hands dirty. But even if she told him that, Mercedes doubted he would believe her. He wanted to set her apart in everything, as though they could never be on the same level.

Mercedes remained near the sale ring until the hammer fell on the last lot number auctioned for the day, then left the building. When she reached the camping area where their rig was parked, she found Gabe outside, charcoaling wieners on a small pit.

"Mmm. Those smell good," she declared as she walked up behind him. "Been here long?"

He glanced over his shoulder at her, then turned his attention back to the sizzling planks of meat. "Only a few minutes."

With a tired sigh, she pulled up a lawn chair and sank into it. As she stretched her long legs out in front of her, she said, "The auction producers are having a shindig tonight. Cocktails and dancing at a ritzy downtown hotel. We're invited."

He let out a mocking snort. "You're invited. Not me."

Mercedes pushed her fingers through the hair at her temples. "Wrong. The both of us were invited."

"Sorry. I'm not up to that sort of—job."

"Thanks for making attending an event with me sound like a job," she said dryly.

"Don't miss it on my account. I'm sure you'd enjoy the evening. You'll feel right at home with those people."

"So would you. *You've* worked with enough of them."

He began to fork the franks onto a paper plate. "Wrong again, Mercedes. I worked *for* them."

The moment she'd walked up, she'd been struck by the fact that he was wearing a plain white T-shirt. His usual long-sleeved shirt was gone and the scars on his forearms were exposed. Apparently he was finally beginning to feel comfortable around her. At least, comfortable enough not to hide the marks of tragedy on his forearms. The idea made everything inside her smile.

"Don't bother splitting hairs," she commented. "And I'm not about to go. Unless you go with me—as my date."

He ran a hand across the back of his neck, then rolled his head to relieve the tension in his shoulders. "All right. If you really want to go, I suppose I can put on my best and pretend, for your sake. But I'm going to be honest and tell you that I'm beat. I'd rather stay here and relax."

It was almost shocking to Mercedes the pleasure his response evoked in her. He'd be willing to go. For her sake. But more importantly, he'd been honest with his own wishes, instead of putting up a pretense just to please her. And that was much more than John or Drew had ever given her.

Rising to her feet, she joined him at the small brick pit and peered over his shoulder at the last two franks grilling over the charcoal. "I'm glad you said that, because I don't want to go, either. So are you going to invite me to share your supper?"

"I'll share."

She pecked a swift kiss on his cheek, then turned and rushed toward the trailer. "I'm going to change. I'll be right back!"

Thirty minutes later, he watched her swallow the last bite of her second hot dog, then lick the remaining mustard from the tips of her fingers.

The simple yet sensual act only added to his awareness of the woman. He found his gaze wandering for the umpteenth time over the smooth, tanned skin exposed by her jean shorts and skimpy tank top. This evening was one of the few times he'd seen her out of her cowboy boots, and he found that even her dainty toes with their bright pink nails mesmerized him.

"I'm beginning to think you could compete with Cook," she told him. "That was great."

"There are still a couple of franks left if you want another."

With a contented groan, she slid her hand across her midsection. "No thanks. I'm so full I can hardly breathe."

Night was falling fast and he knew he should get up and gather the remains of their supper. But he was loath to move when he was finding such pleasure in watching the long shadows of the evening paint themselves across her shapely body.

A few times today, he'd seen her from a distance, smiling and charming her way through the horsing crowd, most of whom were men. He'd be lying if he tried to deny that he'd been jealous of the interplay between her and the good-looking males of the bunch. Yet at the same time, he had to tell himself that he had no right to feel such an emotion toward the woman. She didn't belong to him. And those precious smiles weren't always directed solely at him.

He pushed away a heavy sigh and asked, "What did you think about the price we got for our two horses today?"

"I was very pleased. The stallion went in the high five

figures and the filly was close to that. I'm sure the whole family will be happy. Especially if the three tomorrow go that well." She slanted him a sidelong glance. "By the way, you did a heck of a job showing both horses. You made them look very good."

Her compliment sent a warm glow through him, one that he desperately tried to ignore. Shaking his head, he said, "I didn't make them look good. They did it all themselves."

She leaned forward and as she did he caught the sweet scent of her perfume drifting on the night wind.

"Do you ever take credit for your work?" she asked.

"When I think I've done something to deserve it."

A grin tugged at her lips. "You know, it's pretty standard for most cowboys to be a little arrogant."

He grunted with amusement. "I'm not a cowboy. I'm a horseman."

He was the epitome of both, Mercedes thought. Yet in many ways, he was no different from the airmen she'd worked with for eight long years. His uniform might be jeans and boots instead of dress blues, but he still had that same toughness, dedication and pride.

"Yes. You are that," she said with sober conviction. Rising to her feet, she stretched her arms above her head. "I think I'll go in and make a pot of coffee. Would you care for some?"

He also stood and began to gather up the remains of their meal. "I'll be there in a few minutes."

His few minutes turned out to be several. Tired of waiting, Mercedes finally poured herself a cup and sat at the small table inside the trailer, sipping the hot drink until Gabe finally entered the tiny space.

"I thought you'd gotten lost on your way to the trash barrel," she teased.

"I went to the barn for one last check on the horses before we retire for the night."

She scooted out of the seat to scrounge around in the cabinet for another mug. "You should have told me your intentions. I could have helped you."

"There wasn't anything to do, except fill their hay mangers."

He was standing directly behind her, so close that if she leaned the slightest bit backward, her shoulders would be touching his chest. Just thinking about having his hard, warm body against hers drugged her senses until she felt as though every movement she was making was in slow motion.

Nervously running the tip of her tongue over her lips, she turned and presented him with the coffee cup. His gray eyes connected with hers and the air around them suddenly seemed to be throwing off erotic sparks.

"Here you go," she said lowly.

"Thanks."

He poured himself some coffee and eased onto one of the benches at the table. Mercedes sat down on the opposite bench and tried to breathe normally as she looked at everything within the eight-foot space except him.

"Have you heard from Geraldine today?" he asked.

She darted a glance at his face. At some point since he'd stepped through the door, he'd removed his hat. Now a hank of black, shiny hair brushed against his eyebrow as his head bent forward over the coffee cup. She desperately wanted to touch it, to spear her fingers into the curls around his ears. Even worse, she wanted to put her mouth over his, to let the dark, erotic taste of him sweep her away.

"No. I don't expect she'll be calling anytime soon. In fact, I hope she totally forgets about us and the ranch. I want this time she has with Wolfe to be special."

The only sound inside the trailer was the faint ticking of an alarm clock, but it was still hard for Mercedes to hear over the blood drumming loudly in her ears. It was impossible to figure why tonight felt so different from the previous one—she only knew that it did. Somehow, she instinctively felt that tonight wasn't for revelations. It was for loving.

He said, "I just hope the guy appreciates Geraldine. She deserves an honorable man."

She peeped at him through her long lashes. "That's very sweet of you to say, Gabe." Then before she could let herself think twice, she reached across the tiny table and gently laced her fingers around his wrist. "And speaking of mothers, I'm—well, I wanted to thank you for sharing your parents' story with me last night. That time in your life can't be easy to talk about."

As she spoke, her fingers moved gently against the uneven surface of the scars on his wrist and his gaze dropped to where she was touching him.

"It's like stepping back into a nightmare," he agreed in a low voice.

His skin was warm and just rough enough to feel very masculine beneath the pads of her fingers. Flattening her hand against his arm, she slid it upward toward his elbow, watching his eyes narrow in response. The subtle reaction pushed her pulse to an even faster rate.

"I like you without long sleeves," she said softly. "I like that you're not trying to hide anything from me."

The corners of his chiseled mouth turned slightly downward. "You like seeing all my flaws?"

"We all have flaws. Inside and out," she whispered. "That's what makes us human."

Something sparked in his eyes and then his hand was suddenly gripping her shoulder, tugging her toward him.

"You don't want to see inside of me," he mouthed against her lips. "It's empty. Very empty."

Like icy drops of rain, anticipation rolled slowly down her spine and shivered in the very depths of her.

"Let me be the judge of that," she murmured. Then, before he decided to back away, she closed the last breath of space between their lips.

The contact was like sticking a match to a bed of dry grass. There was nothing slow, sweet or gentle about the kiss or the violent longing it erupted in Mercedes. With one hand at the back of her head and the other cupping her jaw, he held her fast, forcing her lower body to leave the bench and her upper body to rest upon the tabletop as his lips feasted on hers, his tongue invading the moist confines of her mouth.

In a matter of moments, she was totally lost to him, her mind focused on one thing—getting closer. Having his hands upon her body, his hard strength against her.

Moaning deep in her throat, she thrust her fingers in his hair and tried to match the rough, hungry search of his lips. Somewhere along the way, she felt his hands at the back of her arms urging her up from the bench, and then they were both standing. The front of her body was crushed against his.

She was wrapping her arms around his waist, exploring the warmth of his back through the thin T-shirt when he finally tore his mouth from hers and stared at her in anguish.

"This is all wrong," he muttered. "I can't have you."

Her hand glided over his lean cheek. "Isn't that for me to decide?"

His features twisted as though he were in physical pain and her question was making it a thousand times worse. "We've got to think about tomorrow and the days after that."

A provocative smile curled the corners of her lips as she

brought her forehead against his. "Our days are going to get better, Gabe. Even better than tonight," she promised.

His groan was full of skepticism, but he didn't pull away from her when she pressed her lips back to his. And then nothing either of them had said seemed to matter. With everything inside of her, she wanted this man. If she stopped to worry about tomorrow, then she would miss the love he could be giving her tonight.

To press her point home, she slipped her hands under his shirt and splayed them against his muscled chest. He ripped his mouth from hers and began to press a tiny row of kisses down the side of her neck.

"You don't know what you're doing," he mouthed against her skin. "But I'm tired of fighting you—especially tonight."

His words thrilled her and her heart began to hammer out of control as he caught the hem of her top and began to peel it upward and over her head.

"Oh, Gabe, I do know what I'm doing," she fervently whispered. "All I want is this. You."

The image of making love to her had been going over and over in his mind for weeks, and it was hard to believe that it was actually happening. That he was *letting* it happen. But he had no choice. Not when he was on fire for her and she was melting against him.

Quickly, before sanity could creep into his thoughts, he slipped away her shorts, then dealt even more rapidly with her sexy undergarments. By the time she was standing naked before him, he was on fire, aching to be inside her, to relieve the desire that was wrapping around him, binding him to the charms of her body.

Between kisses on her face and neck and breasts, he somehow managed to shuffle out of his own clothing and kick away his boots. When the cumbersome garments were finally out of the way, he reached for her. "Come here, my lovely," he whispered.

With her hand in his, he stepped backward, drawing her with him until he bumped into the set of bunk beds. He sank onto the bottom mattress and drew her down with him.

The bed was short and narrow, but neither of them noticed. All that Mercedes's senses could register was that she was in his arms. His skin was on fire, bathing her in heat. His lips were on hers, pushing her to a height that she'd not known was possible.

Her hands eagerly raced over his body, familiarizing themselves with every muscle of his back, the scarred tendons in his arms, the bumps of his ribs and the long ridge of his backbone. He was all man and strength, and she wanted to absorb it all, to connect herself to him in every way.

When his hand slipped between the juncture of her thighs, he pulled his head back far enough to peer into her face.

"Are you on any sort of birth control?"

Even though she was a grown woman who'd had a lover before, the question filled her face with heat.

"I— No. This isn't something I—do on a regular basis." Until now, she'd not met any man whom she'd wanted to expose herself to in such an intimate way since John's betrayal, but she didn't want to lay that much importance on the moment and scare him away.

Her short breaths seemed to go on forever as he studied her face. Mercedes's heart slowed with dread as she saw a hint of doubt flicker in his eyes. But just as quickly, it was gone and he gently brushed his knuckles against her cheekbone, making her lips tingle, her eyes close.

"I'll take care of it," he whispered.

He left the bunk and went to find his wallet. Moments later, he returned, his manhood safely sheathed in a condom.

The man wasn't taking any chances, she thought with a tiny pang of regret. But on the other hand, that was good. God knew how much she wanted him. Wanted him for keeps. But not through entrapment. She needed his love, and needed it to be given to her willingly, freely.

Once he rejoined her on the bunk, their bodies became a tangled mass of heated flesh. Mercedes had never had anyone kiss her this hungrily, touch her so boldly or turn her senses to mush. She was nothing without the man, and everything with him. The stroke of his hands empowered her, the feel of his lips upon her sent the very center of her being searching and soaring.

When he finally rolled her onto her back and entered her, Mercedes was stunned with the ferocity of the emotions that stung her from all directions. The physical presence of him inside of her was an incredible sensation, yet it wasn't the reason that her eyes misted with tears, or that her heart felt as though it would burst. She loved this man. Loved him with every fiber of her being.

After his divorce, he'd sworn to always be in control, to never allow anyone or anything to make him give up his will-power and bend him in a direction he didn't want to go. But Mercedes was swiftly dissolving that idea. The feel of her small hands gliding over him, the desperate writhing of her body beneath his, the scent of her and the taste of her smooth skin was turning him into a helpless piece of flesh that he couldn't restrain or direct.

He was hardly a novice at making love to a woman and always before he had found it easy to take his time and push all the right buttons, to give satisfaction before he took it. But with Mercedes there wasn't any plan or artifice. No thinking or maneuvering. His hands, his mind and heart were simply reacting to her. Loving her.

And like a blind man racing toward a promised light, his strokes became quicker, deeper, hungrier. Beneath him, her hips were racing to match his rhythm, her open mouth was hot against his chest, her tongue licking, tasting, driving his senses to places he'd not gone before.

When the end came, he was certain that he was floating above her, that the stars behind his eyes were the same as those twinkling down on the red Oklahoma dirt. Above the deafening roar in his ears, he could hear her ecstatic cries, feel her body clenching around his, and he felt a surge of triumph that she was soaring with him. Like two doves winging upward, together, into the blue, blue sky.

Awareness returned slowly as he sucked long, raspy breaths into his burning lungs. Gradually, the fierce pounding of his heart settled to a rapid thud. His cheek was pressed against her silky blond hair and her damp body was smothered beneath his. The heavenly scent of her swirled about him and her soft breath brushed warmly against his shoulder.

He didn't want to move, to break the connection of their bodies. But he knew he had to relieve her of his weight, so he rolled to his side and took her with him.

She didn't say a word. Instead, her sigh said it for her as she snuggled her cheek against his chest and wrapped an arm around his waist.

Gabe slipped a hand beneath the heavy cape of her hair and stroked the back of her neck, while his mind raced to process what had just taken place between them. His earth had suddenly split open and he was shocked at the free fall he'd taken.

He'd just learned what it was like to make *love* to a woman. And one way or another, he instinctively knew his life would never be the same again.

Chapter Thirteen

It was late the next evening when the two of them arrived back at the Sandbur. Mercedes was tired, but pleasantly so. The trip coming home had seemed much shorter than going. Maybe because the last three horses had each brought an exceptional price in the sale ring and ended their trip on an even brighter note. Or maybe because making love to Gabe had changed the way the world looked to her. Everything seemed more beautiful, and she'd chattered throughout the whole trip like a songbird on a spring morning.

After Gabe parked the big rig in its regular spot inside a storage shed near one of the cattle barns, Mercedes began to gather up her handbag and the other odds and ends that she'd collected during the trip.

Rolling back into the ranch yard had been sobering to Gabe. Throughout the day, he'd allowed himself to pretend. He'd let himself believe that he and Mercedes could actually be lovers, that somehow their lives could merge without a problem. But returning to Sandbur soil had woken him from that impossible dream. She *owned* part of this ranch. He only *worked* here. And if that wasn't problem enough, who was to say that she would actually be here for much longer? Lex had already hinted to him that he expected her to fly soon. Why should Gabe think any differently? Mercedes hadn't bothered to tell him anything about her future plans or even how she actually felt toward him.

"Wow, I didn't realize I'd picked up so many souvenirs," she commented with a chuckle as she stuffed the last plastic bag into her purse. "I hope my family loves me for all the money I spent on them."

Before he could talk himself out of what he was about to do, he reached over the gearshift and wrapped his fingers around her forearm. The touch brought her head around and the tender smile she gave him pierced him right in the heart.

"Mercedes, I—" All of a sudden his words jammed somewhere inside him and refused to come out.

"You wanted to tell me something?" she prompted gently.

He drew in a long breath and wondered why there was such an aching pressure in his chest. This woman didn't love him. She'd never even hinted that she did. "Uh, yeah. I think before you go to the house that we should talk."

Her smile turned impish and even more provocative. He tried to ignore the charming dimples in her cheeks even though all he wanted to do was lean forward and kiss the pretty grooves bracketing her lips.

"Oh," she said. "Well, if you're wondering about giving Mother a report about the auction, I'll call her tonight. She's going to be very happy with the way things went."

Feeling much sicker than he'd expected to, he shook his

head. All through the trip home, he'd not allowed himself to think about the future. He'd purposely blacked it out so that he could simply enjoy the moment of being with Mercedes. But now reality had hit him and he'd not been prepared for this much pain. How could it hurt to end something that had never really started? Why should breaking away from this woman be any different from those in the past?

Because you only had sex with them, Gabe. You never made love until last night. Mercedes filled a hole in you. And you don't want to think of feeling that emptiness again, of losing everything she gave you.

"It's not about Geraldine or the auction." He forced the words from his lips. "I want to talk about you—us."

Her blue eyes widened, then turned dreamy as she leaned slightly toward him. "I hope you're about to invite me out to the line shack tonight," she whispered.

Oh, yes, he could easily imagine her there in his bed, the sheets wet from their sweat, her soft hand resting upon his heart. But he couldn't let that happen. It would only make things harder when she did finally go. And she would go. A woman with her credentials and looks wouldn't stay buried on a dusty Texas ranch forever.

"No. In fact, I—" He looked away from her and swallowed, hating himself for being so weak, for hoping, even in the tiniest way, that she might actually care for him. "Mercedes, last night—what happened between us was a one-time thing. If you were thinking we were going to fall into some sort of relationship, I'm sorry. It can't happen."

She reared back as though he'd struck her. "What do you mean, can't happen?"

He grimaced as pain seeped into places inside him that he'd long believed to be dead. "Just what I said. Us being together can only cause problems. Problems that I don't think either of us want to deal with."

Anger replaced the dismay on her face and her nostrils flared as her gaze raked over him. "You certainly didn't have any problems being with me last night," she accused.

Hot color crept up his neck and onto his jaws. "That was a—lapse in judgment. I let the place, the moment take over. But now that we're back on the Sandbur, I can see things clearly. We're worlds apart. You know it and I know it. To try to fit together would be foolish."

Jerking her arm from his grasp, she glared at him. "What are you doing? Trying to punish me for being the boss's daughter? I can't help it if part of this ranch belongs to me. That's just a happenstance of birth. It should have no bearing on how we feel about each other."

"You're right. It shouldn't matter, but it does. And I—I don't intend to make a second mistake with a woman."

Mistake? Was that how he viewed last night? If she hadn't already been so numb with shock, his words would have sliced her right down the middle.

"If that's how you feel, then why did you sleep with me?" she demanded, her voice wounded and throbbing. "Why did you lie beside me until the sun came up? Why did you act as though you cared? As though you *wanted* to be with me?"

Somewhere during her blast of questions, she began to tremble all over and her eyes misted with tears. Before he could watch her pride crumble right in front of him, she yanked open the door on the truck and climbed to the ground.

She was walking away, fully intending not to say another word to him when his hand came down on her shoulder. Spinning around, Mercedes stared at him in stunned fascination.

"What's the matter? You haven't jabbed me enough? I

suppose you won't be satisfied until you've cut me to shreds."
The shock of his sudden about-face was wearing away, and
in its place anger and pain was shooting through her like
shards of glass. "Why don't you go ahead and put the icing
on the cake? Tell me that last night meant nothing to you."

His fingers bit deeply into her shoulder. "Stop it! You're
saying things that aren't anywhere near the truth and—"

"And I never should have been so gullible," she interrupted
sarcastically. "I guess you think I'm pretty naive for believing that last night was more than just a one-night stand for
you. You must have had a nice little chuckle behind my back."

As she watched his rigid jaw relax, tears spilled from the
rim of her eyes. Last night she'd been certain she'd felt love
in his touch. How had she been so wrong about a man? *Again.*

His fingers reached up and gently touched her cheek.
"Nothing about last night was funny—it meant everything to
me. But that doesn't change anything."

"Why?"

Glancing away from her, he swallowed. "I know what it
feels like to invest your feelings in someone and then have it
all smash into nasty little pieces. That's not for me. Not again."

"If you're talking about your wife, then I don't know how
you could compare the two of us. I—"

Swinging his gaze back to her, he cut into her words, "I'll
tell you how I could make the comparison. Like you, she was
beautiful. Sexy. And rich. Her father was the mayor of Grulla,
and he came from old oil money. They lived in a mansion on
the outskirts of town, they drove luxury cars and traveled
anywhere their hearts desired. I knew the moment that I first
met Sherleen that she was trouble. But she was so easy on the
eyes and it stroked my ego to have someone like her chasing
after me." The sneer on his face was directed solely at himself.

"Can you imagine a poor orphan like me catching the eye of someone like her? It was a fool's dream. And yet I let it happen. I let myself believe that she actually loved me and that we could make a life together."

"What happened?" she whispered hoarsely.

"Hell," he snorted, "do you have to ask? She wanted everything that I didn't. A rich social life, traveling, fun and parties."

"You should have known that when you married her."

"Yeah, I should have and I did. But I thought things would change after we became man and wife. Instead, after three months of marriage I was exhausted. When I tried to slow her down, to make her see that I wanted a regular home life, a family with children, she kept promising that things would be different. That she'd settle down and become a better wife, even give me children. And she tried. But it wasn't her style. She was incapable of changing."

"How can you be so sure she wouldn't have changed? People can and do—when they really want to."

He muttered a curse under his breath. "Because all the time she was pretending to be the good wife, she was lying, keeping things from me, seeing people I didn't approve of, going places where a married woman had no business being."

"So what finally ended it for you?"

"I found her hidden birth control pills. We'd been trying for a baby with no success. And she'd been voicing fears that she might be infertile. Infertile, hell," he sneered. "She was doing everything she could to keep from getting pregnant, and lying to me about it."

Mercedes's head swung back and forth in amazement. No wonder he didn't want a woman in his life. His wife had betrayed him in the worst kind of way.

His ugly revelation had Mercedes viewing him in a whole different light and understanding so much more. Instead of frustration, she felt an aching need to assure him, to make him see that he'd never experience anything like that again. Not with her.

"Why did she want to get married in the first place?" Mercedes asked. "Obviously she wasn't ready to be a wife."

"I thought she was marrying me for love, for all the traditional reasons that couples do. But now when I look back, I think that for Sherleen, our short marriage was all just one more adventure. From the time she was born, her parents made sure she got what she wanted. And for some reason, she wanted me."

Stupid, selfish woman. The three words were on the tip of her tongue, but Mercedes bit them back. To say them would only make him feel worse. Like her—she didn't want or need to be reminded that she'd been foolish enough to pick a loser or a user, either.

"What happened to her after your divorce?"

He grimaced. "She went running back to her family. And with me out of the way, she took up her single life again. Now, I don't know or care where she is."

With a heavy sigh, Mercedes turned away from him and ran a hand through her tousled hair. She supposed that she should be totally insulted that he could compare her to such a woman. But because of the betrayals she suffered with two different men, she understood how deep a hurt like that could run, how it often made common sense impossible to see. Telling him that she wasn't like Sherleen would be useless. He had to see that truth for himself. He had to learn to trust all over again. But how long would it be before that happened? Maybe it would never happen, she thought sickly.

Turning back to him, she said bleakly, "I'm very sorry that happened to you, Gabe. But I'm even sorrier that you think the same thing would happen with me."

Something flickered on his face, but she didn't hang around to read his expression or to wait for any sort of reply. She turned and walked out of the shed before he could see the tears streaming down her face.

More than a week later, long after sundown, Gabe was in the training pen, subtly cuing a horse to side pass, when he spotted Lex climbing onto the top rung of the fence. Figuring the man had come to talk, Gabe nudged the horse over to where Mercedes's brother sat with his hat pushed back and an ever-present grin on his face.

"I see you made it back from Florida," Gabe greeted.

"Yeah, thank God. If I don't see another rod and reel in the next twenty years, I'll be a happy man."

"Too much fishing, huh?"

"Too much everything," he conceded with a chuckle. "But I made a nice sell on a couple of bulls, so I guess the trip was worth it. I heard the horses did very nicely at auction. Way to go, Gabe. Cordero's going to be jealous when he hears how well you've settled into his boots."

Gabe's smile was little more than halfhearted as he crossed his forearms over the saddle horn. "I could never settle into Cordero's boots. We don't wear the same size."

Lex laughed, then studied him a bit closer. "I stopped by to see if anyone had told you about the roundup next week. I figured you'd want time to pick out some ponies to take. Since we'll be doing a lot of roping and branding, it's a good learning experience for them."

Gabe nodded. "Thanks for letting me know. I'll certainly have a string ready. I have several two-year-olds that I'd like to work."

Along with the falling sun, the wind had also died, leaving the evening hot and muggy. Gabe lifted his hat from his head and wiped the sweat from his face with the back of his sleeve. Beneath him, the horse stomped at a pestering nit fly.

He'd already put in fifteen hours today. He should have gone home when the last of the wranglers had left for the bunkhouse, but home only made him think of Mercedes. He still didn't know how to fight her haunting memory. Still didn't know how to rub out the dull pain that breaking away from her had left in his heart.

"I guess I should also warn you," Lex went on, "that all the family goes on roundup, including Mother. In fact, if anyone isn't out of his bedroll by daylight, she'll get him out with a pitcher of water in the face."

Gabe looked at him. "You say all the family goes?"

"Well, I'm not sure about the women. There are so many new babies in the family, it's hard to say. But I think Juliet will be coming along with Matt. And if Ripp can get off duty, he and Lucita will go so that Marti can enjoy the experience of riding and camping out."

And what about Mercedes? Gabe wondered. These past days, he'd spotted her coming and going from her little office, but he'd not approached her or attempted to talk to her. Any work he'd needed for her to do, he'd left with written instructions on her desk, long before her workday started.

It was a cowardly way to deal with her, he realized. But there was nothing he could say to make things better, and to try would only make things worse. He realized she saw him as a bastard who had used her. He hated that and hated himself for ever having made love to her in the first place.

As though Lex could read his mind, he suddenly added, "I'm not sure about Mercedes. She's been acting strangely these days. I don't know what's wrong with her, but it's plain she's not happy. I wouldn't be a bit surprised if she takes that job offer from D.C."

Gabe felt as though Lex had thrown ice water over his head. "D.C.?"

Lex nodded. From the man's expression, he didn't seem all that pleased about the news. Gabe had always gotten the impression that Lex was very close to his sister and resented the fact that she'd stayed away for so long in the Air Force.

"Yeah," Lex said. "At the Pentagon. Some sort of intelligence gathering for Homeland Security. She'd be serving her country well, I can admit that. But I'll be honest with you, Gabe. I'm selfish. I want her here. This is where she belongs. Not behind some desk with military men snapping orders at her. Hell, if that's what makes her happy, I can snap plenty at her."

Gabe felt sick to his stomach. How long had Mercedes known about this job offer? While they'd been in Oklahoma? If so, she'd kept it from him. One more thing proving she wasn't a woman who really wanted to share her life with him. "Well, that kind of work has been a part of her life for a long time, Lex. Maybe it's in her blood—like ranching is in ours."

Muttering a curse, Lex began to climb down from his seat. "Females. They never know what they want or how much they can hurt us."

With a backward wave, Lex walked away. As Gabe watched him head toward the big house, he wondered why God had led him to this ranch in the first place. To hurt him all over again?

It didn't make sense. But then, nothing about love ever did.

* * *

The next morning found Mercedes sitting at her desk. A mound of tasks were waiting to get done, but instead of throwing herself into her job, she was on the telephone, listening to her sister call her a coward.

"It doesn't matter how much you badger me, Nicci," Mercedes replied firmly. "I'm not going to go begging the man— for anything. He doesn't want me in his life. Period."

The irritated breath that Nicci let out was loud enough to be heard over the phone. "I didn't think I wanted to be in Ridge's life, either. But he proved me very wrong. That's what you have to do with Gabe. He *needs* to know that you love him. At least tell him so."

"Nicci, I'm not good at expressing my feelings to a man. And one of these days, I'll tell you why. John is only half the reason. For right now, just trust me when I tell you that I've learned that telling a man things—intimate things—can end up making a woman very humiliated."

"Being humiliated is not nearly as bad as being alone. And you know that I'm speaking from experience."

Passing a hand over her forehead, Mercedes glanced out the office window. So far this morning, Gabe had not appeared within her view. But that didn't mean he wasn't close by, and the thought of confronting him again made her tremble all over. For the past week and a half, she'd literally pined for the man. The night they'd spent together in Oklahoma continually drifted through her mind like a haunting refrain she couldn't mute.

She'd fallen in love with him that night. No—that wasn't true. She'd fallen in love with him well before that. She just hadn't known it until their bodies had connected, until she'd slept beside him and he'd given her kisses for breakfast. That time with him had been euphoric and had given her a glimpse into how wonderful their life could be together, if he would only give them a chance.

When they'd arrived back on the ranch and he'd made that abrupt turnaround, she couldn't have been more shocked. He'd given her no hint or sign that he'd had plans to end things between them. If anything, he'd been more kind and gentle on the way home than he'd ever been to her. She'd been blissfully unaware that her happiness had been one-sided.

"Yes, I know that if anyone knows about a broken heart and a worthless man, you do. But at least you have a wonderful man who loves you now. And a beautiful daughter." Groaning, she pressed fingertips to her closed eyelids. "Oh, Nicci, why did I have to fall in love with a man who doesn't want me? Maybe I should leave. Take the job in D.C."

There was a long pause before Nicci finally replied. "That isn't what you want."

"No," Mercedes choked in agreement. "That part of my life is over. I want the man I love. I want us to have a home and children."

"Then get off the phone and do something about it."

Before Mercedes could make any sort of reply, she heard the line click and knew that her sister had said all she was going to say on the matter. And it was enough.

Dropping the phone back in its cradle, Mercedes rose from the leather chair and hurried out of the room. For the past week and a half, Gabe had deliberately ignored her, but she was about to change that.

She didn't find Gabe outside where he worked, so she headed for his office.

By the time she reached the door, her heart was pounding with nervous adrenaline and her hands were sweaty. She wiped them down the sides of her sundress then knocked on the door.

"Come in."

Taking a deep breath, she stepped inside. He was sitting in front of the computer, a telephone crammed against his ear. He was dressed all in dark denim, and beneath the overhead lighting, his black hair gleamed like rich coal. Sensuality seeped from the man like heat from the sun. Yet as she looked at him, she realized there was so much more to him. Beneath all that tough brawn, he was a man who'd loved and lost, fought and scratched his way up. He'd endured rejection and loneliness. Just like her.

As she moved into the room, he glanced up casually, then instantly stiffened the moment he saw that it was her.

"Uh, there's something I need to tend to, Jim. I'll call you back in a few minutes," he said to the person on the phone. "Yeah. Thanks."

After hanging up the receiver, he leaned back in his chair as though he were a principal and she a naughty student waiting to confess her wrongdoing.

"Sorry," she said. "I always seemed to be interrupting."

With slow, deliberate movements, he reached for a pencil. She wanted to tell him he didn't have to worry about taking notes. She planned on making everything crystal clear.

"If you're here about the list for Matt's auction," he said curtly, "I don't have it ready."

Summoning all the courage she could find, Mercedes walked over to his desk and rested a hip on the corner. All the while, she could feel his eyes sliding over her face and neck, down the thrust of her bosom and on to her thigh. Desire snaked through her, reminding her of the deep effect the man had on her.

"I'm not here about the list."

His gray eyes traveled back to her face. In their depths, she saw a gentle warning to back away, to leave him and his emotions alone. She stood her ground and clung to her sister's advice. *He needs to know how much you love him. And you need to find the courage to open up to him, to trust him to be different from the men who hurt you.*

He said, "If this is personal, I—"

"I know," she interrupted. "You don't want to hear it. But I'm going to say it anyway. I've had a job offer. It's a prestigious position at the Pentagon."

He balanced the pencil between his hands and Mercedes thought about how fragile the tiny piece of wood appeared against his strength. He didn't realize that in those same hands, he held her heart, her very life. He didn't have a clue that he could snap her in two just as easily as that pencil.

"I already know about the job. Lex told me."

Dammit, she thought, Lex never could keep his mouth shut. There was no telling what her brother had added or taken away from the facts. He'd always had an irritating way of relaying information as he saw it. And what the hell was he doing telling Gabe about it, anyway?

"I'd have a great salary," she went on. "A cushy office. A big staff to do my bidding."

He shrugged as his gaze dropped to the desktop. "Sounds like a dream come true."

Stung by his indifference, she asked, "Is that all you can say?"

Without looking at her, he rose from the chair and walked over to the coffeepot. "What do you want me to say?" he asked as he splashed the strong liquid into a foam cup. "I wish you the best. I hope you'll be very happy in D.C."

The fact that he could so easily assume that she was leaving the Sandbur, leaving him, was enough to send fury ripping through her. Instantly, she marched over to him, snatched the cup from his hand and slammed it down on the table. "You might know exactly how to treat a horse, Mr. Trevino, but you damn sure don't know about handling a woman," she said tightly.

His black brows pulled together in a puzzled frown, which only infuriated Mercedes more.

"What is that supposed to mean?" he questioned. "I'm trying to be nice about this and—"

"Nice! You think I want nice?" Groaning with frustration, she threw up her hands. "You've got to be the most thick-headed man I've ever met!"

His jaw clenched. "Look, if you came over here thinking I'd start begging and pleading for you to stay, then forget it. We both know that your leaving is—for the best."

Mercedes had never thought she possessed much of a temper. She might be feisty, but she never got angry. Not raging angry as she was now.

"You really believe that?" she asked through gritted teeth.

Turning his back to her, he muttered sharply, "I have to believe it!"

Catching him by the arm, she tugged him around to face her. "If that's the way you feel, then I've made a big misjudgment in you. I thought—" She struggled to swallow as tears began to burn her throat. "Deep down I thought you were capable of loving—of loving me. But I can see now that you're only concerned about yourself. That I've been no more than a passing distraction to you." Unable to bear touching him for another second, she jerked her hand away from his arm. "You're no different than the bastard who broke my heart eight years ago! Which only proves what a bad judge of men I am!"

Whirling away from him, she started to leave the room, but his hand caught her shoulder. The touch of his hand on her bare skin sent streaks of fire racing up and down her arm.

"Maybe you ought to explain that," he demanded in a steely voice.

Biting down on her lip, she slowly turned and met his gaze. "Eight years ago, the affair I told you about was with one of my professors in college. At that time, he vowed that he loved me and wanted to spend the rest of his life with me. I began to plan a future with him, blissfully unaware that he'd just happened to leave out the part where he was already married," she said bitterly. "So don't be using Sherleen as an excuse to shut me out of your life! I know what lies and rejections and betrayals are all about, too! The only difference between you and me is that I was foolish enough to fall in love again. And this time, it's with a man who doesn't even possess a heart!"

Gabe stared at Mercedes in stunned silence, trying to understand what she'd just said, when she let out a choked cry and ran out the open doorway.

Part of his mind yelled at him to run after her and stop her a second time, but the other part of him was paralyzed, incapable of moving a muscle.

Mercedes had fallen in love with him? Is that what she'd said? That she *loved* him?

His hands shaking, he sank into the desk chair and dropped his head into his hands. All along, he'd convinced himself that she was only playing with him, that a few nights of sex was all she wanted or needed from him. It had been easier to let himself think in those terms, easier to keep his heart at a distance. Or so he'd told himself.

Yet the moment Lex had told him about Mercedes's job offer, a part of him had died, withered like a weed in the desert. And he'd known that he'd been fooling himself all along. He loved the woman. He'd just been too afraid, too proud to tell her so.

And now he was on the verge of losing her. He *would* lose her if he didn't do something, and quick.

Dismissing the call he'd promised to return, Gabe hurried out of the barn to find her.

Twenty minutes later, after stopping at her office and finding it empty, then calling the big house to discover she wasn't there, either, Gabe moved on a hunch and headed back to the horse barn.

Before he entered the cavernous building, he met one of the grooms wheeling out a wheelbarrow full of manure.

"Eddie, have you seen Mercedes anywhere around the ranch yard in the past half hour?"

"Sure have. She left a while ago on that roan gelding."

Anger and fear rushed through Gabe. He'd warned her about riding that horse, but apparently she'd decided his opinion didn't count for much. "You mean, the blue roan—Mouse?"

Eddie took off his straw hat and scratched the top of his head. "Yeah, that's the one. He's as mean as a snake, if you ask me. But she seems to love him. Makes you wonder what women are thinking sometimes, don't it?"

Yeah. Like how she could love him when he'd been as mistrustful as Mouse, Gabe thought ruefully.

"I'd better go look for her," he muttered more to himself than to the groom, then hurried toward the barn door.

Eddie called after him. "Want me to saddle a horse for you, Mr. Gabe?"

Gabe waved a dismissive hand back at him. "No. I'll take care of it."

Five minutes later, he was galloping away from the ranch yard, directing his horse toward the west and the river, a route that he knew she loved to ride. It took him an hour to reach the banks of the San Antonio, but he didn't get so much as a glimpse of her or even Mouse's tracks. And the way back to the ranch was just as fruitless.

Once he unsaddled, he made another visit to Mercedes's office, but it was dark and empty. When he tried the big house again, Cook informed him that she hadn't seen Mercedes since she'd left early that morning.

Feeling frustrated and angry at himself for not coming to his senses sooner, Gabe decided the only thing left for him to do now was wait for her to return and hope that she would be willing to forgive him.

The rest of the afternoon passed at a snail's pace for Gabe. Even though he kept himself busy with a pen of yearlings, he found himself looking up every few minutes, hoping to see Mercedes riding back into the ranch yard.

Where was she? What was she doing? Was she out there sulking somewhere, determined to make him worry and fret? No. Mercedes wasn't purposely mean. She wouldn't want to deliberately hurt him—even out of anger. Dammit, why hadn't he realized that weeks ago? It was something he'd be asking himself for a long time to come.

When sundown came and Mercedes still hadn't appeared, Gabe could only make one conclusion. Something had happened to her.

After giving orders to the wranglers, he punched in Matt's number on his cell phone while he headed for one of the ranch's pickup trucks.

He hated to call the man, but Lex was off the ranch on business today, and Matt was more than the general foreman of the ranch, he was Mercedes's cousin, one that was very nearly like a brother. But Matt's first wife had been killed when she'd ridden a spirited horse away from the ranch. Gabe realized Mercedes's disappearance would only bring back bad memories for the man, but finding her was the most important issue now.

"I rode out earlier today to find her," he explained a few moments later as he related the facts to Matt. "I didn't see her anywhere, but then she could have taken a different trail."

"Let's not panic, Gabe. She could have ridden in an entirely different direction."

Gabe swallowed as fear threatened to overtake him. If something bad had happened to Mercedes, he'd never forgive himself.

With the phone still to his ear, he started the truck and gunned it out of the ranch yard. "She's on Mouse. I told her not to ride him—he's totally unpredictable. But she—well, she was angry with me. She probably rode him out of spite."

A grim silence ensued and then Matt said, "Yeah. I know all about an angry woman," he said ruefully. "But Mercedes can ride probably better than you and me put together. I have to believe she's all right. I'll get some of the hands together. We'll saddle up and fan out over the place until we find her."

"Good. I'm heading toward the river again," Gabe told him. "I'm still thinking she went in that direction."

He snapped the phone shut and drove onward across the rough pastureland. After a half mile passed, he suddenly spotted Mouse loping out of a grove of mesquite trees. The empty saddle on his back caused Gabe's heart to take a nose-dive and he was forced to clench the steering wheel to keep his hands from shaking.

Oh, God, he prayed. *Don't let her be injured. Don't let me lose her like this.*

When the horse noticed the truck, the animal instinctively ran toward it. Gabe stomped on the brakes and jumped out at the same time Mouse trotted up, seeming relieved to finally see a human.

"Whoa, boy. You're all right now," he said soothingly as he latched on to the dangling bridle reins.

The horse was sweating and dancing in a nervous jig. Gabe had to struggle with him for a couple of minutes before he was able to examine him and the saddle. A quick inspection showed no blood or sign of injuries. The lack of evidence should have given him a tiny amount of relief, but it only worried him more. Something had made Mercedes fall. But what? And where was she?

Trying to keep himself calm so that he wouldn't spook Mouse even more, he carefully tethered him beneath a nearby hackberry tree, jumped back into the truck and called Matt's cell number again.

"I've found Mouse," he blurted without preamble. "He's fine, but no sign of Mercedes. I've tied him along the trail. You'll find him when you head this way. I'm going on to search for her."

Gabe tossed down the phone and stepped down on the gas. Unless Mouse had been wandering around in circles, Mercedes had to be close by, he thought desperately.

Fifteen more agonizing minutes passed before he spotted her walking on a cattle trail, heading toward the ranch. He tromped on the gas and the truck bounced wildly over several fire-ant hills until he finally reached the spot where she'd halted on the beaten track.

By the time Gabe braked the truck to a stop and rushed to her side, he was so weak with relief, his legs felt close to collapsing.

"Mercedes! My God, look at you! Are you hurt? What happened?"

Her white shirt and blue jeans were covered in dirt, her straw hat bent into an unrecognizable shape. A bloody scratch across her cheek had dried to a brown mark, but otherwise she appeared safe and sound. She was staring at him as though he were the last person she expected to see, which only made Gabe feel even worse about the things he'd said to her.

"I'm fine," she said in a weary voice. "I'm just ashamed to admit that I got bucked off."

Groaning loudly, he grabbed her by the shoulders and tugged her into his arms. As he buried his face against the side of her hair, he gently scolded, "Mercedes, I told you that Mouse was an outlaw! I told you not to get on him!"

Mercedes suddenly realized he was trembling with fear. She wrapped her arms around his waist and pressed her cheek against his chest in an effort to reassure him. He'd been searching for her, she thought incredulously. He did care for her. He had to!

"It wasn't his fault," she reasoned. "We came upon a rattlesnake in the trail and it struck at Mouse's front leg. Before I could get control of him, he began bucking. I landed in a patch of hedge roses and Mouse ran off. I had no choice but to start walking."

"Damn horse! I found him back up the trail." He eased her away from him and shook his head. "Mercedes, when I saw that horse running across the pasture without you, I was—terrified."

Yes, she could hear the aftermath of his fear quavering in his voice, see the concern on his face. It stunned her, thrilled her, to think he might actually care that much. "I'm sorry, Gabe. I never meant to worry you. After this morning—"

"Mercedes," he blurted before she could say more. "This isn't the time or place, but I don't give a damn if we're standing in the middle of a cow trail. Everything I said this morning was a bunch of hogwash. I don't want you to go to D.C. I don't want you to go anywhere. I love you. I think I've loved you from the moment I danced with you that first night we met. I was just too damned afraid, too proud to admit to myself that I could ever need anybody in my life again. Instead, I tried to convince myself that you were the same sort of rich, conniving woman Sherleen had been. And—"

"Oh, Gabe," she interjected, "I'm not anything like her—"

"Wait. Just wait a minute and let me explain," he gently countered. "You're exactly like your mother. Strong and independent. You don't need a man to take care of you—"

"But, Gabe—"

He held up a hand to thwart her protest. "I can live with that, Mercedes. But after we made love, you never bothered to tell me how you felt about me, about your job, about anything that was important to you. What was I to think? That you didn't care? That you didn't want to share that part of your life with me?"

Tears brimmed from her eyes and spilled onto her cheeks. "I've been afraid, too," she whispered as she reached up and clasped his dear face between her palms. "And I'm sorry, Gabe. I should have talked to you—really talked to you. But I'm—you see, for the past eight years, my job has been keeping secrets. The importance of keeping the simplest details to myself was constantly pounded into me by my superiors. And—" She dropped her gaze from his and swallowed hard. "Once I didn't do that and paid serious consequences for it. Since then, I've become—well, not very good about expressing myself to others."

"Can you tell me about it now?"

She looked up at him and tried to smile through her tears. Yes, she could tell Gabe now. Because finally, finally she'd learned to trust again.

"To make a long story short, I became close friends with a fellow airman. His name was Drew and he was a funny, charming guy that I liked immediately. We both worked in intelligence, but I was one security level higher than him. Time went by and I was beginning to think he was a man I could become serious about. And since I'd had a heck of a time getting over John, this was a big step for me. Apparently Drew must have sensed that I was growing fond of him, because he ultimately used that fondness to pry classified information from me."

"I'm so sorry."

"Yeah. So was I. Sorry that I'd been so foolish as to trust him. Especially when I knew better. He went straight to my superiors with the information, and though it wasn't any data that would have caused serious harm, it was enough to tell them that I couldn't be trusted. The whole thing made me look like Mata Hari and Drew like 007."

"What a bastard."

"No. I don't blame him. I was the one at fault. For trusting him in the first place. For opening my mouth when I should have kept it closed." Her arms tightened around him, and this time when she smiled, her eyes were smiling, too. "But I'm not in the military anymore. And I don't have to guard my heart anymore now that I've found you. You're going to be so sick of me telling you every little thing that you'll probably want to drag out the duct tape," she teased.

"I should be apologizing, too, Mercedes. I wasn't exactly being open and honest with you. I guess we've both got a lot to learn about trust."

Sighing with relief, she said, "If you'd not jumped to conclusions so quickly this morning, I would have told you that I have no intentions of going to D.C., or anywhere else. Now or ever."

His fingertips gently wiped at the tears on her dusty cheeks. "Do you really mean that?"

"Oh, Gabe, I went riding this morning in hopes that it

would calm me down. I was so angry with you because you didn't seem to care. I kept asking myself if it might be better if I took the job in Washington."

His eyes were sober as they roamed her face. "And how did you finally answer yourself?"

"The answer was easy," she softly replied. "The Sandbur is where my heart is. Here with you. Besides, deep down I'm a cowgirl, and that's all I ever want to be. And your wife. If you want me."

Tender awe filled his gray eyes as he stroked a hand over her tangled hair. "With me, Mercedes, what you see before you is all you get. Is that enough to keep you by my side, to give me children?"

Love beamed from the smile that spread across her face. "What I see before me is enough to last me a lifetime and beyond, cowboy."

He swept off her hat, then bent his head to kiss her. Mercedes clung to him tightly, letting her lips convey all the love in her heart.

Finally lifting his mouth from hers, Gabe grinned. "Matt has a posse out looking for you. We'd better get back to the ranch and let everyone know you're safe."

They started to the truck, and with a happy chuckle Mercedes curled her arm around the back of his waist.

"And I'd better call Mother and tell her that she has a wedding to plan."

Suddenly concerned, Gabe glanced at her. "What do you think she's going to say?"

Laughing, Mercedes leaned over and kissed his cheek. "That it damn well took us long enough."

* * * * *

Turn the page for a sneak preview of
AFTERSHOCK, *a new anthology*
featuring New York Times *bestselling author*
Sharon Sala.

Available October 2008.

n●cturne™

Dramatic and sensual tales of paranormal romance.

Chapter 1

October
New York City

Nicole Masters was sitting cross-legged on her sofa while a cold autumn rain peppered the windows of her fourth-floor apartment. She was poking at the ice cream in her bowl and trying not to be in a mood.

Six weeks ago, a simple trip to her neighborhood pharmacy had turned into a nightmare. She'd walked into the middle of a robbery. She never even saw the man who shot her in the head and left her for dead. She'd survived, but some of her senses had not. She was dealing with short-term memory loss and a tendency to stagger. Even though she'd been told the problems were most likely temporary, she waged a daily battle with depression.

Her parents had been killed in a car wreck when she was twenty-one. And except for a few friends—and most recently her boyfriend, Dominic Tucci, who lived in the apartment right above hers, she was alone. Her doctor kept reminding her that she should be grateful to be alive, and on one level she knew he was right. But he wasn't living in her shoes.

If she'd been anywhere else but at that pharmacy when the robbery happened, she wouldn't have died twice on the way to the hospital. Instead of being grateful that she'd survived, she couldn't stop thinking of what she'd lost.

But that wasn't the end of her troubles. On top of everything else, something strange was happening inside her head. She'd begun to hear odd things: sounds, not voices—at least, she didn't think it was voices. It was more like the distant noise of rapids—a rush of wind and water inside her head that, when it came, blocked out everything around her. It didn't happen often, but when it did, it was frightening, and it was driving her crazy.

The blank moments, which is what she called them, even had a rhythm. First there came that sound, then a cold sweat, then panic with no reason. Part of her feared it was the beginning of an emotional breakdown. And part of her feared it wasn't—that it was going to turn out to be a permanent souvenir of her resurrection.

Frustrated with herself and the situation as it stood, she upped the sound on the TV remote. But instead of *Wheel of Fortune,* an announcer broke in with a special bulletin.

"This just in. Police are on the scene of a kidnapping that occurred only hours ago at The Dakota. Molly Dane, the six-year-old daughter of one of Hollywood's block-buster stars, Lyla Dane, was taken by force from the family apartment. At this time, they have yet to receive

a ransom demand. The housekeeper was seriously injured during the abduction, and is, at the present time,
in surgery. Police are hoping to be able to talk to her
once she regains consciousness. In the meantime, we are
going now to a press conference with Lyla Dane."

Horrified, Nicole stilled as the cameras went live to where
the actress was speaking before a bank of microphones. The
shock and terror in Lyla Dane's voice were physically painful
to watch. But even though Nicole kept upping the volume, the
sound continued to fade.

Just when she was beginning to think something was wrong
with her set, the broadcast suddenly switched from the Dane
press conference to what appeared to be footage of the kidnapping, beginning with footage from inside the apartment.

When the front door suddenly flew back against the wall
and four men rushed in, Nicole gasped. Horrified, she quickly
realized that this must have been caught on a security camera
inside the Dane apartment.

As Nicole continued to watch, a small Asian woman, who
she guessed was the maid, rushed forward in an effort to keep
them out. When one of the men hit her in the face with his gun,
Nicole moaned. The violence was too reminiscent of what she'd
lived through. Sick to her stomach, she fisted her hands against
her belly, wishing it was over, but unable to tear her gaze away.

When the maid dropped to the carpet, the same man followed with a vicious kick to the little woman's midsection that
lifted her off the floor.

"Oh, my God," Nicole said. When blood began to pool
beneath the maid's head, she started to cry.

As the tape played on, the four men split up in different
directions. The camera caught one running down a long

marble hallway, then disappearing into a room. Moments later he reappeared, carrying a little girl, who Nicole assumed was Molly Dane. The child was wearing a pair of red pants and a white turtleneck sweater, and her hair was partially blocking her abductor's face as he carried her down the hall. She was kicking and screaming in his arms, and when he slapped her, it elicited an agonized scream that brought the other three running. Nicole watched in horror as one of them ran up and put his hand over Molly's face. Seconds later, she went limp.

One moment they were in the foyer, then they were gone.

Nicole jumped to her feet, then staggered drunkenly. The bowl of ice cream she'd absentmindedly placed in her lap shattered at her feet, splattering glass and melting ice cream everywhere.

The picture on the screen abruptly switched from the kidnapping to what Nicole assumed was a rerun of Lyla Dane's plea for her daughter's safe return, but she was numb.

Before she could think what to do next, the doorbell rang. Startled by the unexpected sound, she shakily swiped at the tears and took a step forward. She didn't feel the glass shards piercing her feet until she took the second step. At that point, sharp pains shot through her foot. She gasped, then looked down in confusion. Her legs looked as if she'd been running through mud, and she was standing in broken glass and ice cream, while a thin ribbon of blood seeped out from beneath her toes.

"Oh, no," Nicole mumbled, then stifled a second moan of pain.

The doorbell rang again. She shivered, then clutched her head in confusion.

"Just a minute!" she yelled, then tried to sidestep the rest of the debris as she hobbled to the door.

When she looked through the peephole in the door, she didn't know whether to be relieved or regretful.

It was Dominic, and as usual, she was a mess.

Nicole smiled a little self-consciously as she opened the door to let him in. "I just don't know what's happening to me. I think I'm losing my mind."

"Hey, don't talk about my woman like that."

Nicole rode the surge of delight his words brought. "So I'm still your woman?"

Dominic lowered his head.

Their lips met.

The kiss proceeded.

Slowly.

Thoroughly.

* * * * *

Be sure to look for the AFTERSHOCK *anthology next month, as well as other exciting paranormal stories from Silhouette Nocturne.*
Available in October wherever books are sold.

SPECIAL EDITION™

Tanner Bravo and Crystal Cerise had it bad
for each other, though they couldn't be more
different. Tanner was the type to settle down;
free-spirited Crystal wouldn't hear of it.
Now that Crystal was pregnant, would
Tanner have his way after all?

Look for

HAVING TANNER BRAVO'S BABY

by *USA TODAY* bestselling author
CHRISTINE RIMMER

Available in October wherever books are sold.

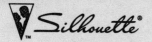

Silhouette®

Romantic
SUSPENSE

*Sparked by Danger,
Fueled by Passion.*

USA TODAY bestselling author
Merline Lovelace

Undercover Wife

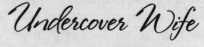

Secret agent Mike Callahan, code name Hawkeye,
objects when he's paired with sophisticated
Gillian Ridgeway on a dangerous spy mission
to Hong Kong. Gillian has secretly been in love
with him for years, but Hawk is an overprotective
man with a wounded past that threatens to
resurface. Now the two must put their lives—
and hearts—at risk for each other.

Available October wherever books are sold.

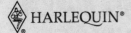

HARLEQUIN®

American ★ Romance®

HOLLY JACOBS
Once Upon a Thanksgiving
AMERICAN DADS

Single mom Samantha Williams has work, four kids and is even volunteering for the school's Thanksgiving pageant. Her full life gets busier when Harry Remington takes over as interim principal. Will he say goodbye at the end of his term in December…or can Samantha give him the best reason to stay?

Available October 2008 wherever books are sold.

LOVE, HOME & HAPPINESS

REQUEST YOUR FREE BOOKS!

2 FREE NOVELS PLUS 2 FREE GIFTS!

SPECIAL EDITION®

Life, Love and Family!

YES! Please send me 2 FREE Silhouette Special Edition® novels and my 2 FREE gifts (gifts are worth about $10). After receiving them, if I don't wish to receive any more books, I can return the shipping statement marked "cancel." If I don't cancel, I will receive 6 brand-new novels every month and be billed just $4.24 per book in the U.S. or $4.99 per book in Canada, plus 25¢ shipping and handling per book and applicable taxes, if any*. That's a savings of at least 15% off the cover price! I understand that accepting the 2 free books and gifts places me under no obligation to buy anything. I can always return a shipment and cancel at any time. Even if I never buy another book from Silhouette, the two free books and gifts are mine to keep forever.

235 SDN EEYU   335 SDN EEY6

Name		(PLEASE PRINT)	
Address			Apt. #
City		State/Prov.	Zip/Postal Code

Signature (if under 18, a parent or guardian must sign)

Mail to the Silhouette Reader Service:
IN U.S.A.: P.O. Box 1867, Buffalo, NY 14240-1867
IN CANADA: P.O. Box 609, Fort Erie, Ontario L2A 5X3

Not valid to current subscribers of Silhouette Special Edition books.

Want to try two free books from another line?
Call 1-800-873-8635 or visit www.morefreebooks.com.

* Terms and prices subject to change without notice. N.Y. residents add applicable sales tax. Canadian residents will be charged applicable provincial taxes and GST. Offer not valid in Quebec. This offer is limited to one order per household. All orders subject to approval. Credit or debit balances in a customer's account(s) may be offset by any other outstanding balance owed by or to the customer. Please allow 4 to 6 weeks for delivery. Offer available while quantities last.

Your Privacy: Silhouette is committed to protecting your privacy. Our Privacy Policy is available online at www.eHarlequin.com or upon request from the Reader Service. From time to time we make our lists of customers available to reputable third parties who may have a product or service of interest to you. If you would prefer we not share your name and address, please check here. ☐

SSE08R

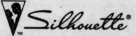
SPECIAL EDITION

#1927 HAVING TANNER BRAVO'S BABY—Christine Rimmer
Bravo Family Ties

Tanner Bravo and Crystal Cerise had it bad for each other, though they couldn't be more different. Tanner was the type to settle down; free-spirited Crystal wouldn't hear of it. Now that Crystal was pregnant, would Tanner have his way after all?

#1928 FAMILY IN PROGRESS—Brenda Harlen
Back in Business

Restoring classic cars was widowed dad Steven Warren's stock in trade. And when magazine photographer Samara Kenzo showed up to snap his masterpieces, her focus was squarely on the handsome mechanic. But the closer they got, the more Steven's preteen daughter objected to this interloper....

#1929 HOMETOWN SWEETHEART—Victoria Pade
Northbridge Nuptials

When Wyatt Grayson's elderly grandmother showed up, disoriented and raving, in her hometown, it was social worker Neily Pratt to the rescue. And while her job was to determine if Wyatt was a fit guardian for his grandmother, Neily knew right away that she'd appoint him guardian of her own heart any day!

#1930 THE SINGLE DAD'S VIRGIN WIFE—Susan Crosby
Wives for Hire

Tricia McBride was in the mood for adventure, and that's just what she got when she agreed to homeschool Noah Falcon's two sets of twins. As she warmed to the charms of this single dad, Tricia realized that what started out strictly business was turning into pure pleasure....

#1931 ACCIDENTAL PRINCESS—Nancy Robards Thompson

Most little girls dream of being a princess—single mom Sophie Baldwin's world turned upside down when she found out she was one! As this social-worker-turned-sovereign rightfully claimed the throne of St. Michel, little did she know she was claiming the heart of St. Michel's Minister of Security, Philippe Lejardin, in the process.

#1932 FALLING FOR THE LONE WOLF—Crystal Green
The Suds Club

Her friends at the Suds Club Laundromat noticed that something was up with Jenny Hunter—especially Web consultant Liam McCree, who had designs on the businesswoman. Would serial-dating Jenny end up with this secret admirer? Or would a looming health crisis stand in their way? It would all come out in the wash....

SSECNM0908

The scream rising in my tight throat. My stomach heaved in protest. Pressing my hand against my mouth, I backed away, unable to tear my eyes from the grisly sight. I kept backing away until I bumped into the door. I tore it open and ran outside.

I kept running until I hit the fence at the edge of the parking lot. Clutching the cool chain links with one hand, I swayed. My stomach violently rejected all I had eaten. I continued to heave long after there was nothing left to expel. When I was finally able to stop, I collapsed with my back against the fence. At first I concentrated on breathing deeply, on regaining some control over my shaking body.

When the trembling ceased, I tried to put my thoughts in order.

Galen Crawford was dead.

★ ---

ILSA MAYR

A TIMELY ALIBI

W⬤RLDWIDE®

TORONTO • NEW YORK • LONDON
AMSTERDAM • PARIS • SYDNEY • HAMBURG
STOCKHOLM • ATHENS • TOKYO • MILAN
MADRID • WARSAW • BUDAPEST • AUCKLAND

Recycling programs
for this product may
not exist in your area.

A TIMELY ALIBI

A Worldwide Mystery/December 2010

First published by Thomas Bouregy & Co., Inc.

ISBN-13: 978-0-373-26735-4

Printed in U.S.A.

This book is dedicated to my librarian friends—
mystery lovers all—who are, in alphabetical order,
as librarians love alphabetical order: Mary Lue Binning,
Helene Evans and Berneice Wilson.

ONE

TERRANCE ARIOSTO WAS rumored to be the richest man
in Westport, Indiana.

He was arguably the stingiest man.

He was definitely the meanest.

I had helped his daughter, Annette, squeak through
our algebra class in high school, and so I'd had lots of
chances to observe him up close and personal. Every
time I'd gone to the estate, I'd prayed that his fearsome
temper outbursts and his snide, sarcastic remarks
wouldn't be directed at me.

So, knowing all that, why was I sitting in his elegant
study, waiting for him to get off the phone? Because
he had asked for me specifically when he hired the
Keller Security Agency to investigate a problem for
him. Barney Keller, my uncle and boss, gave me the
assignment. This was my first chance to prove myself
as an apprentice investigator. I was impatient to get on
with it. Ariosto must have sensed this.

Covering the mouthpiece of the phone with his hand,
he mouthed, "I'll be with you in a minute."

I nodded and crossed my legs. Touching the fine
wool of my skirt, I reassured myself that my suit looked
professional. For what it had cost, it should. Not that I
had paid the original, inflated price. Although I adore
clothes, I never buy anything in the department stores

lining Chicago's Miracle Mile unless it has been marked
down three times. Thinking of my favorite store, I realized I hadn't been shopping in a little over a year. Not
since… I jumped on the memory hard.

I moved in the chair slightly so that I could steal a
quick look at the photo on the antique pedestal desk.
It was a portrait of Pauline Ariosto, his fourth wife.
She was probably my age, thirty. That made her a good
thirty-five years younger than her husband and the same
age as his only daughter, Annette. It was fortunate that
none of my psychology professors had been disciples
of Freud. That saved me a lot of speculation about com-
plexes originating in Greek mythology.

Ariosto hung up the phone. He removed his wire-
rimmed glasses and looked at me.

"All right. Let's get down to business, Cybil. Or shall
I call you Mrs. Quindt?"

"Cybil is fine." For a man his size his voice struck
me as unusually high and reedy. I don't like high voices,
but that wouldn't keep me from doing my very best for
him.

"I asked for you because I've heard that you are a
first-rate investigator."

"Mr. Ariosto, I work for my uncle's agency, but I'm
not a licensed investigator," I felt obligated to point out.
"At least not yet."

He waved his hand dismissingly. "That doesn't matter.
From what I hear, you get results. So, after working in
my warehouse for several days, what do you have to
report?"

"Your suspicions were right."

"I'm being ripped off. I knew it!"

He smashed his fist on the desktop. The photo of Pauline toppled over. He didn't bother to set it upright.

"Who the hell is stealing from me?" he demanded.

A dull, angry red color suffused his skin. I could almost hear him grinding his teeth, and I wondered uneasily if I was about to witness one of his famous temper tantrums. Bracing myself, I said, "Let's get a couple of things straight, Mr. Ariosto. I won't do anything that's illegal, and when I discover who the thieves are, I'll call the police before I call you."

A hint of a grim smile pulled at his thin lips. "Afraid I'll take them apart limb by limb?"

"Something like that."

"You're right. I'm angry enough to go after a grizzly with a stick."

To underscore his words, he cracked his knuckles. I believed him and wanted no part of this. When I made a move to stand up, he waved me down.

"Hold on. I am angry, but I'm not stupid. As much as it would pleasure me to kick…rumps, I won't risk going to jail on an assault charge."

I must have looked skeptical.

"You have my word on that."

Since he had a reputation for keeping his word, I leaned back in my seat.

Ariosto lit a fat cigar, not bothering to ask me if I minded the smoke. *I* did, but since I was in his house and he was an important client, I kept my mouth shut.

"Well, I've known for some time that profits at the Tri State Warehouses were down, but I blamed it on the recession we'd been having. When things didn't perk up but got worse this summer, I knew something was fishy. How bad is it?"

I glanced at the figures in my small notebook. "I estimate you're losing about twenty thousand dollars worth of goods a month. Of course, that's only an educated guess."

For a second he sat as if struck by lightning. Then a stream of expletives spewed from his mouth that would have gladdened the heart of a drunken sailor. After he paused for breath, he demanded, "Who's stealing me blind?"

"Pilfering on this scale must involve an organized theft ring."

"Does that make discovering the thieves more difficult?" he asked.

"No. It would be harder, if not impossible, to catch the random individual sneaking out a pound of butter or a couple of steaks."

Ariosto nodded. "We expect some petty pilfering. That's built into the nature of the business. But not twenty thousand dollars worth. You must have some idea who's doing it."

"Yes, but we want the man or the men who organized the operation, who contacted the places that receive the extra cases of caviar, veal and lobster. We need proof of who gets the payoff."

"Exactly. I want to nail their thieving hides to the warehouse doors." He puffed forcefully on his cigar. "It's going to be hard to find out who these men are," he muttered.

"Not necessarily. An organized group has to meet occasionally to make plans and divvy up the money.

That's how we'll nab them. Uncle Barney says that it's the extra income that gets people caught. If they would salt the money away, they'd be free and clear but most of them don't. They buy things. It's not difficult to spot someone living above their legitimate income."

"Where will you start? How will you do it?" He held up his hand. "No, don't tell me. Just do it. Bring me proof and report to me here at the house. I can't be sure who's in on this at my office. Seems I can't trust anybody."

Since the food distribution warehouse was only one of his many business ventures, I doubted that his entire staff was involved but didn't say so. We shook hands, and I left.

On the portico I almost collided with Pauline Ariosto rushing into the house. Judging by her red, puffy eyes, she had been crying. Life on top of the hill was apparently not any more Edenic than it was in the valley where the rest of us lived.

MY UNCLE'S AGENCY takes up the second floor of a building whose designer had obviously liked Renaissance architecture. This preference was especially apparent in the frieze below the roof and in the treatment of doors and windows. I love the architect's disregard for the purely functional.

Lynn, which is the Americanization of her Vietnamese name she insists on using, was arguing with Glenn, one of the investigators, when I entered the office.

"No receipt, no reimbursement. You know that," the efficient office manager said coolly.

"I already explained it to you. I didn't have time to

get the receipt. The subject I was following had already paid the toll and was speeding toward Chicago."

"Too bad. Next time follow more closely."

Discussion closed, Lynn swiveled her chair to face the computer. Moments later the furious tapping of the keys filled the room.

I looked at Glenn with sympathy. The only way he would get reimbursed was to appeal directly to my uncle. Barney Keller is the one person for whom Lynn will break the elaborate set of rules and procedures she has set up for running the office. I'm not sure, but I think my uncle met Lynn in Vietnam during the war. Sometimes I wonder if they were, or still are, lovers. If so, they are extremely discreet.

Like a penitent, I stood in front of Lynn waiting for her to acknowledge my presence. Sometimes that takes several minutes. When she finally raised those beautiful, black, almond-shaped eyes, I asked, "Is my uncle in?"

"Yes."

"May I see him?"

"I'll announce you."

She always does that, even if his door is wide open.

After murmuring into the phone, she said, "He will see you."

"Thank you," I said, playing along with her formal ritual.

My uncle waved me to his visitor's chair. "So, what did Ariosto say?"

I reported my meeting as succinctly as I could. Barney Keller retired from the army after thirty years to open this agency. He insists on brevity and clarity.

"We are to contact him only at his home," I said in conclusion.

Barney raised an eyebrow. "His house?"

"Yes. He insists on absolute secrecy. He wants only the three of us to know about this. I suspect he's at least as embarrassed as he's furious that someone is ripping him off."

"Yeah. He's the kind of man who can't stand anyone betraying him in any way. His ego won't stand for it."

"I told him I'd continue working at Tri State until I knew the identity of the organizers and had solid proof."

Barney frowned. "I don't like you doing undercover work. If anyone suspects anything, you could be in danger."

"Nobody will suspect me of being anything but an employee. I'm careful and discreet. You know I have the kind of face that inspires people to confide in me without me having to do more than drop a hint or two."

"That's what makes you a natural investigator. But be careful anyway. Your grandmother would skin me alive if anything happened to you. If there's even a hint of danger, you get out. Agreed?"

"Agreed." I rose to my feet.

"Have you seen Mother yet?"

"She's here? Oma's here?"

"Upstairs, waiting in your office. Didn't Lynn tell you?"

She hadn't. If she thinks a message is of a personal nature she often holds it until the end of business hours. I clamped my teeth together to keep from saying anything disparaging about Lynn. However much she irritates me, I keep quiet for Uncle Barney's sake. Outside my immediate family, he's my favorite relative. Always has been.

"If it's okay, I'll go see Oma."

Barney smiled and nodded.

Although I call my grandmother Oma, which is the Austrian equivalent of granny, in my mind I refer to Maximilianne by her shortened first name, Maxi. Like her name, there's something regal about her. Perhaps it's the way she carries herself, or the set of the white-haired head. She's also tough. She had to be to leave her native Austria in 1938 with the prominent Jewish family for whom she worked as an assistant nanny. At age fifteen she'd kissed her mother and her siblings goodbye, not knowing when or if she would see them again.

I paused in the doorway to look at Maxi. Deeply engrossed in one of the paperbacks she always carried with her, she wasn't aware that I studied her with anxious eyes, looking for, and fearing to find, signs of ill health and decline. I released the breath I'd been holding. She looked just fine, her white hair coiled into an elegant twist, one of her cameo brooches pinned to the lapel of her lavender jacket. That told me that her hands hadn't hurt too much from the arthritis that plagued her from time to time.

"Hi, Oma."

Maxi smiled even before she looked up from her book and that sweet smile enfolded me with warmth like heated flannel sheets on a bitter cold winter night.

"There you are, *Schatzi*. Barney told me you went to meet with a client."

I nodded. "Why didn't you let me know you were

coming into town? I might have been able to arrange for us to go to lunch."

"I will next time. I keep forgetting that you're a working woman again. Do you still like working for Barney?"

Scooting my chair from behind the metal desk, I sat down facing her. "I still like working as an investigator. Maybe even more now that I know what I'm doing. Uncle Barney's been training me. It's exciting. The days fly by where before they didn't seem to want to end. I'll always remember that you and Uncle Barney did this for me." I reached for Maxi's hand and held it against my cheek. She smoothed my hair with her other hand. "Thank you again, Oma."

"You're welcome," she murmured. "We couldn't stand by any longer and watch you grow paler and more withdrawn each day. So Barney hit on the idea of hiring you. He always claimed you were the brightest of my grandchildren. And you know what? He's right. What is that American saying? It takes one to know one?"

I nodded.

"Of my six children Barney's also the one with the kindest heart and that makes him a good man." Maxi stroked my hair one more time. "How about some tea? You still have that hot pot in your file cabinet?"

"Yes. I'll get the water from the cooler in the hall."

When I returned, she had set out cups, sugar, and napkins. I set the pot on top of the cabinet and plugged it in. "What brought you into town today?"

"The anniversary. The same thing that drove you to the cemetery first thing this morning."

I must have looked surprised because Maxi felt it necessary to explain.

"Luke told me. He saw you at the cemetery. Though I would have known that the yellow roses were from you."

I nodded. "Yellow was Ryan's favorite color. It suited him, don't you think? He was such a sunny, even-tempered child." My voice broke. The pain in my throat from suppressed tears was excruciating. I busied myself with the box of tea bags, opening it, closing it, repeating the gesture until I could speak again.

"I went at six this morning. It seemed right. Ryan always woke up at that time, full of energy, ready to face all the exciting discoveries a new day would bring." Of the many things my sweet little boy would never experience were his fourth birthday, the new tricycle we were planning to give him, his first day in preschool, camping out that summer in Oma's meadow... I bit my lower lip hard, welcoming the physical pain.

After a while I asked, "You said you saw my husband. How is Luke?"

"He seemed okay. He has his work. I suspect he leaves the hospital only long enough to sleep and change clothes."

"Then why doesn't he understand that working is important to me, too?" I poured the boiling water over the tea bags. "He hates my working here."

"He's afraid. He's lost a son. He can't bear the thought of losing his wife, too," Maxi said softly.

"I understand that, but it's so illogical. The chance of me being killed in a car crash or an accident in the home are so much greater than anything happening to me on the job. Luke wants us to be like we were before Ryan's death and that's impossible. We're not the same people now we were then. Why can't he accept that?"

"He will, just as he will come to terms with your work. He has to. It's kept you from—"

"Oma, you can say it: from having a nervous breakdown. From going off the deep end." I poured the tea. We sipped it silently, each of us pursuing our own thoughts. After a while I heard Maxi sigh.

"Any chance of your moving back in with Luke?" she asked.

"Not any time soon. I need to be on my own. I can't live in a house that holds all those memories."

"That's why you bought and moved into that fixer-upper's dream. Or nightmare, depending on how you look at that house. I think I understand," Maxi said.

"Well, that's more than Luke does."

"I repeat, give him time, *Schatzi*."

"I'm sorry I'm such a wet blanket today."

"You're never that." Changing subjects, she said, with a sigh, "I'm having dinner with your mother and her husband tonight."

"Ah."

"I'm ashamed to admit this, but I would rather finish my book than listen to Justin Merriweather pontificate about banking and investments. The only thing that will make the evening bearable is the excellent food. Your mother has always managed to hire first rate cooks."

We smiled at each other in perfect understanding.

"What are you reading?"

"Actually, I'm rereading. One of Jane Austen's. I wish she had written more books."

"There *are* some good modern writers," I said.

"I know, and I've tried them, but somehow I always return to Jane." Maxi shrugged, smiling apologetically. She stuffed her book into the seemingly bottomless knitting bag she uses for her everyday purse.

We hugged each other before I walked her to the door of the agency.

After Maxi's visit I sat at my desk, staring out the window, remembering, brooding. Then I forced myself back to the task of trying to figure out a way to get proof of the pilfering.

THE NEXT MORNING I ran a little late and hurried into the warehouse just as the bell rang, announcing the beginning of the shift.

"Hey, Elsie Timms!"

Belatedly I remembered that Elsie Timms was the alias I was using at Tri State. I stopped and turned. The foreman crooked a finger, signaling me to join him where he stood, clipboard in hand.

"I'm assigning you to work permanently with Wilma's team."

"Yes, Mr. Walters," I said.

"My, my. Ain't you the polite one. Call me Subby."

Not if I could help it. He had a dirty, leering grin that made my skin crawl.

"You get along with Wilma, don't you? She's the one in the wheelchair."

I nodded. How could I not remember Wilma? I hadn't expected a physically handicapped person to work in a warehouse. Rail-thin and fragile-looking, Wilma zoomed around in her mechanized chair as if she were in training for the Indy 500.

On cue, she sped toward us, braking on a dime in front of Subby. He jumped back.

"Jesus, Wilma, watch out. You're dangerous in that thing."

She merely grinned, looking like a pixie.

"If you have any questions or complaints about anything, I'm the man who'll take care of you." Subby hitched up his pants in that swaggering, typically male gesture before he turned and headed toward the back of the warehouse.

"Don't worry about him," Wilma said. "He's mostly hot air." She plucked an order form from the pile in her lap and handed it to me. "Pick up the items and group them on the conveyer. Most of them are arranged alphabetically."

I KEPT AN EAGLE EYE on the orders I filled, but nothing out of the ordinary happened during the next two days. Or I didn't see it. On the third, I paused to watch one of my orders being loaded onto the truck. I could have sworn that the invoice called for only one carton of coffee, not four. I retrieved and examined the carbon copy of the order.

"Something wrong?" Latoya asked.

She was part of Wilma's team. "Just double checking," I said.

"Don't," she warned in a low tone. "Not if you want to keep your job."

Wilma joined us.

"Even if I think something extra's been added to the order?"

She shrugged. "That's up to you. A guy got fired for mentioning that. Me, I got three kids to support."

"What was the guy's name who got fired?"

Latoya suddenly spotted something she had to do and hurried off.

"Hiram Greene," Wilma said and moved away before I could ask her anything else. While I worked on my next order, I kept wondering how to get the women to talk about what they obviously suspected.

When the lunch whistle blew, I went to my car to fetch the peanut butter sandwich I'd left there deliberately so that I could use my cell phone to report to Uncle Barney. I told him about Hiram Greene. He promised to run a check on the man and get his story. Anticipating that I might have to stay at the warehouse after everyone had left, I moved my rented car out of Tri State's lot and parked it down the block.

My arms and back hurt from all that lifting. I was glad of the chance to sit down in the lunch room, even though the mismatched chairs were hard and the room ugly and uncomfortable.

"The women sit together," Latoya said. "The men prefer to sit by themselves so they can lie and brag without being called on their exaggerations. Tell you the truth, I'd just as soon not have to listen to all that b.s." She rolled her expressive black eyes.

"Not all the women sit together," I said, nodding toward a redhead who had joined the men. "Is that her husband next to her?"

Latoya snorted.

"Cathy's husband doesn't work here anymore," Wilma said.

I saw that Wilma looked pale, almost stricken and sensed a sudden tension around the table.

"Good thing Tom Carnes quit. We'd have nothing but brawls because of her flirting," Latoya said.

A couple of the women snickered. I thought her statement had been an attempt to break the tense silence. What had happened at Tri State when Cathy's husband had worked here?

By the end of the shift, I didn't see any noticeable changes in the orders on the conveyor belts. Most of the pilfered items had to be added after hours. That made sense.

I clocked out, and pretending I'd left something in the lunch room, I walked back in that direction. On the way I angled toward the conveyor belt nearest the wall. There I ducked behind the boxes I had stacked earlier so that they formed a crude hiding place from where I could watch the conveyors.

The warehouse grew silent. The minutes crept by like somnolent snails. My stomach growled with hunger. I was hot, and my neck was going to have a painful crick in it from holding my head at the unnatural angle necessary to peek through a crack in the wall of boxes.

Hearing footsteps, I froze, hardly daring to breathe. In my haste to build the hideout, I hadn't calculated the angle of my vision. All I could see of the thief were his jean-clad legs and feet. Fortunately he wore somewhat unusual shoes: black lace-up work shoes with metal caps over the toes.

It took him forever to add the pilfered goods to the piles on the dock. Or so it seemed to me in my anxiety-ridden frame of mind. If he discovered me, I had no idea what explanation I could offer that had even a slight chance of being believable. My best bet would be to play an irrational, hysterical woman. I could do that.

When I heard the dock doors being closed and the lights went out, I forced myself to count to one hundred before I flicked on my pencil flashlight. By its meager beam I made my way to the ladies' room where I climbed out through the window.

DURING OUR COFFEE BREAK the next morning, I sat beside Wilma. In a low voice I asked her, "Do you know who wears metal-tipped, black work boots?"

She looked at me for a moment before she answered. "Subby has a pair."

That made sense. As the foreman of the warehouse, it would be hard for him not to be involved.

"Why do you want to know about Subby's special work boots? There's something going on around here, isn't there?"

"What makes you think that, Wilma?"

"I don't know."

"But you have some idea," I suggested.

She seemed to be debating with herself. Finally she said, "There have been times when I thought an order was lots bigger than it should have been. Is that what you think, too?"

I nodded.

"Who are you? A cop?"

"No."

"The FBI?"

"No."

"Can I help?"

Her voice was filled with youthful enthusiasm and sounded as though she thought this might be fun. I had to disabuse her of that notion. "No, Wilma. Forget that I asked you anything."

"Why? Because I'm a cripple in a wheelchair?"

"No, because I don't want you to lose your job just because I'm incurably nosy." I shrugged. "My grandma is always quoting the old saying to me about curiosity killing the cat." I excused myself and went to the ladies' room.

There I took a pair of opera glasses and a camera from my shoulder bag. Then I opened the window, stood back, and focused the opera glasses on the truck backed up to the dock. I wrote down every item that was loaded. I intended to compare my inventory to the official invoice. Remembering that Uncle Barney is a firm believer in the saying that a picture is worth a thousand words, I took several photos of the loading process and the license plate of the truck.

Now all I had to do was find out the destination of the trucks. Since lunch wasn't over yet, the warehouse was deserted. I'd seen where Subby had placed his clipboard with the invoices. Quickly I located the right invoice and photographed it. The truck with the added items went to the Neapolitan Restaurant and then to St. Anne's Retirement Home.

I was on the board of Eldercare, a watchdog agency for the elderly. If the home was in on this scheme, we hadn't been very good watchdogs.

I headed toward my place on the assembly line just as the whistle blew, announcing the end of lunch.

AFTER WORK I STOPPED at the hardware store and picked up some nails, paint stripper, and sandpaper. By the time I stepped on my front porch, it was getting dark. When I caught a movement in my peripheral vision, I let out a startled yelp. Then I recognized my husband's lean runner's body.

"Luke! You scared me half to death."

"You should be scared. This is not the safest neighborhood. Why didn't you at least leave the porch light on?" he demanded.

Because it didn't work. Many things in my old Victorian house didn't work. I didn't tell him that. He hadn't been inside the house yet, so I knew he would find lots to criticize. I didn't need to give him additional ammunition. Unlocking the front door, I motioned for him to enter. I flipped the light switch.

"That's some chandelier," he said. "And it's in perfect condition. Was it like that?"

"No. Fortunately, the one in the upstairs hall had the same crystal teardrops so I combined the two to make one chandelier."

Luke glanced around curiously.

I had stripped half the paint off from the banister, so it looked truly hideous. The floor of the foyer was lined with newspapers to protect the wood underneath. I followed his glance as he assessed the living room where the wallpaper had been removed down to the dingy walls.

"There's lots of work to be done yet," I said defensively.

"Did you come to help?" He turned and gave me one of his penetrating stares. "I guess you didn't, so what can I do for you?"

"How long is this farce going to go on?"

"If you're talking about my life, I don't consider it a farce."

"Not your life, Cybil. This house. It'll take years to whip it into shape. That or tons of money which I know you don't have. If you needed a place of your own, why not rent an apartment? Or get a nice, new condominium?"

I set my bag down. "Something about this house called out to me. It needed rescuing." Like me, but I didn't say that. "I can't explain it."

"Maxi said you were on a new assignment. In a warehouse?"

"Yes."

Luke ran his hand through his dark hair, a gesture of frustration I knew well. I could see him struggle for composure before he spoke.

"Jesus, Cybil, I don't understand you. You're a first-class social worker and school guidance counselor. You're on the boards of several important committees that help kids and old people. If you want to work, why not in your own field?"

"I'm not up to that emotionally."

"But you are up to working in a warehouse."

Luke was more upset about this than I had first assumed. "What's really bothering you? Are you embarrassed? Is it a disgrace for a doctor's wife to work in a warehouse? Don't worry. I used an alias." His eyes narrowed dangerously.

"You know me better than that. I wish to God you'd never started with this investigation stuff."

"Now we're getting at the truth. You were all for it in the beginning. What's changed?"

"When your uncle offered you a job, I thought it was a good idea. It got you out of the house. For the first time since Ryan's death, you showed an interest in something. But I didn't anticipate you'd actually go out and personally investigate criminal activities. I thought your uncle would keep you busy with some office work—"

"Ah, you thought I'd be playing at the job. Now it's my turn to say 'you should know me better than that'. I don't do things halfway."

"How long are you planning to work as an investigator?"

"I hadn't thought about it, but now that you mention it, I have no intention of quitting. I like the work and oddly enough, I'm quite good at it." We looked at each other, neither of us prepared to back down. "What bothers you about my job?"

"It's potentially dangerous. Don't tell me that it isn't because I know better. I work in the ER and I see the victims of violence daily. Don't tell me that men are going to let you snoop into their business without getting furious or maybe even physical. I don't want you hurt. Is that so difficult to understand?"

"No," I admitted, feeling guilty and defensive. Still, I couldn't back down. We stood facing each other, much farther apart than the few feet between us.

"If the tables were turned, wouldn't you worry about me?"

He had me there and he knew it. "Damn it, Luke. I

hate it when you're so infuriatingly logical and right."
I moved my head. Pain shot through my neck. I must
have grimaced because Luke noticed.

"What's wrong?" Luke touched my neck, my shoulders. "You're as stiff as a side of frozen beef. Come, lie
down."

I let him lead me to the couch in the living room and
lay down on it, face down. Luke massaged my neck
and my shoulders. I could feel the stiffness ease. We
hadn't resolved our disagreement about my work or the
house, but I was beginning to feel too relaxed to pursue
the subject. I don't know precisely when Luke's touch
changed, but it did.

"Turn over," he murmured after a while, his mouth
tender against my nape.

The telephone rang before I could comply with his
seductive request.

Luke muttered something and got up to answer it. A
moment later he said, "It's for you. Barney."

My uncle didn't waste words on small talk.

"The woman you mentioned? Wilma Johnson? I just
heard a police report. She's dead."

TWO

I SAT DOWN HEAVILY in the nearest chair. My mind was numb as I listened to my uncle relate the scanty bits of news he had. According to Sam Keller, my cousin on the Westport police force, Wilma's wheelchair plunged down a flight of stairs in her apartment building. The medical examiner pronounced her dead at the scene. My cousin thought it was an accident.

"That's hard to believe," I said more to myself than to Uncle Barney.

"Why?"

"Because Wilma maneuvered that wheelchair the way the Unsers drive race cars."

"Accidents do happen."

The more I thought about it the less I believed it was an accident. "The way she guided those wheels through the narrow aisles in the warehouse and up and down the loading ramps…no, it doesn't make sense for her to careen down an ordinary flight of stairs."

"If it wasn't an accident, can you think of any reason why someone would push her?"

Briefly I told Uncle Barney about my conversation with Wilma. Feeling guilt nibble at my conscience, I said, justifying myself, "I didn't ask her to help me. I pretended to be casually nosy."

"Do you think she bought your explanation?"

My mouth was dry. I had trouble speaking. "I thought so, but she wasn't dumb. She probably suspected that something was wrong in that warehouse. I'd feel better if I knew where Subby Walters was at the time of her death."

"So would I." He was quiet for a moment. "We're going to have to tell the police about our investigation. I'll call Ariosto about it."

"He isn't going to like that."

"We have no choice but to involve the cops if someone helped Wilma down those steps."

I agreed with him.

"Uncle Barney, did you ever get a hold of Hiram Greene? The guy who was fired from Tri State for asking questions?"

"I met him at the bar of his choice. At first he didn't want to talk, but after a couple of Coronas, he opened up. Like you, he noticed that some orders got considerably larger by the time they reached the truck."

"Did he mention any specific places?"

"Joe's Steak Emporium. Miami Bar and Grill. The Coterie. The Neapolitan, and Mom's."

"Isn't Mom's a diner?"

"It is. Open twenty-four hours a day. Mom's probably didn't get any lobster or veal, but can you imagine how many burgers and hot dogs they serve?"

"Did he mention to whom he told his suspicions?" I asked.

"Subby Walters, the foreman, and Lyle Novak, the supervisor of the warehouses."

"What did they say?"

"They told him he better find another job, and if he

mentioned this to anyone else, he wouldn't get a recom-mendation. He'd never work in Westport again," Barney said.

"And he believed them."

"He did."

"I think someone higher up in the company hierarchy has to be involved as well. Someone in accounting."

"I agree," Barney said. "You be careful. When this much money is involved, people get ruthless. I've seen it happen time and time again. And keep me posted."

"I will, Uncle Barney." I hung up, unable to believe that Wilma was dead. Had she checked some of the invoices and been caught snooping?

"Are you going to be all right, staying here by your-self?" Luke asked.

For a second I was tempted to ask him to stay, to hold me, but that would be a mistake. We hadn't resolved any of our differences.

"I'll be okay," I said, trying to sound convincing.

Luke touched my face briefly and walked out the door. I'm not sure he believed me, but obviously he thought it was best that he left.

For the next hour I exercised on my floor mat. The slow hatha yoga postures require intense concentration. Ordinarily I can dismiss everything from my mind, fo-cusing on the stretches, on the particular muscles in-volved, on proper breathing, but not tonight. Wilma's young face with the old, old eyes kept intruding, kept making me wonder if my investigation had caused her to become curious and say something to the wrong person.

Guilt doesn't promote sleep, so after a while I

showered. Wrapped in the quilt Luke's grandmother
had pieced for me, I curled up on the living room sofa
to read. Toward morning I must have fallen asleep for
several hours because at six I woke up, feeling groggy
and stiff.

WHEN I ARRIVED AT THE warehouse people stood in
groups, somber-faced, discussing Wilma's death. Suddenly the p.a. system crackled and a man's voice, one
of the top executives, I suspected, informed us of her
loss, adding the name of the funeral home and the date
of the viewing.

Subdued, Latoya and I set to work. Even though
I hadn't known Wilma well, I missed her. The place
wasn't the same without her zipping around in her mo-
torized chair.

During our morning break, Subby Walters joined us.
"You ladies are on your own today. Farrell promised
to hire someone to replace Wilma as soon as possible.
Until then, do the best you can."

He didn't look shocked by the tragedy or especially
affected, I thought, but that wasn't necessarily a sign of
guilt. He could be one of those men who pride themselves on never showing their deeper emotions.

"I like the way he offered to help us, don't you?"
Latoya frowned at Subby's broad, retreating back.

Pouring coffee into the cup of my thermos bottle, I
debated briefly with myself before I decided to question
Latoya. "How did Wilma end up in a wheelchair?"

Latoya blew on her coffee to cool it. "Car accident
last December. During the first major snowstorm we
had. Remember it?"

I nodded. The first storm of the season usually causes lots of fender benders because people have forgotten how to drive on snow and ice.

"It was a miracle that either one of them survived," she added.

"Did Wilma drive?"

"Yeah. Tri State has a women's bowling team. Wilma and Mae Carnes, Cathy's mother-in-law, always rode together. We bowled that night. When we started it was just drizzling a little, but three hours later five inches of snow had fallen on top of the icy streets. It was real bad. Wilma's car hit a patch of ice and went over the embankment on the bypass. Mae was badly hurt, too. She never came back to work. I guess she qualified for early retirement or disability or something. And then a couple of weeks ago she passed away."

A bowling alley. I have been in one maybe three times in my life but I remember that most of them serve beer. Had Wilma been drinking? As if she read my mind, Latoya continued.

"We won that night, so we had a few beers to celebrate, but nobody was drunk."

"Did Wilma just move into the building where she fell down the stairs?"

"No. She's lived there since June when she returned to work. What are you getting at?"

"I thought if it were a new place it might explain why someone who handled a wheelchair as expertly as she did would plunge down the steps."

Latoya looked at me, her face as expressionless as an Ashanti mask. She drank some coffee before she spoke.

"I wondered about that, too. She could pilot that thing in her sleep."

"Any ideas? Explanations?"

She shook her head, setting her dreadlocks in motion. "Wilma didn't drink anymore, and she didn't do drugs."

"Did you know her well?"

"Yeah. Sometimes she'd come to my place for a meal or to play cards. Once in a while she'd watch my kids so I could go out. And as I said, we bowled together."

"Did she live alone?"

Latoya nodded. "Her momma remarried. Wilma didn't want to be in the way. That's what she said, but I suspect she didn't much like her new stepdaddy, so when she was ready to come back to work, she moved into an apartment. She was proud of her place. Fixed it up nice."

Could Wilma's dislike of her stepfather have escalated into domestic violence? Since they didn't live together, I doubted it. "Did she have a boyfriend?"

"Not since the accident."

"Did she have trouble with anyone here at the warehouse?"

"Not that I know of."

We were eliminating possible suspects right and left. All except Walters and his fellow thieves. "Did she say anything to you about the pilfering here?"

Latoya finished her coffee in one long pull and screwed the top back onto her thermos in a decisive motion. "No, she didn't, and I ain't saying nothing either." With that she went back to work.

I MET UNCLE BARNEY at the Ariosto estate. Our meeting with Ariosto was shorter than the time it took to drive to his house. The butler, Brazier, led us into the study. Ariosto agreed somewhat sourly that we should tell the police about our investigation if it became absolutely necessary.

Having settled that, Ariosto demanded, "What have you found out so far?"

"After comparing the official invoice with what actually went on the truck, I think our original estimate of losses might be too conservative. Even though this is only one delivery, I don't see what would keep the thieves from being less generous with the other orders," I told him.

"Where did this shipment go to?"

"The Neapolitan restaurant."

"God dammit," Ariosto yelled. "That son of a gun, Guiseppe. I bailed him out three years ago when his restaurant was going under. Now he's ripping me off. That's gratitude for you."

"He might not know anything about it. His chef could be buying the stolen goods and pocketing the profit," I said, trying to placate Ariosto's fury. One look at his thin-lipped mouth and his glittering eyes and I shut up. He was obviously fighting to control his anger.

"I want his ass on a platter, and I want it fast. Are you documenting this?" he demanded.

"Yes," I said, surreptitiously crossing my fingers. Those photographs had better turn out okay.

Ariosto dismissed us, anger clearly boiling in him.

"I hope he doesn't do anything foolish to Guiseppe," I said to Barney.

"If he does, there's nothing we can do about it."

We stopped at my car.

"Where did you get this?" Barney asked, looking at the beige Ford Escort.

"I rented it. I couldn't very well apply for a job in a warehouse driving my Volvo." Barney nodded his approval. I trusted he would put in a good word for me when I presented the rental charge to Lynn.

"When will you be ready for a surveillance team?" he asked.

"Soon. I haven't yet identified all the truck drivers who are part of the operation."

"Are you going home now?"

"No. I want to take a look at Wilma's building. I need to check out those stairs."

"Good idea. I'll follow you."

Wilma's apartment, located on the third floor of a remodeled factory, featured ramps and an elevator with a bench. Inside, the halls were extra wide to accommodate wheelchairs. Wilma's corner apartment was located a good distance from the elevator and the stairs.

While we were studying the layout, my cousin, Lieutenant Sam Keller, came out of Wilma's apartment. Like most of the Keller men, Sam is tall, fair-haired, blue-eyed. Unfortunately, he has also inherited the family tendency toward baldness. At thirty-five his hairline has receded noticeably.

"What are you two doing here?" Sam asked. He opened a flip-top box, pulled out a cigarette and lit it with a disposable lighter.

"We wanted to take a look at the stairs," Barney explained. "Are you officially calling it an accident?"

"There's nothing to indicate that it was anything else. The brakes on the wheelchair were off, and no one saw or heard anything out of the ordinary."

"Why would Wilma have gone near the stairs at all?" I asked Sam. "Even if she'd been waiting at the elevator, she would have been too far from the stairs to have tumbled down accidentally."

"She could have been on her way to visit someone down that end of the hall. Everybody said she was friendly and sociable. Maybe she waited for someone at the top of the stairs," Sam answered.

"That still doesn't explain how she fell down," I insisted.

"Maybe she miscalculated. Maybe she pushed the wrong button on the chair. Maybe she got dizzy. Hell, Cybil, there could be a dozen reasons."

I shook my head emphatically.

"Lord, you're still as stubborn as you always were," he said.

"I'm not stubborn per se, but when I'm convinced I'm right about something, I don't back down easily," I corrected him.

"I remember when we were kids," Sam said with a rueful expression, "how you used to dig in your heels like a little mule to get your way, but it's not going to work this time. There's not a single solid shred of evidence that it was anything but an accident."

Ignoring my cousin's incorrect and unfair interpretation of my character, I asked, "Uncle Barney, do you want to tell Sam or should I?"

Barney filled him in on the pilfering at Tri State.

"Is Ariosto going to call us in on that?" Sam asked.

"Not yet."

"Then there's nothing I can do."

Sam lifted his hand to forestall my objections.

"Give me proof of foul play or probable cause or anything at all, and I'll actively pursue the case. Nice to have seen you again, Cybil. Let's have lunch sometime. Uncle Barney."

With a casual wave of his hand Sam left us. Silently we watched him take the stairs down, two at a time.

"Sam's right, you know. We have nothing but your suspicions," Barney said.

"Not yet, we don't." I punched the down button with more force than necessary. Moments later the elevator doors opened. Downstairs we met an old woman struggling with two grocery bags.

"Let us help you, ma'am," Barney offered.

He took one bag, and I the other.

"Well, bless you," she said, breathing hard. "I live on the second floor, right by the stairs."

Uncle Barney and I exchanged a look. As casually as I could, I asked, "Isn't that where Wilma Johnson had her accident?"

"Yes. Terrible thing, what happened to that nice young woman." She made a disapproving clucking noise. "I found her, you know," she confided, somewhat self-importantly.

"How awful for you," I murmured.

"I thought my heart was going to give out right then and there. I have a bad ticker, you know," she said, pressing her right hand against her thin chest. The gesture reminded me of Maxi who suffers from angina, and I felt again the stab of worry surge through me.

The elevator stopped on the second floor. We followed her down the hall. "Tell us what happened," I suggested. She didn't need much encouragement. I suspected it wasn't macabre eagerness that prompted her to talk, but loneliness. I made a promise to myself that I would come back to visit her.

"I was sitting by the kitchen window, peeling apples for a pie I was planning to bake for the church supper when I heard an awful racket in the hall. This is usually such a quiet place what with most of us being old, so naturally I went to see what happened."

She paused at her apartment door, rummaging through her black plastic handbag for the key. The cardboard name plate above the doorbell identified her as Ferne Lauder in spidery handwriting. Preceding us into the apartment, she continued.

"The first thing I saw was the wheelchair. It was upside down with the wheels still spinning. I knew right then that something dreadful must have happened. I looked to my left and saw Wilma at the bottom of the stairs, crumpled up like a rag doll. I called her name, but she didn't answer, so I rushed to the telephone and called the manager. She phoned the ambulance and the police right away, but it was too late."

"Did you see anyone in the hall? Or at the top of the stairs?" I asked.

"No. Not right away. Later other tenants came out to see what was happening."

We carried the groceries into the surprisingly roomy kitchen. The table stood in front of a large window overlooking the street where several cars were parked. That gave me an idea. "Mrs. Lauder, did you look out the window while you peeled the apples?"

"Sure. Peeling doesn't take much concentration."

"Did you notice cars parked on the street that aren't usually seen in this neighborhood?"

She wrinkled her forehead in thought. "Like what kind?" she asked after several seconds.

"Oh, I don't know. Something sporty or expensive."

She shook her head. "My grandson drives a sporty-looking car. A Trans Am. I didn't see anything like that out there."

"How about a black, four-door Cadillac?"

She shook her head. "We don't see big, expensive cars like that in this neighborhood." She thought for a moment. "You know, there was a red jeep parked catty-corner across the street that I don't remember seeing there before."

"Well, we'd better go and let you put your groceries away," I said.

"If you think of anything, Mrs. Lauder, please give us a call. Here's my card," Barney said.

"Are you with the police?" Ferne asked.

"No. I'm a private investigator." Barney showed her his I.D.

I envied him that I.D. Not that it was so difficult to get one. I knew it wasn't because I had inquired. What kept me from actively pursuing my own license was that I knew Luke would go through the roof if I became a full-fledged P.I. Still, sometime in the future....

"My, my, just like on television," Ferne said, impressed, looking at the card. "Well, thanks for helping me with the groceries. Can I offer you a beer or something?"

That took me back a bit. I hadn't expected the fragile-looking, white-haired woman wearing a lace collar with a string of pearls to keep beer in her refrigerator. She looked like the perfect ad for a fancy tea commercial. Darjeeling or maybe my favorite, Earl Grey.

"No, thank you," Barney said.

"Maybe some other time. Drop in if you're in the neighborhood," Ferne said, walking us to her door. She smiled at us until the elevator doors closed.

"The cars you asked about belong to Walters and Novak?" Barney asked.

"Yes. Of course, the car could have been parked farther down the street or even in the next block."

"True. And the murderer, if there is one, had a chance to get away unseen. Did you catch that?"

I nodded. "When Ferne went back into her apartment to phone the manager." Uncle Barney looked at me approvingly. That cheered me for about five seconds. Then I remembered our discouraging situation. "Do you realize the murderer may go free? What with the police insisting it's an accident and us not having any evidence to the contrary."

"No, we don't have any evidence yet. But we do know people who have a motive. If this is really murder. It could be a freak accident. Don't dismiss that possibility completely," he cautioned.

On that note, we parted—Barney to go to the office and I to go home and get ready for a dinner benefiting Eldercare. Putting off dressing as long as I could, I looked through the mail, walked through each room downstairs to water the plants facing the east windows, and read the newspaper.

Finally, I could procrastinate no longer. If I had a choice, I would rather come down with a good case of poison ivy than attend one of these functions. Since I didn't sprout an itchy rash, I took a bath, applied makeup a little more heavily than I ordinarily do, and slipped into my electric blue silk dress.

I added the string of fine pearls Luke had given me for our third wedding anniversary. He thinks of me as the pearl type, but I don't. My mother, on the other hand, is. Pearls complement the shimmer of her golden blond hair and the sparkle of her clear, sky-blue eyes. But then, being a truly beautiful woman, everything looks good on her.

Looking at myself in the mirror, I noticed again that I bear no resemblance to Elizabeth Keller Kruger Diver Merriweather, my much-married mother. When I was little, I used to think that I was a changeling until I saw myself in profile. At thirteen a straight nose offers small comfort.

Maxi tried to console me by saying that I had intelligence and character, qualities more valuable in the long run than golden hair. That was even less comforting. I couldn't think of a single boy in junior high who even noticed those qualities, much less found them attractive. Come to think of it, I haven't met too many mature men who prefer them to a sexy body and a flawless face.

ON THURSDAYS restaurants receive their weekend deliveries. Not surprisingly, the orders for each of the eateries mentioned by Hiram were padded with unbilled items.

I documented these with my camera. I even got a shot of Subby carrying a carton of olive oil, but I suspect a court won't consider this admissible evidence. What it will do, I hope, is soften him up for a confession when he is confronted with the photo.

So far I had identified eight truck drivers as part of the local operation. What I didn't have yet was the name of the top executive participating in the thefts and the individuals buying the pilfered goods.

After work I went home long enough to boil a handful of penne, heat the frozen marinara sauce, fix a salad, and eat my dinner while watching the evening news.

Then for the second time that day I drove to the Tri State Warehouses. Dressed in black slacks and a black pullover, my longish hair hidden under a black knit cap, I matched the darkness. I felt like a second-story jewel thief. On cue, my uncle's Oldsmobile and Glenn Brown's Toyota pulled up beside me.

Uncle Barney divided the tasks among us. While he unlocked the trucks with a skeleton key, I placed a bug under the dash, reciting "Mary had a little lamb" to test Glenn's receiver. The whole procedure went off like a perfectly executed top-level military operation. We were out of the parking lot in fourteen minutes.

Tomorrow an investigator with a receiver in his car would pick up a designated truck, tail it and photograph the receiver of the pilfered goods. Uncle Barney had arranged for round-the-clock surveillance of Subby and Novak. We would each take a shift.

THE SURVEILLANCE TEAM had nothing to report on Friday morning. Neither man had left his house during the night. Neither had received a visitor. After a hurried conference, Uncle Barney suggested I attend the T.G.I.F. with my Tri State coworkers.

Alfonso's Bar, where the thank-God-it's-Friday crowd met after work, catered to Tri State personnel as well as to the employees of several small factories near the warehouses. The saloon didn't pretend to be anything but a strictly functional drinking place, featuring a long bar, several booths and tables facing it. The bartender, a man with pronounced jowls and sad eyes which lent him the mournful look of a bassethound, had probably heard of a Brandy Alexander and a Singapore Sling, but hadn't been asked to fix either since bartender school. His clients drank beer and shots with an occasional gin and tonic thrown in.

Not to tax his ability and also to keep a clear head, I ordered a gin and tonic minus the gin for me and one with gin for Cathy Carnes. Since I had invited her, I paid for both. I figured I could hold her attention until one of the men had gained enough courage from a bottle to approach her. I offered her my condolences on the death of her mother-in-law.

Cathy thanked me offhandedly, at the same time lifting her shoulders in a shrug. "Her spine got hurt in that accident with Wilma. We had to put her in a nursing home where she drove everybody nuts."

"Maybe she was in pain."

Cathy flashed me a contemptuous look out of bottle-green eyes. "That's what she claimed. But how come the pain disappeared as soon as Tom got there and waited hand and foot on her?"

I had obviously struck a raw nerve. Without waiting

for me to respond, had I even known what to say, she continued, her voice vehement.

"Her complaints stopped the minute Tom got there each day right after work and didn't start again until he got ready to leave her at ten o'clock. He even gave up a good paying job at Tri State to be a short-order cook so that he could have more time to take care of the old biddy."

She paused to light a cigarette. "Do you know what it's like to have your husband spend every free minute with his mother? Do you?" she demanded.

I shook my head.

"Well my husband did that for the past nine months. Nine friggin' long months. It's so unfair. She was a selfish, demanding old witch." Dropping her cigarette to the floor, she crushed it viciously with her shoe. "You think I'm unfeeling and mean, don't you?"

"No." Part of me understood her bitterness. Tom's exclusive, almost compulsive devotion to his mother puzzled me. It was unusual, to say the least, for a grown man to fixate on his mother to that extent.

A truck driver, who seemed hardly old enough to drive much less entertain hopes of winning an experienced woman like Cathy, approached. His clean-cut features and his black cowboy hat made him look a bit like a very young George Strait. The redhead turned her killer smile in his direction which rendered him almost speechless. He stuttered out his offer to buy her another drink. Accepting his offer, Cathy led the bemused man to one of the booths.

Several men bellied up to the bar, including Subby.

"Hey, Elsie," he said, "congratulate me."

"Sure. On what?"

"Our bowling victory. Man, we smoked those guys from Whitman Electric."

"Congratulations." I lifted my glass in a toast. "So, when did this victory take place?"

"On Tuesday evening."

"This past Tuesday?"

"Yup. We bowl every Tuesday, come rain or come shine."

If that was true, it gave him an alibi. "Are all of you on the bowling team?" I asked the men around Subby, trying to verify his whereabouts.

"Yeah. And so's Tully Smith and Lyle Novak. But none of us was as hot as Subby. He bowled a three-hundred game."

"When you're hot, you're hot," Subby crowed.

Tuning out their rehashing of each frame they'd bowled, I considered this new information. Since both my prime suspects had alibis for Tuesday night, a freak accident causing Wilma's death was looking more likely. My gut instincts refused to believe that, but my logical mind couldn't argue with iron-clad alibis.

Several gray-suited men entered the bar. The executives of Tri State joined the workers at the bar. As soon as their notion of propriety allowed, the drivers and loaders withdrew to the tables, leaving Subby and me with the suits. Lyle Novak joined us. If anything was going to change hands, I believed, it would do so in the next hour. I turned slightly away, my body signaling disinterest, but I was short enough that I could catch their partial reflections in the part of the mirror behind the bar not obscured by bottles.

Cathy's young driver dug quarters out of the front pockets of his tight jeans and fed them into the jukebox. The twangy, despairing wails of a female country singer added to the steadily increasing noise level so that I only heard snatches of Subby and Novak's conversation.

"Tonight?" Novak asked.

"Yeah. That damn…"

I couldn't understand the mumbled name.

"…wants it tonight," Subby added.

"…have no choice…."

"…meet at the warehouse at nine."

Expectancy tightened my scalp. I hardly dared to breathe for fear that I might miss something. What was going down at nine? Whatever it was, I planned to be there to see it.

Another wave of happy-hour patrons entered, crowding the bar. Now I was not only unable to overhear Subby and Novak, it was getting increasingly difficult to keep a watch on them. Just as I was getting seriously alarmed, I spotted Uncle Barney. Wearing a conservative business suit, he blended into the crowd of unwinding executives. We both watched for twenty minutes before we saw Novak move toward the far end of the bar to get the bartender's attention. He called loudly for another drink. As he did so, he leaned against the bar, close to a man I had once glimpsed in the main offices of Tri State. Novak's left hand skillfully took a white envelope from his inside jacket pocket and passed it to the man who slipped it into his suit coat. The transfer took perhaps three seconds, suggesting practice. Very smooth.

I looked at Uncle Barney. He inclined his head slightly, signaling that he had also seen the transaction.

Noticing Cathy head for the ladies' room, I followed her. While she repaired her makeup and I brushed my hair, I popped the question.

"Cathy, do you know the guy's name at the bar who works at the main office? He's in his late forties, trim, wearing a gray plaid suit and gold-rimmed glasses?"

"That's Crawford. Galen Crawford. Head accountant. Did he hit on you?"

"No."

"You aren't...um...interested in him, are you? He's married, but that doesn't keep him from flirting and hitting on women whenever he can," she warned.

I saw her giving me an assessing look in the mirror.

"He...um...usually likes 'em younger."

At thirty, I wasn't exactly over the hill, but I didn't say so. "Does he have children?" I asked.

"Yeah. Two boys in college." She turned to look at me directly. "He's not a bad guy, if you're interested. He's rumored to be generous to his women, though a little rough. A friend of mine in real estate just sold him a cottage up at Emerald Lake. Galen's got money."

"I just wondered who he was," I said and shrugged. While Cathy finished applying russet-colored lipstick two shades lighter than her hair, I locked myself into a stall to write a note to Uncle Barney. He needed to know Crawford's name to start the investigation on him. Passing by him on the way back to the bar, I slipped the folded piece of paper into his hand. I thought I was almost as smooth in doing this as the men had been.

I left the bar, a signal for Uncle Barney to follow me. I sat in my car, listening to a symphony on the university's radio station. I think it was one of Mahler's symphonies. Uncle Barney joined me a few minutes later.

Bending his tall frame to look through the car window, he said, "I'll start with Crawford's bank account."

I told him about the conversation I'd overheard. After a short discussion, I reluctantly agreed that Glenn, my favorite coworker at the agency, could join me at nine—even though this sounded a bit like having a baby-sitter.

My first night of surveillance. I could hardly wait for night to fall.

THREE

I ORDERED A CARRY-OUT pizza at the Neapolitan. It wasn't just curiosity that took me to the restaurant. Guiseppe made great pizzas. My favorite is the double cheese with fresh basil.

After I ate, I met Glenn in the Kroger parking lot where we left our cars. We jogged past several dark factories, skirted the edge of the airport, and arrived at Tri State five minutes later. Crouching in the shadow of the truck parked nearest the office building, we caught our breaths.

"Damn. I'm going to have to work out more," Glenn panted.

"And quit smoking," I said. Being married to a physician for seven years makes you health conscious.

We sat and waited. Instinctively we shrunk back when the bright headlights heralded the arrival of a car. It stopped. The driver extinguished the lights. Apparently he was waiting for someone. Glenn and I decided that the car was probably a top-of-the-line Buick. It was too dark for us to see the logo. Two other cars arrived, one right after the other.

"Subby and Novak," I whispered, recognizing their vehicles.

The three men converged, then walked toward the main warehouse which Novak unlocked. They came back out a few minutes later, each carrying a large carton.

"Are they taking food home?" Glenn asked.

"That would be stupid. How could they explain having commercial-sized goods if they got caught? You can't buy those at your local grocery."

They loaded the cartons into the Buick.

"We've got to find out who the third man is," I said to Glenn. "I'll follow him and you follow Subby. If we run to our cars now, we should be able to see which way they turn when they pull out of the industrial complex."

Glenn nodded. We ran in a crouch until we reached the edge of Tri State's parking lot. Then we sprinted. Guard dogs barked furiously in one of the factories we passed. I hoped their racket wouldn't summon a squad car.

We made it. Glenn blinked his headlights to show that he had seen Subby's Trans Am turn and was following it. I flashed back that I was on the tail of the Buick which drove north. Keeping a hundred yards back, I doggedly pursued it. The driver kept going north. Consulting my fuel gauge, I hoped he wasn't headed for Michigan. After two miles he turned east on Grover, then south.

The street he took led to only one place: Westport University. I didn't want to believe that someone at the school was buying stolen goods. When he passed the two main dining halls and the student union without stopping, I was both relieved and puzzled. My confusion increased when I tailed him down the main street leading to the residence halls. If I stayed this far back, I would lose him for sure in the maze of buildings once the security guard passed him through the check point.

Making a quick decision, I grabbed my raincoat from the back seat. I flung it over my shoulders, placing its hood over my hair. It wasn't much of a disguise, but the man obviously wasn't expecting to be followed. I pulled up behind him as the security guard raised the guard bar for the Buick. It was too dark to be sure, but I thought the driver was Galen Crawford.

"Hi. I'm visiting Teresa Lister in Beaumont Hall," I told the guard, handing him my driver's license. As far as I knew my friend Teresa was still director of the hall. He placed a visitor's sticker under my windshield wiper and waved me on.

As soon as I was out of the guard's sight, I sped up, praying that a jogger would not decide to dart into the dark road. On the winding road around the lake, I periodically caught a glimpse of the Buick's glowing tail lights. When I reached the straight stretch of the road, I knew I had lost him.

He must have taken one of the side streets. I turned around and drove into the first one. It dead-ended in a cul-de-sac lined by three residence halls: Alpha, Sancerre and Phillips. Two were men's dormitories, the other a women's. What if the man was involved with a coed, wooing her with jumbo-sized cans of green beans and corn? Unromantic, but possible. If it was Crawford, perhaps his sons lived in one of the male residence halls, and he was taking them food. Why would he? There were no cooking facilities there. Even as I dismissed these ideas as ludicrous, I couldn't come up with a better explanation for his presence on campus.

Slowly I drove along the half-circle. Although I didn't expect to find the Buick parked out front, I wanted to rule out that possibility before I searched the large parking lot in back. Once again his brazenness amazed me. The gunmetal gray car sat in a no parking zone, the trunk open, the motor running. Naturally there was no legitimate parking space in the entire cul-de-sac. I pulled up to a fire hydrant, hoping a campus cop wouldn't choose to patrol the area at that moment.

I rolled down my window. The air was filled with the smell of wet, fallen leaves, of burning charcoal, of youthful laughter, and the sounds of a Rolling Stones song. I hummed along with "(I Can't Get No) Satisfaction." Two young men passed, each carrying a case of Old Style beer. They headed toward the back of Alpha Hall. Moments later three coeds followed, their arms filled with bags of munchies. It didn't take Sherlock Holmes to figure out that a cookout was in progress. I looked at my watch every few minutes. After the third check, the man I awaited came bounding out of Alpha Hall, pulled off heavy, quilted mitts, and slammed the trunk lid shut. The reason he had worn the mitts was to protect his hands from the frozen goods he'd been handling. Probably the steaks which would soon sizzle on the barbecue grills.

When he turned, I saw his face clearly in the light from the nearby street lamp. I had been right. The man who had just delivered the stolen steaks was Galen Crawford.

Subduing my joy at being right, I pondered what to do next. There was no reason to follow Crawford further. Nor could I enter the hall and demand to know

who had received three cartons of hot groceries from
the head accountant at Tri State. Well, I could, but I had
no leverage to force anyone to answer me.

ON SATURDAY MORNING everyone involved in the Tri
State case met at the agency. Lynn made a large urn of
coffee, set out two dozen assorted doughnuts, a bag of
bagels and a tub of cream cheese. Watching her swish-
ing around in her size four slacks, I ignored the pastries,
virtuously reaching for a plain bagel. I even passed by
the cream cheese without a second glance.

Uncle Barney tacked photos of the receivers of stolen
goods on the cork board. Most of the shots were surprisingly good, thanks to the photography course he insists
every investigator take. The men stopped milling around
the food and sat down. The briefing began.

"We've identified all these men except one: the buyer
for the Neapolitan." Barney pointed to the snapshot of a
short man with a pencil mustache wearing black slacks
and a white shirt, taking a carton of coffee from the Tri
State driver. "From the description we have, this could
be Guiseppe."

"It isn't," I spoke up. "I've seen Guiseppe at the restaurant. He's older and his mustache is much thicker.
Makes him look sort of like a walrus. But this man looks
a lot like him. Maybe they're related."

"Okay. We'll attack it from that angle. Jerry, you
follow up on the identity of Guiseppe's look-alike,"
Barney instructed.

One by one the men from the surveillance team reported. Their statements were similar. The recipients of
the padded orders signed the official docket and paid

for the stolen goods in cash. Half of the drivers handed the cash to Subby, the other half to Novak. Each driver was paid his cut on the spot.

"That way there's no bookkeeping, no record of the illegal transaction. Whoever set this up did a damn good job. And so did you, men. And Cybil. If you've finished your written reports and your expense vouchers, you're free to leave. Thanks."

Lynn spoke up before the men could get out of their seats. "Some of you haven't turned in your listening devices. I must have those before you leave," she said, positioning herself in the doorway as if to block it with her petite body.

Electronic bugs are expensive. One of Lynn's commands is that if you use a bug, you retrieve it no matter how difficult or risky doing so might be. Or you pay for it.

"Cybil, I want to see you in my office," Barney said.

I followed him.

"Glenn reported that his subject stopped off at a bar for a couple of beers and then drove home. How about your man?"

I told him about Crawford's trip to the university. "I thought perhaps he was taking the food to his sons, but they're not listed in last year's directory. Of course, they could have enrolled this fall. The new student list isn't out yet and my contact on campus is out of town for the weekend."

Barney tapped his pipe against his chin thoughtfully. "We've got Crawford as the head honcho in the scheme. Even a quick look at his financial situation indicates that he's spending considerably more money than he earns legitimately. We don't have to solve this little puzzle. He may break down under police questioning and explain it. Still, it's a loose end."

I knew exactly how Barney felt. I hate loose ends, too. "Give me the rest of the weekend to see if I can't resolve this."

"You got it. I plan for us to meet with Ariosto on Monday or Tuesday at the latest to present him with our report."

Back in my office I looked up Crawford's home number. If he answered I'd hang up and try again later. His wife picked up the phone.

"Mrs. Crawford? I'm calling from UMAC Insurance," I ad libbed. "We're offering a special college tuition savings plan for your children. You do have children, don't you?"

"Yes. Two. But they're both in college already."

"Really? May I ask what university they chose?" I wasn't sure she would answer that, but she did.

"My oldest is at Purdue and his brother is at I.U. Both are doing really well."

"That's great. Since you won't need our services, I'll let you go. Thanks for your time." I hung up hurriedly. I suspected she was on the verge of telling me in great detail how well her sons were doing.

So, Crawford hadn't visited his children on campus last night. To whom had he taken the food? I stared out the window for a long time without finding either an answer or a plan of action. The only idea I came up with was to search his office. I would probably find out more at his house, but I wasn't ready to add breaking and entering to my list of investigative accomplishments. Without a doubt, Ariosto would give me permission to search the office. Would that permission stand up in court? I didn't know. Ariosto owned the building, but Crawford occupied the office.

My best bet to get into Crawford's office without arousing suspicion was to masquerade as a cleaning woman. I telephoned Ariosto, told him of my plan without going into details and asked him whether the cleaning crew did the Saturday cleaning that evening or on Sunday. He didn't know, but assured me he would find out fast. He called back within five minutes. The cleaning crew started on Sunday evening at eight.

That worked well with my weekend plans.

WEARING JEANS AND A flannel shirt over a T-shirt, a kerchief tied around my head and yellow latex gloves on my hands, I let myself into the main building. I spotted the cleaning crew, three men and one woman, seating themselves around a table in the lunchroom. A full pot of coffee and a plate of sandwiches told me that they would be there for at least ten minutes.

Crawford's desk was locked. However, the lock was a joke. Even wearing the thick latex gloves, it took me only a minute to open it with my skeleton keys. I searched the contents quickly but methodically. The only interesting thing in the desk was a half-empty bottle of Absolut vodka. Flipping through his appointment calendar, I noticed personal notes. One red, "Get b. gift for Mary." The notation, "Flowers—Ardway," appeared at least every other week. Someone was being showered with flowers from the most exclusive florist in town. That could be a lead, I thought.

I checked his closet, emptied the pockets of the raincoat hanging there, flipped through the half dozen books on finance and accounting on the bookshelf, crawled under the desk to see if anything had been taped to the bottom, turned the umbrella stand upside down and found nothing.

Refusing to believe that there was nothing to be found, I sat in Crawford's chair, letting my eyes examine each wall, each piece of furniture. I had checked them all. I even looked under the blotter, a place so obvious that no one would hide anything there. When I lifted it, the photo of his family tipped over. As I picked it up, I noticed that the fall had dislodged the cardboard backing. My fingers were clumsy because of the protective gloves. I couldn't get it back into the frame. Curious, I looked under the backing and eased out what had been hidden there. The folded piece of paper, roughly three by five inches, contained dates in the left-hand column with sums of money in the right column. At the bottom he had written the four-digit number 5682.

I knew I was taking a risk when I made a photostatic copy. No sooner had I returned the original to its place than I heard voices in the reception area. Frantically, I looked around. There was no place for me to hide except in the closet. Standing as far back in the corner as I could with the raincoat pulled in front of me, I heard footsteps, trash cans being emptied, the vacuum cleaner springing into action. My heart plummeted to my toes when the closet door opened and the sweeper made three half-hearted passes into the closet. Even after the door closed and the sweeper stopped, I could feel sweat pouring down my back.

Although the crew had finished Crawford's office, it would take them an hour or more to finish the other offices on this floor. I would have to dart in and out of rooms to reach the exit to the parking lot undetected. Halfway down the hall I heard a door open. I crouched beside the water cooler. Fortunately the man in matching gray work pants and shirt turned back to the room to speak to his companion. That gave me enough time to duck into the conference room, praying that this was not next on their agenda to be cleaned.

Standing beside the closed door my heart pounded so loudly I feared the man passing by would hear it. His footsteps continued past the door and out into the parking lot. Great. Now I was trapped until he returned. The room was faintly illuminated by the powerful security light just outside the window. I turned to evaluate my surroundings.

My heart stopped when I saw the figure sitting at the head of the conference table.

Caught.

When I started to breathe again, my heart hammered against my ribs so hard my chest ached. My knees almost buckled, my mouth dried up, my voice failed. I waited a beat, but the figure at the head of the table said nothing. Although I couldn't distinguish his features, the breadth of his shoulders suggested to me it was a man.

I tried to speak again. "Good evening." My voice sounded weak and squeaky. The figure remained silent, unmoving. I have a keen sense of smell which isn't always a blessing. What I smelled made my scalp tighten and the hair at my neck stand up. It was a purely atavistic reaction for I could not identify this odor. I took several steps toward the man. His eyes were open, staring at me.

"I came in here by mistake. I'm sorry." His unblinking stare unnerved me. "Are you all right?" I walked up to him. It was Galen Crawford. "Are you ill?" I reached out and touched his shoulder.

His body fell forward, as if filmed by a slow-motion camera. Or so my brain perceived it. When his face hit the table, I winced. For a moment I didn't recognize the wet-looking stain covering his neck or the gray-white wormlike substance that protruded where his hair should have been. Then I knew. The scream rising in me couldn't squeeze through my tight throat. My stomach heaved in protest. Pressing my hand against my mouth I backed away, unable to tear my eyes from the grisly sight. I kept backing away until I bumped into the door. I tore it open and ran outside.

I kept running until I hit the fence at the edge of the parking lot. Clutching the cool chain links with one hand, I swayed. My stomach violently rejected all I had eaten. I continued to heave long after there was nothing left to expel. When I was finally able to stop, I collapsed with my back against the fence. At first I concentrated on breathing deeply, on regaining some control over my shaking body.

When the trembling ceased, I tried to put my thoughts in order. Galen Crawford was dead. There was no question about that. Nobody could live with only half a head. Remembering, nausea rolled through me, threatening to make me sick again. I shut my eyes, fighting it. Although I eventually managed to subdue the nausea, I knew I would never be able to forget the ghastly image of that bloody body.

The police. I had to report Crawford's death. No, I couldn't do that. They would want to know what I had been doing in the building. On the other hand, I didn't have to tell them my name. Grabbing the fence, I pulled myself to a standing position. My knees almost buckled under me. I clutched the wire mesh and hung onto it. Taking deep breaths, I willed myself to stop shaking. Then I staggered unsteadily to my car and managed to drive to the public phone booth outside the Kroger store. I didn't dare use my cell phone. The cops undoubtedly had Caller ID.

My voice sounded surprisingly steady when I reported the location of the body. When the police dispatcher asked my name, I hung up. Digging through my purse I found another quarter. Uncle Barney's line was busy. Damn. I had to talk to him, to ask his advice. Realizing that discussing a dead body would be better done face-to-face, I got into my car and drove to his house.

Uncle Barney lives in the old, elegant part of the city. Ordinarily I enjoyed looking at the giant oaks shading the Victorian mansions, but not tonight. I willed myself to see the pavement, the traffic signs, not Crawford's bloody head. When I reached his front door, I pounded the lionhead door knocker against the oak until he opened the door. I practically fell into his arms.

"Cybil? What's wrong?" Putting his arm around my waist, he half-carried, half-dragged me to the leather armchair in his living room. "You look awful. What happened?"

"I found Crawford. He's dead. Murdered."

"Good God. Are you sure he's dead?"

I nodded. "The back of his head is missing."

"Jesus." Barney crossed to the liquor cabinet. He poured a half inch of amber liquid into a glass and held it to my lips. I drank the bourbon, feeling a fiery, welcome warmth spread all the way to my toes.

"Now tell me everything from the beginning," Barney said.

I did, ending with the anonymous telephone call to the police. "Did I do all right?"

"Yes. Yes." Glancing at my hands, he said, "You obviously didn't leave any fingerprints."

I hadn't realized I was still wearing the latex cleaning gloves.

"Did anyone see you run out of the building?"

Shutting my eyes, I pictured my headlong flight. "I don't think there was anyone in the hall."

"Good. We'll leave it as is for now. If someone ties you to the scene, we'll say you panicked."

"Which happens to be the truth. All I could think of was to get away from that sight as fast as I could. I'm sorry. I should have telephoned the police from one of the offices."

"It's okay. This was your first encounter with a dead body. Most people would panic."

"I bet you didn't."

"You would lose that bet, Cybil. It happened in 'Nam. I staggered off the road and threw up like a sick puppy."

It was good to hear that my reaction hadn't been unnatural or particularly cowardly. "What do we do now?"

"I'm taking you home. Everything else we'll face tomorrow. I have to make a quick phone call before we leave. Excuse me, Cybil."

I leaned back in the chair. Uncle Barney was back in a minute.

"I expect I'll rate a visit from Sam since we told him about our investigation at Tri State," he said.

I groaned. Sam and I rarely saw eye-to-eye on things and now that I was working for Barney, we disagreed even more often.

"I'll try to keep him away from you as long as possible," Barney promised as he drove me home. I don't remember anything about the drive to my house.

When we got there, Luke was waiting for us.

"I phoned Luke," Barney said, his voice apologetic.

Luke took one look at my face and his eyes grew bleak. I don't know what Barney said to him, but Luke helped me undress and put me under a hot shower. When I had warmed up, he helped me into a flannel nightgown and brought me a mug of hot milk with cinnamon sprinkled on top. I tasted it. "What else is in here?"

"A few drops of brandy."

I looked at him questioningly, knowing he doesn't approve of hard liquor.

"For medicinal purposes," he explained. He watched me drink the doctored milk, waiting.

"Want to tell me about it?" Luke asked after a while.

I shook my head.

"Do you think that's fair, Cybil? You come home in shock, looking like death warmed over, and expect me to go on as if nothing has happened?"

He was right. I told him about finding the body, omitting everything else. To his credit, Luke didn't ask questions or deliver a lecture. He put his arms around me and held me until I fell asleep.

I HAD HOPED THAT THE bright morning sunshine would mitigate the horror of the night before, but it didn't. If anything, violent death seemed even more obscene in the face of daylight. Involuntarily, I shuddered.

"I made breakfast," Luke announced, setting the tray on the nightstand.

"Thanks. You stayed the night?"

"On the sofa."

He filled a cup with coffee and gave it to me. It was strong, the way we both like it. Luke set a toasted whole-grain English muffin before me. "Luke, I can't eat."

"Yes, you can. It's easy. Watch me."

His strong white teeth took a bit bite out of his muffin. Then he pushed the pot of honey toward me, his eyes challenging me to refuse to eat. I broke off a tiny piece and put it into my mouth. Eventually it disintegrated and I swallowed it.

"I can't eat," I repeated. "Just because you're used to seeing torn-up human beings doesn't mean the rest of us are."

"Whose fault is it that you found that body?" Luke countered. "Your own. If you'd taken a suitable job you would have spared yourself this ordeal."

"Look, I'm not complaining or whining about my

job. All I'm saying is that I don't feel like eating, and missing one meal isn't going to have any long-range negative effect on my health."

"Suit yourself. I have to get to work." He walked toward the door.

"Luke, thanks for staying. I appreciate it," I called after him.

He stopped and turned. He looked at me with unreadable eyes. Then he nodded and left.

I'd hurt his feelings. I felt like the ingrate he probably thought I was. I'd have to find a way to make it up to him.

FOUR

I SHOWERED, MADE A HALF-HEARTED attempt at curling the ends of my hair with the curling iron, dressed in moss green corduroy slacks, a matching silk blouse and low-heeled suede boots. From the hall closet I grabbed a jacket.

Since I'd left the rental car at Uncle Barney's house, I drove the Volvo. I had forgotten what a comfortable ride it provides.

Lynn was measuring coffee into the filter when I entered the office. She paused to survey me.

"You're early. The coffee should be ready in a minute. How are you feeling this morning?"

From the way she asked, I knew Uncle Barney had told her about last night. "I'll make it."

"I'm sure you will. Most of us do."

And that's all the sympathy I'd get from her. Frankly, I was surprised she had even asked how I was. I watched the dark liquid begin to trickle into the pot.

"I still remember my first air raid," Lynn said, her voice low.

I wondered if the planes had belonged to North Vietnam or to the U.S. To the dead that had undoubtedly not mattered. Lynn seemed lost in thought, so I kept quiet. The only sound in the room was the dripping of the coffee. When it stopped, I held out my mug, the one

Maxi had given me with the chubby Kliban cats on it for her to fill. I took it to my office.

Since I'd taken on this assignment a week ago, two people had died violently. One accidentally. Maybe. The other… I raised my hand to the back of my head, holding an imaginary gun.

"What are you doing?"

Uncle Barney stood in the open door. I hadn't heard him approach. "Trying to see if Crawford could have shot himself."

"And?"

I shrugged. "I'm no expert on gun shots, but blowing off the back of one's head is an awkward way to commit suicide."

"It would be more natural to hold the gun to the temple or fire it into the mouth," he said.

"If I'd kept my wits about me, I would have looked around for a gun."

"What else did you notice last night?"

I thought about the still figure sitting in the chair and it hit me. "He didn't shoot himself. If he had, he would have fallen forward, or sideways, wouldn't he? Somebody arranged him in that chair, and that rules out suicide," I said, pleased with my reasoning.

"I'd say so. It'll be interesting to find out if he was shot in that room or somewhere else."

"But why bring him back if he was killed at another location?"

"Because the murder scene might point to the identity of the murderer. Or maybe he or she thought the body wouldn't be found until sometime today. It's unlikely that the conference room would have been cleaned unless it was used, and it's doubtful that a meeting was held on Saturday. From what we know of the Tri State operation, only a skeleton crew works on weekends and that's mostly in the warehouses. Crawford, as the chief accountant, wouldn't have been expected in the office. Perhaps the murderer needed time to establish an alibi. He or she couldn't know that you would stumble on the body."

I sat, thinking about what Barney had said.

"By the way, what makes you think Crawford was shot?"

"I guess I assumed he was," I admitted. "What else could have been used to take off part of his head? It didn't look bashed in. "I felt a little queasy thinking about that head.

"Never mind. The police will establish what killed him. Come and help me work on the report."

From the way he changed the subject, he must have noticed my reaction. "Wait. There are two more things you ought to know." I told him about Crawford's flower orders and about the hidden slip of paper. I took it out of my shoulder bag and handed it to him.

"It looks to me like blackmail payments he received or paid."

"Received, I think. One of the women at work said that he recently bought a cottage on the lake, and that he has a reputation for being generous to his women. At least to the ones he cheated on his wife with. What do you think that four-digit number means?"

Barney squinted at the number thoughtfully. "It could be a locker number. Maybe a safety deposit box. It's too short for a zip code, a phone number, a lottery ticket or the combination to a safe. I'll have Lynn make a photocopy and place the original into the vault. It could be something simple and obvious that escapes both of us right now."

"Before we start the report, I want to call the florist and try something." Glancing at my watch, I said, "They open in five minutes."

Barney nodded and left. That's the great thing about him. He doesn't insist on knowing the methods his investigators use, so if one of us does something that backfires or misses, we don't have to confess our failure. He trusts us to stay inside the law, but how we get results is up to us.

Promptly at eight I dialed the florist's number. Pretending to be young and flustered, I said, "Hi. I wonder if you can help me. I'm sort of in a tough spot. I'm filling in for a friend and her boss, Galen Crawford, told me to order the usual flowers from you on Friday, but I forgot. And I forgot to ask him who gets the flowers. If I ask him this morning, he'll know I messed up and he'll be so mad at me. Can you help me out?"

"Let me check the rolodex. Yes. Galen Crawford. A dozen red roses to Jennifer Wooster. I can send them first thing this morning. No problem."

"Oh thank you. You saved my life."

Asking for Jennifer's address might have aroused the woman's suspicions. I reached for the phone book. There were only three Woosters listed. Fortunately, Jennifer was one of them. Since I'd done so well with the florist, I decided to try something with Jennifer. I dialed her number.

"Good morning. This is the Central Consumers'

Club. We're going a survey and if you could answer three questions it would help us tremendously. Also we'll send you a free gift. First, are you between the ages of twenty and thirty-five?"

"Yes."

"Are you married or single?"

"Single."

"Where do you work?"

"Tri State Personnel Department."

Surprise, surprise. An office romance and red roses. Galen Crawford had not been an imaginative man.

"Thank you so much. Have a nice day," I crooned, hanging up before she could question me about anything.

When I went looking for Uncle Barney, Lynn informed me that he was in conference and that I was to start on the report alone. Writing reports isn't my favorite thing to do but it's part of the job. By noon I had finished the rough draft. I placed it on his desk before I went to lunch.

Since I was alone, I bought two Cambodian egg rolls and Jasmine-flavored tea from the little booth in the square. I carried my lunch to the bench in the courtyard, enjoying the perfect late autumn day. Most likely there wouldn't be many more.

I brooded about the Tri State case. I wasn't happy with it. Barney had decided to close it. And he was right. We had accomplished what we had been hired to do: expose the theft ring. But two people had died violent deaths during our investigation. That's what bothered me.

Even though I knew the police would mount an

inquiry into Crawford's death, they were satisfied with
the ruling of accidental death in Wilma's case. I was
not. She wasn't careless with her wheelchair. And she
wasn't suicidal. I had been a counselor long enough to
spot the signs of suicidal depression.

Before driving to Ariosto's house, I brushed my hair
and freshened my makeup. A protective act, I reflected.
If I ran into Pauline I didn't want her perfectly groomed,
pampered appearance to make me feel inadequate.

Expecting Brazier's thin, bent body to open the mansion's door for me, I was caught off guard when I came
face-to-face with the best looking young man I'd ever
see outside the movies. I suspect I stared at him round-
eyed until he spoke.

"You must be Mrs. Quindt. My stepdad is holed up
with his lawyer for another ten minutes. Will you come
in and wait? I'll keep you company."

He flashed me a smile of singular sweetness that
made me swallow twice. I was married and ten years
older, but still the young man caused me to catch my
breath. I felt a rush of compassion for all those twenty-
year-olds out there who had few if any defenses against
his beauty.

"I'm Harry Ariosto."

"Cybil Quindt." We shook hands. I followed him into
a game room down the hall.

"I remember you," Harry said. "You were one of my
sister's friends. Well, Annette isn't my blood sister, but
I always think of her as my big sis."

I was flattered he remembered me. Vaguely I recalled
a boy of seven or eight, hovering in the background, shy

and perhaps a little lonely in this huge house peopled by adults. He certainly wasn't shy anymore.

"Can I get you a drink?" Harry asked.

"A soft drink, if you have it."

Harry busied himself at the elaborate wet bar flanking the south wall.

"Aren't you going to offer me a drink, too?"

Startled, I turned in the direction of the voice. A big armchair swiveled around to face us. In it Pauline Ariosto lounged, her legs crossed, her thighs scantily covered by her short denim skirt. With the third button of her white silk shirt undone she looked, I thought, like a woman trying to be deliberately provocative.

"Don't you already have a drink?" Harry asked.

"Not anymore." Pauline raised an empty glass and wagged it at him. The movement caused several bracelets to clink against each other.

"It's still early. Don't you think you ought to go easy on that stuff?"

His voice sounded pleading, I thought.

"Don't you tell me what to do, too. Just fix me the damn drink."

Harry's face flushed, his eyes narrowed. For a second they glowered at each other, the tension between them almost palpable. Then Harry took a decanter, splashed some of its colorless liquid into a glass, added tonic water and a slice of lemon. He brought me my cola before he handed the vodka tonic to his stepmother who thanked him with exaggerated politeness. I felt acutely uncomfortable as if I had walked into an ongoing quarrel.

Harry took a can of beer, popped the tab, and drank deeply, almost defiantly.

No one said anything. I wanted to be almost anywhere but in that tension-filled room.

Ariosto came in, looked pointedly at his wife's drink, his mouth thinning with disapproval. "Isn't this a little early, even for you?" He turned to Harry. "Don't you have classes today?"

"Yes. I came by so Sidney can look at my car."

"Sidney's my chauffeur, not your mechanic. Take your car to a service station."

I could sense Harry's embarrassment clear across the room.

"Cybil, are you ready?" Ariosto asked.

"Yes." All I wanted was to get out of that house.

Without another word, Ariosto started toward the door. I murmured goodbye to Harry and to Pauline and followed him. The man would never win a prize for manners or warmth.

In his study I handed him the report. While he read it, I watched his face turn livid, his hands tighten on the sheets of paper. I was glad we no longer lived in an age when the messenger of bad news was summarily executed.

Whipping his glasses off, he tossed them on the desk. "There's one thing I regret—that Crawford isn't alive so I can have the pleasure of firing him and pressing charges. That rat. One of my top men, and he screws me."

An interesting reaction, I thought. Ariosto considered the pilfering a personal affront. No regret over Craw-

ford's death, only that Ariosto could not administer the
punishment himself.

"You did a good job, Cybil. I won't forget that."

No, he wasn't a man to forget anything. The moment
he handed me the check covering our fee and expenses, I
left that tension-filled mansion as fast as I could without
actually breaking into a run.

AT THE AGENCY Lynn pounced on me the moment I
walked through the door.

"About time you got here," she hissed, her black eyes
snapping. "Barney's had to face them alone."

"Face whom?"

"The police."

Uncle Barney stood up when I entered the conference
room where he was meeting the police. He doesn't do
this in the ordinary course of a business day. I suspected
he wanted to convey a message to Sam and his companion about how to treat me. Both men stood. Sam
introduced me to Sergeant Griffin, a thin-faced man
whose red, raw nose indicted he was suffering from a
head cold. Being susceptible to colds, I sat as far away
from him as I could.

"Did you submit the report to our client?" Barney
asked.

"Yes. The account is settled."

Barney nodded, satisfied.

Sam broke into the conversation. "As I said before,
this is a murder investigation. The usual client confi-
dentiality mumbo-jumbo doesn't apply."

Sam looked ill-tempered, harried. Maybe the investigation into Crawford's death wasn't going well. Or maybe he was catching his partner's cold.

"I realize that," Barney said, his voice quiet. "But it would be helpful if you gave us some information in return. You know, the old 'you scratch my back and I'll scratch yours'."

"All right," Sam agreed, not too graciously.

Barney reported our findings. The only time he consulted the pages in front of him was to get the name of the drivers and the receivers of the stolen goods.

Sergeant Griffin was taking notes furiously.

"That could be a motive," Sam said, "thieves falling out among themselves."

"From our superficial check on his finances, it seems to me he took in more money than could have been his share from the pilfering," Barney said.

"What are you suggesting? Blackmail?"

"In a setup like that, it wouldn't be impossible. By the way, what killed Crawford?"

"A shotgun blast. He must have been in the act of turning his head. He was hit from the side."

"Was he killed where you found him?" Barney asked casually.

Fortunately Sam wasn't very perceptive and so he didn't catch that keen interest masked by a nonchalant tone. I kept quiet. When you have something to hide, be inconspicuous.

"No. He was killed somewhere else," Sam said.

"Time of death?"

"Sometime early Sunday evening. You certainly are interested in details," Sam said, his eyes narrowed in suspicion.

"Professional curiosity." Barney kept his face blank.

"A woman reported finding the body. Would you know anything about that, Cybil?"

"Me? Find a murdered body?" I asked, injecting disbelief in my voice. I met his eyes squarely. Then I shivered visibly, hoping to put him off without actually having to lie.

"You worked at Tri State. What's the gossip about Crawford?"

I decided to tell the truth about this. Crawford's womanizing could be a motive. Some cuckolded husband or lover could have decided to put an end to his tomcatting. "Well, he's supposedly cheated on his wife and according to rumor, he is…was generous to his lovers."

Between sneezes the sergeant made a note of that.

"Were any of the women at Tri State involved with him?"

"You'll have to ask them that yourself," I said.

Sam sent me one of his hard looks which did absolutely nothing to intimidate me. I suppose someone brought to the police station might feel a stab of fear, but it's hard to be intimidated by someone you remember wetting his pants at age five while running away from a spooky house on Halloween night.

"Where were you Sunday night?"

I had braced myself for that question from the moment I entered the conference room. "Let's see," I said, pretending to think back. "I cooked supper, cleaned up after I ate, drove to the store, read and went to bed around eleven." Except for omitting a couple of things, all of that was true.

"Any witnesses?"

"At home? No. At the store? I don't know if the cashier will remember me or not."

"What do you suspect Cybil of?" Barney asked. "Surely you don't think she shot Crawford?"

"No. But I wouldn't put it past her to find the body, phone in a report, and then disappear."

"Are you charging Cybil with anything?" Barney demanded, a hint of steel in his voice.

Sam backed off. "No. I have no proof. The cleaning crew saw and heard nothing."

That was welcome news. I was careful to keep my face blank. I looked at the carpet. It really was a lovely Oriental rug.

As soon as they left the conference room, I slumped in relief.

"Do you think Sam will check my alibi?"

Barney shook his head. "No. He didn't even ask the name of the store."

"Phew. I'm glad that's over."

"You did very well."

"Thanks. So, where do we go from here?"

"A new case."

"But we can't," I protested and then shut my mouth. Officially we were finished with Tri State.

"What's bothering you?" Barney asked.

I shrugged, feeling foolish. "I guess I want to get everything solved, including Crawford's murder, but I know that's now up to the police."

Barney fiddled with his pipe, clearly waiting for me to get something off my chest.

"Oh, all right. Crawford's unexplained trip to the university still bugs me and so does Wilma's death."

"That's been ruled accidental, so unless you come up with concrete, new evidence, we'll leave that alone. As to Crawford's visit to Alpha House, you can pursue that but in down time."

"Thank you."

IT HAD BEEN SEVERAL days since I'd seen my grandmother.

I dialed Maxi's number on my cell phone. She was at home, baking apple strudel.

"If you have time, why don't you come by for a piece? As late as you eat supper, you won't spoil your appetite."

"I'll have to finish some paperwork, but then I'll be there." For Oma's strudel I'd walk the five miles to the farm. Barefooted, if necessary.

I finished the reports and took them to Uncle Barney's office. When I told him that I was on my way to Maxi's farm, he told me to give his mother a hug from him.

Maxi lives on a small farm south of town. Until I got married and had a home of my own, her house was the place I loved most in all the world. Memories of my father who was killed when I was four, are dim at best. The only places I remember are the apartment my mother rented before she remarried and the three houses each subsequent husband provided for her. They were houses, not homes. I know the difference well.

Even though Maxi bakes delicious pastries and bread from scratch, she's not the typical old-fashioned storybook grandmother. For one thing, she holds strong opinions on everything, informed opinions, because she reads all the time. She always has. Years before feminism came into its own, Maxi refused to allow men to congregate at one end of her living room and women at the other. She had six children whom she loved fiercely, but she refused to allow them to become her one topic of conversation or the sole focal point of her life.

"Being a mother ought to make you more knowledgeable of the world around you, not less," Maxi has said many times. "How else can you guard your babies and raise them to become intelligent, worthwhile human beings?"

I had planned to raise my child like that but I wasn't given the chance. Quickly I flipped on the radio. The sweet strains of a Haydn piece washed over me, not lessening my pain, but distracting me a little from it. I concentrated on the music, listening for the woodwinds. I focused so hard I almost missed the turnoff to Maxi's farm.

The house looks like old farm houses did before brick ranches replaced them: narrow, tall in front with a couple of one-story additions in the back. The wooden frame was painted white, the roof covered with green shingles.

Automatically I walked around to the back. The only time I can remember entering through the front door was when I brought Luke to the farm for the first time.

Maxi was waiting for me.

"The coffee is ready and so is the strudel," she called to me from the kitchen sink where she dried her hands on a dishtowel.

"Mmm...nothing beats the aroma of freshly brewed coffee, apples and cinnamon."

"Sit, sit." Maxi had cleared the table after her frugal evening meal and covered it with one of her lovely embroidered cloths. She poured the dark liquid into the fragile porcelain cups with the gold border. Delicate violets ringed the outside. I remember impatiently waiting for the day when I would be old enough to drink out of this cup.

"Uncle Barney sends his love," I said, accepting a piece of strudel.

"So, why didn't my son come?"

"He was still busy at the office."

"Ha! With that *Drachenliebchen*, no doubt."

There's no good translation for that word. Perhaps dragon lady comes closest. Maxi, who is a truly accepting, tolerant person, does not like Lynn. I think Lynn feels the same way about Maxi. Maybe it's because both women are fiercely protective of Uncle Barney. Maybe it's because neither wants to share him with the other. Maybe it's because they're both strong women who are a lot alike. Sometimes I suspect that the dislike is rooted in something that happened in the past.

"How is work?" Maxi asked.

"Fine."

"But?"

I can hide little from my grandmother. Her intelligent blue-gray eyes miss nothing. I told her about the Tri State case and my reservations about it. I could see she was thinking furiously about something.

"What is it?"

"Wilma Johnson. That name is so familiar."

I told Maxi about the accident.

"Of course. Mae Carnes. That's the connection. I'll get my scrapbook."

Ever since she retired as reference librarian from the Westport Public Library, Maxi has been keeping scrapbooks of newspaper clippings on people she knows. Having lived in Westport for over forty years, she knows a lot of people.

"Here it is," she said, carrying over a big album. She removed the clipping and handed it to me.

"Did you know Mae died last week, Cybil?"

"Yes. Her daughter-in-law told me."

"That still surprises me. That Tommy got married. That he broke away long enough from his mother to find himself a wife."

"How well did you know Mae?"

"Not well, and that was a long time ago. Her husband and mine worked together at Studebaker. Before that they'd been friends in high school. The men wanted us to be friends, too, so we could go out together, but Mae couldn't bring herself to leave Tommy with a baby-sitter. He was too frail and too high strung, she claimed." Maxi shook her head.

"If you ask me, the only thing wrong with the boy was that Mae spoiled him rotten and smothered him. I used to see them at company picnics over the years. Tommy was a real mama's boy, hardly left her side." Maxi refilled my cup. "So, what are you going to do about Wilma?"

"I don't know. I have no evidence, just a hunch."

"Don't fret, *Schatzi*. If there's something fishy about

her death, someone will make a mistake, and you'll spot it."

"Thanks for the vote of confidence." Maxi has always supported me in whatever I've wanted to do. Sometimes I think she believes there's nothing I can't do. I saw her glance at the kitchen clock. It was almost time for the PBS evening news. Maxi never misses it. She doesn't even answer the phone or the doorbell while the program is on.

"I'd better get home. I have to do some laundry," I said.

"I wrapped up some strudel for Luke and for Barney." Maxi handed me two foil-wrapped packages from the counter.

Was this a ploy so that I had to go and see Luke? I looked at Maxi carefully. No. She simply liked him, and knowing how much he loved her baking, she wanted to share it with him.

"Thanks, Oma. This will make both of them happy." I kissed her cheek.

I STOPPED AT THE CAMPUS cafe and bought two take-out lattes. Then I drove to the hospital, taking a chance on Luke's still being there. He was. I'd forgotten how good he looked in the lime green scrubs.

"Are you all right?" he asked, his voice concerned.

"I'm fine."

"No aftereffects from the shock of finding that body?"

"None that I'm aware of. I visited Maxi. She sent you some strudel. And I brought a couple of lattes. Do you have time to take a break?"

"For strudel? Are you kidding?" He turned to the nearest nurse. "Marlene, I'm taking a break in my office. So unless there's a catastrophic emergency, don't call me."

The nurse promised, giving me a sly look.

Luke led the way. He moved a bunch of medical journals from the visitor's chair and motioned me to sit.

I set out the coffee and handed him the foil-wrapped plate. He sniffed and sighed happily. I watched him eat the strudel with so much enjoyment it made me smile.

"When was the last time you ate?" I asked him.

"Strudel? Not since the Labor Day picnic at Maxi's farm. Cafeteria food? At noon, I think. It was so unmemorable that I'm not sure."

"Hospital food hasn't improved any, huh?"

"No."

Our eyes met. We both remembered the years of his residency and the countless times I'd come to the hospital to eat the tasteless food so that we could spend some time together. I felt the burning ache in my throat that always preceded tears. Quickly, I suppressed the memory of our early years.

"Would you like this last piece?" Luke asked.

"No, thanks. I ate so much strudel at Maxi's that I'm not only going to skip dinner, but I'm also going to the YWCA to swim laps. I can't afford any more calories."

"You look just fine to me."

The way he looked at me, made me feel warm all over. Time to leave.

"I'd better go. Maxi gave me some strudel to deliver to Uncle Barney."

"Cybil, thanks for bringing me this treat. I'll call Maxi to thank her."

"She'll like that. She always enjoys talking with you."

I spent Tuesday in front of the computer, doing research for other cases the agency handled.

On Wednesday Maxi phoned, saying she had to come to town and could I meet her for lunch at her favorite place, the restaurant in the Nightingale Hotel? Of course, I agreed.

We chose a booth in the corner. When we were seated, Maxi looked around.

"When I first came to Westport, the Nightingale was the best hotel in town. It was during the last years of the depression, so not too many people could afford to stay here. I remember once the Laubensteins invited me to lunch on my birthday. I thought there couldn't be a fancier place than this hotel in all the world."

I watched Maxi's face soften with her memories.

"It's a shame the city let the hotel degenerate into a… well, during the sixties it was little more than a trysting place for illicit lovers. It's now trying to make a comeback."

We ordered hot tea with our chef salads. Maxi considers most restaurant coffee undrinkable.

"What a coincidence," Maxi said, craning her head. "There is Tommy Carnes. We were just talking about him the other day."

I turned my head in the direction of Maxi's gaze.

"Behind the counter," she prompted.

"Cathy, his wife, told me he worked as a short order cook so he could spend more time with his mother."

"That figures. She was the type to use whatever she could to get her way," Maxi said.

Wearing a chef's hat and apron, Tom looked younger than I had pictured him. He would have been a good-looking man except for his petulant expression and his big ears.

"Excuse me, dear. I'll just go and say hello."

I watched Maxi talking to Tom. She returned within minutes.

"He remembered you from the Studebaker picnics?" I asked.

"From his mother's funeral. I would have recognized him anywhere though."

"How is he?"

Maxi looked thoughtful. "That's hard to say. He always was a bit of an odd duck. He's…distracted. Like only part of him is here. There's also a gray aura about him. I don't like that gray aura."

I waited for Maxi to elaborate. She didn't. From what I remembered about auras, a gray one wasn't good. Poor Cathy. I hadn't liked her at first, but after I found out about her home life, I understood her better. All her flaunting was a desperate attempt to reassure herself as a woman.

We enjoyed our lunch. Maxi talked about her early years in this country. I never tire of listening to her.

LUKE'S PARENTS HAD GIVEN us season tickets each year to the football games at the university. Since our

separation, we split the tickets. I had invited Joan, whom
I've known since high school. She's a loan officer in
Westport's biggest bank and an avid football fan. The
home team pulled an upset, giving everyone hope for
an invitation to the Fiesta Bowl. Afterwards we dined at
the Brauhof Restaurant, drinking imported Stiegl beer
and eating excellent pot roast.

THE RED LIGHT ON THE answering machine blinked
furiously when I arrived home. The two messages were
from Terrance Ariosto, asking me to come to his house
as soon as possible. The first had been left at five-thirty,
the second an hour later. I thought his voice sounded
urgent, perhaps even worried, but with an authoritative
voice such as his, it's hard to tell.

I exchanged my suit for jeans, a white turtleneck with
a jewel-toned challis scarf, and a suede jacket. Looking
in the mirror I thought I looked all right except for my
hair. It was beginning to rain which always makes my
hair go out of control. Something about the humidity.
I gathered it up, twisted it into a knot at the back of
my head and fastened it with half a dozen hairpins. I
grabbed my shoulder bag and my raincoat and drove to
Ariosto's.

On the way I tried to guess what he wanted with me,
but had no clue. Crawford's murder was a police matter
and the pilfering case had been solved. At least to Uncle
Barney's satisfaction, if not to mine. All that was left
unexplained was Wilma's death which kept bothering
me like a hard to reach mosquito bite.

I parked the car in the circular drive and walked up

to the door. I rang the bell. No one came. I knocked harder. To my surprise, the door opened a few inches.

"Hello," I called out. No answer. I called again, louder this time. I was sure I could be heard in the far reaches of the house. Hesitantly I pushed the door open. The elegant entry before me was dimly lit by two tapers on the wall but empty. The house was silent. That was odd.

The house was unlocked with the lights on; and somebody ought to have been home. Certainly Ariosto, who had phoned me twice, asking me to come. Where was Brazier? Besides him, the household staff included the cook, Mrs. Dougherty, as well as the chauffeur whose name escaped me just then.

I proceeded toward Ariosto's study down the hall. Here the door was ajar, too, light spilling out into the hall.

"Mr. Ariosto?" After waiting a few seconds, I pushed the door open wide enough to step inside. I sensed movement to my left but before I could turn, I felt as if the roof had collapsed on my head, burying me in darkness.

I DON'T KNOW HOW MUCH time passed before I became aware of pounding pain in my head.

From far off I heard groans. It took a while before I realized they were mine. Raising my head, I saw the polished hardwood floor pitch and heave. Nausea surged through me, forcing me to close my eyes and lower my head back down to the floor.

I fought the nausea, the dizziness, the pain. My fingers burrowed under the twisted knot of hair to find a throbbing lump that seemed to grow even as I explored it with gentle fingers.

Great. I probably had a concussion. Luke was going to love this.

The smooth floor felt cool beneath my cheek. As long as I didn't move, I could endure the pain. Tempting as it was, I couldn't remain there. Who had hit me? Ariosto? No, that made no sense. He had summoned me. Who then? Was that person still in the house? For the first time since I'd regained consciousness, alarm surged through me. I had to get up. Find Ariosto. Phone the police and report the assault on me.

Slowly, inch by inch, I pulled my upper body into a sitting position, fighting nausea all the way.

When I opened my eyes, I wished I hadn't. A few feet away from me sprawled the body of a man. Even though he lay face down, I knew it was Ariosto.

I half scooted, half crawled toward his outflung arm, searching for a pulse. Finding none in his wrist, I touched his throat. Nothing. That's when I saw the puddle of blood under his upper body. At the same time I became aware of that sweet, sickly smell I had noticed in the conference room where I had found Crawford.

My heart started to pound painfully, echoing the pounding in my head. Still, I wouldn't, couldn't, panic this time. Carefully I lifted up Ariosto's shoulder and looked at his chest. That was a mistake. The room spun crazily. I let my head drop back onto the floor. I wasn't going to pass out, I vowed.

I looked at my watch. Surprised, I discovered that I'd been unconscious for mere minutes. I was fairly certain that the person who hit me was gone. Why should he, or she, stick around? Still, I listened intently for several seconds. The only noise I heard was the humming of the far-off furnace.

The telephone. I pulled myself up, using the desk. Leaning halfway across the desktop, I dialed the emergency number, requesting an ambulance and the police. While I was still holding the phone, I dialed Uncle Barney's number, praying he would be home. He picked up the receiver on the third ring.

"Uncle Barney, I'm sorry to bother you at home, but I need your help," I said, speaking slowly and carefully. I heard a low voice in the background. Female. Not pleased by the interruption. Lynn?

"Is this really important?"

"You tell me, Uncle Barney. I'm in Ariosto's study. He's lying in his blood on the floor. I have a lump the size of a ping pong ball on my head, and I've called an ambulance and the police, but I don't know if I'm going to pass out before they get here."

"Is Ariosto dead?"

"Yes. His chest...." I gagged and pressed the back of my hand over my mouth. "There's so much blood," I said, my voice weak.

"Hang on. I'll be right there."

SIX

Knowing that Uncle Barney was on his way, I immediately felt better. Not much, but some. I had to concentrate on something other than the body on the floor.

Looking around the study I saw a cart by the window loaded with glasses, decanters and an ice bucket. I zeroed in on the bucket. Removing the scarf from around my neck, I wrapped ice cubes in it and placed it on the bump on my head. The throbbing in the lump lessened.

All the glasses on the cart were placed upside down on a snowy linen napkin. All except one. It was empty. Ariosto's glass? I doubted that because on his desk sat a squat tumbler containing a small amount of amber liquid in it.

The deep windowsill behind the cart was covered with travel brochures. Most of them advertised ocean cruises. Was Ariosto planning to take Pauline on a cruise? Where was Pauline anyway? Where was the rest of the household?

I took a pencil out of my bag and used it to move the brochures around. I could explain my fingerprints on the telephone and the desk, but not on the brochures. I found a slip of paper with a telephone number on it and some notations that looked like dates and times of departure. I copied them into my little notebook. There was also a program of the Chicago Symphony, my very favorite.

I noticed that it featured Daniel Barenboim conducting Beethoven.

The last time I'd found a body I panicked and ran. This time I would use my chance to look around until the police arrived. Was anything out of place? Missing? I had been in this study several times. The room obviously hadn't been ransacked.

Using my pencil I pulled out the middle drawer of the desk. It contained nothing out of the ordinary. The left drawer held a metal cash box. I expected it to be locked but it wasn't. After a quick count I estimated that it contained about eleven hundred dollars in cash. The motive for the murder had not been robbery. The right drawer was locked. That piqued my interest. Why lock it and leave the cash box open?

I studied the lock. For a wealthy man, Ariosto certainly hadn't paid to have good locks installed on his desk. It took only three keys on my skeleton ring to open the drawer. Somewhat surprised, I stared at the hanging file folders. What was so important in them that they had to be locked up?

Ariosto was…had been an orderly man. Each file was labeled with a tab. Reading them, I discovered that they referred to members of his family and household. I scanned the contents of the folders until I heard the distant sound of a siren. Quickly I closed the drawer, locked it, and scooted around the body without looking at it.

The first person who entered the house was Lieutenant Sam Keller, my cousin.

Two medical attendants carrying a stretcher rushed in behind him. I directed them to the study.

"Cybil. What are you doing here?" Sam demanded. "The dispatcher said somebody's been hurt or killed. Who?"

"Terrance Ariosto."

Sam whistled. "Boy, you don't fool around with small fry, do you?"

I opened my mouth to reply, but thought better of it.

"Follow me," Sam ordered.

I did. Sergeant Griffin, blowing his nose, trailed close behind me. In case I decided to bolt? Both men entered the study, but I waited in the hall. The sight of Ariosto's body was indelibly imprinted on my brain. I didn't need to see it again.

I walked to the bottom of the elegant, curved staircase and collapsed on the second step. That's where Uncle Barney found me a few minutes later.

"You okay?" he asked.

I nodded. "The body's back there." I pointed down the hall, "and so's Sam."

"I'll be right back."

Uncle Barney returned shortly and sat down beside me. "Let me look at you." Gently he touched the back of my head, feeling for the bump. He couldn't miss it. "Maybe we ought to have this looked at before anything else."

"No. Later. Maybe."

"Do you see double? Have trouble focusing?"

"No. If I have a concussion, it's a mild one. Remember, I'm married to a doctor. I've learned a few things in our years together."

"I just wanted to be sure. Ariosto's not a pretty sight. Sure you're okay?"

"As okay as anyone can be under the circumstances. Do you think he was killed with a shotgun like Crawford?"

"Seems that way to me. The autopsy will say for sure."

"Both deaths have to be connected, but how?"

"I have no idea. Yet. Tell me exactly what happened."

"Yes, I want to know that, too," Sam said, walking up to us. "Let's go into the parlor or whatever this room is called." He led the way into the living room. "Sit down," he said, pointing to a sofa.

I sat.

"Well, I'm waiting," he prompted.

Sergeant Griffin flipped his notebook open, ready to record whatever I had to say. I told them exactly what had happened, starting with the telephone message on my machine.

"What did Ariosto want with you?" Sam demanded.

"I don't know. We finished our investigation for him days ago. Unless it had something to do with Wilma's death. Or Crawford's."

"I told you there was no evidence of foul play in her death," he snapped. "And we're investigating Crawford's murder. Anybody else hear this so-called telephone message?"

"It isn't so-called, and it's probably still on the answering machine tape. Why don't you go and check it out?"

"I might just do that." Sam paced the length of the room. "Let's go over this again."

"Let's not. My head hurts."

"You might have left something out."

I groaned, pressing my hands against my temples.

"Okay, okay. Let's skip to when you got here. Are you sure there was no one else here?"

"I was at the time. Now we know that the person who hit me over the head was still in the study. He or she was probably the same person who killed Ariosto."

"Anything to indicate whether it was a man or a woman?"

"No."

"Did you hear a shotgun blast?"

"Is that what killed him?" I couldn't repress a shiver.

"Probably. Did you hear it?"

"No. When I arrived, everything was quiet, but all that means is that the murderer had already shot Ariosto."

"Let's try to pin down the time you arrived. When did you get here?"

"I didn't look at my watch when I left home, so I can only guess. I must have left between seven thirty-five and seven-forty. It takes fifteen minutes or so to get here. That would make it seven-fifty or fifty-five."

"Then what? Wait. Why don't you show us what you did and we'll time you."

Reluctantly I went back outside and reenacted my arrival.

"Okay." Sam looked at his watch. "That took only two minutes. The dispatcher recorded your call at five after eight." Sam paced some more. "Cybil, think back carefully. You said you checked Ariosto's pulse. Was he still warm?"

I must have looked sick, because Uncle Barney protested the brutal question.

"Look, we're trying to establish time of death. Usually we have to rely on the autopsy report which gives us a range of hours at best. This time, though, we lucked out. The way I figure, Cybil must have arrived moments after the shotgun blast. Think, Cybil."

"I don't know. He...he wasn't cold or stiff."

"What color was the blood?"

I pressed my hand over my mouth, fearing I might get sick.

"Look here, Sam. Cybil's in shock and in pain. Ease up."

"I can't. This is too important."

I waved my hand for them to stop. "I'll answer. I remember that Ariosto's white shirt was bright red in front. Not rusty brown."

"Good work, Cybil. That means the blood hadn't started to coagulate. That puts the time of death as no earlier than seven-forty and no later than seven-fifty-five. Good, good."

Sam seemed inordinately pleased. I was fairly certain that no physician would narrow down the time of death that closely based on the evidence he had, but I said nothing.

"Cybil, what did you see when you pushed the door to the study open?" Sam asked.

"Nothing. The world caved in on me."

"Are you sure? Think back."

"I saw the door. The dark wood. I pushed it farther back…then nothing."

"He or she must have stood pressed against the wall, arm raised." Sam demonstrated. "As soon as you pushed the door open, wham!"

I flinched when his arm came down forcefully. "What do you think the assailant hit me with?"

"The skin wasn't broken on your scalp," Barney mentioned, "but that's because your thick coil of hair protected you. Could have been almost anything. The butt of a shotgun even."

"The murder weapon?" I asked.

"Could be," Sam agreed. "Did you hear anything when you came to?"

"No."

"You didn't hear a car start?"

"No. But I was out cold. He could have driven off during that time."

"Was there a car parked out front when you arrived?"

"No. But it could have been parked in back where the family's cars are kept. Or even farther back by the stables. You wouldn't hear a whole fleet of cars start from there."

"Where does that back road lead to?" Barney asked.

"Out to Locust Road. I remember leaving once that way after I'd gone horseback riding with Annette."

"Locust connects with major roads going east and west," Sam added. "The murderer could have gone any-where from there. Sergeant, make a note to check that area first thing in the morning. Get it roped off now."

Sergeant Griffin left immediately.

"Okay. You didn't see or hear anything. What did you touch in the study?"

"The edge of the desk. I needed it to help pull myself up. And the telephone."

"Anything else?"

"No. I used my scarf to remove the lid to the ice bucket." I told Sam about the improvised ice pack which since had turned into nothing more than a sopping wet scarf.

"You called the operator and Barney. Why did you call him?" Sam demanded.

"Because I was scared, alone, and in pain. I needed a friendly face."

"Why not call your husband?"

A fair question, I thought, but Luke was the last person I would call under such circumstances. He hated my job and would never forget this incident. Aloud I said, "You know Luke and I are separated. I don't call him when I have a problem."

"Why did Ariosto call you?"

"I already told you. I don't know why. He just left a message to come here."

"Isn't it unusual for him to call you to his house?"

I shrugged. "Not really. I reported to him at his house when we investigated Tri State. He liked meeting here. When you have as much money as he does, you can summon people anywhere you want."

Sam grunted.

Just then two men wheeled a stretcher through the hall. On it lay Ariosto's wrapped figure. The last time he'd leave his house, I thought. Tears rose in my eyes.

For no reason that I could fathom, I started to cry. Seeking to comfort me, Uncle Barney put his arm around my shoulders.

"I have to take Cybil home. Luke will have my hide if she doesn't get medical attention right now."

That seemed to work. Sam gave permission for Uncle Barney to escort me home. He helped me into his car.

"I'm taking you to the emergency room," Barney said.

"No! Under no circumstances. Uncle Barney, I don't have the kind of concussion that needs hospitalization."

"Then I'll call Luke to come to your house to have a look at you. I don't want to hear any argument about that."

Whenever Uncle Barney used that tone of voice, it was useless to argue.

I must have dozed off, for the next thing I knew, he had pulled into my driveway. He led me onto the porch where he took the key from my purse and unlocked the door.

"Wait," I said, knowing I had left a ladder in the foyer. I switched on the light and headed straight for the sofa in the living room.

"You've made some progress," Barney said, looking at the walls from which I had stripped four layers of wallpaper. He used his cell phone to call my husband.

Luke arrived only a few minutes later. He must have been at the hospital which is only six blocks from my house.

To my shame, I used my injury to act more groggy than I really felt. It saved me a lot of questions I didn't want to field. Luke was great. He examined my lump, shone a light into my eyes, checked my reflexes and announced that I had only a minor concussion, which I already knew. I perked up some. Suddenly I wanted to talk.

"Who do you think killed Ariosto and why?" I asked Uncle Barney.

"That's hard to say. Any man who acquires that much wealth also acquires enemies."

"Business enemies?"

"Probably. Personal, too."

"Ex-wives," I murmured.

"There are times when a husband is justifiably tempted to do in not only an ex-wife, but a current wife as well," Luke muttered meaningfully. He unpinned the knot of hair that had saved me and placed an ice pack on my head. He raised my hand and put it on the bag to hold it in place.

His hands were gentle, I noticed, though his voice was not. I grabbed his hand and pressed it. "Thank you."

"You're welcome."

"Not too many people will benefit financially by Ariosto's death," I said. "Certainly not Pauline."

"How do you know that?" Luke asked.

Uncle Barney leaned forward, waiting to hear my answer as well.

"I saw the prenuptial agreement she signed."

"Where did you see that?" Barney asked.

"In his desk. Don't worry. I didn't leave any prints."

"Jesus," Luke said, staring at me as if I'd suddenly sprung horns.

"Good girl. What else did you see in the desk?" Barney asked, directing a brief, apologetic look at Luke.

"That's it, Barney. It's bad enough that you encourage Cybil in this investigating business, but now you've gone too far. She should have been resting an hour ago, not answering asinine questions and doing God knows what." Luke stood up, glowering at Barney.

"You're right. I'm sorry," Barney murmured, his voice meek. "I got carried away. I'll talk to you tomorrow, Cybil. Now you've got to rest."

I didn't want to rest. I wanted to talk. I was all wound up. Luke put an end to that speedily. Next thing I knew he'd shoved a pill into my mouth, forced water down my throat and had me lying in bed, wearing nothing but my underwear. The last thing I remember was him tucking the down comforter around me.

Time passed in a haze of headaches, interrupted sleep, and brief moments of wakefulness. During these moments I remember Luke checking my eyes, asking me how I felt and Maxi putting damp, cold cloths on my forehead with murmured, calming words.

When I finally woke up with a clear head, I could tell by the light in the room that it was late. I turned. My head still hurt and my mouth felt cottony but the nausea was gone. The glittery hands of the crystal clock on my nightstand told me it was eleven-fifteen; the date indicated that it was Monday.

Luke had kept me in bed around the clock, justifying his decision by his belief that rest is a great healer. Maybe so, but I had a lot to do. Just to be on the safe side, I called his name twice. When he didn't answer, I crawled out of bed. If I hurried I could be up, dressed and looking perfectly well by the time Maxi came to check on me.

I took a shower, turning the water to lukewarm because hot didn't feel good on my bump even though it wasn't as large as it had been the night before. Even so, I shampooed gently around it. By the time I had dried myself and put on a robe, I didn't feel that great anymore. I curled up on the love seat in my bedroom. The air will dry my hair, I thought, closing my eyes and drifting off.

The moment Maxi walked into the room I woke up.

"Stay put," she said. She sat down beside me, checked the back of my head and my eyes. Then she stroked my hair.

"How do you feel?" she asked.

"So-so," I answered truthfully.

"Luke said to keep checking your eyes. He also said to remember that the human skull is pretty sturdy, but not indestructible."

I nodded slightly.

"Can you eat something?"

The idea didn't appeal to me particularly.

"At least a bowl of soup," she cajoled. "I'll go and fix it."

It was about noon. I had hoped to make it to the office by one. Maybe if I ate something, I might feel stronger. Holding onto the walls, I inched my way into the kitchen.

"Cybil, I was going to bring the food into the bedroom," Maxi said, her tone chiding.

"You know I don't like to eat in bed. Food always gets on the sheets." Looking at the crackers she'd placed on a plate, I added, "I hate crumbs in my bed. They feel like pebbles."

I sat down at the kitchen table which faces the backyard. The brilliant red of a cardinal caught my eye. I looked for his mate. I spied her sitting on a branch of the lilac bush.

"Here it is. Chicken soup. Doesn't it smell good?"

"Yes, it does." I managed to eat most of it, pleasing Maxi tremendously. Afterwards I lay down on the sofa, planning to get up as soon as Maxi finished cleaning up. I didn't. When I awoke again it was four. I felt better. I telephoned the office, asking Lynn to let me speak to Uncle Barney.

"So, you got yourself in trouble again," she said in lieu of a greeting. "Barney has been on the phone with the cops most of the day. And we had to send someone to fetch your car from the Ariosto place and drive it to your house."

Her tone implied unmistakably that all that was my fault. Before I could stop myself, I murmured an apology, but at least she put me through to Uncle Barney without further comments.

After answering his inquiries about the state of my health, I asked, "What's new on the Ariosto case?"

"Officially the cause of death is a gunshot wound, as we suspected."

"Where was everybody last night?"

"Pauline and Harry were in Chicago. They returned late. The staff had the night off."

"All at the same time?"

"Yes, and it struck me as being strange, too," Barney admitted.

"Maybe Ariosto wanted everybody out of the house when he talked to me. But why would he?"

"I don't know unless it was something of a sensitive nature."

"Such as?"

Barney was silent for a beat. "It would have to be personal, I think."

"About his family?"

"Yes. Maybe about Pauline."

Now I was getting where he was heading and I didn't like it. "You don't suppose he wanted me to follow her?" To spy on lovers was a truly repugnant idea. Even if the lovers were carrying on an illicit relationship. My instant, relieved reaction was that I wouldn't have to do it now.

"It could have been about an employee in his house," Barney added.

"True." Brazier? Unthinkable. Mrs. Dougherty? Unlikely. The chauffeur? I hardly knew him. That automatically moved him to the top of the list. Pauline and the chauffeur? No. The idea was ridiculous. What's-his-name was hardly a handsome youth, as I remembered him. Pauline wouldn't risk her marriage and its bejeweled compensations lightly. She had struck me as a shrewd, levelheaded woman not given to rash impulses.

"You mentioned a prenuptial agreement last night. What else did you see?"

"As I said, Pauline doesn't profit by Ariosto's death.

Harry's got a hefty trust fund, so he gains nothing either."

"Not unless Ariosto disinherited him."

"He couldn't. Harry's adopted. In our state you can't disinherit adopted children," I reminded Barney.

"True. Who else was mentioned?"

"Ariosto's nephew, Ramsey, who gets a chunk of cash but also receives a block of stock for each year he works for Ariosto. I doubt that he would cut off that desirable perk."

"And his daughter?"

"Annette inherits big, but I can't see her shooting her own father. Besides, she married money." I thought for a moment. "You think the two murders are connected?"

"Crawford's and Ariosto's? They could be."

Uncle Barney was silent. I imagined him toying with his unlit pipe, the way he does when he's concentrating.

"I keep thinking about Crawford's blackmail. If only we knew what that four-digit number was. That has to mean something," I said.

"I agree. We'll keep working on it. In the meantime, you stay home and get well."

I remained seated by the telephone, thinking. After a while I removed the notebook from my bag and stared at the mysterious numbers: 5682. I added the digits. I subtracted them. I averaged them. I pretended they stood for letters of the alphabet which gave me EFHB. That didn't mean anything either. At least not to me.

Feeling physically better but thoroughly frustrated, I pulled on jeans and a sweater and drove to the nearest place with public lockers: the airport. Identifying myself to the head of security, I asked him about the locker numbers. My digits were out of his range. The same thing happened at the bus station and at the post office. I phoned my friend Joan. Even though she was a loan officer and didn't deal with safety deposit boxes, I thought she would know. She told me that the safety deposit boxes at her bank consisted of four digits and one letter of the alphabet.

Passing one of Westport's high schools, I made an illegal U-turn and went to consult with the assistant principal. Their lockers consisted of three digits only as did the lockers of the other four high schools in the city. I had ruled out all public places in less than two hours. With my strength flagging, I drove home for another nap on the sofa.

Maxi brought supper from the farm, claiming that there was nothing in my larder fit to cook. From a gourmet's point of view, she was probably right.

SEVEN

AT THE AGENCY Glenn and the other operatives were solicitous, Lynn distant. I tried to explain to her that if Ariosto had called Uncle Barney he would have gone to his house, too. Somewhat frustrated by her lack of response, I added that it wasn't my fault our client got himself killed. On a logical level Lynn had to agree with me, but she wasn't ready to let me off the hook yet.

At the staff meeting Barney wrote the puzzling number on the board, soliciting everyone's input.

"A numbered account in a Swiss bank," Glenn guessed.

"Too short," Barney said.

"Maybe the number of a receipt," I offered. "You know, like from a pawn shop. Maybe a place that repairs things."

"Could be," Barney agreed. "Glenn check it out."

That damned number had to be important. Why else hide it behind a picture?

Barney asked me to go to lunch with him which earned me a reproving look from Lynn. Since it was a working meal and I wasn't wasting my uncle's time with personal matters, I smiled blithely at her as we left.

We went to The Upstairs, an excellent restaurant catering to the business crowd. The place was jammed with dark-suited men. The occasional woman present was also conservatively attired, but not me. I was wearing a paisley-print challis dress in shades of blue and purple with a dirndl skirt and ruffles around the high neckline, topped with a short boiled-wool jacket the same color as the brightest violet in the dress. I felt like a cheerful peacock among a flock of somber crows.

After we ordered, a turkey club sandwich for Barney and a spinach salad for me, we concentrated on our problem.

"We've got two men killed with the same weapon, presumably by the same person. The connection between the victims is Tri State. One of them is involved in theft and blackmail," Barney summarized.

"The question is, whom is he blackmailing and why?" I added. "At first I thought Crawford might be blackmailing Ariosto who got fed up with the blackmail. They had a confrontation, and Crawford killed him, but his own murder rules that out."

"I agree. There's a third person involved with both of them."

"Our only clue to that person so far is that mysterious number and the money paid to Crawford. Then there's Wilma's accident," I answered.

Ignoring the reference to Wilma, Barney said, "Sam found out that Crawford opened a savings account in his name only in July. All the deposits to this secret account were made in cash."

"Blackmail money."

The waitress served our food. A few minutes later she brought me a folded piece of paper bearing a telephone message. "Annette Ariosto has called twice. She wants to see me urgently," I read aloud.

"Finish your salad first," Barney ordered. "She can wait a few minutes."

"I wonder what she wants," I murmured. Thoughtfully I speared a hot bacon dressing-covered piece of spinach. "I'm sure it's not a social call." We ate in silence, each of us wondering about Annette's call. Neither of us lingered over lunch or asked for dessert.

Back at my desk I dialed the number Annette had left. Like her father she came straight to the point when she answered.

"My attorney advised me to hire you, Cybil. Are you free to accept the assignment?"

"Well, yes, I think so, but why does he want you to hire me? Annette, your father was murdered. This is a police matter."

"They suspect me and Ramsey," she blurted out.

"You're… I was going to say kidding, but naturally you aren't. Are you sure about their suspicions?"

She laughed bitterly. "I only wish I weren't."

"Why do they suspect you?"

"Can you come to Dad's house? I don't want to talk about this over the phone. There are too many extensions in this house. Someone might eavesdrop."

In her suspicions, too, she was like her father. "Sure. When do you want me to come?"

"Right now."

"I'll be there in less than thirty minutes." Briskly I brushed my hair, applied lip gloss and ran to Uncle Barney's office, bypassing Lynn's desk. I heard her hissed exclamation but ignored it because I knew he was dying to know why Annette had called.

"Her attorney advised her to hire us. She's a suspect, she claims, and so is Ramsey."

"Interesting. What does she want you to do?"

"She wouldn't tell me over the phone. I'm on my way to the house now."

"Our legal system provides for the defense of all suspects, even the guilty ones."

I waited for Uncle Barney to continue. When he didn't, I said, "I'll tell her that if I find evidence pointing to her guilt and if the D.A. or the cops ask me about it, I'll have to reveal it."

"Yes. She needs to understand that."

"If after I talk to her I think she's guilty, I'll turn down the case. Is that acceptable to you?"

"Eminently."

"Good. I'll report to you after I get back." I was glad Uncle Barney isn't one of those unethical private investigators who give the profession a sleazy reputation.

ONCE AGAIN I PARKED THE Volvo in front of the mansion. Brazier let me in. He even remembered my name. As he escorted me to the morning room, I asked, "Brazier, what's your regular day off?"

"Sunday. You are wondering where I was Saturday night?"

"Well, yes. When I arrived none of the staff were here to let me in."

"Mr. Ariosto insisted we all take the evening off."

"Did he insist on that often?"

"No, ma'am. I recollect that happening maybe two or three times in the twenty years I worked for him."

"Did he say why he wanted you all to have the night off?"

"Mr. Ariosto wasn't in the habit of explaining his orders, Miss."

Of course, not. How dumb of me to think he might have had the courtesy to do so.

Annette stood by the bay window gazing out over the covered swimming pool. She was smoking one of her long, thin cigarettes. We greeted each other, but she didn't offer to shake hands. I didn't think she had changed a lot, but then her tall, angular, well-groomed, expensive look ages well. Compared to the hard glamor of Pauline who lounged in a love seat, Annette appeared understatedly elegant.

"You mind going for a walk?" Annette's question was a mere formality. Already she was reaching for a mink-lined car coat.

"No," I said, not having a choice. Not that I minded the walk.

Outside she set off quickly toward the stables, her shoulders hunched against the wind, her hands buried in her coat pockets. I pulled the hood of my coat over my head, waiting for her to speak.

"I can't believe any of this is happening," Annette burst out at last. "It's like a nightmare. First Dad gets himself killed. Then the cops are continuously around, snooping, prying, insinuating."

At the stables, Annette pulled the huge door open. Even though there hadn't been horses around for several years, the stables still smelled faintly horsy.

"I wish Dad hadn't sold the horses. Some of my happiest times were spent here."

Annette walked past the empty stalls, obviously re-membering their former occupants. I followed her, still waiting for her to tell me what she wanted me to do.

"But I guess without anybody riding them, there was no sense in keeping horses."

"Harry didn't like to ride?"

"No. As a boy he was afraid of them. Dad tried to cure him of his fear by putting him on Red Thunder, but Harry ended up bawling like a baby."

That must have been the equivalent of tossing someone who is afraid of water into the deep end of the pool. Head first. I remembered Red Thunder as a nasty-tempered, overfed, baleful-eyed beast whom I avoided at all cost. Whenever I saw Ariosto at the stables which, thank heaven, hadn't been often, he slyly offered to saddle up Red Thunder for me. His idea of a joke, I guess.

Stopping at the last stall, Annette lit another cigarette, sucking at it greedily. I stepped back to avoid being enveloped by smoke.

"You asked me why the cops suspect me. One reason is that I inherit most of Dad's property."

She said that defiantly as if expecting me to cluck disapprovingly or make some guilt-inducing comment. When I didn't, she continued.

"My God, as if I were poor!"

"There's more to it, isn't there, though?"

"How clever of you," she flung at me.

Her tone was mocking. Now I remembered that she'd been sarcastic and sharp-tongued in high school. I ig-nored her sarcasm. After all, she was paying for my services, she was still in shock from her father's murder, and she was scared. I remained silent, waiting for her to continue.

"All right, if you must know," she added, her voice and expression testy, "Dad and I had a row the last time I was here."

"A row?"

"Okay, a fight. A shouting match. But we always shouted at each other when we argued. Naturally the hired help overheard and told the cops. Couldn't wait to tell them I'm sure."

"What was the fight about?"

"Do you have to know that?"

"Since it seems to be the reason the police suspect you, yes."

"It was about money. See, as soon as I mention money you get that aha-she-did-it look in your face, too."

"You must admit it's an unfortunate coincidence."

"Tell me about it." She took another deep drag on her cigarette before she ground it out with her high-heeled boot. "Anyway, it wasn't as if I needed or wanted the money for myself. I had an opportunity to invest in a really promising venture and I didn't have enough cash of my own."

"And your father refused to lend you the money."

"Yeah. He claimed the investment was too risky. That's just because he was so conservative and he didn't know Sasha who is a great designer. His clothes are really fabulous. All he needs is a little capital to get his first collection out and he'll be off and running. It was practically a sure thing."

Personally I didn't think that anything in fashion was a sure thing. From what I'd heard, haute couture was almost as risky a venture as opening a new restaurant. "How much did you ask for?"

"Only five hundred thousand. It wasn't as if Dad couldn't afford that. But no, he didn't trust my judgment."

Because she was involved with this Sasha? Judging by her passionate tone and expression the designer must mean a lot to her.

"Anyway, Sasha managed to get by on the two hundred and fifty thousand I had, so it didn't matter in the end. I certainly couldn't kill Dad for a measly half a million."

I believed her. Anyone who could refer to half a million dollars as measly, didn't need the money desperately. Besides, I always thought she loved her father. "Is that all the police have on you?"

"Well, no."

I hadn't thought so. "What else is there?"

"I don't have an alibi for that evening."

"Since you live in Detroit, it would take longer than an evening to get to Westport and back."

"I was alone that evening and that night."

I kept looking at her, waiting for an explanation.

"The kids were staying with my husband's parents, and he was on a business trip. I gave my housekeeper the night off. I felt like being alone."

She was lying about that. Her body language betrayed her.

"You don't believe me, do you?"

"I believe you did not kill your father."

"But?"

"You're not telling the complete truth about your alibi."

"Thanks for believing me about Dad."

"Annette, I can't help you if you don't level with me."

"I'll tell you this much. I...I wasn't alone."

The implication was obvious. She'd been with a man. Sasha?

"I won't admit that to the cops. I just can't. You've got to help me."

"I'll try. You said the police suspect Ramsey, too. Do you know why?"

"Uh-huh. He had an argument with Dad at the office. Dad threatened to fire him, but he did that regularly, every two months or so for the past ten years. Ramsey didn't shoot Dad. Except for me, my cousin was one of the few people who really liked my father. Dad argued with everybody. That in itself didn't mean a thing."

"How did he get along with Harry?"

Annette shook her head. "Harry never learned that you had to stand up to Dad. If you didn't, he rode rough-shod over you. Grit was the only thing he respected."

"And Pauline?"

With a dismissing gesture, Annette snorted. "I gave that marriage another six months at most. She didn't care about Dad. Only about what she could get out of being Mrs. Terrance Arioso. Just like his third wife."

Annette's mother, the second Mrs. Arioso, had been killed by a fall from a horse. I don't remember her. In high school when I used to come to the house, the third Mrs. Arioso had been in residence. She had reminded me of a small, compact dynamo, always in motion.

"What was your stepmother's name?" I asked.

"Which one? Mrs. Committee?" Again Annette's laughter was bitter. "Lucinda. That woman had time for everything and everyone except the people in this house. Convenient for her to forget that charity starts at home. Harry could have used a mother a whole lot more than Westport needed a super committee woman."

"Where is she now?"

"I thought you knew. She died six years ago, so you can scratch her off your list of prime suspects. Besides, I can't imagine her capable of enough passion or anger or hate to kill anyone."

"Whom can you imagine as the murderer?"

"That's just it! I've thought and thought about that. There isn't anyone except…."

"Except?" I encouraged.

"Dunn, the chauffeur. I guess Dad finally had enough of his unreliability and fired him. He told Dunn he wouldn't work in this town again. He was lucky Dad didn't call the cops on him."

"Why should he have?"

"Dunn was a thief. Dad suspected him for quite a while but he could never catch him. He'd order two cases of Beefeater Gin but received only one. Guess who had the other case?"

"Who would know Dunn's last address in town?"

"Brazier keeps the staff records. Are you going to check on Dunn?"

"Yes. I'll start with him." Mostly because I didn't know where else to begin.

She walked back to the house with me and left me in

the servants' sitting room off the kitchen. Brazier donned wire-rimmed spectacles to look through a file.

"Here we are. Sidney Dunn. 503 South Fourth Street."

"What kind of car does he drive?"

"A Pontiac sedan. Navy blue."

"License plate?"

Brazier looked through the form. "Hmm. Sidney didn't fill that part in."

One of the bells mounted on a board on the wall rang. Brazier glanced at it. "Excuse me," he said, "Mrs. Ariosto needs something."

Though Brazier's face was schooled not to betray any emotion, his voice suggested ever so subtly that Pauline rang that bell quite often.

"Thank you, Brazier. I'll wait for Mrs. Dougherty."

He nodded and left. Moments later she walked in.

"There you are," Mrs. Dougherty said with a smile. She carried a tray. "I saw you walking with Miss Annette. You looked cold. I made us some tea like in the old days."

"Thank you." I gladly accepted the cup she handed me. The tea looked rich like polished mahogany, just the way I like it. "Mmm. Good enough to drink without anything in it," I said, declining her offer of sugar and lemon.

"I'll just take a bit of sugar."

The cooks's bit consisted of two heaping teaspoons. She settled her ample body into the armchair, prepared for a leisurely chat. I had always enjoyed our tea visits while waiting to tutor Annette who was never punctual.

"Miss Annette hire you?" she asked, stirring her tea.

"She did. Do you think Sidney Dunn is a thief?"

Mrs. Dougherty winced at the word. "That's a mighty hard label to pin on a man. I think maybe he wasn't as careful about what supplies belonged to the house, but in an establishment like ours, few employees are that scrupulous about whether they paid for the bar of soap they're using or not. Employers know and expect that. I don't know why the boss suddenly turned on Sidney. He wasn't any worse than anybody else."

"How long have you worked here?"

"I was hired by Annette's mother when she came here as a bride. Now there was a fine woman." Mrs. Dougherty sipped her tea, sunk in memories. Then she roused herself. "You want some cookies? They're store bought, I have to confess, but it doesn't pay to bake in a house where everybody watches calories. Except Harry, and he was never partial to sweets."

"Harry lives on campus, doesn't he?"

"Yes, but he's back here a lot."

Watching her closely, I tried to interpret the undertone in her voice. She really liked Harry. The shy little boy had probably spent his happiest hours in Mrs. Dougherty's kitchen. She would have been happy to have him come home. Yet I sensed…reservations? Disapproval? I couldn't pinpoint the emotion.

"How's Harry doing in school? He's a senior now, right? I saw him the other day for the first time since he's grown up. He's certainly a fine-looking young man," I said.

"Isn't he, though?" she remarked, pleased. Then she sighed. "He's a senior, and he was doing real good

till the spring semester. Then his grades took a dive."
Mrs. Dougherty shook her pink-beige, fluffy curls
sorrowfully.

"What happened?" I asked.

"Near as I can tell, Harry fell in love."

"That happens a lot in college. But grades don't usually drop through the floor."

"When you fall for the wrong woman, everything goes wrong."

Brazier returned, effectively stopping whatever else she might have said.

"Mrs. Ariosto wants a small steak and a salad for dinner, and Miss Annette wants a poached egg and steamed broccoli," he told Mrs. Dougherty.

"A real challenge to my cooking skills," she muttered.

Knowing that I couldn't learn anything else, I thanked her for the tea and left.

Brazier saw me to the door. "Miss Annette has hired me to look into what's happened. Tell me about Dunn's leaving," I requested. Brazier obviously didn't want to answer my question, but knowing that Annette had hired me, he did.

"Well, there was a case of gin still in the trunk of the limousine when Dunn went off duty."

"He could have left it there by mistake."

"Maybe." Brazier shrugged.

"So Dunn might have been fired even though he could have been innocent?"

"Innocent isn't a word I would associate with Sidney."

From Brazier's expression I knew he wouldn't say anything else except goodbye.

EIGHT

My next stop was Dunn's apartment. His was the up-stairs part of a small frame house that needed a coat of paint. The entrance to the upper half had been added to the side of the building, consisting of unprotected stairs leading to a small landing. I climbed the worn wooden steps and rang the doorbell. When no one answered, I pounded on the door. He apparently wasn't home.

Maybe the people downstairs knew something about his whereabouts. Mounted on a post of the sagging front porch was a wooden box with Dunn's name stenciled on it: a mailbox without a lid, overflowing with mail. Glancing around to see if anyone was watching, I flipped through the contents of the box, rationalizing that look-ing at the outside of envelopes wasn't tampering with the U.S. Postal Service.

Most of it was junk mail, with a few bills. A phone bill. Master Card. An envelope marked Airport Inn that looked like it contained a bill. Why would he get a state-ment from a sleazy motel on the outskirts of town? I tossed the mail back into the box and knocked on the front door.

An enormously obese woman opened the inner door, leaving the torn screen door latched. Even the short waddle to the front door had left her wheezing. "What do you want?" she asked, her tone less than cordial.

"Are you Sidney Dunn's landlady?"

She looked me over as if she wondered if I had a machine gun tucked under my coat. Finally she nodded.

"I'm looking for him."

"He ain't here."

"I discovered that already."

"What do you want with Sidney?"

"When will he be back?"

"Don't know. He didn't say."

"Do you know where he is?"

"Nope."

Her voice indicated that she wouldn't tell me if she knew. "How long has he been gone?"

She shrugged. "Three, four days." She looked at me through slitted eyes, partly the result of layers of fat, partly due to suspicion. "You that ex-wife of his who's been dogging him?"

Suddenly the landlady looked even heavier, like an outraged mother hen with her feathers ruffled.

"No. No. The Ariostos want me to talk to him. He used to work for them."

Her tiny eyes glared at me balefully. "Those bloodsuckers? A man works long hours for them with never a word of appreciation and at the first sign of trouble they give him the boot. The rich ain't fit to spit on."

Her version of Dunn's firing was different yet, but like Mrs. Dougherty, she seemed to like the chauffeur.

"I only want to ask Sidney a couple of questions," I said. "Here's my card. If he comes home, please have him call me."

Suspiciously she opened the screen door just wide enough to stick out her pudgy hand for my card.

She didn't say anything but closed the inner door decisively.

Now what, I wondered, standing on the sidewalk. When in doubt, pursue the routine set up for finding missing people. I pulled into the nearest fast food restaurant which happened to be a Burger King and bought a medium diet cola. The place was quiet in the interim between lunch and dinner.

I sat by the window, making notes on the Dunn investigation. It wasn't that I suspected Sidney Dunn of the murder of his boss. I still thought that someone connected with both Crawford and Ariosto had to be guilty of that. But as Ariosto's driver he could possess some vital piece of information.

The Airport Inn. What was Sidney's connection with this questionable establishment? Since I had no other leads, and since I was in the western part of the city, I decided to pay the inn a visit.

Up close the Airport Inn looked even more seedy than it had driving by at forty-five miles per hour. I parked in front of the office. One of the *f*s had been smashed in the neon sign that identified the motel's headquarters. Quickly I scanned the area, hoping no one I knew saw me enter this hot-sheet establishment.

There have been times when I've found the smell of popcorn enticing beyond resistance. This wasn't one of them. Possibly because the butter used in the machine in the corner had been rancid. Possibly because the popcorn maker hadn't been cleaned in recent history. I tried not to breathe. The office was empty, giving me a chance to look around.

Cluttered beyond belief, I almost stumbled over a low

magazine rack. When I noticed the type of literature it held, I gave it a wide berth. The T-shirts hanging on a rack bore slogans I hadn't known were legal to print. Hearing heavy footsteps approach, I faced the counter. That was a mistake. The array of "love aids" as they were advertised in the display case was astonishing: everything from erotic oil to reputed aphrodisiacs to crotchless underwear to black leather items I was too embarrassed to look at closely.

The man's jaded eyes assessed me briefly but thoroughly. Just to set the record straight, I showed him my business card.

"Security Agency, huh? Well, cookie, we don't need no security. There's two of us on duty at all times. We're security enough."

He flexed his arms, threatening to split the Budweiser University T-shirt's sleeves, to emphasize his claim. He probably pumped iron every other day, but that didn't mean he could fight. Still, he looked formidable enough physically that few would challenge him.

"We've got to have our own security, what with our rentals and all."

The rentals he referred to were shelved behind the desk. From what I could see they were all so-called adult videos.

"I'm looking for someone," I said.

"Ain't we all." He grinned briefly, humorlessly, displaying big, yellow teeth.

"His name's Sidney Dunn."

"Never heard of him."

"That's strange. You sent him a bill. Judging by your

establishment, I don't think you give credit unless you know someone."

"Still ain't heard of him."

"Maybe the other security person has."

"Nope. Him neither."

Not only was he lying, he wasn't even pretending not to. That made me angry. "He's wanted for questioning in connection with a murder case. If you'd rather talk to the cops, I can arrange that. Of course, they'll be interested in how many of your guests aren't old enough to buy cigarettes or your magazines or rent your adult videos. Not to mention how many of them have liquor and grass in their rooms." That got his attention.

"Hold on. Let's not be hasty. I know Sid."

"That's better. Where is he? Look, I only want to talk to him. I don't care who he's with."

"Room 21."

"Thank you." For a tough guy he caved in quickly, but I also had a hunch that he would phone Room 21 as soon as I was out of sight. I left my car parked where it was and sprinted around the corner to my destination. I knocked on the door. I thought I heard a flurry of motion behind it before a male voice answered.

"Who is it?"

I identified myself, telling him I wanted to talk to him about Ariosto.

Cautiously he opened the door. The first thing I noticed was that Sidney was alone. The door to the bathroom was closed though. The second thing I noticed was that the room had a definite lived in look: beer bottles and pop cans overflowed from the inadequate trash can, a greasy pizza carton leaned against the wall and the small table was littered with filled ashtrays and crumpled fast food sandwich bags. The room could stand a thorough airing.

I watched Sidney turn down the volume on the television set, silencing a rerun of a game show. Sidney wore brown slacks, a tailored yellow shirt open over a snow-white T-shirt and white tube socks.

Straightening, he faced me, hands on hips. His small, bright, clever eyes watched me with a predator's gleam. The eyes and the ginger hair gave him a slightly fox-like appearance, I thought.

"You heard that Terrance Ariosto was murdered?"

"Yeah. It was on TV. Couldn't have happened to a more deserving guy." Realizing how that sounded, he added, "Hey, that don't mean I killed him. I didn't like him, but I don't know anybody who did. He was a mean, spiteful s.o.b., if you'll pardon my French."

"He fired you, didn't he?"

"Yeah. After fourteen years of toting his skinny butt all over creation he fired me without a recommendation. It ain't easy at my age to get another job without references."

Could that have set him off to come back and blow a hole into Ariosto's chest? I doubted it, but still it was possible.

"Look, lady, I didn't kill him. Sure, I hated his guts. Who wouldn't?"

"Why did he fire you?"

"What did they tell you up at the house?"

"They said Ariosto caught you with a case of gin that belonged to him. Expensive gin."

"Oh, sure. I don't even like the stuff. I'm…"

Why did he look as though he realized he'd said something he shouldn't have, I wondered. "Did you take the gin?"

He lifted his shoulder in a gesture that could mean anything. That, coupled with his closed, obstinate expression, told me he wasn't going to elaborate.

"Where were you on the night of the murder?"

"I don't have to tell you."

"That's true, but you can tell Lieutenant Keller. I'm sure he's looking for you as is your ex-wife." At the mention of the ex, his ruddy complexion paled, it seemed to me.

"That's hitting below the belt."

"Where were you the night Ariosto was killed?"

Sidney sighed. "Right here."

"Can anybody corroborate that?"

"No."

The bathroom door opened a foot. "Sid, we'd better tell her before she sets your ex loose on us."

The female speaker remained behind the door.

"Would you please come out, Miss...?"

"Ms. Clark. Donna Clark," she said, pushing the door open all the way.

A woman in her forties, I judged, whose body was just beginning to thicken around the middle, but who was still attractive. Donna came and stood next to Sidney.

"Sid didn't kill nobody. He was right here with me. I'll swear to that on a stack of Bibles ten feet high."

I wondered what it was about Sidney that made women like him. Then he smiled at Donna, and I knew.

"How can you be sure he didn't sneak out?" I asked.

"The television said Ariosto was killed before midnight. Well, we'd rented a bunch of videos which we watched till two in the morning. You can ask the desk clerk. He writes down the time you rent them and when you return them," Donna said. Then she smiled, recalling something. "That was also the night the VCR broke down and the guy had to come fix it. That must have been around eight or so, wasn't it, hon?"

"Yeah, it was," Sidney agreed. "He saw the both of us right here."

I believed them. "Why did Ariosto fire you?" I persisted.

"Why is that important?" Sidney asked.

"You've been around enough to know why." From his expression I could tell he knew it established motive. I also thought he was casting around swiftly for an answer.

"Well, as they said, the gin. Ariosto didn't need a reason to get rid of somebody. He chose the gin. It was as good as anything."

Sidney looked relieved that he'd hit on a reason that sounded plausible. I knew he was lying.

"That's all I'm going to say about it."

His fox-like features, sharp and in control, told me that he meant that. I wouldn't get anything else out of him. I gave him my card in case he had a change of heart. On a hunch I asked, "Did either one of you know Wilma Johnson? She worked at Tri State."

Both said they didn't know her.

I thanked them for their time and left.

Sidney had slipped up. Instead of confirming without hesitation that the theft of the Beefeater was the reason he got fired, he had initially denied it. Moreover, his denial rang truth. I was certain Ariosto hadn't fired him for something that paltry. What had been the real reason and why hide it? What was he trying to gain? A guy like Sidney never did anything without an eye toward profit.

On the way back to the office, I stopped at a Mobil station. While the attendant filled my tank, I reported my conversation with Sidney to Uncle Barney.

"I'm certain he knows something that has bearing on the murder, but he isn't going to spill it. At least not yet."

"What do you want to do? Call in Sam?"

"Sidney isn't going to tell Sam either. I know as sure as I'm standing here, the guy's hoping to profit from what he knows."

"Blackmail?"

"Or extortion." I could never remember the legal distinction between the two.

"You want me to put a tail on him and see whom he contacts?"

"Yes, but not yet. I don't think he's quite ready to pounce on his victim. He's not keyed up enough for that step."

"Good. Right now all the men are out. What's your next move, Cybil?"

"Make an appointment to see Ramsey Ariosto."

"Keep me posted."

I called Ramsey's secretary who put me right through. He was tied up the rest of the afternoon and most of the next day but could meet me for breakfast.

BUSINESS REPLY MAIL
FIRST-CLASS MAIL   PERMIT NO. 717   BUFFALO, NY

POSTAGE WILL BE PAID BY ADDRESSEE

THE READER SERVICE
PO BOX 1867
BUFFALO NY 14240-9952

NO POSTAGE
NECESSARY
IF MAILED
IN THE
UNITED STATES

Send For
2 FREE BOOKS
Today!

I accept your offer!

Please send me two
free Mystery Library™
novels and two mystery
gifts (gifts worth about $10).
I understand that these books
are completely free—even
the shipping and handling will
be paid—and I am under no
obligation to purchase anything, ever,
as explained on the back of this card.

About how many NEW paperback fiction books have you purchased in the past 3 months?

❑ 0-2   ❑ 3-6   ❑ 7 or more
E9FL   E9FW   E9F9

414/424 WDL

Please Print

FIRST NAME

LAST NAME

ADDRESS

APT.#   CITY

STATE/PROV.   ZIP/POSTAL CODE

Visit us online at
www.ReaderService.com

WD-MYS-511 ▲ Detach card and mail today. No stamp needed. ▲

FOR OUR BREAKFAST MEETING I chose my good navy wool suit. To liven it up I selected a tailored shirt, slate-colored and slubbed with beige and navy stripes. I liked the shirt a lot but the silk-cotton combination fabric was a bear to iron.

The coffee shop of the downtown Holiday Inn was crowded, but Ramsey had reserved a booth where he was waiting for me, sipping coffee.

"Can we order right away?" he asked after shaking hands politely. "I have a meeting at nine-thirty."

"Sure. I only want coffee." Since I'd gotten up early, I'd already eaten a bowl of cereal with skim milk. I noticed that Ramsey studied me intently.

"You know, I remember you now. You knew Annette. Your name didn't ring a bell, but your face does. What I recall most vividly about you is your skin."

"My skin? How odd."

"Not really. The rest of us in high school bought benzoyl peroxide cream by the pound, but your skin was completely unblemished and clear. I envied you that flawless complexion. And you had long, long hair."

"Didn't we all?" I asked, smiling.

"Yeah." Ramsey smiled back, patting his thinning top.

"The reason I called you," I said after the waitress poured me a cup of coffee, "is because Annette hired me. She feels that you two are suspects in the murder of your uncle."

"I know. We discussed hiring you."

"Did you and your uncle have a fight?"

"Oh yeah. We had a humdinger of an argument Friday afternoon and no, I have no alibi for the time he was killed. The woman I was going to take to dinner Saturday night canceled. She'd come down with a bad cold. So, I spent the evening and the night alone in my apartment."

"Did anyone see you? Call you?"

"No."

"Did you order anything to be delivered? A pizza?"

He shook his head regretfully. "No, I popped a frozen pie in the oven. Believe me, if I'd known I'd need an alibi, I would have called Pizza Hut. As it was, I worked all evening on a report. Nobody even telephoned."

"What was the argument about between you and Mr. Ariosto?"

"Business. I wanted to change a procedure and he didn't. But it isn't…wasn't unusual for us to argue. Terrance had a confrontational personality. The only way for a man to keep from getting stomped into the ground was to yell back as loud as he yelled."

"You said for a man. What was the best way for women to get along with him?"

"Cater to him shamelessly. Flatter him. He was sharp enough to see through these tactics, of course, but he still enjoyed them."

"Is that what Pauline did?"

"Yes. At least at first. After she felt secure, she sloughed off but never enough to alienate Terrance. She's a clever and calculating woman where men are concerned."

"Annette thought the marriage was bound to fail. Do you agree?"

"Yeah. Terrance wasn't the long-term, faithful type.

He liked variety and change. But he was getting older which might have prolonged Pauline's tenure as his wife. Why are you asking about her?"

"If neither you nor Annette shot him, someone else did. I'm desperately looking for candidates. You care to nominate anyone?"

Ramsey wrinkled his forehead, his gray eyes thoughtful. At that moment I discerned a marked resemblance to his uncle.

"There is someone. Terrance and he have locked horns for years. Still…" Ramsey shook his head.

"Why now, right?"

He nodded.

"But something happened recently that could have heated up the conflict?" I guessed.

"Yup. You could say that. We were awarded a bid worth twenty-five million dollars in new construction."

"I didn't realized you were into building."

"Frontier Enterprises is an Ariosto subsidiary. One of our most profitable ventures."

I had seen many building sites marked by Frontier placards. "Whenever a big project is up for competitive bidding, somebody, several somebodies as a matter of fact, lose. They don't usually kill the winner. What happened?"

"Well, Alan Fettner, Terrance's arch rival, lost the bid to us by only a few thousand dollars. At the Rotary luncheon on Friday he and Terrance engaged in a shouting match which ended with them shoving each other until a couple of other Rotarians separated them."

I watched him carefully. I was certain he knew exactly what happened. "Okay. What happened? Why did they fight?"

"Accusations flew and one thing led to another."

"Ramsey, please don't make me drag this out of you. What you mean is that Fettner made accusations. About what?"

"Fixed bids."

"What made Fettner think that?"

Ramsey searched my eyes. I had the feeling he was weighing his words carefully.

"Fettner was paranoid. When he learned what our bid was, he hit the ceiling, telling everyone that Terrance had conspired to fix the bid. You see, the bid was only a little lower than his."

"How do you explain that?"

"We both figured the cost closely. We thought we could do it for what we entered. If you're going to fix a bid, it's less suspicious if you make the difference to the nearest bid bigger."

"He had no evidence? Just accused Frontier Enterprises of that?"

"Yes. Well, he hinted that the guy taking the bids was a friend of Terrance's who'd leaked the Fettner bid which was turned in ahead of ours."

"What was Ariosto's reaction?"

"First he said that if Fettner really believed that, he should bring charges against us. If not, he should shut up or we'd sue him for slander. That's when things really heated up and they got physical with each other."

"Do you know Fettner well?"

"Yes."

"Do you think he's capable of waiting for over twenty-four hours and then shooting your uncle?"

The waitress interrupted to serve breakfast, giving Ramsey a chance to think about his answer.

"I don't know. Fettner's got a temper, but I just don't know if he'd be capable of murder."

"How badly did losing this bid hurt him financially?"

"Nobody likes to lose a contract of that dimension. Still, I haven't heard any rumors that Fettner Enterprises is in trouble."

"How soon would you hear that sort of thing?"

"Pretty fast. At least rumors of trouble. Things like he was postdating checks to pay for supplies or taking out a loan, or being slow to meet his payroll. Those things leak quickly in a town our size."

"But you didn't hear anything like that?"

"No. Fettner did lose bids to us several times recently."

"Exactly how many and over what period of time?" I asked, pulling out a pad to make notes.

"Let me think. One in the spring and one last summer. And once before that. Maybe twenty months ago."

"That adds up to a lot of money."

"True. But we've lost bids, too. You figure for every three bids you make, you're doing great if you win one."

While Ramsey finished his eggs, I tried to decide what else to ask him. "Can you think of any other business competitors or of people who worked for your uncle who held a grudge against him?"

"Not the kind you murder for. Terrance wasn't liked

by people, but he paid well and that goes a long way to make up for bad manners and a hot temper."

"Even with you?"

He smiled at me. "Yes, even with me. Call it being perverse or something, but I liked the old pirate. We understood each other. Besides, he took a serious interest in me when my father died. He paid for me to get my MBA at Indiana University, taught me the business, and promoted me as I deserved it. He was also generous in his rewards. No, I had no reason to kill him."

"I know."

"Thank you, Cybil. I don't mean to look a gift horse in the mouth, but how do you know I didn't kill him?"

"You had no reason. Not a killing reason anyway. But most of all, you lost out financially with your uncle's death. I know about the shares you received for each year you worked for him."

"You're well informed."

"Do you know anyone in his personal life who would hate him enough to shoot him?" Again Ramsey chose his words with care.

"As I said, Terrance wasn't liked by many people. Not that he cared what people thought about him. I imagine it would have been easier to live with a hungry grizzly than him. But he was exceedingly generous and he could be charming when he set his mind to it."

He had to have been to accumulate four wives, not to mention a string of lady friends between marriages, I thought.

"What about Annette?" I asked.

"No way. She spent a lot of her life trying to win his approval. Or at least get his attention."

"How would he have felt if her marriage had broken up?"

"Are you speculating or do you know something?"

"Just answer my question, please."

"That would depend on the reason for the break up. If her husband had mistreated Annette, which I can't imagine, Terrance would have been the first to urge her to leave him. Any other reason...I don't know. Terrance was crazy about his grandchildren and proud of Annette's settled family life. I suspect in part because his own had been rather a mess. My guess is he would have been disappointed if her marriage had broken up."

I had been thinking of Sasha or whoever the man was she spent Saturday night with. Terrance would have disapproved of her infidelity, but that was no reason for her to shoot him. I was clutching at straws.

"Why are you asking me about Annette?"

I shrugged and changed the subject. "Have you been married?"

"Once. It didn't last. It was mostly my fault because I was too busy building a career to take the time to work on the relationship."

Ramsey was a nice guy, I thought. Not that nice guys don't occasionally kill someone. He could have gotten fed up with the constant arguments with Ariosto and his threats to fire him, brooded about it and...no, I couldn't buy that theory even as I formulated it.

"So, your prime candidate is Alan Fettner?" I asked.

He didn't look happy about that statement. "I'd hate to put it that strongly. Fettner's the only one who had a serious enough quarrel with my uncle recently. That's all I'm implying."

"Fair enough. Thanks for the coffee. May I call you if I have further questions?"

He said I could. He parted with a handshake in the parking lot.

At the agency I typed up a report on my meetings with Ramsey and Sidney. Then I reread everything in the Ariosto file, making notes of things to do. One of the items to pursue was the phone number listed among the travel brochures. Five minutes later I knew it wasn't a number used in the Westport area. Logic suggested that it had to be a number near Westport. Why would anyone call a travel agent halfway across the continent? What I had to do was take a map and draw ever widening circles around our town, prefix the various area codes to the number I had and place the calls. It sounded like a long, tedious job so I put it off till later.

The phone number reminded me of the mystery number I'd taken from behind Crawford's picture frame. Checking with Glenn, I learned that he'd struck out with all the possibilities we'd come up with. What could the blasted number be? More and more I leaned toward the notion that it was some kind of a code. If that was true, we'd probably never discover what it meant.

Discouraged, I looked at the next item on my list: the used glass on Ariosto's drink cart. If I took Sam to lunch would he tell me if they found prints on the glass? It was worth a try. He agreed pleasantly to meet me at the Casa Grande at noon. My treat.

NINE

SAM KELLER WAS IN THE BAR when I arrived at the Casa Grande. He finished his draft beer in one thirsty pull and joined me.

"Cousin, don't look so disapproving," he told me. "It's only on television that cops never drink while on duty. Besides, I don't consider one beer as drinking."

"I don't disapprove. Stop being so defensive."

Sam placed his hand against my back and nudged me in the direction of the dining room.

"I'm starved," he confessed. "The baby is teething and kept crying off and on all night. I overslept this morning and didn't get any breakfast."

"Not even a single donut?" I asked, knowing how addicted he is to sweet rolls.

"One donut doesn't count. A guy my size needs something more nourishing."

"How's Peggy?"

"Making noises about not waiting till the baby is two before she goes back to work. Claims her brain is turning into mush."

I smiled at the idea of Peggy's brain being anything but razor sharp. She's a first class accountant who does our taxes each spring.

"Do you need to look at the menu?" Sam asked as soon as the waitress appeared to pour water.

"No. We can order right away." For all his brave talk about drinking on duty, I noticed that he ordered coffee with his burrito.

"So, what is it that you want to know?"

I wasn't even tempted to pretend that this was anything but a business lunch. "Annette Ariosto Stevens hired me on advice from her attorney. They think that the police favor her or her cousin Ramsey as the murderer."

"Is that what they think?"

"How much truth is there to her suspicions?"

"Some. Neither has an alibi, and both gain financially." Sam raised his hand authoritatively to stop my rejoinder. "I know about the stock Ramsey gets each year. But he also gets a quarter of a million from the estate. That can buy a hell of a lot of stock."

"True, but I'm convinced that he didn't shoot Ariosto and neither did Ariosto's daughter. Have you found the murder weapon?"

"No. And not because we haven't tried."

"Any information about it?"

Sam told me about gauge and velocity and other technical things that didn't mean much to me.

"One thing's for sure. The shotgun as a choice of weapon indicates premeditation. Nobody walks around with a loaded shotgun. The killer went to Ariosto's loaded for bear."

I thought about that for a while. "There was no sign of forced entry, was there?"

"There wasn't."

"So, Ariosto must have let his killer in."

"Or he had a key."

Ignoring the implications of that, I said, "I can't picture Ariosto admitting the murderer into the house if he was carrying a shotgun. The man wasn't a fool."

"It was raining, remember? The murderer could have had the weapon hidden under his raincoat. Or he could have used a sawed-off shotgun which can be carried under a jacket."

"Then it could have been someone outside the family," I insisted.

"Anything's possible," Sam admitted but seemed skeptical.

"Have you talked to the ex-chauffeur?"

Sam raised a pale golden eyebrow. "Should I have? Why?"

I could have bitten off my tongue for mentioning it, but I'd been sure Sam knew about it. "Ariosto fired him on Friday."

"How did you find out about that?"

"From the staff." I wasn't about to mention names.

Scowling, Sam took out a small notebook. "Wait till I talk to them again," he muttered.

"You can't blame them for not volunteering information to the police. Most of the time you guys aren't exactly diplomatic or overly friendly."

"Name of the chauffeur," he demanded.

I told him, but revealed nothing else about Sidney. The arrival of our food calmed Sam. Like most of the Keller men, he loves to eat. While he attacked the huge, cheese-covered burrito as though a seven-year famine lurked outside the door, I picked at my taco salad.

"How about a little give and take," I suggested when

he paused for breath. "What about the used glass on the drink tray in the study?"

"No prints on it. The residue in it was gin and tonic."

"It couldn't have been Ariosto's drink since that was on his desk with some amber liquid in it."

"Scotch."

"He must have offered the murderer a drink."

"Or the killer poured himself a gin and tonic afterwards."

I shuddered at the idea of anyone cold enough to fix a drink while the body was lying a few feet away, bleeding and still warm. "Any prints on the decanters?"

Sam nodded. "Ariosto's and the butler's."

Summing up, I said, "What we have here is a murderer who drinks gin and tonic. The glass had to be his. Nobody else would wipe off their prints. It's someone Ariosto knew, and it's a man."

"Why a man?"

"The shotgun. It's such a…my feminist friends will disown me for saying this, but it's such a masculine weapon. Big. Unwieldy. Loud. It's a gut reaction, nothing more," I admitted.

"I have the same gut reaction. Physically a shotgun is unwieldy, especially if it has to be hidden against the body of the person carrying it."

"Did you find anything else in the study? Something that shouldn't have been there?"

"You know I can't reveal anything specific." Pushing his empty plate away, Sam lit a cigarette.

"But you can answer with a yes or a no, right?"

"Maybe. Depends on the question."

"Did you find any fingerprints you can't account for?"

"No."

"Anything under Ariosto's fingernails?"

"No. He was shot at close range but the murderer wasn't close enough for Ariosto to grab him while falling."

"I picture the killer standing by the decanter, his back toward Ariosto. He takes the shotgun out from under his raincoat, turns and shoots."

Sam nodded. "He probably took a couple of steps toward Ariosto before he let him have it."

"Can you put a face on the murderer?"

"No. But that's off the record. Can you?"

"No. I wish I could."

"Is that enough give or take?"

"Yes, thank you. Unless you want to volunteer something?"

Sam ignored that. Pushing back the sleeve of his navy blazer, he glanced at his watch. "Cybil, I hate to eat and run, but I've got to be at the courthouse in thirty minutes."

"That's okay. Go ahead. I'll have another cup of coffee."

"Thanks for lunch. Be careful, Cybil. This is murder. That raises the ante considerably."

"I'm always careful."

I asked the waitress for a refill and the check. Somehow I had to get in to see Fettner. I was fairly sure he wouldn't agree to see me if I telephoned for an appointment. Ramsey had given me a good description of the man as well as his business and home address.

Deciding to try a long shot, I drove to his business. The offices took up the entire, flat-roofed building. I parked so that I could see the reserved executive parking spaces. Fortunately, they all seemed to be still out to lunch or away on a construction site. I took the copy of my latest hatha yoga magazine and flipped through it. As much as I wanted to read it cover to cover, I didn't dare, knowing how caught up I get. If it's something interesting, the whole world could pass by and I wouldn't notice.

A white BMW arrived. The driver parked in a reserved spot. Unfortunately, of the four men who got out none was Fettner. They were too short and not nattily enough dressed to fit his description. Slowly all the spaces filled but one. Fettner didn't arrive at the office until three o'clock. By then I had shifted my body into every position permitted by the car seat, had balanced my checkbook, had finished the crossword puzzle in the *Chicago Tribune,* and had studied the wallpaper swatches long enough to have picked the one I wanted for the dining room. I wrote down Fettner's license plate number as Uncle Barney insists we do just in case we'll need it.

Since the only clue I could work on in the office consisted of tracing the phone number, I lingered in the parking lot, speculating that since Fettner, who'd arrived carrying a hard hat, might have worked through lunch and might take off early. He did, a few minutes later, having exchanged his dark gray suit for tailored cords, a sweater whose V-neck was filled by an ascot tie and a wind breaker with a famous logo on the pocket. I followed his black Lincoln at a discreet distance.

Fifteen minutes later we arrived at the Riverview Country Club. Fettner took a golf bag from his trunk, checked his watch, and sauntered inside. From his pace I figured he was early and this was as good a time as any to talk to him. Being a Riverview member, I strolled right in.

My quarry was at the bar, ordering a drink. When I sat down on the stool beside him, he looked at me, surprised. His surprise changed to pleasure. Seeing his dove-gray sweater up close, I knew it was cashmere.

"Can I buy you a drink?" he asked in a low, coaxing voice when the bartender placed a Bloody Mary in front of him.

"Thank you. I'll have one of those," I said, indicating the tomato juice concoction, "but without the vodka."

"A virgin one, huh?" he asked, amused.

Since I wanted information from him, I decided to be friendly. I smiled. We introduced ourselves.

"You're a builder, aren't you?" I asked, all but batting my eyelashes at him.

"Why, yes," he said, pleased. "How did you know that?"

"Don't be so modest. Your company's signs are all over the county. Yours and Frontier's are practically on every construction site in the city. Is Frontier your biggest competitor?"

"It was. I don't know what'll happen in the future."

Pretending to remember, I said, "That's right. The owner of Frontier was shot last Saturday night. Ariosto was his name, wasn't it?"

"Yes, God rest his soul."

His pious sentiment struck a wrong note.

"You knew him?"

"Sure. For years."

"Isn't that something, him getting shot like that?"

"Probably some hopped up drug addict looking for something to steal." He downed a third of the good-sized Bloody Mary.

"But the paper said robbery wasn't a motive. It could have been an angry competitor."

That startled him. "That's a hell of an idea. If every angry businessman killed his competitor that would put an end fast to free enterprise as we know it." Staring at me hard, Fettner added, "You didn't just drop in for a friendly drink, did you?"

"No. I followed you."

"Who are you?" His eyes narrowed suspiciously.

I told him.

Considerably less friendly than before, he asked, "What do you want?"

"I understand you leveled serious accusations against Ariosto before the two of you indulged in a shoving match at last Friday's Rotary luncheon."

"So what? That doesn't mean I shot him the next day."

"No, but I would like to make certain you have an alibi. I have to rule out suspects or add them to my list. Where were you Saturday evening between seven and eight?"

"I don't have to tell you that."

"True. But then the police will be here to ask you that before you can tee off." That wiped the belligerent expression off his face.

"I have nothing to hide from anybody except my wife."

"I'm discreet. It's a prerequisite of my job."

"I won't deny that I was ticked off at Ariosto. But that wasn't so much because he underbid me by a few lousy bucks, but because he gloated over it. He had to rub my nose in it. Ariosto may have been a good businessman and he may have pulled himself up by his bootstraps financially, but socially he never left the gutter he grew up in. He was boorish, ill-mannered, crude and profane." Picking up the small cocktail napkin, Fettner patted his mouth with a precise, fastidious gesture.

I didn't think there were more than two or three people who would disagree with that assessment of Ariosto.

"That still doesn't tell me where you were Saturday evening when he was killed."

"I was right here. Not in the bar but in one of the private rooms."

That surprised me. Fettner seemed too refined to partake of the profanity-laced, smoke-filled, high-stakes poker games that take place in the private rooms on weekends.

"My wife is violently opposed to any kind of gambling, but I enjoy a good game of baccarat once in a while."

Baccarat. Of course. How could I have ever suspected him of anything as vulgar as five-card stud?

"Can anyone verify that?"

"Baccarat's scarcely a game you play by yourself," he informed me, just a trifle condescendingly. Calling to the bartender, Fettner asked, "Is Lou here yet?"

"No. He won't be in till five."

"Lou was the dealer that night."

Several men entered the bar. Fettner motioned to one of them to join us. "Kirby, where did you see me Saturday night?"

"Right here," Kirby answered, looking at me with undisguised curiosity.

"Here in the bar?" I asked.

"Yeah, and elsewhere," Kirby said, trying to guess how much he should reveal.

"Kirby, tell her exactly where we were between seven and eleven."

"In room 117, playing cards."

"Thanks, Kirby."

Dismissed by Fettner, Kirby joined his friends.

"This better not get back to my wife."

"It won't. Thanks for your time." Placing a five dollar bill on the bar for the jazzed up tomato juice, I left.

AT THE OFFICE I TRIED to trace the phone number by dialing various area codes first. After thirty minutes I decided there had to be a more logical way to proceed. If for some reason I didn't want to use a local travel agency, where would I go? To a large city. Using this theory I dialed the area code for Indianapolis and the number. A recorded male voice informed me that I had reached the True Church of the Light whose shepherd was out at the moment. The voice blessed me mechanically before inviting me to leave a message.

In Chicago, which I realized in retrospect was the city I should have called first, I reached the A-Z Travel Agency. Pretending to double check arrangements for the Ariostos, I found out that Mr. and Mrs. Ariosto had reservations on the S.S. Oslo for a Caribbean cruise starting December 27th. Interesting, I thought, but didn't see how that helped me clear Annette of suspicion. As a matter of fact, at that moment I had absolutely no idea what to do next to clear her.

Since I always think better when I walk, I grabbed my coat and set out for a prowl through the historic section of the city that adjoins the downtown area. The cobblestone streets, gaslights and big, old houses appeal to me. I had wanted to buy a house here but Luke wouldn't hear of it. These houses, he claimed, were impossible to heat in our near-arctic winters. Not only that, they needed continuous repair. So, when we separated, I bought an old house in the area.

I wanted a house that was as different from the suburban home I'd shared with my little boy as I could find. The familiar ache settled on my chest, making breathing difficult. Maxi assures me that one day the memory will hurt less, but I wonder. I walked fast, as if my pace could outrun the pain. It couldn't, of course. After a while I turned around and went back to the office.

"Where have you been?" Lynn demanded, pouncing on me the moment I walked back into the agency.

I glanced at my watch. "I've only been gone twenty-five minutes."

"It doesn't look good for the agency if the police are always camping on our doorstep."

I looked around pointedly. "The police?"

"One Sergeant Griffin. I put him in the small conference room. He says he won't leave without you. What have you done now?"

She made it sound as if I were a habitual offender. "What does he say I've done?"

"He doesn't. 'It's routine'," she mimicked.

Ah. Lynn was as upset by the inspector's refusal to confide in her as she was by his presence. She loves being privy to all that's going on.

"Are you sure you don't know what he wants?"

"Would I lie to you?" I gazed at her as guilelessly as I could manage.

She looked at me, uncertain whether I was serious or facetious. "I guess I'd better go and face the music."

As I entered the conference room, a series of sneezes greeted me. "Gesundheit."

Sergeant Griffin's face appeared from behind a large crumpled handkerchief. "Thank you." Rising from the straight-backed chair he'd been sitting on, he said, "Mrs. Quindt, Lieutenant Keller wants to see you."

"That's what Lynn told me. When?"

"Now." His cocker spaniel eyes looked apologetic.

"This very minute?"

"Yes, ma'am. I'm not to return to the station without you."

Sergeant Griffin's long, perpetually melancholy face didn't look too happy at the possibility of having to drag me against my will to the police station. "Why does the lieutenant want to see me?"

"It's routine."

"That's such a convenient phrase. Covers everything, doesn't it?" I smiled at him, adding to his discomfort.

Marching past Lynn with my police escort, I said, "You will inform Uncle Barney of my trip to the police station when he gets back, okay? And get the bail money ready, just in case." I saw an alarmed expression settle on her face.

The sergeant escorted me to an unmarked sedan.

"Sergeant, that can't be a cold," I said after he had sneezed his way to the driver's side of the car. "What are you allergic to?"

He made a dismissing gesture with his hand. "What aren't I allergic to, that's the question. My doctor says that in twenty years of practicing medicine he hasn't seen a case worse than mine," Griffin said, clearly proud of that distinction.

It always amazes me that people love the superlative even if it pertains to something bad. "What are you doing for it?"

"Everything." During the short trip to the station, he recited the highlights of his complicated health regimen. Then he escorted me to Sam's cubicle in the upstairs squad room.

"Mrs. Quindt," he announced with a gravity that would have done an imperial herald proud.

"Thank you, Griffin." Sam fixed me with cool, blue eyes. "Have a seat, Cybil."

I sat. When the sergeant positioned himself behind me, notebook in hand, I knew this was an official occasion.

"When was the last time you saw Sidney Dunn?" Sam asked.

"Day before yesterday."

"Where did you see him?"

"At the Airport Inn." That rated a surprised stare.

"I'll probably regret asking, but how did you locate him there?"

"Brilliant deductive reasoning." Sam was about to snap at me for that but controlled himself. "Are you looking for him?"

"Not anymore."

I didn't like the sound of that. "You found him?"

"Yes."

Getting answers from Sam could be like quizzing a brick wall. Sam was in one of his famous stubborn Keller moods. I tried a different approach. "Since you've found Sidney, why do you want to talk with me? He can tell you anything you want to know."

"I wish that were true," Sam mumbled.

"Sam, don't be cryptic. It's not your style. What's going on? Either tell me or charge me with something or I'm leaving."

"What did you and Sidney talk about at the Airport Inn? Does Luke know you went to that sleazy place?"

"What my husband knows or doesn't know is beside the point!"

"Temper, temper, Cybil. I repeat what did you and Sidney talk about?"

I took two deep, calming breaths before I answered. "We discussed the reasons for him getting fired."

"Which were?"

"I don't know. Sidney implied it was over the theft of a case of gin, but he wasn't telling the truth. Or at least not all of it."

Sam sat, waiting for me to explain further. "I thought he knew something about Ariosto's murder that he wasn't saying. I had a hunch he might try to raise money with that knowledge."

"Blackmail?"

"That's how I read the situation. Sam, what happened?"

"Dunn's dead. Shot like Ariosto and Crawford."

"Oh, my God."

"A glass of water, sergeant," Sam yelled.

"I'm okay," I managed to say. "I should have asked Uncle Barney to put him under surveillance. If I had, Sidney Dunn might be alive today."

"Maybe and maybe not. Even if we'd pulled him in for questioning, there's no guarantee that he'd have come clean. He probably would have attempted the blackmail anyway and wound up just as dead. Don't blame yourself."

"Drink this," the sergeant said, pressing a paper cup into my hands. Dutifully I sipped some.

"If you feel faint, put your head down between your knees," the sergeant advised.

"I'm not going to faint. I never faint. Sam, where did you find Sidney's body?"

"In his apartment."

"Did his landlady call you?"

"Yeah. She was coming home from the grocery store when she saw the upstairs lights on. She hadn't seen him for several days so she went up."

"Have you notified his girlfriend?"

"Donna Clark? Yes."

"Poor woman."

"How do you know her?"

"From the motel. She was there."

"You do get around. Any idea what Sidney held back?"

I shook my head. "He drove Ariosto as well as other

members of the household. Obviously he saw or heard something that pointed to the murderer. Or to someone else who could be embarrassed if that piece of information came out. Unlike Brazier and Mrs. Dougherty, Sidney didn't feel as loyal as they did."

"Anything else you have forgotten to mention? Any little old thing?"

Usually I'm impervious to Sam's heavy-handed sarcasm, but I was feeling burdened with guilt about Sidney, so I told him about my conversation with Alan Fettner. I couldn't handle another murder that I might have prevented if I'd done something.

"I'm going to have another talk with everybody connected with this case." Anger threaded Sam's voice.

"Try the polite approach. It gets more answers than your abrasive manner," I advised.

"Thank you, Miss Manners. You may go."

He didn't have to give me permission twice. I practically shot out of my chair. At the door I paused. "I remember something else," I said. "Sidney was hiding out from his ex-wife."

"Thank you for sharing this. Is there anything else that conveniently slipped your mind?"

"No."

"Cybil, the count's up to three murders. I hope you're telling me all you know."

I didn't care for the threat in Sam's voice but I managed to answer calmly. "I am. Honestly. But the count's up to four. Don't forget Wilma." Sam waved his hand dismissively. "Can I have Donna's address? I'd like to send her a condolence note. She was in love with Sidney."

Sam hesitated.

"Oh, for heaven's sake! The woman must be devastated. I only want to do the decent thing."

Grudgingly he supplied it with the caution, "But if she lets anything slip that seems pertinent, I expect you to pass it on. Promise, Cybil."

"I promise."

I walked back to the agency. Since Uncle Barney wasn't back yet, I drove home. Too restless and agitated to think clearly and productively, I decided to join my hatha yoga group. That decision made, I flung off my suit, pulled on silver-gray tights, a mauve leotard, sneakers and jeans and took off again.

Two hours later I emerged feeling tranquil and at one with the universe. The harmonious mood stayed with me while I stir-fried vegetables and tofu for my dinner. Hatha yoga classes always inspire me to embrace an innocent vegetarian diet.

The phone rang. A woman's voice spoke to me, but it was difficult to understand the words because she was sobbing.

TEN

"DONNA?" I ASKED, guessing her identity.

"I'm sorry. I thought I was done crying for a while." She broke off, sobbing again.

"That's okay." Donna's raw pain tore at me.

"Have you heard about Sidney?"

"Yes, and I'm sorry. Can I do anything for you?"

"That's why I called. Sidney left an envelope I'm supposed to give to you."

For an instant I was speechless with surprise. "Donna, do you know what's in the envelope?"

"No. It's sealed. Sidney said to call you right away if…if anything happened to him."

"How awful for you. Do you have someone who can stay with you?"

"My sister is on her way."

"Do you have a doctor?"

"No."

"I'll be over as fast as I can." I hung up. Then I called Luke to ask if there was anything I could give Donna to calm her down.

"I can't prescribe anything for her without having examined her. Give her chamomile tea with honey. It has a mild sedative effect. Offer her sympathy. Listen to her. You're good at that."

"Luke, if she's completely falling apart, may I call you again?"

He sighed. "Yes. Even after seven years of marriage I have a hard time resisting your pleas. Maybe because you only plead for others and never for yourself."

"Thank you, Luke."

DONNA LIVED IN THE southern part of the city. I drove around for fifteen frustrating minutes looking for her street. This was the oldest subdivision in the city where the only logic visible in laying out the streets was the use of Indian tribes in naming them. Kickapoo was a one-block street between Apache and Huron. Indians of the Great Plains, the New England woodlands and the Southwest were placed cheek-by-jowl, so not even the names adhered to any kind of order. Disgusted by the unnecessary delay, I muttered a few uncomplimentary things about city planners.

The house was a tiny square box, distinguished from its neighbors by the flower box under the picture window which was filled with plastic pink geraniums. Donna opened the door. Her eyes were nearly swollen shut from the tears which were still pouring down her face. I couldn't help but hug her. Feeling the agony of her loss, the memory of mine threatened to break through. I fought my tears hard.

After a few seconds, Donna gained control over her weeping. With a soggy tissue pressed against her face, she asked me to come in.

"How soon do you expect your sister?" I asked.

"Any time now. She had to get the kids ready to bring them along. I guess they'll all spend the night."

"That's good. You shouldn't be alone."

Donna nodded. Apparently remembering why I was there, she picked up an envelope from the coffee table.

"Sidney gave me this right after you spoke to us on Tuesday."

"Thank you." Eagerly I ripped it open. The business-sized envelope contained a key with a plastic tag attached to it. The lettering on the tag, which had been originally golden, was mostly rubbed off. I took the key to the lamp on the end table. Even though the bulb wasn't overly bright, I managed to decipher the printing. "The Dolphin #18," I read aloud. "Does that mean anything to you?"

Donna shook her head. "When I went to Florida, we stayed in a motel by that name but that was four years before I met Sidney. There couldn't be a connection."

"I agree. What exactly did Sidney say when he gave you the envelope? Think, Donna. It's important."

"He said, 'Give this to Mrs. Quindt if anything happen to me.' I asked him what he thought might happen to him. He laughed and hugged me but told me nothing. Just gave me a flip answer like in case his car went down into the river or something like that, I should call you. I begged him to stop what he was doing but he wouldn't. He said we deserved something, that he was tired of other people having everything."

"Do you know what he was up to?"

"No. He just said that soon we'd be living on easy street. No more kowtowing to rich people. He knew something that was worth a lot of money. I told him

I didn't want the money if he could get hurt, but he wouldn't listen."

"Did Sidney know a lot of rich people beside the Ariosto family?"

"I don't think so."

Just as I suspected. Sidney had something on one of the family members.

"Mrs. Quindt, all I ever wanted was Sidney. Maybe he didn't look like much to you, but he was good to me. He never hit me. He never even yelled or lost his temper. And he didn't get falling down drunk or do drugs. He was kind and gentle and...." Donna started to cry again.

"When did he leave today?"

"At six when I went to work. He took me. I do the breakfast shift at the Pancake Shoppe. I didn't see him again. The cops arrived right after I got home. I still can't believe Sidney isn't going to walk through that door."

She sobbed harder now. I sat on the couch beside her. Placing my arm around her shoulder I murmured comforting things. Eventually she calmed down enough for me to ask her more questions.

"Did he talk about Mr. Ariosto's murder?"

"We heard it on the Saturday evening news. Sunday morning Sidney got up early to buy the newspaper. He sort of chuckled after he'd read the article about the murder. He said something like 'for two cents I'd call the cops and tell 'em what I know.' Then he got that funny look on his face. He winked at me and said, 'I know how we'll come into a lot of easy money, babe.

No more driving for me, and no more hash slinging for you.' Does that help?"

"Some. He never said anything specific? Like from whom he was going to get this money?"

"No." Donna shook her head.

"Were you together the whole time since Saturday?"

"Yeah. Except when I was working. I had Tuesday off. Sidney didn't want to stay at his place because his ex-wife was bugging him about back alimony and my daughter was home that day. That's why we were at the motel," she explained.

"When you two were here, did he ever go out alone?"

"Yes. On Monday."

"Did he say where he was going?"

"No. Just said to wish him luck." Donna thought for a moment. "Wait. After he'd gone I went into the kitchen to start dinner and that's when I put the stuff away he'd left on the kitchen table. He'd been looking at a map of the university. I couldn't figure out why."

"A map of the buildings on campus?"

Donna nodded.

Crawford had driven to campus with me tailing him to the Alpha House complex. Sidney, contemplating blackmail, studied a map of the university. This was too odd to be a coincidence.

The doorbell rang, followed by a female voice calling Donna.

"That's my sister."

Donna opened the door and threw herself at a

younger woman loaded down with blankets, pillows and a teddy bear.

"It's going to be okay, sis," the newcomer said. "I'm here. Come on in, kids, and close the door," she yelled behind her.

I tried not to look at the children, but, of course, I did. One appeared to be six. The other, too bundled up to give a clue to its sex, was younger. Perhaps four, the age my Ryan would be had he lived. One of my secret fears is that some day a mother is going to light into me, suspecting me of God knows what because I look at her child with hungry eyes. Switching my gaze to the women, I saw that Donna's sister was the take-charge type. Relieved, I bid the women goodbye and left.

I PHONED UNCLE BARNEY who asked me to report verbatim which I did, having a fairly good memory. He does that when he wants to get the underlying nuances of an interview.

"I'm fairly certain Sam doesn't suspect me of the Dunn killing," I concluded. "Sorry I didn't call sooner, but Donna's really broken up. From what she says, she tried to stop Sidney from going after the easy money, but he wouldn't listen. If only I had asked you to put him under surveillance he might still be alive."

"I doubt that. Cybil, if he was set on blackmail he would have proceeded with it no matter what, and that's a dangerous crime. If you want to keep on doing this kind of work and not develop ulcers, you'll have to stop taking on the guilt of the world."

"I know."

"Tell me what Donna had to say."

"All she knows is that Sidney studied a map of the campus and left an envelope for me in case something happened to him. The envelope contained a key attached to a plastic tag engraved with The Dolphin #18."

"What does the key look like?"

"It reminds me of the kind motels and hotels used to have."

"What are you planning to do with it?"

"First thing in the morning I'm going to the main branch of the public library and start checking their telephone directories for hotels and motels. I'll start with the towns closest to Westport and work out from there. There can't be that many places in the Midwest named The Dolphin."

"Let me know what you find out."

"I will," I promised before I hung up.

I took a shower. Wrapped in a pink fleece robe I looked through the television offerings. An old movie with Melina Mercouri caught my eye. This reminded me of the first time I saw Luke. It was at a campus film festival. I think I fell in love with him when we discussed one of those heavily symbolic Ingmar Bergman films over coffee in the student union. Sometimes that seems a lifetime ago.

While I was waiting for the movie to start, I wondered if I really would be satisfied with merely clearing Annette. Deep down I wanted the murderer caught, justice done, and order restored. And I had to admit to myself that I would be happy if I could help bring about these things.

THE WESTPORT PUBLIC LIBRARY had celebrated its hundredth year and had outgrown the present facility some time ago. The out-of-town telephone directories stood tightly wedged behind the computerized card catalogue. I worked with them there, seated in a comfortable chair, until the smell of unwashed bodies and dirty clothes drove me to a far corner table. With cold weather settling in, the library became a favorite place of the homeless.

After checking all the towns within a hundred-mile radius, I found one motel named The Dolphin. Quite logically it was located near Lake Michigan.

My next step was to drive to The Dolphin and take a look at it. Since it was a sunny fall day, I decided to drive north before turning west on Michigan State Road 12. It's a lovely drive. My only regret was that the trees had already lost their colorful fall foliage.

After expecting the place to be more on the order of the Airport Inn, The Dolphin was a pleasant surprise. The swing set in the play area indicated that this was a family-oriented establishment, so what connection could it have with murder?

Before I did anything else I had to find out if the key fit the lock to Room 18. The parking space in front of that room was empty. Gambling that the occupant had left by now, I walked to the door, knocked and announced, "Maid service." When no one answered, I tried the key. It unlocked the door smoothly, silently.

The room had either been made up already or it hadn't been rented the night before. Still, I decided to check to see if anything had been left behind. The wastepaper basket in the bathroom was empty, as were the dresser drawers and the closet. I closed the door and returned to my car where I sat for a while trying to guess the significance of Sidney's clue. Since I couldn't solve the puzzle, I returned to the agency.

Uncle Barney was having lunch with a client. That gave me time to think some more about the key. Obviously Sidney had believed that I would be able to come up with the right solution or he wouldn't have left it for me. The only thing vaguely useful that popped into my mind was to stake out Room 18 and see what happened.

Surprisingly, Uncle Barney agreed with my plan when I broached it. He assigned me the eight to midnight watch. That way I could attend Terrance Ariosto's funeral which was scheduled for two o'clock that afternoon. I came close to pleading with him to send someone else, but managed to restrain myself. He obviously thought I could handle going to the funeral. I couldn't disappoint him.

Since wearing slacks to such a solemn event seemed tacky, I hurried home to change into a full-skirted, loden green wool suit with a large matching fringed shawl and brown dress boots. My attendance served a dual purpose: I represented the agency in paying our respects, and more prosaically, I was there "to note who else was attending," as Uncle Barney put it. Not that any of us believe that a lightning bolt would strike the murderer at the grave site. Still, it wouldn't hurt to observe reactions and expressions.

The closer I got to the cemetery, the shakier I felt. When Uncle Barney asked me to attend the funeral I agreed because I wanted to prove to myself that I could do this without falling apart. My horror of funerals goes as far back as I can remember. I'm told that as a four-year-old attending my father's burial, I screamed when his coffin was lowered into the ground. Perhaps that explains my unreasonable fear of shut-up, dark or small places like elevators, cellars, and rooms without windows. What going through a long tunnel does to me is difficult for anyone untroubled by claustrophobia to understand. Having to place my sweet son's body into the cold earth did nothing to decrease my terror of funerals.

Suddenly deeply buried memories burst through the surface of my consciousness. I felt my heart skip a beat, then kick into a fast, hard rhythm that was as painful as it was scary. My breathing grew shallow and rapid. I felt as if I couldn't get enough air. I pulled into the cemetery parking lot, my hands frozen on the steering wheel. I couldn't move. *Breathe deeply, slowly,* my mind urged, not yet completely overtaken by panic and anxiety.

Closing my eyes, I envisioned my hatha yoga teacher and heard her say, "Breathe in to the count of four, hold, and breathe out to the count of eight." Doing this, I stopped myself from hyperventilating. By the time I had conquered my anxiety and could breathe normally, perspiration dotted my forehead. Several minutes later I was able to get out of the car. Though my legs felt weak, I was able to follow the mourners to the grave.

Standing to one side, I watched the family members arrive and be seated on the folding chairs arranged for them. Annette, wearing a beige cape trimmed with rich brown fur, undoubtedly mink, irritably brushed aside the solicitous hand of a black-clad attendant holding a chair for her. Her banker husband appeared self-assured and trust-inspiring even as he contemplated the copper

casket. In direct contrast, Harry looked absurdly vulnerable, young, and uncertain. My heart went out to him.
He waited until his stepmother took her seat before he
hunched down into his.

Pauline drew the magnificent black, full-length fur
coat around herself, whether for warmth or psychologi-
cal protection, I wasn't sure. I was sure, however, that the
sunglasses she wore didn't hide tear-swollen eyes. No
emotion was visible on her face except a slight defiance
as if she dared anyone approach her for not pretending
to be grief-stricken. The only tears I saw shed at the
service coursed down Mrs. Dougherty's broad, kind
face.

Listening to the minister read the Twenty-Third
Psalm, I dug my fingernails into the palms of my hands
to retain control. Mercifully the service was brief.

Ramsey Ariosto caught up with me on my way to the
parking lot. He relayed Annette's invitation to join them
for a drink at the house. Although I wasn't in the mood
to socialize, I reminded myself that as an investigator
I might garner something that would shed light on the
three murders that had us baffled.

I took my time getting to the Ariosto mansion, giving
the family a chance to get ready for the reception—if
that was the right word for the occasion. Wake implied
camaraderie and conviviality, neither of which I expected to find at the mansion.

Brazier, even more solemn-faced than usual, opened
the door and took my shawl. I waited my turn to go
through the receiving line, murmuring condolences.
The only ones who seemed to need them were Annette
and Harry. The former was pale under the blush that sat

prominently on her gaunt cheeks and the dark circles under her eyes no amount of makeup could conceal; the latter's handsome face was ashen, the blue eyes constantly darting from one object to another, searching for...I had the disquieting feeling that not even Harry knew what he hoped to find.

In the dining room a lavish buffet was spread out on the long table. Even though I had skipped lunch, I couldn't bring myself to take food. Instead I accepted a glass of orange juice without gin from the young man behind the bar which was set up in a corner of the room.

Since Annette had murmured to me that we needed to talk, I had to wait until her hostess' duties were done. Not feeling like making small talk with people I didn't know, I went to the kitchen where I saw two women replenish trays of food. Since Mrs. Dougherty wasn't one of them, I went to the servants' sitting room.

"May I come in?" I asked her.

"Oh sure. I'd be glad of the company," Mrs. Dougherty said. "Come and have some of this food. It's catered, so I can't guarantee its quality."

On the coffee table sat a tray of assorted, small sandwiches, chicken wings, shrimp and relishes. I watched her pick up a sandwich, look at it critically, and take a bite.

"Just as I thought. They used store-bought bread. For what they charge they could at least get bakery bread."

"Any cucumber sandwiches among those?"

"No, but I'll fix us some."

Before I could request for her not to go to any trouble,

she'd gone. She came back within minutes, carrying a chopping block, a golden loaf of homemade bread, mayonnaise, a pepper mill and a long, English cucumber. I watched her skilled hands assemble four cucumber sandwiches, two of which she put on a plate for me.

I thanked her, suddenly discovering that I was hollow with hunger. Between bites I asked her about her plans for the future.

"Mr. Ariosto, God rest his soul, set up a pension plan for me years ago. I think I'll retire and do some volunteer work in the community. Brazier's retiring, too, so I don't know what Miss Annette will do with the house."

"What about Mrs. Ariosto?"

"Her?" Mrs. Dougherty shrugged. "She gets a generous allowance each month. My guess is that she'll spend it in Chicago or New York among the bright lights and excitement. She never liked Westport. Always complained that there was nothing to do here."

"She seems to be holding up well."

Mrs. Dougherty uttered a sound that was a cross between a snort and a sniff and all pure contempt.

"Why shouldn't she hold up well? It isn't as if she'd been crazy in love with her husband. Her kind rarely is."

"Was she in love with someone else?"

Mrs. Dougherty eyed me shrewdly. "She might have been. Something's the matter with her, that's for sure. She doesn't act like herself."

"How does she act?"

"Skittish. Drops things when you walk up behind her. Drinks way too much."

"It's only natural that her husband's murder would upset her."

"It started before that."

"Oh? How long ago?"

Mrs. Dougherty thought for a minute. "It's hard to pinpoint exactly when someone starts to change, but I think it happened this summer. Some days she'd be real up and happy. Other's she'd snap and bite your head off for no reason. Sometimes I suspected she'd been crying and she's not the crying type."

"How had Pauline acted before this summer?"

"Sort of lady-of-the-manor like. She enjoyed giving orders and being waited on."

"And Mr. Ariosto? How did he treat her?"

Mrs. Dougherty shrugged. "The way he treated all his wives."

In other words, abominably, I thought. "Did he notice the change in her?"

"He noticed the drinking, and he didn't like it. I don't know if he was aware of anything else."

From the way she said this, I knew she wouldn't elaborate.

We finished our sandwiches in silence.

"Harry doesn't look well. Have you noticed that?" I asked after a while.

"My poor lamb. He doesn't eat much even when I fix his favorite foods, and I suspect he sleeps even less. I would never have thought his stepfather's death would hit him so hard. But then Mr. Ariosto was the only family he had left since his mother passed away. Poor boy."

"I talked to Sidney shortly before he was killed," I began but Mrs. Dougherty interrupted.

"Wasn't that just awful? I can't believe what's going on out there. Poor Sidney."

"He told his lady friend that he was going to come into big money. Sidney suggested it was going to come from someone in this house. Do you know what he was hinting at?"

"Sidney was always talking about making it big. I can't remember how many times he sat at my kitchen table, filling in a racing form or studying the winning lottery numbers. Each time he placed a bet he was sure he'd win a bundle. I wouldn't put any store in anything Sidney said about coming into money. Nothing but wishful thinking, if you ask me."

Brazier interrupted us to tell me that Annette was ready to see me in the morning room.

"Have you found out anything?" she demanded as soon as I crossed the threshold.

Sensing her agitation, I answered from the doorway. "Yes, we've learned several things, but they're not conclusive. We're still working on our leads."

Annette sucked on her cigarette almost fiercely, dragging the smoke deep into her lungs.

"Where were you yesterday around noon?" I asked. Since she didn't believe in beating around the bush, I didn't either.

Annette peered at me through the smoke drifting from her cigarette. "Why?"

"The police will ask you that, probably before the day is out." She didn't look happy at the prospect. For a beat I thought she was going to refuse to answer my question.

"I went to the funeral home to make sure everything was in order. Then I met my husband at the airport. He came in on the noon flight from Detroit."

"Good."

"Cybil, I insist on knowing why I need an alibi."

"Sidney Dunn was shot around noon. His head was practically blown off with a shotgun."

Behind me I heard something that sounded like someone gagging. I turned in time to see Pauline running into the downstairs powder room.

ELEVEN

ANNETTE JOINED ME IN TIME to see her father's widow run into the bathroom. Our eyes met. She raised an eyebrow and shrugged one elegant shoulder.

"Pauline was perfectly composed during the funeral and the reception, so why should news of the chauffeur's death upset her?" Annette wondered.

I wondered, too. If Pauline had shot Sidney, she would have prepared herself to receive the news of his death with the correct mixture of polite shock, horror and surprise. But if Sidney had been blackmailing her and somebody else had killed him, Pauline's natural reaction would be one of relief. For her to become physically ill made no sense. But it was interesting, interesting enough for me to pursue further. Turning to Annette, I asked, "How long have you had seats in Orchestra Hall?"

"We've had season tickets for twenty years or more. I think Dad's first wife was a music lover. I suspect she's the one who started the subscription."

"Are the seats the same ones each year?"

"Yes. For as long as I can remember we've had two seats in the twelfth row. Why do you ask?"

"No special reason," I murmured.

Annette went back into the morning room, crushed her cigarette in an ashtray and immediately lit another. I lingered in the doorway long enough to see Pauline drag herself upstairs, white-faced and ill-looking. As soon as I decently could, I left Annette with assurances of informing her of my progress.

I went into the kitchen where the same caterer's employees fixed sandwiches. Neither woman objected when I put the kettle on and prepared a tray. When the tea had steeped, I carried the tray upstairs. Assuming that the master suite was still in the same location, I knocked on its door.

"Go away."

Pauline's voice sounded muffled. "I brought you some tea. I'm coming in." Before she could object, I opened the door. The sitting room was opulent and even though it was twice the size of my living room, it seemed smaller because it was crammed with antique furnishings. It was also empty. I didn't know whether her bedroom was the one on the right or the one on the left.

"Pauline," I called.

"Leave me alone."

The voice came from the room to the left whose door was slightly ajar. I knocked on it perfunctorily and went in. Pauline was lying face down across the queen-sized bed. Setting the tray on the round table covered with a cloth that matched the flowered drapes, I poured the tea.

"This will make you feel better," I said, walking to the bed.

Pauline sat up, glowering at me. "I doubt that," she snapped. "The least you could have done was bring me a vodka tonic. Annette, that skinny witch, is watching me like a hawk, daring me to take a drink."

"Sorry, I didn't know that's what you wanted." Her husband's murderer had taken a gin and tonic. Casually I asked. "Do you ever drink gin and tonic?"

"Only if there's no vodka. Why?"

"Just wondered. Here's your tea. It's better for you than alcohol since you'll have to go back down to see your guests."

"Oh God," she muttered, burying her face in her hands. "Why don't they go home?"

"They will. In an hour it'll all be over. You can hang in there till then. You can do it. Here. Drink this."

She looked up at me, her strange, yellow-green eyes distrustful, yet I sensed she wanted to trust, to reach out to someone. Who in this house would show her any kindness? After a moment's hesitation, she took the cup from me, sloshing a little tea into the saucer. Ignoring that, she took a couple of sips. Shuddering, she said, "This stuff is as vile as medicine."

I had never thought of orange pekoe in those terms but to a non-tea drinker it might taste that way. Up close, I noticed that Pauline had aged in the past week. The strain probably accounted for the downward slant of her mouth, and the exhaustion in the set of her shoulders suggested sleepless nights. Perhaps she wasn't as unfeeling and tough as she pretended to be.

"What are your immediate plans?" I asked. Her answer was prompt.

"Get away from here. This house. This town. Go some place where the sun shines. A cruise, maybe. Yeah, a cruise through the Caribbean islands."

I tried to hide my shocked reaction. She was going on the cruise she'd planned to take with her husband. This struck me as completely insensitive if not downright macabre.

"Alone?" I asked.

"Of course, alone. What kind of question is that? Who did you think I'd go with?"

I saw my question had made her both angry and defensive.

"My husband just died, for Christ's sake."

I studied Pauline closely, observing the tremor of her hands that hadn't been there before.

"I have no family. Who could I take? Answer me that."

"I don't know, but you don't seem the type who would enjoy a cruise alone. I thought maybe you'd take a girlfriend."

She leaped on that suggestion. "That's a good idea. I might just do that."

Pauline was lying. She was taking someone on that cruise, and it wasn't a woman. Had she been carrying on a love affair all along? Had my hunch been right when Ariosto summoned me to the house on the day of his murder? Had he been ready to hire me to find out who his wife's lover was? I hadn't like the idea then and I didn't like it now, but that would provide Pauline with a motive to kill her husband. Or more likely, to have him killed. I didn't want to believe that even as the thought wormed its way through my brain.

"You may take this back down with you," she said, dismissing me as if I were the upstairs maid.

"I'll take it when I leave." There was one more subject I needed to discuss with her. "So, you're a lover of classical music," I said casually.

"What?"

"The Chicago Symphony." Watching her eyes, I knew the moment she realized where I was headed. It didn't seem to frighten her.

"Oh, yeah, the symphony. When Terrance couldn't go, Harry volunteered. He really knows a lot about classical music. Did you know he wanted to study music? But Terrance wouldn't let him. Said it was a waste of time because there's no money in it. I suppose he was right about that. Terrance was always right about money if nothing else." Her voice was bitter.

"Did you take the toll road to Chicago?" I asked.

"Yes. We parked in a garage on Randolph Street and walked to Orchestra Hall."

I wondered why she volunteered that. To strengthen an alibi for the night her husband was shot? "Did you drive?"

"No. Harry did. He made good time in that car of his."

"What does he drive?"

"A Ferrari." Pauline was silent, lost in thought. After a while she said, "I never imagined…"

"What?" I prompted.

She pulled herself together. "Nothing. Why are you asking me these questions?"

I shrugged. "Making conversation. You looked ill and upset. I thought you might want someone to talk to." I rose from the chair and picked up the tray.

"I'll go down with you, if you wait a minute." Pauline crossed to her dressing table which looked like a display counter in Marshall Field's cosmetic section. With somewhat unsteady hands she reapplied burgundy lipstick, dusted her cheeks with blush, fluffed up her silver streaked hair and announced she was ready to face the mob downstairs.

After I deposited the tray in the kitchen, I looked for Harry. When I couldn't find him, I drove to the agency, forming theories and discarding them as fast as I made them.

I reported to Uncle Barney. Since I had surveillance duty that night, I dashed home right after that and fixed a turkey sandwich and a thermos of strong coffee.

At The Dolphin I parked next to Glenn's car. He formed a zero with his thumb and index finger, signaling no activity had taken place in Room 18. Then he threw me a brisk two-finger salute and drove away.

Settling in as comfortably as I could, I picked up the sweater I was knitting for Luke for Christmas. Since I was working on the back which called for nothing more complicated than alternating rows of knit and purl, I could do this in the near-dark of the car. It helped pass my four hour stint and kept me from nodding off.

At midnight Uncle Barney took over. I drove home, went to bed, and read for an hour before I turned the light out.

Loud pounding woke me. Glancing at my clock, I saw that it was three minutes to seven. Who on earth was making that racket? I ran downstairs and flung the front door open.

"Luke?" I managed to say after I recovered from my surprise. "What are you doing?" I paused. "I mean I *see* that you're hammering on my porch railing, but why?"

He paused and straightened up. "Because your railing

is loose. One of these dark nights you might stumble, grab for it, and it'll collapse. You could get hurt."

"Oh. I know it's loose. My handyman promised to fix it. He must have forgotten."

"Don't tell me you hired Muttering Manny as your handyman?"

"Okay, so I won't tell you. And don't glower at me."

Luke shook his head. "Cybil, the man is unreliable. Half the time he doesn't know where he is. The other half he thinks he's waiting for orders to go to 'Nam."

"He's not that bad. If he were, the V.A. Hospital wouldn't have released him. And he needs the money."

"No, he doesn't. He only spends it on cheap liquor."

"I don't actually give him cash. Usually I feed him a meal as part of his payment and send the rest to Father Joseph who looks out for him."

Luke nodded approvingly. "But Manny is still unreliable. You need to hire someone who'll actually show up when he's supposed to."

"I have. Several times. I never realized how hard it was to hire good help…." My voice trailed off. That's exactly what Luke had told me years earlier when I had wanted to buy the old Victorian house one street over. From the gleam in his dark eyes I knew he remembered that. "Are you going to say 'I told you so'?"

"No, I'd never say that to you."

Luke grinned at me. He really has an adorable grin. I had almost forgotten that. He hammered a nail into place.

"I'm surprised you were still asleep. You're usually up with the sun," he said.

"And you sleep until the last possible minute. Why are you up so early?"

"I couldn't sleep."

I looked at him carefully. "How come? You're usually asleep thirty seconds after your head hits the pillow."

"I'm changing shifts. It always takes me a few days to adjust."

I didn't believe him. Or not entirely. I also knew from the set of his shoulders that he wouldn't elaborate. Luke isn't a stubborn man ordinarily, but once he's made up his mind, he usually doesn't budge. By the way he stood, I knew this was one of those times. Had I contributed to turning him into an insomniac?

"How about you? Why were you still in bed at seven in the morning?" he asked. "Couldn't you sleep? How long have you had this problem again? I don't want to give you pills, but I know of a clinic that deals with sleep disorders and has had good results with other methods."

"I just went to bed late. That's all. I don't need a clinic." Luke didn't look as if he believed me. "I had surveillance duty last night and didn't go to bed until nearly two."

"Surveillance? Alone? In the middle of the night?"

Luke whacked the nail with unnecessary force. The railing shuddered. Another whack like that one and I would need a whole new railing. "Luke, I was in no danger. Do you think Uncle Barney would send me some place where I could get hurt?" He gave me a long, hard look.

"No, I guess not."

"You want to come in for coffee?" I asked.

He glanced at his watch. "I'd love to, but I better get going." He picked up the bag of nails and turned to go.

"Luke?" He turned back. "Thanks for fixing the railing. And thanks for caring." He looked as if he wanted to say something but changed his mind. He waved and walked to his car. I watched him drive away.

UNCLE BARNEY AND THE OTHER agents who'd been on watch at The Dolphin had nothing to report when I went to the office.

I puttered around for a while, cleaned out my in-basket, straightened out some files in my drawer and filled out my expense account. When my desk looked as bare as Mother Hubbard's cupboard, I realized I couldn't stand not doing anything.

Even though I knew Sam had sent Sergeant Griffin to check Pauline's alibi, I would double check it. I had no other leads to follow, no clues that meant anything to me. Besides, I like Chicago. Spending a couple of hours there wouldn't be a hardship at all.

I took the toll road as far as Lake Station, swung off onto the Chicago Skyway to Stony Island and hit Lake Shore Drive after passing the Museum of Science and Industry. I know Sandburg called Chicago the "hog butcher of the world" but in the years that have passed since then, enormous changes have taken place. This city is now as exciting and elegant as any in the country. At least to me it is.

I parked in the same garage on Randolph Street

Pauline used. Unfortunately, the two men on duty Saturday night wouldn't report for work for another three hours. It was also too early to visit Orchestra Hall. Glancing at my watch, I knew I couldn't get back in time to cook dinner and be ready for the stakeout at eight. Thank heaven for take-out food and delis.

I retrieved my car and drove toward the Lincoln Park area and my favorite deli which specializes in central European imports, including Austria's Stiegl beer. I also stocked up on sausages, cheeses and the pungent black bread Maxi and Uncle Barney like. Anticipating their pleasure, I smiled.

When I returned to the parking garage, the two attendants, their hair cropped close with initials shaved into it, had arrived. Both in their early twenties, they exaggerated their cool walk until it was a parody of itself. I identified myself and told them why I needed the information.

"Do you remember parking an unusual car with Indiana license plates last Saturday night?"

They exchanged a significant look.

"What's the matter?" I asked.

"Somebody else asked about that," the shorter of the two said. The initials on his head read "ALM".

"A cop? Tall, thin, sneezes a lot?"

Both nodded. I took out two ten-dollar bills and held them up. "What about the car?"

"Italian wheels. Real cool," ALM said.

"Most expensive sports job I've seen around here," initials DRG added.

"Blood-red with jet black leather interior."

"Do you remember the make?" I asked.

"Uh-huh. Sonny Crockett wheels."

"Pardon?" I saw them exchange a look that clearly conveyed their opinion of my ignorance.

"Sonny Crockett on 'Miami Vice' drives a car like that."

"A Ferrari," ALM added with exaggerated patience.

"Oh." "Miami Vice" had to be on reruns somewhere. "This Ferrari. Did it stay in this garage all evening?" I asked.

"Sure did. The young dude driving it gave us twenty bucks each to keep an eye on it."

"What did he look like?"

ALM shrugged. "All whities look alike."

They laughed uproariously at this witty observation. I waited until they recovered.

"Was someone with him? A woman perhaps?"

"The dude was alone."

"When did he drop the car off?"

"About ten to eight," DRG said.

"When did he pick it up?"

"Around eleven-thirty."

According to Sergeant Griffin's report, Pauline and Harry had stopped for a sandwich and a drink after the concert. That accounted easily for the time that elapsed between the concert and the time they retrieved the car.

"Thanks." I handed each a bill and walked south to Orchestra Hall. I told the woman in the office what I needed. Obligingly she looked up the usher who worked that section of seats.

"That's Thelma Young's area, but this is her day off."

"I've got to speak to her. It's really important." I

exaggerated a little, saying that an innocent woman might go to jail if I couldn't talk to Thelma. "I know you can't give out addresses of your employees, but could you call her? I'll pay for her time if she'll see me."

"Well, I guess I could do that."

Five minutes later I was on my way to the garage. My two attendants had taken good care of the Volvo for which I tipped them generously.

Thelma lived in Rogers Park. After consulting the map of the city, I drove north on Lake Shore Drive, then swung west. Apparently Thelma had been watching from the window. She opened the door before I had a chance to knock.

"Come in," she said, tying the belt on a green satin robe. "I just got up. Don't mind the mess."

Her efficiency apartment seemed anything but efficient, probably because of the mess she'd referred to. I wondered if she ever hung up any of her clothes or just tossed them into piles of dirty, so-so, and clean. She lit a cigarette.

"Want some coffee?" Thelma asked. "It's only instant."

"No, thank you," I said hastily. I watched her dump a half teaspoon of instant coffee powder into the mug, add water from a kettle that couldn't be anywhere near boiling and sip the weak-looking brew. Maxi would be horrified at what Thelma called coffee.

"So, you want to pay me for information," she said, looking at me over the rim of the mug.

"No, I want to pay you for your time while I ask you questions, the answers to which I expect to be truthful."

Thelma shrugged. "Have it your way. I have no reason to lie. How much are you paying? Not that I wouldn't cooperate without it, but a girl can always use the extra cash. I'm going to school part time. Another year and I'll be a dental hygienist."

"Will twenty dollars for five minutes of your time cover it?"

"Could you make it twenty-five?"

"Sure," I agreed and pulled the bills from my wallet.

"What do you want to know about Saturday?" she asked.

"Whether two people attended the symphony that night. The family's had the same seats for years. In your section, twelfth row, seats five and six. The same people don't necessarily attend each time."

"Last Saturday," she said, closing her eyes in concentration. "Yeah. The woman arrived first. She had this gorgeous silver cape slung across one shoulder." Thelma sashayed across the room, her hips swaying in imitation of the woman's sensuous glide. "He didn't get there until the last minute. Slipped me a five, so I showed him to his seat even though I should have made him wait in the foyer." She paused a moment. Then she giggled. "The movie star. Or gigolo."

"Pardon?"

"It's a game I play. Trying to guess what people do. He was so good-looking he could have been a movie star."

"What about the gigolo?"

"He could have been that, too. The woman he was

with wore enough jewelry to be able to afford him. She was also older than him. Not much, but a few years."

"Did they stay for the entire concert?"

"That I don't know. All I know for sure is that they were there at the beginning. That I can swear to in a court of law."

It didn't really matter if they stayed for all of the performance or not. They couldn't have driven back to Westport, shot Ariosto and returned in time to get the car out of the garage at eleven-thirty. Besides, the Ferrari had remained in the garage. Even if Pauline had driven a second car to Chicago and they had used it, there still wasn't enough time.

"Well, thanks a lot." I handed Thelma her twenty-five dollars which she folded carefully and placed into the pocket of her robe.

So much for long shots. And double checking. And filling in time with action.

I MADE IT HOME IN JUST a little under three hours and in time to take the deli items to Maxi's farm. She insisted on grilling a couple of the sausages for us. I didn't try to talk her out of it. She added some of her cabbage cooked with white wine and dark bread for a simple but tasty meal. Armed with a thermos of her delicious coffee, I drove to The Dolphin.

This being Friday night, the motel filled up rapidly, but Room 18 remained unoccupied.

It was a perfect Bulwer-Lytton night: the wind howled and intermittent rain squalls hurled sheets of water against the windshield, rendering the dark night even more impenetrable. I turned on my tiny reading light, certain that its meager beam couldn't be seen outside the car. With it on the seat next to me, I could knit. During one of these downpours, a car slid into the parking slot before Room 18. Dropping my knitting on the passenger seat, I slipped out of the Volvo. Carefully I closed the door with a soft click. I skirted the parked cars and dashed to the relative protection of the stairs leading to the rooms. From there I could see the room without getting blinded by the rain.

The figure emerging from the light-colored Mercedes struggled briefly with a wind-tossed umbrella before hurling it back into the car. Mentally I reviewed the list I'd made of all vehicles belonging to the Ariosto family. It included an off-white Mercedes. I watched the dark shape run to the door. From the small waist, accentuated by the tightly belted raincoat, I was certain the Mercedes' driver was a woman. My guess was confirmed when she pushed back the hood to unlock the door. Just before entering, she looked around nervously and I recognized her: Pauline Ariosto.

Even though part of me half expected her, I was still dismayed. I didn't want it to be Pauline. When I realized what I was doing, I chided myself. My job wasn't to approve or disapprove of people and their activities. I'd been hired to clear Annette. Nothing more.

Grimly I stepped farther into the recess behind the stairs to wait. I took the camera from my pocket and slipped the strap around my neck. Chances were I wouldn't recognize Pauline's lover. A photo would help us identify him. If the light spilling from the open door was strong enough for a photograph.

Burying my hands deep in the pockets of my raincoat,

I shivered. It seemed to turn chillier by the minute with the kind of wet cold that penetrates all layers of clothing. Whoever Pauline's lover was, I hoped he was the impatient type.

He wasn't. Twenty-six minutes elapsed before I heard footsteps. Pressing myself as far into the dark corner as I could, I hoped my chattering teeth wouldn't betray my presence.

From the way he moved, he was young and in a hurry. As soon as his rapid strides moved past the stairs, I stepped forward to watch him approach Room 18. From the back I couldn't tell much about him, but his lean, jean-and-black-leather jacket-clad body reinforced my opinion of his youthfulness. Stealthily I followed him a few steps.

Pauline must have been waiting by the door for as soon as he knocked, she flung it wide open and threw herself into his arms. When she pulled back to look at him, the light from the room fell full on his face. I gasped, feeling as if someone had knocked the air out of my lungs.

TWELVE

HARRY ARIOSTO.

Stepmother and stepson. Lovers.

I couldn't believe it, not even after I saw them exchange a passionate kiss before Pauline pulled Harry into the room. I kept staring at the spot where they had stood long after the door closed behind them.

Eventually I roused myself to action. I had to call Uncle Barney. There was no sense now in him driving all the way to the motel to relieve me. I dashed back to my car and phoned him. He wasn't in, so I left a message on his machine, asking him to wait for me at my house.

I got the car's heater going full blast. Water squeaked in my loafers. My jeans flapped soggily against my calves. Few things are more uncomfortable than cold, wet denim, I reflected, trying to wring water from the stiff material.

After the car was toasty, I switched the motor off. There was no real reason for me to stay, yet I was reluctant to leave. The temperature dropped quickly inside the car, forcing me to run the motor at fifteen-minute intervals.

At ten-thirty the lovers emerged. Harry waited solicitously until Pauline drove off before he turned up his collar and darted toward the far parking lot. Something compelled me to follow him with my headlights off. Fully expecting to see the Sonny Crockett car, I was surprised when Harry unlocked a blue 1986 Mustang. I entered the license plate number in my notebook. I didn't know quite how, but Harry having access to a second car might be important in solving the case. If we ever solved it.

Before I left the motel, I had to find out in whose name Room 18 was rented and what the arrangement was. Pauline had arrived, key in hand. I had the other key, left to me by Sidney who, I suspected, pilfered it from one of the lovers.

A glimmer of an idea came to me but it involved use of a phone book. I drove toward Michigan City. At a well-lit convenience store I spied an inside pay phone. Luck was with me. A telephone directory with all pages intact was chained to the wall. After I located what I needed in the florists' section of the yellow pages, I dialed the motel's number.

"Hello. This is Blossoms Unlimited. We have a delivery for the party in Room 18 but I can't read the name. My assistant's writing looks like chicken scratches. Honestly, it's impossible to get good help anymore," I complained.

"I know what you mean. It's the same in the motel business. Did you say Room 18?"

"Yes, sir." I pressed the receiver against my ear, praying the man on the other end wouldn't change his mind. He didn't.

"Let's see," he said. "Room 18 is reserved for Paul Greco."

"Thank you so much. This is very kind of you."

Paul Greco was certainly a more imaginative alias than the usual Brown, Smith or Jones. Driving toward Westport, I kept wondering how he'd hit upon that name.

At home, Uncle Barney's car was parked in front of my house. He joined me. I lit the fire I had laid earlier. The heat from the fire warmed my outstretched hands. Despite its warmth, I shivered.

"What's wrong, Cybil?"

Even though I had my back turned to Uncle Barney, he could tell that I was tense. I turned to face him. "Room 18 had visitors tonight. A pair of lovers."

"I'm not surprised," he said wearily. "Who?"

"Pauline Ariosto. Subconsciously at least, I expected her to show up."

"Why didn't you tell me?" Barney demanded.

"It was only a hunch. Maybe only half a hunch, if that's possible."

"It is. Never discount hunches, Cybil. Not even partial ones." Barney took his pipe from his tweed jacket and fiddled with it. "Who joined her?" he asked, his curiosity carefully restrained.

"Now that's the kicker. I never even considered this man for the role of her lover." Though I knew he was waiting for my answer, I had to take a couple of deep breaths.

"Who, Cybil?" Barney asked again, but his voice was gentle.

"Harry Ariosto."

"Jesus H. Christ!"

Uncle Barney is the cleanest-mouthed man I know.

This exclamation came as close to swearing as I've ever heard him come.

"Pauline's stepson?"

"Yes. It's like that Greek story of Phaedra. Do you remember it?"

"No."

"As I recall, Phaedra fell in love with her stepson." I shook my head, bemused. "I wonder how long ago that's supposed to have happened." I walked to the adjoining library whose only furniture consisted of the glass-fronted, built-in bookshelves. I reached for a dictionary of mythology. "It says here that the accepted date for the Trojan War is around 1290 B.C. The Phaedra story occurs in the generation preceding the war. How many years ago is that?"

"Around three thousand," Barney said.

"Imagine. All those centuries between then and now and still we see the same triangle situation, the same passions." I shook my head.

"I've found that human nature is pretty much the same the world over. I guess it's timeless as well." Barney tapped the bitten end of his cold pipe against his jaw. "I don't suppose you could be mistaken about the nature of their relationship?"

"No. The kiss I witnessed was anything but familial. Besides, why would they need a motel room if they weren't lovers? I wish I were mistaken," I heard myself add somewhat wistfully.

"Why?" Barney wanted to know.

I hadn't thought about that before. I shrugged. "I don't know, except I like Harry. And it's not only because he looks like a Greek god."

"A Greek god?" Barney's left eyebrow rose.

"We were speaking about Greek mythology," I said quickly.

"Well, that certainly gives both of them a strong motive for murder," Barney said.

"Yes, but no opportunity. There's no way they could have come back to Westport, shot Ariosto, and returned to Chicago. It's not possible."

"Don't be so sure," Barney warned. "Just because we haven't been able to figure out how it was done, doesn't mean it can't be done. Do we have anybody else whose motive is anywhere near as powerful?"

"No. For a short while Dunn and Fettner looked like good candidates but both have alibis. I'm sure neither Annette nor Ramsey did it, even though Ramsey has no alibi and Annette is unwilling to name hers."

"Get her to disclose it to you. We have to clear Annette completely. Recheck Ramsey Ariosto also. Somebody must have seen him or spoken to him that evening. Then we'll take the Chicago trip apart. In my experience, criminals always make a small mistake. The trick is to find it."

"All right."

"What do you know about Harry?" Barney asked.

"Very little. He's a senior at the university. Drives a Ferrari. Didn't stand up to Terrance Ariosto according to Annette. I saw Harry and his stepfather together once. Ariosto treated him shabbily but then he treated most people that way. Mrs. Dougherty likes Harry. She said he did well in school until the spring semester when he…" I paused, knowing now with whom he fell in love. "When he fell in love."

"So, we know approximately when the affair started. Since it's lasted this long, it's apparently more than a little fling," Barney said, his voice thoughtful.

The words "little fling" didn't strike me as being appropriate, not when the fling seemed to be connected to the deaths of three men. With that horrendous toll, nothing less than the term grand passion would do.

"Cybil, didn't you used to know someone on campus?"

"I still do."

"See what you can find out about Harry. Discreetly, of course. We don't want to spook anyone into doing something foolish."

"I can't see either Pauline or Harry using a shotgun to kill three people. At least not personally."

"You think they hired someone?"

"Yes."

Barney clamped his teeth around the stem of his pipe the way he does when he concentrates. After a while he said, "I don't think so. It's not as easy to hire a hitman as television programs suggest. I doubt that either Pauline or Harry have the kind of connections it takes to find an assassin."

"What about those awful macho survival magazines? Some of their ads are very suggestive," I pointed out.

"True. Still, I don't think these murders were committed by professionals. The weapon's all wrong, for one thing."

"For another?" I queried.

"At least two of the victims probably opened their doors to the murderer. None of the three put up a fight which suggests that they knew the killer and didn't anticipate danger." Barney glanced at his watch. "It's getting late. Tomorrow we'll concentrate on this case exclusively. If you need help with the legwork, let me know."

I walked Uncle Barney to the front door.

THE NEXT MORNING I drove to the YWCA and forced myself to swim thirty laps. I needed the physical exertion to balance the emotional stress of the case.

After that I drove to Ramsey's apartment. I had left a message on his machine the night before, so he knew I was coming.

Ramsey opened the door promptly, freshly shaved and showered judging by the smell of soap and aftershave that wafted from him. He wore jeans with paint stains that seemed to have withstood repeated laundering and a red-and-white Indiana University sweatshirt.

"I'm making coffee. Do you mind talking in the kitchen?"

"Not at all."

He offered me orange juice which I declined. Ramsey sipped his while setting out mugs, spoons, milk and sugar on the small butcher block table in the breakfast nook. As soon as the coffee maker stopped dripping, he brought the pot to the table along with a box of chocolate chip cookies. He held the opened box toward me. I shook my head, suppressing the shudder his idea of breakfast evoked.

"What can I do for you?" Ramsey popped a whole cookie into his mouth.

"We would like to eliminate you from our list of suspects. Let me finish, please," I said when he stopped chewing and looked at me wide-eyed. "I don't think you shot your uncle but my believing that isn't good enough. We need proof. We have to verify your alibi. I want you to concentrate on last Saturday. Tell me everything you did from the minute you woke up to the moment you fell asleep."

Ramsey munched a couple of cookies before he spoke. "I slept late that morning because I'd been to a party the night before. When I got up and looked in my fridge for something to eat, all I found was beer, a small tub of margarine and a bottle of ketchup. I decided it was time to go to the grocery store. On my way back, I stopped at the International House of Pancakes for brunch. After I put the groceries away I did a couple of loads of laundry."

He paused in his recitation to eat another cookie and think. I sipped my coffee.

"I don't remember in what order I did these things, but I wrote checks to cover some bills, took out the garbage and bundled up a bunch of newspapers for recycling. Later I watched the Notre Dame-U.S.C. football game. After that I popped a frozen pizza in the oven and worked on my report. I had reservations at the country club for dinner, but as I told you, my date got sick. So I stayed home. That is, until the police called me, wanting to know where the rest of the family was. I told them about Pauline and Harry being in Chicago and the staff having the evening off."

"Think back to the early part of the evening. Did anyone phone you? Come to the door to sell you something?" I could tell by the surprised look on his face that Ramsey had remembered something.

"How could I have been so dumb?" Ramsey looked at the cookie box, stunned. Then a wide, happy smile settled on his face. "Cybil, I have an alibi! During the crucial half hour I bought cookies from a girl and allowed her to use my phone."

"Back up, Ramsey. Start at the beginning. What girl? How old?" It wouldn't help much if she was very young, I thought.

"She said her name was Nancy and she was selling cookies for their church. The profits would be used to pay for the youth group's travel expenses to a summer camp for underprivileged children where they would work as junior counselors. With a story like that how could I buy less than six boxes?"

"Right." I grinned back at him. "Tell me more about the girl."

"I didn't look at her that closely. She looked like all twelve or thirteen year olds look, I guess. You know, braces on her teeth. Wearing blue jeans and a parka."

"I bet if she'd been twenty-two instead of twelve you could describe her in great detail," I muttered. "What about the phone call?"

"I was her last customer. I got the impression that she'd stayed out longer than she'd planned and it had gotten dark. She asked if she could use the phone to call her mother to come and pick her up. Naturally, I said it was okay. Her mother wasn't home when she called the first time. I could tell she was afraid to go outside so I asked her to wait in my living room which she did. When she called home again a few minutes later, her mother was there and came right away."

"What time did she arrive?"

Ramsey smiled again. "Seven forty-five. I remember

I looked at my watch when she knocked on the door. Seven forty-five, Cybil. There's no way on earth I could have driven to my uncle's house and shot him."

"No, you couldn't. What is Nancy's last name?"

Ramsey's smile shrunk a little. "I don't know."

"What was the name of her church?"

This question killed his smile. "I don't remember."

"Think, Ramsey."

He shook his head, looking unhappy. "United something. Maybe."

"Don't give up. We'll figure it out yet. From what you said, Nancy was walking from apartment to apartment?"

"Yes."

"How long did it take her mother to get to your place?"

"Ten minutes at the most."

"And she came up to your apartment?"

"Yes."

"Mmm. Let's see. She got Nancy's call, grabbed her purse and car keys, drove over, parked and walked up here. If she did all this in ten minutes, she can't live very far away."

"True, but how does that help?"

"At the agency we'll call every church in town till we find the one whose youth group is selling these cookies. I'm sure there won't be more than one Nancy in that age bracket. We'll get in touch with her and have her verify your alibi. Simple, isn't it?"

AND IT WAS. With four of us telephoning, it took only thirty minutes to locate the church using cookies as a fundraiser. Fortunately, Barney knew the pastor whom he persuaded to disclose Nancy's last name and address.

The Taylors lived on the near northeast side which meant I was there in less than fifteen minutes. The pastor had phoned Mrs. Taylor. She shooed the two girls watching television out of the living room and invited me to sit in the best armchair. Perching on the edge of the matching couch, she looked at me anxiously.

"I won't take much of your time," I said with a re-assuring smile. "I only need to verify something. Did you pick up Nancy at Ramsey Ariosto's apartment two Saturday nights ago at seven forty-five?"

Mrs. Taylor nodded, her face growing more anxious. "I've told that girl time and again to get herself home before dark. Anything could happen to her out on the streets. This town isn't as safe as it used to be when I was Nancy's age." She shook her head and sighed before she continued. "But she's bound and determined to sell the most cookies and win the contest. When she called from that nice Mr. Ariosto's apartment, I rushed right over to pick her up."

"Did you look at your watch to check the time?"

"Well, no. I'm allergic to every kind of watchband I ever tried, so I gave up wearing watches. But Mr. Arioso's clock on the wall chimed the time when we were there. I remember thinking that I'd have to get the lead out if I wanted to finish decorating the cupcakes for Sunday school."

I'd seen the antique clock in Ramsey's living room. "Well, thank you so much, Mrs. Taylor. I won't hold up your lunch any longer."

I had cleared Ramsey Ariosto. One down and one to go. Glancing at my watch, I decided to grab a bite to eat before I tackled Annette and got her to admit she hadn't spent the night of her father's murder alone.

The Horn of Plenty, Westport's only natural foods cum vegetarian restaurant, is always crowded which is the only thing I hold against it. This being Saturday with the downtown area relatively deserted, I had to wait only ten minutes for a table. I used the time to phone Uncle Barney and report on my interview with Mrs. Taylor. After enjoying the Horn's marinated vegetable plate and multigrain muffins, I drove to the Ariosto estate.

Once again Annette asked me to join her for a walk even though it was a cold, overcast late October day.

"I know why you're here," she said.

"Oh?"

"Ramsey called. He talked to your uncle who confirmed that his alibi has been established. I figured you're here to verify mine."

"Yes." I saw Annette shiver and zip up her coat.

"I don't want anyone to hear what I have to tell you."

"I understand."

"I don't know how to say this exactly."

"Straight out is usually the best," I encouraged.

Looking at me, she asked, "Are you still married to that good-looking doctor?"

"Yes, but we're separated." I didn't know what my marriage to Luke had to do with anything.

"Maybe then you'll understand. Or maybe you'll condemn me." Annette laughed, but it was a joyless laughter.

"I've been married for eight years. My husband's a good man, but..." She shrugged. "Anyway, I never planned to cheat on him. It just happened. I met this man and before I knew what happened, we were involved. It was so heady, so exciting to feel young and desirable again. At least, it was then. But if I get through this with my marriage in one piece, I'll break off the affair as soon as I get back to Detroit."

"You spent that Saturday night with this man, didn't you?"

"Yes."

We continued to walk in silence, rounding the tennis court.

"Do you have to know his name, Cybil?"

"Not now. Maybe not even later. I'll let you know." Annette didn't display her emotions often but this time she was visibly relieved. "How long do you plan to stay in Westport?"

"Until this is cleared up. The police politely but firmly advised me not to leave town. My husband and children are flying back tonight."

"Let's hope you can join them soon. I have to speak to Pauline. Is she here?"

"No. She went to the Sports Club a while ago."

We walked toward the back door.

"I came across an odd thing," Annette said. "I was paying the household bills, including charges to various charge accounts. My father's gold card listed the purchase of a shotgun. The kind used to kill him."

I stopped walking. "That is strange. What was the date of the charge?"

"The Monday before my father was killed."

The day after Crawford was shot. "Is the shotgun in the house?"

"Yes."

"Did you report this to the police?"

"Yes. They had already examined all the guns in the house."

Strange indeed. Why would anyone buy a gun identical to the one used to kill the head accountant? No reason unless…yes, that made sense. To replace the murder weapon taken from the gunrack. That meant that someone from the house had shot Crawford which brought me back to Pauline and Harry.

At the backdoor I said goodbye to Annette.

THE SPORTS CLUB IS an exclusive organization dedicated to the pursuit of the more esoteric sports. That's all I knew about it. That and its approximate location out in the fields northeast of the city. I found the club with only a few wrong turns.

Driving slowly around its perimeter, I saw that it was enclosed by a tall fence warning against trespassing. I suspected that the fence was electrified. At the entrance gate an armed, uniformed guard stood watch. He didn't look friendly, I thought, as I drove past.

I parked on the nearest side road. Across from the entrance the large corn field was bare but the bushes lining the ditch bordering the road offered enough protection to hide my approach. At least I hoped they did as I ran in a low crouch to a spot across from the gate. Keeping low, I watched.

The guard checked the identification of the driver
and any passengers before raising the ramp to admit the
vehicle. Why such tight security? Probably to protect the
privacy of the members who no doubt paid a big enough
fee for it. But why use an armed guard? His presence
intrigued me enough to make me determined to take a
closer look at the club.

The arrival of a laundry truck gave me the idea of
how to get in. I had to wait an hour before the right
vehicle pulled up to the gate. The pickup truck deliver-
ing salt for the club's water softeners was ideal. At it
slowed down, I sprinted across the road. I caught up
with it as it came to a full stop. Swinging myself over
the tailgate, I fell on a bag of salt. I held my breath,
fearing the guard might have heard the thump with
which I'd landed.

"You're late today."

The guard's voice.

"Yeah. This is my last stop."

This accounted for the few sacks on the truck. Lucky
for me. If the truck had been fully loaded, I couldn't
have hidden in it. I only hoped the guard wouldn't decide
to spot check. I flattened against the sack as much as
possible, hardly breathing until the driver put the truck
in gear. When I was sure the truck was out of sight of
the guard, I risked a look.

We were approaching the back of a building, obviously the truck's destination. As soon as it slowed
down, I climbed over the tailgate and dropped to the
ground. Even though I landed hard, I managed to roll
and sprint to the cover offered by a parked van. When

no one raised the alarm, I brushed off my slacks and headed for the center of the complex as though I had every right to be there.

THIRTEEN

TWO MEN PASSED ME, shotguns resting easily on their shoulders. Intrigued, I followed them at a discreet distance. We passed a sign pointing north, labeled skeet shooting. Just about at the same time I heard shots at equally timed intervals. We walked through a wooded area for about two hundred yards, I estimated, before we reached the target range.

I had no trouble spotting Pauline. She wore a yellow down vest over an olive-green jumpsuit. With the gun at her shoulder, I heard her yell "pull". A fraction of a second later the saucer-shaped clay target splintered in the air. In the time I watched her, which must have been a good five minutes, Pauline didn't miss a single target. The woman was a deadly accurate shot.

Apparently the round or whatever it was called, was over for Pauline lowered the gun. I took advantage of the lull to speak to her.

"You do this very well," I commented.

Pauline jumped, startled by my voice. She wheeled around. From the scowl on her face I deduced that she wasn't glad to see me, but she forced herself to be civil. She even managed a brittle smile when she greeted me.

"Have you been shooting long?" I asked.

"Terrance introduced me to the sport. Seems like it comes naturally to me."

"Do you enter competitions?"

"Sure. I've won quite a few trophies over the years."

She said this with obvious pride. Pauline looked better than she had the last time I saw her. The cold, fresh air had put color into her cheeks and her hair glittered silvery. She must have had it freshly streaked, I decided.

"How did you find me?"

"Annette told me where you were."

"Well, I'm busy. What do you want?" Pauline turned away, preparing to shoot again.

"Why did you buy a shotgun to replace the one missing from the gun cabinet in the game room?"

Pauline whirled around, the gun pointing at my head. For a terrifying moment I wondered if she was going to shoot. Involuntarily, my body arched away from her. After a tense moment, Pauline slowly lowered the gun.

"I don't know what you're talking about. What makes you think I bought a gun?" she demanded, her eyes and voice flat.

"Because you made the mistake of charging it. My guess is that you phoned the order in and the company demanded a credit card number. That shows how desperate you were to get a look-alike gun into the rack. Why? What happened to the original? The one used to kill Galen Crawford? It was never reported stolen."

Pauline paled a little but otherwise retained remarkable control. This was one cool woman, I thought with a trace of admiration. Not that I had expected her to fall apart and confess on the spot.

"I repeat. I don't know what you're talking about."

Knowing I wasn't going to get a thing out of her, I acknowledged temporary defeat with a small nod in her direction. Then I turned and walked away. At the edge of the wood I paused. I heard Pauline call "pull". This time the clay target fell to earth unscathed. Out of the next ten shots she missed six. My questions had rattled her more than a little.

On my way back to the center of the club, I spotted a familiar figure, one I had left only hours earlier. Ramsey, bow in hand and quiver slung from a belt, disappeared around the corner of a building. Was the entire Ariosto family members of this club? Before I consciously realized what I was doing, I was in full pursuit of Ramsey.

Staying well back from the archery range, I watched him. In a flowing, continuous movement he fitted an arrow, raised the bow, aimed, anchored his right hand against his cheek and released the arrow smoothly. It pierced the target with a sharp thunk. I looked on, fascinated, as he repeated the process with a deliberate rhythm and astonishing accuracy that suggested a shooting machine. After a short time the bull's eye looked like a porcupine's back. Could the accuracy with a bow and arrow be transferred to a shotgun? The question made me uneasy.

Adding to my unease was the problem of getting out of the club unseen. The salt delivery pickup was long gone, but the laundry truck, back doors wide open, was still parked near the spot where I'd jumped out of the pickup. I looked around casually before I leaped into the van. Crouching behind a canvas laundry hamper I waited. Five minutes later two bags were tossed in, the doors closed and the motor revved up. I stayed hidden until we passed through the guard ramp.

Unless I wanted to ride all the way into Westport, which would leave me with the problem of retrieving my car, I had to get out of the truck soon. Unfortunately, the driver was going too fast for me to jump out. I would have to wait until he reached the four-way stop at Spruce Lane. As soon as he slowed, I opened the door a little. Only the fact that I had braced myself in anticipation saved me from being flung out onto the asphalt. The moment he stopped, I jumped out and started hiking back to my car.

It was a good three mile walk and despite my brisk pace, I reached the Volvo thoroughly chilled. All I wanted was a long hot bath and a pot of steaming Darjeeling tea.

SUNDAY I MET TERESA LISTER for lunch in the faculty dining room on campus. We'd been roommates during our freshman year and probably would have lived together all four years except that I participated in the sophomore-year-of-study abroad which threw us out of sync. Absorbed in the Sunday *Inquirer,* Teresa didn't notice my approach until I sat next to her in the reception area of the dining room. We greeted each other affectionately before proceeding into the high-ceilinged, oak-paneled, vaguely medieval-looking dining room.

Over fruit salads topped with delicious frozen raspberry yogurt, we caught up with each other's lives.

Teresa told me that she'd been promoted. She'd leave Beaumont Hall for the dean of students' office and part-time lecturing on women's studies at the end of the fall semester. I congratulated her.

"So, what can I do for you?" Teresa asked the moment she had emptied her plate.

I grinned at her. "Some things never change. You're still as direct as ever, and you still inhale your food in record time," I said, glancing at my half-full plate.

She shrugged. "I don't see the point in changing either habit. Both save time."

"And you're still preoccupied with time. Don't you ever just vegetate?"

Teresa shook her head, setting her short, black curls into motion. Once again I observed that she was better looking now than she had been at eighteen. She had grown into the harshly attractive lines and planes of her face which had struck a discordant note in her youth. I could envision her as a stunning looking silver-haired, black-eyed septuagenarian when the rest of us looked merely faded and worn.

"Are you still sleuthing, Cybil?" Teresa asked.

"Yes."

"Good for you. I bet that's why you asked me to lunch even though there's no lecture or concert on campus, isn't it?"

I started to protest but had to admit that her shrewd observation was correct. We only met when there was also another reason for me to come to the university.

"It's okay, Cybil. I understand. I don't meet you in town either."

"That could change now that you live off campus,"

I hinted. Spooning up the last of the yogurt, I wished there were more. "Anyway, I do want some information from you. It's connected with a case I'm working on."

"What do you want to know?"

"Information on a student."

Teresa's straight, black eyebrows curved.

"It's nothing confidential," I assured her. "I know what sort of grades he's made. I want to know something about him as a person."

"What's his name?"

"Harry Ariosto."

"Ah. You're investigating the murder of his step-father."

"Yes. Do you know Harry?"

"As a matter of fact, I do. We make it a policy to talk with all students who've lost a family member."

"What did you think of Harry?"

Teresa was quiet for what seemed to me a long time. I finished my salad while waiting for her to speak.

"Have you met Harry?" Teresa asked.

"Yes."

"Then you know how handsome he is. The secretaries look sort of shell shocked every time he comes to the office."

"You've seen him several times? Why?"

"Because he's a troubled young man."

"I noticed the change in him, too," I murmured.

"What do you think caused the change?"

Guilt over committing adultery with his stepfather's wife, I thought. Aloud I said, "Guilt. Terrance Ariosto treated Harry abominably. I would guess the young man had some nasty thoughts about his stepfather while he was alive and now feels badly."

"I worked with Ariosto on several fundraisers," Teresa said and grimaced. "I've never met a more odious, obnoxious man. I confess I had a few unpleasant thoughts about him myself. You want to go to my office with me? I'll look at the notes I made during my meetings with Harry."

Naturally I agreed. Teresa insisted on driving. Since visitor's parking spaces around the administration building are usually filled even on Sunday, I didn't object. However, when she headed west, I was puzzled. "Isn't the Ad Building north of here?"

"It's faster this way. We miss two traffic lights."

I suppressed a smile.

In Teresa's office books not only filled the shelves, they were stacked on every conceivable surface. I moved a stack off her straight-backed visitor's chair and sat down. Index cards stuck between the pages marked the passages Teresa was researching.

"What are you working on?" I asked.

"The role of feminism in Latin America."

Teresa took a manila folder from the filing cabinet and studied it before she spoke. "I noted here that Harry appeared to be almost distraught the first time I spoke with him. During his subsequent visit he had himself more under control, but I had the impression that deep down he was still anxious and upset."

"What did he say about his stepfather?"

"That struck me as odd at the time. Harry's answers were… I don't know how to put it except to say that they were carefully formulated. You know, as though he had thought out each answer beforehand. The most spontaneous remark he made was about working for his stepfather during the summer."

"Oh? Where did he work and in what capacity?"

"Let me see." Teresa scanned the page. "At Tri State. Seems he was some sort of overseer at a warehouse."

Harry was the connection to Crawford. He had to be.

"In what residence hall does Harry live?"

"Alpha."

I must have looked stunned because Teresa asked if something was wrong. I shook my head. Harry had been in on the pilfering. He had to have been for Crawford himself to deliver the steaks to Alpha the evening I had tailed him.

"Well, that's about all I know about Harry that I'm at liberty to disclose," Teresa said, shutting the folder.

"Does Harry have a roommate?"

"Yes." Teresa glanced at the folder again. "Joe Martinello. Room 141, Alpha Hall. Their phone number is 5682."

"What? What was that number?" When Teresa looked a little surprised at my insistent tone, I apologized. "I'm sorry. I didn't mean to yell. Did you say 5682?"

"Why, yes."

How could I have been so dense? The prefix for all campus phones is 242. Everybody in Westport knows that. Everybody in northern Indiana knows that and that's why only the last four digits for a university phone are usually given. When I thought of all the time our agency spent trying to figure out what the number could be, I felt like laughing and crying at the same time. I thanked Teresa for her help but declined her offer to drive me back to my car. I had to think. Walking helps me sort out my thoughts.

It all had to have started this past summer when Harry worked at Tri State. Had he uncovered the pilfering and demanded a cut? Had he organized it? He could have, but I didn't think so. It didn't quite seem in character. More likely Crawford had tumbled across the illicit love affair and had blackmailed Harry into looking the other way while he organized the theft ring. Of course, Crawford had undoubtedly blackmailed Pauline and Harry into forking over silence money as well. According to the piece of paper I found behind the photo, the sums were considerable.

What had happened then? Had Crawford's demands escalated into the realm of the impossible? Uncle Barney said blackmailers often become so greedy that they back their victims into a corner where they have no choice but to turn against their exploiters. While all that made sense, I couldn't picture Harry shooting Crawford.

Maybe Harry's handsomeness blinded me to some character flaws. I didn't think so, but it wouldn't hurt to meet him and look at him with hard, unflinching eyes.

Ten minutes later I parked my car near Alpha Hall.

From the lobby I phoned Harry's room. He was out, but his roommate agreed to come down to talk to me. Joe Martinello, handsome in a dark-eyed, black-haired, Mediterranean way, was as unsuspicious and friendly as Harry probably had been before he got involved in adultery and murder.

"Have you noticed any changes in Harry?" I asked

Joe after we'd arranged ourselves in the uncomfortable, modern chairs grouped around a low glass-topped table.

"Yeah. He's as tightly wired as a coil. I keep telling him to lighten up, but he can't. I'm getting worried about him."

The concern Joe felt for Harry was clearly mirrored in his eyes. "How long have you known him?"

"We started rooming together at the beginning of our junior year, but I met him the year before."

"When did you notice Harry getting uptight?"

Joe answered without hesitation. "When I arrived on campus at the end of August."

"Has his anxiety increased since then, or remained the same?"

"It's gotten worse. Especially lately. With his father being killed and all..." Joe broke off, shaking his head.

Since he was obviously glad to have a chance to talk about his concern for Harry, I continued to probe. "Did his anxiety increase even before his father's death?"

Joe wrinkled his forehead in concentration. "Yeah, it did. I'd been attributing it all to his father's murder, but you're right. He got more nervous and worried even before his dad died."

"About a week earlier?"

Joe stared at me, eyes widened in surprise. "How did you know that?"

There was no longer any doubt in my mind: Harry was involved in Crawford's death. Maybe nobody could come up with any hard evidence, but he was involved. Given Harry's volatile emotional state, would he break down under police questioning? But for that to happen Larry Keller had to have a good reason to haul the young man in. Maybe I could provoke Harry into doing something foolish. I caught Joe glancing at his watch.

"If you stick around, you can speak to him yourself. Harry took Tweety-Bird up but he should be back in ten, fifteen minutes."

"Tweety-Bird?"

Joe grinned. "That's what he calls his single-engine Cessna. He keeps it at the Westport Flight Club."

I simply stared at Joe. It hadn't even occurred to me that Harry could be a pilot. *Some investigator,* I thought, disgusted with myself. Having access to a plane changed everything. Harry could have flown the Cessna to a small airport in Chicago, such as Meigs, established an alibi with Thelma Young, left Orchestra Hall immediately after that, taken a cab to the airport, flown back to Westport, shot his stepfather, clobbered me over the head when I showed up unexpectedly, and returned to Chicago in time to reclaim the Ferrari from the parking garage at eleven-thirty.

I felt ill. Then the cold-bloodedness of the scheme hit me and made me furious. Fighting my anger, I asked Joe to give Harry a message from me.

"I'll be happy to pass on anything you want me to."

"Tell him that I know all about The Dolphin." Noting Joe's perplexed expression, I added, "Harry'll know what I mean. Believe me." I thanked him for his help and stalked off. As soon as I got home, I called Uncle Barney and told him what I'd found out.

"His own plane, huh? Well, I'll be. I didn't think of

that either, but then it's not as if every college kid could pilot a plane, much less own one."

"Do you think I did right by mentioning The Dolphin?"

"It might prod somebody into doing something rash, which is what we want. I think it's time to put a couple of people under surveillance. I'll let you know what shift I want you to take."

"How about checking out the small airports?"

"I'll put Glenn on that. You've done enough for a Sunday. Enjoy the rest of the weekend, Cybil."

I tried to do that, but didn't quite succeed. I felt uneasy and jumpy, expecting something to happen. Since I couldn't sit still long enough to listen to music or to read, I put on my work gloves and started to strip off the uglier-than-sin wallpaper above the chair railing in the dining room.

GLENN'S PRELIMINARY INVESTIGATION on Sunday had netted nothing except the information that Harry hadn't taken Tweety-Bird up on the Saturday Ariosto had been killed. I hadn't expected him to be so careless as to use his own plane.

On Monday morning Barney looked at the list of small airports in a hundred-mile radius of Westport and assigned one to each investigator. Mine turned out to be a surprisingly large airfield located west of the city just over the countyline. The receptionist directed me to a hangar where the manager-owner worked on some dial in the cockpit of a plane named Lily-Oh II.

"Mr. Dawson, could I speak to you for a minute?"

He raised his head. "Sure."

Dawson swung himself out of the cockpit with the grace of a gymnast. He was tall, lean, and long-legged. When he came closer the countless lines crisscrossing his weathered face belied the youthfulness of his movements. The World War II leather bomber jacket he wore looked like the real thing, though I suspected he wasn't old enough to have been a flyer in that war. When I told him what I needed to know, it turned out he knew Harry.

"Nobody took a plane up that Saturday night. The weather was bad. Rainy and windy," he said.

"Could anyone have gone up despite the weather?"

"Yeah. Somebody with lots of experience. Or a natural-born flier."

"Is Harry one of these natural-born fliers?"

"He sure is. Too bad his old man nixed the boy's aspirations to join the Air Force. Harry wanted to run away and sign up when he hit eighteen, but I encouraged him to go to college, graduate, and then join up. In the meantime he logged as much flying time as he could."

"How did Harry acquire his plane since Mr. Ariosto was opposed to him flying?"

"He used the money his mother left him. Ariosto had a fit, but there was nothing the old man could do about it. Tweety-Bird had been bought and paid for."

"You're sure Harry didn't take one of your planes that evening?"

"Positive. I was here till midnight. I wanted to stick around to turn the clocks back from daylight savings time. Then I went for a beer at Lynn's Tavern which is just down the road a piece, parallel to the runway. I'd have heard any plane taking off or landing."

I believed him, thanked him for his time, and left.

From my car I phoned the agency. Uncle Barney had heard from the other investigators. Harry had not used a plane that night. At least not in the tri-county area that would have enabled him to shoot Ariosto and establish his alibi in Chicago.

"So, that's that," I murmured, feeling defeated.

"For the moment. We'll examine all the facts again and look for what we missed or misinterpreted," Barney said. "Are you coming in?"

"In a little while. Since it's on the way, I'll stop at the Ariosto mansion. I have the nagging feeling that I've overlooked something important."

I had no idea what I could have missed, but it bothered me enough to pay the family another visit.

As soon as Brazier opened the door, I was hit with the noise of unusual activity. Cartons were stacked three high in the hall outside the study.

"What's going on?" I asked Brazier.

"Miss Annette has put Mr. Ramsey in charge of everything."

Looking at Brazier's face closely, I couldn't detect anything, and yet I was sure I'd perceived a hint of disapproval. "Are you staying on?"

"No, ma'am!"

This time the butler didn't hide his emotion. Brazier might as well have shouted that nothing on earth could induce him to serve Ramsey.

"Is Miss Annette here?"

"No. She had to fly to Detroit but she'll be back tomorrow."

"Oh. Then I'd like to talk to Mrs. Dougherty for a minute."

"She's in the kitchen. I know she'll be glad to see you."

Brazier's gloomy expression and tone of voice hurried me to the back of the house where I found a red-eyed Mrs. Dougherty moving through the kitchen aimlessly, wringing her hands. She was so discomposed that she allowed me to make the tea. Only after I had settled her into her favorite chair and dosed her cup liberally with sugar was she able to tell me what was wrong.

"He fired me, that's what's the matter. After all these years, he fired me!"

"Who fired you?"

"Mr. Ramsey. But I told him I had already retired, so he couldn't sack me. Imagine the nerve of that upstart! Offering me two months' salary and showing me the gate!"

Her shelf-like bosom heaved in agitation. "When did all this happen?"

"The lawyer came yesterday and announced that Miss Annette put Mr. Ramsey in charge of everything."

"I suppose that makes sense," I murmured. "She lives in Detroit and Harry is too young and inexperienced to take over."

"Well, he finally got what he always wanted."

"Who?"

"Mr. Ramsey. More than once I heard him hint around that he wanted to live here at the mansion but Mr. Ariosto wouldn't have him."

"Why not? Surely there was room for one more."

"Room to spare."

"Then why?"

Mrs. Dougherty shrugged. "Mr. Ariosto must have had his reasons. I only know that Mr. Ramsey's two-faced. Oh, he was always polite to us, the servants I mean, in front of people, but he treated us like dirt when no one was watching."

Maxi, speaking of the exemplary employers she had followed to the United States in her youth, said that the true test of someone's character was revealed in their relationship to servants or employees.

"Anyway, my sister's coming this afternoon to pick me up. I can't wait to leave this house," Mrs. Dougherty said.

I wondered what Pauline was going to do. Had Ramsey thrown her out too? I stayed with Mrs. Dougherty long enough to calm her down and listen to her plans for her retirement. After promising to keep in touch, I hugged her goodbye. Then I set out to find Pauline.

Ramsey's voice stopped me as I passed the study.

"What are you doing here, Cybil?" he asked, coming to the open door. He was carrying the small landscape painting that had hung behind the desk.

Determined to keep my eyes off the floor in front of the desk even though all traces of blood had been removed, I said, "I dropped by to see Pauline."

"She's in the morning room."

"I understand congratulations are in order."

Ramsey smiled. "Yeah. You're looking at the director of Ariosto Enterprises."

"And owner of this house?"

"No. Just the caretaker."

I sensed he would have loved to own the house. Ramsey already acted like the lord of the manor. "You're not wasting any time redecorating the place," I said, looking pointedly at the painting. He didn't even have the grace to look embarrassed.

"Terrance had no taste where art was concerned. Look at this kitsch."

"I've seen worse," I said.

"There's a phone call for you," Pauline told me, joining us.

"You can take it in here." Ramsey gestured towards the desk in the study.

It was Uncle Barney. I listened, not wanting to hear or believe what he had to say. "Are you sure?" I asked, knowing in my heart he would be. "Sweet heaven above," I murmured, replacing the receiver.

"Are you okay?" Ramsey asked.

"You look as pale as a ghost," Pauline said.

"Harry's plane crashed. He's dead," I blurted out.

FOURTEEN

PAULINE DIDN'T UTTER A SOUND. Her eyes rolled back in her head and before I could so much as open my mouth to speak, she crumpled to the floor like a rag doll.

"What the hell!" Ramsey yelled.

Both of us kneeled beside the still figure. I searched for her pulse, reassured when I located its beat.

"Pauline," I called. When she didn't respond, I unfastened the wide belt of her dress. "Ramsey, get me that pillow from the couch." After he did, I placed it under her feet.

"Does that help?" he asked.

"It's supposed to. Allows the blood to flow back to her heart."

"Pauline," Ramsey called to her.

She moaned. Her eyes fluttered open. They focused on me and she remembered. "No," she whispered through pale lips. "Tell me it's not true."

"I wish I could."

"Harry isn't dead. He can't be. No!"

The word became a long wail of agony that cut right through me. I was sure it could be heard in the far reaches of the mansion. Pauline rolled over onto her stomach, beating her fists against the wooden floor.

"Let her be," I told Ramsey, who tried to restrain her. I knew from experience that sometimes emotional torment can be borne only if it's matched by physical pain. "Get Brazier to phone her physician. She'll need a tranquilizer to get through this."

After a few minutes Pauline's screams dulled into a heartbroken keening that was even more terrible to hear. I stroked her hair, unable to murmur the traditional, meaningless phrases that I knew too well could bring her no comfort in her loss. When the first terrible wave of her pain receded momentarily, Pauline turned to look at me.

"How did it happen?" she asked between sobs.

The investigator assigned to shadow Harry had witnessed the crash, so I knew. When I hesitated, Pauline again demanded to know how her lover had died.

"According to several witnesses, the plane nose-dived to earth and exploded on impact." Though the words were brutally frank, the truth was usually less devastating than the images the mind invents if allowed to speculate. Pauline stared at me, trying to absorb this information, her tears stilled for the moment. Then what little color was left in her face drained away. She swayed. I grabbed her by the shoulders and shook her.

"Pauline, don't you dare faint again," I ordered. Although losing consciousness is a natural response to great shock, it still scared me.

"He killed himself. My Harry killed himself. He said he might, but I thought I'd talked him out of it. It's my fault. All my fault. Oh, my sweet, sweet Harry."

She began to sob, great gasping sobs that shook her body. Pauline collapsed against me. I held her until Ramsey returned.

"Her doctor said he'd prescribed Valium for her already. Brazier went to get it."

Moments later Brazier returned with the prescription bottle and a glass of water. I read the instructions, noting that I could give her two pills. Pauline was crying so hard it took both Brazier and myself to get her to swallow the pills before we persuaded her to rest on the sofa. Then I pulled up a chair beside her and sat down.

I don't know whether the pills started to take effect quickly or whether Pauline was too exhausted to continue to weep, but a curious resignation settled over her. She began to speak in a soft voice.

"It's all my fault, all of it. Harry didn't do anything wrong except help me move him. I kept telling Harry not to worry. I'd take the blame, but it bothered him so badly he could hardly eat or sleep."

Suddenly I knew what she was talking about. "Harry didn't shoot Crawford, did he?"

"No. He only helped me move the body. I phoned him. I didn't know what else to do."

"Where did you shoot Crawford?"

"In the park. Down by the river where he always met me to collect the money."

"He was blackmailing you?"

Pauline nodded. "He found out about Harry and me. By a stupid coincidence. We were so careful except for that one time. After the Tri State picnic at Lake Michigan, we didn't go home to switch cars. It seemed so dumb to drive to Westport when we were practically at the motel already. Crawford saw Harry's Ferrari and my Mercedes pull off the highway and followed us."

"From whom did Harry borrow the mustang?" I asked to satisfy my curiosity.

"From his roommate."

"Why did you shoot Crawford?"

"Because I was desperate. He demanded more and more money. I couldn't come up with any more. I probably would have started to pawn my jewelry and continued to pay him, but he taunted me. He laughed and called me names and then he hit me. I guess I panicked. I grabbed the shotgun and pulled the trigger."

"Why did you take the gun with you? No, maybe you'd better not answer that," I added, conscious of Ramsey standing behind me. Her answer could prove premeditation and that was something I didn't want to have to report to the police. Making a conviction stick wasn't part of my job.

"It doesn't matter," she continued, her whole body acknowledging defeat. "Without Harry nothing matters anymore."

"The gun," Ramsey reminded her.

"It was in the car. I'd just been to the Sports Club. I'd taken it to the gunsmith there to check. I never meant to shoot Crawford."

"Why didn't you leave the body there and call the police? With Crawford hitting you, it would have been self-defense," I said.

"I didn't think. I drove to the nearest phone and called Harry. He came and we decided to put the body into the conference room. We didn't think it would be found before Monday. Maybe not till Tuesday. That would have given us time to decide what to do."

"You could still have told the police after they found the body."

"We thought about doing that, but then the gun disappeared from the rack, and we didn't know what to do."

"When did you notice that the gun was gone?"

"On Monday afternoon. That's when I ordered the replacement just as you guessed."

"Pauline, think carefully. Who was in the house from the time on Sunday evening when you put the gun back into the rack and Monday afternoon when you noticed its disappearance?"

"Don't you think you should let her rest?" Ramsey asked.

"In a little bit. Think, Pauline. Who else was in the house?"

"Everybody in the family. Harry, Terrance, Ramsey, and me. And all the staff."

That didn't help much. "Did Sidney Dunn blackmail you?"

"Yes. But not until after Terrance was shot. He found out about Harry and me. I don't know how he got the key to the motel room. He was an awful snoop, so it wasn't hard for him to find things."

"Did you shoot Sidney?"

"No. When I heard you say he'd been shot, I thought Harry might have shot him. But when I'd had time to think, I knew he couldn't have."

"And you didn't shoot your husband either, did you?" I asked.

"Shoot Terrance? Heavens, no. I was much too afraid

of the man to pull a gun on him. Besides, I didn't have the shotgun anymore. And Harry didn't either."

I believed her. "What were you and Harry planning to do?"

"We were going to run off together as soon as Harry graduated. We never planned to fall in love. It just happened. We both tried to fight it. We really did. You've got to believe me, Cybil."

"I do." I could see her eyes grow heavy. "Sleep now," I murmured.

"Harry," she whispered. Tears trickled silently down her cheek even as she fell asleep.

I rose from the chair, feeling as if I'd been through the proverbial wringer.

"You believe she didn't kill Terrance and the chauffeur?" Ramsey asked.

"Yes. Don't you?"

"No way. She killed all three men."

His certainty and the barely suppressed satisfaction I detected in his voice appalled me. I clamped my teeth together and counted to ten. Brazier's return saved me from an argument that could easily have become ugly.

"Mrs. Quindt, could you look in on Mrs. Dougherty? She's mighty upset over Mr. Harry's death."

"I'll go see her right now."

I found Mrs. Dougherty sitting at the kitchen table, her face buried in her hands. "I'm so sorry. I know how fond you were of Harry." I laid my hand on her shoulder.

Looking up with tears in her eyes, she said, "My poor lamb. He never had a chance. Not with a woman like her."

"You knew about the affair?"

"I suspected it."

"Did anyone else?" I asked.

She shook her head. "I don't think so. I only suspected because I've known Harry since he was a little boy. He never could hide things from me."

Taking a deep breath, I said, "Mrs. Dougherty, we still don't know who killed Mr. Ariosto. Now that Pauline has confessed to killing Crawford, everybody will try to blame her for the other two deaths as well. That will implicate Harry."

"No! Harry is innocent. He could never kill anyone. There isn't a mean bone in his body. I mean, there wasn't." She pressed her hand over her mouth to keep back the sobs.

"I think he is innocent, too, but I need your help to prove that. Think back to that Sunday night and Monday morning. Who was in and out of the house?"

"This will help my boy?"

"Yes."

Mrs. Dougherty wiped her eyes with a tissue and blew her nose. Then she was ready. "Well, let me see. On Sundays we have the main meal at noon, so I don't have to cook in the evening. I just make sure there are plenty of snacks and sandwich fixings in the refrigerator."

I let her tell it in her own way, hoping this method would best trigger her memory.

"After I got back from visiting my sister, Mr. Ariosto asked me to fix him a turkey sandwich, which I did. Then Mr. Ramsey arrived and joined Mr. Ariosto in the study. He stayed there until Mrs. Ariosto and Harry came. They didn't want anything from the kitchen. Just drinks from the bar."

"Did Mr. Ariosto join them?"

"No. Only Mr. Ramsey. Later I heard them go out and Mrs. Ariosto came back in."

"Did all three go out at the same time?"

"No. Mr. Ramsey left a couple of minutes earlier. Let's see. Where was I? Oh yes. Sunday evening. When the police called, Mr. Ariosto went to the warehouse."

"What did Mrs. Ariosto do?"

"When she came in after seeing Harry off, she went straight upstairs."

"Did Mr. Ariosto tell everyone that Crawford had been killed when he returned?"

"Brazier, Sidney, and I were sitting in the kitchen. Mr. Ariosto came in and told us. Then he said he was going to phone Mr. Ramsay with the news."

"Tell me about Monday."

"Mr. Ariosto got up early as always, had a light breakfast, and left. Mrs. Ariosto got up early too, which was unusual. Harry came home."

"Wasn't that unusual, too?"

Mrs. Dougherty shrugged. "He said he left a book here."

"Did he talk to Mrs. Ariosto?"

"Yes. They went for a walk together. I saw them from the kitchen window. No sooner had they gone, when Mr. Ramsey arrived, saying he forgot some papers. You want me to go on with who was here for lunch?"

"No, that's not necessary. Thank you."

"I hope this helps clear my poor lamb."

"It will." Mrs. Dougherty's face brightened.

Now I knew who killed Terrance Ariosto and Sidney Dunn. I even had an inkling what the motive in the Ariosto murder was and how the alibi had been rigged, but I had absolutely no tangible proof. Zero. Zilch. Uncle Barney claims that there's no such thing as a perfect crime. The perpetrator always makes at least one mistake, even if a very small one. Obviously I had to find it. I wasn't about to let Pauline be accused of committing two premeditated murders.

On my way to the study to check on Pauline, I met Ramsey.

"I phoned Annette. She's taking the next flight. She was pretty broken up about Harry."

Why that should surprise him, I couldn't imagine. After all, Annette had known and cared for Harry since he was a boy. She'd stood up for him, even to her father.

"I also called the police."

"You didn't waste any time, did you," I snapped, not hiding my annoyance. "Pauline's just had a tremendous shock. Couldn't you have waited?"

"Why? She'll have to face the authorities sooner or later. You want a drink, Cybil?"

"No, thank you."

"I think I'll have one."

I waited until Ramsey entered the study before I hurried into the game room. Standing before the gun rack, I wondered how the murderer had smuggled the shotgun out of the house. Uncle Barney suspected that he'd hidden it under his raincoat when he came to kill Ariosto. Could he have smuggled it out the same way? In broad daylight on Monday morning with people coming and going? If he had nerves of steel he could and there was no hint that the killer lacked those.

I crossed to the nearest of the two windows. Both faced the rose garden. Unlatching the window, I noticed that it opened soundlessly and that the screen was the type that could be removed by pulling out two screws on each side, something that took mere seconds. It would be a cinch to lower the gun out the window and pick it up on the way to the car, a raincoat casually thrown over it.

Where was the murder weapon? Scrutinizing the shotguns again, I realized that their size alone eliminated many of the most common hiding places. He could have thrown it into the river. If he had, we could never prove he committed those murders. But if Sidney saw him take the gun from the house, the murderer might have been reluctant to risk being seen with the weapon again.

The impatient, authoritative pounding on the front door could only mean one thing: Sam Keller and his men had arrived.

Sam took one look at Pauline before storming back to the living room where Ramsey and I waited.

"Who gave her the sedative?" Sam bellowed.

"I did."

"I might have known it was you, Cybil."

"We had her physician's permission," I told him. "Besides, a couple of hours can't make much difference to you, but they will help Pauline.

"What if she recants her confession when she wakes up feeling better?"

"She won't. But even if she did, you're no worse off

than before." I could see Sam struggle with his temper. In the end he merely glowered at me.

"Who all heard the confession?"

"Ramsey, Brazier, and I."

"And she confessed to all three murders?"

"She did not!" I shot Ramsey a slit-eyed look. He had obviously intimated that over the telephone. "She only admitted shooting Crawford and from what she said, she acted in self-defense."

"Is that what you heard, too?" Sam asked Ramsey.

"More or less. If you believe Pauline."

"You don't?"

Ramsey shrugged. "She's a clever woman. She probably figured you'd nail her for the Crawford murder so she confessed, hoping to get away with pleading self-defense. Or maybe she thought if she owned up to one murder, you'd forget about the other two."

"That's pure bilge, and you know it," I told Ramsey. "Pauline didn't have to confess at all. The police weren't exactly breathing down her neck."

"Calm down, Cybil," Sam said. "Nobody is going to railroad anybody. However, it's a fact that all three men were killed with the same gun which strongly points to the murderer being the same person. Even you thought that."

"Up till now. Pauline says the gun was stolen. Probably that Monday morning. I believe her. She isn't lying, not when she feels the way she does."

"And how's that?" Sam asked.

"That she's got nothing left to lose."

Ramsey snorted. "Nothing left to lose? Only her

freedom. Possibly her life." His voice resounded with sarcasm.

"I didn't realize you disliked Pauline that much, Ramsey."

"I don't, but I'm not taken in by her dramatics."

"I'd hardly describe losing somebody you love as dramatics." I could feel red-hot anger rise in me.

Sam stepped between us, addressing me. "Tell me about the gun being stolen."

I told him about Pauline charging the purchase of a replacement.

"That doesn't prove anything either way. We've got to find that gun," Sam muttered.

"Do you still need me here?" I asked.

"No. You can go, but come by the station later so we can take your statement. You won't forget, will you?"

"I'll be there."

In the hall I nodded to Sergeant Griffin who leaned against the wall opposite the study, keeping an eye on Pauline.

I drove straight to the airport, the nearest place that had what I needed. First I telephoned Uncle Barney. I ended my report with a request. "I want a tail on Ramsey Ariosto right away."

"I thought you cleared him," Barney said.

"I did. Now I have to destroy that alibi I worked so hard to build for him. What makes me absolutely furious is that he played me as if I were a fish at the end of his line. Pretending not to remember the girl who sold him the cookies the first time I interviewed him. Ha! He knew damned well his alibi would look stronger if I established it than if he told it to me or the police. Ramsey used me, and that's something I can't stand!"

"Calm down, Cybil."

It irked me that everybody was telling me to calm down when I really didn't feel like calming down. I wanted to yell at the top of my lungs. I wanted to throw things, like a stack of big, white stoneware plates against a cement wall. Since I didn't have plates handy and since I wouldn't dream of creating a scene by yelling, I took several deep hatha yoga breaths.

"I'm calm," I said through half-clenched teeth. "If Ramsey hasn't ditched the murder weapon yet, I strongly suspect he'll try to get rid of it the first chance he gets. I want one of us to catch him in the act."

"I'll assign someone to shadow him. Where's Ramsey now?"

"At the mansion. I'm sure he's going to stay there until Pauline is arrested and taken to jail, the whole time trying to persuade Sam that she's guilty of all three murders."

"Where'll you be?"

"As soon as I rent a car, I'll watch the mansion from Locust Road. Ramsey's Chrysler Imperial is visible from there, so that's where I'll park."

I rented an inconspicuous beige Chevy, left my Volvo in the airport's long-term parking lot, and took Locust Road to the side street nearest the Ariosto estate. It was really just a lane but wide enough for a car to get past me. Ramsey's car was still parked in the same spot. As I waited for the operative from the agency to arrive, I tried to come up with a plan of action.

After a while I got out of the car and paced. By the

time Glenn's Toyota parked behind me, I knew what I had to do.

On the phone Mrs. Taylor agreed to see me if I could get to her house before one when she took her daughters back to St. Mary's Elementary School. I told her I would be there in half an hour. I beat that by four minutes.

"I hope you don't mind talking while I fix lunch for the girls," she said, leading the way to the kitchen.

"I don't mind."

The counters and appliances were arranged in a U-shape with the kitchen table placed in the open part of the U. The girls, sitting at the table side by side, cast curious but shy glances at me from time to time, while their mother sliced Spam into a frying pan.

"Mrs. Taylor, you said you knew what time it was when you picked up your daughter by looking at Mr. Ariosto's wall clock. Did you look at any other clock when you arrived home?"

"No. I went straight to the kitchen to decorate the cupcakes. As you can see, my clock on the range doesn't work. My husband keeps promising to fix it but something else always comes up."

"Did you listen to the radio in the car or in the kitchen?"

"No. Nancy always listens to loud music and the girls have the television on full blast. Frankly, I enjoy the quiet."

"So, your only source of information on time was Mr. Ariosto's clock?"

"Yes. Until we went to bed and I set the alarm. I'm not real hung up on time," she confided, dividing the fried Spam between two plates. She added two slices of white bread and placed the plates before her daughters. Mrs. Taylor uncapped a bottle of ketchup, upended it and hit the bottom. She paused, wrinkling her forehead. "You know, later on that evening I was surprised how much I'd gotten done by nine. Was Mr. Ariosto's clock wrong?"

"Something like that," I said evasively. Mrs. Taylor would undoubtedly be called to testify, so I was careful not to put words into her mouth. "Thank you for your time. Please stay. I can find my own way out." I left her trying to dislodge the ketchup from the bottle.

Before returning to the office I used the drive-through of the nearest fast food restaurant to pick up a hamburger with lettuce and tomato and a small soft drink.

Lynn, looking stunning in a crimson charmeuse tunic over black pants, frowned at my carry-in lunch. She thinks eating at my desk isn't upscale enough for the image she wants the agency to project. I ignored the frown, wishing I could wear that shade of red without looking completely washed out.

Fifteen minutes later I met with Uncle Barney.

"I talked to Sam. Pauline Ariosto has been arrested for the murder of Galen Crawford," Barney told me.

"He didn't waste any time, did he? Did Sam say anything about the other murders?"

"Just the standard reply: they're following leads."

Which meant they'd be questioning Pauline until she dropped.

"Don't look so unhappy, Cybil. The Westport police do not use rubber hoses. Besides, Pauline has an attorney to protect her rights."

Barney mentioned the law firm which was prestigious enough, but their expertise didn't extend to criminal proceedings, I thought.

"They'll bring in some big name criminal lawyer before the trial, I'm sure," he added. "What did you find out this morning?"

I told him about my visit to Mrs. Taylor.

"You think Ramsey set the clock ahead?"

"Yes. When Mrs. Taylor came to pick up her daughter, it was only six forty-five, not seven forty-five. That gave him time to get to the Ariosto estate and back. If she had commented on the time difference, he could have claimed to be confused about the imminent daylight savings standard time change. He was lucky. Since it was a rainy day, it was dark out, so Mrs. Taylor accepted the time shown on Ramsey's fancy clock. He took a chance and it worked."

"You're convinced Ramsey shot Ariosto and Dunn?"

"Yes. If you'd seen and heard Pauline, you would have believed her, too. She admits shooting Crawford in self-defense. From what Cathy said about him, he had a reputation for being rough with women."

Barney fiddled with his pipe. After a while he said, as if thinking aloud, "Harry is dead. Sidney is dead. You've ruled out Annette. That leaves Ramsey. He had opportunity and motive which I think was greed. Would you agree with that?"

"Yes. Greed and love of power. You should have observed him at the mansion. He loves running the whole show. But I don't think his motive was only greed. Something else happened. Something in his relationship with his uncle contradicts Ramsey's claim that he and Terrance were close. If that had been the case, why would Terrance have refused to allow his nephew to live on the estate? That building is big enough to house a dozen people without crowding anyone."

"Mrs. Taylor's testimony won't be enough to bring him to trial unless we come up with some additional proof, preferably physical proof," Barney pointed out.

"I know. If only we could find that blasted gun." We were both silent, thinking about this problem. Suddenly I remembered something. "Pauline said she'd taken the gun to the gunsmith at the Sports Club. I think I'll talk to him."

"You might as well. Maybe he'll know something we can use to trace it."

I phoned the Sports Club. The gunsmith, Mr. Mueller, was on the shooting range but was expected to be in his workshop shortly. I left a message, stating that I would be there by two-thirty to pick up a gun he had repaired. I was fairly certain that this would get me into the club without trouble.

MR. MUELLER WAS A BEAR of a man. Not only was he physically huge, he was hairy. He'd tied his long black hair with a thick leather thong. His sideburns met the bushy beard that hid his lower face.

"What can I do for you?" His voice rumbled from his deep chest.

"Mrs. Pauline Ariosto brought in a shotgun for you to look at. What can you tell me about that?"

"It was her favorite shotgun. I gave it a general tune-up so to speak."

"What's distinctive about Mrs. Ariosto's gun? How could I identify it among a whole rack of similar shotguns?"

He worked his fingers through his beard, thinking. Then he grinned. "It's got a nick in the stock. It's a tiny nick, but big enough to make it stand out from other guns."

"Where on the stock?" I asked, hardly daring to believe this lucky break.

The gunsmith picked up a gun and showed me. "Run your hand over the butt plate like this and just onto the stock. You can't see the nick unless you know what you're looking for, but you can sure feel it."

"Would you be willing to repeat this to the police and in a court of law?"

Mueller looked alarmed, but that didn't mean he was necessarily guilty of anything. Most people were not too eager to face the police.

"Will it help Mrs. Ariosto?" he asked.

"Yes."

"Then I will. She has a real appreciation for a fine gun. Don't find too many women like that."

I thanked him profusely.

At last we were getting some place. Not that I knew where to start looking for the gun, but at least I'd know when I found it. That was not quite true, I realized with a start. I knew exactly where to start the search. He might no longer have the gun. On the other hand, he was arrogant and cocky and a shotgun wasn't as easy to get rid of as a handgun. In any event, a search was definitely in order.

I took a deep breath to tame the butterflies cavorting in my stomach. What I was about to do was just a tad risky.

FIFTEEN

DRIVING THROUGH THE PARKING LOT of Ramsey's apartment complex, I searched for his slot. Although I'd been fairly certain he wouldn't be home yet, I had to make sure. I parked the rented Chevy in the visitors' lot. Palming the skeleton keys, I sauntered casually to the back door of his building. In a complex almost exclusively occupied by young professionals, four o'clock in the afternoon is dead time which suited my purpose perfectly. Even so, I quickly glanced in all directions before I tried the door. It was unlocked.

I met no one as I walked up the flight of stairs or in the hall, but passing the apartment next to Ramsey's, I heard piano music. Chopin, I thought. Praying that occupant would stay put for the rest of the prelude, I studied Ramsey's lock. The second key I tried opened the door. I slipped inside quickly and found myself in total darkness.

In his haste to take custody of the Ariosto mansion that morning, Ramsey had left all the drapes closed. Chastising myself for not bringing a flashlight, I decided it was quicker to turn on some lights than to open all the drapes. Hopefully no one would notice if a little light spilled out from beneath doors and around windows. Adjusting the surgical gloves I had borrowed from

Luke's emergency supply, I glanced around, looking for places he could have hidden the shotgun.

Before I searched any of the rooms, I thought it best to make a quick survey of the entire apartment. Remembering the kitchen, I merely swept it with a brief glance. There was no sign of the cookie box he had used to dupe me. Ramsey Ariosto had spoiled chocolate chip cookies for me forever.

The navy-blue-and-white tiled bathroom featured a tub-shower combination and sleek Euro-style cabinets and washbasin. Unless he had put in a secret trap door, there was no space to hide a shotgun. On the way out I had to stop myself from automatically picking up the pile of wet towels on the floor.

Ramsey had left his king-size bed unmade, something Maxi considers the height of slovenliness. Naturally, I consequently never leave my bed unmade. One wall of the room consisted of floor-to-ceiling closets which would take some time to search.

The second bedroom served as a sort of den-cum-storage area for his sports equipment. I recognized the bow he'd used at the Sports Club. A golf bag rested in a corner next to tennis racquets, baseball bats and mitts, a jumble of shoes including basketball high tops, nylon running sneakers, and cleated baseball shoes. I could have imagined that. I turned and caught my breath. A gun rack, much like the one in the Ariosto game room, stood between two windows, holding three shotguns and a rifle.

Had Ramsey read "The Purloined Letter"? Was he clever and reckless enough to hide the murder weapon in plain view? There was only one way to find out. The gun cabinet was locked and being an antique, it wouldn't yield to the first half dozen keys I tried. I felt sweat bead on my forehead. The clock in the living room chimed the half hour. Four-thirty. As head honcho of Ariosto Enterprises, Ramsey could decide to come home early. That possibility sent my heart racing. Unfortunately, it also made my fingers tremble.

Closing my eyes in concentration, I willed my hands to become steady. Just when I was tempted to force the lock, my pick worked. The door to the gun cabinet opened with a click that sounded unnaturally loud.

I removed the shotgun, running my fingers over the butt plate and the stock as the gunsmith had showed me. Nothing. I checked again. The wood was smooth and unmarred. I replaced the gun and tried the next one. When the living room clock announced four forty-five, I paused for a moment, knowing I had to get out of the apartment. With almost feverish haste I examined the second gun. I couldn't believe that it, too, was unmarked. Could I have been wrong?

With some trepidation I reached for the last gun. The nick was there! Tiny, not easily visible, the damaged spot was exactly where Mr. Mueller said it would be.

"All right!" I murmured, feeling immense satisfaction. Now all that was left for me to do was tell Sam to come to the apartment with a search warrant. Carefully I set the gun back in its place. As I reached for the glass door to shut it, I thought I heard a noise in the living room. I froze, listening intently. My heart jumped into my throat, my blood roared in my ears when I heard the unmistakable click of the front door closing.

"What the hell...."

Ramsey's voice. I had left the lights on. He had to realize someone had been or was still in his apartment. Even though I knew there was no place to hide, my eyes frantically searched the room. His footsteps, though muffled by the carpet, closed in on me, trapping me.

Ramsey stopped in the open doorway, the revolver in his hand pointed at me. His eyes jumped to the half-opened cabinet and back to me. He knew, I thought, horrified.

"How'd you figure it out?"

"Figure what out?" I bluffed.

"Cut the crap, Cybil. Why else would you be looking at my guns except to find Pauline's? Step away from the gun rack."

To underscore his order, he motioned the gun in the direction he wanted me to go. I did as I was told, though I asked, "Are you afraid I'm going to jump you and take the revolver from you?"

Ramsey ignored that. Without taking his eyes off me, he shut the glass door. With his left hand he located a small key on the key ring he'd taken from his pocket and locked the cabinet.

"Who knows you're here?"

Ramsey was thinking about shooting me, I thought, not quite believing it.

"Answer me."

His gray eyes, cold and calculating, impaled me, and I knew he meant to kill me. Fear shot through me, paralyzing me. I couldn't even speak.

"So, nobody knows," he said, reading my reaction correctly. "Excellent. That'll make it so much simpler."

Ramsey's sarcastic remark roused me. I'd be damned

if I was going to make anything simple and easy for him. "Uncle Barney knows I'm here," I lied brazenly, looking him straight in the eye. My voice was surprisingly strong, lending credence to my claim. I knew he half believed me.

Ramsey shrugged. "It doesn't matter."

Glenn should be parked outside. Unless he lost Ramsey while tailing him, but that was highly unlikely. Somehow I had to get Ramsey outside. "You're not going to shoot me in here, are you? Your music-loving neighbor is bound to hear it. I know this particular prelude. It doesn't rise to the kind of shattering crescendo that would cover the sound of a shot." I could tell he was thinking this over.

"You're right. We'll wait until dark before we leave."

Reprieved for an hour or so.

"Walk into the living room and sit on the couch," he ordered.

I did. He perched on the edge of an easy chair, facing me, the revolver steady in his hand. A low coffee table stood between us. The only thing on it heavy enough to be used as a weapon was a large glass ashtray. I eyed it longingly. Ramsey would have to turn his head long enough for me to grab it, leap across the table and smash it on his head hard enough to stun him and wrest the gun away from him.

No, I didn't just want to stun him, I discovered. I wanted to put a large bump on his head. That would be poetic justice. Of course, the chances of my doing that were minimal. Once outside, they improved somewhat. Maybe we'd meet people coming home from work.

Maybe I could break away and run. Would he shoot me with witnesses around? I didn't think so.

But what if no one came? What if we were alone in the dark parking lot? What if he succeeded in forcing me to drive his car to a lonely spot where he'd raise the gun and… My mouth felt parched and dry, but the palms of my hands were damp. I'd have to take any chance I got, even a lousy one, before we reached his car.

"You never answered my question, Cybil. How did you tumble to me as the guilty party?"

"What?" It took me a moment to focus on his question. "Oh, that. Logic, I guess."

Ramsey frowned. "I don't understand. Explain."

"Pauline didn't shoot Terrance. That left you, so you had to have done it. It's perfectly clear and logical."

"I don't get it. Pauline could have been lying. How could you be so certain she was telling the truth?"

In her pain Pauline was beyond lies. The agony of her loss burned away all other emotions, all other concerns until nothing else existed but the shattering awareness of what she'd lost. But I knew Ramsey would not understand that, so I didn't bother to explain. All I said was, "Sometimes the truth is startlingly obvious."

Ramsey looked unconvinced.

"Why did you kill your uncle?" I wasn't sure Ramsey would answer that, but he did.

"Because I was tired of being jerked around like a yo-yo. I worked and slaved for that man but do you think he ever acknowledged my contribution? No way. And he never got tired of telling me how he took me in after my father died and raised me like his own son and how much money he'd spent on me. He repeated that over and over until I could recite it in my sleep. God protect us from that kind of charity. Well, that Friday it all came to a head. I told him that I more than repaid him with years of had work. Do you know what he had the gall to do?"

I shook my head, afraid that if I spoke Ramsey would stop his confession.

"He gave a position that he'd dangled in front of me like a carrot, a position he'd promised me, to someone else. Can you believe that? For two years I've worked my tail off in hopes of getting the vice presidency, and he gave it away. Just like that." He paused, as if he still couldn't believe what had happened.

"Not that the guy who got it was any better than me. Far from it. He wasn't nearly as qualified. No, Terrance did it for the sheer pleasure of tormenting me. Nothing gave him the charge that besting someone or doing someone in did, not even sex. Giving that job to someone else killed two birds with one stone: Terrance knew it would eat away at me, and it gave him a new victim in the newly promoted guy. The man couldn't possibly handle the job, and Terrance knew it. Terrance Ariosto was the biggest bastard that ever lived. He deserved to die."

"So, when Crawford was shot you saw your chance. How did you find out about Pauline and Harry's involvement?"

"That was easy. I saw them come in that Sunday and knew something drastic had happened. So I waited outside for them and overheard enough to know what had happened when Terrance told me about Crawford's death."

"How did you know about the shotgun?"

"I saw Pauline with it at the Sports Club that afternoon. I came back to the house on Monday and took it."

"That's when Dunn saw you?"

"That damned snoop. He saw me carry something to my car. He must have seen the empty spot in the gun rack and put two and two together. Blackmail is about as low as you can sink."

Personally, I thought murder deserved that distinction, but I wasn't about to argue with a man pointing a big revolver at me who'd already killed twice.

"It was you who hit me over the head in the study?"

"Yeah. You arrived a couple of minutes too early. I was at the house in the morning and found out that Terrance was going to be alone that evening. I didn't know he had asked you to join him. You almost wrecked everything."

There was actually an accusing note in his voice. I couldn't believe it. "Ah, but then I established an alibi for you. You must have enjoyed that."

"I did. You were wonderful. So earnest, so concerned, so eager to help."

Ramsey had the nerve to grin. At that moment I understood the urge to slug someone. I clenched my hands in helpless fury. Ramsey glanced at the clock on the wall. It wasn't time yet. I wasn't ready. I had to keep him talking.

"What was Terrance's reaction when you pointed the shotgun at him?" I asked.

"He laughed at first, claiming I'd never have the guts

to shoot him. What was so funny about that was that in my fantasies I'd killed the bastard a thousand times."

I'd been wrong about one thing. It hadn't been a dispassionate murder. The suppressed anger and humiliation of a dozen years had fired that shot. A shiver ran down my spine.

"Let's go. It's dark enough."

Startled, I looked into his eyes. Cold determination had replaced the feverish emotions I'd seen there moments earlier.

"For what it's worth, Cybil, I never intended to hurt you," Ramsey said. He stood up, the gun steady in his hand.

"But a man's got to do what a man's got to do?"

"Something like that. Move it, Cybil."

I was still afraid, terribly afraid, but anger coursed through me and with it came the determination to thwart Ramsey. I was not going to be a meek victim. I'd put up one hell of a fight, and I would win.

The hall was empty. Passing his neighbor's door, I noticed that Chopin had been replaced with a piece from the Renaissance. Not Vivaldi, but a contemporary of his. With a gun pressed against the small of my back, that was an odd thing for me to notice.

Nearing the door to the parking lot, I tensed for action. Glenn was somewhere out there, but probably too far to help me. I was on my own. I stopped, waiting for Ramsey to open the door. When he did, I gained two steps on him. The moment I set foot on the brightly lit landing, I cast a quick look around. Two women approached us. Without hesitation and without warning, I flung myself forward and rolled down the three steps.

"Oh my God. Are you hurt?" one of the women shrieked, rushing to my side.

"My ankle. I'm sure I've broken it," I cried out piteously.

"Are you sure?" the other woman asked.

"My husband is Dr. Luke Quindt. He's in charge of the emergency services at Westport Hospital so I know something about these things." The more information about me I could reveal before Ramsey forced me to go with him, the better my chances of survival were. I groaned for effect. Several other people joined the circle around me, I noticed, pleased. The bigger the crowd, the better. Ramsey faded farther to the rear.

"Cybil? Please let me through."

"Glenn?"

"I saw you fall. Are you okay?" Glenn squatted beside me.

In a voice no one but he could hear I said, "I'm fine. Do you see Ramsey?"

Glenn glanced around. "No. I saw him come through the door behind you, but I don't see him now."

"Good. Help me up. We have to make an urgent phone call."

Two HOURS LATER, after Sam had removed the shotgun from Ramsey's apartment, after he'd taken my statement and had put out an all-points bulletin, we learned from the highway patrol that Ramsey Ariosto had run a road-block in Michigan. He had been killed instantly.

I went home then. The house was empty and quiet. I longed for company, but it was too late to disturb Maxi. Luke? I was tempted, but if I called him, he would expect more than being merely a sympathetic listener. I wasn't ready to be what he expected me to be.

I fixed a pot of Darjeeling tea, lit a fire, and listened to Beethoven's Ninth Symphony. Eventually the music washed away the dregs of fear and horror that still clung to me.

BECAUSE OF THE CASE, I had missed going to the cemetery on All Saints' Day. It's an Austrian custom to honor the dead with a visit on this day, a custom Maxi has always kept. I bought a huge bouquet of mums which I divided and added to the ones Maxi had already placed on the graves of our dead: my son's, my father's, my grandfather's and my Aunt Elise's, Maxi's daughter whom polio took in the early fifties.

I kept one perfectly petaled white blossom for Wilma. Though she wasn't a member of my family, I had liked her.

Although the caretaker had given me directions, it took me a while to find Wilma's marker. I stood before it, remembering her: quick, efficient, friendly and unfailingly cheerful except for the one time when the Carnes, mother and son, had been mentioned.

My breath caught. I recalled Maxi's words. She had been truly surprised that Tom had escaped his mother's overpowering hold long enough to get married. I added Cathy's description of the mother-son relationship to Maxi's. What emerged was the portrait of an unhealthily strong attachment. What would happen if such an attachment was suddenly severed?

Suddenly I knew, though again I didn't have a shred of evidence, only my suppositions.

Then I remembered something Ferne Lauder had said. I telephoned her from my car. After the usual exchange of greetings, I asked, "Do you remember the day my uncle and I came to talk to you?"

"Of course, I do. Not much happens around here, so I remember anything that's out of the ordinary."

"Good. I asked you then if you'd seen cars parked on the street that you hadn't seen there before."

"Yes. And I told you there hadn't been a Trans Am like my grandson's or a big Cadillac."

"But what had you seen?"

"A red jeep."

"I thought you'd said that, but I had to be sure."

"Does that help you, dear?"

"It does. Thanks a lot."

"Listen, why don't you come by some time for a beer?"

Hearing the loneliness in her voice, I said, "I will before the week is out." And I would go see her, but first I'd pick up a cold six-pack to take along.

A red jeep.

Flipping through the phone book I located the address I needed. It was near the cemetery. I saw the jeep sitting in the driveway from half a block away. I parked behind it. When I knocked, Cathy opened the door.

"My goodness. I didn't expect to see you again," she said. "I just got home from work. Come in."

"Thanks. Is Tom home?"

She stared at me with a mixture of alarm and surprise. "He's in the den. He hasn't been himself lately. Is something wrong? What's he done?"

"We'll let him tell us." I followed her to the den.

When I saw Tom, I was shocked. He looked shrunken, as if his clothes had grown too big for him. He seemed listless, barely looking at me when I greeted him.

"Cathy, I'd like you to stay," I said, sitting in a chair facing Tom. She sat beside him on the sofa.

"Maxi sends greetings. You remember her, don't you, Tom? She was your mother's friend," I said, my voice gentle as if I addressed a sick child.

He nodded indifferently.

"Do you also remember Wilma?" A change came over him. His eyes focused on me. I shrank from the exultant, triumphant expression gleaming in them.

"She's the one who drove the car that hurt Mama."

"So you decided to hurt her."

"Yes. Mama told me to."

"Tom, what are you talking about?" Cathy asked, horrified. "I can't believe Mae told you to—"

"—push Wilma down the stairs," I finished the sentence for her.

"She didn't tell me how to do it. The stairs were my idea."

Tom seemed to be proud of that.

"I don't believe your mother told you to kill Wilma," Cathy said, now as pale as the white wall behind her.

Tom turned on her. "That's how little you know. She told me every night until I did it. Now Mama can rest. The guilty have been punished."

Cathy and I stared at each other.

"Let me get this straight," Cathy said. "Mae talked to you after...after she died."

"Sure." Tom rubbed his temples as if he felt pain there. "I heard her voice every night until I pushed

Wilma down the stairs. Now everything's quiet." His hands fell away from his temples, resting relaxed in his lap. An almost angelic smile hovered around his lips.

"May I use your phone?" I asked Cathy.

"Sure. It's in the hall."

She joined me there just as I completed my call to the police.

"What'll happen to him?" Cathy asked, nodding her head in the direction of the den.

"The police are on their way. My guess is that he'll be placed in a mental institution."

Cathy sighed. "I knew he was growing weirder by the day, but I had no idea he'd done that to Wilma."

"It's not your fault," I reassured her, touching her arm.

She looked at me, her expression grateful. "Thanks. I needed to hear that."

After that there was nothing left to say. She returned to sit with her husband. I went outside and stood on the porch, waiting for the police.

REQUEST YOUR FREE BOOKS!

2 FREE NOVELS
PLUS 2 FREE GIFTS!

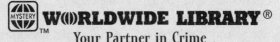

WORLDWIDE LIBRARY ®
Your Partner in Crime